BOUND BY DESIRE

SERPENT'S KISS SERIES BOOKS 1-3

SHERRI HAYES

Bound by Desire (Serpent's Kiss, Books 1-3)

By Sherri Hayes

ISBN (ebook): 978-1-948471-13-8

ISBN (paperback): 978-1-948471-14-5

Cover Design by Miblart.

This is a work of fiction. Names, places, characters and incidents are the product of the author's imagination and are fictitious. Any resemblance to actual persons, living or dead, events or establishments is solely coincidental.

BURNING FOR HER KISS

SERPENT'S KISS #1

BURNING FOR HER KISS
SERPENT'S KISS SERIES BOOK 1

SHERRI HAYES

About The Book

Beth Davenport has no interest in getting involved with another man for the foreseeable future. To say her last relationship ended in disaster would be a colossal understatement. The only reason she agrees to put in an appearance at Serpent's Kiss, a private kink club in downtown St. Louis, is because her best friend, Nicole, won't quit nagging her. When she walks in the door that night, the last thing she expects to do is meet a man who will have her reconsidering her ban on men.

As a captain with the St. Louis Fire Department, Drew Parker is used to being in charge. His crew relies on him to make sure they know what they're doing and return home to their families after every shift. It isn't, however, what he wants in a relationship. Drew decides to join Serpent's Kiss to see if what appeals to him in fantasy is something he wants to explore in the real world. He's also hoping that he'll be lucky enough to meet a woman with whom he can explore his desires. The night Beth walks into the club, he is intrigued. Drew has to get to know her better.

After what happened to her, Beth is reluctant to get involved with Drew. It doesn't matter that he is sweet and charming. She's been burned before and Beth doesn't think she can survive having her heart crushed again. Drew, however, won't take no for an answer. He wants a relationship and is determined to chip away at her defenses until she relents. Will she give him a chance, or did her ex leave her with scars too deep to heal?

Chapter One

Drew Parker had finally drummed up the courage to come to Serpent's Kiss by himself four weeks ago. He'd been anxious about walking into a kink club. The idea of going alone terrified him. In the end, after a lot of internal arguments, he'd done it. He'd made the leap into the unknown.

In the months leading up to his first trip to the club, Drew attended a few local munches. That had been daunting in and of itself. He hadn't known what to expect, but the people were more welcoming than he'd thought they'd be—especially John and his mistress, Allison. They seemed to sense his need for guidance and had taken him under their wing, so to speak.

It was through John and Allison that Drew found out about the club. Serpent's Kiss was a private club in the heart of downtown St. Louis. On the outside, it appeared to be an old warehouse. No one would know it was a BDSM club unless they paid close attention to the people who came and went on Friday and Saturday nights.

With the help of his new friends, he was introduced to the club and its owner, Mistress Katrina. Drew was a little surprised a woman owned and ran a kink club. He wasn't sure why, but he'd just assumed a man would be in charge. The joke was on him, however. If he'd ever been in doubt as to his submissive tendencies, they'd disappeared after his interview with Mistress Katrina. The moment she began questioning him from behind that big wooden desk, her tone of voice changed and he felt his heart pick up its pace. She seemed to get a kick out of his reaction, and after a few more questions, she'd shown him around the club.

While Mistress Katrina's dominant nature got his blood pumping, that was where his reaction to her ended. There was no physical attraction. He was confident part of that was because the dungeon mistress was a busty blonde. He preferred leggy brunettes with a little extra cushion in the back end.

Thinking of his first meeting with the club's mistress made him squirm in his seat. She was certainly nothing like he'd expected her to be. Then again, most of the Dommes he'd met weren't what he'd expected. Allison was a perfect example. The Dommes he'd seen in online videos barked orders at their submissives, and seemed to take pleasure in humiliating them at every turn. Allison was nice. Drew had no doubt that, if pushed, she could be hard as nails, but she'd been nothing but pleasant to him. She'd even offered to do a scene with Drew if he wanted. Although it was tempting, he wasn't sure if he was ready for that step yet. For the time being, he was content to watch. Everything was still so new to him.

To be honest, Drew was relieved to discover not all Dommes were like the ones he'd seen online. While he wanted his lover to be in control in the bedroom, public humiliation wasn't on his list of desires. He wanted to serve his partner—to worship her body and mind. Meeting Allison and John gave him hope.

As Drew glanced around the main room, he spotted some familiar faces. It was a typical night. The main room was scattered with people talking and sipping on drinks. Submissives were in various stages of undress. Some were on leashes kneeling on the floor next to their masters or mistresses. Others were sitting beside or on top of their master's or mistress' laps. Mistress Katrina was near the bar talking to a male Dom and his female sub. Drew recognized both of them, but he didn't know their names.

There were also a handful of people Drew had met at the munches he'd attended. While he'd met a few others since coming to the club, the atmosphere was different. Munches were for socializing. Serpent's Kiss was for playing.

The club was divided into sections, which was one of the things Drew liked the most. There were plenty of seating areas scattered around the main floor, as well as a bar along one wall, a small dance floor, and a raised platform. He'd been told the platform was used for demonstrations, but he'd yet to witness one of those since he'd been a member. As for kinky play, very little beyond the occasional spanking or some other light impact play occurred in the main room. Everything else took place upstairs.

A couple of weeks ago, he'd drummed up the courage to climb the stairs and take a look around. The upstairs rooms looked completely different with people in them than they had when Mistress Katrina had shown him around during the club's off hours. The sounds alone charged the atmosphere.

Although Drew didn't consider himself a voyeur, he couldn't help himself. He was drawn into watching some of the scenes. Most of the items in the rooms were things he'd seen online in his initial research into the lifestyle. Some of them appealed to him. Some of them didn't.

Drew had the desire to submit to a mistress, but he wasn't looking for just the physical aspects of submission. Maybe that sounded cheesy, but he'd done the whole sex-only thing in the vanilla world. There was physical gratification, yes, but he'd never truly felt connected to a woman before. Drew knew part of that was his desire to give up control to his partner. He was twenty-eight, and he wanted someone he could share his life with.

As a firefighter, he saw death and tragedy on a regular basis. He didn't want to wake up ten years into the future and still be searching for someone who could give him what he needed. That was why he'd decided to plunge headfirst into this new lifestyle instead of dragging his feet in the regular dating pool. Even still, Drew knew it was going to be an uphill battle. There were more male subs than there were female dominants. Even at the club, there were five male Doms to every one Domme. But as his new friend John had reminded him on multiple occasions, if Drew didn't put himself out there, he'd never find the woman he was searching for.

Drew watched as John sat at his mistress' feet with his head in her lap. It wasn't demeaning in any way. It was affectionate, and Drew wanted that for himself.

Allison moved, getting John's attention. "Get me a drink, my boy."

John was swiftly on his feet. "What would you like, Mistress?"

That was the last of their exchange Drew heard because his attention had shifted to the door. He vaguely registered John leaving the cozy sitting area, but Drew was too focused on the woman who'd walked through the club's main entrance.

The new arrival surveyed the room. From the way she was carrying herself, Drew was almost positive she was a Domme. If he was being honest with himself, he was hoping she was a Domme. Whether she was or not remained to be seen.

She looked to be about five foot six or seven, but the black heels she had on added a good three to four inches to her stature. Her long hair was pulled up into a high ponytail and looked almost black in the dim club lighting. The black corset and jeans she wore accented her curves to the point where Drew was afraid he might be drooling.

Only a few seconds passed before the woman strolled with confidence over to the bar and ordered a drink. Drew continued to stare. She chatted with the bartender for several minutes, even after he'd handed the woman her drink. Drew didn't recognize the woman as anyone who'd been to the club since he'd joined, but the bartender seemed to know her. Of course, that didn't mean anything. For all Drew knew, the mystery woman and the bartender lived next door to each other. Then again, this was a private club. In order to be here, she had to be a member. Especially since she'd come alone.

Drew's eyes followed the woman as she headed to a booth across the room. She sat down with another group of people similar to the one he was with. He recognized most of them. They were all regulars.

Abruptly, John sat down next to him on the couch having returned with his mistress' drink. "I wouldn't get your hopes up."

Drew reluctantly pulled his gaze away from the woman. "What?"

"Don't *what* me. You're staring at Lady Beth."

Then what John said registered. "What do you mean I shouldn't get my hopes up? She is a Domme, right?"

"Oh yes, definitely a Domme."

"She doesn't like male subs?"

"She does." John drew out the two words, and Drew knew there was a 'but' coming.

He sighed, frustrated. "Then what's the issue?"

John lowered his voice to a whisper so no one around them could hear the information he was about to disclose. Drew doubted his friend would tell him anything ninety percent of the club didn't already know, but he decided to play along. One of the first things Drew learned was that word traveled fast in the small community—especially if it was something bad. "She used to come here all the time with her sub, Ben. They'd been together for years, from what I heard, before Mistress and I began getting involved in local events. Then, three months ago, they both suddenly stopped coming. To the club. To munches. Everything."

Drew couldn't help himself. He was intrigued. "What happened?"

"Ben traveled a lot for his business. Sometimes he was out of town for weeks at a time going to all sorts of places. Apparently, his trips weren't business related. At least, not completely. Lady Beth found out he had a wife and daughter in Florida."

"That's insane. It's like something you hear on TV." Drew shook his head, trying to digest the information he'd received.

"I know. He'd lied to her the entire time."

Drew's gaze drifted back to Lady Beth. He couldn't imagine what it would be like to have trust broken in such a way.

John's voice pulled Drew out of his musings. "I don't know if she's ready to dive back into a relationship, man, and I know that's what you want."

It was true. Drew did want a relationship, but he was willing to work for it. One step at a time, right? So the first thing he had to do was find a way to introduce himself.

❧

BETH DAVENPORT TRIED TO IGNORE ALL THE STARES SHE RECEIVED WHEN she entered the club. It had been three months since she'd stepped foot inside Serpent's Kiss. She knew showing up would mean she'd be the hot topic of gossip for the evening. Her best friend and fellow Domme, Nicole, had warned her about the rumors floating around. They were surprisingly accurate as far as rumors went except no one knew how Beth had come to find out about Ben's lies. Only Nicole knew the whole truth, and Beth wanted to keep it that way.

Domme or not, finding out a large portion of the life you'd been living for the last three years was a lie left Beth broken in a lot of ways. She wasn't even sure why she'd come to the club. Oh, that's right. It was Nicole's hounding over the last two weeks. Nicole had insisted three months was enough moping.

Every Friday afternoon for the last month, Nicole had called Beth asking if she was going to put in an appearance at Serpent's Kiss. Each time, Beth had weaseled out of it. Her friend had even enlisted Katrina's help more than once.

The club mistress was a formidable woman in her late forties. She'd been married to a man who wanted no part in her kinky ways. Beth didn't know her back then, but the way the story went was that at forty-four, her husband was diagnosed with a rare form of cancer. He'd died within two months. The sudden change in Katrina's life prompted her to take stock. Six months later, she opened Serpent's Kiss.

While Beth admired Katrina and her take-the-bull-by-the-horns attitude, Beth wasn't sure she was ready to be back at the club. Unfortunately, when Katrina had put her on the spot, Beth hadn't been able to say no. Both Katrina and Nicole had been incredibly supportive after what had happened with Ben. While Beth had no desire to put herself back out into the dating world—it was the last thing she wanted at the moment—Nicole and Katrina had convinced her that she needed to get out and mingle. She had friends here, and it wasn't right for her to turn her back on them because Ben had been a class-A jerk.

So here she was, sitting with Nicole and a group of their friends. Beth was the only Dominant in their group without a sub. It was a little awkward, but she tried to ignore it and have a good time. Nicole was right about one thing, Beth had missed her friends. She wasn't going to let what Ben did tarnish that.

"I think you have an admirer," Nicole whispered in Beth's ear, jarring her from her thoughts.

"What?"

Nicole scooted closer to her. "There's a guy across the room that hasn't been able to take his eyes off you for the last fifteen minutes. I'd say he's interested."

Beth didn't even bother to look. "I'm not."

"Oh, come on. He's hot, and I happen to know he's a sub."

"That doesn't change anything. I'm not ready to get back into the dating pool again."

Her friend rolled her eyes. "Well, you don't have to date him, you know."

She shook her head. "I'm not into playing with random subs and you know it. Even if I was, I don't think I could even do that after everything."

Nicole frowned. "You have to get back on the horse sometime."

Beth sighed in defeat. "I know. Maybe in a month or so—"

Her friend placed a hand on her arm, stopping Beth mid-sentence. "I don't think he's going to wait a month or so. He's coming over."

"What do you mean he's coming over? Here?"

Nicole nodded and turned back to their group, effectively leaving Beth to fend for herself. Taking a deep breath, Beth prepared herself for whatever line this guy was going to try to sell her.

Her heart pounded as she felt him drawing closer, but Beth refused to show any outward signs that she was aware of the man. It would only encourage him.

To her surprise, instead of coming over and trying to sweet-talk her, the guy sat down in the chair to her right and said nothing. It was odd to be sure, but since she wasn't interested in the slightest anyway, Beth decided to ignore him and refocus on her friends' conversation. Maybe he'd eventually get the idea and go away. Or maybe she was only being paranoid and he didn't walk across the room for her at all.

Ignoring him turned out to be more difficult than Beth originally thought. Although he didn't attempt to engage her in conversation, she felt his presence beside her. Even with her eyes purposely averted, Beth knew he wasn't a small man. She'd seen enough in her peripheral vision to know he was tall and nicely proportioned.

No matter how aware she was of his presence, Beth outwardly ignored him. That was until she finished off her drink. She scooted forward in her seat, preparing to head to the bar for a refill, but he moved, too, inevitably drawing her attention. "May I, ma'am?"

Beth tilted her head to look at him for the first time, and all the moisture seemed to disappear from her throat. Cute did not begin to describe the man sitting next to her. He was tall and lean, but she wouldn't call him lanky with his broad shoulders and muscled arms. His hair was a light brown and he was clean-shaven, but it was his eyes that drew her in. They were the most amazing baby blue.

When she didn't respond, he repeated his question. "May I get you a refill on your drink, ma'am?"

"Y-yes." Then, catching herself, she spoke again with more confidence. "Um. No. Thank you. I don't know you from Adam."

He extended his hand. "Drew Parker."

She raised an eyebrow.

"Allison and John will vouch for me. No funny business. I promise." He tilted his head toward another Femdom, Allison, and her longtime boyfriend and sub, John. Beth knew them both, although not well.

Beth waited until Allison looked in her direction, and gave her a questioning look. Allison smiled and nodded.

Reluctantly, Beth handed her glass to the man sitting beside her.

"What would you like?" he asked.

"The bartender knows. Just tell him it's for Beth." Her answer came out more clipped than usual. She wanted him to take his leave as quickly as possible before she went and did something stupid. Beth kept her gaze on him as he walked away. Her stomach was doing flip-flops and she didn't like it one bit.

He returned a few minutes later and handed her a small glass filled with half Coke and half Sprite. Beth rarely drank alcohol, and never at the club. Whenever she came to Serpent's Kiss, she was either playing with Ben or she was alone where she'd have to drive home. Either way, she didn't drink.

After taking the glass from Drew, she turned back to her friends, effectively ignoring her unwanted admirer once more. Nicole had a knowing smirk on her face that Beth desperately wished she could wipe off. Maybe she could borrow one of the club's floggers. It had been a while since she'd thrown one, and she had to admit the thought of having the leather in her hands again was appealing.

For the next hour, Drew continued to sit beside her in silence as she chatted with her friends. Everyone in their small group brought Beth up to date on what was going on in their lives. Meanwhile, her new admirer said nothing. And although he did little more than sit there, he was making her uneasy. Every one of her nerve endings seemed to be aware of him.

Finally, Beth couldn't take it any longer and turned to face him. "I don't know what you're looking for, but let me spell out exactly what I'm *not* looking for. I'm not looking for a submissive and I don't play with random partners."

"I understand." His voice was smooth, and it sent tingles down her spine. This was not good.

She quirked an eyebrow at him. "You understand?"

"Yes, ma'am."

Beth waited for him to leave, but he remained where he was. "So if you know I'm not looking for a relationship or a play partner then why are you sitting here?"

"I'd like to get to know you, if you're agreeable." He sounded sincere.

"You want to be friends?" she asked.

"Yes, ma'am."

"Why?"

He shrugged. "You seem interesting."

Beth gave him a hard look trying to decide if he was telling the truth or not. She never used to question her judgment, but after Ben, everything was different. "Do you have a mistress?"

"No, ma'am. I'm pretty new to the lifestyle."

"How new?"

"A few months." His gaze never left hers.

"Have you ever played with a Femdom before?" Why she was asking was beyond her. It wasn't as if she ever planned on playing with him.

"No, ma'am."

Again, she had no idea why she was pressing for information, but the questions kept coming to the forefront of her mind and she kept asking them. "No vanilla girl out there for you?"

"I've tried vanilla relationships and they don't work for me. I want a woman to take control."

The image of him tied to a bench completely at her mercy flashed in her mind before she squashed it. No. She would not go down that path.

If he wanted to be friends, she could try, she supposed. But there would have to be ground rules—no seeing him outside the club being the number one. She had no idea if he frequented the local munches or not. If so, she would have to be careful. Munches were more laid back. That could open up a whole new set of problems—especially since she was already having a physical reaction to him.

Theirs would have to be a lifestyle friendship only. If Drew had questions about BDSM or needed help finding a Domme, she could maybe give him advice. That was it, though. Beth wasn't ready to get tangled up in another web of emotional attachment.

Taking a deep breath, she offered her hand, and introduced herself. "I'm Beth. Beth Davenport."

He wrapped his fingers around hers almost reverently. "It's nice to meet you, Beth Davenport."

Chapter Two

Drew's alarm woke him bright and early at six. He didn't get in until almost two, and he was feeling it. Originally he'd planned on leaving the club at eleven —he had to work Saturday, after all—but after laying eyes on Beth, getting a full night's sleep became less of a priority. She'd stayed until one thirty, so he had as well. The thought of leaving before her didn't cross his mind.

Padding into his bathroom, Drew stepped into the shower, and turned on the spray. He adjusted the temperature so it was a little cooler than normal hoping it would help wake him up.

As the fog lifted from his brain, he recalled the end of his night. When he'd offered to walk Beth to her car, she'd looked at him with shock, and then panic. He wanted to comfort her, but he was at a loss. She wasn't his mistress. They'd agreed to be friends, and he'd gotten the impression she wasn't entirely comfortable with that much. He had to be cautious. As much as he wanted to touch her, he knew it wouldn't be a good idea.

Drew smiled as he rinsed the shampoo out of his hair. Turning off the water, he grabbed a towel, and swiftly dried himself off. Beth hadn't sent him away. Friendship wasn't exactly what he wanted, but he could work with it. She'd been hurt. He could understand that, too. Drew's last girlfriend, Mya, hadn't understood his need to relinquish control. Although at the time he didn't completely understand it himself, he'd tried to explain it to her. She'd lashed out at him, and they broke up.

Their fight was the driving force behind Drew's exploration into BDSM.

He needed someone who understood what he needed, what he craved. Trying to fake it wasn't working for him anymore.

Drew pulled up to the fire station with five minutes to spare. He parked his car and grabbed his duffel bag from the backseat. He worked in one of the larger stations in St. Louis, and they were in the middle of a shift change. People were coming and going from all directions. Everyone he passed acknowledged him in some way. Being a firefighter was like being part of a large family. Sometimes it even reminded him of a college frat house.

"Parker!"

He whirled around and looked up. Chief Franks was leaning over the second-floor railing. "Morning, Chief."

"I need you to grab your crew and head down to Crawford Street ASAP. Madison's crew is still there holding a scene until an inspector gets there."

"Is the fire out?"

"Yep. All I need you and your guys to do is sit on your pretty asses until the inspector gets there and takes over the scene."

"Arson?"

Chief Franks nodded. "Looks like."

"Let me put my things in my locker, and I'll grab the guys."

Without another word, Chief Franks headed back into his office.

Drew worked his way to the locker room. Baily and Irwin, two of the guys on his crew, were already there. "Hey. We need to grab our gear and head over to Crawford. Shawn and his crew are holding a scene until one of the inspectors show up, and we need to go relieve them."

"The fire's already out?" Baily asked.

" 'Fraid so."

Both Baily and Irwin sighed and shut their locker doors.

Drew focused on putting his own things away. "Do you know if Romeo's made it in yet?"

"Looking for me, Cap?" Eddie Romero—otherwise known as Romeo—strolled into the locker room right on cue.

"Put your things away, and then grab your gear. We've got to go relieve Shawn's crew."

"Fire?"

"It's already been put out, man," Baily said.

Since Drew had an SUV, they all piled in and drove over to the scene. The mood was a lot more somber than it would have been had there still been a fire to fight. As it was, all they would be doing was standing around twiddling their thumbs.

The warehouse was less than five miles from the station. A lot had changed in the area over the last ten years. Most of the old warehouses had been converted into apartments and storefronts. Drew supposed they were lucky the building the arsonist chose was still abandoned.

He parked along the curb behind the truck. His buddy and fellow captain, Shawn, and his crew were lounging against the side, waiting. When he saw Drew pull up, he pushed off the truck and sauntered over to meet them. "I was hoping you'd be the inspector."

"Any idea what's taking so long?" Drew asked as he rounded the vehicle to unload their gear from the back.

"Not a clue. Dispatch said they were on their way, but so far nothing."

With their gear unloaded, Drew handed his car keys over to Shawn. "I guess we wait, then."

Thirty minutes later, they were still waiting. Drew was about to radio dispatch again to see what was going on when a dark blue sedan pulled up in front of the fire truck. A woman exited the vehicle, her head tilted down looking at something. He began striding over to her, not sure who she was or what she was doing at the scene.

She looked up, and Drew nearly tripped over himself. It was Nicole from the club. Beth's friend. And someone he knew for a fact was a Domme. From the way her eyes widened, Drew guessed Nicole was as shocked to see him there as he was to see her.

Nicole recovered quickly and walked toward him. "Good morning, gentlemen."

His crew mumbled hello while Drew got his bearings. He wasn't sure what to say or how he should handle the situation, so he decided to play dumb, remembering what Mistress Katrina had told him about the privacy of the club's members. "Can I help you, ma'am?"

Drew didn't miss her smirk. "Nicole Owens. I just transferred to the Fire Marshal's office. I understand we have a suspected arson."

"You're the fire inspector?"

Amusement lit Nicole's eyes at his question. "Yes."

"Okay." Drew was still shaken, but he knew he needed to buck up and do his job. "Baily, Irwin, stay with the truck. Romeo, you're with me and the inspector."

They spent the next few hours combing through every inch of the building. The pictures, or what he could see of them through the digital camera Nicole was using, downplayed the damage, in Drew's opinion. It looked as if the building had been in the process of being remodeled. All the new internal structure was ruined. The building was only safe to be walking around in because of its brick exterior and the quick reaction time of the responding stations.

Nicole followed them down, out of the building, and back onto the sidewalk. "Thank you for going over everything with me. I think it's safe to say this was arson. I'll get this turned over to bomb and arson so they can take it from here."

Romeo smiled, and Drew realized his friend was smitten with the new fire investigator. Too bad he was married and Nicole was currently spoken for. "It was our pleasure, ma'am."

During their walk through the building, Drew and Nicole had done their best to keep things professional. They spoke when needed, but that was where it ended. It was for that reason the next words out of her mouth stunned him. "I'm starving. What would you guys say to some lunch? I know a little place around the corner."

Before Drew even had a chance to respond, Baily was answering for all of them. "Sounds great. Lead the way."

BETH HAD BEEN RUNNING AROUND LIKE A MAD WOMAN ALL MORNING. SHE hadn't gotten nearly enough sleep, and Tommy showed up late. Of course, the lack of sleep was entirely her own fault. Beth should have left the club well before midnight. She didn't want to dwell too much on why she'd stayed until almost one.

It was a little before noon and the Saturday lunch rush was already in full swing. Half the tables in her café were occupied and they had several patrons at the counter waiting on their orders. What she wouldn't do for a break, or even better a nap, right about now. Too bad that wasn't likely to happen in the next two hours. Lucky for her it wasn't a weekday. They were so busy sometimes during the week that she didn't make it home until almost dinnertime.

She piled the roast beef on a slice of still warm rye bread. Most of Beth and Tommy's customers were locals. They were lucky. Even on Saturdays they were usually busy. With the revitalization going on in the area, they were hoping to stay that way for many years to come.

The bell above the door jingled announcing another customer, and Beth tried to hurry. Getting behind would only make it worse.

"Hey, B. You have a visitor," Tommy yelled.

Beth sighed. She hated when he called her that, but telling him did no good whatsoever. Tommy was twenty-three and felt the need to give everyone a nickname. She had to admit B was better than the first nickname he'd come up with for her—Bumble Bee.

Cutting the sandwich in half, Beth placed it along with chips and a homemade pickle on a plate and brought it out with her to give to Mr. Keller. "Here you go."

He smiled back at her and took the sandwich. "Thank you, dear."

Beth wiped her hands on her apron and started toward the counter where Tommy was chatting with someone. When she saw who it was, she grinned.

Then Beth noticed the man standing behind Nicole. Drew Parker.

No. No, no, no, no. This was not supposed to happen. He wasn't supposed to be here. He wasn't supposed to know anything about her life outside the club . . . the lifestyle.

The only thing that made her feel a little better was the look on Drew's face. Clearly, he hadn't been expecting to see Beth any more than she'd been expecting to see him.

"Nicole. What are you doing here?" Beth asked through gritted teeth.

Her friend acted as if nothing were amiss. "We were working in the area and got hungry. I told Captain Parker and his crew that I knew of a great place for lunch, so here we are."

Beth was going to strangle her.

Putting on her best hostess smile, she tried to keep the irritation out of her voice. "What can I get you?"

Nicole ordered her usual, turkey on wheat, and then stepped aside so Drew could order. Beth tried really hard not to react to him, but it was impossible. Her heart was hammering in her chest. She hadn't missed that he was wearing a polo shirt with the St. Louis Fire Department logo on it. They hadn't talked about jobs the night before. Beth wasn't sure how she felt about him being a firefighter.

That thought brought her up short. What the heck was she doing? What did it matter if he was a firefighter or not? It was his life. It had nothing to do with her.

"Hi," Drew said.

"Hello." She adjusted the straws displayed on the counter, and then stopped herself. Why was she fidgeting?

He smiled and cleared his throat. "I've never been here before. What's good?"

"Everything's good. We bake all our breads and pastries fresh daily."

"Hmm." Drew glanced up at the menu behind the counter. "I think I'll try the pulled pork."

"Make that two," the man standing behind him said. The sad part was, Beth had completely forgotten about the rest of them.

"Sure. Two pulled pork sandwiches coming right up." Beth swallowed and looked to the other two men. "And what can I get you two?"

The one on the far left spoke up first. "I'll take a roast beef sandwich."

"Turkey, please, ma'am," the blonde said. In response, his buddy rolled his eyes.

Beth nodded absentmindedly. All she wanted to do was get out of there as soon as possible. "I'll be out in a few minutes with those."

Disappearing into the back, Beth helped Tommy with the sandwiches, and then made him take them out front. She hid in the kitchen until Tommy yelled for her again. "I'm busy."

"Oh no, you're not." Beth looked up to find Nicole standing right inside the kitchen with her hands on her hips.

Reaching for the nearest towel, Beth began tidying up. "Yes, I am. Tommy was late this morning, and we're behind. I'd like to get out of here at a decent time today."

Nicole propped her hip against the metal counter less than a foot away from where Beth was pretending to clean. "That may be true, but it's never stopped you from coming out to visit me for a few minutes."

"You have people with you today. You don't need me interrupting."

Her friend shook her head and clicked her tongue in disapproval. "You can't fool me, Beth Davenport. The only reason you're hiding in here like a chicken is because of that man out there."

"I don't know what you're talking about."

Nicole went on as if Beth hadn't said anything. "Which tells me that, as much as you claim to have no interest in him, you do. A lot of interest, if I'm not mistaken. So stop being a coward and go out and say hi to the man."

Beth dropped the towel and hunched her shoulders. "It's not that easy."

"Oh sweetie, yes it is. He's not Ben."

"You don't know that. You don't know any more about him than I do."

Nicole edged closer. "I know he's been a firefighter for seven years and was recently promoted to captain. I know he's got an eye for detail. When we walked through a building today, he spotted a few things that both me and his buddy missed. And I know from the looks he was giving you last night and how he kept glancing over his shoulder to see if he could catch a glimpse of you throughout lunch that he's interested."

"I can't. I'm sorry. I know you mean well, but I just can't. It's too soon."

Her friend sighed. "Okay. I don't agree with you, but . . ."

"Thank you."

"Well, I'd better get back out there. Don't want them to think I ditched them or something." Nicole winked and turned to go.

"Nicole?"

"Yes?"

"You don't think he'd say anything, do you? I mean, he's new. He knows not to . . . I mean . . ."

Nicole grinned. "I don't think he'll say anything. We were both shocked when we met this morning. I figured if he was going to let the cat out of the bag, he would have done it then. He didn't say anything. Didn't even act like we knew each other. I'd say you're safe."

"Okay."

"Anything else?"

"Yeah. If you ever pull anything like this again, I'm going to ask to use Katrina's cat-o'-nines."

Nicole laughed and ducked out of the kitchen. "You'd have to catch me first."

Beth threw the towel in her friend's direction. She missed, and it landed on the tile floor a few feet shy of the doorway. Sighing, Beth ambled across the room to retrieve the towel. Throwing it in the hamper, she went to the closet to get a clean one.

The door closed behind her and she was alone in the small supply closet. Instead of going to the back of the room, she lowered herself onto the step stool they kept right inside the door. Moisture welled up in her eyes, and before Beth knew it, she was crying uncontrollably. It made no sense, and yet it did. The tears weren't for Ben or her lost relationship. Beth was scared. Terrified. Nicole was right. Drew was interested, and Beth couldn't deny she was attracted to him as well. And he was a sub. It should be perfect. It would be perfect if not for the nightmare she'd experienced with Ben.

She wiped at the tears, but for every one she banished two more came in its place. Interested or not, Beth couldn't risk it. If Drew hurt her, she didn't know if she'd be able to survive it. Ben, and his wife and daughter, nearly killed her. Beth took her role as a mistress seriously. It wasn't a game to her. She not only wanted the physical connection it provided, but the emotional one as well. Beth had loved and trusted Ben, and he'd taken both and trampled it.

There was a knock on the door, and Beth jumped up. "B? You in there?"

She rushed to the back of the room to get the towel she'd originally come to retrieve. "Yeah. I'm just getting a clean towel. I'll be there in a minute. You need some help with something?"

When she emerged from the storage room, Tommy was washing dishes. He paused mid wipe, and frowned. "Are you all right?"

Beth knew she must look a mess. She quickly turned her back to him. "I'm fine. Did you need me to watch the counter for a while?"

"Beth?"

"Hmm?"

"It's two thirty. There's only a few tables left, and they're finishing up."

She glanced at the clock on the far wall. Sure enough, it was two thirty. Beth had been in that supply closet for almost two hours.

"Are you sure you're okay?" Tommy asked.

Beth nodded. "Yeah. I'm fine. Really. I'll just go check on the tables we have left and then I'll be back to help you."

Tommy was right. Guests at one table were getting up, and the other two were almost finished with their lunches. Beth walked over and asked if she could get them anything else. It was the least she could do after abandoning Tommy and her business for two hours.

Chapter Three

Beth felt horrible. Tommy had been swamped with customers throughout the lunch rush. So much so that he didn't have time to search for her. Luckily, since it was a Saturday, most of the lunch-goers were regulars. She had no idea what would have happened if she'd flaked during a weekday.

As soon as the last customer was out the door, Beth sent Tommy home. He'd protested, of course, but she put her foot down and made him leave. Besides, she needed a little time to herself.

It took her twice as long to wipe everything down and prep for Tuesday. Most of it was mindless work—cleaning surfaces, filling containers. Things she could do in her sleep. It gave her way too much time to think.

Drew had been in her café. He knew where she worked. And thanks to Nicole, he'd breached the careful boundary Beth had placed upon their relationship without even trying.

Nicole. Beth was still cursing her best friend. Then again, maybe she should be rethinking their entire friendship after Nicole threw Beth under the proverbial bus. She didn't understand why Nicole was pushing so hard for her to get back in the dating scene. It wasn't as if she had a vested interest in anything. It was Beth's life, after all.

By the time she headed home, Beth was on edge. She'd promised Nicole she'd put in an appearance at Serpent's Kiss later, but she was rethinking that plan. All she wanted to do was go home and curl up on the couch with a bowl of ice cream.

Beth was still debating the issue three hours later when there was a knock on her front door. It was Nicole. "What are you doing here?"

Nicole brushed past Beth into the two-story house. She'd bought it the year before as a present to herself for her café making it past the five-year mark. At the time, Beth had envisioned kids running through the house laughing—kids she'd planned to one day have with Ben. Realizing having children might never happen for her was depressing. She was thirty years old with no real prospects on the horizon.

The memory of Drew sitting beside her the night before flashed in front of her eyes. Her pulse began to race thinking about him. It was crazy. Nuts. She had to be out of her mind reacting like this to a man she didn't even know.

"Penny for your thoughts?" Nicole asked.

Beth shut the front door and forced the memory of Drew out of her head. She leveled a not-so-pleasant look at her friend. "I'm thinking of all the ways I can torture you for the stunt you pulled today. What the hell were you thinking bringing him to my café?"

Nicole shrugged as if it were no big deal. "We were in the area and it was lunchtime. Where else would I take them?"

"Why not let them fend for themselves? They seem capable enough. I'm sure they could handle it all on their own."

Her friend chuckled. "I'm sure they could. But where would be the fun in that?"

Beth threw her hands up. "Why are you doing this?"

"I don't know what you're talking about. Doing what?"

"Trying to throw this guy at me."

Nicole turned on her heel and headed in the direction of Beth's bedroom. "Did you already have something picked out to wear tonight?"

Beth followed. "I haven't decided if I'm going or not. And stop avoiding the question."

"I'm not avoiding anything. What I'm doing is making sure you get out of this house and back into the land of the living."

Nicole's comment hit its mark. Beth had been living like a hermit these last three months. When she wasn't at the café, she could usually be found at home, sitting in front of the television. Beth couldn't say how many movies she'd watched in that time. More than she'd probably watched the first thirty years of her life.

"I'm not ready." It sounded feeble even to Beth's ears.

Her friend threw several items onto the bed, and lowered herself to the floor to go through Beth's shoe selection. "No one says you have to do anything more than socialize. Not even with Drew, although I could tell by the way you reacted to him last night and today he must do something for you. Be that as it may, Drew's working tonight so he won't be there. You're safe."

For some reason that made Beth feel better. She wasn't ready to see him again.

"Besides, I need some company. Jeff had to go help his sister move into a new apartment, so I'm on my own tonight."

Beth sighed and picked up the dress Nicole had selected. It was sexy, but certainly not the most provocative thing Beth owned. "Girls' night?"

Nicole smiled. "Girls' night. Now come on. Katrina is giving a demonstration tonight, and I don't want to miss it."

❧

AN HOUR AND A HALF LATER, BETH WAS SITTING IN THE CLUB'S MAIN ROOM with a drink in her right hand. The furniture had been rearranged for the evening's activities. While they were waiting, a few people wandered over to say hi. Everyone was friendly, saying they were glad to see her back.

It wasn't until Nicole got up to get another drink that Daniel, a Dom in his early fifties, came to say hello.

Beth smiled when he lowered himself into the chair beside her. "How have you been?"

"Can't complain. What about you? It's good to see you back."

Daniel was one of the nicest men Beth had ever met. He'd been in the lifestyle for over twenty years, and he was full of helpful advice. It was too bad she wasn't a submissive. Daniel was one of the few men Beth trusted.

"I'm good."

He raised one eyebrow. Beth had seen him give that look to subs many times.

"I am. The café is doing well. I'm keeping busy." Beth took a sip of her drink.

Daniel didn't beat around the bush. "Have you heard from him?"

Beth didn't need Daniel to clarify who 'he' was. She knew he was referring to Ben. "No. Not since I kicked him out."

He nodded. "Maybe I shouldn't say anything, but if it were me, I'd want to know. He came by the club about two months ago."

Beth spat out her drink.

"Don't worry. Katrina asked him to leave and made it very clear he was no longer welcome. In fact, I think she promised him the end of her whip should he make another appearance." Daniel grinned.

Although Beth knew she shouldn't ask, she couldn't help herself. "What did he want?"

Daniel shrugged. "No idea. Katrina didn't let him get more than a few feet inside the door. The only reason I know as much as I do is because she asked Sam and I to back her up."

Beth rolled the glass between her hands, looking down into the dark brown liquid. "Thanks for telling me."

Nicole sat down on the other side of Beth. "Hey, Daniel."

"Nicole. How's the new job?"

"One word: paperwork."

They all laughed.

Before any more could be said, the lights dimmed and Katrina made her way to the front of the room. "Thank you all for coming to our demonstration tonight. We've had a number of individuals ask about wax play, so tonight we're going to go over all the dos and don'ts. I'll stop periodically to see if there are any questions, but I ask that everyone please wait until those specific times so as not to break my, or my submissive's, concentration during the scene."

Katrina motioned toward a man who had been standing off to the side. He looked to be about Beth's age, maybe a little younger. Beth had never seen him before, which surprised her. Katrina didn't have a single submissive she regularly played with but in the past she'd usually used Ryan for stuff like this. Then again, Beth had been out of the loop for a while. Maybe things had changed.

The man walked over and knelt down in front of Katrina. She walked around the man, taking her time. Once behind him, Katrina ran a hand down the length of his back, and then back up into his short-cropped hair. "As with many other forms of play, touch is extremely important. It can tell you things you might miss otherwise. Is your sub tense? Are they scared? Excited? Learning to read your partner is one of the greatest gifts you can give yourself and them."

She moved to retake a position in front of him. "Go lie facing up on the table, Wes."

The man stood and strolled over to the table. Doing as he was told, he lay down with his back on the padded surface.

As Beth continued to watch the scene, she couldn't help but think about

Drew. What would he look like laid out like that? Did he have as many muscles under his shirt as he seemed? What would he feel like under her hands?

Wes sucked in a deep breath as the wax hit his chest. Other than that, however, he didn't react. Knowing Katrina as Beth did, she smirked as the club mistress redirected the candle lower. Wes cried out as hot wax dripped down his stomach to his cock. It was fully erect. He was obviously enjoying Katrina's torture. From the look on her face, Katrina was having fun as well.

"I might have to try that," Nicole whispered.

Beth snorted, but otherwise let it go. Her mind was still on Drew. Nicole said he was working. He could be out fighting a fire as they sat there watching Katrina hold a burning candle over her willing victim.

Without thinking, Beth sent up a silent prayer Drew would be kept safe. She wasn't sure she wanted a relationship with him, but she was quite certain she didn't want to see him harmed either.

৩৩৩

DREW DIDN'T HAVE MUCH TIME TO THINK ABOUT BETH DURING HIS SHIFT. They'd not been back fifteen minutes on Saturday afternoon before they were called out to a car accident. Once they got that cleaned up, the guys headed back to the station. They were less than a minute away when the call came in for a small grease fire.

By the time they got back and cleaned their gear, they were all ready for some downtime. Unfortunately, there was still work to be done. His lack of sleep the night before was beginning to wear on him. As soon as the clock struck nine thirty, Drew made a beeline for his cot, and crashed. Lucky for him, the next call didn't come until four hours later. He rolled out of his bunk and hit the ground running.

Shawn cornered him the next morning. "I heard it was a busy shift."

"All minor stuff." Drew shrugged. It had kept him occupied. That was probably a good thing.

"So. What's with you and the lady at the café?" The two of them were alone, but they wouldn't be for long.

"Nothing."

"Sure. I heard you were craning your neck all throughout lunch trying to get another glimpse of her. You gonna ask her out?"

"Gonna ask who out?" Johnson, one of the stations EMTs, asked.

Two other guys followed Johnson in and Drew became the center of attention.

Drew sighed. The last thing he wanted was to draw the guys into this. For one thing, he couldn't explain how he knew Beth. Or how he knew she wouldn't be thrilled if he asked her out.

Before he could figure out how to answer, Shawn did it for him. "Parker here had to babysit a scene yesterday until the inspector got there, and apparently the new inspector took them all to lunch at this little café. Rumor has it he was taken with the woman behind the counter."

"Was she hot?" Martinez asked.

Romeo chose that moment to join the conversation. "An eight or a nine, I'd say."

The guys whistled.

Drew shook his head. It was useless. "I'm outta here. See you guys tomorrow."

On his way home, Drew took a detour and drove by the café. All the lights were out and the doors locked. According to the sign, they were closed on Sundays and Mondays.

He wasn't sure if he was disappointed or relieved. Drew wanted to see Beth again, but what exactly would he say? He supposed he could apologize for the day before, but even that sounded lame. Nicole had blindsided them both.

Drew didn't know what to make of Nicole. Never in his wildest imagination had he dreamed of running into her, or anyone else from the club for that matter, on the job. Maybe that was naïve of him, but it had thrown him for a loop.

He had done his best to remain professional throughout their examination of the building. She hadn't brought up their connection, even when Romeo was out of earshot. Katrina had explained to him the importance of privacy for many of the club's members when he'd joined. He was completely on board with that. Drew couldn't imagine the ribbing he'd get from the guys if they ever found out he wanted a woman to dominate him. He'd never live it down.

The week seemed to drag. It had nothing to do with work. They had plenty of calls to keep them busy. Most of them were medical, but something was better than nothing.

Drew did a lot of thinking over the course of the week, and most of it revolved around Beth. It had been a while since he'd pursued a woman. Being a firefighter had its perks. When he was younger, it was great. Find a pretty woman in a bar, tell her how you rushed into a building and saved someone's life, and more often than not, she was enamored.

It was great for the first five years or so. He'd been more concerned with getting laid than finding a long-term relationship. Drew wasn't sure if it was because he was getting older or not, but he was ready for something more meaningful. He didn't want to wake up ten years into the future and not have someone waiting for him at home. He wanted a wife—a family. Was Beth the right woman? He didn't know, but he wanted to find out.

Friday night Drew put on his best black jeans and a dark blue T-shirt his ex-girlfriend always said made his eyes pop. He was hoping Beth would be at the club. Drew still wasn't quite sure how to cross that line Beth had drawn in the sand regarding their relationship, but he knew he had to figure out something.

The first thing he did when he walked in the door of Serpent's Kiss was look for Beth. It took a minute, but he found her in the corner laughing with Katrina. Drew smiled. She looked happy. Relaxed.

As if Beth could feel his eyes on her, she turned her head in his direction. Her smile faltered, and his heart sank. She wasn't pleased to see him.

A second later, Nicole was in front of him. "Don't get discouraged."

He blinked. "What?"

"Beth. Don't let her attitude discourage you."

"Oh. Okay."

Nicole smirked. "Come. Let's get a drink."

Without a better option, Drew allowed Nicole to lead him across the room to the bar. She ordered herself a drink, and he did the same.

They found two bar stools and sat down. "You handled last Saturday well. If I didn't know any better, I would have thought we'd never met."

"Well, we hadn't. Not officially."

She smiled. "True."

The bartender placed their drinks in front of them, and Nicole twirled the little umbrella between her fingers. "What are your intentions, Drew Parker?"

He nearly choked on his drink. "Excuse me?"

"You heard me. I'm sure you've heard Beth's story. Or at least part of it. I don't want to see her hurt. So I'll ask again. What are your intentions?"

Drew thought for a moment. He could refuse to answer, but he wasn't sure that was the best idea. So far, Nicole had been his best ally. "I want to ask her out."

"And?"

"And I don't know. As I'm sure you know, I'm new to this. I don't really know what comes next. Or if I'm overstepping some unwritten rule. All I know is that I'm attracted to her. I'd like to see if there's more."

"Are you looking for a relationship, or someone to scratch your itch?" Nicole asked.

Drew had to hand it to her. She wasn't pulling any punches. "I'm looking for a relationship. Is Beth that woman? I don't know yet."

Nicole took a sip of her drink and grinned. "Fair enough. And honest. Okay, I'll help you. But if you break her heart, I'll break your balls. Got it?"

The look she gave Drew had him swallowing nervously. He had no doubt she meant it. "Got it."

"Good. Now, go mingle with your friends. In about an hour, find her and say hi. Keep it light."

"Anything else?" he asked.

She slid off the stool and patted him on the back. "Turn on that firefighter charm all you boys are famous for. It might make a small dent in that wall of hers."

Drew snorted, and watched as Nicole strolled across the room to join Beth and Katrina. They spoke for a few minutes before the club owner excused herself. Beth leaned in and whispered something to Nicole. He figured Beth wasn't happy he and Nicole had been chatting.

Following Nicole's advice, Drew went to find John and Allison. They were upstairs watching a scene in one of the semiprivate rooms. The Dom had his submissive in a spread-eagle on a Saint Andrew's cross. It was obvious he'd been working on her for a while. Her back and ass were red, and he was in the process of inserting a butt plug.

"You made it." John smiled, and nodded toward the large viewing window. "Mistress wanted to see the scene. You just missed the flogging. Very intense."

"Looks like it."

"Daniel is one of the best at flogging, especially Florentine," Allison supplied.

They stood there watching the rest of the scene, which concluded with the sub hanging limp in her bindings after several screaming orgasms. By the time it was over, Drew was hard as a rock. He knew he couldn't seek out Beth with his cock straining against his jeans.

He excused himself and headed back downstairs. Instead of going into the main room, he turned the corner, and found a spot along the wall. He leaned back against the vertical surface and took several deep breaths. He had to calm down—a difficult feat in a club shrouded in sex.

It took a while, but he got himself under control. He strolled out into the main room of the club and scanned for Beth. She was sitting next to Nicole near the center of the room.

Taking his time, he made his way over to her. "Hello again."

Beth glanced up.

He wasn't sure what to make of the look on her face. "May I sit down?"

"Um. Sure."

"Thanks." Drew sat beside Beth on one of the love seats. "How have you been?"

Instead of answering, she said, "You didn't tell me you were a firefighter."

"No. I suppose I didn't. You didn't tell me you worked in a café either."

"I don't work there. I own it." Her voice held an edge he didn't understand.

"Impressive. The food was great, by the way." He had no idea what had caused her sour mood.

Beth relaxed her shoulders a little. "Thank you."

"So are you going to answer my question?" he asked.

"And which question is that?"

He smiled. "How have you been?"

She glanced down at his crotch. Drew didn't need to follow her gaze—he already knew what she would see. He was hard again. Not as bad as he'd been after watching the scene, but enough that it would be noticeable.

Beth smirked. "Probably a little better than you at the moment."

Chapter Four

Beth was having difficulty containing her amusement. As she continued to stare at Drew's lap, the bulge in his jeans became more pronounced. She knew she should probably look away, but she was enjoying the show too much.

"Sorry. I was watching a scene upstairs. Guess I'm still a little worked up."

She forced herself to meet his gaze. He seemed embarrassed, although she couldn't fathom why. Most of the males walked around the club in various stages of arousal. It was par for the course given the club's vibe.

Beth knew she should let it go, but she couldn't help herself. "And what about the scene had you worked up?"

He shrugged. "I don't know. The whole thing, I suppose."

"Do you know who it was?"

"I don't know the Dom's name, but I've seen him around the club. I didn't recognize the submissive. John said I missed a pretty impressive flogging."

Although Beth was curious to know more of the specifics, and to dig deeper into what had aroused him about the scene, she let the subject drop. She was already having too many thoughts of her own about what she'd like to do to Drew. The last thing she needed was to add to it.

Silence stretched between them for several minutes. That didn't mean she wasn't extremely aware of him. She'd been too aware of him from the moment he'd sat down beside her.

Beth was scrambling, trying to figure out how to break the lull in conversation when he cleared his throat. "So what do you like to do for fun? When you're not here at the club, I mean."

As topics went, Beth figured this was a relatively safe one. "I like history."

"History?" His eyes widened in shock.

"Not what you were expecting?"

"No, it's just . . ." He shook his head. "Okay, yeah, I wasn't expecting that."

"I'm sure there are a lot of things about me that would surprise you." As soon as the words left her mouth, Beth wished she could take them back. She didn't need to be flirting. It would only encourage him, and that's not what she wanted.

He smiled, and her stomach did a little flip. "I'm sure there are."

Beth needed to regain control of the conversation, and fast. "What about you? What do you like to do when you're not here or out fighting fires?"

"Anything outdoors—hiking, camping, that sort of thing. Have you ever been camping?" he asked.

"Not since I was ten. That's when I started realizing the importance of dry clothes and a warm bed." Beth cringed again. Why did she keep putting her foot in her mouth?

Drew grinned. "The last part is only an issue if you're sleeping alone."

"Well, seeing as how that would be the case, I don't see where it matters." Her words came out sharper than they should have.

"I'm sorry. Did I say something wrong?" He was frowning, and Beth hated to admit how much she wanted to see him smiling again.

She sighed. "Drew, we can't be anything more than friends."

"I know."

"Do you?" she countered.

"Yes."

Beth raised her eyebrows, broadcasting her doubt.

He met her gaze. "I'm not going to lie."

"That's good, because I detest liars."

Drew nodded. "Would I like to take you out on a date? Yes. But if friendship is all you're offering, then I'll take it."

She wasn't sure what to make of his statement. Was he telling the truth, or was it only a ploy to get her to let her guard down? "Why?"

"Why what?"

Was he intentionally being dense? "Why would you be okay with friendship? And why are you wasting your time sitting here with me when you could be off finding yourself a Domme?"

He shrugged. "I enjoy talking to you."

Beth was expecting him to elaborate, but he didn't. "Are you not interested in finding a mistress? If you sit here all night talking to me, that isn't likely to happen."

Drew smirked. "I'll take my chances."

She looked him over, head to toe. "Are you sure you're a sub?"

"Pretty sure, yeah. Why?"

Beth was trying to figure out a nice way to say it, but decided to throw caution to the wind. There was no reason to hold back. She was who she was, and if he didn't like it, he could take himself somewhere else. "Because you're awfully cocky for a submissive."

He laughed. "That's probably the firefighter in me. We tend to be a rather cocky bunch."

If what he said were true, whomever his mistress ended up being would have her hands full. Too bad it wouldn't be her. "How did you decide to become a firefighter?"

His smile grew wider. "I used to go camping with my dad when I was younger. By the time I was eight, I was begging him to let me build the fire. I'd take my time, making sure it was just right, and then once I had it perfect I'd sit there and watch it burn until my dad would tell me it was time to turn in. Dad said I was so fascinated with fire I'd either grow up to be a firefighter or an arsonist."

"I'm betting he's happy you chose firefighter."

"Yeah." Drew chuckled. "So what about you? What made you want to own a café?"

She began to relax. This was the kind of stuff friends talked about. This was safe. "That's a long story."

He shifted his weight, which brought their legs closer together. "I've got time."

Beth hated to admit it, but she was more aware of him than she'd like—even when having such a mundane conversation. "Um. Well, the short version?"

"Sure."

"I used to work in a bakery, but after the owner died it closed up. I was trying to figure out what to do with myself. One day I was having lunch with a friend at a little restaurant across town. When they brought out our sandwiches, they were less than stellar."

"And you thought you could do better?" Drew asked.

"Not exactly. My friend thought I could. And by the end of our lunch, she had me thinking seriously about opening up my own place."

He grinned. "And you did."

Beth couldn't help but grin back. "I did. It was the best decision I ever made. Lots of hard work, but definitely worth it."

Drew cleared his throat. "I should apologize for last week—for just showing up in your café like that. I had no idea you'd be there."

Beth sighed. "I know you didn't. It's fine."

"So you're all right with me maybe stopping in to get a bite to eat once in a while?"

Was she? To tell him no would be rude, but look at what happened the last time. She'd ended up hiding out in the supply closet for two hours.

"That was the wrong thing to ask, wasn't it?"

"No. I mean, of course it's fine. Why wouldn't it be?" Oh, maybe because his appearance had thrown her off for the rest of the day? She couldn't tell him that, though.

"Okay. Good. I'm glad." He gave her a smile that had her heart racing.

"Nicole told me you've been a member of the club for a little over a month." She needed to get their conversation back on track.

"Yes. It's been a good experience so far."

"You said you're new to BDSM."

"That's right."

Before either of them could say any more, Nicole sat down across from them. "My feet are killing me. I never should have worn these new boots."

"That's why you never play in new shoes," Beth said.

Nicole slipped off one of her boots and began massaging her arch. Her submissive, Jeff, appeared a moment later with a drink for her. She took a sip and sighed. "Thank you, love. That's just what I needed."

Without words, she lifted her foot slightly and rotated it. Jeff got the message and lowered himself to the floor. He adjusted Nicole's foot so that it was resting in his lap, and he began gently kneading her flesh.

The rest of the evening was spent with the four of them talking about an upcoming spanking event scheduled the following week. Nicole and Jeff dominated the bulk of the conversation. Spanking was one of their main kinks, and both of them were looking forward to the event.

While Beth enjoyed spanking, she didn't get as into it as some of the other Femdoms. There were other things one could do to a sub that were a lot more fun, in her opinion.

As the conversation continued, she found herself watching Drew's reactions. He seemed interested. Beth wondered if he'd ever had an erotic spanking before. It was a foolish train of thought, but one she was beginning to realize was inevitable. She was attracted to him. No matter how much she tried to deny it, facts were facts. That didn't mean she had to act on it.

By midnight, Beth was ready to call it a night. Like last weekend, Drew offered to walk her to her car. She opened the driver side door and turned around to face him. "Thank you for the escort."

Drew smiled. "You're welcome."

There was a moment of tension before Beth broke it by sliding behind the wheel. "Good night, Drew."

"Good night, Beth."

❧

Drew continued to replay the conversation he had with Beth in his head the next day as he did some laundry and tidied up his apartment. Was he being too aggressive in his pursuit of her? Did that make him less of a submissive? He didn't know the answer to that.

But what was the alternative? Beth had made it clear she wasn't interested in anything more than friendship. He, of course, was, and Beth knew that. Still, he'd been honest. If friendship was all she was comfortable giving him, then he'd take it and hope she grew to trust him enough to make herself vulnerable again.

As the day wore on, he grew more and more restless and all he could think about was going to the club again that night. Would she be there? And if so, would she be happy to see him? He didn't know the answer to either of those questions and it was slowly driving him insane. Maybe he was more of a masochist than he thought.

All his worrying had been for nothing. When he arrived at the club a little after eight, he realized Beth wasn't there. By nine thirty, he knew she wasn't coming. Whether or not that had anything to do with him, he didn't know. He hoped not.

By the time Monday rolled around and he returned to the station for his next shift, he was running scenarios in his head of what he'd do the next time he saw her—what he'd say. His mind was so full of Beth it had taken him twice as long to finish the paperwork on his desk. Most of the guys hated this part of the job, but Drew didn't mind it. Not usually. The thing with Beth was playing havoc with his brain, though. He couldn't concentrate.

As he was settling into his cot for the night, he remembered how she'd smiled when he told her about camping with his dad. Beth was beautiful—and even more so when she let her guard down.

Although there'd been some tension on Friday night, it was less than the week before. He wondered if that would have held true had Nicole not interrupted them. It seemed as if Beth was more comfortable keeping the conversation casual. Anytime it began getting too personal she would tense up, which was the last thing he wanted. Then again, he also wanted to know everything about her.

Taking a deep breath, Drew tried to push his inquiries out of his mind. He needed to rest. It was already after midnight.

Unfortunately, his sleep was interrupted two hours later by the alarm. Jumping out of bed, he joined the rest of his crew down on the main floor as they donned their gear. Although they'd all been awakened from sleep, it didn't take long for the adrenaline to take over as word came over the radio from dispatch about the blaze. They were sending eight trucks, which meant it had to be of significant size. It would probably keep them busy for the rest of the night.

Sure enough, Drew and the other firefighters on the scene spent the next four hours putting out the flames and making sure all the hot spots were extinguished. He hadn't been able to spend much time analyzing the burn patterns, but given the location and what little he'd seen, Drew wouldn't be surprised if it turned out to be another target of the arsonist.

By six, the scene was secure, a fire inspector was on scene, and they were ready to head back. Drew grabbed hold of the rigging to pull himself up onto the truck when his gaze landed on two people watching from about three blocks away. Even though she was wearing a pink apron with what looked to be flowers, he recognized her instantly.

Hopping down from the truck, he hollered to the guys that he'd be right back, and then jogged over to where Beth stood. "Hi."

"Hi." Her eyes were wide, although her voice was steady.

He looked down at himself and took in all the soot. Only then did it occur to him how he must look after spending the last four hours inside a burning building. He shouldn't have crossed the street to her. "I'm quite a sight, aren't I?"

It was the young man beside her who answered. "We couldn't believe it when we came into work this morning. I wasn't sure I would even be able to get to the café with the roads blocked off."

Drew didn't want to take his eyes off Beth, but he didn't want to be rude either. "Yeah, it was a hot one, that's for sure. It was safer to keep everyone back until we got it under control."

"Was it the arsonist?" Beth asked.

"Too early to tell." Of course she would know about the arsonist. She was friends with Nicole. Besides, it wasn't as if they could keep something like this out of the news. Several camera crews were on scene during the fire, but luckily, the officers who responded had kept them away from the action.

She nodded.

"I should probably get back. Need to get the truck ready to go before the next shift comes on at eight."

"Cool." There was a little more enthusiasm in the young man's voice than was warranted. Drew could see a bit of hero worship in the man's eyes as well.

Drew turned to go. He'd taken two steps when Beth stopped him. "Drew?"

He met her gaze, and realized there was still something about the way she was looking at him. "Yeah?"

"I have some muffins about to go in the oven. They should be ready in a half hour or so. If you're free."

A slow smile spread across his face. "Good to know. Thanks."

"Yo, Parker. Come on man. You can flirt on your own time," Baily yelled from inside the fire engine. His voice echoed off the surrounding buildings even from so far away.

Drew took another long look at Beth, and then hustled to rejoin his crew. The whole way back to the station he couldn't wipe the cheesy grin off his face. Beth had invited him to return to her café for muffins after his shift. He tried to remind himself not to get his hopes up—it was only breakfast. It didn't mean anything. Maybe if one of the other guys had trotted down the street she would have extended the same invitation.

Even as the thought crossed his mind, he knew it wasn't true. He could maybe see her handing out something already made as a thank you, or even offering to have all the guys stop in later, but that's not what she'd done. She'd given him a personal invitation.

With that in mind, he worked quickly to clean and stow his gear so he could head back over to Beth's café as soon as possible. His crew noticed his rush and had to give him a hard time about it. He laughed it off and concentrated on what he was doing.

It was after eight thirty before Drew made it back to the café. He'd had to take a shower, which slowed him down, but he didn't want to show up smelling, and looking, like a burnt piece of charcoal.

He opened the door and walked into the brightly lit space. There were a handful of customers seated at the small tables, and one at the counter talking to the young man who'd been standing beside Beth earlier. As Drew strolled toward him, he noticed the man was wearing a nametag that said Tommy.

"Hey, you made it," Tommy said, catching sight of Drew.

"I couldn't turn down the offer of fresh baked muffins, could I?"

"Beth makes the best muffins," said the woman standing beside him, waiting for her order.

"Is that so?" Drew had to admit he was curious as to what this woman had to say. Clearly, she wasn't a first-time customer. The way she said Beth's name was too casual.

"Oh, gosh, yes. There's nothing like one of her blueberry muffins hot out of the oven and a cup of coffee. The best way to start your day, I tell ya."

Drew's stomach took that moment to protest. He hadn't had anything to eat since dinner the previous night.

The woman giggled as Tommy handed her a brown paper bag. She patted Drew's arm as she went to leave. "Get one of the cinnamon rolls. I promise you won't regret it."

With the woman gone, Drew turned his attention back to Tommy. "You have some loyal customers."

"Beth does. She has a talent for baking. I just help her out and follow her recipes."

Although he knew he shouldn't, Drew had to ask. "Have you two been working together for a long time?"

"I used to work with her at the old bakery when I was in high school. She was starting this place up, and found out I was looking for work, so she asked if I wanted to come help her. I've been here ever since."

Drew was about to ask another question when Beth came through a set of swinging doors. She stopped when she spotted him. "You made it."

"An offer of fresh muffins is hard to pass up." He smiled, hoping it was having the effect on her he wanted.

"I suppose it is." Beth slid a tray of chocolate chip cookies into a glass case and wiped her hands on her apron. "Did you want some coffee? Or we have milk or juice."

"Coffee sounds great."

She nodded. "Why don't you go sit down and I'll bring it out to you."

Before he could say anything else, she disappeared through the swinging doors again. He shook his head and went to find a place to sit as far in the back as he could. When Beth brought his breakfast out, he was hoping she might stay and visit with him for a few minutes. A guy could dream, right?

Chapter Five

What had she been thinking? After completely freaking out the last time Drew came into her café, she went and invited him to come have muffins? Was she crazy?

Apparently.

As she placed two muffins on a plate—one blueberry, one banana nut—she tried to regulate her breathing. She could do this. She would do this. It was only breakfast.

After seeing him earlier that morning in his firefighter gear and covered in dirt and grime, Beth had experienced a jolt of fear. Whether it was fear for him or fear of what could have happened had they not been able to contain the fire, she didn't know.

The fire he'd help to put out was a little over two blocks from her café. She was no expert, but Beth knew in places with buildings so close together it wouldn't have taken much for the fire to spread. What would have happened if it had made it to her café?

Carrying the muffins and a carafe of coffee out to the dining room, Beth tried to push her thoughts about the fire aside. She and Tommy were safe, as was her café—thanks to Drew and the other firefighters.

He grinned as she walked toward him. Beth felt a fluttering in the pit of her stomach seeing him sitting there in his white T-shirt and jeans. The thought of what he would look like naked flashed through her mind. She ignored it, and set the plate down in front of him.

"Thank you," he said.

"You're welcome. I hope you like them." Crazy as it sounded, Beth really wanted him to like her muffins. It was completely irrational, but there it was just the same.

She cleared her throat. "Well, I'll let you eat. Just let Tommy know if you need anything else."

As she turned to go, his voice stopped her. "Will you join me?"

"I don't . . ."

"Please? I won't bite. I promise."

Beth chuckled. "I thought you preferred being the bite-*e*."

Almost instantly, she started to blush. Why in the world had she said that?

Drew glanced down, and then back up to meet her gaze. "Touché."

Their eyes locked for several moments before Beth lowered herself into the chair beside Drew. "Sorry about that. I shouldn't have—"

"It's all right. Besides, it's the truth. At least, I think it is."

Drew picked up the blueberry muffin and took a large bite. While he chewed, Beth was drawn to how his throat moved as he swallowed. His skin was smooth. He'd shaved before he came.

She lowered her gaze to the T-shirt he was wearing where it was pulled tight against his muscles. For some reason, Beth was having trouble looking away.

"Wow. This is amazing." His exclamation roused her from her thoughts.

Beth felt the blood rushing to her cheeks again. "Thank you."

He took another bite, chewed, and then took a drink of his coffee. "Do you mind if I ask you something?"

She had no idea what he wanted to know, but given the gratitude she was feeling, Beth figured she'd take a chance. "All right."

"Is it me, personally, that you don't want to date, or is it men in general? Because of what happened, I mean."

Looking down at where she had her hands clasped on the table, Beth thought about how she should answer. If she told him it was only him, she was fairly positive he would go on his way and not bother her anymore. But could she do that? As much as she didn't want to date anyone at the moment, Drew had revived something in her she thought was dead.

Taking a deep breath, Beth glanced up. "It's not just you."

He nodded and took another bite.

As Drew was tearing into his second muffin, the timer she had attached to her apron went off. "I need to go check on something in the kitchen."

"I'll let Tommy know if I need anything. Thank you again for breakfast."

"You're welcome." As she stood to go, Beth felt reluctant to leave. It made no sense, and it certainly wasn't what she wanted. Too bad her mind and body weren't on the same page.

Forcing her legs to move, she hurried into the kitchen, and leaned back against the wall. She needed to get a hold of herself. He was only a man, and other than him being a firefighter and a sub, she knew very little about him. Getting too involved could land her in a world of hurt. Again. She couldn't let that happen.

Her secondary timer went off on the oven, and Beth rushed over to remove the bread before it burned. She didn't know what she was going to do about Drew. She really didn't.

A little after noon the next day, things became even more complicated when a man showed up with a bouquet of spring flowers for her. The flowers were beautiful. Simple, yet lovely.

"Who are they from?" Tommy asked as he followed her into the back.

"I don't know." It was true. She didn't know. She hadn't dared look at the card yet. That didn't mean she wasn't ninety-nine percent sure.

Tommy huffed. "Well, open the card already. The suspense is killing me."

She laughed. "It's killing you?"

"Yes."

Beth shook her head and plucked the card from where it was nestled in some baby's breath. "Well, I don't want you falling dead on my kitchen floor, so . . ."

He rolled his eyes. "Come on, B. You never get flowers. I bet it's that hunky firefighter. I saw the way he was looking at you."

"And just how was he looking at me?"

"Like he was imagining what you looked like with your clothes off."

"Tommy!"

He chuckled. "Well, it's the truth. Now, are you going to open the card or not?"

Beth toyed with the idea of not opening it for about two seconds, before running her finger along the envelope's seam. Whether she liked it or not, she was curious.

Slipping the card out of the envelope, she flipped it open.

Beth,

Thank you for breakfast.

Drew

"Well?" Tommy demanded.

She fought a smile, and lost the battle. "They're from Drew."

"The firefighter?"

"Yes."

Tommy did a fist pump. "I knew it."

It was Beth's turn to roll her eyes.

"So?"

"So what?" she asked.

He sighed. "Sooo. Are you going to go out with him?"

"Just because he sent me flowers doesn't mean we're going out on a date."

"Pfft. A guy doesn't send a woman flowers he doesn't have the hots for."

Beth moved about the kitchen to get some water for her flowers. "Don't you have customers to wait on?"

Tommy gave her a hard stare. "Yes. Probably. But, B, give this guy a chance. I like him."

"Why? Because he's a firefighter?"

"No. Because I've met him three times now and not once has he talked down to me."

She knew what Tommy was saying. Ben would often come into the café for free meals when he was in town. Whenever Tommy was at the counter, which was almost always, Ben would make Tommy feel as if he were little more than a child—at least that was Tommy's view. Whenever Beth would ask Ben about it, he would deny doing any such thing. And, of course, Beth never witnessed the interactions personally. Ben was always on his best behavior when she was out front.

"I'll think about it, okay?"

Tommy smiled.

"Now, get out there and take care of our customers," Beth ordered.

He stuck out his tongue, and jogged away.

Alone with her flowers, Beth read over Drew's card again. It wasn't anything fancy—very direct and to the point. But if she was honest, she liked that he wasn't all about the frills. If Beth did this again, she wanted real. She wanted honest.

Placing her flowers on the table beside where she was working, Beth went back to preparing the mixes they'd need for the next day. As she worked, her eyes kept going back to the flowers. Could she take a chance on Drew? Could she trust him not to break her heart?

The problem was she didn't know the answer. There were too many what-ifs—too many unknowns.

By the time she and Tommy closed everything down for the day, Beth was finally coming to a decision. Although she'd told Drew they could be friends, she'd kept him—and their friendship—at arm's length to protect herself. Maybe that wasn't the best idea.

She and Ben hadn't been friends first. They'd jumped into a relationship right from the start. She'd trusted everything he'd told her on blind faith. That obviously hadn't worked well, so maybe it was time to change things up.

As she drove the short distance to her house, Beth knew she and Drew would need to sit down and talk, really talk, if he was truly interested in her. She would offer friendship. A *real* friendship. They could see where things went from there.

Pulling into her garage, Beth turned off the engine, and retrieved her flowers from the passenger seat. She hoped Tommy was right—that Drew was different. Only time would tell.

❧

DREW HAD ARRANGED FOR THE BOUQUET OF FLOWERS TO BE DELIVERED TO Beth around noon on Wednesday. He'd watched the clock all morning. Then he spent the entire afternoon wondering what she'd thought of them.

When he'd asked her the day before if it was him or guys in general, her answer gave him hope. She'd been burned, and he understood her caution. That didn't mean he was willing to give up. There was something about her that sucked him in. He couldn't explain it. Yes, she was gorgeous, but it was more than that. The way she gave him that look—the one that made him excited and edgy all at the same time. It was damn close to how he felt when they were responding to a fire. He could only imagine what it would be like to play with her.

He'd watched a few scenes with Dommes and their male submissives. One he witnessed stood out above the others. It wasn't so much what was being done, but more the connection between the players. He'd later found out that the two had been together for almost twenty years. Drew wanted that.

Shawn found him on Thursday morning as Drew was filling up his coffee mug. "Saw your girl yesterday."

"What?" Drew wasn't sure he'd heard Shawn correctly.

Shawn took a mug out of the cabinet above the sink and reached for the coffee pot. "You heard me. I stopped in at that café you had lunch at last week. The one on Crawford Street."

As curious as Drew was, he tried to play it cool.

When he didn't respond, Shawn continued. "Yeah. And your girl was there. Looks like you may have yourself some competition."

"Really? How's that?" Drew said, leaning back against the counter.

Shawn raised his eyebrows up and down several times. "Someone sent her flowers."

"And?"

"And? Come on, man. Don't try to tell me you're not interested. If half of what Romeo and Baily are saying is true, you were practically drooling over her. Heed my advice, if you want in on that, you're going to have to make your move, but quick." Shawn had ten years on Drew, but the two had developed a friendship over the last few years. It was Shawn who'd encouraged Drew to apply for the captain's position when it opened up.

"I'll keep that in mind." Drew tried not to let it show how pleased he was that not only had Beth received his flowers, but that it was done in such a way that her customers had noticed. He needed to change the subject, though, or he was going to give himself away. "So what brings you in early? Didn't you want that extra hour's sleep?"

His buddy smiled. "Chief called. You and me have a meeting in his office first thing. Hope you didn't have any plans this morning."

"Just a date with my bed," Drew said as he pushed himself away from the counter and headed toward the chief's office.

"Be better if you had someone there to keep it warm for ya."

Drew gave Shawn a playful shove. "Sure. Keep rubbing it in that you have a woman at home."

Shawn laughed. "Could be you, too, buddy. Just saying."

"Yeah, yeah. Come on. Let's see what the chief wants."

Turns out, the chief wasn't the only one waiting for them. Nicole was also in Chief Franks' office along with the other captains assigned to the station, and another man Drew didn't recognize.

The meeting was brief. The man he didn't know was from bomb and arson. It had been confirmed that both the fire from two weeks ago and the one over the weekend had been arson, and they looked to have been set by the same person. The mayor was all over this. So far, they'd been lucky—the arsonist seemed to be targeting abandoned buildings. Sooner or later, someone was going to be in the wrong place at the wrong time. The mayor wanted the guy caught before that happened.

By eight thirty, Drew was headed out to his car with his duffel bag. He tossed it in the backseat and was about to get behind the wheel when someone called his name.

He pivoted to see Nicole striding toward him. "I'm glad I caught you."

"Something wrong?"

She smiled. "Nope. Not a thing."

Drew was confused. She'd sought him out to tell him everything was good?

"Don't give me that look. I just wanted to let you know that I think the flowers you sent to Beth were perfect."

"Thanks."

"I wanted to find out what your next move is." she said.

"I don't know. I haven't really thought that far ahead. The flowers were a gamble."

Nicole looked serious. "You got any plans for today?"

He shook his head. "Just sleep."

"Good. Why don't you stop into the café for a late lunch—say, around one thirty?" There was a gleam in her eye Drew wasn't sure he liked.

"Why one thirty?"

The evil look in her eye spread to the rest of her features. She had a wicked grin on her face. "Because the café closes at two. It will give you enough time to eat and linger. Maybe you can offer to help her close up. Show off some of those service skills."

He snorted. "You're pushing awfully hard for this relationship. Why?"

Nicole's face fell. "You didn't see her . . . after. Although she's been cautious with you, there's finally some life in her again."

Drew guessed that made sense. "I'll see what I can do."

Before Nicole could add anything more, Drew lowered himself into the driver's seat.

"Take care of my girl," she said.

He nodded and drove away.

When he arrived at his apartment, Drew was struck at just how bare it was. Some of it could be explained by him being a bachelor with no woman in his life. Even that, however, was a stretch. His one-bedroom apartment didn't contain more than the basics. He had a bed, a dresser, a small table with two chairs, a television, and a recliner. That was about it when it came to furniture. He'd always intended to make more of an effort, but had never gotten up the energy to do it. After all, who was going to see it?

If he was thinking about pursuing a relationship with Beth, maybe he should finally do something about the place—spruce it up a little. He couldn't imagine she'd be all that impressed.

Strolling into the kitchen, he downed a glass of water before going into his bedroom. Although it was almost nine in the morning, he quickly went through his bedtime routine. Lowering himself to the bed, he reached over and set his alarm for twelve thirty. It would only give him a few hours' sleep, but given the option of catching a few extra hours of sleep and seeing Beth again, he'd pick the latter.

Slipping between the sheets, Drew leaned back onto his pillow. His bed was the one thing he'd splurged on when buying furniture for his apartment. Although the cots at the station weren't horrible, they certainly didn't scream luxury. The mattress and box springs had cost him a pretty penny, but it had been worth it. Settling in, he enjoyed how the material conformed to his body.

Drew closed his eyes and sighed, letting sleep take him.

His alarm went off waking him from an amazing dream. He was lying on his bed, hands tied to the headboard with Beth sitting astride him. She had this look on her face that sent his heart racing and had his cock stiff.

Reaching down beneath the sheets, he wrapped his hand around the part of him that was aching. It had been months since he'd been with a woman—something he couldn't have imagined a couple of years ago. This was different, though. It wasn't a faceless woman he was imagining. It was Beth.

Closing his eyes, he let his mind wander as his hand worked up and down his shaft. The pressure in his balls built quickly, and before he knew it, he was on the verge of exploding.

Throwing the sheet off him with his free hand, he ran his thumb over the head of his cock as he pulled up once . . . twice . . .

A surge of energy sprang up as he released, covering his hand and stomach. Tilting his head back, he took several deep breaths to calm himself down before reaching over to grab the towel he'd taken to keeping beside his bed.

With the majority of the mess cleaned up, Drew made his way into the bathroom. After throwing the soiled towel into the hamper, he turned on the water, and stepped into the shower. As the spray pounded his back, Drew couldn't shake the memory of Beth on top of him. His dreams of being with her got more detailed as time went on.

He had to hope the reality would be better than the fantasy. Drew had never wanted to get his hands on a woman more, and knowing that, even if they did end up in a relationship, she could deny him was driving him even madder. But it was also thrilling.

Drew knew he had to be patient. His dad always told him that the right woman was worth the effort, and Drew had a feeling Beth was that woman. At least, for him.

Chapter Six

Drew had to admit he was a little nervous as he stepped inside the café. He homed in on Tommy behind the counter. When the man saw him, he smiled. That eased some of Drew's anxiety. At least Tommy was glad to see him.

"You come for lunch, or to see Beth?" Tommy asked.

"Both, actually."

Tommy beamed. "Tell me what you want to eat, and then I'll run back and get Beth for you."

After placing his order, Tommy gave Drew his change, and handed him a glass.

"Go ahead and have a seat. I'll let Beth know you're here and have her bring your food out to you."

"If she's busy, I can wait." The last thing Drew wanted was to take her away from her job.

"No worries. We're slowing down. She's probably starting to clean up already."

Before Drew could say another word, Tommy had disappeared into the back. What was it with people lately?

Shrugging it off, Drew went to get his drink and find a table. He chose a spot in the back again. Although there weren't many people in the café at this time of day, Drew still wanted them to have some privacy. That, of course, was all based on the assumption that Beth was going to come out and talk to him.

As the minutes ticked by, Drew watched most of Beth's few remaining customers file out of the café. By the time Beth appeared with his sandwich, only one other table near the front was occupied. As far as Drew was concerned, it was perfect.

Without saying a word, Beth set the plate down in front of him and took a seat.

"Thank you," he said.

Beth nodded. "Thank you for the flowers. They were lovely. And rather unexpected."

He smiled. "You're welcome. I'm glad you liked them."

Silence filled the space between them as he dug into his lunch. He wasn't sure how much he should push and how much he should let her lead.

Luckily, before he came to a decision, she spoke. "I don't know how much you know about what happened. With me and my ex, I mean."

"Not much, but I know enough."

"Do you?"

There was an edge to her voice, and Drew was hoping he hadn't overstepped again. "I know you were hurt, that he betrayed your trust."

"I see. And did Nicole tell you that?"

"No. John did that first night I met you at the club."

She sighed. "I guess I'm not surprised. Bad news travels fast."

"John said he didn't know the details, but he wanted to give me a heads-up since . . ."

Beth smirked slightly, and then frowned. "Since he realized you were interested in me."

Drew met her gaze. "Yes."

She was quiet for a several minutes, and he took the opportunity to finish his meal.

When she spoke again Drew had the urge to hug her, but he resisted. "I can't offer you anything more than friendship right now. I'm sorry. I just can't."

"I understand."

"You keep saying that."

"And I mean it. Like I told you before, I'm willing to take what you're offering. No strings," he said.

Beth snorted. "You sent me flowers."

"So?"

"So that isn't exactly something a friend would do."

He pretended to be offended. "Says who?"

She chuckled and shook her head. "Says me, that's who."

"You've never had a friend send you flowers?" he asked.

"Not the point." She rolled her eyes at him.

Drew had to admit he was having fun, and since she seemed to be right there with him, he continued. "Sure it is. You mean to tell me Nicole has never sent you flowers?"

"Yes. She has. For my birthday. But Nicole is not you." There was a light in Beth's eyes—a sparkle—and he loved seeing it.

"Ah. So I'm not special enough to send you flowers. I see how it is."

Beth rested her face in her hands and laughed. "You're impossible."

He grinned. "Am I?"

She looked up at him, amusement the most dominant emotion on her face. "Yes. You know exactly what I mean, and you're intentionally missing the point I'm trying to make. You're a guy. Guys don't send flowers to women they're friends with."

His expression sobered. "Would you rather I not have sent them?"

Beth paused and seemed to consider his question. "No. I liked the flowers. I just don't want you to get your hopes up."

"I'm not." He'd said it before, and if she needed him to, he'd repeat it every day until she believed him.

❧

Beth wasn't sure if she should believe what Drew was saying or not. It was obvious he wanted more than friendship from her. Looking like he did, she couldn't imagine why he'd be willing to settle for friendship when he could probably go down to the local bar and find several women willing to give him whatever he wanted.

It irked her how much that thought turned her stomach. Although she wasn't ready for a relationship with Drew or anyone else, the thought of him with another woman made her ready to pounce. Even she knew that wasn't fair. Beth had no claim on him. He was free to date, and even sleep with, whomever he wanted.

She stood quickly, sending the chair scraping along the floor. "I should get back to work if I want to get home at a decent hour."

Drew arose and picked up his plate. "Want some help?"

"That's all right. Tommy and I—"

"Please? I took you away from what you were doing . . . put you behind. Let me help."

Beth tilted her head to the side and considered his offer. If Nicole had offered to help her close down for the day, Beth would have jumped at the chance and would have immediately put her to work. If she was going to allow Drew into her circle of friends, shouldn't she treat him the same?

"All right. Follow me."

Without looking back, Beth made a beeline for the kitchen. Tommy was already at the sink doing dishes. When he saw Drew behind her, he winked.

She rolled her eyes and grabbed the tray they used to close down the dining room. Filling up the small bucket with warm soapy water, Beth handed it over to Drew. "Think you can handle wiping off all the tables and filling up the salt and pepper shakers?"

"Yeah. I think I can handle that."

"Good. I'll be out to check on you in about twenty minutes. And don't forget to check underneath the tables."

Beth thought she heard Drew chuckle before he headed back out to the dining room.

"Going a little hard on him, aren't you?" Tommy asked.

"No."

"Come on, B. Don't play that game with me. I've known you for too long. You like the guy. Admit it."

Picking up a clean towel, she wet it and began scrubbing the kitchen counters. "Yes, I like him. I know I shouldn't, but I do. Satisfied?"

"Maybe."

Beth groaned. "You're as bad as Nicole, do you know that?"

Tommy laughed so hard he had trouble catching his breath. "I'll take that as a compliment. I like Nicole."

As much as she wanted to comment, Beth kept her mouth shut. Tommy knew a lot about her life, but he had no idea that both she and Nicole were into BDSM. Tommy was young. Okay, he was twenty-three. Still, he was young enough for her to feel the need to keep that part of her life away from him. She'd known him since he was sixteen, and in many ways, she still viewed him that way.

Trying her best to ignore the satisfied grin on Tommy's face, Beth concentrated on getting her work done. Once she had everything cleaned and put away, she went out to the dining room to see how Drew was doing.

She found him near the front of the café. Even though she hadn't told him to, he'd flipped all the chairs upside down and placed them on the tables. To her knowledge, he'd never been to her café after hours. Maybe he'd worked in a restaurant when he was younger. That or he paid attention to details. When she'd worked at the bakery, putting the chairs on the tables was something all the new employees had to be told. More than once someone would just try to vacuum around the chair legs and call it done.

"You put the chairs up. That's good."

He glanced up. "Figured it was easier to do it as I went. I didn't see a sweeper anywhere, though."

Beth took a long look at the table she was standing next to. The salt and pepper shakers had been filled and arranged neatly at the center of the table beside the sugar. She walked to the window and flipped the sign to closed before turning her attention back to Drew. "It's in the supply closet. I'll show you."

She turned on her heel knowing he'd follow her. When she heard his footsteps behind her, Beth grinned.

Opening the door, she stepped into the small room, and turned on the light. Everything for the restaurant that wasn't food-related was stored in this room. She spotted the vacuum on the far wall and was about to retrieve it when Drew brushed past her. The area he'd touched—albeit briefly—left behind an almost electric charge.

He must have felt it, too, because he stopped and turned to face her.

They stared at each other for several moments before Drew cleared his throat. "Do I need anything else while I'm in here?"

She swallowed and shook her head. "No. The vacuum should be it."

Not waiting for a response, Beth left the room, and went to find Tommy. He was up front stocking supplies behind the counter. "Having fun with the firefighter?"

"Shut it. Now, what else needs to be done up here?"

Tommy chuckled and pointed to the large display case.

"Left that for me, did you? Thanks so much." Beth took a wet rag and began cleaning the large glass case they used to display the baked goods. It was perhaps her least favorite part of running the café. Everything had to be taken out of the case, wiped down, and put back. Sounded simple enough, but when jelly or icing dripped and then dried on the metal racks, it sometimes meant scraping it off.

As she was prying some icing from the center rack, she heard the vacuum turn on. Beth didn't need to look up to see Tommy was smiling—the amusement was vibrating off him. He was enjoying this thing with her and Drew way too much.

Before long, everything was as it should be, and Beth found herself standing outside the back door with Drew and Tommy. Beth knew she and Drew needed to talk, and figured this was as good a time as any. "Thanks, Tommy. I'll see you in the morning."

He glanced back and forth from her to Drew, and then nodded. "Call me if you need anything."

She didn't miss the thumbs-up Tommy sent her way as he was getting into his car. Beth sighed as she faced Drew and tried to prepare herself for what she was about to do. "Would you like to take a walk with me?"

"Sure."

Drew seemed a little surprised, but he followed her down the alley and out onto the sidewalk that ran along the front of the café. She turned left, setting a leisurely pace. As they continued to walk, Beth realized he was intentionally keeping himself a step behind her. "You can walk beside me. I'm not your mistress, and we aren't playing. There's no protocol."

Beth actually thought she saw him blush.

"Sorry. I don't . . ." He shook his head. "Sorry."

He lengthened his step a little and fell in beside her. "Thank you."

"It's my fault. I feel like I keep screwing this up," he said.

"You're not. If it were anyone else, I'm sure it wouldn't be this complicated."

Drew shot her one of his killer smiles. "Maybe I like complicated."

She laughed.

They passed several more storefronts before either of them spoke.

Beth took a deep breath. "I want to apologize to you."

"For what?"

"I told you we could be friends, but so far I've done a really crappy job at holding up my end of things."

"That's not true."

"It is." There was no room for argument in her tone. "Although I said it, I didn't mean it. Truthfully, I was hoping you'd lose interest and go away."

"Is that what you want?" Beth didn't miss the hint of disappointment.

She groaned. "This isn't coming out the way I wanted it to. I wanted to apologize, and then offer for us to start again. Somehow I've even managed to screw up the apology."

He stopped, so she did, too.

Drew's brow was furrowed. It looked as if he was deep in thought about something. "So what does that mean, exactly?"

Beth released a harsh breath. "It means that before when I said we could be friends I didn't really mean it."

"And now?" he asked.

"And now? I'd like for us to try to be friends. Real friends. I still can't offer you more than that right now, but . . ."

He didn't answer right away. "How would this *real friends* thing work? As opposed to the fake friends thing."

When she realized he wasn't upset, she relaxed a little. "I suppose it means we would talk, hang out, that sort of thing. Isn't that what friends do?"

"It is. I guess I'm just wanting to make sure I know the ground rules."

Beth nodded and started walking again.

Drew fell into step beside her.

"Okay. Rule number one. While we can hang out, it can't be anything remotely like a date."

"So no showing up at your door with flowers. Got it."

She grinned. "Exactly."

"All right. What else?"

"Let's see. No inappropriate touching. Or kissing, of course."

"Of course."

One side of his mouth pulled up, and she knew he was fighting a smile. He was taking this much better than she thought he would. Maybe this could work after all.

"Is there anything besides no kissing or date-like behavior that's off the table?" he asked.

Beth shook her head. "Not that I can think of. If something comes up, I'll let you know."

"Fair enough."

They'd covered almost six blocks when Beth turned left to head toward the local farmers' market. She rarely bought anything, but she liked to stroll through the stalls to see what the vendors were selling—especially the ones hawking baked goods.

She knew the moment Drew realized where they were going. "Do you come to the market a lot?"

Beth shrugged. "I try to get here once a week. It's good to check out your competition once in a while."

"Ah. Good idea."

As they strolled through the stalls, Beth wondered what was going through Drew's mind. She'd laid out their friendship, and on the surface, he appeared to be content with the arrangement. But was he? She knew he wanted more. How long would he be happy with what she was willing to give before he became fed up with her and moved on?

"May I ask you a question?"

They were passing by a vendor who was selling a variety of apples. "Sure. And you don't have to ask permission. We're friends. You can ask me whatever you want. If I don't want to answer, I'll tell you."

He nodded. "How long have you been a . . . a . . ."

Beth smiled. "About six years."

"So you were in your early twenties?"

She chuckled. "Are you fishing for my age?"

"Maybe." Drew's eyes sparkled with mirth.

"I'm not like some women. I have no issues telling my age. I'm thirty." Beth glanced over at him. "And you?"

"I'm twenty-eight. My birthday is next month, though."

"So you're a young thing," she said, teasing.

"Not that young."

Beth nodded.

"Does me being younger bother you?"

"Not at all. Why would it?" Beth asked.

"I don't know. Just thought I'd ask."

"Are you asking as a friend, or are you asking if it would bother me if we were more than friends?" She was fairly sure she knew, but she wanted him to spell it out for her.

"I'm curious if it would make any difference if this thing between us did develop into more. Eventually," he hurried to add.

She made him wait for her answer, and as they rounded the corner to the last row of stalls, she could feel his tension growing. "No."

"No?"

"No. It wouldn't matter to me."

Beth heard him release a large burst of air from his lungs. "Okay. Good."

The two of them finished at the farmers' market and headed back toward the café. When they arrived at her car, Beth leaned against the metal to face Drew. "Thank you for walking with me."

"No thanks needed. I had fun. It was a good way to spend an afternoon."

"When do you have to work again?" she asked. If they were going to be friends, she should probably get an idea of what his schedule was.

"Tomorrow. I work twenty-four-hour shifts. One day on. One day off. After three days on, we get four days off. It's a nine-day rotation." When he saw her confused look, he shrugged. "I know it's a little confusing at first."

"That's okay. I think I get it."

They stood in silence for several moments.

"Any plans for tonight?" Beth had no idea why she was asking.

Drew shrugged. "Not really. I'll probably watch a little TV and turn in early."

It sounded a lot like the evening Beth had planned for herself. "Well, I'll let you get on with it, then."

She moved to get into her car, but he stopped her. "Beth?"

"Yes?"

"Does this new friends thing include us exchanging phone numbers?"

Beth thought about it for a moment. Although giving him her phone number gave her pause, she wasn't as nervous about it as one might think. Katrina was really good at screening applicants for the club. She'd even found Ben's marriage certificate when they'd applied for membership. The problem was Ben was good at lies and procuring fake documents. When the subject came up, he was able to produce a very legal-looking certificate of annulment dated about a month after the marriage. Unfortunately, neither Beth nor Katrina had thought to question it. They'd both learned a very hard lesson.

No, nerves had nothing to do with Beth contemplating Drew's request. Even without the background check Katrina would have done on him, she knew he was a firefighter. She knew where he worked, and even if he hadn't told her, with Nicole's help she would be able to find out. What was holding her back was the thought that it would be one more thing linking them together—one more step into opening herself up to trusting a man again.

"You don't have to if you're not comfortable," Drew said.

"It's not that. Okay, it is that. A little. But you're right. Friends do typically exchange phone numbers."

Before she could second-guess herself, Beth took out one of her business cards and a pen. Flipping it over, she scribbled both her home and cell numbers onto the card and handed it to him.

He looked it over, and then tucked it into his wallet. "Do you have another one of those? I don't have anything with me to write on."

Beth gave him another one of her cards, and he quickly jotted down his numbers. "The cell number is usually better. As long as I'm not out on a call, I'll answer."

She took the card and slipped it into her pocket. "Thanks."

"I should let you go. Thank you again for this afternoon. I had fun."

He waved, and she waved back before getting into her car. Every time she saw Drew, she got in deeper. How long would this 'just friends' thing hold?

She didn't know the answer to that. But for the first time since Ben exited her life, she was beginning not to care. Drew wasn't anything like her ex, which was good. The last thing she needed was another fake submissive who played with her and her emotions. She wanted real, and for all of Drew's cockiness and his inexperience with being a sub, he was real.

Driving home, Beth tried not to let the possibilities weigh too heavily on her mind. She would let this thing with Drew play out. Hopefully, if he turned out to be another Ben, she'd find out before it cost her another broken heart.

Chapter Seven

After she got home from the café Beth second-guessed giving Drew her phone number. Although the rational side of her brain kept trying to talk her down, the irrational part wouldn't shut off. Thoughts of her phone ringing every five minutes soared through her head the entire drive.

By the time Saturday night rolled around, Beth began to calm down. Drew hadn't called. Not once. It had only been two days, but for some reason she'd expected him to utilize her phone number or show up when she least expected it. He did neither and she was adamantly ignoring the tinge of disappointment it caused.

As Beth dressed to go to the club, she eyed her phone where it lay on her dresser. She knew that in all likelihood Drew would be there, and she was trying to convince herself that she wasn't anxious to see him.

Readjusting her necklace, Beth took a final look at herself. She'd chosen one of her more provocative outfits—not for Drew's benefit, of course. Her top wrapped around her torso, coming to a deep V that ended a few inches above her navel. It showed off her breasts nicely as well as her waist. The leather skirt she'd chosen clung to her hips, and ended roughly four inches above her knees. It covered everything it needed to, but also showed off her long legs. To enhance the effect, she'd chosen black stockings and her favorite boots. The boots were also leather and had a three-and-a-half-inch heel.

She picked up her jacket and slipped it over her blood-red top, which also happened to match her lipstick. The outfit made a statement, and on some level Beth knew she was playing with fire. But for the first time in more than three months, she didn't much care. She was going to enjoy herself. She was going to prove to herself, and to everyone else, that Ben no longer had any sway over her life. Tonight had nothing to do with Drew. It was about her taking control of her life again.

Now, if she could just believe that, she'd be all right.

Twenty minutes later, Beth pulled into the parking lot outside Serpent's Kiss. The space was nearly full. From the look of it, there would be a decent crowd inside the club. Then again, it was Saturday night, so that was to be expected. Katrina had created a safe, fun environment for kinksters to both socialize and play.

Beth crossed the short distance to the club's entrance, and stepped inside the small foyer. She removed the red and black plastic card from her purse, and slid it through the card reader beside the door. Two seconds later, the light on the reader turned green and the interior door unlocked, allowing her to enter.

She stepped into the second room—this one larger than the first—and was greeted by Ali, a woman not that much older than Beth herself. Ali had been a member at the club for a little over a year. She didn't have a Dom, but every now and then she would volunteer for a demonstration. Beth knew Ali was on the lookout for a more permanent play partner, but as far as Beth knew, she hadn't set her sights on anyone specific. "Good evening, Lady Beth."

Beth removed her jacket and handed it to Ali, who was manning the coat check for the evening. "Thank you, Ali. Looks like the club is rather busy tonight."

"It is. There's been a steady stream of people for the last hour or so." Ali paused and glanced down for a moment. "I believe I even saw that new sub, Drew, come in a short while ago."

"Is that so?" Hearing he was inside made Beth's heart rate kick up a notch.

"Yes, ma'am."

Nodding, Beth headed for the door that would lead her to the club itself. Squaring her shoulders, she opened the door, and entered the main room. She immediately began searching through the crowd. Beth told herself she was only looking for her friends, but that wasn't entirely true. Sure, she was looking for Nicole and the other members of the group she typically hung out with, but she was mainly scanning for Drew. Ali said he was there, which also told Beth that everyone in the club knew he'd set his sights on her. For some reason, knowing that didn't bother her as much as it probably should.

Ignoring her nerves, Beth continued her search. She wanted to find him first. She wanted to be the one to set the tone this time around.

Right when she was about to give up and head to where she'd seen Nicole and Jeff sitting across the room, she spotted Drew. He was sitting with his friends, Allison and John.

Beth hesitated, but then Drew looked up. She knew the exact moment when he found her in the crowd. His eyes went wide, and his lips fell open. Before she could lose her nerve, Beth took a deep breath and walked toward him.

DREW ABOUT LOST IT WHEN HE CAUGHT SIGHT OF BETH. HIS COCK JUMPED to attention and began straining against the confines of his jeans. The closer she got to him, the worse his condition became. Beth was wearing a curve-hugging leather skirt and black boots that ended right below her knees. He couldn't see the rear view, but his imagination had already taken over and then some.

If the skirt and boots weren't enough, the top she had on was downright sinful. It was deep red and dipped low, showing off her cleavage. Drew knew he was going to need some serious alone time later. He only hoped he could make it home first.

When she was about ten feet away, he stood. He had to ball his hands into fists to keep from reaching for her. The fact he couldn't touch her at all was driving him crazy—especially when she showed up looking like this.

She came to a stop in front of him and smiled. "I was wondering if you'd be here tonight."

He shrugged, trying to appear calm even though he was anything but. "I try to come on my nights off. Gets me out of the house and keeps me out of trouble."

Drew had meant it as a joke, but when Beth's eyes sparkled with amusement he knew something was coming. "You come to a kink club to stay out of trouble?"

Heat rushed to his face, and Drew couldn't believe she was actually making him blush. "I guess you have a point. Maybe that was the wrong choice of words."

Beth chuckled. "Maybe."

He felt something nudge his foot, and glanced down. Although John wasn't looking at him, Drew knew his friend must want an introduction. It wasn't as if Drew had talked about anything besides Beth the last few weeks. Considering John was the only friend Drew had he could talk to about her, he'd taken full advantage.

Clearing his throat, Drew angled his body so Beth could get a clear view of John and Allison. "I don't know if you know my friends. This is Allison and John."

Allison nodded in Beth's direction. "We've met. It's good to see you back at the club."

"Thanks. It's good to be back," Beth said.

Allison grinned and tilted her head toward John. "I'm not sure if you've met my boy before."

"No. I don't believe so."

"Did you want to join us?" Drew asked.

Beth turned her attention back to him. "I was thinking about getting something to drink and then heading upstairs."

Although Drew knew he shouldn't, he couldn't pass up the opportunity to spend time with her. "Care for some company?"

"Sure."

They said a quick goodbye to Allison and John before making their way across the room to the bar. Drew hadn't missed the encouraging look John had given him as they strolled away. His friend was one hundred percent behind his pursuit of Beth.

Drew followed Beth's lead as they stepped up to the bar. Katrina was very picky about who ran her bar. She had a strict policy of no more than two of what she considered 'soft' alcoholic beverages and one of what she considered the hard stuff per person per night.

Although he wasn't much of a drinker, he'd found out on his first night at the club just how serious Katrina was about the policy. He'd been nervous and needing a little liquid courage, so he'd ordered a shot of whisky. When he joined, he'd been told about the rules, but at the time, he hadn't really thought much about it. That was until he was told all they could give him for the rest of the night were drinks that contained absolutely no alcohol. It had made for a very long first night.

Beth rested her forearms on the bar, stretching her top even more, and Drew had to bite back a groan. She was killing him. Absolutely killing him.

The bartender, Brandon, strolled over to them. "Hey, Beth. What can I get you?"

"Just the usual for me."

She turned to Drew, waiting. "I'll take a water, please."

"Coke and Sprite, and a water. Comin' right up."

As they waited, Drew searched his mind to come up with something relatively safe to say. What he wanted to do was ask if he could kiss her, but he knew that probably wouldn't go over well.

He was still pondering when Brandon returned with their drinks.

Beth reached for her membership card.

"Let me get it?" Drew asked.

She stopped, met his gaze for a long moment, and then nodded.

He handed over his membership card. Within a few seconds, Brandon had swiped the card, and handed it back to him.

They took their drinks and headed upstairs. He wasn't sure if Beth wanted to watch a specific scene, or if this was a purely voyeuristic venture. Either way, he was happily along for the ride as long as it meant he was by her side.

The first room they came to had two people inside he didn't recognize. It was a male Dom and a female submissive, but unlike the scene he'd witnessed the week before, this one seemed a little awkward. The Dom's movements were less fluid, and the submissive didn't appear to be completely relaxed.

"First public scene."

Drew jumped a little at the sound of Katrina's voice. He hadn't noticed her come up behind them. "Oh."

"Have they been playing together long?" Beth asked.

Katrina shook her head, but didn't take her eyes off the couple in the room. "No. They're both fairly new to the lifestyle."

The Dom selected a blindfold from the table and secured it over the sub's eyes. She tensed, and he placed his hand on the top of her head in a comforting gesture.

"Decent instincts," Beth said.

"Yes. I didn't get any bad vibes from either of them. They're just very new. It will take time for them to establish a rhythm," Katrina agreed.

As he stood there, Drew tried to take it all in. Although the couple was still feeling their way around, he could also see the hidden connection there in the way the sub reacted to her Dom's touch. She might be unsure of what he was going to do, but it wasn't that she lacked trust in him. It was most likely trust in herself she was struggling with.

Drew could relate to that. Since he'd never participated in a scene before, he had no idea how he'd react. Even though he wanted to give up control to his partner, actually doing it was something altogether different. In all honesty, as much as he and Beth being friends frustrated him, he was grateful for the opportunity to get to know her before they ventured into anything like what he was watching unfold before them. He needed to be able to trust her completely, and no matter how much a person said they trusted another, true trust didn't happen overnight. It was built and tested over time.

Several more minutes passed as the Dom inside the room circled his submissive with a crop. Every now and then, he'd swat her leg, arm, or breast. It was completely random, and the sub was having a hard time keeping still. She was anxious. But what shocked Drew was that he was, too. His skin was tingling with every hit the crop made to the submissive's flesh.

Someone came up behind them, pulling Drew out of the moment. He took a deep breath and tried to find his balance again.

The man addressed Katrina. "Sorry to interrupt, but your presence is being requested in room five."

She nodded and then turned to Beth and Drew. "If you'll excuse me?"

A moment later, Katrina was gone, and he and Beth were alone again.

When Drew turned back around to look into the room, the Dom was kneeling in front of the sub. From this angle, he couldn't tell what the Dom was doing, but then he saw the sub's intake of breath and knew clamps were most likely being attached to her nipples. Drew had heard the reaction often enough in the club.

"What are you thinking?" Beth asked.

Drew met her gaze. "Wondering what it will be like. My first scene, I mean."

She stared up at him, and Drew once again felt that spark that always seemed to be lurking when Beth was near. He wondered if she felt it, too. When he noticed the vein in her neck pounding, he knew she did. It gave him courage. He took a step forward—the scene they'd been watching totally forgotten. "Beth . . ."

Before he could do anything else, a door slammed shut at the end of the hall, jarring them both. Beth blinked and stepped back. She edged past him and hurried down the hall.

Not knowing what else to do, he followed after her. She kept moving until she reached the last door on the right. Stopping for only a moment to glance inside, Beth hurried through the doorway and out of his sight.

Drew had to admit he was worried. Everything had been going well until a moment ago.

When he arrived at the open door, he looked inside. She was standing in the center of the room with her back to him. He wasn't sure what to do, so he stood a foot or so inside the door and waited.

Beth didn't react outwardly to his presence although he knew she had to realize he was in the room. Just when he was ready to break the silence, she spoke. "Shut the door, please."

Startled, he did as she asked without thinking. The door clicked as it latched into place, the sound echoing off the walls. Drew felt as if he were missing something.

Several minutes passed before Beth set her drink down, strolled over to the wall, and removed a crop. It looked identical to the one used in the scene they'd been observing.

She held the crop in her right hand, and ran her left down the length of it. "Do you know this is the first time I've picked up one of these in four months?"

Drew wasn't sure what to say, so he remained silent.

"We were in the middle of a scene."

He was confused. "I'm sorry?"

Beth turned around to face him. "Ben and I. We were in the middle of a scene when his wife showed up."

Drew felt bile rise in his throat. "You don't have to tell me this."

"I want to. You need to know what you're signing up for."

He still wasn't sure he wanted to hear it, but he nodded anyway.

She returned the crop, and reached for some items he wasn't familiar with —a few of which looked as if they could be painful. "We were in my bedroom. I had him secured to the bed, and I was flogging him."

Although he knew about her previous sub, it was weird hearing her talking about playing with another man.

"Someone rang my doorbell. At first, I ignored it since we were in the middle of playing, but the person persisted. I figured it must be pretty important, so I released one of his cuffs, and threw on a robe to go see who it was."

She sighed and dropped her hands down to her sides. "When I opened the door, I came face-to-face with a very angry woman I didn't know. She pushed me out of the way and began searching my house. I was furious, of course. I followed her, demanding to know who she was and why she was in my house."

During the few weeks Drew had known Beth he'd never seen her look as vulnerable as she did at that moment. He couldn't imagine what she'd been thinking when the woman burst into her home.

"Eventually she found Ben in my bedroom. He was still in my bed—both feet still secured to the bedposts." Beth looked up to meet his gaze. "After that the details get a little fuzzy. There was a lot of shouting as she released the remaining cuffs. But it ended with her slapping me, calling me a pervert, and telling me to leave her husband alone. She dragged him out of my house in his underwear."

"I take it that he never mentioned he was married."

Beth snorted. "No. He didn't."

Drew felt helpless. He wanted to comfort her, but wasn't sure how.

"Ben showed up at the café the next day. He tried to apologize. Explain himself. That's when I found out that he didn't only have a wife, but a daughter as well."

When Drew heard the catch in her voice, he threw caution to the wind. Leaving his water on a long table right inside the door, he crossed the room to her in three long strides. He stopped a foot in front of her, and opened his arms in offering—giving her the choice to take his comfort or not.

She hesitated for only a moment before stepping into his embrace. It was the first time he'd been so close to her. While he hated seeing her in distress, he couldn't help but take in the feel of her body against his. If only he could take the hurt and betrayal he knew she must have felt away from her, the moment would have been close to perfect.

"Thank you," she whispered.

"Any time."

She pulled away, and he couldn't help but feel the loss. "I haven't told that to anyone besides Nicole. Katrina knows some of it, but . . ."

"Thank you for telling me." He felt honored that she'd shared something so personal with him.

"I figured you should know, in case . . ." She took a deep breath and released it. "In case it changed your mind about me."

He was confused. "Why would it change my mind? He lied to you. He betrayed your trust."

Beth looked down at her hands, and then back up at him. "He broke me, Drew. I know you want a mistress. And I know you're hoping I can be that for you one day. I just don't know if that's possible. I don't know if I can . . ."

Drew extended his hand, and she took it. He gave her fingers a squeeze. "I'll take what you are willing to give."

She opened her mouth to speak, but he cut her off.

"Whatever you're willing to give, all right?"

Beth studied him for several moments before nodding. It was a small step, but he'd take it.

Chapter Eight

They retrieved their drinks and made their way downstairs. Drew was acting as if what she'd told him didn't matter. Maybe it didn't, but it still didn't change the facts. She wasn't ready to be anyone's mistress again.

As they neared the bottom of the staircase, she took in the number of available Femdoms in the club that would be willing to take on a new male sub. There were at least three that she could think of off the top of her head. If Drew was a masochist, she could add a couple more to the list.

Beth knew she should encourage him to shift his attention to one of these Dommes, but the thought of actually speaking the words made her feel as if she'd eaten something that didn't agree with her. Ready or not, she wanted him for herself. Even though she had no idea how long it would take her to feel up to a relationship again, she couldn't bring herself to suggest another mistress.

"Is something wrong?" Drew asked.

It was only then that Beth realized she'd come to a dead stop at the bottom of the stairs. "No. I'm fine. I should find Nicole, though. She's probably wondering where I am since I told her I'd be here tonight."

He nodded and glanced down at her glass. "Did you want me to get another drink for you?"

"I think I'm good for now." She paused and considered her next words carefully. Although she wanted to spend time with him, she didn't want him to feel obligated to stay by her the entire night. "It's all right if you want to go hang out with your friends. I don't mind."

If she hadn't been watching him as closely as she was, she would have missed the disappointment that flashed in his eyes. "Is that what you want?"

She swallowed, and looked him square in the eye as she spoke. "No."

He grinned, and the butterflies were back to fluttering in Beth's stomach. Why did she have such a strong reaction to him? It would be so much easier if she didn't.

Before Beth could lose her nerve, she stepped forward, and leaned in close to whisper in his ear. "Thank you."

The muscles in Drew's neck moved as he swallowed. "For what?"

She tipped her head enough to meet his gaze. "For having patience with me."

Drew closed his eyes. "Beth."

"Yes?" She knew she was teasing him, but she couldn't help it.

He opened his eyes, and the look in them nearly burned a hole in her soul. "I so want to touch you right now."

Her only response was to lick her lips.

Beth heard him groan, which caused her to chuckle. She'd missed this. She'd missed this a lot.

Backing away, she shot him a heated look, and then turned on her heel.

She had a huge grin on her face as she strutted across the room toward Nicole. Her friend must have seen at least part of the exchange, because she smirked at her as Beth sat down.

"Having fun?" Nicole asked.

"As a matter of fact, I am."

Nicole snapped her fingers, and Jeff crawled to her side. She brought his head into her lap and began running her fingers through his hair before turning her attention back to Beth. "About time."

Beth felt Drew lower himself into the space next to her. He didn't say anything, but she could feel the energy flowing off him. She knew she was on dangerous ground, but it didn't matter.

They passed the rest of the evening talking about some new toys Nicole had acquired. Although her friend could sometimes be slightly more sadistic than Beth, she and Nicole had a lot in common when it came to play. When Beth had been with Ben, she and Nicole had often shared ideas. Since the demise of Beth's relationship, Nicole had toned it down. Yet another thing Ben had taken from Beth that she wanted back.

During most of their conversation, Drew had sat beside her and listened. He didn't need to be the center of attention. That was good. Beth wasn't into bratty, attention-seeking submissives.

By the time Drew walked Beth out to her car at the end of the night, she was feeling pretty good. They'd had a nice time. She hadn't felt pressured to be anything other than herself.

Beth was still riding her high on Tuesday morning when she strolled into the café. Tommy picked up on the change in her mood. "Tell me you have a date with that fireman?"

She laughed and shook her head.

He groaned. "What in the world are you waiting for?"

Beth shrugged and slipped her apron over her head.

Tommy rested his hands on his hips and sighed. "Do I have to have a talk with him? Is he not stepping up?"

She stopped what she was doing and leveled a hard stare at him. "Don't you dare. This is none of your business. Do you hear me? You stay out of it."

He rolled his eyes, and stuck out his tongue at her before reaching for a bowl. "I just don't get it. He's single, right?"

"As far as I know."

"Then what's the problem?" Tommy asked.

"I don't know if I'm ready." Her reply was barely above a whisper, but she knew he heard her.

"If I ever see Ben again, I'm going to punch him. I should have done it the day he came in here begging you to hear him out." Tommy rarely got angry. He was one of the most easygoing people she knew. But she had no doubt if Ben were to walk through the door at that moment, Tommy would follow through on his threat.

Beth dropped the dough she'd just removed from the refrigerator on the counter, and pulled Tommy in for a hug. "Thank you for caring, but I'll be okay. I promise. I just need some time."

Tommy snorted. "I still want to punch him."

She smiled. "I know you do, and that means a lot."

Sighing, he went back to work on the mix he'd been making when she'd come in. "I just don't want to see you miss out on something because of him."

There wasn't really anything Beth could say in response to that, so instead she nudged him with her hip to lighten the mood. It worked. He grinned back at her, and hip checked her in return.

The two of them worked quickly to prep for the morning rush—neither one bringing up Beth's relationship issues. Once the doors opened, the steady stream of customers seemed to keep coming nonstop. By ten thirty, they were nearly wiped out of all their pastries. She hated to tell people they were out of something, so it was a good thing it was almost lunchtime. Even though they occasionally sold a muffin or two during the afternoon, most customers made their selections based on what was left in the case.

She disappeared into the kitchen to remove the last two loaves of bread from the oven when Tommy peeked his head in the back. "You have a delivery."

"What?" She looked toward the back door, but it was secured, as it should be.

He chuckled. "Nope. Out front."

Before she could respond, he was gone.

Sighing, Beth placed the bread on the cooling rack, and then went to see what he was talking about.

There on the front counter sat another bouquet of flowers. These were purple and white with some greenery mixed in. Unlike with the previous delivery, Beth didn't hesitate to reach for the card. She knew they were from Drew.

Beth,

Thank you for trusting me.

Drew

The grin that spread across Beth's face made her cheeks hurt.

"Tommy, can you watch the front for a few minutes?" She took her flowers, and the card, into the back without waiting for a response. Digging through her purse, she found Drew's number, and dialed before she could have any second thoughts.

"Hello?"

"Drew, it's Beth. I didn't catch you at a bad time, did I?"

There was a hesitation, and then the sound of a door closing. "Not at all. I was just hanging out with some of the guys from the station. We were getting ready to start up the grill."

"Oh. Okay. Well, I won't keep you, then. I only wanted to let you know that I got your flowers, and I wanted to say thank you. They're beautiful."

"Don't apologize. I love that you called me. And that you like the flowers. Lunch will wait. You can call me anytime you want. As long as I'm not in a burning building, I'll answer."

"Still, you're with your friends. I won't keep you."

"Beth?"

"Yes?"

There was a long pause. "Thank you for calling. I'm glad you like the flowers."

Drew was flying high when he stepped out onto the deck in Romeo's backyard. That was until three sets of eyes turned in his direction and seemed to be waiting for something. "What?"

"Got something to tell us, Parker?" Baily asked.

"Not at all."

All three of them scoffed.

"You ran out of here with that phone to your ear awfully fast, Captain. You got a hot date you aren't telling us about?" Romeo teased.

Drew strolled over to the cooler and grabbed a bottle of water. He downed it before answering. "Why would I tell you knuckleheads if I did, hmm?"

Luckily, Sophia, Romeo's wife, chose that moment to bring a large platter of meat outside. Conversation pretty much became nonexistent as everyone focused on the food.

His reprieve didn't last long, though. About five minutes into the meal, the eating slowed, and the conversation resumed. Of course, his phone call was still at the top of the subject list.

"At least tell us if it was a woman? It was a woman, right?" This time it was Baily who chimed in.

Drew sighed. Not answering would only work the guys up more, but he didn't want to say too much either. His relationship with Beth, whatever it was, was private. "Yes, it was a woman. Your sister, actually. She wanted to know if I was free tonight."

Irwin and Romeo laughed. Baily scowled. "Not funny, man."

"Yeah, it really was," Romeo said.

With a few well-placed comments, Drew was able to deflect the conversation away from his phone call. He doubted it would last indefinitely, though.

Sure enough, the next day the guys started in with little comments. First it was Baily asking if he needed to sit down and have a heart-to-heart with Drew about the birds and the bees. Then it was Romeo with an offer of dating advice. The only one who kept his opinions to himself was Irwin.

"Come on, guys. It was just a call."

"Yeah, 'cause I go running for privacy when my friends call," Romeo hollered from the top of the truck.

"Maybe I just didn't want to make them listen to all your whining," Drew shouted back.

There was a collective laugh.

Before the guys could get started again with the questioning, the alarm went off and they all abandoned cleaning the rig to respond to a small kitchen fire a couple of blocks from the station. The entire call took a little over an hour. It was enough to get the guys' minds off Drew's personal life, but he knew not to get his hopes up. That's why as soon as they were back at the station, he cleaned his gear as quickly as he could, and then barricaded himself in his office.

Throughout the afternoon, there were knocks on his door from not only his crew, but nearly every one of the guys at the station. It was almost as if they'd developed a rotation and brainstormed excuses to bother him. He wasn't sure if they were waiting for him to extend an invitation for one of them to come in and talk, or if they were hoping to catch him on the phone again. Either way, they were disappointed. He would answer their question and then send them on their way. After a while, he began thinking of assignments to keep them busy. Once they realized bothering him was getting them more work, the interruptions became less frequent.

When dinnertime rolled around, Drew grabbed his food, and headed back to his office. He wasn't in the mood to socialize even though he knew doing so would only invite more questions. What he really wanted to do was talk to Beth, but he didn't think calling her so soon would be a good idea. He didn't want her to think he was a stalker or anything.

Sleep was a long time coming that night. He'd waited until most of the guys had gone to bed before heading for his assigned cot. Even then, he'd heard a couple of coughs and mumbled words as he made his way to his bed.

Although he wished the guys would let it go, Drew knew that wasn't going to happen. It wasn't the way things were done. He was acting strange, and they all knew it. Drew was going to have to figure out something to tell them. It would be different if he and Beth were already in a relationship. This friendship of theirs was a little more complicated to explain.

If he and Beth did end up in a relationship, he was sure she'd meet the guys eventually. It was sort of inevitable. He wasn't worried. Beth could hold her own. Drew had no doubt about that. It was the fear that if his buddies found out what Beth was—what he was—Drew had no idea if it would change how they viewed him.

It ended up being a slow night. They'd been called out a little after one to a possible heart attack. The EMTs had taken the man to the hospital, and then they'd all returned to the station. Nights like that were rare, so Drew counted his blessings.

Five days later, he walked into his apartment around nine with an arm full of groceries. Before leaving for his shift the day before, Drew noticed his refrigerator was disturbingly empty. Granted, he didn't cook much outside the station—it was only him, after all—but that didn't mean he wanted to eat peanut butter on stale bread for every meal. Plus, he was off for the next four days, and the last thing he wanted to do was eat frozen dinners the entire time.

Setting the bags down on the counter, he went to work putting everything away. Drew placed a couple of tomatoes on the counter beside a bag of onions and some garlic. One of these days he hoped Beth would let him cook for her. Of course, there were a lot of things Drew was hoping she'd let him do for her.

His thoughts began drifting into X-rated territory when he heard his phone beep. Digging it out of his pocket, he checked the message he'd just received. His heart skipped a beat when he saw it was Beth. He hadn't heard from her since they'd spoken on the phone the week before, and he hadn't been able to make it to the club on Saturday. When he hadn't heard from her again, he'd debated calling her, but had hesitated. He was trying to let her set the pace.

I hope I didn't cause you any problems with your friends. - Beth

Drew quickly typed out a response.

You didn't. I was happy you called.

Okay. - Beth

Her reply didn't give him much to work with, but he wasn't willing to end their conversation yet—even if it was only via text.

The café is closed today, isn't it?

Yes. - Beth

He took a deep breath, and plowed ahead. She'd made first contact. He was going to take a leap of faith.

Do you have plans?

Not really. - Beth

Did you want to catch a movie?

She didn't answer back immediately.

Together? - Beth

Yes.

There was another extremely long break in the exchange, and Drew was thinking he'd put his foot in his mouth again.

Friends? - Beth

He released a loud sigh of relief.

Of course.

All right. What time? - Beth

Drew was shaking with excitement. He could barely type his response back to her.

I just got home. Let me check movie times, and I'll text you back. Anything you want to see?

I hate to admit this, but I don't really know what's out right now. Been a while since I've gone to the movies. -Beth

Okay. I'll put together a few options.

As quickly as he could, Drew finished putting away his groceries, and then went to the bedroom to retrieve his laptop. It took him a few minutes to pull up movie times for nearby theaters. He wanted to give Beth as many options as possible, so he chose a location that boasted twenty-four screens. They had five different movies all starting within a half hour of each other. He figured he and Beth could find something suitable to watch from the choices.

He texted her back with the movie names and times.

Did you want me to pick you up?

She answered almost immediately.

No. I'll meet you there. What time? - Beth

Now? LOL

Didn't you work last night? Don't you need to sleep? - Beth

I can sleep anytime.

You need your rest. 2? - Beth

Okay. I'll see you at 2.

Sleep well, Drew. - Beth

I will. Now.

By the time Drew plugged his phone into the charger on his nightstand and slipped into bed, he felt as if his face would fall off from grinning so much. He had a date with Beth. Okay. Not a date. It was two friends going to see a movie together. Still, he was going to be spending time with Beth outside her work or the club. He couldn't see a downside.

Unfortunately, his enthusiasm for his afternoon with Beth made for a restless sleep. Thank goodness it had been slow at work the night before or else he might have found himself dozing during the movie. That was unacceptable. Drew would have begged on his hands and knees for this time with Beth. He wasn't going to waste it.

The entire time he was getting ready, he kept telling himself that he needed to calm down. They were going out as friends. It wasn't a date.

That was true enough. He also knew that if the outing didn't go well this afternoon, then the chances of him ever getting her to agree to go out on an actual date with him were slim to none. Talk about pressure.

Drew threw on a nice pair of faded jeans and a T-shirt. He had thought about stepping it up a little, maybe nice khakis instead of jeans, but decided that might not be the best idea. He couldn't do anything that would suggest they were on a date.

After swiping his keys, he made the short drive to the movie theater. Getting out of his car, he saw her already waiting on a bench not far from the main entrance. She was beautiful, but she always was. Her hair was down, and for the first time he saw how it looked as it framed her face. He wanted to run his fingers through it and see if it felt as soft as it appeared.

He made it halfway to where she was before she saw him. Drew picked up his pace and crossed the parking lot. "Sorry I wasn't here sooner. Did you have to wait long?"

She smiled, but it seemed off somehow. "No. I got here a few minutes ago."

They stood in awkward silence for a moment.

"Should we go inside?" he asked.

"Yes. I mean, no. I mean . . ." She shook her head and huffed. "I hate feeling so out of sorts."

Disappointment began to take hold. "Did you change your mind?"

"No. I agreed to see a movie with you, and that's what I'm going to do. But we've agreed this isn't a date, correct?"

"Correct. It's just two friends going to see a movie together."

Beth nodded. "That means I pay for my ticket, and you pay for yours. I don't need there to be any blurred lines."

Although the notion of him not paying for Beth's ticket rubbed him the wrong way, he agreed, and motioned toward the ticket counter. "Shall we?"

She looked up at him with a much more relaxed expression. "You know, I was thinking maybe that action flick. You like action movies, don't you?"

"Come on. I'm a guy. Of course I like action movies. What's not to like? Fighting? Guns? Explosions?"

Beth laughed, and Drew felt a warmth spreading through his chest. So far so good. He had one goal for the day—to make sure Beth had a good time—and he was going to do everything he could to make that happen.

Chapter Nine

Beth didn't know what to expect when she'd accepted Drew's invitation. All she knew was that when he'd asked, she really wanted to go. So throwing caution to the wind, she'd texted him back agreeing to meet him at the theater.

It turned out to be a very good decision. After getting their tickets, Drew had guided her over to the concession stand saying that they had to have popcorn. He'd gotten a large bucket—insisting he hadn't eaten anything since breakfast—and a large soda. She'd ordered herself a drink, and tried to get him to let her pay half for the popcorn as well, but he was adamant that it wouldn't be fair since he'd most likely eat the majority of it himself. Short of arguing with him in the middle of the cinema, Beth let it go. Sometimes Drew didn't act very submissive.

While they were waiting for their movie to start, they munched on popcorn and commented on the theater ads that were showing. It was laid-back and natural. After a while, Beth started to relax.

The movie turned out to be pretty good. As advertised, there was a lot of action. What she hadn't expected, however, was the tearjerker ending. The credits began rolling on the screen, and Beth was sniffing and wiping tears off her cheeks. How utterly unattractive.

"You okay?"

Beth nodded and reached into her purse for a tissue. "Yeah, I'm fine. I don't know why they always make these movies with endings that make me cry."

Drew shrugged. "They probably figure they've gotten the men with all the violence, so they need to appeal to the women as well with something emotional."

She chuckled. "That's rather sexist, you know."

"Or honest."

Beth had to give him that. And he was probably right in any case. Ninety percent of the movie was all about killing and blowing things up. While she had nothing against an action-packed movie, Beth preferred if there was a little more to it—a little heart. Which, of course, explained the tears she was currently wiping off her face.

They waited until everyone else had exited the theater before leaving. It gave her time to pull herself together and get rid of any evidence of her emotional outburst.

As they left the cinema, the bright sunlight nearly blinded Beth. Her eyes were extra sensitive after spending such an extended time in the dark. She had to blink several times before her vision returned to normal.

Drew stayed close by her side, but made sure he kept a friendly distance. While there was a part of her that wanted to close that gap, she was pleased that he was respecting her wishes. Maybe he wouldn't make such a bad sub after all.

"Um." He cleared his throat. "I'm still kinda hungry. That popcorn didn't really fill me up. Did you want to grab a bite to eat?"

Here they were on shaky ground once more. "What did you have in mind?"

He released the tension in his shoulders, and she realized he must have been anxious about asking her. "There's a burger joint around the corner?"

"It's a little early, but I could probably eat."

And there was that smile of his again—the one that had her stomach all tied up in knots the other night. It was having a similar effect now.

"Lead the way."

Drew didn't waste any time guiding her the short distance to a restaurant that looked as if it had been transported through time from the 1950s. There were even little jukeboxes on the tables. A sign right inside the door indicated that customers were to seat themselves. He paused for a moment, taking in their options. "Booth or table?"

"Booth." Beth was impressed he'd asked.

They settled into a booth along the back wall, and a server came over to get their drink orders and give them menus. After the woman returned with their sodas, Beth and Drew put in their orders. Listening to him rattling off what he wanted to the server made her realize he hadn't been exaggerating about being hungry. Even if she were starving, she wouldn't be able to eat everything he'd ordered. Not by a long shot.

"Are you really going to eat all that?" she asked.

He grinned. "Probably."

They both grew quiet for a few moments. There was an awkwardness hanging between them, and Beth knew it was mostly her fault. She'd placed parameters on their relationship, and now they were both trying to figure out how to navigate without overstepping.

Beth took a sip of her water. "Do your parents live in St. Louis?"

Drew shook his head. "They live on a farm about an hour away, but I have a brother that lives here."

This was the first time Beth had thought to ask about his family, and to say she was interested was an understatement. "Is he a firefighter, too?"

He laughed. "No. Seth is ten years older than I am, and he enjoys his comfy job at his law firm."

"So he's a lawyer?"

"Yeah. Corporate law, mostly. He's tried to explain it to me, but to be honest, I usually end up tuning him out. While I don't mind the paperwork that comes with my job, I couldn't imagine weeding through pages of contracts looking for loopholes and technicalities. Seth loves it, though."

They both leaned back as their food arrived. Beth had kept it simple ordering a turkey club and fries. In contrast, three plates were set in front of Drew—each completely full. She guessed she had to hand it to him that at least one of those plates contained a salad, even if it looked as if lettuce was a minimal ingredient.

For the next several minutes, they both concentrated on their food. When the conversation resumed, it was Drew who broke the silence. "What about you? Do you have any family in the area?"

"No. I grew up in Ohio, and my parents still live there, along with my brother and sister."

Drew took another bite of his burger and swallowed. "Are you the oldest?"

Beth nodded.

"What brought you to St. Louis?"

She swallowed before answering. "School. I had no idea what I wanted to do, so I applied to a dozen or so schools all across the country. I got into most of them, but the University of Missouri offered me a partial scholarship."

"So you came here." His smirk was back.

"So I came here." She twirled her straw between her thumb and index finger with a glint in her eye. "What about you? Did you go to college?"

"Community college. I knew I couldn't join the fire department until I was twenty-one, and my parents refused to let me sit around and do nothing for four years."

Beth chuckled. "Smart parents."

"They are. And they completely supported my decision to become a firefighter. You should have seen my mom when I was promoted to captain. You would have thought I'd won an Oscar or something."

It was obvious by the look on Drew's face that he loved his parents. "She was proud of you. As she should be."

"Thank you."

Drew finished off his food, wiped his mouth, and laid his napkin on the table. "Can I ask you something?"

The tone of his voice had her a little worried. "Sure."

"Does my job bother you?"

She had to admit his question had caught her off guard. "No. Not really, anyway."

When he gave her a questioning look, she knew she was going to have to elaborate, even though she really didn't want to. "Yes, I've worried a little on occasion, but in the general sense, no. I figure you must know what you're doing."

He released a heavy breath. "I do. We're always training and making sure safety procedures are followed."

Beth smiled, hoping it came across as encouraging.

"I mean, I didn't think you had a big issue with it, but I figured it was best to ask. I've had women in the past who, while they initially loved the idea of dating a firefighter, the reality of it was too much for them."

"But we're not dating." The statement was said with less conviction than she knew it should.

"I know, but I'm hoping . . ."

Drew let that linger in the air as they stared at each other.

Despite all her reservations, Beth felt that pull toward him she always did. It was getting harder and harder to keep him at bay when there was a voice in her head—that was getting stronger by the minute—telling her to take a leap of faith and go for it.

As much as she wanted to do just that, the fear of another broken heart still made her question whether or not it was smart to get involved. "I like you, Drew. A lot. I really do."

"Is it because I'm new to this . . . the lifestyle, I mean?"

"No. If anything it helps." She gave him a weak smile. "I enjoyed today. Maybe we can do it again sometime."

He gave her a grin that made her heart skip a beat. "How about tomorrow? I'm off for the next three days."

Beth shook her head and laughed. "You're incorrigible, do you know that?"

"Is that a yes?"

"I have to work tomorrow." She was dragging her feet to see what he'd do.

"I can wait."

Grabbing her purse and the bill the server had left on the table for her food, she slid from the booth, and stood. "It's good practice for you."

He picked up his ticket and followed her toward the front of the restaurant. She could tell he was dying to press her, but kept his mouth shut.

Beth made him wait until they were standing in front of her car. "I'll meet you here at three thirty. Don't be late."

Before he could respond, she got behind the wheel and shut the door. Beth spared him a glance in her rearview mirror as she drove away. He looked pretty pleased with himself, and Beth wondered if she really knew what she was getting herself into. And for the first time she considered what would happen if she couldn't get past her fear. Drew had made his interest in her clear—his desire for a relationship. What would happen if she couldn't deliver? She'd been so afraid that he'd break her heart, but what if she broke his instead?

છ₩ઝ

DREW WAS HUMMING AS HE WALKED JOYFULLY TO HIS CAR. HE HAD another movie date with Beth the next day. Okay, not a date, but that was a technicality. She was opening up to him, and his mind was racing with the possibilities.

"Hey, Parker."

Turning, he came face to face with one of the guys from his crew. His good mood quickly dwindled. Although he normally wouldn't care, Drew wasn't ready to share Beth with the guys. They'd want to know everything about her, and well, he was still trying to figure her out himself. "Hi, Baily."

Baily looked around as if searching for something. "You meeting someone?"

Before Drew could answer, the little girl standing next to Baily spoke up to get her father's attention. "Daddy, are we going to go see the princesses now?"

Taking advantage of the opportunity, Drew opened his car door. "I don't want to make you miss your movie. I'll catch you later."

"You coming by Romeo's house tomorrow to help with the pool?"

Crap. He'd completely forgotten about that. "Got something in the afternoon, but I'll be there for a few hours. You?"

Baily, of course, didn't let it go. "Got a hot date?"

Drew decided to make a joke of it. He winked at Baily, and slid in behind the wheel of his car. "Something like that."

The next morning, Drew contemplated the wisdom of showing up to Romeo's at all. Sure, he said last week that he'd help, but that was before Beth had agreed to spend any kind of time with him outside the club. He had no doubt that by the time he got there his 'hot date' would be the main topic of conversation. Drew had to figure out what he was going to tell his crew about the woman he wasn't actually dating.

Pulling up in front of the two-story house, he could see that Baily and Irwin were already there. Taking a deep breath, he turned off the engine, and made his way into the backyard where he knew they'd be waiting.

The teasing began as soon as they saw him.

"Hey, hey. He made it," Baily said.

"Up late last night?" Romeo asked wiggling his eyebrows up and down suggestively.

Drew ignored their comments, and reached for one of the blueberry muffins laid out on a table set up along the back of the house. "You said eight thirty, didn't you?"

The guys chuckled, but settled down some when Sophia stepped into the backyard carrying a pitcher. "Thought you boys might like some juice to go with your breakfast. I've got some coffee brewing as well. I'll bring it out when it's ready."

Romeo took the pitcher from her and kissed her cheek. "Thanks, baby."

She smiled and disappeared back inside the house.

After stuffing their faces with muffins, coffee, and the apple juice Sophia had provided, the four of them got to work. By the time lunch rolled around, they had the ground cleared and leveled with sand, and the pool lying in parts on the lawn. Overall, it was a very productive morning.

At noon, Romeo fired up the grill and cooked some burgers and brats. They lazed on the back patio eating and shooting the bull. It was then that the subject of his upcoming afternoon activities resurfaced.

"You going to tell us what's so important that you're abandoning us this afternoon?" Irwin asked.

Kyle Irwin was the quietest guy on his crew. He usually kept his head down and went along with whatever was going on. For him to be speaking up, Drew knew what the main topic of conversation had been before he arrived that morning.

He shrugged. "I just have plans, that's all."

"Girl plans?" Baily asked.

"Not exactly."

There were a lot of suggestive noises followed by Romeo lifting his beer in salute. "Well, don't let us get in the way of you getting some pussy."

While Drew knew he shouldn't let the guys get to him—especially since it was nothing he hadn't dished out before himself on occasion—it irritated him all the same. Beth wasn't some random hookup. "It's not like that. We're friends."

"You're blowing us off to go hang out with a girl you're not banging? Something wrong there, man," Baily said.

Drew let it go and finished off his burger. He tossed his trash in the garbage bag Sophia brought out earlier that morning, and headed into the house to use the bathroom. On his way back out, he ran into Sophia. She had her arms full with two more pitchers. The sun was beating down on them, and they'd been downing water almost as fast as she could bring it out to them. "Here, let me help you."

She smiled, and handed him one of the pitchers. "Thanks."

He opened the sliding door for her, and waited until she was outside before following. The rest of his crew, already several feet away, was huddled around the various parts that would eventually make up the pool.

Sophia took the pitcher from him and laid it on the table. "Eddie tells me you've got a hot date this afternoon."

"Not you, too."

She chuckled. "You know they'll find out eventually. The more you keep it from them, the more they're going to tease you."

"I know."

Going up on her tiptoes, she kissed his cheek. "You're a good guy, Drew Parker. I hope whoever she is that she's good to you."

Drew nodded. "I should probably cut out. I need to stop at home and grab a shower. Thank you again for keeping us in food and drinks."

"Anytime. You know that."

After saying a quick farewell to Baily, Romeo, and Irwin, Drew jumped in his car and drove to his apartment. Once inside, he peeled himself out of his dirty clothes, threw them on top of the washer, and padded naked toward his bathroom. He took his time taking a shower, making sure to wash off all the dirt and grime.

Satisfied he was once again clean, he dried himself off, and then wrapped the towel around his waist so he could shave. Date or not, he wanted to look his best for Beth.

By two thirty, he was ready. Unfortunately, that meant he still had an hour before he needed to meet Beth at the movie theater. He thought about driving to the café and seeing if maybe she wanted to ride to the cinema together, but he wasn't sure how she'd react to that. The last thing he wanted to do was mess things up.

He lowered himself onto a tan couch, the newest addition to his living room, and tried not to let his nerves get the better of him. Needing a distraction, he pulled out his phone and dialed his parents' number. His dad was most likely out in the barn, but he was hoping his mom would be home.

"How are you, sweetheart?"

Drew smiled when he heard his mom's voice come through the phone. "I'm good. How about you?"

"Same old, same old. Not much changes around here."

He knew that all too well. It was one of the many reasons why he'd left the farm for the city. Although Drew enjoyed the space, he had no desire to shoe horses or milk cows for the rest of his life. "Is Dad staying out of the heat?"

"Oh, you know your father. Ain't nothing going to keep him away from his animals."

"Yeah, I know."

"Don't worry too much about your dad. He can take care of himself. And when he can't, he's got me." She was full of confidence. His mother had always been a take-charge type of woman.

"I still worry about you guys."

"And you don't think we worry about you and your brother?" she asked.

"I know you do."

"Speaking of worrying, are you coming home for the barbecue this year?"

Drew knew she was talking about the annual Memorial Day barbecue his parents held at their house. It was a big deal. All his cousins would be there, as well as many of the surrounding farmers. "I'm not sure yet. I'm going to try to make it, but if I come, I'll have to leave before dark. I have to work Tuesday."

"Don't worry about that. We just want to see our son."

"I'll see what I can do."

He talked with his mom for a few more minutes before he realized it was already after three and he needed to go. "I'm sorry, Mom, I'm meeting someone at three thirty, so I need to go."

"A woman?"

Drew bit back a groan.

"Andrew Raymond Parker, are you holding out on me? Have you met someone?" He could hear her hope.

"She's just a friend."

Of course, his mother heard what he didn't say. "But you're hoping it will eventually be more than that, right?"

He didn't answer.

"Invite her to come to the barbecue. I'd love to meet her."

"Mom, I can't—"

"Yes, you can. You said she's a friend, right? Well, we'll have a bunch of friends here. She'll fit right in."

Drew wasn't so sure about that.

"Well?"

"I'll think about it."

"You do that. Now, go meet this girl of yours. If she's the right one for you, she'll know what a catch you are."

He laughed. "You're biased, you know?"

"Of course I am. Doesn't mean I'm wrong, though."

Drew shook his head.

"What are you still hanging on the phone for? Go. Scadoodle. I want grandbabies one of these days before I'm too old to enjoy 'em."

"Goodbye, Mom."

It was her turn to laugh. "Goodbye, Drew. Take care of yourself. We love you."

"Love you, too. I'll call back soon."

He hung up the phone and lowered his head. So much for keeping Beth a secret for a while, until they figured everything out.

Chapter Ten

Most days flew by for Beth while she was at the café. There was plenty of work to keep her busy, and for the months since the fallout with Ben her business had been the only real bright spot in her day-to-day life. Her customers were always able to lift her spirits.

Today had been different. From the moment she awoke, Beth's mind was on her upcoming meeting with Drew. She'd enjoyed her time with him the day before, and despite her reservations, she was looking forward to seeing him again.

She worked doubly hard to stay on top of her work throughout the day so that she could leave a little early. Even Tommy noticed and commented that she must have a date with her firefighter. Beth tried to ignore him, but inside she felt a little giddy. Every time she caught herself getting too worked up, she'd remind herself that she still didn't know all that much about Drew. But even she knew that excuse wasn't going to hold true much longer. He'd told her about his job, his family, and some of his hobbies. How much more did she need to know?

The sad reality was that no matter how cautious she was, there was always the chance that he'd hurt her—especially now that he was worming his way into her heart. It was crazy really. The man would be a handful for whatever mistress chose to take him on. So why was she beginning to consider it?

Even with the extras she'd done throughout the day, it was after two thirty by the time she was able to leave the café. Having rushed home, Beth jumped into the shower and got herself ready as quickly as she could for her non-date with Drew. She chuckled to herself as she pulled one of her favorite pairs of shorts up over her legs and took a glance in the mirror to see how they made her backside look. Each meeting with him felt more and more like a date no matter how much she insisted otherwise. She cared about her appearance. She cared what he *thought* of her appearance.

After a final check in the mirror, Beth grabbed her purse off the table and headed for her car.

She spotted him standing near the entrance of the movie theater as soon as she pulled into the parking lot. After finding a place to park, she went to meet him. "Hey."

"Hey." He smiled, but it wasn't the full of life smile he normally flashed her. This one didn't set off butterflies in her stomach.

"What's wrong?" she asked.

Drew shook his head. "Nothing. Are you ready to go in? There are a couple of movies starting soon."

"I'm not concerned about the movies at the moment. I want to know what's wrong."

"I told you. It's nothing."

She gave him a look that made it clear she wasn't buying what he was selling.

He ran his hand through his hair. "Look, can we not talk about this here?"

Beth glanced around. While there weren't a lot of people in their general vicinity, there were enough within hearing distance.

"Where would you feel comfortable talking?" She tried not to think too much about the leap of faith she was taking. Or what it would mean in regards to their relationship.

"We don't—"

"Where?"

Drew sighed. "There's a park a few miles from here. Would you be up for a hike?"

"I'll follow you there." Without further comment, she turned back toward her car, and waited until he maneuvered his own vehicle out into traffic.

The drive wasn't far. As Drew said, the park was only a few miles away. There were three other cars in the small lot, but no sign of people. She guessed they were already on the trails.

Beth turned off the engine, exited her vehicle, and joined him a few feet away. "Lead the way."

He released another loud sigh, and began walking across the parking area to a marked trail.

They trekked down a small hill and around a bend before Drew started talking. "I want you to know that I've been completely honest with you in regards to our friendship. I'm completely okay with us being friends."

A tinge of unease began creeping up her spine. "Why am I sensing a *but?*"

"I called my mom before I came, and I sort of let it slip that I was meeting you this afternoon."

He looked incredibly guilty. While Beth wasn't sure how she felt about his mom knowing about her, she didn't understand what was causing him to react the way he was.

"I tried to explain that we're just friends, but you know how mothers are." He stopped to meet her gaze. "Anyway, I'm supposed to invite you to my family's Memorial Day barbecue. It's a huge affair with all my cousins and many of the surrounding farmers."

Not what she'd been expecting.

"I don't expect you to go . . . not that I don't want you to . . . I do . . . but . . ." He shook his head and began walking again. "Mom will want to know if I asked you the next time I talk to her, and I don't like lying to my mom."

"So you knew you needed to ask."

"Yes."

They strolled side by side in silence for several minutes. Beth didn't know what to think of the invitation. Of course, she knew that his mother thought they were an item even if Drew had told her otherwise. And Beth thought it was incredibly sweet that he was nervous about saying something to her, yet he did it anyway because he didn't want to have to lie to his mother. It said a lot about him.

"I'll think about it and let you know."

He stopped again. When he faced her, his eyes were wide with disbelief. "What?"

Beth tried to stifle her laugh. "I said I'd think about it. I'm assuming it's on Memorial Day, correct?"

"Well, yes. It's—"

"So I have about three weeks before I have to make a decision."

When he realized she was really considering going to meet his family, he perked up considerably. "You mean you might actually want to go?"

This time she restarted their forward progress. "This *thing* between us. I've been thinking a lot about it. I'm not sure I'm completely ready yet, but I'll admit, I'm getting there. At this point, I think we should play it by ear and see what happens."

Drew groaned.

"What?" Beth couldn't imagine what she could have said that would make him react like that. She thought he'd be thrilled. Wasn't that what he wanted?

"I have an insane urge to kiss you right now."

This time she didn't hold back her laughter.

It took a few seconds, but eventually he joined her. "Sorry, but it's the truth."

When she got a hold of herself again, she was feeling lighter than she could remember being in a long time. "I know it is, and believe me I appreciate it. I'm getting there. Just please be patient."

He reached out and touched her arm, causing her to halt her movement. The look in his eyes caused her breath to hitch, and all thought of patience and waiting flew out the window. She took two steps forward, closing the gap between them. Beth could feel his warm breath brush against her face.

She lifted her right hand and ran her index finger along the seam of his lips. They were soft, and they parted as she continued to rub back and forth. It was as if something was drawing her in . . . something unseen yet irresistible.

Drew closed his eyes, and her gaze fell to his mouth. Despite her earlier assertion, she wanted to kiss him. It was almost a craving it was so potent. She'd never felt anything like it before.

Beth was moments away from succumbing to what she wanted when the sound of someone coming jarred her back to reality. With it came the knowledge of what had almost happened . . . what she'd almost allowed to happen.

Allowed. That was comical. She'd pursued it. She'd let her growing feelings for him and the situation to completely unarm her. What was happening to her?

Frustrated with herself, Beth took off at a faster than natural pace. It didn't take long for her to hear Drew racing to catch up.

"Beth. Wait. Please."

As much as she wanted to run away and forget it ever happened, that wasn't her style. She slowed down and waited until he was beside her again.

"I'm sorry."

She looked over at him, but didn't stop walking. "Why are you sorry? You didn't do anything."

"I stopped you. None of that would have happened if I hadn't—"

"Drew, you have nothing to apologize for. That was all me. I set up these rules for our relationship and, apparently, I can't seem to follow them. That's my fault, not yours."

"Still."

They were coming to the end of the trail. She wasn't sure if she was glad about that or not. "Maybe there are a few things we need to talk about."

"Okay." He sounded as if he were waiting for her to chastise him or something.

"What you did—stopping me—was perfectly normal. I'm the one who stepped over the line and didn't stick to the limits we'd both agreed to. Just because you're a sub doesn't mean you have to be the one always to apologize. It's me who should be apologizing to you, not the other way around." She was hoping he understood the weight of what she was saying. Although they were technically alone, she didn't want to get into a full-scale discussion about the lifestyle out here in the middle of the woods.

"I understand what you're saying but, Beth, I just told you that I wanted to kiss you. I'm pretty sure that would qualify as a green light on my side of things. And it was your limit, not mine. I have no issues with you kissing me anytime you feel the urge."

When she glanced up at him, the sparkle in his eyes was back. "Fair enough. But still, if I mess up, now . . . or later . . . don't hesitate to call me out on it."

"I can agree to that."

"Good."

The trail opened up and Beth realized that they weren't back at the parking area as she'd originally thought. It was a large open space. The grass had been mowed, and there were a couple of tents along the opposite tree line. Apparently, their hike wasn't over.

DREW HAD WALKED THE PATH THEY'D TAKEN MANY TIMES OVER THE YEARS. It led to one of his favorite local camping spots. Granted, he had a few, some a lot more remote, but this was where he liked to come if he was limited on time but needed to get away for a day or two. It had seemed logical to bring Beth here.

She glanced up at him and then back at the campsite. "Do you come here a lot?"

"At least once a month when it's nice. It's not too far from home, but it's away from the noise of the city."

Without further comment, she started toward the small pond on the far side. It was a good distance away from the tents, and it would give them privacy to continue their conversation.

She found a large rock and sat down. Instead of joining her—because if he did he was afraid they'd end up right back where they'd been a few minutes before—he strolled over to the bank and knelt down. "I've spent many hours fishing here."

"Did you use to fish with your dad when you were younger?" Beth asked.

He picked up a stick that had washed up along the bank, tossed it out into the water, and stood. "Almost every Saturday morning when there wasn't snow on the ground."

"I've noticed that you never mention your brother when you talk about these trips with your dad. Why is that?"

Drew waited to answer her until he was back at her side. She scooted over to make room for him. He sat down, and he instantly felt that electric pull toward her. Taking a deep breath, he looked out across the pond, and tried to concentrate on the conversation. "He used to go when I was younger, but as Seth got older, he lost interest. By the time he was sixteen, he was off doing his own thing, leaving me and Dad on our own."

"You would have been six then, right?" Beth smiled, and he felt the muscles in his stomach clench.

"Right." He swallowed and pressed his hands into his thighs to keep from reaching for her like he wanted to. "The age difference meant we didn't have much in common. I think that was part of the reason he didn't want to go camping and fishing with us. I mean, what fun is it when you have your six-year-old little brother tagging along?"

"I bet you were cute when you were younger."

He drew back and pretended to be offended. "Are you implying I'm not cute now?"

Beth pressed her lips together and studied him in a way that had his entire body vibrating.

The air around them felt as if it could ignite at any moment. Drew didn't know what it was about Beth, but being with her was both comfortable and excruciatingly frustrating at the same time.

She closed the gap between them once more. This time her lips came within an inch of his. Drew held his breath waiting to see what she'd do.

Her eyes met his. "I'm not sure I'd use the word *cute* to describe you."

His palms were itching, but he tried to remain still. All those years of learning to work under pressure were coming in handy. Who knew he'd be relying on his crisis management training to navigate a relationship? "What word would you use?"

"Hmm. I have a few words I could use, but I think I'll keep them to myself for now."

The look in her eyes had him desperate to close the distance between her lips and his.

Right when he thought he couldn't take it anymore, Beth's mouth made contact with his own. Before he knew what was happening, she was framing his face between both of her hands and straddling his lap.

Instinctively, he brought his arms up to embrace her.

"Hands on the rock. Keep them there," she ordered.

It was absolutely insane, but her words caused his cock to swell. He groaned in frustration, but did what he was told.

She plunged her tongue inside his mouth and took what she wanted. It was the hottest thing Drew could ever remember experiencing in his life.

The kiss didn't last more than a minute or two, but it was long enough for him to know he wanted more.

Beth rested her forehead against his. She was breathing just as hard as he was. Her chest was heaving up and down, brushing against his chest. Not to mention that she was still straddling his lap.

"Please tell me you want to do that again."

She laughed. It was so nice to see her happy and carefree.

"Is that a yes?"

"Don't get cocky on me now." She ran a single finger down the side of his face and over his lower lip.

He closed his eyes, trying not to push.

"Open your eyes," she whispered.

When he met her gaze, he noticed the amusement was gone. He was instantly on alert. "What's wrong?"

Beth shook her head. "Nothing's wrong. I'm just . . . considering my options."

"Options about what?"

"You."

"Oh." He wasn't sure he liked the fact that thinking over her options had banished the fun they'd be having.

Before he could formulate another question, she explained. "Things between us are moving faster than I thought they would."

"Is that bad?" He needed to know. In his opinion, things between them weren't moving fast enough.

She sighed. But Drew also noted that she hadn't removed herself from his lap. That was good, wasn't it?

"I don't know. Maybe. Maybe not."

Since they were no longer in the heat of the moment, he took a chance and brought his hands up to rest on her hips. She didn't protest, so he settled in and enjoyed finally being able to touch her. "We're friends, right? So talk to me."

Beth released a single, rather sarcastic-sounding laugh. "Last time I checked, friends didn't do what we just did."

He decided to try to lighten the mood. "Well, some friends do. At least, that's what I've heard."

She gave him a small smile. "I don't do friends with benefits."

"Good," he said in all seriousness. "Neither do I."

They were both quiet for several minutes. As much as he wanted to say something, he knew she had to process this thing between them in her own time. He was hoping after the kiss they shared that she'd be ready to move to the next level with him. As much as he enjoyed their friendship, he wanted more with her. And after that kiss, he knew the potential was there.

Beth sat back, resting her ass on his thighs. The serious look was still there, and he wanted to wipe it away. He wanted to go back to when he'd seen the passion and teasing in her eyes.

"What's your schedule this week? I know you said you had the next couple of days off."

He had no idea why she was asking, but he'd gladly tell her anything she wanted to know. "I work Friday, Sunday, and Tuesday. Then I'm off for four days."

"So you don't have to work this Saturday?" she asked.

"No. I get off around eight in the morning and don't have to be back in until about seven Sunday morning."

She nodded, and he waited to see what she'd say next. "Did you still want to go out on that date?"

Was she serious? "Yes. Of course I do."

Beth nodded. "Okay."

He tried to contain his excitement. "Does this mean you want to go out on a date with me Saturday? A real date? Not just meeting up at the club?"

"Yes, if you want to."

Without thinking, Drew pulled her against him and gave her a solid kiss.

Luckily, she didn't seem upset.

"Thank you. For trusting me, I mean."

She wrapped her arms around his neck and gave him another kiss. It wasn't as heated as the first one, but this time he was able to hold her in his arms. Drew couldn't imagine it got much better than this.

Chapter Eleven

They sat for a little longer, enjoying their peaceful surroundings before making their way back to the trail. Drew couldn't wipe the smile off his face. Never in a million years could he have imagined that a short hike to talk about an invitation to his family barbecue would result in Beth agreeing to go out on a date with him. And that kiss. Heaven help him, but he wanted more of those. Well, he wanted more, period, but he had confidence that it would come in time. He only had to be patient.

Beth walked quietly beside him as they wound their way back down the path that led to their cars. She seemed . . . pensive.

"Something wrong?"

She glanced over at him and then back up at the trees. "No. Just thinking."

"About?"

There was a twinkle in her eye when she met his gaze this time. "I'm trying to decide how fast I want to take things with you versus how far . . . and fast . . . you'd want to go."

Although she said it with a hint of levity, Drew knew she was being serious. They would need to talk about things if their relationship was changing. Given the BDSM aspect they both wanted, it would mean a more detailed conversation. "I'll be honest. Other than the basics and what I've seen at the club, I don't know much. And the more I do learn, the more I'm realizing most of what's online is wrong."

Beth nodded. "If you don't know the specific sites to look for, you mostly end up with porn. It's a bad example of what the lifestyle really is."

He snorted. "That's for sure. I was so nervous the first time I got up the courage to go to a munch."

"It was nerve-racking for me as well, even though I didn't go by myself."

"Was it with . . . Ben?" he asked, almost afraid saying his name would somehow shatter the progress they'd made.

"Yes."

They both grew quiet as they reached the top of the hill and stepped out onto the grass surrounding the parking area. He could see their vehicles parked side by side about thirty feet away. Soon they would be going their separate ways, and it was the last thing he wanted. Drew wasn't ready to say goodbye to her yet. "Did you still want to catch a movie?"

Beth didn't answer until they were in front of their cars. She shook her head. "I'm not really in a movie kind of mood anymore."

"Hungry?" He didn't want to sound desperate, but let's face it—he kind of was.

She chuckled. "I could probably eat."

"So could I. Would you care to join me? I know a place not far from here. We could ride together and I could bring you back to your vehicle when we're done." He paused. "Or you could follow me."

After a moment's consideration—Drew thought it was more to toy with him than anything else—she sashayed over to the passenger side of his vehicle. He grinned and went to unlock her door. Beth smiled a thank you, and then slid inside.

While he could cook for himself, he was no stranger to eating out. Being a bachelor meant he knew a lot about the local places to eat. For their date on Saturday, he planned to take her some place nice, but he figured he should keep it casual for tonight. This wasn't a date. Or officially it wasn't.

They pulled up in front of a small family-run restaurant, and he turned off the engine. "Ever been here before?"

She looked up at the sign. "I think so. But it's been a while."

After exiting the vehicle, they met around front before heading toward the entrance. As soon as they were through the door, an older lady greeted them. "Welcome. Two of you this evening?"

"Yes, ma'am," Drew answered.

The hostess escorted them to a table along the wall and handed them menus.

Beth scanned the dining room and grinned. "I have been here before. I remember that green counter along the wall."

He glanced over to see what Beth was referring to, and had to chuckle. Most of the décor in the place had been done in the seventies, including the mint green counter that separated the kitchen from the dining room. "I guess it doesn't hurt business."

She took in the other diners. "I guess not. You'd think it would, though. I mean mint green?"

Drew couldn't argue with her. The décor was tacky at best.

Their server came a few moments later, and they put in their orders. Once they were alone again, Beth clasped her hands together on the table in front of her. "Are you sure you want to go forward with this?"

When he tilted his head to the side in confusion, she clarified. "The non-vanilla part, I mean. Did you want to keep things . . . normal for a while first, or—"

"I've done *normal*. Normal doesn't work for me."

Beth nodded. "Okay. Katrina has a limits list on the club's website that you can download. Fill it out and bring it with you Saturday. We can go over it and see where we want to go from there. Sound good?"

"I can do that." Nervous excitement was coursing through his body. This was really happening.

She smiled as the server brought their salads. When the woman walked away, Beth cleared her throat. "Were you surprised that I kissed you?"

He nearly choked on his food. After taking a sip of water, he met her gaze. "A little. But I'd be lying if I said I wasn't hoping for a repeat performance when I drop you off at your car."

Beth smirked and dug into her salad again. "I might be able to arrange that."

Drew turned his attention to his food, but inside he was counting down the minutes until he would be able to get his hands on her again.

"Why don't you tell me more about your family? I should probably know what I'm getting myself into if I decide to spend Memorial Day with them."

"Not much to tell. I mean, we're a fairly normal bunch. Dad farms and takes care of his animals. Mom runs the house." Drew shrugged, not sure what else to say. Overall, his family was pretty boring.

Beth shook her head. "There has to be more to it than that. I mean, you grew up on a farm. What was that like? Were your parents strict or did they let you get away with everything? Inquiring minds want to know."

He finished his salad and pushed his plate to the side. "It was a lot like you'd expect. It was just my parents, Seth, and I, until Seth went away to college. Our nearest neighbors were almost a mile away, so until I was old enough to go to school I didn't play with other kids my age much. We went to school, did our homework, and our chores."

"Did that bother you?" she asked. "Being so far away from other kids, I mean. Given there was such a big age gap between you and your bother, I imagine it could be pretty lonely."

"Not really." He paused as their server returned with their meals. When they were alone again, he continued. "There was always plenty to do. If I wasn't helping Mom or Dad, I was running around the farm pretending to protect our home from approaching enemies and wild animals."

She laughed.

"Then, once I started school, I made a few friends and they'd come over on the weekends and they'd help me defend the farm."

"It sounds like a very normal childhood."

"It was. I was very lucky. My parents have been together since they were in their early twenties and are as much in love today as they were then. I couldn't ask for better."

They grew quiet for several minutes as they ate. After talking about his own family, Drew couldn't help but wonder about hers. "What about you? Was your childhood normal?"

Beth shrugged. "I suppose you could call it *normal*. My parents didn't get married until they were in their early thirties. They had me seven months later."

"Were you the reason—"

"That they got married? Yeah." Beth hesitated. "I mean, they loved each other—still do—but I sort of rushed things along."

"And your siblings?" he asked.

"I think they were more planned than I was." She took a bite and swallowed. "We were all loved and cared for. Even when my dad lost his job and we had to move in with my grandparents for a few months, they made sure we had what we needed."

It was nice to hear more about Beth and her life. Although he'd gotten to know her some over the last month, he loved that she was opening up to him.

They lingered over coffee and shared a piece of apple pie. Being with Beth was easy.

Although he didn't want to, Drew let her pay for her dinner. When they went out on their date on Saturday, he was paying and she'd just have to deal with it.

The drive back to her car was too short. They'd spent the last five hours together, yet it wasn't enough. He felt as if he'd only scratched the surface and he wanted to know more. He wanted to know everything.

When she got out of the car, he followed her. They were alone in the parking lot. All the other vehicles were gone.

Drew was trying to decide whether to ask if he could kiss her or just do it when she reached up to cup the back of his head. She pulled his mouth toward hers, and he didn't resist. Seconds after their lips connected, he had her pressed back against her car, and her leg was wrapped around his waist. This time he didn't hold back. His hands were on her back, her legs, her ass. She felt amazing, but there were too many clothes between them.

Beth was the first one to break the kiss. When her mouth left his, she trailed her lips down his jaw to his neck. She grazed her teeth right where his pulse was pounding beneath the skin. Part of him wanted her to bite down so he could know what it felt like. Instead, she teased him, holding him on the edge, not giving him what he wanted.

He dug his fingers into her hips and ground his pelvis into the heat he could feel coming from between her legs. Ever since he noticed her across the room that first night, he'd wanted to get his hands on her. Now that he was able to touch her, he didn't want to stop.

Finally, she clamped down on his neck with her teeth, and his cock pulsed almost painfully. He was hoping she wouldn't make him wait too long before he was able to feel her pussy surrounding his cock. But thinking about her pussy did nothing to help calm him down. Neither did her snaking her hand between them to cup his erection and give it a squeeze.

"Mmm," she hummed against his neck.

He swallowed. "I want you."

"Patience." Her breath ghosted along his neck, sending a chill down his spine.

He moaned.

She ran her fingernail down the side of his neck, and released her hold on his cock. He didn't know if that was better or worse.

Drew took a deep breath and nodded. It would be getting dark soon, and he knew she should be on her way. The park closed at dusk. "I should let you get home."

Beth rose up on her tiptoes and brushed her lips against his. "I'll see you Saturday. And . . . you can call me." She was teasing him, and he loved it.

"I'll call. Let you know what time I'm picking you up for our date." He hadn't let go of her, and she didn't seem anxious to pull away.

She nodded and brought their mouths together once again.

This kiss was all soft lips and gentle suction. It did nothing to dampen the fire inside him.

She pulled away before he was ready, so he followed her with his mouth, seeking more.

Beth laughed. "I promise the wait will be worth it."

"My cock feels like it's about to explode."

As if to test his assertion, she wrapped one hand around his cock and the other cupped his balls. She squeezed each three times, and he nearly fell over. He dug his fingers into the sides of her hips and closed his eyes. "Beth . . . please."

"Please what?" she asked against his lips.

Before he could form a coherent thought, her hands were gone and she was moving away from him. He opened his eyes to find her slipping behind the wheel of her car. She grinned up at him and waved. "Call me."

Drew stood without moving as she drove away, his cock painfully hard. Making it to Saturday was going to be torture. Pure torture.

❧

BETH WAS PULLING INTO HER DRIVEWAY WHEN NICOLE CALLED. "HEY."

"Hey, yourself. How'd your movie date with Drew go?" Nicole asked.

Tucking her purse under her arm, Beth hurried inside, and kicked off her shoes. "It didn't."

"What do you mean it didn't?" Nicole demanded.

Beth sighed, and flopped down on her couch with the phone to her ear. "I mean we ended up going for a walk instead. Apparently, he let it slip to his mom that he was meeting me this afternoon, and was told to extend an invitation to me to the family's Memorial Day barbecue."

"Meeting the family, huh? That's a big step. You gonna go?"

"I haven't decided. I told him I'd think about it." Beth rolled over and propped herself up on her elbow. "Oh. And we're going out Saturday."

Nicole got real quiet for several moments. "Going out as in meeting up again to hang out or going out as in going on a date?"

Beth didn't answer right away. She wanted to let Nicole stew a while. "The second."

"Finally!"

"It's only been a month."

"A very long month," Nicole insisted.

"If you say so."

They both chuckled.

"So tell me, how did a walk turn into plans for a date?"

Beth eagerly filled her best friend in on the details of her time with Drew, including what turned out to be the first of several kisses. Nicole was riveted, and pumped her for details. Her friend burst out laughing when Beth relayed the heated good-night kiss she'd shared with Drew. "I would have paid to see that."

"I don't think we're ready for an audience."

"Beside the point." Nicole released a contented sigh. "I'm happy for you."

"Let's not get ahead of ourselves. It's just a date."

"And several kisses. Rather passionate kisses. We can't forget those," Nicole said.

Beth rolled her eyes. "Whatever you say."

"So does that mean you'll be coming to the club together Saturday night?"

The thought had crossed Beth's mind. "I don't know. We have a lot to talk about. That is, if the date goes well."

"Don't jinx yourself. Why wouldn't it go well?" Nicole asked.

"I don't know. Just nerves, I guess. Look, I should go. I have a few things to do before I turn in."

"All right. Sleep tight. And dream of that hunky fireman of yours."

Beth shook her head. "Good night."

"Good night."

Disconnecting the call, Beth headed for her bedroom, placed her phone on the charger, and booted up her computer. She located her limit list and opened the file. It had been a while since she'd read over the list, let alone updated it. She and Ben had been together for three years. At the beginning, it had been a useful tool in helping them navigate the kinky side to their relationship, but after a while they'd foregone their lists entirely and relied solely on verbal communication. If something came up that interested one of them, they brought it up and discussed it. It showed a level of comfort . . . of trust.

Beth snorted. *Trust.*

She took a deep breath and pushed Ben out of her thoughts. This wasn't about Ben. It was about Drew. Her and Drew. And in situations like theirs, lists were good. They had to start somewhere, and knowing what kinks interested each of them was better than guessing. She needed to know what Drew wanted to explore. Who knows? They might find out that their kinks weren't compatible. It wasn't as if they'd talked about them in any detail.

As it turned out, most of the changes she made were minor. They consisted of changing things from 'want to try' to 'like' or 'dislike'. The vast majority of it, however, stayed the same. What happened with Ben made her more cautious, but it didn't change what she enjoyed.

She saved her new list and logged off the computer. Knowing she needed a little me time before turning in for the night, Beth headed for her bathroom and began filling her tub with water.

Once she made sure the temperature was right, she opened the bottom drawer of her vanity. Tucked into the back underneath several hand towels were two of her treasured bathroom accessories. One was a dildo. The other a vibrator. Both were waterproof and perfect for some underwater fun. There was nothing like a nice long soak in her bathtub, and two of her favorite toys, to relax her.

With her bath ready, Beth removed her clothes, twisted her hair up into a bun, and lowered herself into the tub. The warm water surrounded her. Baths were something she cherished. Before she'd bought her house, she'd lived in a one-room apartment that only had a small shower. The only time she was able to take a bath was when she went home to Ohio, and that wasn't often. One of these days she was going to have one of those soaker tubs installed so she could stretch out and still have the water come up to her chin.

Beth leaned back and closed her eyes, letting her mind drift. It didn't take long for Drew's image to flood her vision. She could still feel his hands on her back, her hips, her butt. His cock pressing against her, wanting desperately to be let out.

She ran her hands down her torso, lingering on each one of her breasts, tugging at her nipples. What would it feel like to have him sucking and licking every inch of her? Beth planned to find out.

By the time she grazed a finger over her clit, she was ready. Beth reached for her toys and positioned them exactly where she wanted them. The soft hum of the vibrator could be heard even through the water as it massaged her pussy. It felt good, but she needed to be filled. Since she didn't have a real cock at hand, a fake one would have to do.

The silicone dildo stretched her inch by inch as she pushed it inside. While she enjoyed toys, there was nothing like the real thing. Beth let her imagination take over and pretended it was Drew pushing his way inside her. Drew making her breath hitch. Drew pumping in and out of her faster and faster.

She approached her peak and increased the pressure against her clit. It was enough to send her barreling over the edge.

As her high faded, she was struck with a fit of giggles. Over the last few months, she'd pleasured herself plenty. None of them had been as intense as what she'd just experienced. She had no idea if it was because of the afternoon she'd spent with Drew, or if it was because she'd imagined it was him, instead of some faceless man who happened to have a very talented appendage. Either way, she was feeling extremely sleepy.

Beth opened the drain and forced herself out of the tub. As she dried herself off and got ready for bed, she began humming. It was crazy how happy she was. Nothing had even happened with Drew yet. Okay, that wasn't true. They'd kissed. And, boy, what a kiss it was. There was definitely chemistry there. She'd felt it down to the tips of her toes.

She strolled naked into her bedroom and plucked one of her favorite nightshirts out of her dresser, humming the entire time. After running a brush through her hair, she slipped under the covers. There was a lot she'd need to do before her date on Saturday, but she'd worry about that tomorrow. Letting her eyelids close, she fell into a peaceful sleep.

The next morning started normal enough. Her alarm went off at five, and by six thirty she was elbow-deep in bread dough. She was in the process of taking a fresh loaf of bread out of the oven right before noon when Tommy popped his head back in the kitchen. "Delivery."

Beth made sure nothing was in immediate danger of burning before going out front. She had a feeling she might be getting more flowers, and she was right.

"Are you going to read the card?" Tommy was in his element.

"Well, of course I am."

She had her hand poised inches above the card when it dawned on her that every customer had their eyes trained on her. Every one of them stared at her full of curious anticipation. Mrs. Carlisle—an older woman who came into the café almost every morning—was sitting at a table not far from the counter with her husband of nearly forty years. She held her hands clutched to her chest, a huge grin on her face. They were all waiting.

Heat flooded Beth's cheeks. She grabbed her flowers and made a mad dash toward the kitchen.

Unfortunately, she didn't get far before she heard a familiar voice. "Who sent the flowers?"

She looked up and all signs of her blush vanished. There, standing near the door, was Ben.

"You need to leave." Beth resumed her path toward the kitchen and didn't look back.

She heard some rustling and raised voices, but remained hidden. Maybe it was cowardly, but Ben was the last person she wanted to deal with. Not now. Not when she was finally getting her life in order.

Beth had no idea how much time had passed, but she didn't think it was more than a few minutes when Tommy came back to check on her. "Are you all right?"

She nodded. "I'm fine. Is he gone?"

"Yeah."

"Thank you."

Tommy reached for some gloves, and she realized he was planning to work on the sandwiches she was supposed to be making.

"I can get those," she said. "Why don't you go back out front and make sure no one needs a refill on their coffee. I'll make sure everything is taken care of back here."

He looked unsure. "I can help."

Beth shook her head. "I've got it. Promise."

The smile she gave him was weak, but it was the best she could do. Ben showing up had thrown her. The last time she'd been somewhat prepared. This time . . .

She placed the fresh loaf of bread in the slicer and began assembling the sandwiches for her customers. Why was he here? Why now?

As quickly as she could, Beth rushed the sandwiches out to the customers who ordered them. She didn't miss the sympathetic looks she received from her regulars. Many of them had been around when she and Ben had been a couple. They all knew things had ended between them. Some even knew it ended badly. She hated their looks of pity.

Plastering a smile on her face, she finished her task, and then returned to the kitchen. Her gaze fell on the flowers Drew sent. Ben had taken that moment of joy away from her and she hated him for it.

She ran her fingers over the delicate blooms—tulips this time—and extracted the card.

Beth,

I hope you enjoyed our hike as much as I did.

Drew

Simple and to the point. So why did her chest clench? Drew seemed to know exactly what to say and do to break through her defenses. She felt moisture trail down her cheeks, and swiftly wiped it away.

Before she could second-guess herself, she dug her phone out of her pocket, and shot Drew a text.

Got the flowers. They're beautiful. Thank you. - Beth

Only seconds passed before he responded.

You're welcome. Call you tonight?

She didn't hesitate to reply.

Yes. - Beth

Smiling, she laid her phone down on the counter, and got back to work. Ben was her past, and as far as she was concerned, he was going to remain there. She had the potential of a new relationship with Drew. A relationship that wasn't built on lies. She was going to concentrate on that and forget Ben ever existed.

Chapter Twelve

"You holding out on me?"

Drew shoved his phone back in his pocket and picked up the nail gun he'd been using before answering Beth's text. "Why do you say that?

Shawn had called Drew late the night before and asked if he could help put on a roof. He used to work with Shawn a lot on his days off back when they were on the same crew. Now, more often than not, they had conflicting schedules.

His former captain and friend dropped another bundle of shingles onto the roof and leveled a stare at Drew. Shawn raised his eyebrows. It was a look Drew had seen often. It was the you're-full-of-shit look.

While he was reluctant to tell anyone about Beth, he knew he could trust Shawn. "Her name's Beth."

"Is it serious, or just fun?"

It was a valid question. Shawn knew all about Drew's wilder days. He also knew Drew had settled down over the last two years. "Hopefully serious. We'll see what happens Saturday."

Shawn began laying down another row of shingles. "Big date, huh?"

Drew grinned and continued to work. He'd been thinking a lot about his upcoming date. It couldn't be overly complicated since he had to work the next day, but he wanted to make sure it was memorable at the same time. "I've been trying to figure out where to take her."

They worked side by side for several minutes before Shawn responded. "What does she like?"

"She likes history." Drew shrugged. "We haven't talked about it all that much. And I know she likes movies. I guess I could take her to a museum, but she doesn't get off work until three. That doesn't leave us much time."

"This is a first date, right?" Shawn asked.

"Yeah."

Shawn nodded. "And you want to make a good impression?"

"Of course."

"Take her to a concert in the park. You can pack a picnic dinner for you both. Women love that sort of thing. Plus, unlike the rest of us, you can actually cook."

They both chuckled. Drew had taken some ribbing from the guys at the station when they found out he wasn't a total slouch in the kitchen. That was until they were the ones benefiting from his knowledge.

The more Drew thought about Shawn's suggestion, the better it sounded. It would be nice to spend the evening under the stars with Beth, listening to music.

The sun was dipping low in the sky by the time they'd finished the roof and cleaned things up. Drew said goodbye to Shawn and drove home. As soon as he walked in the door, he stripped out of his clothes and headed for the shower. Once he didn't feel as if he were sporting a second skin of dirt and sweat, he fully intended to call Beth. He'd been dying to talk to her all day. Seeing her the previous two days had spoiled him.

He rushed through his shower and threw on some shorts before settling in on the couch with his laptop and his phone. After he'd pulled up information on concerts in the park, he scrolled through the contacts on his phone until he found Beth's name. He smiled as he pushed the call button.

"Hello." Beth's voice was husky. His mind began racing with the possibilities. The only time he'd come close to hearing her like that was after their kiss when they'd both been breathing hard.

"Did I call at a bad time?" He really hoped she would say no.

She sighed. "Not at all."

"Okay. It's just . . . you sound . . ." Funny? Weird? Incredibly sexy?

Beth giggled. "And how do I sound exactly?"

"Um . . ."

"Yes?" She was clearly enjoying tormenting him.

"You sound . . . you sound like you're really turned on." There. He'd said it.

This time she laughed. "You're close. I just finished spending some quality time with my favorite vibrator."

Drew's head fell back against the couch and he groaned. All thoughts of his Internet search went out the window. Without conscious thought, he moved his hand closer to his groin where his cock was tenting his shorts.

"Does that turn you on? Knowing that I was pleasuring myself?" she asked.

He swallowed. "You have no idea. Just imagining you touching yourself like that makes me hard."

"Mmm. I remember what you felt like all hard and ready."

"You'd think I hadn't jacked off in weeks," he admitted.

She hummed. "I'll take that as a compliment."

Drew shifted in his seat. Her voice still had that husky tone and it wasn't helping his current condition. "You most definitely should."

There was a long pause, and then her voice dropped even lower. "What do you think about when you're getting yourself off? Anything you want to share?"

"You." Was he imagining it, or did he really sound out of breath?

"What about me? Am I doing anything special?" Her voice was barely above a whisper.

He cupped his hand over his erection and pressed down. "This morning, I imagined that I was tied to the bed, and you were sitting on my face."

"Hmm. I like the sound of that. Is that something you'd like me to do to you?"

"Yes." It was one of his many recurring fantasies. Most involved him being tied up. Everything else varied. Sometimes she was riding him. Other times she had her pussy covering his face . . . grinding against his tongue until he couldn't smell or taste anything but her. That's what had filled his vision earlier that morning.

"Are you alone?" she asked.

"Yeah. I'm home. In my living room."

"Good. If you're wearing any clothes, take them off." She was completely serious.

"Now?"

Beth sounded amused by his question. "Something wrong with now?"

"No. I just . . . give me a sec." He picked up his laptop and placed it safely on the coffee table, then stood and removed his shorts before resuming his place on the couch. "Okay."

"Put me on speaker and get comfortable. I want your hands free, but I still want to be able to hear you."

It took Drew a minute or so to get everything situated. In a way, the whole situation was a little strange. He'd had phone sex before, which he was pretty sure was what was going to happen, but always in the past he'd been the one giving the instructions. This was different. Different, but not in a bad way. "Okay, I'm good."

"I want you to spread your legs as wide as you can. With one hand, I want you to hold your cock against your stomach. With the other hand, I want you to touch your balls."

She paused a moment, giving him time to do as she'd instructed.

His balls were heavy in his hand. It was crazy how worked up he was considering he came both the night before, and then again that morning. He shouldn't be this hard.

Whether he should be or not was irrelevant. He was.

"Now, I want you to roll your balls around in your hand. And every now and then I want you to give them a little tug."

He did what she said. It was something he'd done before. He was sure most guys had. When your junk was right there in front of you every day, you got curious. But for some reason, Beth telling him to do it made it feel ten times better.

"How does that feel?"

"Good." More than good, if he was being honest. The only thing that would make it better was if he was pumping his cock at the same time.

She must have read his mind. "I want you to take the hand holding your cock and begin moving it up and down. Slowly. We don't want you to come too fast now, do we?"

A groan escaped his throat before he could stifle it.

Beth chuckled. "If you're going to be my submissive, you're going to have to learn patience."

He closed his eyes and tried to concentrate on not coming.

"Tell me what you're thinking about right now."

That was easy to answer. "I'm imagining it's you touching my cock and balls."

"What am I doing? Am I between your legs? Straddling you?"

"You're between my legs."

"Mmm. I think I like that." She sounded as if she was smiling. "I'm going to lick your cock now. Run your thumb over the head of your cock and imagine it's my tongue."

"Gah! I don't know how much longer I can hold on. Beth, please."

"Please what? Tell me what you want." She was taunting him. Teasing him.

And he found that he loved it. He was hard and pulsing in his hand. His balls were full and tight, ready to explode.

"I want to come. Please. I don't want to disappoint you, but I don't think . . . I don't . . ."

"Let it go. Let me hear you come for me," she whispered.

Drew picked up speed, pulling and pumping like a mad man. It didn't take long. He saw red and white and . . . well, he couldn't quite remember. Light flashed before his eyes as he spilled out his cum over his hand and stomach.

"You still with me?" she asked.

He breathed deep. "Yeah."

Beth laughed. "Go clean yourself up, and then we can talk."

"Be right back." He jumped up off the couch and raced into the bathroom. It took a few minutes to get everything back to normal again. He had to admit it was the best phone sex he'd ever had.

As he returned to the living room and slipped back into his shorts, it dawned on him that Beth hadn't come. At least, he didn't think she had. Granted, he'd been a little distracted at the time.

He took the phone off speaker and held it to his ear, his joyous euphoria fading. What kind of a jerk didn't make sure a woman he cared about got hers first? "I should probably apologize."

❦❧

BETH WAS FEELING PRETTY HAPPY AFTER LISTENING TO DREW. SURE, SHE could have joined him—her toys were still out and easily accessible—but that hadn't been the point. She'd wanted to see how he'd react to being dominated, even if it was only over the phone. From her end, he'd seemed to enjoy it, which was why she was confused by his comment. "For?"

"I should have made sure you came first. I didn't even think—"

Out of all the possibilities that had been swirling in her head, that hadn't been one of them. "It's fine."

"No. It isn't." He blew out a loud breath. "It's been a long time since I've left a woman hanging like that."

"I'll let you make it up to me. How about that?" She hoped he could tell she was teasing.

"I guess I can deal with that."

She laughed. "I'll look forward to it."

Neither said anything for several moments.

Beth stretched out on her bed, and then raised herself so she was sitting up against her headboard. "So tell me, Drew Parker, have you ever had phone sex before tonight?"

"Maybe a time or two." He chuckled. "Okay, maybe more than that, but it's been years. Since being out on my own, in-person encounters are much more desirable."

"Agreed."

"That's not to say that I didn't enjoy what we just did. Or what I just did, I guess. Because I did. Enjoy it, I mean."

It was cute to see him nervous. "I'm glad you liked it. In your past experiences with phone sex, had you ever had your partner tell you what to do?"

He snorted. "No. Not at all. Usually it was me telling her what to do."

"What did you think of the role reversal? Other than our kiss, this was your first real taste of domination, wasn't it?" From what he'd told her in the past, she was almost positive this was the case.

"Unless you count the one time I tried to talk my last girlfriend into tying me up and having her wicked way with me."

"This would be the same girlfriend who broke up with you because you wanted to be dominated?"

"One in the same," he said.

"Then no, that doesn't count."

There was a pause, and when he began speaking again Beth could tell he was smiling. "I'm glad my first experience with this will be with you."

Was he being honest or trying to butter her up for something? She hated that her mind automatically went there. Another by-product of Ben. Drew had never given her any reason to question his sincerity.

He must have noticed her silence. "Was that the wrong thing to say?"

"No. I was just thinking. Maybe . . ." She glanced up at the ceiling. "Maybe this isn't such a good idea."

"Don't say that."

She closed her eyes and took a deep breath. "Do you know what my first thought was when you said that you were glad your first experiences would be with me? I wondered if you were telling the truth or trying to pull the wool over my eyes about something."

"That's understandable, I guess. I have to earn your trust. But Beth, I promise you that I'm not like him. I mean, I invited you to come meet my family. If I had something sinister to hide, why would I do that?"

Beth took a moment, and he waited for her to gather her thoughts. Damn Ben. He was still screwing up her life. His showing up at her café hadn't helped either. She had no idea what he wanted, and quite frankly, she didn't care. She just wanted him to go away and let her get on with her life.

"Don't back out of our date. I promise we'll have a good time. If we don't, I'll go away. If that's what you want."

It didn't take a genius to know how hard those words were for him to get out. She'd seen the look on his face when she told him that she'd go on a date with him—something she knew he'd been wanting since they met.

Pushing down her fear, she tried her best to get things back on track. It wasn't fair to keep making Drew pay for Ben's mistakes. "Have you decided where we're going Saturday?"

"I have something in mind, but I'm still hashing out the details." She didn't miss his sigh of relief.

"Anything you'd like to share?"

"I'd rather surprise you."

"I guess that would be acceptable." She was trying to bring back the teasing atmosphere from before her anxiety had put a damper on their conversation. "Should I dress up?"

"Not if everything goes as planned. I'll text you once I confirm everything."

"I'll need to know what time you're picking me up, as well. Don't forget I have to work Saturday." Although he knew that already, she felt the need to remind him. A part of her wondered if maybe it was her way of keeping things on a level she could handle. Everything with Drew was moving so fast.

"I remembered." He grew quiet. "I've been working on my list."

Beth knew there had to be a question in there, so she gave him some time.

"What if we compare lists and we're not . . . compatible? What happens then?"

There wasn't any question of their chemistry. After the kiss they shared, that question had been answered loud and clear. Kinks, however, were a different thing entirely. His question was valid. What happened if he wanted something she couldn't give, or vice versa? "I guess we'll have to cross that bridge when we come to it."

He snorted. "I don't think I've ever felt so unsure of myself in a relationship before. You'd think I was a teenager again fumbling my way around the backseat of a car with my first girlfriend."

That made her laugh. "I wouldn't go that far."

"It's true."

"Drew, just be yourself. Do what comes naturally—what feels right. Everything else will figure itself out."

"So what you're saying is that I need to relax."

She chuckled. "Something like that."

"I should let you get ready for bed. It's getting late, and I know you have to be up early."

Beth glanced at the clock and realized that it was already after ten. They'd been on the phone for almost two hours. Her gaze landed on the bouquet he'd had delivered to her earlier that day. She'd put the flowers in a vase with some fresh water and placed them on the stand beside her bed. "Thank you again for the flowers."

"You're welcome."

There was a long pause, and she wondered what he was doing. "You have to work Friday, don't you?"

"Yep. I have to be there at seven."

As things with Drew heated up, that little voice in the back of her head that worried about his safety got stronger. "Be safe, okay."

"Always."

She reached over and ran the tips of her fingers along one of the petals. "Good night."

After Beth hung up the phone, she scooted off the mattress, and began getting ready for bed. That included cleaning the toys she'd used earlier. As she washed the silicone dildo, her thoughts returned to Drew masturbating to her instructions. Hearing him had been such a turn on. She couldn't wait to get her hands on him.

Unfortunately, that thought was quickly followed up by another memory of Ben. Why wouldn't he leave her alone and why had he shown up wanting to talk to her? It had been bad enough when she'd found out he came to the club months ago, but if he'd been looking for her, why hadn't he sought her out at her house or the café then? Why had he waited until now? Did he hear she'd found someone else? And if so, how? As far as she knew, he was living in Florida with his wife and daughter. Was someone feeding him information? Was he trying to destroy her new relationship before it even got started?

Beth felt the beginning of a headache coming on.

Gritting her teeth, she finished what she was doing, and left her toys out on the counter to dry. It was one of the advantages of living alone.

She finished going through her nightly routine, and snuggled beneath her sheets. Beth forced her mind to more pleasant thoughts, such as Drew and the fantasy he'd shared with her. Rope bondage wasn't something she excelled at, but she knew the basics. She also had several sets of leather cuffs. If he liked to be bound, she could work with it. And if rope was something he wanted to explore more, she could certainly find someone at the club to help her expand her skills. She had no idea what else would be on his list, but so far he hadn't revealed anything she viewed as a hard limit.

Releasing a deep breath, she closed her eyes and let thoughts of Drew tied to her bed fill her mind. She was dying to know what he looked like underneath all that clothing. To have him at her mercy caused her body temperature to rise and moisture to pool between her thighs.

Before she could change her mind, she snaked her hand beneath the sheet. Saturday night couldn't come soon enough for Beth. She had no idea if they would attempt to play that night, but if things went well, she had every intention of taking Drew up on his offer and letting him return the favor.

Chapter Thirteen

By the time Saturday afternoon rolled around, Beth was becoming nauseous from all the ups and downs she'd experienced in the last day and a half. One minute she was looking forward to her date with Drew. The next minute, she was debating whether or not to call it off.

Nicole had been her saving grace. Every time Beth started to get cold feet, she'd call her best friend and get reassured that she wasn't being stupid by giving Drew a shot. Honestly, she was making herself sick with all the dependency, but she needed a shoulder to lean on and Nicole got the luck of the draw.

"You ready for this?" Nicole asked.

It was four fifteen and Beth was standing in front of her bathroom mirror fixing her hair and makeup. She had her friend on speakerphone so she could get ready and talk at the same time. Drew had sent her a text on Friday letting her know that he'd pick her up at five on Saturday evening. Giving him her address had taken more resolve than giving him her phone number, but she'd done it. His reply back to her, including a smiley face and a 'see you tomorrow', had her grinning and all feelings of unease disappeared.

With less than an hour until he was due to show up on her doorstep, she'd needed Nicole's support yet again. "I think so. I just hope I'm making the right decision. The friends thing was working well. What if this ruins it?"

"What if it makes it better?" Nicole countered.

"I know. I'm just worried about all the what-ifs. I can't help it."

"Considering what that jackass Ben did to you, it's not surprising. Speaking of which, he hasn't shown up again, has he?"

Beth had told Nicole about Ben showing up at the café earlier that week. Her friend had wanted to track him down and have a nice long chat with him. It was a sweet notion, and Beth appreciated it, but she also knew it wouldn't help anything in the long run. If Ben showed up again, she would most likely have to look into getting a restraining order. That wasn't a pleasant thought, but she couldn't have him continuing to show up at her shop and disrupt her and her business.

"No." She finished running the brush through her hair, and debated whether or not to put it up or leave it down. "I just wish I knew what he wanted. First the club, and now the café? And why so much time in between? It doesn't make sense."

"No, it doesn't. But you know what they say. Curiosity killed the cat."

She laughed. "Thanks. I'll try and remember that."

Deciding to leave her hair loose, Beth cleaned up the counter, and went to her bedroom to start getting dressed. Drew said they would be keeping things casual, so she was opting for shorts and a fitted T-shirt.

"Just remember to relax and have fun. It's just a date. And Drew seems like a nice guy."

Beth waited until she'd pulled her shirt over her head before answering. "So did Ben, at first."

"You have to learn to trust again sometime."

"Maybe I need to have that tattooed across my forehead or something."

"Nah. If it was on your forehead, you'd only see it when you looked in the mirror."

As usual, talking to Nicole had lightened her mood considerably. "Okay, I think I'm ready. And . . . ." Beth glanced at the clock beside her bed. "I have over twenty minutes to kill. Just enough time for me to psych myself out again."

Nicole snorted, and Beth could almost see her rolling her eyes. "Do you have any idea where he's taking you?"

Beth strolled into her living room and took a seat on her couch. "I asked, but he said he wanted to surprise me."

They spent the next several minutes throwing out ideas on where Drew might be taking her on their date. It had started with things such as dinner and a movie, but by the time a knock sounded on her front door, they were both giggling and making jokes about outrageous costumes and scavenger hunts.

"I think he's here."

"Relax, and have fun. Oh, and call me tomorrow. I want details." With that, Nicole hung up, not giving Beth time to respond. Sighing, she tucked her phone into her purse before going to answer the door.

Drew stood on her front porch with a small bunch of red flowers. They looked a little like lilies, but she'd never seen lilies that color before.

"Hi."

"I hope I'm not too early. I couldn't wait any longer." He gave her that smile she loved so much.

"Eager, huh?" Was it wrong that she had the urge to grab him by his shirt and yank him inside?

"Just a little." He handed her the flowers. "These are for you."

She took his offering and brought them close enough to inhale their scent. "They're beautiful. Thank you."

Drew surprised her when he reached up and ran his hand along the side of her face. His fingers left tingles in their wake where they touched her skin. Her body heated, and her desire to kiss him overruled everything else. Throwing caution to the wind, she grabbed hold of his shirt with her free hand and pulled him to her.

He offered no resistance as her mouth sought his.

The kiss was brief but intense. When she took a step back, they were both breathing hard. Her body and her mind were at war. They'd been dancing around their attraction for over a month. Her body knew what it wanted. But she had to be strong. Things needed to be discussed before they went any further—what they both wanted, what each expected.

She released him and backed away. "Let me put these in water, and then we can go."

Beth took a few extra minutes in the kitchen to calm herself down. Her libido was in overdrive.

When she walked back into the living room, Drew was mumbling to himself.

"Everything all right?"

He snapped his head up to meet her gaze. "Yeah. Fine. Are you ready to go?"

"Sure."

Beth locked up and followed him out to his vehicle. He opened the car door for her, and waited until she was settled in the passenger seat before closing it and rounding the car to get behind the wheel. Drew was being a gentleman, and she had to say that so far, she was impressed. Not that he hadn't been a gentleman before. He'd always been polite and attentive when they were together, but this was more than letting her walk through a door first. She felt valued. Beth really hoped it wasn't all an act.

"So do I get to know where we're going?" she asked.

He shot her a quick smile before refocusing on the road. "We're having a picnic. There's a concert at the park tonight celebrating the beginning of summer."

Definitely not what she'd been expecting. But the more she thought about it, the more appealing it sounded.

It didn't take them long to arrive at their destination. The park was divided up into various areas. Given it was a beautiful Saturday evening, there were a lot of people milling about. Most of them, however, were congregated around the soccer fields.

"Did you want to walk around a little first, or we could scope out a spot near the stage?"

Although Beth would have loved to have taken a look around—it had been a while since she'd been to this park—she'd been on her feet all day. "I think I'd like to find a place and sit. It's been a long day."

Drew headed to the back of the car to gather the blanket and food he'd brought. "Did something happen?"

She shook her head as they made their way around most of the people to a grassy area not far from a small stage. "No. Just busy. The warmer weather means more people are out and about. I really shouldn't complain. It's great for business. But I think I'm going to have to hire some help soon. It's getting to be too much for Tommy and me by ourselves."

He laid out the blanket a good distance away from where the band would be playing. While they were here to see the concert, he also wanted them to have a little privacy. It was a date, after all. "That's probably a good idea. I mean you've had a good number of people in there every time I've stopped by. Have you even had a vacation since you opened?"

Once he had everything on the blanket, he motioned for her to have a seat.

"No. The only days I have off are the days we're closed. Tommy's taken a few days here and there, but not many. We've both been working hard to make the café a success."

"It sounds like it worked." His grin was back, and Beth felt that fluttering in her stomach.

She swiftly looked away, trying to keep a hold on her emotions. Besides, they were in public. "So what about you? How was work yesterday?"

Drew began removing items from the cooler he'd brought. "Slow. We had a few med calls, but that was about it."

"Is it like that a lot?"

He quirked an eyebrow at her.

"Slow, I mean." He held out a container filled with tiny sandwiches, offering her one. "Thanks."

After removing a sandwich for himself, he replaced the container inside the cooler. "Water? I would have brought some wine, but they don't allow glass here, and I've never felt it quite right to drink wine out of a plastic cup. It reeks of high school kids sneaking into their parents' liquor cabinets."

He wrinkled his nose, and she chuckled. "Water's fine."

Drew twisted the top off the bottle and handed it to her. The whole situation was quaint and different, but she found she liked it. This was something she could see them doing over and over again.

❧

SHAWN HAD THOUGHT A CONCERT IN THE PARK WAS A GREAT DATE IDEA, and Drew was beginning to think his friend was right. The longer he sat next to Beth on their blanket, the more he realized that he owed Shawn. Drew had picked a spot in the back near a cluster of trees to give him and Beth a little privacy. He knew, as the time for the concert got closer, every inch of grass in front of the stage would be packed with people.

"Wow."

Beth's exclamation brought his attention back to her. She'd bitten into one of his sandwiches and was staring at it with wide eyes.

She met his gaze. "This is amazing. Where did you get this?"

"I made it." A feeling of pride spread through him.

"Remarkable. Do you cook, too?" she asked.

He shrugged. "A little. When I have the chance. I wouldn't call throwing together a picnic cooking, though. It was mostly just slicing, chopping, and mixing."

Before he knew it, she was on her knees. "What other goodies do you have in there?"

He motioned toward the cooler and sat back as Beth opened it to look inside.

A few moments later, Beth had pulled out and opened several containers. She took a bite of each of their contents. "This is really good."

"Thank you."

"No, Drew, I mean seriously good. Are you sure you're a firefighter?"

He laughed. "Pretty sure."

She shook her head as if she'd heard some private joke, and then lowered herself back down next to him. "Where did you learn to make stuff like this?"

"Desperation, mostly." He picked up a strawberry and popped it in his mouth.

"Most of the guys I've met either order takeout or warm up TV dinners when they get desperate for food." He wasn't sure if the look she was giving him was one of pride or skepticism.

As they continued to eat, he explained. "I guess my mom spoiled me. She used to cook these amazing meals when I lived at home. Then I came to the city and . . . well, like you said, it was mostly takeout and TV dinners. After a while, I couldn't take it, so I asked my mom if she had any simple recipes I could make. Things kind of grew from there. I found it wasn't as hard as I thought it was."

"I'm impressed. I mean you could open your own café and give me a run for my money with these sandwiches."

He grinned. "That's nice of you to say, but I think I'll stick to my day job. Cooking is just a hobby."

She surprised him with a hard kiss that lingered.

When she pulled away, he took a deep breath, inhaling her scent. "Not that I'm complaining, but what was that for?"

It was her turn to shrug.

Deciding to test the waters, he leaned in and kissed her this time. She didn't resist in the slightest, and their lips mingled together for several minutes before they broke apart.

"Thank you for agreeing to tonight," he said as he picked up his sandwich again.

Beth didn't comment, but there was a twinkle in her eye. He had no idea what the night would hold for them, but he wasn't going to worry too much about it. They were together—on a date—something he hadn't thought would happen for a good long while. He was going to enjoy every minute of it.

By six thirty, they were still nibbling on the food he'd brought as the area in front of the small stage began to fill in with people. Some brought blankets like Drew and Beth had, while others had lawn chairs. As the number of people grew, so did the noise. Even the hint of privacy had disappeared.

"There're more people than I thought there'd be."

She glanced in his direction as she took a sip of her water. "How did you find out about it?"

"Shawn. He's a good friend, and he was my captain for seven years." Drew couldn't help smiling as he remembered some of the crazy stuff that had happened to them during the time they'd worked together. Shawn was like a brother to him. He was the same age as Drew's brother, but unlike Seth, Shawn hadn't pushed Drew aside. Shawn had taken Drew under his wing when he'd joined the fire department. Drew didn't know if he would have made it through that first year if it hadn't been for Shawn.

There was a knowing look on Beth's face. "You're close."

"We are. I used to work with him a lot on our days off. It doesn't happen much anymore, though."

"That's too bad. You should always have time for friends," she said.

He nodded. "What about you? I know you and Nicole are pretty tight."

Beth snorted. "Yeah. You could say that. I mean we were close before, but after . . . well, let's just say if not for her, I'd still be sitting in front of my television in my PJ's with a quart of rocky road ice cream."

Drew wasn't sure what to say to that. He knew she had to be referring to her ex, but the last thing he wanted to do on their first date was talk about what he knew was a sore subject for her. "Did you meet at the club?"

"We did. It didn't take long for us to start hanging out outside Serpent's Kiss, though. A girl always needs a shopping partner."

He was glad to see that sparkle back in her eyes. The sun still glowed bright in the sky, and created a sort of halo around her face as she stared back at him.

"You're so beautiful." His voice was soft . . . reverent. "The way the sun is shining down on you, you look like an angel."

She looked over her shoulder, and then leaned in close to whisper in his ear. "Is that what you want? For me to be an angel? I thought you were looking for something a little . . . naughtier?"

Her breath washed over him, and he shivered. Or maybe it was her words that caused his reaction.

Before he could figure it out, the band took the stage, and welcomed everyone to the show. Drew was listening, sort of, but he couldn't take his eyes off Beth. She was smirking back at him. "Beth . . ."

She placed a single finger over his lips. "Later."

There was a part of him that wanted to drag her back to the car and make out like a couple of teenagers. He wasn't sure how well that would go over with Beth. It was the only thing that stopped him.

Taking a calming breath, he nodded.

Beth grinned and removed her finger.

The band began to play, and she turned her attention toward the stage. Drew, however, continued to watch her. Everything about Beth was appealing to him. He loved her eyes. When she looked at him, he felt as if he had an acrobat inside his stomach doing somersaults.

Of course, that didn't lessen the effect her body had on him. Everything from the silkiness of her hair and how it flowed down around her shoulders, to the way the clothes she wore seemed to accentuate her curves. Whenever he was near her—and even when he wasn't—he wanted to bury himself in her softness.

As if she knew he was thinking about her, Beth reached for his hand and brought it to rest on her lap. It looked completely innocent. And at first, it was. Then she shifted a little, spreading her legs. Heat he had only dreamed about radiated from between her legs. He closed his eyes and tried to keep from embarrassing himself.

"You okay?" she asked.

"Yes." He didn't open his eyes. He couldn't. But he also wasn't willing to remove his hand either.

"You sure?" He didn't miss the amusement in her voice.

He glanced over at her. "You're enjoying this."

"Just a little." There was no hiding her smile.

Drew sighed and tried to concentrate on the band. He couldn't say he was very successful since it was impossible to ignore the woman sitting beside him.

It was getting close to eight thirty, and he could tell the concert was winding down. A few people who had chosen to sit closer to the back had already begun packing up their things.

"Did you want to stay 'til end?" he asked, hoping she was as ready to go as he was.

Without a word, she began gathering their things. He took the cue and finished packing everything into the cooler he'd brought.

Once they had everything, Beth and Drew made their way back to the car. The parking lot was less crowded than it had been before. The soccer fields were empty, and with the exception of two young kids with their mother, so were the playgrounds. He went to the back of the vehicle and opened the trunk.

No sooner had he tossed everything into the trunk, he felt her press against him from behind.

He sucked in a breath, unsure of what to do. They weren't exactly alone.

All thought left him as Beth cupped his erection—the one he'd been trying to tamp down for the last two hours. "We need to talk about our lists. Are you up for that?"

She squeezed him a little, and he nodded.

"I can't hear you." She squeezed again. Harder.

"Yes. Please."

Beth chuckled and released him.

He groaned when the cool air hit him as she moved to her side of the car. Never had he wanted a woman quite like he wanted Beth. Then again, he'd never wanted a woman like Beth before.

Giving himself a moment, he made sure he wasn't going to be giving anyone a show before closing the trunk. The sooner they went over their lists, the sooner he could get some relief. At least, he hoped.

Chapter Fourteen

Beth tried to stay calm as Drew parked his car in front of her house and they strolled up the walkway to the front door. She'd been stupid pushing the physical like she had when they needed to talk about things. But they'd been dancing around their attraction for a month. When given the chance, she hadn't been able to keep her hands to herself.

Which was what had led to her current dilemma. They needed to talk, but doing so with their adrenaline pumping wasn't smart.

"Something wrong?" he asked.

She shook her head and opened the door.

When they stepped inside, she started to walk toward the kitchen, but he stopped her. "What's wrong? And please, don't tell me it's nothing. I can see it in your face. Something's bothering you. Are you having second thoughts?"

Taking a slow, deep breath, she stepped toward him. Without saying a word, she reached up and pulled his head down to hers.

Drew responded by wrapping his arms around her waist and pulling her closer.

As she slid her tongue inside his mouth, she felt his body respond. Blood surged through her veins, and she knew there would be no way to have a rational discussion until they released some of the sexual tension that had been building since the night they met.

She took a step back, urging him to follow her. He met her step for step, not releasing his hold on her. It was almost as if he were afraid she'd disappear if he eased up. That was perfectly fine with her. She didn't want him going anywhere either.

When her knees hit the back of the couch, she pulled away, and lowered herself down. He followed her, not allowing her to get too far away.

Drew hovered over her, his face inches from hers. She turned his head slightly and nipped at his earlobe.

"I seem to recall you promising to make it up to me."

"What did you have in mind?"

Beth wiggled her shirt up over her head and tossed it to the side. His gaze went directly to her breasts. She wondered if he could tell how hard her nipples were behind the black bra she wore.

Running her hand along his face, she directed his attention away from her chest and back to her face. "I want you to know that I'm clean. I've been tested twice since . . . well, since everything happened. I—"

"So am I, Beth."

She cut off his words by smothering them with another kiss. He began kissing her back in earnest. Her body was pulsing, and all she could think of was what his mouth would feel like in other places.

With that in mind, she leaned against the cushions and arched her back, pushing her breasts against him.

He took the hint and moved his lips down along her neck until he reached her bra-covered breasts. Beth didn't waste time once he arrived at his destination. She reached behind her to unhook her bra, and with a little maneuvering, it was out of the way without too much effort.

Drew took the removal of her bra as all the invitation he needed, and latched onto one of her nipples. She tangled her fingers into his hair and held him tight to her chest while he licked and sucked.

"Harder," she demanded.

He did as instructed and drew her flesh further into his mouth. It felt amazing. She'd dreamt of feeling his tongue lave at her tits for weeks.

Ripping his mouth away from her left breast, she guided his attention over to the one on the right. The cool air hit her wet nipple, causing it to stiffen even more. Both of her breasts were aching for his attention, and she needed it from him—now.

He brought his hand up to cup the breast he'd just abandoned, and began massaging it. Every nerve ending in her body was tingling, and her pussy was begging for attention. She just wasn't sure if she was ready for him to stop playing with her breasts yet. He didn't show any sign of getting bored or frustrated with his current endeavor, so she decided to let him worship them for a while.

With every tug his lips made, Beth felt herself getting wetter. She scraped her nails along his neck and back, encouraging him. "Do you know how many times I've imagined what your mouth would feel like?"

Drew groaned, but otherwise made no move to change his position or what he was doing. That was good. She wasn't ready for him to stop.

Reaching between them, Beth popped the button on her shorts, and lowered the zipper. When Drew realized what she was trying to do, he used his free hand to help her push her shorts down her legs.

Naked, she pressed her pelvis up against his clothed body letting him feel the heat and wetness. His hand gripped her hip and held her against him. "Do you like that?"

He hummed.

She let him dig his fingers into her hip while she ground against him for several minutes. Then, when she couldn't take it any longer, she pushed his head away and repositioned herself on the couch so she was lying down with one leg bent against the back of the couch and the other spread wide with her foot flat on the floor. She was completely open to him. "I want you to make me come with your tongue."

Apparently, she didn't have to ask twice. As soon as the words left her mouth, he was there between her legs. He spread her open further and ran his nose along the inside of her thigh before slowly licking up her slit. Beth knew she was wet, but she hadn't realized just how wet she was until he reached the top of her cleft and met her gaze. Already his lips were glistening with moisture.

He swirled his tongue around her clit, and her body responded in earnest. The pulsing in her belly began building into a pressure she knew would eventually explode into the most wonderful orgasm.

Cupping his head, she let his tongue work its magic. Beth hadn't had many lovers, but she'd had a few. The best one at cunnilingus had been Ben. That, however, was after lots of practice. Drew wasn't as skilled, but he showed great promise. That and he seemed to love having his mouth on her pussy.

As she got closer, she dug her hands into his scalp and began grinding her pussy against Drew's face. He held tight to her hips, securing himself, and kept licking as if his life depended on it.

Beth felt her orgasm coming and embraced it completely. She tossed her head back and let out a strangled cry.

For a few moments, she felt as if she were floating. It was heavenly.

A gentle pressure drew her attention as she came back down to earth. Drew was still between her legs, his tongue massaging her still swollen flesh. She reached down and ran her fingers through his hair. "Thank you."

Only then did he look up and meet her gaze. The entire lower half of his face was covered in her juices. "No, thank you. Just say the word and I'll do it again."

Beth grinned. "Good to know."

Pushing herself up on her elbows, she looked down at the erection he had pressing aggressively against his pants.

He followed her gaze.

"That seems to be a habit when I'm around," she said, smirking.

Drew chuckled. "What can I say? He likes you."

"Mmm. Well, let's do something about that, shall we?" She sat up, and he followed suit.

Without giving him time to process what was going on, Beth straddled his lap, took his face between her hands, and drove her tongue into his mouth. Her scent was everywhere. Not only could she taste herself, but she could also smell her heady odor as her nose brushed against the side of his face. She loved that she'd marked him. Whether she liked it or not, she wanted him. Not just his body. She wanted to mark him as hers and watch him lose himself in his submission to her.

He clutched at her hips, holding tight to her ass.

"Do you like my ass?" she asked, having noticed he went for it every chance he got.

"Yes. I love your ass. Then again, I can't think of any part of you I don't love. You have a fantastic body."

She ran a hand down his chest. "Trying to suck up, are you?"

Drew shook his head. "Not at all. I could touch you for hours and it wouldn't be enough."

"Yes, well, you've done a fair amount of touching tonight. I'd say it's my turn."

Scooting back, she took hold of the hem of his shirt and lifted. He leaned forward to make it easier for her to get it up his torso and over his head. Once removed, she threw it over to join her discarded shirt.

She backed herself up further until she could place her feet on the ground. He looked a bit disappointed that she was no longer within his reach, but that would soon be remedied. Placing her hands on his knees, she knelt down in front of him and went for the button of his pants.

It didn't take long before Drew figured out that the evening's tryst wasn't over yet. He helped her shimmy his pants down his hips and legs, and then watched intently as she laid them nearby.

Beth placed her hands on his knees again, and this time she pushed them wide apart. Looking him straight in the eye, she ran her palms up his legs until they were settled on either side of his erection. "I'm going to suck your cock now. You'll have to let me know if I do better than your hand."

⊷❦⊶

HE WATCHED AS BETH LOWERED HER MOUTH TO HIS COCK. THE anticipation of her lips made it feel as if it were happening in slow motion. When she finally made contact, he sucked in a sharp breath.

She ran her tongue along the slit in the top of his cock, and then along the ridge of its head. Even when she did finally take him into her mouth, it was only the very tip. She seemed perfectly content to take her time.

His palms itched with the want to touch her, but he didn't know if he should. They hadn't talked about anything yet. Hell, at the moment he was doing good to think, period.

Beth snaked one hand between them and began playing with his balls. It was just like what she'd had him do when they were talking on the phone. The difference, however, wasn't lost on him. This time it wasn't his hand milking his cock. It was her very warm, and very wet, mouth.

When he couldn't stand it any longer, he placed one hand on top of her head and tangled his fingers in her hair. She didn't object, but she did take him in a little farther and scraped her teeth along his length. He got the message loud and clear. Even though it might seem as if she was in a subservient position, she was still in charge. It was crazy how much knowing that turned him on.

Drew closed his eyes as she worked his cock and balls. He didn't even care as she gradually increased the pressure and the suction. Everything felt right.

She bobbed her head up and down taking him in until he felt the head of his cock hit the back of her throat. He knew he should feel a sense of power knowing all it would take would be a quick thrust of his hips to plunge his erection down her throat, but instead he felt vulnerable. Beth held his cock in her mouth. She could cause him pain or pleasure. It was completely up to her.

He moaned as he felt his orgasm building. "Beth . . ."

She didn't let up. If anything, she increased her efforts.

Within a few moments, he was no longer able to hold back. "I'm coming. Beth, I'm . . ."

She gave a gentle tug to his balls, and he felt a burst of energy shoot straight up his cock. He groaned as he released into her mouth, letting go of all the pent-up sexual frustration he'd been experiencing since seeing her walk into the club over a month ago.

Beth glanced up at him from her spot between his legs and grinned. "Well?"

He huffed out a laugh. "Oh yeah. Definitely better."

Pushing herself up onto her feet, she sashayed across the room to get her clothes. Drew's eyes went right to her behind. He'd had that ass in his hands, and it felt as good as it looked.

She bent over and wiggled her backside. "Enjoying the view?"

"You have no idea. I've been trying to picture what you'd look like naked for weeks now."

Slipping her panties up her long legs, she pulled them over her hips before walking back to where he sat on the couch. She placed one knee on the cushion beside his thigh, and then the other, straddling his lap. Her breasts were inches from his face before she lowered herself down onto his legs. Drew couldn't help himself. His hands went immediately to grab that perfect ass of hers.

She grinned and leaned in to brush her lips against his.

He pulled her to him, enjoying the closeness. It was strange. In some ways he already felt closer to Beth than he had his last girlfriend. He attributed that to the fact that he didn't have to try to hide what he liked, or at least that he preferred the submissive side of things. Being able to let go and know that she would lead was liberating and arousing at the same time.

"We should get dressed," she whispered. "We have things to talk about."

Drew wasn't quite ready to let her go. "Why can't we talk like this?"

Beth chuckled and sat up. "As appealing as that sounds, we do need to talk about our lists and doing so when we're in a sexualized state isn't wise. Being aroused alters your thought processes. We both need to be thinking rationally."

As much as he hated to admit it, what she said made sense. When she'd had her mouth on his cock earlier, he would have agreed to just about anything.

He let his hands drop to the couch, releasing his hold on her. Beth ran a hand down the side of his face and placed one last kiss on his lips before backing off his lap and standing up. She went back to gathering her clothes and getting dressed. He reluctantly did the same.

Once they were fully clothed again, he followed her into her kitchen.

"Have a seat, and I'll get us both some water," she said.

Drew pulled out a chair and took a seat. While she busied herself getting their drinks, he realized that not once had he pondered what the inside of Beth's house would look like. All his dreams about Beth had revolved solely around her and maybe a single piece of furniture such as a bed or a couch . . . or even a table. And even now, as he sat in the middle of it, he was trying to mesh what he was seeing with the woman he'd gotten to know over the last month.

She set a glass of ice water in front of him, and sat down on the opposite side o the table. "You seem to be thinking hard about something."

He took a drink and shook his head. "Just looking around. Your house is very . . ."

"Normal?" she offered.

While that wasn't exactly what he'd been trying to say, he supposed it was as good a word as any. "I guess you could say that. It doesn't look that much different from my mom's. She has a similar setup. The table is even in the same location."

"Ah. I thought maybe you were thinking I'd have floggers on the wall for decoration or something."

Her tone was lighthearted, joking, and he found himself smiling at how relaxed he was with her. "Not exactly. Although I am curious. I mean, you did say you played in your house, right?"

She took a sip of her water before answering. "I keep a chest in my bedroom with the majority of my toys. Most are portable, though."

There was that glint in her eye again. He was feeling himself becoming worked up again despite the distance between them. "That's . . . good."

Beth stood and strolled over to the refrigerator. She poked her head inside and returned to the table with a container of fruit and cheese. "We might as well have a snack while we talk."

He swallowed and nodded. As much as he didn't want to admit it, he was a little on edge.

"Did you bring your list with you?" she asked.

"Yes. It's out in the car." He should have thought to bring it in with him, but he'd been distracted at the time. The only thing he'd been able to think about the entire way back to her house was how long he'd have to wait before he would get to touch her.

"Why don't you go get it? I'll grab mine, and we can sit here and go over everything."

She smiled down at him, and then walked out of the room, leaving him sitting at the table. He wondered if it was intentional.

Taking a huge gulp of his water, he placed the empty glass back on the table and stood. This was what he wanted. Now all he had to do was hope he didn't chicken out when they both laid all their cards out on the table.

Chapter Fifteen

Beth had printed her list out the night before, so all she had to do was retrieve it from the drawer where she'd stashed it. She heard the front door open and close as she pulled the sheets of paper out of their hiding place. Drew had presumably gone out to get his list.

She took her time as she made her way back downstairs to the kitchen. Setting the papers on the table, Beth picked up both their glasses and refilled them. They might as well be comfortable while they discussed things.

It was hard to believe that she wasn't more nervous. Leading up to their date, she'd nearly driven herself crazy with all the what-ifs. Sure, they were still there, but they weren't nagging at her as much as they had been. Okay, that wasn't true. She was still worried. About the future. About whether they could make things work between them. But what they were about to talk about—their limit lists—that wasn't worrying her so much. Given their fun on the couch, she guessed they'd be able to figure out how to make a sexual relationship work pretty easily. It was the rest that was questionable.

Drew walked back into the room as she was returning their glasses to the table. She could tell he was more anxious than he'd been before, but he also looked resolute.

"Have a seat," she said.

He released a heavy breath and lowered himself into the chair he'd been in earlier.

Beth joined him at the table. "I know you've never done this before, but I have to say this is one of the things about this lifestyle that I like the most. Honestly, I think if more vanilla couples did this, they would be much happier."

Drew smiled and relaxed his shoulders a little. "I'm trying not to stress too much about it, but it's strange putting all your wants and desires out there even though I know you're already aware of some of them."

"The first time is always the hardest. It will get easier." She picked up her list and scanned the first page. "Let's start with something simple. As far as the D/s dynamic is concerned, what are you interested in? Given what I know about you so far, I can't see you wanting something 24/7."

He grinned. "No. Not only would that be difficult with my job, I just can't see myself being submissive all the time. I'm not even sure I could be that way most of the time. My fantasies usually revolve around bedroom activities, so I think I'd like to confine it to that. For now, at least."

Beth nodded. "So bedroom only. That works for me, although I would be interested in expanding that some in the future if that is something you want. A 24/7 relationship doesn't appeal to me either. Frankly, it's too much work. But I do like the idea of you kneeling at my feet while we watch a movie, or maybe even having you do things around the house while I keep you in line with my crop."

"That could be interesting."

"Very." Beth couldn't help but picture Drew on his hands and knees cleaning up some mess she'd intentionally made for the sole purpose of watching him do her bidding. He'd be naked, of course, and she'd have fun playing with him while he was busy trying to get her floor spotless.

Drew cleared his throat. "If I'm working, we can't play. I can't jeopardize my job."

"I would never want to put your career in danger, Drew. Nor would I want you distracted when you're working. Your job is dangerous enough as it is."

He frowned. "My job still worries you."

Beth sighed. "I'm not sure that will ever change. I mean, if I were rushing into a burning building as part of my job, wouldn't you be concerned about me on some level?"

"You're right. I would."

She grinned, trying to lighten the mood a little. "Let's get back to our discussion. We've figured out when we don't want to play, so now we need to figure out when we do. I know your schedule is . . . well, for lack of a better word . . . strange."

He chuckled.

Beth rolled her eyes. "It's the truth. I'm going to need a calendar to keep track."

"You get used to it."

"I suppose I will." She reached for a couple of grapes and popped them into her mouth. "But that still leaves the question as to *when*. Between your schedule and mine, it could get a little hairy."

Drew picked up a cheese square and took a bite. "My single days off can be hectic. Also, I have to be at work by seven in the morning."

"So I'd say those days are out."

He frowned again.

"What?" she asked, not understanding his reaction.

"I want . . ."

"Yes?"

"Beth, I want a relationship with you. I want the other stuff, too, but I want us to date and . . . and be together as a couple."

She knew this. If all he'd wanted to do was play, she was sure he would have been able to find another Domme at the club to experiment with. The man was easy on the eyes and she'd seen more than one Femdom looking him over. She wasn't sure what his wanting a relationship had to do with their playtime, though. "I know."

He grinned. "Good."

"So it's agreed that we only play during the stretches when you have at least four days off, and during the rest of the time we're just a regular couple."

"Agreed." He paused. "That means we can still do normal couple things during the non-play times, correct?"

It took her only a moment to get what he was asking. She burst out laughing. "Are you asking if we can still have sex if we're not playing?"

Drew's cheeks turned a bright shade of pink.

Beth shook her head. "You are such a guy."

He puffed his chest out. "I would hope so."

This only made her laugh harder.

Drew joined her.

It took them several minutes to regain their composure. When they did, it was Beth who spoke first. "I think tonight we proved that we can have perfectly good sex without getting kinky."

His eyes widened. "Good?"

"What? You didn't think what we did tonight was good?" she asked.

He snorted. "Tonight is probably up in my top five sexual experiences ever, and I didn't even get my cock inside you. Plus, it still felt as if you were in control, and I liked that. I don't want that to change."

"Good. Me either." She looked down at her papers and tried to hide how much his words thrilled her. *One of his top five.* She wouldn't deny she was feeling pretty pleased with herself. "So we've talked about the when. We should probably talk about the what."

Drew pushed his list across the table in her direction. "Being that I work mostly with guys, I figured there wouldn't be any sexual term I hadn't heard before. This proved me wrong."

She chuckled and did a quick scan of what he'd marked. It was what she'd expected for the most part. He was interested in bondage, although he had no personal experience with it. Impact play was also on his *want to try* list as well as sensation play. She was happy to see that humiliation and degradation were listed as 'not interested'. The one thing she was surprised to see, however, was that he'd marked 'maybe' beside CBT. She hadn't pegged him for an interest in cock and ball torture.

"CBT?" she asked.

He shrugged. "I've seen it done at the club. It looks extremely painful."

"It can be."

"I made a comment to John once saying how I couldn't understand how a guy could want that done to him. He explained that there was a heightened sense of giving up control associated with it. She quite literally has you by the balls and can do with you what she wants." He leaned forward and picked up another piece of cheese. Instead of eating it, he rolled it between his thumb and index finger. "I don't know if I'll like it, but it's something I'd like to try. Eventually."

Beth could take or leave CBT. It had its place, and it was fine once in a while, but it wasn't something she normally did. "Maybe we can explore that in stages. There are many different types of CBT. We'd have to discuss the specifics and just how far each of us wanted to go with it."

He took a deep breath and ate the cheese he'd been toying with.

She handed her list to him and picked up several more grapes. "I don't see any major conflicts. Many of the things you want to try I've done before."

Drew nodded as he looked over her list.

"Do you have any questions?" she asked.

"How do we know where to start?"

Beth grinned. "I'd like for you to leave your list with me. I'll look over it in more detail tomorrow and come up with a game plan."

"Okay. That makes sense."

"Is there anything specific that you'd like to try first?"

"Bondage." He had the answer out almost before she was able to finish asking the question.

Beth chuckled. "I think that can be arranged. You're off on Monday, correct?"

"Yes. But I have to work Tuesday. Then I'm off Wednesday through Saturday," he said.

"Why don't you come over on Monday? I'll make us dinner and we can talk some more. You can take my list home and look it over in more detail as well."

"I like the sound of that," he said.

"Good. I can have dinner ready by five. That will give us plenty of time after."

❧

DREW WAS RELUCTANT TO LEAVE BETH ON SATURDAY NIGHT, BUT HE HADN'T felt comfortable asking if he could stay the night. They weren't there yet. Besides, he had to work the next morning. With her work schedule, Sundays and Mondays were her only days to sleep in. He didn't want to take that away from her just to satisfy his own selfish want.

His apartment was dark when he arrived home. He must have forgotten to turn on the outside light in his haste to get out the door. Turning the key in the lock, he pushed open the door, and flipped on the light.

The sight that greeted him was not what he'd expected. His buddy, Shawn, was curled up on his new couch with a blanket draped over him. "Shawn?"

Shawn rolled his large body to face Drew and then sat up slowly. It was only then that Drew noticed several empty beer cans beside the coffee table. "Hey. You're back."

Drew shut and locked the door behind him. "What happened?"

"My old lady kicked me out. Said I'm afraid of commitment or some shit." Shawn ran his hands through his hair, causing it to stick up in all directions. "Do you think I can crash here for a few days? I start my rotation tomorrow, so I won't be able to look for a new place until Friday."

"Sure. Whatever you need."

"Thanks."

Walking into the kitchen, Drew realized he still had Beth's list in his hand. He quickly folded and tucked it into his front pocket. The last thing he needed was for Shawn to get curious. Trust was one thing, but he didn't want to have to lie to his friend. He also wasn't ready to put his sexual preferences out in the open to be scrutinized.

"Were you out with your girl tonight? The one you were telling me about?" Shawn asked.

Drew took two glasses and filled them with water. He had no idea how much Shawn had had to drink, but if what he could see on the floor was any indication, his friend was going to be feeling it tomorrow.

Handing one of the glasses to Shawn, Drew sat down a few feet away on the recliner. "I was. And before you ask, it went well. She's making me dinner Monday night." He couldn't hide his joy about that, so he didn't even try.

"I'm happy for you. You deserve it."

"Thanks."

They were both quiet for several minutes.

"I hope you don't mind that I used the spare key you gave me," Shawn said.

"Of course not. I gave it to you to use if you needed it. You obviously needed it tonight."

Shawn gulped down half the water in his glass. "Yeah."

"You want to talk about it?" Drew asked. Shawn had certainly listened to Drew's women troubles over the years.

"Not much to tell." Shawn shook his head and downed the rest of his water. "I was over at Mickey's helping him set up a swing set for his girls for most of the day. Came home around five and Jill had my bags packed and waiting for me at the door. Everything was fine last week. I don't know what happened."

"Did you mention she'd been out of town or something?" Drew asked, trying to help his friend make sense of what appeared to be the end of his relationship. Shawn and Jill had been together since Drew had been a firefighter—longer.

"Yeah. Her sister's been sick, so she was in Denver helping take care of her sister's kids. She got back late last night. I was hoping we'd get to sit down and enjoy a nice evening together before I went back on rotation."

Drew didn't know what to say. "I'm sorry, man. I really am."

Shawn nodded and looked around the apartment. "Are you sure you don't mind me crashing here for a few nights?"

"Of course not. We're both on duty tomorrow, then between sleeping and having dinner at Beth's, I won't be here much Monday either."

"I owe you."

"Pfft. How many times did you save my skin in the last seven years?" Drew asked.

His friend laughed. It was good to hear.

"Exactly. So don't sweat it. Crash here as long as you need."

Considering it was going on eleven, Shawn helped Drew clean up some of the clutter and downed a few ibuprofen before climbing back on the couch. After making sure everything was locked up tight and that the lights were out, Drew made his way into his bedroom. Only then, with the door closed, did he fish Beth's list out of his pocket.

She had very few things marked as 'want to try'. Then again, she'd been in a BDSM relationship before. Although he knew that, seeing it in black and white was quite different. He felt the jealousy peak inside him and tried his best to push it away. It was completely irrational. She was with him now. *Officially.* There wasn't any use getting upset about her being and doing things with another man. Especially a man who ended up being a lying, cheating bastard.

Drew was so caught up in his internal argument that he almost missed something Beth marked on her list as 'love'. He ran his finger down the page to be sure he wasn't reading it incorrectly.

He wasn't.

Beth loved knife play.

Racking his brain, he tried to remember what he'd put for that. Dislike? Hate? He couldn't remember. During his two months as a member of Serpent's Kiss, he couldn't recall ever witnessing knife play.

Before he lost his nerve, he pulled out his cell phone and sent Beth a text.

Knife play?

It took her a few moments to respond.

Yes. -Beth

It sounded crazy to admit it, but he was curious.

Why?

Instead of her sending another text in response, his phone rang. He answered it quickly and held it up to his ear. "Hey."

"Hey, yourself."

"You didn't have to call. I was a little shocked, that's all. I wasn't expecting you to be into that," he said.

Beth hummed. "I noticed you marked it as *dislike* on your list."

He guessed that answered his question. "I've never seen it done, but I'm not sure I'd like something like that."

"I didn't think I would either until I saw a demonstration. Once I tried it myself, I was hooked." She paused. "If you're not comfortable with knife play we can take it off the table for now. There's no pressure, Drew. I get that this is new to you."

While he understood and appreciated that, he felt he needed to be honest. "I'm torn. A part of me is curious since you ranked it so high on your list, but having a blade that close to my skin . . ."

"It isn't about that. Or at least for me it isn't. It's a mind game. I'm not going to cut you, but I could. The possibility is always there."

"Thanks."

She laughed. "Just being honest, remember."

He was quiet for a moment. "I'll think about it."

"Fair enough."

A knock sounded on his bedroom door and it caused him to jump.

"Yes?" he yelled in the direction of the door.

"Do you have an extra toothbrush lying around somewhere?" Shawn asked through the door.

"Yeah. Just give me a minute and I'll get it for you," he responded back to Shawn. To Beth he said, "Can you hang on?"

"Sure. But I can let you go if you—"

"No." He hesitated. The last thing he wanted to do was sound desperate. "I'll be right back."

As swiftly as he could, Drew headed out into the hall to the bathroom, dug through his linen closet until he found an unopened toothbrush, and then grabbed the tube of toothpaste from the medicine cabinet. It was one of the few lessons his brother had imparted to him. Always have a spare toothbrush in your closet for overnight guests. The last thing you want is to French kiss a girl goodbye in the morning when she hadn't yet brushed her teeth.

With Shawn's issue taken care of, Drew rushed back into his bedroom. He made sure his door was shut firmly behind him, and then went to the bed to resume his phone call with Beth. "I'm back."

"Everything okay? I didn't realize you had houseguests."

"It was a surprise to me, too." Drew debated how much to tell her. "Shawn was here when I got home. His girlfriend kicked him out."

"That's horrible."

"Yeah. It is. They've been together for years," he said.

Beth grew quiet. "Does that mean you're going to need to cancel for Monday night?"

"No. Shawn can take care of himself. I'll be there."

"I guess I'll see you then." He could tell she was smiling, and he wished he were there to see it. "Good night, Drew."

"Good night, Beth."

With a spring in his step, Drew plugged his phone into the charger, and then went to get ready for bed. It had been an amazing day, and he couldn't wait for Monday when he could see Beth again.

Chapter Sixteen

When Drew's alarm woke him up at six the next morning, he jumped out of bed with an excess of energy. He loved his job, but it had been a while since he'd had such a spring in his step. The renewed energy he felt was an obvious byproduct of his date with Beth. Or Beth herself. Things had gone better than he'd expected, and they were moving forward with a relationship. He couldn't have asked for more than that.

His mind on other things, Drew opened his door and headed toward the bathroom. It wasn't until he heard movement in his kitchen that he remembered he had a houseguest.

Seconds later, Shawn turned around and caught Drew standing there buck-naked. Shawn smirked and pointed a piece of toast at him. "I like you, Parker, but not that much."

Drew held up his middle finger and continued on his way to the bathroom.

Figuring he'd get his shower out of the way, he turned on the water, and stepped into the spray. As he worked the soap down his body, he smiled remembering Beth between his legs. He had no idea what the future held for them, but he knew he'd do just about anything to feel her mouth on his cock again.

Although it was tempting, Drew decided it probably wasn't a good idea to jack off in the shower with Shawn in the other room. Besides, his friend would most likely want to shower as well before heading into the station, so he probably shouldn't use all the hot water. Finishing up, he dried off, and wrapped a clean towel around his waist.

Shawn was just finishing his breakfast of toast and orange juice when Drew strolled out of the bathroom. "It's all yours."

His friend nodded, and Drew darted into his room to get dressed.

They drove separately to the station. Shawn wasn't ready for the guys to know that Jill had kicked him out. Drew could relate to that. These guys were family to him, but there were some things you didn't even want family to know.

It was midmorning before they got their first call. There was a gas leak in an assisted living facility. All seventy apartments had to be evacuated. Since the residents were over the age of sixty-five, many had to be helped out or even carried. Once everyone was safe, it was a matter of securing the area until the leak could be fixed.

When they arrived back, everyone fell into their normal routines making sure the trucks and all the equipment were cleaned and ready for the next call. Drew gathered his crew for a quick debriefing, and out of the corner of his eye he could see Shawn talking to his guys as well. Everything had gone well, all things considered, so there wasn't much to discuss. When he dismissed his crew, though, he glanced over to where Shawn had been but he was gone.

Drew found his friend in the kitchen. It was lunchtime, but given they'd all been out on a call for the last two hours nothing was ready. He washed his hands and pitched in to help.

"Thanks," Shawn said.

The two worked together to get lunch on the table as soon as possible. Drew didn't know about everyone else, but he was starving. He'd learned long ago to make sure he ate well at every meal. A call could come in at any time, so you took advantage of the food put in front of you no matter what it was.

They'd barely taken a few bites of the lunch they prepared when another call came in. It looked as if it was going to be one of those days. He shoved a last bite in his mouth while he listened to the dispatcher rattle off the information they would need. Then they were off—their half-eaten lunch left sitting on the long table.

Three hours later, Drew worked alongside his crew as they finished their daily chores around the station. It was only then that he had time to think on Shawn's situation. Jill had complained that Shawn was afraid of commitment. The two had never gotten married. They weren't engaged. Yet they'd been together for over seven years. Drew had always thought that was a mutual decision, but apparently it wasn't.

Thoughts of Shawn's relationship inevitably led back to Drew's newly established one with Beth. He knew she'd been hurt by her last relationship, and that she had trust issues. Would that translate into a fear of commitment? She hadn't showed any signs of that last night, but things had moved rather quickly. Maybe once she had time to ponder everything she'd change her mind. He really hoped not.

Shawn came up on his left. "You got a minute?"

"Sure." Drew tossed his rag onto the bench and followed his friend outside.

Shawn kept walking until they were several feet away from the open bays. It wasn't likely anyone would hear them out there.

"I got a text from Jill while we were out earlier."

From the look on Shawn's face, she hadn't been messaging to ask him back. "What did she say?"

He leaned back against the building and ran a hand over his face in frustration. "She wants me to come get the rest of my stuff tomorrow. Says she wants a clean break so she can move on with her life before it's too late."

Drew moved to stand beside Shawn. "I'm sorry."

For the first time in the seven years Drew had known him, he thought Shawn might break down.

He didn't. Instead, he took a deep breath and looked across the street where a couple of kids were playing. "I know you have a date tomorrow night with your new girl, but do you think you can go with me to move my stuff? It shouldn't take more than a few hours. Most everything in the house is hers anyway."

"Sure. Did you want to go first thing in the morning, or would you rather get some sleep first?" Drew asked.

"I think I'd rather get it over with, if you don't mind."

"Of course not."

Shawn nodded. "I'd ask some of the other guys but . . ."

"But you'd rather they not know yet. I get it."

Shawn snorted. "I suppose you do. How long do you think you're going to be able to keep your new girlfriend from everyone? Given that cheesy grin I've seen on your face a few times today, and your late night phone call . . . I'm thinking a week, tops." The change in subject had brightened Shawn's mood considerably.

Drew rolled his eyes. "We'll see."

"She must be something if she has you mooning after her already."

He smiled. "She is."

"I'm happy for you." Sadness crept back into Shawn's features.

"Do you think you and Jill can work it out?" Drew asked.

"I don't know. She seems pretty determined it's over." Shawn bent down, picked up a stick from the sidewalk, and began tearing off the bark. He'd quit smoking about six months ago, and Drew figured he was probably trying to distract himself from wanting a cigarette. "Tell me about Beth. What's she look like?"

Drew grinned and lowered himself down beside Shawn. "She's about five six. Long, dark brown hair. It's almost black it's so dark. Her curves are what dreams are made of, and her legs . . ." Drew sighed as he remembered having his hands on her hips as he licked her pussy and watched as she shuddered around him.

Shawn whistled. "You've got it bad. Maybe a week's too long."

Drew shoved his friend, stood, and brushed himself off. "We'd better get back in there before someone comes looking for us."

Nodding, Shawn threw the battered stick down on the sidewalk. Drew thought he'd push himself up off the wall and that would be the end of their conversation. He was wrong. Shawn looked up at him, squinting in the sunlight. "If she's the one, don't let her get away. Don't make the same mistake I did."

Before Drew could respond, Shawn was up and headed back into the station. Drew had no choice but to follow him. Shawn always had liked to get in the last word.

Aside from an EMS call around nine that night, things were quiet. Drew settled into his cot a little before eleven. He closed his eyes and tried to relax. It had been a busy day. He should've fallen asleep in minutes, but at eleven thirty he was still awake. Of late, he would have blamed it on his libido, but that wasn't the problem this time.

He was worried about Shawn. His friend had gone through the motions during their shift. Normally he was a pretty laid-back kind of guy. He could be serious when the situation warranted it, but otherwise he didn't let much bother him. The apparent end of his long-term relationship was weighing on him. Shawn's parting words rang through Drew's head once more. He knew his friend was right. If Beth was the one, then he had to do everything he could to hold onto her. He had to show her she was appreciated and that he wouldn't take her for granted.

Rolling over, he dug his cell phone out of his pocket, and scrolled through his contacts until he found Beth's name.

I hope you had a relaxing day. I'm looking forward to tomorrow night.

There was no reply. He hadn't expected there to be. Beth was most likely asleep.

Feeling better since he'd reached out to her, Drew tucked his phone back into his pocket, and tried to get some sleep while he could.

❧

SHE FOUND DREW'S MESSAGE THE NEXT MORNING WHEN SHE CHECKED HER phone. Beth smiled at his words. If she wasn't careful, she could see herself falling for him. Who was she kidding? She was already well on her way.

After making herself a quick breakfast, she headed to the grocery store. There were a few items she would need if she was going to make dinner for the two of them this evening. She was going to keep it simple—steak, baked potatoes, and salad. What meat-loving guy didn't like that?

Beth was on her way out of the store when her phone rang. The moment she saw Drew's name on her screen, her stomach did a little flip. "Morning."

Drew chuckled. "Good morning. I didn't wake you, did I?"

"Nope. I've been up for a while. I was just doing a little shopping for our dinner tonight."

"That's actually why I'm calling." His voice took on a serious tone.

She frowned. "You aren't canceling on me, are you?"

"No. Not at all. But I had to do something this morning, and it's taking longer than expected. I haven't even been home yet to change out of my uniform," he said.

It was on the tip of her tongue to ask for details, but she held back. "Is everything all right? Are you okay?"

"Yeah. It's nothing like that. A buddy of mine just needed my help with something." He paused. "I need to go. I'll see you tonight. I promise. I just might be a few minutes late."

"Okay. I'll see you tonight."

He seemed reluctant to hang up. She was about to ask again if everything was all right when she realized he'd disconnected their call.

Trying not to let it bother her, Beth put her shopping bags into her car, and drove home. She had a lot to do before he arrived, including going through her toy box. While they wouldn't be playing tonight, she did want to talk about what their first scene would be. If all went well, and he agreed, their first session would be Wednesday evening. It was the start of his four days off, and it would give him some time to deal with any lingering effects of their play.

The hours passed quickly as she worked around the house and prepped dinner. By the time five o'clock rolled around, everything was as ready as it could be. All she needed now was Drew.

Only twenty more minutes went by before she heard a car pull up out front. She watched as he climbed out of his vehicle and made his way up the driveway. He had a small bouquet of flowers in his right hand.

When he reached the front porch, Beth opened the door to greet him. He looked up at the sound, and smiled as soon as he saw her standing there. Despite his smile, she hadn't missed the worry that had creased his features before he realized she was there. Something was troubling him. While their relationship was still new, she hoped he would open up and share whatever it was with her. If they were going to have the type of relationship they both claimed they wanted, communication was key. Especially if they weren't only going to be play partners.

He stepped through her door and extended his arm, offering her the flowers. "Sorry again. I was hoping I wasn't going to be late, but . . ."

"It's fine. Why don't you come into the kitchen with me while I finish putting everything together?"

Drew grinned and motioned for her to lead the way.

She strolled over to the refrigerator while he took a seat at the table.

"Anything you need me to do?" he asked.

"Nope. I cooked the potatoes and made the salad earlier. All I have to do now is cook the steaks." She glanced back at him and smiled. "Thank you for offering, though."

He sat patiently as Beth removed the potatoes from the oven and then adjusted the setting to broil. She seasoned the steaks and laid them aside before going back to the refrigerator for the salad. It was a simple meal, but one she thought he'd enjoy.

Once everything was cooking, she joined him at the table. She was trying to come up with the best way to broach the subject that had been eating at her all day when he spoke up. "I guess you're probably wondering what all that was about today."

"I am a little curious." A *little* was putting it mildly.

Drew sighed. "Remember when we were talking Saturday night and I told you what happened with Shawn and his girlfriend?"

Of course she remembered. "Yes."

"Well, she sent him a text Sunday while we were working wanting him to come by today and clean out his stuff. He asked if I'd help him."

"That was nice of you." It was nice, but from everything she'd learned about Drew so far, it fit his character.

He shrugged, brushing off the compliment. "He'd do it for me."

Beth figured that since he'd brought up the subject, she'd go ahead and jump in with both feet. "Is that what you were thinking about then, when you were walking up to the door?"

"Yes and no."

He was quiet for a few moments, and Beth took the opportunity to get up and put the steaks in the oven. When she turned around to return to her chair, Drew was standing behind her. Without a word, he reached out, pulled her into his arms, and kissed her.

"I missed you," he said, resting his forehead on hers.

She wasn't sure if she wanted to admit it yet, but she'd missed him, too. Everything seemed to be happening so fast between them. "I'm here now."

Drew took a deep breath and then lowered his mouth to hers once more. She wrapped her arms around his neck and gave as good as she got. If she wasn't ready to say she missed him, she had no problems showing him.

Things quickly got out of control as their tongues mingled and hands explored. Beth ran her fingers through his hair as he lowered his mouth to her neck. All thoughts of food quickly left her mind until she began to smell the meat as it broiled in the oven. She placed her hands on his shoulders and pushed a little to get his attention. He pulled back with a questioning look on his face.

Beth smirked and held up one finger.

Turning her back to him, she leaned over and turned off the oven. As appealing as dinner sounded, Drew was even more so. Sure, she could wait, but she didn't want to. And from the looks of it, Drew didn't either.

When she faced him again, she had a plan. "I know we agreed that we wouldn't play when you have to work the next day, but are you up for a little mild bondage?"

His eyes lit up, and she could have sworn she saw his cock twitch. "Yes."

She nodded and placed her palm flat against his chest.

He got the message and began walking backward. Within a few steps, his knees hit the edge of the chair he'd been sitting on a few moments before.

Beth ran her hand down the length of his chest until she reached the hem of his shirt. She took hold of it and worked it up over his torso. When he realized what she was doing, he raised his arms over his head to help her remove it.

Then she went for the button on his pants. He kept his hands out of the way as she worked. Normally she would take her time if she was undressing a sub as part of foreplay, but she wasn't worried about either of them being ready for the main event. She was already wet and aching to feel his cock inside her, and from the way his erection stood at attention, she would guess he was more than ready as well.

Once he was completely naked, she directed him to sit down. She could tell he was curious, but eager as well.

She walked around behind him and opened a drawer where she kept various items. Beth had learned not long after she and Ben had started playing that it was a good idea to have kinky items, or at least pervertables, in each and every room. Toward the back of the drawer, she found what she was looking for. It was an old scarf. Someone had given it to her years before at a Christmas party. It was orange and rather ugly looking. She'd found it one day and was going to throw it out, but then had gotten inspiration to keep it for times such as this.

Grasping the scarf in her hand, she went back to stand behind Drew. She took hold of his arms and guided them behind the back of the chair. "I'm going to tie your wrists. If something doesn't feel right, just say red and we'll stop. I'll untie you and that will be it."

He nodded. "Got it."

Beth waited a spilt second before she bent down and secured his wrists with the scarf. "How does that feel?"

"Amazingly good."

She chuckled.

Moving around to his front, Beth released the top button of her blouse. The muscles in his jaw flexed a moment before she saw him swallow hard. Oh yeah, this was going to be so much fun.

Chapter Seventeen

Drew couldn't believe this was happening. His heart was pounding in his chest as the reality of what was about to occur sank in. Beth stood before him slowly unbuttoning her top. He could already see a hint of the purple bra she was wearing. She toyed with the next button that would give him a full view of her chest. He wanted her to hurry. He wanted to see, to touch, to taste.

In reaction to his thoughts, he leaned forward. The motion tugged at the scarf that bound his wrist to the chair—reminding him that he wasn't, in fact, free to touch. He groaned and the burning in his groin increased. His reaction didn't make any kind of sense, but it was there just the same.

Beth must have heard him groan. She stepped forward and bent over to whisper in his ear. Her breast was inches from his face. "See something you like?"

"Yes." It was all he could do to get out that one word when she was so close to him.

Without moving away, she popped the button she'd been playing with a few moments before. He took a deep breath as he watched her work through the remaining buttons before discarding the shirt. She hadn't backed away during the process. Her tits were right there. So close, yet far enough away that he couldn't easily reach. Not with his arms bound as they were.

Her chest vibrated, and he glanced up to find her grinning down at him.

This teasing was torture.

He loved it.

She cupped the back of his head and positioned herself so that his face was nestled between her breasts. He wasted no time nuzzling his nose into her cleavage and running his lips along the seam of satin and lace. Beth wasn't overly endowed in that area, but she had more than enough in his opinion. Her bra pushed her tits together, and he ran his tongue along the valley it created.

Beth reached up with her free hand and pushed one satin cup out of the way. He didn't need an engraved invitation. In less than a second, his lips were covering her nipple, sucking it into his mouth. She dug her nails into his scalp as he continued to lick and suck and tease. With only her body, she told him what she wanted and how she wanted it.

Somewhere along the line, she released her hold on him long enough to reach behind her back and unclasp her bra. It fell away, and she guided him to the other side. He'd never been a breast man, but there was something about having Beth's tits in his mouth—feeling her fingers in his hair—that turned him on more than playing with a woman's breasts ever had in the past.

The sound of a zipper caught his attention. He stopped and began to pull away.

"I don't remember telling you to stop." Her voice was firm but breathy at the same time.

He went back to what he was doing, but he had to admit that he was imagining what that sound meant and the fact that he was tied to a chair and not able to get his hand on her luscious ass.

"Something wrong?" she asked.

"No. I was just . . ."

She tilted his head up and brushed her lips against his. "Did you not want me to take off the rest of my clothes?"

There was a gleam in her eye, and Drew realized that he'd screwed up. Even though all they'd agreed on was some light bondage, he'd told her he wanted her to take charge when it came to the bedroom. "Sorry. I guess old habits are hard to break."

Beth hummed and trailed her mouth along his jaw until she captured his earlobe between her teeth. "I shall forgive you." She bit down enough to cause a slight measure of pain. "This time."

He got the message. Tonight was only a little fun and exploration of something he'd wanted to try. In the future, there would be consequences.

Before he could dwell too much on what had just happened, she lowered her mouth over his again, and thrust her tongue inside. There was no sweetness to this kiss. Teeth clashed as she continued her assault, holding his head in the exact position she wanted it.

Gradually she eased her grip, and softened the kiss. There was still no doubt, however, as to who was in control. He met every caress of her tongue with one of his own.

Drew was so lost in the kiss that he almost missed the movement of her hips as she straddled him. It was only then that he realized her skirt and panties were gone. He'd heard the zipper, yes, but how had he missed her shedding the rest of her clothing?

His breath caught in his throat as she rubbed her bare pussy over his cock. Her juices covered him as she rocked her hips and continued to kiss him. He wanted to be inside her. He wanted to feel that heat surrounding him.

"Beth."

He tried to break free from their kiss, so she moved her mouth lower to his neck. Drew didn't know if that was any better as she ran her teeth along his skin, biting and sucking as she went. He was on fire and he felt as if he would go mad if he didn't have her soon.

When he didn't think it could get any worse, it did. Beth reached down between them. He couldn't see from the position he was in, but he could feel it. She lifted enough to fit her hand between them, and plunged her fingers into her pussy. Drew couldn't tell how many, but it didn't matter. She was fucking herself right there on his lap.

"Please. Please, Beth. I want to be inside you. I need to . . ."

The next thing he knew, those same fingers that had been in her pussy were at his lips. He eagerly opened his mouth and took the offering. Tasting her only made him want her more. He was so aroused, he was afraid he might not last long even if she did give him what he wanted.

She removed her fingers from his mouth and brought his lips to meet hers. He moaned deep in his throat and his nostrils flared as he tried to keep himself in check. At the same time, he didn't want to. All he could think about was her.

Beth pulled back enough to rest her forehead against his. Her eyes were dilated and she was breathing hard. The tips of her nipples brushed against his chest, sending sparks through him with every touch.

"I'm going to fuck you now." It was all she said before she took hold of his cock and lined it up with her entrance.

He gritted his teeth and closed his eyes as she lowered herself down.

"Open your eyes. I want you looking at me."

Drew did as she said, and he was so glad he did. Her eyes glazed over as she took him all in. He wouldn't have wanted to miss that.

Once she had taken every inch of him, she began to move. First it was only a rocking motion. Then she rested her hands on his shoulders and began lifting and lowering herself on his cock. It was only by watching her face, knowing that he wanted her to get there first, that he kept his orgasm at bay.

Seeing her pleasure build was a fascinating sight. As she got closer, her eyelids drooped. Her head fell back, breaking their eye contact, and her mouth opened to form a silent O.

Her speed picked up and he had to close his eyes again to keep himself from coming. It was the only way.

Again, he felt it when she slipped her hand between them to touch herself. This time she used two fingers—one on each side of his erection—to rub. He forced his eyes open so he could see the motion of her hand as it moved.

Watching her hand was nearly his undoing. Knowing she was touching herself combined with the movement of his cock sliding in and out of her pussy made all the moisture leave his mouth. For the first time since she'd bound his wrists, he made a conscious effort to get free. He wanted to touch her. He wanted to hold her hips in his hands and impale her with his cock over and over until she exploded all over him.

Not only did her tie hold, but also his actions weren't needed. Beth took what she wanted from him. She ground herself against him with a fierceness and abandon he'd never seen from a woman before outside porn. He knew porn was fake. Beth wasn't faking. She was as caught up as he was.

Her breath hitched and her fingers picked up their pace. A few moments later, she released a strangled moan as her muscles pulsed around him. Her orgasm seemed to go on forever.

When she finally stilled and opened her eyes again, he was still hard and teetering on the edge. It wouldn't take much to make him come.

Beth smiled and gave him a long, languid kiss. And while she kept their bodies joined, she remained amazingly still. He needed friction.

In that vein, Drew lifted his hips.

She broke the kiss and stood.

He nearly cried.

That is until Beth turned herself around and began to lower herself onto him again—this time giving him a prime view of her ass.

BETH HAD ALMOST FORGOTTEN HOW MUCH FUN THIS WAS. OKAY, THAT wasn't true. She hadn't forgotten. Not really. But she didn't realize how much she'd missed this feeling of being in complete control of her pleasure as well as her partner's.

Given that she had Drew exactly where she wanted him at the moment, she figured she'd provide him a nice view as she milked his cum from him. They'd talked about him being an ass man, and he'd more than proven it to be true over the short time they'd been together. At every opportunity, his hands went straight for her backside.

As soon as she seated herself on his cock again, his breathing picked up, and he began to buck his hips. She could only imagine how badly he wanted his hands free. It would be interesting to see how he felt about the restriction . . . after.

She braced her hands on his knees, and rocked in time with him. It felt good, and another orgasm began to build low in her belly.

His thrusts became more aggressive and she knew he was getting close. She shifted her weight to one hand and began massaging her clit.

"Please tell me you're close. I don't know if I can hold on much longer," he panted.

Beth was close. Closer than even she realized.

Her second climax hit her without much warning. One moment she was climbing the peak, and then the next she was flying. She cried out as her orgasm claimed her.

A few moments later, as she was coming back down to earth, she realized Drew was chanting her name. Running her hands along his inner thighs, she nudged his balls out of the way, and began rubbing his perineum.

He went off like a rocket—her name left his lips in a gasp.

She gave him some time and then twisted around so that she could see his face. He looked up at her and blew out a shaky breath.

Beth chuckled and reached behind the chair to loosen the scarf. "I'm going to go clean up. I'll be back in a minute."

Drew nodded, and she lifted herself from his lap.

The loss she felt was frightening. She'd always enjoyed sex . . . even more so after she'd discovered kink. This was something altogether different.

Trying not to dwell too much on what she was feeling, she gathered up her discarded clothes, and strolled into the half bathroom right off the kitchen. She took a few minutes to go to the bathroom and clean herself up.

When she walked back into the kitchen with a damp cloth, Drew was standing beside the chair, still naked, with a huge grin on his face. She laid the cloth on the counter and took a quick look at his wrists. There were a few red marks, but nothing that would last more than an hour or two.

After her brief inspection, he glanced down at both his wrists.

"You may want to roll your shoulders a few times. It will help prevent stiffness," she said, reaching for the cloth and handing it to him.

"Thanks."

Once he'd cleaned himself, he did as she suggested and rolled his shoulders several times. She took the opportunity to go back to preparing dinner. It was already after six thirty. Now that she wasn't ready to jump his bones, her body was making its other needs known.

She heard him moving around behind her as she turned the oven back on to warm the steak and potatoes. The potatoes would be fine—she wasn't worried about that. The steak was a completely different story. It had only been cooking for four or five minutes before she'd turned everything off. Hopefully, it wouldn't be too chewy.

Turning around, she came face to face with Drew. Before she could say anything, he wrapped his arms around her, and buried his nose in the crook of her neck.

Beth didn't hesitate to return the hug. It felt good to have a man's arms around her again. Even if she was still scared of getting hurt.

"That was amazing," he murmured against her skin.

"So you enjoyed your first experience with bondage?"

He pulled back enough to see her face, and ran a hand along her cheek. "It was . . . well, it's hard to describe. Not being able to touch you when I wanted to was frustrating. But knowing you could do anything you wanted to me and I couldn't stop you"—he brushed his lips against hers—"I'm not sure I've been so turned on in my life."

She smiled. "So you'd like to do it again?"

Drew kissed her. He took his time, and she felt herself melting into his embrace. "You can tie me up anytime you want."

Beth laughed and circled her arms around his neck. "Good to know." They stood there for several minutes touching and kissing until the timer she'd set went off.

Drew laid out the plates and silverware while she got the food out of the oven and brought it to the table. By the time everything was in place and they were ready to sit down and eat, it was almost seven. He held out her chair for her. When he'd set the table he'd made sure to seat them side by side rather than across from each other as they'd been on Saturday night. Throughout the meal, he continued to touch her. Sometimes it was little more than a brush of her hand or arm. With every caress, she felt her libido revving up again.

She cleared her throat. "We should talk about tonight."

He took a bite of his food. "What about it?"

"Was there anything I did that you didn't like?"

His answer was immediate. "No."

"Nothing?" she asked.

"I'll admit you did a few things that surprised me, but considering I don't remember the last time I came like that . . . no, I can't say there was anything you did that I didn't like."

She was quiet for a few moments. "Speaking of coming, I know we didn't really talk about protection. I get a shot every three months, but we still should have talked about that. I'm sorry. I got caught up—"

"It's fine," he said, laying a hand on her arm to stop her rambling. "We'd already talked about us both being clean and I trust that you'd be careful about pregnancy."

"Still, it was irresponsible of me."

He finished the rest of his dinner before he responded. "I could have said something, too. It wasn't as if you had me gagged or anything. I am an adult, remember. I have a condom in my wallet. My dad taught me always to carry one. Just in case."

She grinned. "Very good advice."

"It was. And it came in handy more than once over the years." He turned to face her. "When I realized that you weren't going to use anything, the only thing I felt was happiness that there wouldn't be anything between us. I'm twenty-eight and I've never had sex without a condom. The main reason for that was that I've never been in a relationship before where I intended it to last for any length of time. It was something I'd considered with my last girlfriend, but then things fell apart and I'm glad I decided not to go there. Maybe, deep down, I knew how she'd react to my desires and that's why I never broached the subject."

Even though he didn't say it, she knew what he was implying. Drew was making a commitment to her. To them. He didn't have plans to go anywhere anytime soon. It left her with mixed feelings. She didn't want him to go anywhere, but at the same time it was a big step given they'd only been on one official date.

Deciding it was best not to dwell on it, she changed the subject. "Wednesday starts your four days off. Did you want to try a scene or would you rather wait?"

"If it means you having your wicked way with me again, then yes. I want to try a scene."

Beth ignored his flippant response. "I was thinking we should keep it simple. Since you enjoy bondage, we could work that in as well as some impact play. Are you up for that?"

He must have realized how nervous she was because he clasped her hand and squeezed. "Beth, I trust you. I wouldn't be here if I didn't. As long as it's not a hard limit, I want you to do what you want. I promise that I'll use my safewords if it gets too much. That's what they're there for, right?"

She nodded. "Right."

Drew was quiet for a moment. "You're not having second thoughts about us, are you?"

"No." She smiled and gave his hand a reassuring squeeze. "Ben and I had been dating a few months before we started playing."

"I get it. It took me four months to get up the courage to bring up something as simple as bondage in my last relationship."

"And I tied you to a chair on the second date."

He laughed. "Yeah."

Drew hadn't let go of her hand. Their eyes met, and he moved closer, drawing her in.

"Did you want to spend the night?" she asked as his lips drew closer to her mouth.

"I have to work tomorrow," he whispered. "I have to be in at seven, and I don't have any clothes here."

She placed her palms flat on his chest and began moving them lower. "What I have in mind wouldn't involve clothing. And besides, my alarm goes off at five. Surely that would give you enough time to get home and change."

His response came in actions rather than words. He stood, taking her by the hands. "How fast do you think we can get this cleaned up?"

Cleaning up was the last thing she was worried about given the heated look he was giving her. "It can wait until tomorrow."

The words were barely out of her mouth when he began leading her toward the stairs.

Chapter Eighteen

While the alarm had gone off at five, they hadn't made it out of bed until after five thirty. Saying goodbye to Beth had taken another twenty-five minutes—not that he would have changed anything. It was the first time in the last seven years that he'd wanted to call in sick. He knew his crew was counting on him, however, so he made himself do what he had to do.

He made it home at six twenty-four. Shawn was already gone. Drew took one of the fastest showers of his life, threw on his uniform, downed a bagel and some orange juice, and jogged back out to his car.

The station was buzzing with activity when he arrived at ten after seven. Several of the guys greeted him as he made his way to the locker room. It was in the locker room that he ran into Shawn.

"Good morning." His friend shot him a knowing smile.

"Morning." Drew tried to act normal as he stowed his keys and wallet into his assigned locker, but the writing was already on the wall. Shawn was aware that he hadn't come home last night. He also knew Drew had had a date with Beth. It didn't take a rocket scientist to put the two together.

His friend waited until the other guys exited the locker room before he started in with the questioning. "Last night went well, huh?"

"Yeah."

Well didn't begin to cover it. After they'd gone to her bedroom, they'd had another round of hot and heavy sex. That time he was able to touch her to his heart's content. Afterward, they'd talked more about what they wanted to explore when it came to the BDSM side of their relationship. For some reason, he'd always envisioned negotiations taking place across a table like you see on those cop shows—stark interrogation room, harsh lighting, that sort of thing. This was about as far removed from that as could be. They'd talked for hours tangled in each other's arms.

Shawn whistled, causing Drew to look up. "Must have been some night if you're daydreaming about it already."

Drew felt the heat surging in his cheeks. He turned his head so his friend couldn't see.

Patting him on the back, Shawn walked toward the door. "I'm happy for you. Enjoy it."

After shutting his locker and taking a deep breath, Drew went out to meet with his crew—and maybe get a little more breakfast. They had work to do, and if they weren't too busy with calls, he wanted to get some training in as well. The training was more for his benefit than theirs. Drew needed to keep busy. The faster the next twenty-four hours went, the better.

NORMALLY WHEN BETH WAS LATE TO WORK, IT THREW HER ENTIRE DAY into a tailspin. She hated being late.

Tommy, who had known her for nearly seven years, knew this about her. That was why he immediately became suspicious when she floated around the kitchen humming to herself during morning prep, even though she'd come in nearly twenty minutes late. He stopped what he was doing and stared her down.

"What?" she asked when she noticed him looking.

"I'm trying to figure out why you're so cheery this morning."

She grinned as memories of the night before came back to her.

"Ah." Tommy smiled and nodded. "Things are going well with the firefighter."

Beth had no reason to deny it. "They are."

"Good. I'm glad." He reached around her to grab a large mixing bowl from the shelf. When he returned to his position beside her, he nudged her with his hip. "Make sure he treats you right."

Although she didn't comment, the look on her face must have been answer enough for Tommy.

When the doors opened at seven, people began flooding in. Almost every week they were busier than the one before. She'd been considering hiring another employee, if for no other reason than to give her and Tommy a break every now and then.

It was as they were closing the café down that afternoon that Beth broached the subject with Tommy. "What do you think about me hiring someone to help us around here?"

He looked up from where he was wiping the front counter. "You mean another employee?"

She nodded.

"I think it's a good idea. If things keep picking up, you and I aren't going to be able to handle it on our own."

"I know. And with summer just around the corner, it's probably going to get even busier."

On her way home that evening, Beth swung by the store and picked up a help wanted sign for her front window. Maybe she'd get lucky and have someone see the sign and apply. If not, she'd have to place an ad in the local paper. She had plenty of foot traffic, though. Odds were someone who frequented her café was either in need of a job or knew someone who was.

That night she opened her toy chest and laid everything on her bed. Beth sorted the items based on what Drew had put on his checklist. Everything not on his list she tucked away in the bottom drawer of her dresser. The rest she cleaned and then returned to the chest so they would be easily accessible when she needed them.

With that accomplished, Beth made herself some dinner, and then curled up on the couch to call Nicole.

"Well, how was it? Please tell me you fucked that boy senseless."

Beth laughed. "Well, hello to you, too."

"Pfft. Save the pleasantries for later. Come on. Spill. You two did have sex, didn't you?"

She rolled her eyes. "Yes."

"And?"

"And . . . we'll be doing it again tomorrow." Beth picked up the bowl of ice cream she'd brought into the living room with her.

"It's about time."

"It was only our second date."

"Maybe technically. But tell me you didn't want to see him naked the first time you laid eyes on him."

Beth chuckled as she licked the ice cream from her spoon. "I think half the women in Serpent's Kiss wanted to see him naked."

"You think that's changed? Something tells me the first time you two scene at the club you're going to have an audience."

"I figured. Somehow, I don't think Drew is all that into exhibitionism."

"He'll get over it."

Although Drew didn't strike her as a man who had issues with his body, it was one thing to be comfortable in your own skin. It was another to have a dozen people watching you get your rocks off. "We'll have to talk it over. Honestly, it's not even something I'm thinking about yet. We need to get through our first scene before we add anything else to the mix."

"Something holding you up? I would have thought you two would jump right into it."

"His schedule. He's in the middle of a rotation," Beth said, figuring Nicole would understand since she knew how their scheduling worked.

"Makes sense. It wouldn't be good if he experienced subdrop in the middle of a shift."

The thought had crossed Beth's mind. She worried about his safety enough as it was. It was one of the reasons she'd asked him to spend the night. "We're going to try on Wednesday evening. He's coming over for dinner, and then we'll see how things go from there."

"I'm happy for you."

"Yeah, well, don't count your chickens yet. He might realize after he gets a full taste of submission that he doesn't like it."

Nicole let out a noise that sounded somewhere between a whine and a snort. "You actually believe that?"

"It could happen."

"And pigs could fly."

She was right. It was a long shot. Especially given his reaction to being bound. "I know you're right. I just—"

"Stop worrying. Things are going great, right? Just go with it."

"I'll try."

Nicole sighed. "Don't try. Do."

Beth rolled her eyes. "Okay, Obi-Wan."

"I supposed I should give you credit for at least getting the movie reference."

"Why, thank you so much for your generosity." Beth chuckled and went to put her empty bowl in the dishwasher. She glanced over at the clock and was surprised to see how late it was. "I should probably let you go and get myself ready for bed."

"You do want to be fully rested for your big night tomorrow."

Beth groaned. "Don't put more pressure on me than I already feel."

Nicole laughed. "Good night."

"Good night."

It took Beth several minutes to walk through the lower level of her house and make sure everything was turned off and locked up for the night. As her day wound down and she got ready for bed, she couldn't help remembering the previous night.

She slid beneath the covers and reached for the pillow Drew had used. A faint hint of his smell still lingered on her sheets. And if she closed her eyes, she could almost imagine him there, lying beside her again.

Beth was surprised how right it had felt for him to be in her bed. The first time Ben had spent the night with her, it had been awkward. He'd been restless, which in turn had caused her to be restless as well.

Drew, however, had no issues falling asleep in her bed. He'd rolled over, curled up against her back, and fallen asleep within minutes. His comfort had in turn made it easy for her to relax and drift off to sleep herself. She hadn't been plagued by self-consciousness or uncertainty as she had with Ben. Then again, all her cards were on the table with Drew. He knew she was a Domme and liked to be the one calling the shots in their sexual relationship. She hadn't tried to downplay her desires. Instead, she'd embraced them and so had he.

Tucking the pillow he'd used the night before under her chin, Beth turned onto her side, and closed her eyes. Drew would most likely spend the night tomorrow after their scene. While she realized it wasn't good to be overly attached to him so soon, she already knew she was going to be helpless to stop it. Wise or not, her heart wanted Drew. She'd welcome him into her bed as often as she could have him.

❧

"Any plans for your days off?" Baily asked to the room at large. The new shift had arrived so Drew and his crew were about to head home.

Romeo clasped the necklace he always wore around his neck when he wasn't on duty. Once it was secured, he tucked the gold cross beneath his shirt. "I'm sure I have a 'honey-do' list waiting for me when I get home."

All the guys laughed. Whenever Romeo had his four days off, his wife always had a new project . . . or two waiting for him.

Baily nodded toward Irwin. "What about you? Got any plans?"

"Nah. Not really. I might see if my brother-in-law needs some help at the restaurant."

"Trouble in paradise?" Romeo asked.

Irwin shrugged. "I don't know. Maybe."

They strolled out of the locker room and headed toward the parking lot.

"What about you, Cap? Got a hot date with your café lady?" Baily asked.

Drew tossed his duffel bag into the backseat of his car and shut the door. He waited until he was opening the driver door and about to slide into the seat before answering. "As a matter of fact, I do. See you all bright and early Sunday morning."

While they were still gaping wide-eyed back at him, he started the engine, and drove away. He knew there would be hell to pay during his next shift, but for the time being, he couldn't wipe the grin off his face.

He was about to slip into bed an hour later when Shawn ambled through the door. "Hey."

Drew leaned against the doorjamb outside his bedroom. "Hey."

Shawn walked into the kitchen and reached into the refrigerator. He pulled out a beer and took a large swig.

"You all right?" Drew asked.

"Yeah. I'm fine."

He didn't buy that for a second. "Something happen? Is it Jill?"

His friend took another long pull on his beer before turning around to face him. "I figured I'd go by the house this morning. See if maybe Jill and I could talk."

"And?"

"I pulled up to the curb in time to see a guy I didn't recognize stepping out to get the morning paper."

"Oh, man. I'm sorry."

"Yeah. So am I." Shawn stared down at the floor. "How could I have missed this? How could I not have known she was seeing another guy?" He looked at Drew as if hoping he had an answer for him.

"I don't know."

Shawn nodded as if he had expected Drew's response.

Silence filled the air for several minutes before Drew cleared his throat. "I'm supposed to go over to Beth's tonight. I can call her and cancel if—"

"Don't you dare. Go. Spend time with your woman."

"Are you sure?" Drew asked.

Shawn drained the rest of his beer and threw the bottle in the recycle bin. "Sure I am. No reason why we both have to spend the evening wallowing in self-pity."

"That isn't reassuring."

"I'm fine. Really. Or, at least, I will be." Shawn sighed and headed toward the bathroom. "Go get some rest. I'm sure you'll need it for tonight."

Drew stood there and watched his heartbroken friend disappear into the bathroom. He was torn. Tonight would be his and Beth's first real foray into BDSM—and his first ever. It was something he'd dreamt about since laying eyes on her. But Shawn was one of his closest friends.

With a sigh, Drew stepped into his bedroom and closed the door. Aside from the call that woke them all up at five o'clock this morning, he'd gotten a decent amount of sleep during his shift. His anxiety over his upcoming evening with Beth had made it a bit difficult to fall asleep, but after that, he'd been out until the alarm sounded. He figured it was a good idea to try and get at least a couple more hours of sleep, given the evening they had planned. Shawn was right. If things went well with Beth later, he would need all the rest he could get.

He rolled out of bed a little before two in the afternoon. Although he was still concerned about Shawn, at least he felt rested.

Drew stretched, feeling the pull of his muscles. As he laced his fingers behind him to stretch his arms and back, a knowing grin pulled at the corner of his mouth. He wondered if Beth would tie him up again.

The thought of Beth caused him to look over at his phone. It was showing he had a voice mail message.

Holding the phone up to his ear, he checked his messages.

It was Beth.

"Good morning. I hope you're ready for tonight." There was a level of seduction in her voice, and he felt his pulse quicken in anticipation. *"Be at my house at five. Bring an overnight bag. I don't plan on letting you out of my bed before morning."*

He swallowed and instinctively reached down to cup his groin.

She lowered her voice, but instead of lessening the effect, it did the opposite. *"No touching yourself until I say."*

There was a long pause in her message, and he could feel the blood pumping through his veins. He removed his hand from his growing erection even though it was the last thing he wanted to do. This was what he'd signed up for. This was what he'd wanted.

After several moments of silence, she finished her message in a lighter tone. *"I'm looking forward to tonight. See you at five."*

Beth's message ended, and the automated voice came on asking if he wanted to save or delete the message. He hovered over the delete button, but then changed his mind and saved it instead. There was no real reason to. She hadn't left a list of instructions he was unlikely to remember. If he was being honest with himself, it had more to do with having access to her voice whenever he wanted it. And the best part about the message was that she showed both sides of herself—the Domme and his girlfriend.

He chuckled as he laid the phone back on his dresser and went to get some coffee and a light lunch. Drew was still grinning when he strolled into the kitchen. He stopped short, however, when he saw Shawn sitting dejectedly on the couch.

Shawn opened his eyes and sent Drew a weak smile. "Sleep well?"

"Yeah." Drew walked over to the coffeemaker and flipped it on. "You?"

His friend shrugged.

"You need your sleep. You have a shift tomorrow."

"I'll be fine," Shawn said, waving him off. "We weren't that busy last night, so I got a good four hours at least. That's enough."

While Drew wasn't convinced, he wasn't Shawn's babysitter either, so he let it go. Instead, Drew moved about the kitchen gathering what he'd need to make scrambled eggs and bacon. He somehow figured he'd need the extra protein later.

Shawn folded the blanket he was using and placed it, along with his pillow, at one end of the couch before joining Drew in the kitchen. Falling into the same routine they were used to at work, Shawn gathered what was needed to set the table. Drew carried the food over when it was ready, and they dug in.

"What time are you supposed to meet your girl?" Shawn asked.

Drew was still unsure if he should leave his buddy alone, but if Shawn didn't want him there, he wasn't going to push. "Five."

Shawn shoveled in a few more bites. "Want to head over to the gym before you go? I feel the need to pummel something."

"Sure." Drew lowered his head so Shawn couldn't see the smirk on his face. There was no doubt in Drew's mind whose face his friend would be picturing as he planted his fist in the gym's punching bag.

Chapter Nineteen

Beth had everything ready for Drew's arrival, even the food. She wondered if he'd gotten her voice mail, and how he'd reacted. They'd discussed orgasm control as they lay in her bed on Monday night. Although their arrangement was bedroom only, he'd liked the idea of her deciding when he would be allowed to come. If it came to their sex life, he wanted her to be the one in charge. She'd experimented some regarding that aspect of domination with Ben. He didn't much care for it, so it was put in the strongly dislike column.

A knock sounded on her front door and she shook off the memory of her ex. Tonight was about the future—hers with Drew. The rest was water under the bridge.

Butterflies began swirling in her stomach when she drew closer to the entry. She paused for a moment with her hand on the knob to steady herself before opening the door.

Drew stood on the porch smiling at her—a duffel bag slung over one shoulder and a single daisy in the other. "Hi."

"Hi," she said, moving out of the way so he could come in.

He brushed past her into the foyer. She shut the door and turned around to find him close.

"I brought you a daisy."

Beth could feel his breath on her face and it had her head whirling. Drew was all man. There was no doubt about that. "It's beautiful. Thank you."

"It means loyalty. Commitment. I thought it was fitting given our plans for tonight."

"You seem to know a lot about flowers. Are you trying to impress me?" Beth didn't know if she wanted him to say yes or no. She didn't need frills, but she had to admit it was nice.

Drew's lips curled up into a sheepish grin. "Maybe a little. My mom loves flowers. She has a wide variety growing around the farm. I used to help her weed the beds when I was younger and she would tell me all their different meanings."

"Does she still have them? The flowers, I mean?" Beth asked.

"Yes. When she's not in the house cooking, you can usually find her in her flower beds."

Hearing this new insight into his family relaxed Beth even more. Drew was sharing things with her about himself and his childhood. Taking the offered flower, she raised it to her noise, and inhaled its fragrance. "Does your mom have any daisies?"

"She does. Daisies are one of her favorites."

Beth went up on her tiptoes and brushed her lips against his before giving him a soft kiss. "I can't wait to see them, then."

He blinked. "Does that mean you're going to the barbecue with me?"

She nodded.

Before Beth knew what was happening, he had dropped his duffel bag to the floor and picked her up. She laughed as he twirled her around.

When he finally set her feet back down on solid ground, he was grinning from ear to ear.

"I'll make sure you're not back too late. I know you have to work the next day," he vowed.

Beth gave him another hard kiss, and then began walking toward the kitchen. "Don't you have to work as well?"

"Well, yes, but I'm not worried about that."

She glanced back at him. "I just don't want you getting hurt because you're dead on your feet."

He chuckled and took the plate she'd picked up off the counter out of her hand. "Not to worry. I once pulled a twenty-four-hour shift with zero sleep."

When she gave him a questioning look, he continued. "Right when things were beginning to settle down for the evening, we got a call for a possible injury accident. Took us about an hour to get that all cleaned up and head back to the station. We were about ready to head up to our bunks when the next call came in. It pretty much kept up like that all night. I think we rolled into the station at around six in the morning. By that time, there was no point in going to bed. We all chipped in to get things prepped for the next shift, and then started on breakfast."

"Wow," she said, taking the food out of the oven and placing it in the center of the table.

"Luckily, that doesn't happen often. It was a rare night."

Beth grabbed the pitcher of ice water and sat down.

Drew followed. "It smells great."

"Thank you." She motioned that Drew should help himself while she filled both their glasses. "Are you ready for tonight?"

"I think so. I'm more anxious than anything."

"Anything in particular you're anxious about?" she asked.

He shrugged. "The usual, I suppose. I don't want to mess up."

"If you *mess up*, then we'll deal with it. You're learning. It's to be expected. Who knows? I could be the one to mess things up."

Drew snorted before taking a bite of his food. "I doubt that."

"It could happen."

He watched her for several moments. At first, he looked as if he was going to comment, but then he must have changed his mind.

Beth decided to jump on her chance to change the subject. The last thing she wanted to do was get into the self-doubt Ben had left in his wake. "Do you have any questions before we get started?"

"When will we start?"

It was a good question. "When we've finished eating, I'll show you to the guest room. You can put your stuff in there and do anything else you need to do. Once you're done and ready to get the evening underway, I want you to meet me in my bedroom."

Drew blew out a heavy breath. "Okay. Anything else?"

She reached over and ran her hand up the inside of his thigh. "When you come to me, I want you naked. You will enter the room with your gaze on the floor. After that, you just need to do what you're told."

The muscles in his throat contracted as he swallowed.

"Drew?"

He looked up to meet her gaze.

"We're going to have fun tonight."

"We haven't started yet, right?" he asked.

"Right."

Without warning, Drew placed his hands on either side of her face and brought his mouth down on hers. She moaned as her body reacted to the feel of his lips, and heat spread throughout her body.

Just as suddenly as he began the kiss, he ended it. They were both panting, and Beth was tempted to say forget about the scene and take him in the kitchen chair as she'd done before. The only thing that stopped her was a curiosity to see just how powerful their connection could be in a full scene. "I'm going to make you pay for that, you know."

He chuckled. "I can't wait."

Beth glanced over at his empty plate. "Finished?"

"With food."

She felt her body temperature rise a few degrees more. "Follow me. I'll show you to the guest room."

Not waiting for a response, Beth stood, and made her way to the stairs. She knew he was behind her even though she didn't look back.

At the top of the stairs, she made a left. When she'd bought the house, there had been four bedrooms. The master, of course, had its own bathroom, but the other three shared a communal bathroom at the end of the hall. That was why one of the first things she did after buying the house was to renovate the upstairs. She lost a bedroom in the deal, but gained two additional bathrooms. It was a fair trade, and given the nature of their relationship, Beth had felt Ben needed to have his own space—including his own bathroom.

Beth strolled into the guest room. She stopped a few feet inside the door and waited for Drew to enter.

He threw his bag on the bed and took in his surroundings. "Nice. But I think I like your room better."

His cocky smile was back. She was going to have some fun with that attitude of his. "If you're good, I promise you'll be seeing the inside of my bedroom a lot."

"Promises, promises."

She shook her head and turned toward the door. "You have ten minutes. Don't be late or I'll have to punish you."

Drew's smile grew bigger. "I'd better hurry, then."

Beth rolled her eyes and walked to her bedroom where the night's activities would take place. She removed her shirt and skirt, leaving her in a purple corset with a matching set of panties. Going to her closet, she retrieved the black boots she'd worn to the club a few weeks ago. They were her favorites. Satisfied with her attire, Beth took a final look around to make sure everything was in place.

She was closing the lid on the small cooler filled with ice that she'd brought upstairs earlier when she heard Drew enter the room. Beth looked in his direction and saw he had followed her instructions. The erection he was already sporting told her how excited he was. Heat flared in the area between her legs. She couldn't wait to get her hands on him.

DREW WANTED TO LOOK UP AND FEAST HIS EYES ON BETH. HE'D ONLY gotten a peek at what she'd been wearing as he'd entered the room and then dutifully lowered his gaze. Even that small glimpse was enough to have his cock standing at attention.

"Come over here," she ordered.

He obeyed, keeping his head down.

Beth cupped the side of his face with one hand and looked into his eyes. She must have seen whatever it was she was looking for because she nodded, released her hold on him, and took a step back. "On your knees."

Lowering himself to the floor, he waited to see what she'd do next.

Nothing happened for several moments. All he could hear was his own breathing. Her scent was all around him, though, and as she moved closer to him, he could smell it even more. She was aroused and his mouth moistened in anticipation of being able to taste her again.

Placing a hand on the top of his head, she began to move. Beth combed her fingers through his hair and then down his back as she walked to stand behind him. Her touch felt so good. It was exactly what he needed after everything that had been going on with Shawn and work and . . .

He must have tensed or something, because the next thing he knew she was whispering in his ear. "Shh. Whatever's going through your mind, let it go. Tonight you are mine. You're here to serve me. Nothing outside this room matters. It will still be there later to worry about."

"Yes, ma'am."

"Good."

It sounded as if she was pleased with his answer. He wondered if she was smiling.

She went to her dresser and retrieved something before returning to stand behind him. "Raise your chin."

He did as he was told. Seconds later he felt something wrap around his neck. A collar.

"This is a training collar. I thought it might help you get into your submissive mindset. To remind you that your body belongs to me tonight."

She waited.

Drew realized she wanted him to answer. He decided to try out her new title. They'd talked about it. She was going to be his mistress, after all. Still, this would be the first time he'd actually called her that. "Thank you, Mistress."

A moment later, he felt something slide against the back of the collar followed by a click. He realized it was a lock.

Taking several slow deep breaths, he relaxed and let and what she'd said sink in. As he did so, he felt the stress of his day begin to fade. This was their time and he was going to savor it.

Beth stood before him and he was able to get his first good look at her. She was stunning. The corset she was wearing hugged her curves and lifted her tits. He wanted to bury his face in her cleavage. Then there were her panties. The tiny scrap of material that covered her front made him salivate for a view of the back. Drew could only imagine how her ass would look.

"Had a good enough look?" she asked.

He met her gaze and saw that she was amused by his perusal. "I could stare at you all day."

"I'll keep that in mind." Looping a finger in the O-ring he hadn't noticed on the front of his collar, she pulled up. "Stand."

There was a part of him that fought against her ordering him around, but there was a larger part that wanted this.

She led him over to the wall. It was then he noticed the large X with cuffs attached to it. "Stand facing the wall with your arms raised and your legs spread."

He got into position and held still as she secured his arms and legs. There was still plenty of room between him and the wall. Beth took advantage of the space by grasping his cock. "Did you touch yourself today?"

"No, Mistress."

She ran her hand from base to tip three times, making his cock swell even more.

He had to bite back a groan when she took her hand away.

"Tonight we are going to do some experimenting," she said.

Drew had no idea what that meant, but he'd told her that he was up for trying anything he'd marked on his list and he'd meant it. There was a lot he'd seen at Serpent's Kiss that he was curious about. This was his opportunity. He had what he wanted—a relationship with a woman willing to dominate him.

A sting to his behind brought him back to the present. It didn't hurt exactly, but it had returned his focus.

The first sting was followed by several others in various places on his ass and thighs. Only when Beth trailed the flat leather tip along his spine before landing another blow to his butt cheek did he realize she was using a crop on him. It felt different than he'd expected. As she continued to hit different places on his body, he felt his skin warming.

Beth pressed herself against him from behind and ran her nails over his ass. It wasn't the first time she'd touched him like this, but it felt different after she'd used the crop. Everything was very sensitive. He could feel every movement—every scratch.

"Did you like that?"

"Yes."

Beth allowed her hands to drift lower. She raked her nails along the inside of his thighs, and he sucked in a breath.

He felt her lips against his back. "Don't worry. We're just getting started."

To his great disappointment, she removed her warmth from him and went to grab something else. This time he knew what she was using with the first strike—a flogger. The falls licked at his flesh, making his already sensitive skin tingle. She mixed soft, almost tickling caresses with hard blows that thudded soundly against his back, ass, and legs. He felt the stress of the day leaving his body completely as he became lost in the sensation.

Drew was so caught up in what he was experiencing that the feel of something much firmer hitting his backside caused him to snap his head up.

Beth laughed. "That got your attention."

She hit him with it again and he felt the bite of the leather. It hurt, but it wasn't altogether unpleasant. His body was singing at that point and whatever she was using only added another note to the symphony.

After ten strokes with whatever she was using, something soft caressed his overly sensitive backside. He closed his eyes and let the feeling take over.

Right when he was getting used to the gentle touch of whatever she was using, the flogger was back. Then, moments later, the softness returned. It was a game trying to anticipate which he would feel as she moved back and forth between the two. He found that he yearned for the feel of both.

Hands splayed across his chest and trailed down over his abs to wrap around his cock. Lips pressed against his back as the hands pumped his erection. It felt wonderful, but it wasn't enough. He needed more. In that vein, Drew flexed his hips into the hands.

Almost instantly, the hands were gone.

"Uh-uh. None of that." Beth's voice grounded him.

"Sorry, Mistress."

"Hmm. It's just as well. I have other plans for you this evening." She bent down and released his ankle cuffs, and then stood to free his wrists as well. "How are you feeling?"

"I think every nerve ending I have has been awakened."

"Does that mean you're ready to continue?" she asked.

"Yes. Please."

Beth smiled. "Remove my panties."

He eagerly dropped to his knees and looped his fingers in the sides of the purple underwear he'd been admiring earlier. Inching them down her legs, he worked them over her boots, and deposited them on the floor.

She lifted her leg, resting it on the blanket chest at the end of the bed. The new position opened her up to him and her pussy was staring him right in the face.

No words were spoken as she laced her fingers through his hair and guided his mouth to where she wanted it to be. He'd been dreaming since their date about the next time he'd get to taste her. Drew would be happy to do this for her every day if she'd let him.

Beth rested her hand at the base of his neck and began grinding her pussy against his tongue. Her wetness coated his face as he licked and sucked her, drawing out her pleasure.

He knew she was close when she shifted her hips, placing his tongue directly over her clit. Drew flicked his tongue rapidly, edging her closer. Her grip on his neck tightened and her hips jerked moments before her breath hitched and he felt a flood of moisture on his chin. There was such a sense of satisfaction in serving her this way. And when he gazed up into her eyes, he knew he was exactly where he wanted to be—on his knees serving her.

Chapter Twenty

Beth tried to catch her breath as her orgasm faded. Drew's head was still in between her legs, licking and nuzzling her pussy. She had half a mind to let him get her off a second time. But as much as she wanted to come by his mouth again, she wanted him inside her more. Reaching behind her, Beth retrieved the leash she'd placed on the end of the bed, and attached it to his collar.

Drew froze and looked up.

She smiled down at him and gave the leash a firm tug. "Get on the bed and lie down with your hands behind your head."

He hesitated briefly and then did as she'd instructed. This was going to be a test to see how well he obeyed without being bound.

Beth climbed onto the bed and straddled his waist. The end of the leash was wrapped around her hand. She kept enough of a pull on it to remind him it was there.

She brushed her mouth against his before running her tongue along the seam. He groaned and parted his lips. Beth took the offering and dipped her tongue inside his mouth. The taste of her arousal filled her senses. Drew was hers and tonight she was going to claim him.

Their kiss continued. She was in no hurry. They had hours to play, and she planned to enjoy every minute of the time they had.

After a while, though, he became impatient and started to reach for her. Beth broke the kiss and jerked on the leash. "Did I tell you to move your hands?"

Drew blinked up at her as if waking from a daze.

She knew the moment her words sank in. He placed his hands back into position and lowered his gaze. Beth remained where she was, waiting to see what he'd do. It was almost as if she could see the words forming in his mind as he centered himself once again.

Releasing her hold on the leash, she got up off the bed, and went to fetch the items she'd placed on the dresser. Drew's eyes followed her movement. Normally for sensation play, she'd blindfold her partner, but since this was his first time, she decided that she wanted him to see what she was doing to him. Tonight's exercise was about obedience.

Beth set the cooler, flogger, nipple clamps, and cock ring next to the bed. She made sure to lay each item down slowly so he could see them. Other than furrowing his forehead some when she opened the cooler, he didn't react.

The end of the leash laid flat against his stomach. She left it there and chose to grasp the leather about a foot from where it connected to the collar around his neck. Pulling his head up away from his hands an inch or so, Beth gave him a hard kiss before releasing him. She left the leash in place, however, just in case.

"Keep your hands where they are. If you move them again, I will have to punish you."

"Yes, Mistress."

Satisfied, she placed her palm on the inside of his thigh. "Spread your legs."

She stood by the bed while he moved his legs. Once he was where she wanted him, she took his cock and worked the silicone ring down the length of his erection. The constriction caused him to harden further and she dipped her head down to lick the tip of his penis.

He sucked in a breath as she ran the tip of her tongue through his slit. "Like that?"

"Yes, Mistress."

Beth covered the head of his cock with her mouth and circled it with her tongue before releasing him. "If you're a good boy, maybe I'll use my mouth on you more later."

Drew nodded, and she could tell he was trying very hard not to move. He wanted more and he was used to calling the shots in the bedroom. She had to remember that this was all new to him.

With the cock ring in place, Beth reached for the nipple clamps. Although he'd seen them used many times, this would be his first experience with them. She placed them both on his chest so he knew exactly what was coming next, and then began rolling his nipples between her fingers. He didn't react much when she gave a gentle tug, so she decided to increase the pressure. Beth wanted to see how much pain it took for him to respond.

She got her answer on her third try. Based on his responses she knew she'd have to tighten the tweezer clamps almost completely. If he liked them, she might try something stronger next time.

Pinching his nipple, she placed one of the clamps on either side, and then slid the band of metal up the two arms until she saw him wince. Then she did the same on the other side. With both clamps in place, she noticed he had a look of total concentration on his face.

Beth placed a hand on his cheek, drawing his attention. "You doing all right?"

"Yes, Mistress."

"Remember you have your safewords if it becomes too much."

He nodded.

She reached for the small flogger. Unlike the larger one she'd used on him earlier against the wall, this had more of a stinging sensation. With the ring driving all the blood to his cock, it would be fun to see how he reacted to the flogger on that part of his anatomy.

Glancing up at his face to make sure he was still okay, Beth began working the flogger in random movements over his chest and legs before she took aim at his erection. With the snap of her wrist, she struck his cock right above the silicone ring.

He flinched, but then settled himself.

Beth took that as the green light to continue and began a series of blows on his cock, balls, and inner thighs. By the time she was done, the entire area had a nice pink hue to it. She tossed the flogger onto the floor and took hold of his balls in her left hand while lowering her mouth to lick and sooth the flesh she'd just abused. He moaned as her tongue made contact and widened his legs even more to give her better access. Beth saw his chest begin to rise and fall faster as she continued. His cock was hard and pulsing.

Before she moved on, Beth placed a wet kiss on the tip of his cock. It bobbed a little, which made her smile. He seemed to be enjoying what she was doing to him.

She stood, stuck her hand in the cooler, and removed an ice cube. Drew had his eyes closed. He seemed lost in everything he was feeling, so he startled a little when she brought the cold object to his lips.

He opened his eyes and looked up at her.

Beth rubbed the ice along his lips, and he slid his tongue out to lick the cool liquid. She held it there, letting him drink. When the ice melted enough, Beth allowed him to suck it into his mouth while she went to retrieve another cube. This one she ran along his forehead and then down his neck and collarbone. As she moved lower, she followed the path of the ice with her mouth—licking and biting—warming the skin she'd cooled moments before.

As she worked her way to his chest, she circled his nipples with the ice, and then one by one removed the clamps. Drew arched his back. He breathed through his nose as she eased the hurt with her tongue.

She palmed what remained of the ice cube and wrapped her hand around his cock while she continued to kiss her way across his abdomen. He gasped and tensed. Beth knew keeping still had to be killing him, but he was doing it.

Slowly she ran her hand up and down his length letting the warmth melt the ice. She looked up to watch his reaction and was pleased to see that he had his eyes closed and his head tilted back.

When she arrived at her destination, Beth straddled his hips. She waited until the ice was completely melted, and then guided his cock to the entrance of her pussy.

His eyes flew open as he felt her heat envelope his cock.

◈

DREW HAD ENTERED INTO THE NIGHT WITH NO ILLUSIONS. HE WAS GIVING up control to Beth and he knew what that meant. Because of that, Drew didn't know if he'd get to be inside her.

She lowered herself down onto his erection with excruciating slowness. Watching his cock disappear inch by inch into her pussy and not being able to touch her was torture—but he couldn't look away.

If that weren't enough of a visual, Beth released the hooks that held her corset together. He held his breath as she shed the garment and threw it down beside the bed.

"Give me your hands."

He moved quicker than he thought possible. She laced their fingers together, using their connection as leverage. When she moaned, he transferred his attention from where she was grinding away on his cock to her face. Beth's eyes were closed and her head was thrown back. She was totally assured in what she was doing. It was amazing to watch.

Her breathing became more labored. She picked up her paced, slamming down onto him as she chased toward her goal.

The fevered pace had all the blood rushing to his groin. He felt his balls tightening, readying for climax. But he didn't know if that was going to happen. Again, that decision belonged entirely to Beth.

He didn't want to look away from her. Them. But he had to. If he didn't concentrate, he was going to come whether he wanted to or not. It was right there—he could feel it beckoning.

Suddenly, Beth tore her right hand from his, and reached between them. A second later, he felt the vibrations. "Shit!"

Her only response was to place both his hands on her tits. Drew was so thrilled to be touching her that he began playing with them in earnest. From their previous encounters, he knew what she liked. It amazed him how focused he was on her considering his body was so close to betraying him.

"More," she said. "Pinch my nipples."

Drew did as she asked, doing his best to give her what she needed.

The intensity continued to build as she rode him. He was sweating but it was the least of his worries. Like it or not, he was going to come if she kept up the way she was. Between the feeling of her wet pussy pulling and squeezing him and the vibrations at the base of his cock, he was seconds away from losing it.

Beth must have realized how close he was because she leaned down, bringing their foreheads to rest against each other. Her mouth hovered only centimeters from his—so close their breath mingled together. Their eyes met and held as Beth matched her breathing with his. Everything outside the two of them fell away.

Her breath hitched in her throat and he felt it deep in his core. Beth caressed the side of his face as she continued to move against him. He could feel every intake of breath, every exhale.

"Come," she whispered.

Instinct took over. Drew released his hold on her breasts and dug his fingers into her ass, thrusting his hips. They both gasped, and he felt Beth's muscles clamp down. Her face contorted with pleasure as her orgasm claimed her.

Seeing her come undone—feeling it—was the last straw. With one last jerk of his hips, a burst of energy shot up his cock as he experienced one of the most explosive climaxes of his life.

He was vaguely aware of Beth reaching between them to turn off the vibration and remove the cock ring before she collapsed on top of him. Neither of them moved for a while after that. Her chest rose and fell with his. Feeling her against him in the aftermath of what they'd shared was almost spiritual. Was it the kink, or was it because it was with Beth? Could he even separate the two? Lucky for him, he didn't have to.

"What are you thinking so hard about?" she asked.

"Is it always like that?" She turned her head to look at him. "So intense, I mean?"

Beth smiled and ran her hand down the length of his chest. "When it's with the right person."

Drew brushed the pad of his thumb along her cheekbone. Her face was flushed and her hair was wild. She'd never looked more beautiful. He pulled her in for a lingering kiss.

She hummed and rested her head against his shoulder. "How are you feeling?"

It wasn't funny, but he laughed anyway. "I'm not sure I could be any better than I am right now."

He felt her smile.

"What about you?" he asked.

Beth gazed up at him with both eyebrows raised. "Did you think I was faking that orgasm I just had?"

Drew grinned. He'd never been this happy in a relationship before. "No. If you were faking it, then you deserve an Academy Award. I meant did I do all right? I've seen scenes at the club, but . . . well, it's different when you're the one that's in it."

"Yes, it is." She propped herself up on her elbow, but kept the length of her body pressed against his. "Did you enjoy what I did to you?"

With their scene over, he took full advantage of his freedom to put his hands wherever he wanted. "I did. It was . . . liberating."

"For me as well."

He cocked his head to the side. "How?"

She ran her fingers through his hair. It made him want to curl up against her and never move. "It's a release for me. I can let go of all my stress and be in the moment."

Drew guessed that made sense. Being a top wasn't something he'd ever desired to be, and after the experience he had, he didn't think it would be in the future—especially if that future involved Beth. "I guess that's good since I very much like being dominated by you."

"Yes, that's a very good thing." Beth kissed him. "We should go get cleaned up."

"I don't want to move. I like lying here with you like this."

"So do I, but you'll thank me in the morning."

Before he could protest, she was getting out of the bed. He felt a sharp pang of loss as she distanced herself from him. It didn't last long, however, since almost as soon as her feet hit the floor, she was reaching for him.

It was in the process of climbing out of the bed that Drew felt the first real signs of soreness. His ass felt as if he'd sat on a heating pad for too long.

"Sit on the edge of the bed and I'll remove your collar."

He looked to find Beth standing only a foot in front of him. "Sure."

Drew lowered himself down on the edge of the mattress. Her hand brushed against his chest as she reached to unclip the leash that he'd completely forgotten was there.

He waited while she walked to the other side of the bed. She returned with the key, and leaned over to unlock him. The position placed her bare breast within an inch of his face. Drew couldn't resist, so he latched on and sucked it into his mouth. Beth moaned, but then leaned out of his reach as she turned the key and the restriction of the collar pulled away.

Beth tilted his chin up so that he could look at her. She was still naked and it was impossible for him not to take notice even though he'd been inside her less than twenty minutes ago. It had never been like this for him before. Granted, he wasn't sure if he could go again so soon—he wasn't Superman after all—but that want was still there.

She gazed into his eyes for several minutes before running her fingers over his mouth. He parted his lips, hoping to convey that he was ready and willing for anything she wanted. Beth closed her eyes and sighed.

Taking her hand, he kissed the tips of her fingers, and then her palm. A feeling of warmth flooded his chest at the tender moment. Beth was different in more ways than he could count, and so were his feelings for her.

When she opened her eyes, he saw the same tenderness reflected there that he was experiencing. He'd known he was falling for her—that he was already halfway gone. Now he was positive that the falling was over. Although he doubted she was there yet, he knew there was no longer a question as far as he was concerned. He loved her, and he would do everything in his power to show her just how much.

Chapter Twenty-One

The next morning Drew woke up to the sound of Beth's alarm. She groaned, rolled over, and hit the snooze button. When she plopped back down on the mattress, he slid up behind her and gathered her into his arms.

"Mmm. Good morning."

Drew kissed her shoulder and nuzzled his nose against her neck. "Definitely a good morning."

"Not too sore?" she asked, turning to face him.

It was true that his backside was still somewhat tender, but overall he felt great. "No worse than I would be after a good workout at the gym."

Beth grinned. "I wish I didn't have to go to work. It would be nice to stay in bed with you like this."

He couldn't agree with her more. Spending the day in bed with her sounded pretty close to perfect to him. "Too bad Tommy can't cover for you today."

"Oh, I meant to tell you. I decided to hire someone else. It's just becoming too much for me and Tommy by ourselves."

"I think that's a good idea. You both need to take some time off once in a while. Plus, I'd like to take you camping with me one of these days and we'd definitely need more than two days." He pressed his lips against hers in a teasing kiss before moving his attention down to her neck.

She hummed. "Camping, huh?"

"Yes," he said between kisses. "Don't worry. I'll be sure to keep you nice and warm at night."

"Is that so?" Beth tangled her fingers in his hair as he worked his way lower.

"Promise," he murmured before tracing around her nipple with his tongue.

Unfortunately, their fun was interrupted by her alarm going off again.

Beth took a deep breath and stared down at him. "I have to start getting ready or I'll be late."

Drew knew he should let her go. He knew how much the café meant to her. Instead, he pushed himself up until he was at eye level with her.

"Be late." The words were whispered, but that didn't decrease the emotion behind them.

Everything around them seemed to stop as he waited to see how she'd react.

She placed her palm flat on his chest. Drew was sure she was going to push him off her, but then she hit the off button on her alarm with her free hand and reached for his cock. "Make it fast. And you don't come until after I do."

His morning wood grew with her words. "Yes, Mistress."

The tip of his erection pressed against her pussy as she guided him right where she wanted him. Beth raised her hips and he took it as an invitation to thrust forward.

She was tighter than she had been the night before. Considering how little experience he had with morning sex, Drew didn't know if that was normal or if it meant that he needed to do more to get her aroused—maybe both. To be sure, he molded his hand to one of her breasts and sucked her nipple into his mouth. Little by little, he kept going until the base of his cock was pressed against her.

"More," she urged as she bent her knees to give him better access.

He gave her more. Releasing her breast, he propped himself up on his knees and grabbed hold of her hips for leverage. The new position drove him deeper, and the look on her face every time he plunged forward had him determined to please her no matter what.

When he noticed her breathing begin to change, he debated whether or not he should provide additional stimulation to her clit. Beth took the decision away from him when she grabbed hold of his hand and positioned his thumb where she wanted it. "Touch me."

Drew had learned a few things in his wilder days. He had no issue putting that to use in making sure Beth felt good. Widening his legs a bit, he timed his thrusts with a firm pressure to her clit. It only took three times before Beth arched her back and came undone before his eyes.

He picked up his pace as she rode out her orgasm. Knowing he didn't have to hold back, Drew concentrated on the feeling of her, hot and wet around his cock. Beth was an amazing woman and she was all his.

A handful of thrusts later, Drew felt his climax within reach. He was right there.

Beth took both of his nipples between her fingers and twisted hard. That was all it took. Drew felt his orgasm all the way down to his toes.

Blood pounded in his ears as he fell forward, bracing himself on his forearms. "Now, that's a great way to wake up."

Lacing her fingers behind his neck, Beth grinned up at him. "Enjoy yourself, did you?"

"With you, always."

"You're good for my ego." Beth shifted beneath him. "But I really do have to get ready."

Reluctantly, Drew flopped over onto the mattress beside her.

He thought she'd scramble out of the bed as soon as he'd removed his weight from her. That's why he was surprised when she turned toward him and ran her index finger from his collarbone to his navel. "Want to join me in the shower?"

"I thought you didn't want to be late."

She shrugged.

It looked as if the morning fun wasn't entirely over.

❧

BETH WAS ALMOST AN HOUR LATE, BUT FOR THE FIRST TIME, SHE DIDN'T care. When she walked through the door, Tommy nearly attacked her. He'd been worried she might have gotten into an accident or something. After she explained that she'd just overslept, he calmed down and they got to work.

The day turned out to be one of the busiest they'd ever had. Beth had no idea how she and Tommy managed, but they did. Somehow. By the end of the day, though, she was dead on her feet. It only reinforced the need to hire some help. If days like this became the norm, she and Tommy would burn out quickly.

As it was, Beth didn't make it back home until after five.

"I was starting to worry."

She snapped her head up to find Drew sitting on her front porch. "Sorry. I probably should have called. Things were just crazy today."

They'd made plans for him to come over again for dinner and maybe even another play session. Beth knew with the way she was feeling there was no way she would be up for playing.

"I can go if you'd rather be alone," he said.

Although Beth was tired, she couldn't bring herself to send him away. "Stay."

He nodded and followed her inside.

Beth kicked off her shoes and started toward the kitchen.

Drew reached for her arm to stop her. "Let me cook for you. You can sit down on the couch, have a glass of wine . . ." He stepped closer and pressed his forehead against hers. "Let me take care of you."

"You don't have to do—"

"I want to." He cupped the side of her face and gave her a soft kiss.

"Okay."

He smiled. "What kind of wine would you like—red or white?"

"White, please."

"Coming right up." Before disappearing into the kitchen, he gave her another kiss.

It had been a long time since someone had offered to pamper her. Sure, there were times when she'd ordered Ben to do something for her, but it wasn't the same.

Thinking of Ben reminded her that she hadn't seen him since the day he'd shown up at her café. While she'd like to think that he got the message and would leave her alone, she highly doubted it. Ben could be very persistent when he wanted something. If he truly wanted to talk to her, he'd keep trying. Next time she would be more prepared. At least, she hoped she would be.

"Here you go." Drew handed her a wineglass that was filled almost to the brim.

She raised one eyebrow at him.

He kissed her nose and chuckled before walking off. "Dinner will be ready in about half an hour."

Taking a sip of her wine, Beth sat down, and stretched her legs out onto the couch. She tilted her head back and tried to relax.

Before she knew it, he was back. Drew placed two plates on the coffee table and then gently picked up her legs so that he could sit down. The care that he took to arrange her legs so that they were draped across his lap warmed her heart. How was she not supposed to fall for him when he did stuff like this?

She accepted the plate that he offered and took a bite. It was baked ziti and it was delicious. "Is there anything you can't cook?"

"I'm glad you like it." His smile melted her as it always did.

They ate in silence for several minutes before she decided that she needed to let him know that their plans for the night would have to change. "I know you were hoping we could play tonight, but I don't think I have the energy."

"I figured as much. You looked as if you were about to collapse earlier." He took a drink of the wine he'd poured for himself—a glass that wasn't even half as full as the one he'd poured her.

"Does that bother you?" She knew it would have bothered Ben. If they'd made plans for a session, then he expected them to play.

"Not really. There will be plenty of other opportunities. I am kind of hoping you'll still let me stay the night, though." That cocky grin was back.

"I don't know. I might have to think about that one," she said as she peered at him over her wineglass. "It's been a long day. I need my rest."

Drew leaned forward and placed his empty plate onto the coffee table along with his drink. Then he turned his attention to her feet. "Guess I'll have to convince you."

Beth moaned when his fingers pressed along the arch of her right foot. "What are you doing?"

"Giving you a foot massage."

He kept rubbing, and it felt heavenly. She soon forgot her food.

"Are you done?" he asked when he realized she'd stopped eating.

"I don't think I can eat while you're doing that to me."

Drew halted. "Do you want me to stop?"

"No. It feels too good."

He laughed and went back to what he was doing.

Beth set her plate and wine on the floor next to the couch, then leaned back to enjoy her massage. He worked every muscle in her feet and ankles with a circular motion that seemed to draw out every bit of stress. When he'd begun, her feet had been throbbing and tight. After his attentions, she was starting to feel normal again. "You're good at this."

"Thank you." He continued by dragging his hands along her calves and then down again.

It had been a long day and with the coaxing of his hands, she was becoming drowsy—so drowsy, she'd missed what he'd said entirely. "What was that?"

Drew dug his fingers into her skin as he traced a path from the back of her knee down to her heel. "I asked if you'd like for me to draw you a bath."

"You're spoiling me. Keep this up and I'm never going to let you leave."

She said the words in a teasing way, but his response and the look on his face were utterly serious. "That's the plan."

Beth swallowed. Was she misreading him? They'd only recently begun dating.

While she was still mulling over his words, Drew lifted her legs and stood. "Let me warm up the rest of your food so you can finish eating, and then I'll go start that bath for you."

He kissed the top of her head before bending down to retrieve her plate. As she watched him stroll out of the room, she tried not to read too much into what he'd said. Beth knew he was looking for something more than just someone to play with. He'd wanted a relationship. Considering she'd only ever played with one other person besides her ex, she was on board with that. While Beth understood that there were a lot of people out there who didn't mind playing casually with other members of the club, it wasn't something that had appealed to her. Then again, neither did casual sex.

She lifted her wineglass to her lips as Drew returned with her warmed dinner. "I'll come get you when your bath's ready."

Beth grinned up at him. "Thanks."

There was a slight hesitation before he jogged up the stairs to see to her bath. She really didn't know what she was going to do. The man had not only wormed his way past her defenses and into her heart, he was taking up residence there. Even though she'd meant it as a joke, she was wondering if it were more prophetic. When she'd found out about Ben's other life, she'd been crushed, but more than anything Beth had been embarrassed—betrayed. How could she not have known?

What she hadn't felt was all that heartbroken over the actual loss. Ben could be attentive, but looking back at the relationship she realized more often than not it was always a means to an end with him. It was a way to manipulate her.

If Ben had been the one waiting for her tonight, she doubted it would have crossed his mind to give her a foot massage. On the off chance that it would have, there would have been strings attached. Since they'd made arrangements to play, he would have most likely ended the massage by asking if she felt up to having some fun then.

Glancing toward the stairs, Beth had to admit that Drew and Ben were very different men. She knew now that Ben had been selfish. He was selfish in everything he did, including how he'd treated both her and his wife. Drew was the complete opposite of selfish. Whenever they were together, he made her feel as if she were the only woman in the world. Even his job reflected his unselfishness—he ran into burning buildings trying to save lives and people's homes.

Whether she liked it or not—and even though it scared the crap out of her —she didn't know what she'd do if Drew left her life. If he ever betrayed her like Ben had, Beth didn't know if she'd be able to recover.

"Hey. Is everything okay?" Beth looked to find Drew kneeling beside her.

She grinned. "Yeah. I'm good."

He still looked somewhat concerned, but he didn't press her. "Your bath's ready."

Beth nodded.

Drew helped her up and took her mostly empty plate from her. "Did you want to finish eating first?"

"No. I'm good. We were so busy, I didn't get to eat lunch until almost two." While that was true, her lunch had consisted of half a croissant and some roast beef eaten in between orders.

They made their way upstairs to her bedroom. Drew went to check the temperature of the water again while she got undressed. Beth was tempted to forego the bath and crawl into bed, but she didn't want to seem ungrateful. She plucked her robe from the closet so she'd have it for later, and trudged into the bathroom.

When she walked in, she could hardly believe her eyes. Drew was on his knees next to the large tub. He had lowered the lights and had several candles lit. It was very romantic and peaceful.

He got to his feet and crossed the short distance to where she stood in the doorway. Without a word, he took her robe from her and hung it up on the door. Then he reached for her hand.

She placed her palm in his and let him lead her over to the bubble-filled water. Drew helped her as she got in and lowered herself down into the tub. It felt wonderful. The scent of lavender surrounded her and she wondered if it was from the bubble bath, the candles, or both.

"Would you like another glass of wine?" he asked.

Beth shook her head. "If I drink much more, I'll fall asleep. I'm not far from it now."

Drew smiled.

"You didn't have to do this, you know." She felt as if she needed to put it out there.

"I wanted to. Besides, you can pay me back one of these days." He brushed a strand of hair from her face and winked at her.

She chuckled.

"Relax and enjoy your bath. I'm going to run downstairs and clean up, then I'll be back to check on you."

Beth sighed and slid further down into the water as she let the warmth pull the tired ache from her body. She loved baths and she wondered how Drew had known, or if it had been a guess.

The sound of something moving off to her right made her open her eyes. It was Drew. He was blowing out the candles. When had he returned?

"You're back."

She stretched. That's when it dawned on her that she must have dozed off. "Guess I was more tired than I thought."

He reached for a towel and then for her. She took the offering, and stepped out of the bathtub. Beth had to admit that she could get used to this type of attention.

After unfolding the towel, he slowly dried her off. It wasn't meant to be erotic, but it was. Although her mind wasn't remotely in the mood for sex, Drew was able to get her body to respond. Like it or not, her body wanted him.

She closed the distance between them and pressed her naked body against his fully clothed one. Drew stared down at her, unmoving, but he was unable to hide his body's reaction. She could feel his erection straining against his jeans. Beth wrapped her arms around his neck and pulled his lips down to hers.

"Beth . . ."

His whispered plea only made her body yearn for him more. "Shh. Take me to bed, Drew. Make love to me."

There was a moment's pause, and then he scooped her up and carried her into the bedroom.

Chapter Twenty-Two

Beth held tight to Drew's hand as they approached the entrance to Serpent's Kiss.

"Nervous?" he asked.

There was no reason to deny it. "A little."

He gave her hand a gentle squeeze.

"What about you?"

"Not at all. In fact, I'm thrilled that I get to walk in there with you." Drew turned her to face him and placed his free hand on her hip. "I've only been dreaming about this since I first saw you across the room."

She rolled her eyes.

"What?" he asked, pulling her closer. "You'd rather have another hot stud by your side?"

"A *hot stud*, huh?"

He shrugged. "Gotta call 'em like I see 'em."

Beth ran the tips of her fingers along his jaw. "I might have to borrow one of Katrina's paddles and spank some of that cockiness out of you."

"My ass is all yours any time you want it." He punctuated his words by palming her behind.

Before she ended up doing something completely inappropriate in public, Beth took a step back and resumed her progression toward the door. "I'll keep that in mind."

They strolled into the foyer and she realized that her nerves had almost completely disappeared. Beth knew she had Drew to thank for that. He'd been able to tease her out of her funk. At every turn, he'd been there for her. Even earlier that day, he'd proved his devotion by showing up at the café in time for the lunch rush. She was able to stay in the back and make the sandwiches while Drew ran them out to the customers and helped Tommy with the soups and pastries.

Later, when they were cleaning up, she asked him why. His answer was simple. *I figured you could use the help.*

He realized she'd stopped again. "Beth, if you're not okay with this—"

She shook her head. "No. I'm fine. Let's get this over with." Not waiting for him to comment, Beth swiped her membership card, opened the door to the lobby, and marched through it.

Bridget was behind the coat check. She smiled, started to say something, and then closed her mouth just as quickly when she noticed Beth was not alone.

Taking a deep breath, Beth decided to acknowledge the elephant in the room. "Drew, you know Bridget, right?"

"Yes. We've met."

"Y-yes," Bridget stuttered.

If Beth was being honest with herself, the young woman's response was almost comical. She kept blinking like there was something in her eyes. Maybe the night wouldn't be that bad if everyone's response was similar.

After checking the light jacket Beth had brought along for later—it was still a little too chilly for her liking late at night—she and Drew made their way into the club. They'd intentionally timed their arrival so that most of the regular patrons would already be there. It would be easier to blend in that way. At least, that's what she'd been hoping.

It took less than a minute for her bubble to burst. One by one everyone in the room turned their attention in Beth and Drew's direction. "I guess this means the cat is officially out of the bag."

He chuckled. "I'd say so."

She straightened her shoulders. "Here goes nothing."

❧

DREW STAYED BY BETH'S SIDE AS SHE WORKED HER WAY TOWARD THE BAR. He glanced around to find that most of the people following their progress had smiles on their faces. When he caught sight of John, his friend gave him a thumbs-up. Seeing confirmation of John's approval, and what appeared to be that of most of the club's members, had Drew grinning from ear to ear. He picked up his pace and placed a reassuring hand on Beth's lower back. She glanced over at him and then continued on.

Chad was behind the bar. Drew had only met him once before. Chad was okay, though. He didn't joke around with the members as much as Brandon did, but he wasn't part of the lifestyle either.

"Lady Beth, what can I get you this evening?" Chad greeted as she stepped up to the bar.

Drew stayed behind her, letting her lead.

"I'll have a Coke and Sprite, please." She turned to Drew. "What would you like?"

"Just a water. Thanks." While he typically had a beer on the nights he came to the club, this evening was all about Beth. He wanted her to be comfortable with their new status—their new, very *public* status.

Chad nodded. "Coming right up."

Beth turned around so that her back was against the bar. "You're sure you don't want anything besides water?"

He traced a line up her arm with his fingers. "Nope. I'm good. Besides, I need to stay hydrated, right?"

"I don't know if I'm up for playing in public yet," she confessed.

"It's up to you. I'm fine with whatever you decide."

"You're being awfully submissive tonight."

"Isn't that what I'm supposed to be—your submissive?" He edged closer, crowding her a little, acting anything but submissive. It was a bold move considering where they were.

She grinned and an evil glint appeared in her eyes a moment before he felt her hand grab hold of his junk. It wasn't painful, but the threat was there. "Make sure you remember that."

Drew smiled. "Yes, Mistress."

Chad returned with their drinks, and she released him. This was a gray area when it came to their arrangement. Outside the club, he was only her sub when it came to sexual things. Inside the club, however, the lines were blurred. He liked serving her last night—rubbing her feet, drawing her bath. Drew had also expressed an interested in kneeling at her feet and having his head in her lap. Before spending time at Serpent's Kiss, he wouldn't have thought something like that would appeal to him, but when he'd seen the level of devotion between John and Allison, it made him curious.

Because of that curiosity, they'd decided to play it by ear for the time being. He was always supposed to show her respect while inside the club walls.

Outside that, they were still negotiating. He promised that he would communicate if he wanted more, and she had done the same.

When he began researching BDSM, he'd thought that everything took off at full speed from the start. Drew supposed that had a lot to do with porn. Of course, now he knew just how inaccurate those videos were. Even still, he'd somehow imagined things with Beth being hammered out swiftly with no question marks. While their relationship had hit the ground running and he had no complaints, it was evolving and changing the more things they tried.

The night before came to mind. Beth had surprised him when she asked him to make love to her. Their sex up until then had always had some element of dominance and submission. He'd worried that their lovemaking wouldn't be as fulfilling for him if he was the one in control—it never had been in the past. What he found, though, was that knowing that he was doing what she wanted, how she wanted it, gave him pleasure. It was submission in a way he'd never imagined it.

He followed her over to where Nicole, Jeff, Daniel, Brandon, and two subs he recognized but whose names eluded him at the moment, were congregated. They all had knowing smiles on their faces as Beth and Drew sat down on one of the love seats.

"I was wondering if you were going to make it," Nicole said.

Beth met her friend's gaze and responded with a level of confidence he knew she didn't feel. "Busy day."

"Well, we're glad you're both here," Daniel said, tipping his glass in their direction.

Trying to divert some of the attention, Drew addressed Brandon. "Enjoying your night off?"

"I am. As much as I like being behind the bar, sometimes it's nice to sit back and let someone else take care of everything for a night."

Nicole leaned toward Brandon and whispered, "That's what you have a sub for."

All the Dominants in the group chuckled. Beth's tension seemed to be ebbing. She was no longer holding herself rigid. Drew rested his left arm along the back of the love seat, and placed his right hand on hers where it lay on her leg. Beth flipped her palm over and grasped his fingers. She leaned back against his chest, and he inhaled the scent of her shampoo.

He was so caught up in Beth that he almost missed the switch in conversation. "There haven't been any more sightings of *you know who*, have there?"

Beth shook her head. "No."

"Do you think he'll show up again?" Daniel asked.

Nicole jumped in before Beth could answer. "You can pretty much count on it. Ben isn't one to give up."

Drew's head was spinning with this new information. Beth's ex had contacted her—or tried to, at least? Why hadn't she said anything?

Eventually, the conversation shifted again but he lost track of what they were saying. He was too busy mulling over the realization that his girlfriend's lying ex had made contact with her. Drew wasn't sure if he was hurt or angry that she hadn't told him—maybe a little of both. Sure, they had only started dating in the last week, but they were supposed to be friends. Her other friends knew about it. Why hadn't he?

It was hard to tell how much time had passed when he felt Beth elbow him. Drew found her staring at him with a strange expression. "What? Something wrong?"

"I was going to ask you the same question."

He frowned. "You didn't tell me about your ex coming to see you."

Beth shifted to face him. She cradled his hand in her lap, caressing the ridge where his palm and wrist met. It was distracting, but he couldn't bring himself to ask her to stop.

"I didn't mean to keep it from you. It just never came up."

"When did he come to see you?" he asked.

"It was almost a month ago. And then I was told that he showed up here at the club two months before that. Katrina kicked him out."

He blew out a breath. "Good."

"I don't know what he wants. But if he's already tried twice, he's likely to do it again."

"I don't like it." That was the understatement of the year. Drew hated it. Although he hadn't known Beth back then, he knew that if he had, he would have wanted to rearrange Ben's face for him. Even thinking the man's name made him see red. He wasn't sure he could be held responsible for his actions if he ever saw him face-to-face.

"I don't like it either. Trust me, I'd much rather go the rest of my life without ever having to see or talk to him again. Unfortunately, I doubt that's going to happen. The first time he caught me off guard. That won't happen next time."

Drew saw movement out of the corner of his eye and realized that their little group had broken away to give them privacy. He glanced down at their hands. "How did this night turn out to be about your ex?"

"Because my best friend doesn't have a filter."

Despite the seriousness of their conversation, he chuckled. Everything he knew about Nicole supported Beth's assertion. "She's worried about you. So am I."

She kissed him. It was one of those barely there kisses, but it still had his heart kicking up a notch.

"You don't have to worry about me," she whispered against his lips. "I can handle Ben."

Their eyes locked, and he was reminded of the night before when she'd been looking up at him as he'd filled her. "I don't think it's possible not to worry about you, Beth."

Neither of them moved until the music changed from the slow sultry number to something with a driving beat that reminded Drew of sex. The air around them began to change, and thoughts of Ben took a backseat to his desire to get his hands on the woman right in front of him.

Beth stood, and Drew followed.

Without a word, she led him by the hand up to the second floor. Had she changed her mind about playing?

They stopped briefly for Beth to talk to Cooper, one of the Dungeon Monitors. It didn't consist of much more than her checking to see if a room was available. He nodded, instructed them to give him ten minutes, and then disappeared through a side door that Drew hadn't noticed before. Less than two minutes later, he reappeared with a large bag and entered one of the playrooms. When he returned to the hall several minutes later, he gave Beth another nod, and she led Drew into the room Cooper had vacated.

He felt he needed to ask. "Did you change your mind?"

She released his hand and strolled over to peruse the implements hanging on the wall. "I thought we needed a distraction. Tonight was supposed to be about you and me."

Drew couldn't disagree. Excited to find out what Beth had in mind, he waited to see what she'd do next.

"I want you to pick out five of these that you'd like to try," she said, pointing to the array of impact devices along the wall. Beth turned to look him in the eye. "No scene. And you can keep your clothes on. But I want you to have an idea what they feel like."

"All right." Walking over to the wall, he scanned his choices. Some of the toys were scarier than others. There was a lot of leather, of course.

He knew he liked the flogger that Beth had used on him on Wednesday night. After their shower, he'd had the chance to get a better look at it. There were a few on the wall that appeared to be of similar construction, but there were plenty that had obvious differences. One had knots tied into the ends of the falls.

"That one has more bite to it than the one I used on you the other night," she said.

Drew nodded and moved on. The thing he'd loved most about being flogged was that it was a solid thud against his back. While he hadn't minded the leather strap she'd used on his ass, it had felt a lot different from the flogger. There was a sting to it that Drew wasn't sure he was crazy about. "I think I'll skip it, then."

Beth hummed.

"What?"

She smiled. "Nothing."

Something told Drew that whatever she was thinking, he wasn't going to like it.

Shaking it off for now, he removed a wooden paddle and a flogger that looked heavier than the one Beth had used. He placed them on the table and then returned to his task. Drew knew from watching what went on at the club that no two implements were exactly the same, even if they looked similar. Every subtle variation made a difference.

For that reason, he tried not to stray too far from what he'd tried on Wednesday. His next two selections were made of leather. One was flat with three flaps that overlapped. The other was also flat, but it had a slit down the middle. Drew couldn't remember what it was called, but he'd seen it used before. Reactions from the subs had varied, which made him curious.

With only one item left to be chosen, he altered his original goal—to stick to the somewhat familiar—and ventured over to the selection of canes. John liked canes. A lot. Then again, John also enjoyed having his testicles tortured. That thought alone almost made Drew reconsider, but again, he was drawn by curiosity. This would be the perfect time to gauge if it was something he wanted to move up on his list or place in the 'hell no' column. Before he could talk himself out of it, Drew took one of the canes from the rack and placed it on the table beside the other toys.

Beth stood at the other end of the table and ran her hand over a couple of the toys. "Interesting choices."

"Good interesting or bad interesting?" he asked.

She ran her hand over three of the toys. "Just interesting. I figured you'd pick a flogger. You seemed to enjoy that quite a lot the other night. Almost as much as you liked me tying you up."

Again, Drew couldn't disagree. Although, there really wasn't anything they'd done so far that he'd disliked. He wasn't sure the leather strap would ever make it onto his favorite list, but one never knew. After conversing with people at the club, he'd learned that preferences evolved over time. What he didn't care for now could be his favorite thing in a few years.

While he'd pondered, Beth had strolled to the center of the room. She glanced up, and Drew followed her gaze to a set of cuffs hanging from chains.

"I'm not going to cuff you tonight, but I do want you to hold onto the ends. It will ensure that you keep your hands out of the way and help you hold position."

That made sense. He walked over to stand next to her and reached up to take hold of the dangling cuffs.

Beth ran a hand down the length of his back before cupping his backside. "I'll give you four swats with each, two on each cheek, so you can tell me what you think of them."

He nodded.

She removed her hand, and Drew wanted to call her back. There was something about her touch that affected him in an elemental way. It made his pulse quicken, yet was comforting at the same time. He'd heard about the intense connection that could develop between subs and their Dominants. Even though their relationship was new, he felt it. Drew could only imagine what it would be like once they'd been together for a while.

"Are you ready?" she asked.

Drew couldn't see her. She was standing behind him on his left side. That didn't mean he couldn't feel her. "I'm ready. Do your worst."

Beth laughed and a second later, a loud smack reverberated in the room as she landed the wooden paddle against his right ass cheek. She rubbed her hand over the area she'd hit and leaned in to whisper in his ear. "It's never wise to tempt your mistress."

Three more quick hits of the paddle and he was beginning to feel the burn. By the time she picked up the fourth implement, he was starting to think she was right. Issuing your mistress a challenge moments before she was going to take a paddle to your ass probably wasn't the smartest decision he'd ever made in his life.

Chapter Twenty-Three

Beth had to hand it to Drew. He'd taken everything she'd given him. Which, granted, would have been worse had she ordered him to remove his clothing. As it was, he'd be feeling the aftereffects of their evening for the rest of the night, at least.

When she'd devised this little experiment, Beth had only planned to give him a few light swats with each of the items he'd selected. After his comment, however, she felt the need to remind him of just what position he held in this relationship. She'd landed four substantial hits to his ass with the paddle and then followed it up with four more of both the flapper and the tawse.

"How are you doing?" she asked when she picked up the cane.

"Fine."

She rubbed the cane across the back of his thigh before flicking her wrist. The rattan snapped against both of his butt cheeks, and she saw him tighten his grip on the cuffs. "Just fine?"

Before he could respond, she made contact again with his backside.

"Yes. Just. Fine."

Sliding her hand over his ass, she ran a finger along the waist of his jeans. "What do you think of the cane? Is it what you expected?"

He shook his head. "No. Not exactly."

"How is it different?" She moved around in front of him, but kept her hand inside his waistband, teasing.

"I wasn't expecting it to be so . . . intense."

"Hmm. Yes. There are subs that take great pride in being able to take their master or mistress' cane."

Drew didn't comment. Not with a snarky comeback, or even a grunt.

"Look at me."

He lowered his eyes and met her gaze.

"Do you want me to stop?" she asked. "You only have two more to go."

It took him a moment to answer. "No."

Beth removed her hand from his jeans and placed it along the side of his face. As he stared back at her, she saw some of that attitude returning to his features. It made her smile. "When we get home, I'm going to tie you to my bed and ride you until you beg me to let you come."

"Whatever you want, Mistress."

She let her hand drop from his face, repositioned herself behind him again, and flicked her wrist twice more in quick succession. He jumped at the unexpected contact of the cane striking his ass. "Remember you said that later tonight."

Ready to end this experiment, she tossed the cane down on the table, and picked up the flogger. It was heavier than what she normally liked to throw, but there was nothing wrong with mixing it up now and then. Taking two steps back, she held the flogger in both hands, and took aim.

His reaction to the flogger was worlds apart from how he'd responded to the cane. As she made contact for the third time with his butt, he dropped his head. Clothes or not, this was feeling more and more like a scene with every passing minute. Beth needed to end this. She needed to end it and get them both back to her place. While Serpent's Kiss was a sex positive club, she wasn't ready to do that with him here quite yet. No, she wanted him completely to herself for a while longer.

Beth lowered her arm and returned the flogger, along with the other implements, to the wall. Drew must have realized what she was doing because she felt him come up behind her.

"Everything all right?" he asked.

She turned and circled her arms around his neck before pulling his mouth down to hers. "No. It's not."

After a passionate kiss, he stared into her eyes as if trying to assess what she'd meant. "You wanna go home?"

She kissed him again. This time their lips barely touched, but the meaning behind it was clear. "Yes. I'm ready to go home."

Drew took her hand and led her out of the room. Although some Femdoms would have had a problem with him doing the leading, Beth couldn't care less. She loved how enthusiastic he was. And she hated to admit it—she certainly wouldn't to him—but she loved his cockiness a little, too.

They passed Katrina at the bottom of the stairs. "Leaving so soon?"

"Yes," Drew said without giving Beth the chance to answer.

Katrina laughed and waved as Drew practically dragged Beth through the club toward the entrance. "Have fun."

When they reached the lobby, Beth dug in her heels and jerked on Drew's arm to get his attention.

"What?" he asked.

She took a single step forward, pressing the length of her body against him. "You're going to have to learn some patience."

When he realized she wasn't upset, he dipped his head and shot her a sheepish grin. "I'll work on it."

Beth responded with a smile that was anything but sweet and then went to retrieve her jacket from the coat check.

Bridget was still in the alcove. The young woman already had Beth's coat in her hand by the time she approached.

"Thank you," Beth said.

"You're welcome. I hope you both enjoy the rest of your evening."

It was no longer light out, and as they made their way to his car, Beth found herself searching the shadows. The conversation about Ben was making her paranoid. It was as if she was waiting for him to jump out from behind one of the bushes or something.

They arrived at Drew's car and he opened her door for her. She gave him a peck on the lips and then slid into the passenger seat.

He waited until he was behind the wheel to say anything. "Did I do something wrong?"

She looked over at him and gave him a curious look. "No. Not that I know of. Why?"

"Just checking." He turned on the engine and maneuvered the car out of the lot. "You seem like you have something on your mind. And to be honest, I'm not sure my ass can take another beating tonight."

Beth let out a loud, very unladylike laugh.

Drew took her hand and brought it up to his lips. "I know I was . . . a little overzealous in there, but I couldn't help it."

"I noticed." She placed her hand on his inner thigh and let it drift closer to his crotch. "But in this case, you're safe. I love Serpent's Kiss, but the things I want to do with you right now . . . well, I'd rather not have an audience."

He swallowed and nodded.

They were both quiet the rest of the drive home. She didn't remove her hand from where it lay less than an inch away from the bulge in his pants. It was only common sense that made her keep her hands to herself, and even that was pushing her limits. Beth pressed her legs together seeking the friction she needed but couldn't have quite yet.

He pulled up to her house a few minutes past ten. Before she could blink twice, he was out of the car and standing there with his hand outstretched, ready to help her out of the vehicle. Beth took his hand, and they made their way up the front steps and into her house.

Once the door closed behind her, she turned to face him. "Go upstairs. Remove all your clothes, and lie face up on my bed. I'll be there in a few minutes."

Drew leaned down and gave her a kiss. It was soft and in some ways it destroyed her defenses more than all the hot and heavy make-out sessions. "Yes, Mistress."

She remained rooted to her spot until she heard him moving around on the second floor. Taking what she hoped was a calming breath, Beth began making her nightly rounds to double-check that everything was secure before she turned in. She took her time even though the urge to race upstairs was eating at her. Drew was addicting, and if she wasn't careful, Beth was going to find herself in a worse position than she'd been in before—a position where she couldn't imagine her life without him.

For good measure, and to prove something to herself, she did a second walk-through of the lower level of her home. Then she strolled into the bathroom, took care of business, and washed up. Beth was stalling. She knew that.

Lifting her head, she took a long look at herself in the mirror that hung above the sink in her small half-bath. The past four months had been quite a transformation. She'd gone from someone who was relatively happy and content with her life, to someone who'd barely been able to get up in the mornings. There were no longer bags under her eyes from the restless nights, and a healthy color had returned to her cheeks. She felt normal again. Better, if she was being honest with herself.

She knew what, or who, in this case, was responsible for the drastic change. Beth had no doubt she would have rebounded on her own, but it would have taken time. Drew had coaxed her back into the land of the living. He'd made her think that there was still a possibility to have that future she'd dreamed of having. Granted, it starred a different leading man, but she was starting to think she'd cast the part all wrong the first time around. Ben wasn't half the man Drew was, and he never would be.

Shooting one last look into the mirror, Beth turned off the light, and walked toward the stairs. She had a submissive waiting. *Her* submissive. And she was going to make sure he knew exactly who he belonged to before the night was over.

❧

DREW LAY ON THE BED LOOKING UP AT THE CEILING. HE WAS TRYING TO slow his heart, which seemed to be trying to beat its way out of his chest. Following Beth's instructions, he'd gone upstairs, removed his clothes, and situated himself on her bed. The sheets scraped against his still tender backside. It added to his awareness. Not only of his own body, but of Beth as well—of what was still to come.

The sound of her feet on the stairs sent all efforts to slow his heart out the window. He turned his head toward the door, and his breath caught in his throat when he saw her enter the room.

She strolled over to where he lay and ran her hand down his chest to his thigh. His cock twitched as her hand came close, but she ignored it completely. Then she turned her back on him and opened the chest where she kept her toys. She'd showed it to him the evening before. It was a small collection compared to what could be found at the club, but more than enough for their personal use.

When Beth faced him again, she held a length of rope in her right hand. She had a knowing smirk on her face as she approached him. "Give me your hands."

Drew didn't hesitate. He presented both hands to her eagerly.

She maneuvered them so that his palms were facing each other and then began wrapping the rope around both wrists, binding them together. As the ropes secured his wrists, Drew felt himself becoming grounded. With the rope in place, Beth lifted his arms over his head and used a second section of rope to connect his bound wrists to the bed.

Beth leaned over him, her hands on his face. She traced the outline of his lips with her thumbs. He wanted to kiss her, but he didn't think that was going to happen. Not the way she was looking at him. Her eyes were almost predatory.

"The ropes aren't too tight, are they?" she asked in that seductive voice of hers. He could listen to it all day. Then, of course, he'd most likely be sporting a permanent erection.

"No, Mistress."

She came closer to whisper in his ear. It sent chills rippling through his body. "Is this how I had you tied up in your dream?"

"Yes."

"Yes, what?" She punctuated her question by pinching one of his nipples. He jerked.

Beth asked her question again. "Yes, what?"

Drew swallowed. "Yes, Mistress. This is how it was in my fantasy."

"Good," she said as she scraped her teeth along his neck before sinking them into his skin. He didn't know whether or not he wanted to push her away or invite her to devour him some more.

It was interesting how being tied up like this made him pay attention to things more. Beth was still fully clothed, and he could feel the scratch of the fabric against his chest. It shouldn't be erotic, but it was. Her tits grazed his abdomen with a featherlight touch.

He was so focused on the feel of her body that he'd almost missed her words. "Tonight we're going to work on patience. Patience and obedience."

When she pulled away from him and climbed off the bed, he had to bite the inside of his cheek to keep from begging her to come back. Drew wanted her to touch him. He didn't care how. As long as her hands were on him in some fashion, he would be happy. It was almost comical to realize that even if it meant her grabbing him by his balls and inflicting some sort of torture on him that he'd take it as long as it meant she had her hands on him.

That line of thought was quickly shelved when Beth shimmied her jeans over her ass and down her legs. His heart had skipped a beat when he'd first seen her in them earlier. They molded to every one of her curves and the first thing he'd done upon seeing her in them was palm her backside and squeeze. Seeing that perfect ass of hers bending over in all its glory made him want to do it all over again.

"See something you like?" she asked.

"Yes." He cleared his throat. "Mistress."

Beth chuckled and continued to remove the bottom half of her clothing. She turned to face him as she removed the sheer top she'd worn over her corset. Before Beth, he'd never understood the fascination with corsets. They covered too much skin and took more time to remove than a bra. Seeing her standing there, though, with her breasts molded beneath the blue satin and lace . . . it made his mouth water.

With all her clothing removed except her corset, Beth sashayed back to the bed and lay down beside him. Drew could feel the heat from her soft skin and all he wanted to do was get closer.

"Shh," she said, caressing his face. "Patience, remember. If you're a good boy, I might even let you come tonight."

They'd talked about orgasm control. And while they both wanted it as part of their relationship, it hadn't been something she'd truly put to the test. Whenever they'd had sex, he'd been allowed to come. He knew that might not always be the case, but he wasn't sure if he was ready for that to be taken away yet. They'd only been together a week. He could still count how many times he'd had his cock inside her and felt that rush of fulfillment.

"Tell me what you're thinking." She searched his eyes as if she could somehow figure out what was going through his mind.

"Just hoping I please you enough to be allowed to come, Mistress." He didn't want to make her think he'd changed his mind because he hadn't.

She scraped the nail of her index finger over his left nipple, causing it to pebble. Again, the sensation was a mixture of both pleasure and pain. "I'm going to push you tonight. Some things you may like more than others."

"I understand, Mistress." A thrill ran through him every time he called her his mistress. She not only owned his body but his heart as well—even if she didn't realize it yet.

As if to test him, Beth scraped a line from his nipple down to his erection. She circled the base of his cock with her fingernail and then cupped his balls in her hand.

Drew held his breath. He had no idea what she'd do next.

The feeling of all five of her nails scratching along his testicles made him stiffen. Instinct made him want to close his legs for protection, but he made himself keep them open for her.

She hummed against his neck. "These belong to me as much as your cock does."

Her nails dug in a little more and he gasped. "Yes, Mistress. Yes."

Right when he thought he might have to safeword for the first time, she moved her attention to the underside of his cock. While it was still a sensitive area, he'd rather have her torturing his cock than his balls. At least, he thought he would. It was just a guess since—

Holy hell!

He arched his back as a single nail started at the base of his cock and trailed upward. Drew thought for sure that he would lose his erection, but that wasn't happening. He was just as hard—or maybe harder—than what he'd been before she'd begun toying with him. His body's reactions made no sense, but the evidence was there standing tall for all the world to see.

Beth shifted, and the next thing he knew she was straddling his face. Her ass was staring back at him. Her pussy inches from his mouth. He took the invitation and tugged at his restraints in order for his tongue to make contact with the moist flesh between her legs. She faltered briefly in her movements when he licked the first bits of moisture from her labia. He did it again, wanting to see what she'd do and needing to please her.

"More," she said as she lowered herself onto his face.

If she wanted more, that was what he would give her. Drew dove in with vigor, fucking her with his tongue and circling her clit.

As he ate her pussy, Beth continued to torture him with her nails. It was as if two things were vying for his undivided attention. He was surrounded by Beth's scent, tied to her bed. His cock was quite literally in her hands to do with what she wished. For the first time in his life, he thought he might be able to come without a hand, mouth, or pussy adding friction. Was that even possible?

Drew knew she was getting close when she started grinding against his face. He doubled his efforts and concentrated on her clit. If he had his hands free, he would have added his fingers to the mix as well.

Out of the blue, Beth leaned forward. He felt her place one hand on his balls, pressing them to the side of his leg. Then, almost all in the next instant, one of her fingers was rubbing the skin on the underside of his testicles and another was skimming his asshole.

Her breath hitched and she jerked her hips violently against his tongue.

"Come," she yelled.

The last thing he felt was her lips wrapping around the head of his cock. After that, he saw a flash of light and then the world fell away.

Chapter Twenty-Four

Beth pulled the sheet over both their bodies and curled up alongside Drew. She had untied his wrists and then dropped the rope on the floor next to the bed before curling up next to him. As she placed her cheek against his chest, she felt a tremor pass through him. "Are you all right?"

He didn't answer right away. She tilted her head up to see his face. Drew had his eyes closed and he was still breathing deeper than was normal. Unsure what else to do until he started talking to her, she held him tighter.

Drew lifted his arm and rested his hand on her hip. With his other hand, he caressed the side of her face. "I don't think I've ever come so hard in my life. Scratch that. I *know* I haven't."

She smiled and kissed the smooth column of his neck. "Are you thirsty?"

He swallowed and then nodded. "Yeah. I could use some water."

Beth reached behind her to grab the bottle of water she'd left on her nightstand. When she turned back around, she saw he'd propped himself up on his elbow. She handed him the bottle and then reached for candy that had been sitting next to the water. "You should suck on this as well. It will help."

There was a slight hesitation before he took the offered candy. "Thanks."

She stayed close, but gave him some space as he downed almost half the bottle of water before unwrapping the hard candy and popping it into his mouth. "Are you feeling lightheaded at all? Cold? Jittery?"

Drew took another sip of water before reaching for her. "I feel a little off balance. And I feel a strong desire to wrap my arms around you."

She smiled. "That can be arranged."

They propped some pillows up behind them so Drew could still suck on his candy, drink his water, and get the connection with her that he wanted. Beth enjoyed being a Domme. There were so many things about it that turned her on. But this was one of the best parts for her. She loved the quiet moments after a scene when everything was still raw. It held an intimacy that she couldn't explain to someone who had never experienced it.

He traced a line with the tips of his fingers down her spine, and then curled his palm around her hip. "I guess I like CBT more than I thought I would."

Beth giggled. "While that may be true, that wasn't really what I'd consider CBT."

"It wasn't?" He seemed shocked by her statement.

"No. That was more me giving you a preview of what knife play is like without the actual knife." Drew was quiet for several minutes, and she remained silent allowing him time to process what she'd said.

"Interesting."

"That's it, just *interesting?*"

Drew grinned down at her. "Well, my head is still spinning from that out-of-this-world orgasm I just experienced. Maybe I'll be able to come up with something better in the morning."

Although she really was curious to hear his thoughts, now that he had more insight on what she had in mind when she'd talked about knife play, she understood that he really did need time to recover.

"Beth?"

She looked up at him. "Yes?"

"I never thought to ask before, but . . . what's your full name? I figure since we're now officially dating and you're going to meet my family soon, I should probably know something like that."

Burying her face in his shoulder, she couldn't help but chuckle. Given what they'd just done it felt silly, but kind of appropriate, too. "Bethany Paige Davenport."

"*Bethany Paige,*" he repeated. "I like it."

She pinched his side and he laughed. "Glad you approve."

Finished with his candy, he slid down lower on the bed, and took her with him. "I'd wondered if Beth was maybe short for Elizabeth, but for some reason, you didn't strike me as an Elizabeth."

Having his arms around her—feeling the warmth of his body—could easily become an addiction all its own. She couldn't seem to get close enough. Luckily, Drew appeared to have the same problem.

"Mom had a friend in school named Bethany. She loved the name, so when she found out she was having a girl, Bethany it was." Beth lifted her leg and wedged it between his, aligning their bodies even more. "Paige was my dad's contribution."

She left it at that, and he seemed to sense there was something more.

"There's a story there."

Beth shrugged. "Dad had a sister that died. From what I understand, she never made it home from the hospital, but they named her Paige. My dad was old enough to remember her."

Drew kissed the top of her head. "It's a good story."

"Whenever someone asks, Dad just says it's a family name. He never goes into detail." She took a deep breath. "What about you? Since we're talking names, is Drew short for Andrew?"

He nodded.

"What about a middle name?"

She felt the rise and fall of his chest beneath her before he answered. "Raymond."

The way he said the name gave her the impression that he wasn't a huge fan of his middle name. "*Andrew Raymond Parker*. I like it."

"You wouldn't if the only time it was ever used was when you were in trouble."

Beth couldn't hide her amusement. "Got in trouble a lot, did you?"

"I was a boy. Of course I got in trouble. It's part of the job description."

"Is that so?" She traced a line from his abdomen and along his hipbone. Placing her hand flat on his left butt cheek, she gave a gentle squeeze. "Sore?"

"Nothing I can't handle. Although, I can feel it every time I move."

"Good. Maybe it will remind you to keep that smart mouth of yours in check."

Drew surprised her by rolling her over. "You love my smart mouth."

"Nope," Beth said trying to suppress a smile. She wasn't doing a very good job.

The next thing she knew, his hands were at her sides, and he was tickling her.

"Drew! What. Do You. Think. You're. Doing?"

By the time he let up, she was gasping for air. And he was beaming down at her. He looked younger and more carefree than she'd ever seen him before, and her heart skipped a beat. This felt so natural. It didn't feel as if they'd only been in her bed together a handful of times.

Before she could analyze what she was feeling too closely, Beth took hold of the back of his neck and pulled his mouth down to hers. She attacked his lips in a not-so-subtle reminder of who was in charge.

Beth didn't release him for several minutes—not until she felt him press his weight against her. Even then, the look in his eyes held things she wasn't ready for, so she averted her gaze and pretended to look at the clock. "We should get some sleep. I still have to work tomorrow."

He moved, bringing his cheek to rest above her right breast. "I signed up to do some volunteer work in the morning, but I should be free after lunch. Would you like some help at the café again?"

"If you keep coming by to help, I'm going to have to put you on the payroll." She ran her fingers through his hair as they talked. "Sure you don't want another job?"

Drew snorted. "Thanks, but I think I'm good. You see, I have this girlfriend that keeps me pretty busy on my days off."

"She does, does she?"

"Oh yeah. She's a real slave driver."

Beth pinched him, and he laughed.

"Remember you said that the next time I have you tied up," she said.

His only response was to dip his head an inch or so and draw her nipple into his mouth.

She could have made him stop, but it felt too good. Besides, it was the perfect distraction to her thoughts and where they were leading. Taking hold of his wrist, she guided his hand between her legs. Beth opened herself to him and stopped thinking for a while.

❦

DREW WAVED TO TOMMY AS HE DUCKED IN BEHIND SOME CUSTOMERS A little before one. Tommy nodded and then turned his attention back to the man standing in front of the counter. As usual, the café was busy. Drew only counted two empty tables and there were four people in line. It said a lot about Beth's food. Since he'd eaten it several times himself, he knew what all the fuss was about.

Beth was standing at the sink washing her hands when he strolled into the kitchen. She looked in his direction.

"You made it." The smile she gave him sent warmth spreading all the way down to his toes.

Unable to resist, he closed the distance between them, and gave her a kiss that was probably a little much for the workplace. Good thing he wasn't her employee.

She released a contented sigh as his lips left hers.

He waited until she opened her eyes and then glanced around the kitchen. "Now, put me to work. What do you need me to do first?"

Put him to work she did. Within minutes, he was loading food on trays and taking them out to customers. Things didn't slow down until it was nearly time to close. He liked working with Beth, mostly because every so often when she'd hand him a tray of food she would rise up on her tiptoes and give him a peck on the lips. It made the running back and forth worth it.

They were closing up when a woman stopped near the front of the café acting as if she wanted to come in but kept changing her mind.

"Beth." Drew yelled loud enough to get her attention in the back.

"Yeah?" She appeared through the kitchen door, wiping her hands on a towel.

He tilted his head toward the front. The woman still looked unsure of herself. "Want me to see what she wants?"

Beth shook her head. "No. I got it."

When the woman noticed Beth was heading her way, she froze. He'd seen that look before from people who were standing across the street watching their home burn. It was a deer in the headlights kind of look—a mixture of panic and something akin to disbelief.

"Can I help you?" Beth asked, cracking the door open.

The woman spoke, but it was too low for him to hear. Beth nodded a few times. Whoever the woman was, she was obviously shy, or nervous, or maybe both. After several minutes, the woman left, and Beth locked the front door again.

"Everything okay?" he asked.

"She was inquiring about the job opening."

Even though the woman was nowhere to be seen, Drew looked behind Beth to where she had been. "Does she realize she'll have to deal with people?"

Beth smiled. "Yes. She worked in a diner when she was in high school."

He went back to the table he was cleaning. "So are you going to hire her?"

"I told her to show up Tuesday morning at seven and I'd give her a trial run."

"That was nice of you," he said.

She took a step forward and brushed the back of her hand along his arm. "I can be very nice. When I want to be."

Drew took a deep breath and met her gaze. "Are we going to the club tonight?"

"I haven't decided yet."

"I doubt it could be worse than last night. I'd say the hard part is over. Everyone knows we're together now. End of story."

Beth shrugged. "Maybe. But that wasn't why I was considering staying home."

He gave her a questioning look.

"It's your last night off. I don't want to wear you out when you have to be at work first thing in the morning." He opened his mouth to speak, but she cut him off. "Plus, I think I might want you all to myself tonight."

It was hard to argue with that.

As it turned out, they did make an appearance at Serpent's Kiss that night. They received a few lingering looks, but it was nothing like it had been the night before. For the most part, they hung out with friends and relaxed.

They headed back to Beth's house around ten thirty. Drew was feeling a little guilty that he hadn't really talked to Shawn since Wednesday morning. Other than a few quick texts, he hadn't communicated with him at all in the last four days.

"What's bothering you?" Beth asked as they lay in her bed that night.

"Just worried about Shawn."

"I've sort of monopolized your time off, haven't I?" She turned slightly so that she could look at him.

"Could be the other way around. I could be monopolizing your time."

Beth rolled so that she was facing him. "This is moving kind of fast, isn't it? I mean, we've spent nearly every minute I wasn't at work together."

He hated to ask, but he felt he needed to. "Are things moving too fast for you, Beth?"

Her forehead wrinkled as she considered his question. "I don't know."

Drew waited.

"I know it should. It's only been a week since our first date, but . . ." She looked him in the eyes. "I missed you Tuesday night when you weren't in my bed."

It didn't take a genius to know how much that admission cost her. The urge to tell her that he loved her was strong, but he resisted. She may have admitted that she missed him, but that didn't mean she was ready to hear that he had fallen in love with her.

"I missed you, too," he whispered. "I was lying in my cot remembering what it had been like to fall asleep with you beside me. It made it hard to go to sleep." Drew flexed his hips against her to make sure she got his meaning.

She gave him a gentle shove. "I'm sure you managed. Don't you have a shower at the station?"

He laughed. "If you think I'm going to go into a public shower room to jack off, you're crazy."

"So you just had to suffer, huh?" she teased.

"Yes." He buried his face in her hair. "I could hear all the guys around me and all I wanted was to be here with you. Tomorrow night is going to be torture."

Drew expected her to laugh, but she didn't. "I know."

Neither said anything for a long time, but Beth finally broke the silence. "What's your family going to think of me? Am I anything like the other girls you've brought home?"

He was grateful for the change in subject. "Yes and no. I've always been attracted to strong women, even in high school, so that won't shock them. I think the biggest difference will be our relationship itself."

Beth stiffened in his arms, and he knew he needed to clarify. "Not what we do in the bedroom. I'm talking about the normal stuff." He laced their fingers together and held them up close to their faces. "Like the fact that I like to be touching you. It doesn't matter if I'm holding your hand or if I have my arm around you."

She squeezed his hand. "So that's different. What else?"

"I've been thinking about sleeping arrangements. There is no way my parents are going to let us share a bedroom—they're old-fashioned that way."

"Mine probably wouldn't either."

Drew lowered their hands, but didn't release her. "What do you think about camping?"

She raised her eyebrows. "I thought we already covered this."

"True, but if you recall I presented you with an alternative that would make camping more appealing."

"You did. Although I'm not one-hundred percent convinced," she said.

Taking the plunge, he told her his plan. "Give me the chance to convince you. Sunday night you and I will camp under the stars. We'd be away from the house and completely alone. And best of all, we can share a sleeping bag."

Beth kissed the hollow at the base of his collarbone. "You think you have it all figured out, don't you?"

"I think I'd go insane if I knew you were sleeping in the same house and I couldn't be there next to you," he confessed. Let her take that however she wanted.

"Your parents won't get suspicious or want to come with us?"

"I don't think so. Mom doesn't camp. And Dad's back gives him issues now and then, so I doubt he'll want to chance it the night before the big party." Drew paused. "The only one we really have to worry about is Seth."

"You think your brother will want to tag along?"

Drew shrugged. "It's unlikely, but maybe. You never know with Seth."

"Do you and your brother get along? I know you've told me some about when you were kids, but what about now that you're older? Does he still treat you like you're his pesky younger brother?"

"I suppose we get along as well as most brothers do. He has his life. I have mine. We don't exactly travel in the same circles." Drew preferred physical work and getting his hands dirty. Seth was just the opposite. Drew was pretty sure the only time his brother broke a sweat was in the gym.

"So no meeting for lunch or dinner even though you both live in St. Louis?" she asked.

"Not really. As I said, we both have very different lives and we're both happy the way things are. I think we've met for lunch a handful of times since I moved to the city."

Beth sighed. "That's kind of sad. I'm not very close with my siblings either, but that's mainly because they're so far away. Still, we e-mail about once a week just to see how each other is doing."

He knew he shouldn't ask, but that little voice inside wouldn't let him leave it alone. "Have you told them about me?"

"Yes."

Knowing she'd told her family about him made Drew smile.

"Don't get all cocky on me." She poked him in the ribs. "It's not a big deal."

Whether Beth admitted it or not, it was a big deal. At least, to him.

He slipped his arm around her waist and cupped her ass in the palm of his hand as he tucked her head into his shoulder. It was a near perfect position and he didn't have any desire to move from it until morning. Drew kissed the top of her head and rested his cheek on her hair. "I'm glad you told your family about me."

She didn't say anything for a long time. He thought maybe she'd fallen asleep. Then, in a soft voice she said, "Me, too."

Chapter Twenty-Five

When Drew arrived for work on Sunday morning, the station was full of activity. The outgoing shift had recently returned from a fire and everyone was busy cleaning equipment and getting debriefed. As he walked by some of the guys, he thought he heard one of them mention arson, but didn't get a chance to question it before he heard his name being called.

"Parker!" He looked up to find Chief Franks peering over the second-story railing.

"Morning, Chief."

"I need to see you in my office at eight sharp." Chief Franks' gaze landed somewhere behind him. "You, too, Cameron."

Willis Cameron, captain of one of the ladder trucks, shot Drew a questioning look as they both headed toward the locker room to stow their things. "Any idea what that's about?"

Drew shoved his duffel bag into his locker. "I thought I overheard one of the guys downstairs mention arson. I'm guessing another building was targeted last night."

"Bomb and arson really needs to catch this guy already. What's it been . . . six buildings now? I wonder if there were any people in this one."

"I guess we're going to find out." Shutting his locker, Drew began walking toward the kitchen with Willis. "And even if this one wasn't, sooner or later there will be. His luck is going to run out."

"True that."

Lucky for Drew, Beth had brought home some of her amazing blueberry muffins on Saturday and he'd enjoyed them and a cup of coffee before leaving her house that morning. She'd gotten up to see him off even though he told her she didn't have to. Sitting there with her at her table eating breakfast had felt very domesticated to him. It had only been a week and yet it felt as if they'd done the same routine hundreds of times.

Drew smiled as he poured himself a fresh cup of coffee. He was taking his first sip when his crew found him.

"There you are. I thought maybe your big date had worn you out and you'd called in sick."

Of course, everyone in the kitchen heard Romeo. They all stopped what they were involved in and turned their attention on Drew.

He took his time, taking another drink of his coffee before he responded. "You think I'd let you off that easy, Romeo? Someone's got to be here to keep you in line."

Some of the guys chuckled. Romeo was a great guy, but he had the habit of talking first and thinking later.

"Come on, Parker. You've got to give us some details here. Let us live vicariously."

Drew took his coffee over to the table and sat down. Although he still felt protective of his relationship with Beth, he knew it was a lost cause to keep it from the guys he worked with, especially his crew—they were like family. Since he was planning to be with Beth for a long time to come, they were going to have to know about her sooner or later.

Before he could figure out what to say, Baily pulled up a chair beside him. "It's the café lady, right?"

"Yes."

Romeo whistled. "Oh man. You've got good taste. That is one hot piece of ass."

Drew gave him a hard stare.

"Oh wow," Irwin said, finally piping up for the first time. "It's like that, is it? Better watch what you say, Romeo. Looks like our captain here has it bad for this one."

Some of the other guys were still paying attention to their conversation. Others were starting to drift out of the room. It was nearing eight and the previous shift was eager to head home—probably to get some sleep since they'd most likely been up all night fighting that suspected arson.

"You should bring her to Romeo's barbecue," Baily said.

They all nodded.

Drew shook his head and stood. He still had a few minutes before he had to be in Chief Franks' office, but he needed a breather from the interrogation. "No can do. I'll be at my parents' Monday for their big shindig."

"I'm surprised you'd want to leave your new girl that long. She may find someone else while you're gone."

Romeo thought he was smart, but Drew was about to make clear the position Beth held in his life. He strolled with coffee in hand toward the door that would lead him out to the bay and the stairs to Chief Franks' office on the second floor. "Not likely since I'm taking her with me."

He knew there would be a price to pay for that kind of admission, but seeing Romeo momentarily speechless had been worth it. For now he needed to concentrate on his job. Cameron was right. If last night's fire was by the same arsonist that would mean six buildings had been hit. So far no one had been hurt—not civilian or firefighter—but set fires were always more dangerous. They tended to burn hotter and spread faster than your typical fire. They really needed to catch this guy.

Four hours later, Drew was working on some paperwork while his guys did some general housework around the station. He shifted slightly and was reminded of Friday night when he'd been able to feel the residual effects of Beth's spanking. His morning had been full between his meeting with Chief Franks and a call about a hydrant not working properly. This was the first opportunity he'd had to decompress.

Every time Beth crossed his mind he would start grinning. It was impossible not to. Drew finally had the kind of relationship he wanted, and with a woman who kept him engaged and interested outside sex. He'd never had that before and he knew, even now, that he was never going to want to give that up. Beth was it for him. He just had to get her to see it, too.

A knock sounded on the doorjamb causing Drew to look up. Jamison, a private on Willis' ladder crew, framed the doorway. "There's someone out front asking for you."

Confused, Drew nodded and set his pen down to go see who it was. Seth had only dropped by once in seven years, so Drew doubted it was him.

When he rounded the corner, he couldn't believe his eyes. It was Beth. "Hey."

"Hey." She looked uncharacteristically shy. "I hope you don't mind that I came."

"No. Not at all." He pulled her out of the main hall and into one of the side rooms so they could have a little privacy. "I'm just a little surprised. Everything all right?"

Beth reached into her pocket and pulled out a watch. *His* watch. "You left it on my dresser."

"Thanks for bringing it to me." He took the watch and secured it on his right wrist.

"You're welcome. I didn't know if you would need it today or not."

"I'm surprised I didn't realize it was missing." Drew was shocked really. It was a gift from his parents upon graduating from the fire academy. He rarely left home without wearing it, and it was as much a part of his work uniform as his dark blue pants and polo shirt were.

"Well, you have it now, so . . ."

Drew was torn. He didn't want her to go, but he knew she couldn't stay either. "Do you have any plans for today?"

It was a weak attempt to prolong her visit. "I'm meeting Nicole for lunch, actually."

He glanced down at his watch. "It's already after twelve."

"I know," she said. "I'm going to be late."

"I'll walk you out."

Beth nodded, and he followed close behind her as she walked down the hallway and out the front door. She turned, hesitating. Beth didn't act as if she wanted to leave any more than he wanted her to go.

Drew felt her press something into his hand. He opened his palm to find a key.

"Come over tomorrow morning when you get off work." Although she didn't pose it as a question, he knew she was really asking.

"Are you sure?" Giving him a key to her house was a big step—especially for her.

"I'm sure."

Drew searched her eyes to see if he could detect any hesitation or uncertainty on her part. He found none.

Closing his fingers around the key, he slipped it into his pocket. "I'll try to be quiet."

Beth took a step toward him. She grabbed a fistful of his shirt in her right hand and twisted, pulling him closer. Her lips were on his before he could think about the consequences. Then there wasn't much thinking at all as the memory of her mouth and her body against him the night before spread through every muscle of his being.

When she finally detached her mouth from his, she looked up at him with heavy-lidded eyes. "Don't be too quiet."

He blinked, and she chuckled before giving him another quick kiss and walking away.

Drew was still trying to get his bearings as he turned to go back inside. That's when he noticed that they'd had an audience. A handful of guys, including Baily and Romeo, were standing outside the bay watching his interaction with Beth. Ignoring them, he opened the door he'd exited a few minutes before and headed back to his desk. He knew what was coming, but he was going to try to hide from it for a few minutes more. At least until he could get his body's reaction to that kiss to go away.

❧

"I gave him a key."

Nicole paused with her fork halfway between her plate and her mouth. Her face was completely blank as she stared across the table. Beth didn't know what to make of her best friend's reaction to her declaration.

"Would you say something? Am I being stupid?" Beth asked.

It took Nicole another few moments. She returned her utensil to her plate and placed her hands in her lap. "That depends."

"On?"

"On why you did it."

At least Nicole didn't immediately tell Beth that she'd lost her mind. "We've spent pretty much all our free time together since our date last Saturday."

"I know."

She glared at her friend. "Are you going to let me finish?"

Nicole waved her hand indicating Beth should continue.

"Anyway . . . I was surprised at how much I missed him Tuesday night when he had to work and that was after he'd only spent one night in my bed." Beth plucked nonexistent fuzz from her napkin. "He has to work tonight and I know I'm going to miss having him beside me."

Luckily, Nicole caught on to her train of thought. "And you don't have to work tomorrow so you were thinking he could come straight from his shift and maybe be there when you wake up?"

It was embarrassing to admit, but there it was. "Something like that."

"Do you regret giving him the key?" she asked. It was just like Nicole to cut to the chase.

Beth sighed. "No."

"Then what's the problem?"

"Everything is moving so fast with him. I mean, we just started dating and I want to be with him all the time. That's not normal," Beth said.

Her friend gave her a knowing smile.

"What?"

"You're falling in love with him."

She sat up straight in her chair, defiant. "No, I'm not."

Nicole picked up her drink and brought it to her lips. "If you say so."

"I can't be. It–it's too soon." When Nicole didn't respond, Beth asked, "Isn't it?"

"Only you can answer that, Beth. But let me remind you that while you've only been *officially* dating for eight days, the courtship has been happening for well over a month."

Beth didn't comment right away. "How did you know with Jeff?"

Her friend's eyes lit up at the mention of her man. "We were sitting in his apartment one evening watching a movie. He looked over at me and asked if I wanted any popcorn."

That didn't sound like an *aha* moment to Beth, but what did she know? With Ben, it had been a gradual thing. There wasn't a single moment she could pinpoint when she'd fallen in love with him. It just sort of showed up one day. "Him asking if you wanted popcorn doesn't sound all that romantic."

"It wasn't. And it wasn't just the popcorn. But it was at that moment when I realized that he wasn't like all those selfish guys I'd dated in the past. He was always asking if he could get me anything, or going out of his way to help me relax after a stressful day at work. It was then that I realized we clicked, and that I wanted to be with him long term. Being with him did, and still does, make me happy," Nicole said.

Beth thought back on her time with Drew. He did make her happy. But was that love or just hormones? She honestly didn't know.

"Look, you don't have to take my word for it. One of these days it will just hit you like it did me. You'll see."

"And if it doesn't? What if Ben broke that part of me and I can't get it back?" It might sound like a stupid question, but in her mind it made perfect sense.

"You gave Drew a key to your house, right?"

She rolled her eyes. "You know I did because me telling you that is what started this whole conversation."

Nicole picked up her fork and began eating once more. "A month ago you didn't think you'd be able to trust another man again. You wouldn't have given Drew a key to your home if you didn't trust him."

This was true. Beth did trust him. Whether that trust was misplaced or not remained to be seen.

⚜

DREW USED HIS NEW KEY TO LET HIMSELF IN BETH'S FRONT DOOR. HE'D hightailed it out of the station as soon as he could, but even still, it was getting close to eight thirty. The house was quiet, so he figured she was still asleep.

Hitching his duffel bag a little higher on his shoulder, he made sure the door was locked behind him, and climbed the stairs. It had been a rough shift. Not because of the calls—they'd only had two after Beth's visit—no, it was due to the ribbing he'd endured from the guys. He tried to take it in stride. It was par for the course when you worked with fifteen other guys. The only thing he wanted to do was crawl into bed with Beth and feel her warm body pressed against his.

When he stepped into her bedroom, he was surprised to find her wide-awake and waiting for him. "I thought you'd be asleep."

"I didn't sleep all that well last night. It was lonely in this bed all by myself."

She threw back the covers. It was only then that he realized she was completely naked. He swallowed and dropped his bag.

"Come here, Captain." Beth spread her legs for him. "There's something that desperately needs your attention."

All the innuendo and suggestive comments he'd had to deal with over the past twenty-four hours disappeared as he crawled onto the bed and took up position between her legs. Her pussy gleamed back at him, already moist and ready for his attentions.

"I missed you, Mistress." He dipped his tongue into her heat and partook.

Beth placed her hand on the back of his head and lifted her hips. "I missed you, too."

He had no idea what she'd been thinking about before he arrived, but whatever it was had her very wet. Her clit was already peeking out from beneath its hood, and he teased it as he sucked and licked every inch of her within easy reach of his mouth. It was the perfect way to end his shift—start his day—however you wanted to look at it.

Her fingers dug into his scalp as she got closer. He flicked his tongue against her clit in rapid succession because he knew how much she liked that. Drew felt her legs begin to tremble, and then her breath hitched. A moment later, she arched her back and released a high-pitched squeal.

When she glanced down at him still perched between her thighs, he knew he had a shit-eating grin on his face.

"Thank you. I needed that," she said, caressing the side of his face.

"Anytime."

Beth sat up and stretched.

He was unsure what to do next. Their arrangement said they would only play on his four-day-off stretches, but they'd already discovered that most of their sexual encounters involved some level of kink, even the more vanilla ones. There was nothing he wanted more after eating her pussy than to sink his cock inside her.

She patted his cheek and then turned to put her feet on the floor as if she was going to get up. "I'll use the bathroom down the hall. Get yourself ready for bed. I'll be back in a minute."

Although he was somewhat disappointed, he didn't argue with her. Drew went to retrieve his duffel bag and dug out his toothbrush and toothpaste. If all they were going to do was sleep, he might as well go through his normal pre-bed routine.

Ten minutes later, Beth strolled into the room still as naked as she'd been when she left. He was in her bed waiting for her. She climbed in beside him and reached for him.

Drew met her halfway, and his heart began to race as she drew his mouth down to hers. "I thought—"

Beth kissed him hard. "You thought what?"

"That you didn't . . . that you didn't want to." Talking was becoming less of a priority.

Any ideas he had of her not wanting to have sex with him this morning fell by the wayside as she wrapped her fingers around his erection and guided it home. Feeling her pussy milking his cock as he pushed inside her had him longing more than ever to blurt out that he loved her, but he knew he couldn't do that. Instead, he buried his face in her neck and repeated 'I love you' over and over again in his mind with each thrust of his hips.

Chapter Twenty-Six

They slept until a little after eleven. Because Drew hadn't been all that busy during his shift, he'd been able to get a decent amount of sleep. That didn't mean that he was going to pass up the chance to spend a few more hours in Beth's bed with her softness pressed against him.

That afternoon, in need of some clean clothes, Drew took Beth with him to his apartment. He was surprised to find Shawn there. The last time he'd spoken to him, it sounded as if he'd found an apartment.

"You're home." Shawn glanced up from the television. When he realized Drew wasn't alone, he clicked it off and stood. "Hello. You must be Beth."

She smiled. "And you must be Shawn. I've heard a lot about you."

"Only good things, I hope."

Beth pressed her lips together, brought her thumb and index finger in front of her mouth, and then acted as if she was locking her lips closed and throwing away the key.

"Ah. So it's like that, is it?" Shawn glanced over at Drew. "I like her."

Drew rolled his eyes. "Glad you approve."

There was a lull in the conversation and a lightbulb seemed to go off in his friend's head. "Did you guys need me to make myself scarce for a while? I can go catch a movie or something. Give you some privacy."

"That's all right. We aren't staying. I just came by to get some clean clothes." Drew leaned in and gave Beth a kiss. "I'll hurry. Make yourself at home."

Leaving Beth in the living room with Shawn, Drew scurried into his bedroom and gathered up enough clothing to get him through the next three days. He was eventually going to run out of clean clothes, but he wasn't willing to sacrifice time with Beth in order to do laundry.

He was zipping his bag when there was a knock behind him. Drew looked over his shoulder to find Beth framing the doorway.

"Do you have a bag or something you could put your dirty laundry in? I have a washer and dryer at my place. You're more than welcome to use them."

"Are you sure?" he asked.

Beth strolled across the room and he was mesmerized by the sway of her hips as she walked toward him. When she came to a stop in front him, Drew had to remind himself that they weren't really alone and that he needed to keep his hands to himself. She traced a line down the outside of his jaw with the tip of her nail, reminding him of Saturday night. Almost instantly, there was a lot less space in his pants.

"I'm sure." The words barely left her mouth before her lips brushed against his.

"Okay." He tried to breathe through the temptation. "Beth?"

"Yes?"

"Shawn's still in the next room." As the moments ticked by, that fact was becoming less important. His friend was an adult and it was Drew's apartment. If he wanted to make love to his girlfriend in his bed, then he would.

To his disappointment, Beth put some distance between them. "I'll wait for you in the other room. Don't be long."

It might not have been a command—they weren't playing—but Drew still flew around his bedroom gathering dirty clothing wherever he could find it. In less than two minutes, he had his duffel bag in one hand and his laundry bag full of dirty clothes in the other. The only thing left to do was get Beth home as fast as humanly possible. If he was lucky, they could spend the rest of the day in her bed.

Over the next few days, the two of them spent what some might call an unhealthy amount of time together. If they weren't working then they could usually be found together. Beth had help at the café so she didn't need his assistance anymore. When Shawn had called to see if Drew could give him a hand moving into his new apartment on Wednesday morning, he'd jumped at the chance. It would be something to keep him occupied while Beth was at work.

Drew had never been in love before. The reality of it—the feeling as if he couldn't get enough of her—wasn't something he was prepared for. He'd experienced lust in the past. The physical attraction to Beth wasn't what bowled him over. It was the wanting to see her roll over and smile at him first thing in the morning or having her give him that look when he was acting a little too playful.

He pulled up to his apartment at noon. Shawn was inside, packing up the few things he'd brought with him. The rest was in a storage unit a few miles away.

The two didn't say much as they loaded everything into Shawn's pickup truck. Drew hopped in the passenger side while his friend got behind the wheel. "Thanks for letting me stay at your place. I appreciate it."

"Anytime. You know that," Drew said. "Not like I've been at my apartment much lately anyway."

Shawn pulled out onto the road and headed in the direction of the storage facility. "Can't get enough of each other, huh? I remember those days."

Drew didn't comment.

The rest of his afternoon was spent hauling the few pieces of furniture Jill hadn't wanted, and helping Shawn get his apartment ready for living. Drew didn't mind doing domestic chores. Housekeeping was part of being a firefighter. That being said, his friend's new place left a lot to be desired. It was a one bedroom like his, but everything in it appeared to have been transported from the seventies.

"I hope you got a good deal on this place," Drew said.

"What? You not digging the shag carpet?" Shawn chuckled and shrugged. "It's the middle of the month. Beggars can't be choosers. Besides, it's just me. I'm not out to impress anyone."

"Yet."

Shawn shook his head. "Not for a while. I think I need to take a break from women for a bit. Jill and I were together for ten years. It's going to take a while to get my mind wrapped around someone else in my life like that. "

At four o'clock, Shawn dropped Drew back at his apartment. Maybe he should have gone inside and stayed put for a while—give Beth some space. He didn't want her to feel smothered.

His good intentions lasted about as long as it took his friend's truck to disappear. Digging his keys out of his pocket, Drew opened his car door and got behind the wheel. With any luck, Beth would already be home.

She was.

Drew hurried up the walkway and knocked. A few moments later Beth opened the door. "Hey."

Without waiting for more of an invitation, he stepped over the threshold, and scooped her up in his arms. "Hey."

Beth laughed until he pressed his lips to hers. It was a slow, deep kiss that said more than words ever could.

She licked her lips and met his gaze. "Why didn't you let yourself in?"

He kissed her again. "I didn't want to assume. You might have been busy or something."

"I was starting dinner." She hadn't made any move to pull away. Hopefully, she didn't have anything on the stove or in the oven that would burn.

"Want some help?" he asked.

Only then did she back out of his arms. "Always."

Drew followed her into the kitchen and they spent the next hour working side by side cooking dinner. He wondered what his mom would think if she knew.

That night as they feel asleep, Drew let the excitement of the upcoming weekend take hold. He was bringing his girlfriend home to meet his family. Drew was almost positive his dad would like Beth, but Dad was easy to please. His mom and Seth would be the real test—Seth especially. His brother was naturally suspicious. Drew always figured it was a lawyer thing.

As Beth's breathing evened out, Drew let himself wonder for the first time what it would be like to be married to her. She was everything he wanted in a woman. He could see himself coming home to her every day for the rest of his life.

The only thing he had to do now was convince her. She'd come a long way, but there were still times when he thought she was second-guessing herself. The only time that didn't seem to happen was when they were in bed. Beth knew her role there the same as he did. It was everything else, the traditional boyfriend-girlfriend stuff that brought that look into her eyes every so often.

He'd noticed it a lot that first week, but as the days passed, it was less and less. Either Beth was beginning to relax and trust their relationship, or she was getting better at hiding it from him. He really hoped it was the former.

❧

ON SUNDAY MORNING, BETH WOKE UP WITH A HUGE SMILE ON HER FACE. Drew was in the middle of another four days off and they'd spent last night having some fun with bondage. She'd had a long day at work and needed a release.

The smile lasted as long as it took her to remember that they would be going to see Drew's parents in a few short hours. It felt like a big moment for her—for them. She wasn't sure why every step forward in their relationship filled her with anxiety, but it did. Maybe it was because, deep down, she knew the significance.

Drew was important to her. Technically, they'd been together only two weeks, but in some ways she felt closer to him than she ever had to Ben. How was that possible? She'd been with Ben for three years. He knew her. Drew . . .

As much as she didn't want to admit it, Drew did know her. Maybe it wasn't in the same way, but considering how things turned out with Ben that was probably a good thing. Drew was honest. It was the only way to describe him. He held nothing back. It didn't matter if they were in bed or out of it, he gave her all of himself and it was hard to combat that.

His eyes flittered open, and when he saw her looking at him, he grinned. "Good morning."

Unable to resist, she drew closer to him.

The feel of his arms around her brought Beth comfort. He'd spent every night he hadn't been working in her bed. She knew some in the lifestyle would feel that there needed to be some separation. Maybe they were right, but she couldn't bring herself to make him sleep in the other room or even go home. Not having him beside her when he was at the fire station was bad enough.

"Are you ready for today?" he asked.

"Not really."

His chest vibrated with amusement. "It'll be fine. You have nothing to worry about."

Beth snorted. "I'll remember you said that when it's time to meet my parents."

"Bring it on."

They lay there for several minutes just enjoying each other. Eventually, though, they had to get up and begin getting ready. There was no use putting it off anymore as tempting as that might be.

Drew's parents lived roughly an hour east of St. Louis. As they drove farther into Illinois, civilization fell away and they were surrounded by nothing but fields. He'd said he grew up on a farm, but Beth was envisioning more along the lines of what she was used to in Ohio. There was nothing except fields for as far as the eye could see. She didn't even think they'd passed a house in the last ten minutes.

"You okay over there?" he asked.

"Yeah. I just thought there'd be more . . . houses."

He smiled. "That's southern Illinois for ya. Fields as far as the eye can see."

"Is it like this where your parents live?"

"Pretty much. There's a small town about ten miles down the road, so there are a few more houses if you head in that direction."

He said it as though it were the most natural thing in the world. Of course, to him it probably was. Beth couldn't imagine living so far out of touch from everything. She'd grown up in the suburbs and that's what she was used to. This felt as if one could get lost.

Fifteen minutes later, they turned onto a road that looked only marginally better than a gravel driveway. They seemed to keep going farther and farther out in the middle of nowhere.

Then she noticed a mailbox up ahead. Drew put on his turn signal even though there was no one behind them. She guessed it was showtime.

Beth reached for his hand as they drove up the long driveway toward the house. That, at least, was how she'd pictured it—an old two-story farmhouse with a wraparound porch. She wondered if Drew's parents ever sat outside on a hot day sipping iced tea.

He pulled up to the house and parked the car alongside a fence. "You ready?"

"No," she said.

Drew squeezed her hand and shot her that teasing grin of his. "Don't worry. I'll protect you."

She rolled her eyes. "So I need a big strong man to protect me from your family?"

"You never know. Mom might have some secret truth serum or something lurking in her cupboards. She'll make you tell her all your secrets."

Beth shook her head and laughed.

"Don't worry. We'll be alone tonight. Camping, remember?" Drew's eyes were sparkling. He loved teasing her as much as she loved teasing him.

Taking a quick look around, Beth confirmed that they were still alone before leaning across the console and whispering in his ear. "I'm going to make you beg for it tonight."

She saw the muscles in his throat move as he swallowed, making her grin. Drew could tease her all he wanted as long as he remembered that she would always get the last word. The only thing that kept her from pushing things right then and there was the fact that any member of his family could come out to greet them at any given minute. Beth didn't think finding her sitting in Drew's car with her hand wrapped around his cock would be a great first impression.

Reluctantly, she pulled back enough to meet his gaze. His pupils had dilated, and Beth wondered if she looked down at his lap whether she'd find him aroused. Her train of thought did nothing to help her current state one bit. "We should go inside. Your mom's probably wondering what we're doing out here."

He looked toward the house. "She's probably at the window watching."

"Oh, goody."

Drew chuckled. "Come on. We should go inside before I start tenting my shorts."

"We wouldn't want that now, would we?" Yet again, Drew had managed to dispel her fears.

Beth met him at the front of the vehicle. He laced their fingers together before making his way toward the house. As they drew closer, she saw the outline of a woman in one of the upstairs windows. Drew had been right. She had been spying on them.

He opened the door and let Beth go inside first. Moments later, they heard someone coming down the stairs. They didn't have to wait long before a woman descended into view. She had brown hair the same shade as Drew's, but it was mixed with a fair amount of gray. Beth knew that this had to be Drew's mother.

The woman greeted them with a warm smile, then walked over to Drew and wrapped her arms around him.

Drew hugged her back.

Beth stood anxiously waiting for the introduction she knew was to come. From the conversations they'd had about his family, she knew this meeting was important. Whether Drew admitted it or not, Beth doubted a relationship between them would last if his family didn't approve. As they pulled apart, his mother's gaze settled on her.

"You must be Beth." Instead of the nod or handshake Beth was expecting, Drew's mother embraced her as well.

Startled, it took a moment for her to return the gesture. Beth looked to Drew for guidance but he wasn't any help as his attention had turned toward the door.

Things happened fast after that. Beth was quickly introduced to Drew's father, Bill, before being hustled over to the kitchen table. Nancy, Drew's mother, placed a towel-covered bowl on the table. "Help yourself. I'm sure you're hungry after the drive. Lunch will be ready soon."

Drew sat down beside Beth while Bill disappeared up the stairs. At home in his surroundings, Drew opened the towel and motioned for her to help herself to a roll. Since neither one of them had been eager to get out of bed, they'd been running late this morning. Because of that, breakfast had been nothing more than a bowl of cereal.

"Thanks," she said, picking up one of the warm rolls.

He smiled. "Mom makes the best rolls. I've tried to duplicate them, but they never come out the same."

Beth pinched off a section of her roll and popped it in her mouth. The moment the taste and texture hit her tongue, she thought she might have died and gone to heaven. The rolls were a perfect balance of sweet and savory. No wonder Drew loved them.

"Good, huh?"

All she could do was nod. Beth's mind was already working to dissect what was in the rolls.

Drew placed his hand on top of her leg as he leaned in to whisper in her ear. "I'll give you the recipe when we get home. Maybe you'll have better luck making them."

She wasn't sure if she was experiencing some sort of high from the carbohydrates or if it was merely the fact that she could feel his breath caressing the side of her face, but Beth felt her temperature begin to rise. Placing a hand over his, she removed it from her leg.

He chuckled.

Unfortunately, anything Beth might have said was silenced when Bill joined them at the table. He reached for one of the rolls, took a huge bite, and asked, "My boy here tells us you're a pretty fine baker. You make anything as good as my Nancy's rolls here?"

Before she could answer, Drew chimed in. "Her muffins are the things dreams are made of."

Nancy appeared beside Beth with what looked to be a large pot of stew. "Yes, dear, we're all aware of how much you like muffins, but I do believe your father was referring to food."

Beth thought her eyes would pop out of her head as she stared up in shock at Drew's mother. Nancy only winked at her and turned to get the salad.

Fingers tangled with hers under the table. She knew it was Drew, but she was too stunned to speak.

He squeezed her hand, and she finally turned her head in his direction.

"They like you," he mouthed.

She swallowed and nodded. They liked her. Okay. That was good. Beth only hoped she could get used to their teasing and not die of embarrassment before they headed home on Monday night.

Chapter Twenty-Seven

Lunch was interesting, to say the least. Beth didn't know what she'd expected, but Drew's parents weren't anything like what she'd been picturing. They were older. His dad had to be close to seventy and his mom wasn't much younger, but they didn't act that way. As soon as they were finished with their meal, Bill got up from the table and offered to help Drew bring in the bags.

"Actually, I brought my camping gear. I figured Beth and I could sleep down by the creek tonight," Drew said.

A knowing smile spread across Bill's face. He knew exactly why his son wanted to camp out instead of spending the night under his parents' roof. "Well, then, I'll help you unload everything and haul it back to the campsite."

"Thanks." Drew stood and pushed in his chair. "Did you want—"

"You men go on ahead. Beth and I will clean up."

There was a finality in Nancy's voice that left an uneasy feeling in Beth's stomach. She didn't know the woman well enough to hazard a guess as to what was coming, but she knew something was.

Nothing was said at first beyond a few polite 'can you hand me that plate' or 'there's a container over there you can use' for the first couple of minutes. It was tempting to let her guard down.

"My son tells me you own a café."

It wasn't the line of questioning Beth had been expecting. "I do."

There was another pause.

"A lot of hard work running a business. Long hours."

"It is," Beth agreed, "but I enjoy it for the most part. Baking has always been a passion of mine."

Nancy nodded, reached for a dishtowel, and began wiping down the counter. Beth could tell there was something on her mind.

Not sure she wanted to know what Nancy was thinking, Beth decided to keep the conversation on food. "Drew tells me he gets his love of cooking from you."

His mother smiled. "My boy is very talented in the kitchen. Could probably have been a chef if he'd put his mind to it." Nancy pulled out a chair and sat down, inviting Beth to do the same. "But he's wanted to be a firefighter since the second grade. I thought maybe he'd grow out of it, find something a little safer he wanted to do with his life, but that didn't happen. Too much of his father in him."

There was no malice behind her words. She was only stating a fact.

"Are you disappointed he didn't choose to do something different with his life?" Beth asked.

"Oh, heavens no. I want my boys to be happy. Both my boys. If that means one of them has to rush into burning buildings on a regular basis, then so be it." It was clear Nancy had come to terms with Drew's choice of profession a long time ago.

"I haven't met Seth yet, but Drew's told me a little about him." In truth, Beth was extremely curious about her boyfriend's brother. Some of the things Drew said made her think Seth had a superiority complex. After meeting Nancy and Bill, however, Beth had a hard time believing that. They were very down-to-earth people. She had to imagine Seth couldn't have fallen that far from the tree. Drew certainly hadn't.

"Seth and Drew are very different. There's ten years between them, and where Drew always wanted to play outside, Seth preferred to have his nose in a book." Nancy smiled but there was a sad element to it. "It's good to see Drew has found someone that makes him happy. I can only hope that one day Seth does as well."

A weight lifted off Beth's shoulders at the compliment. Whatever Drew's mom had been after in arranging this one-on-one time, she seemed to have found it.

Beth was about to ask more about Seth when they heard the front door open. She and Nancy both turned their heads toward the noise. Two seconds later, a man Beth didn't know strolled into the room. He was tall—maybe an inch or two taller than Drew.

Nancy scrambled out of her chair and went to hug the new arrival. "You missed lunch."

The man looked slightly abashed from the mild scolding. "Sorry, Mom. I had to go into the office this morning to pick up some paperwork."

"This is a holiday weekend. You shouldn't be working." Nancy shook her head, a look of disapproval on her face.

It was then that the man whom Beth deduced had to be, Seth, noticed her sitting at the table. "Hello."

Beth stood. "Hello. You must be Seth."

He nodded and gave her a thorough once-over. "I am. And you must be my little brother's new girlfriend."

Before she could answer, Nancy stepped in. "Beth, this is my oldest, Seth. Seth, this is Beth."

His gaze was scrutinizing and he showed no signs of extending the same welcome as Nancy and Bill had done. Trying not to let it bother her, Beth cleared her throat. "Well, it's nice to meet you, Seth. Nancy, thank you for lunch. I think I'll go outside and see if they need any help getting the tent set up."

"Of course," Nancy said.

As Beth reached the door, she thought she heard Nancy saying something about being rude but it was said so low Beth couldn't be sure.

She hurried outside and scanned the large yard. On the other side of the driveway was a huge barn. Beth doubted they were in there, so she headed around to the back of the house.

The first thing she noticed when she rounded the corner were the flowers. Drew hadn't been exaggerating. There were flowers everywhere—rows and rows of them in a variety of colors. Beth took a minute to enjoy the view before continuing her search for Drew.

When she passed the small wooden shed, she spotted them. They were farther away than she thought they'd be. It would be quite a trek in the dark if they needed to visit the house for any reason.

Unsure of her footing, Beth took her time crossing the grassy area that stood between her and the men. They had their backs to her as she approached.

"Seems serious," Bill said. Beth had no idea what they were talking about. Were they talking about the farm? Something to do with Drew's job?

Nope. He wasn't.

"It is. I love her."

At Drew's confession, Beth's heart skipped a beat. She knew then that they were talking about her.

Bill nodded. "I figured as much. Even with your mother's nagging, I doubt you'd bring a woman home to meet us unless she was pretty important to you."

If Beth thought Drew's last statement shocked her, his next one nearly had her running all the way back to St. Louis. "I want to spend the rest of my life with her."

She must have made a sound because they both turned their heads in her direction. A long silence followed and by the look on Drew's face, he knew she'd overheard.

With a subtle cough, Drew's father excused himself and left the two of them alone. Neither spoke right away. What was there to say? How did she respond to that? They hadn't even been together for a month yet. He couldn't love her. And he absolutely couldn't be thinking about marriage so soon. They didn't even know each other that well.

"Beth? Will you say something, please?" Drew asked.

"I'm trying to convince myself that I didn't just hear what you said."

He looked down at the ground and then back at her. "I do love you."

"How—"

"I've loved you for a while. Probably since before our first date. I didn't think you were ready to hear it so . . . so I didn't say anything."

She was trying to take it all in. A voice in the back of her mind screamed that he was lying—that he was saying it to manipulate her—but Beth knew that was only her fear talking. Drew had no reason to lie. She'd committed to their relationship. "And the other?"

Drew took a step closer to her. "The part about me wanting to spend the rest of my life with you?"

Beth swallowed. "Yes. You c-can't . . . you can't mean that."

The next thing she knew, he was standing close enough to touch her. Drew reached for her hands. "I do."

She opened her mouth to protest, and he cut her off. "I know you're not ready. Like you said, this thing between us is still new. But my dad always told me that one day I'd just know. He was right."

So many emotions were racing around inside her. She wanted to believe him. The part of her that had been falling for him since the first time he sat down beside her at Serpent's Kiss wanted everything he said to be true. Experience had taught her different, though. Beth had thought she was closing in on the dream before and had it blow up in her face. Dating Drew had been a huge risk for her. She couldn't give anything more. Not right now. It was just too soon. "I'm sorry. I can't . . ."

He moved closer. "I'm not asking you to. No pressure, Beth. I'll wait as long as you need to feel comfortable."

"And if I never do?"

Drew cupped the side of her face and looked her straight in the eye. "I'll still be here."

❧❦❧

He'd thought she was inside with his mom. If he'd had any idea that she was standing close enough to hear what he'd said to his father, Drew never would have said it.

"You don't mean that."

"Yes. I do mean it." Drew wished he could make her understand. He'd played the field, as it were. At no point in time had he ever felt anything near what he felt for Beth with any other woman.

"Hey."

Drew glanced over Beth's shoulder. Seth was striding toward them.

"I need . . . I need to think," she whispered.

He felt her start to back away. Instinct made him grasp her hands tighter, but then he let go. Whatever was going through her mind, they wouldn't be able to discuss it with Seth there. So like it or not, Drew watched as Beth turned and walked away, leaving him standing alone as his brother drew closer.

Seth tilted his head in the direction of Beth's retreating back. "Lovers' spat?"

"Not exactly." Drew returned to what he'd been working on before Beth's arrival—securing their tent.

His brother surprised him by pitching in to help.

They worked side by side making sure everything was set up properly. Seth was keeping his own counsel for the time being, but Drew knew that wouldn't last. His brother had an opinion about everything. He was sure Beth was no exception.

Finished, Drew tossed their overnight bags inside the tent and began scrounging the area for kindling. It was a warm day and should be a nice night. That didn't mean they wouldn't want a fire if they decided to sit outside the tent after the sun went down. It was always good to be prepared.

Seth followed him over to the line of trees, but made no move to help with the gathering of wood. "A little soon to be bringing someone home to meet Mom and Dad, don't you think?"

"Nope."

"Mom says she owns a business."

Drew shot a glare in his brother's direction. "Yes. A café."

"Is it solid? Have you seen her financials?"

That brought his progress to a halt. Drew turned around to face his brother. "Why in the world would I ask to see the financial records of my girlfriend's business?"

"To make sure she and her business can stand on their own two feet." The way Seth said it made it sound as if that should have been obvious.

"It's her business, not mine."

"I can do some digging when I get home. I'm sure I can find—"

"No." Drew was getting angry.

"No?"

"That's right. No. You stay out of her finances and anything else of hers. It's none of your business." Drew didn't even want to hazard a guess as to how it would look to Beth if she found out his brother had been digging around in her private life. Not to mention the very real possibility that his brother could make a connection with Serpent's Kiss. Katrina was good at keeping the nature of the club under wraps but he wouldn't put it past his brother to stake out the place.

Seth frowned. "You can never be too careful. It's always good to err on the side of caution in these—"

"I said no."

He pressed his lips together in displeasure.

Drew didn't care. All he wanted to do was go find Beth and get her to talk to him. Instead he was here listening to his brother spout off some insanity about Beth and her money.

"Mom wanted me to ask if you and your girlfriend would be joining us for dinner or if you were planning to fend for yourselves tonight?" Seth's voice was tight, but Drew was happy that his brother was dropping the subject.

"We'll be there." At least, Drew was hoping they would be. That, of course, had a lot to do with Beth.

The sound of retreating footsteps was the only indication that his brother had left. While Drew continued to gather sticks, Seth's line of questioning lingered. Why would he care if Beth had money or not? It wasn't as if Drew was wealthy. He made a good living and had some savings, but that was about it.

Eventually he became frustrated with that line of thinking—it wasn't getting him anywhere anyway—and his thoughts drifted back to Beth. She said she needed to think. In his experience, when a female said that it was rarely a good thing. Granted, Beth wasn't like any of the other women he'd had in his life, but he wasn't willing to sit by and watch her fear convince her that they shouldn't be together.

He dropped an armful of wood near the campsite, cleaned the dirt from his hands, and went in search of her. There were a lot of places to hide on the farm. During his childhood, Drew had explored them all. He knew he'd be able to track her down one way or another.

It turned out that she wasn't that difficult to find. She was standing by a fence, petting one of the horses. Drew leaned against the weathered post about a foot away from her and waited. She dropped her hand, and the horse bent his head down to chew on some grass. It was peaceful except for the underlying tension in the air.

"Did you really mean it?" she asked. "That you love me and—"

"Yes."

She nodded.

"Beth, I'm not asking for anything more from you. I like what we have. None of that has to change."

"For now. But eventually you're going to want more." He opened his mouth to speak, but she cut him off. "Don't deny it."

"I wasn't going to." Drew wanted to touch her, but he forced himself to remain where he was. "Can you honestly tell me that you're never going to want more?"

She took a deep breath. "Yes. I do want more. Someday."

With that, he couldn't hold back any longer. Closing the distance between them, he turned her to face him. "Then what's the problem? Me? Can you not see yourself growing old with me?"

A smile tugged at her lips. "You know that's not it."

"I'll make you a promise, okay? When you're ready, you let me know. No pressure."

"No pressure, huh?" she asked, finally beginning to relax.

He circled his arms around her waist and pulled her against his chest. "None at all. But I should warn you. When you do give me the green light, all bets are off. I plan on going all out when I propose."

"It's talk like that that makes my blood pressure spike."

Drew kissed her neck and ran his nose along her jaw up to her ear. "Once we're alone in our tent tonight, I'm sure I can do a much better job at elevating your heart rate."

Beth tilted her head back, giving him better access to her neck. He took the invitation gladly. Within a few minutes, she was grasping the back of his head and rubbing against him. It was making it hard to remember that they were standing in the middle of a field on his parents' farm.

"Where are your parents? Your brother?" she asked.

"Mom and Seth are probably in the house. Dad's most likely in the barn." He said all this in between kisses. Beth hadn't stopped her very suggestive movements against him. He really hoped no one came looking for them anytime soon because he wasn't going to be able to walk if she kept it up.

"So we're alone?" She leaned back to look at him.

Drew glanced over his shoulder toward the house. There was no sign of his family. He had no idea what she had in mind, but at this point he was up for just about anything. "Yes."

Beth sank back against the fence and guided him to stand between her spread legs. With a mischievous smile on her face, she popped the button on her jeans. He swallowed as she wrapped her hand around his wrist and brought his hand to rest on her abdomen. Drew met her gaze, thinking she couldn't possibly want him to do what was going through his mind.

She reached behind his head again and jerked him closer. Beth grazed his ear with her teeth before she whispered her command. "Stick your hand down my pants and finger fuck me until I come."

Holy hell. This was really happening.

The thought that they could be caught crossed his mind for a split second, and then it was gone. After what had happened between them, the only thing he wanted to do was connect with her in the most elemental way. If they couldn't make love, then the least he could do was get her off.

He flattened his palm and slid his hand beneath the waistband of her jeans and underneath her panties. Drew had watched her get dressed that morning so he knew exactly what her underwear looked like—red silk with lace in the front that gave him a glimpse of what was underneath. He'd been trying not to think about it during their drive. Given that he could currently feel the scratch of the lace against the back of his hand, it was at the forefront of his mind yet again.

Moist heat coated his fingers as he reached the junction between her legs. Wanting to make sure she was ready, he circled her clit several times, drawing a soft moan from her before dipping his fingers inside her.

The space in which he had to move was limited, but it didn't seem to matter. Beth dug her fingers into his neck and began moving her hips in time with his fingers. Her breathing became labored as she got closer.

"Harder," she demanded.

Drew shifted a little, hoping to change the angle and get a little more leverage. She responded with a high-pitched whine that resonated from her throat. Then her knees begin to buckle as pleasure took over. With his free hand, he increased his hold on her, keeping her upright.

Less than a minute later, she buried her head in his neck and released a near silent scream. He could feel her heart pounding in her chest. To be honest, his was pounding as well. Drew didn't know a man alive who could do what he had just done and remain unaffected.

She hummed and turned her head to find his lips. The kiss was full of passion and promise. Drew may not have gotten off himself but that was all right. He was able to serve her needs.

He had no idea how long they'd been kissing when a throat cleared behind him. It was only then that he realized his hand was still shoved down Beth's pants. Trying not to make it obvious what he was doing and where his hand had been, Drew turned to the side, blocking his father's view. He was hoping his dad would think his arm was behind her back or even cupping her ass. Both of those options were less awkward than the reality.

"Sorry to interrupt, but I was hoping I could get you to help me with something in the barn before dinner." His father stood at least ten paces away from them, probably not wanting to get any closer once he'd realized they were making out and not merely talking.

Drew nodded, trying to clear his head. "Sure. I'll be up in a minute."

Not questioning why Drew didn't come right away, his father turned back toward the barn.

"Guess it's a good thing I didn't go down on you, huh?" Beth said, smiling.

Laughing, he removed his hand and helped her right herself. "Yeah. Good thing."

When he left Beth to go in search of his father, she was in much better spirits. He was hoping it would stay that way, but he wasn't naïve enough to think that her doubts wouldn't resurface in the future. Drew was beginning to realize that when she felt unsure of herself, Beth tended to go toward the sexual side—the place she knew she had control. He understood it, but he didn't like it. The only thing he could do was hope that one day she felt comfortable enough with him and herself to overcome whatever was holding her back.

Chapter Twenty-Eight

Seth was quiet during dinner, even for him. Drew had no idea what his deal was. He would like to think it was brotherly concern.

Beth, at least, seemed to be better. She was smiling and laughing at his father's jokes. It was progress.

They stayed to help his mother clean up and prep some things for the next day. Usually it was only him in the kitchen with his mom slicing things up the night before. Having Beth there working beside him felt good.

Once everything was as ready as it was going to get for the evening, Drew and Beth made their way back to the makeshift campsite. With a little bit of daylight left, he built a small fire for the two of them. The flames licked at the kindling, catching easily, so he added some larger logs.

She sat down on a large rock to his left. "I'm imagining you doing this as a little boy."

Drew smiled. "It never gets old." He leaned back on his heels and stared into the flame. There was something about fire that had always appealed to him—the way it moved and flowed.

For a long while nothing could be heard but the sounds of the night surrounding them and the crackling of the fire. He knew her mind had to be going a mile a minute and he wanted to give her time to work through whatever it was she was contemplating.

While she was thinking, Drew let his mind drift to the afternoon he'd spent with his father. It had been a while since he'd mucked out stalls and put new hay down, but it had felt good to exert some energy after getting Beth off like that. After he'd said goodbye to her, he'd turned on the hose his mom used to water her flowers and washed his hands. It had helped, but until he'd washed up for dinner there was still a faint scent of her on his fingers.

He heard her move and figured she must be chilly, and decided to scoot closer to the heat of the fire. Then he felt her run her hand along the inside of his leg. She wasn't cold.

Drew turned to face her and that's when she kissed him. This wasn't a kiss where one could mistake its meaning. Her mouth was pressing against his with such force that his teeth were hurting. Even still, his cock responded. How could it not? The memory of her coming by his hand earlier had been on his mind moments before. Of course, it didn't help that her palm was also pressed against his groin.

"Beth?"

She barely removed her lips to respond. "No talking."

Thinking was becoming difficult, but this didn't feel right. He'd let her sidetrack their discussion with sex earlier. Drew couldn't let her do it again. When Beth lifted her leg to straddle him, he knew he had to act quickly or all his good intentions would go out the window.

"Red," he gasped.

Drew knew exactly when what he'd said registered. Her entire body froze. She pulled back and stared at him with eyes wide.

He knew he had to explain. "We can't, Beth. Not like this. You're using this"—Drew gestured down to where her hand still hovered all too close to his erection—"not to talk about what happened earlier."

Without a word, Beth removed herself from his lap and stood. He'd wanted her to stop pushing him away emotionally with sex, not for her to physically go away.

She looked down at the fire. Drew waited, hoping she'd share with him what she was feeling. They would never make it past this if she kept it inside.

As the minutes passed, he began to think that maybe safewording hadn't been the best idea. Instead of opening up, she appeared to be shutting down.

"I'm going to bed. Good night." The words were uttered without looking at him. Drew knew she was hurting, but he had no idea how to make it better so he let her go into the tent without him.

He rubbed his hand over his face in frustration. This wasn't how he'd imagined spending the night with her.

When he couldn't stand it any longer, he doused the fire, and climbed into the tent. Beth was on her side, facing away from him. He kicked off his shoes and lay down beside her. She didn't move—not even a little—so he didn't think she was asleep.

Knowing he was going to have to be the one to break the ice, he rolled over and placed a hand on her hip.

Beth flinched. Any doubt he'd had that she was awake vanished.

Although he wanted to make her talk about it, he knew she had to do it on her own time and in her own way. Drew meant what he'd said earlier. He would wait as long as it took. All he wanted her to do was talk to him.

"I don't . . ." Beth sighed. "I don't want you to think that I don't care about you."

"I don't think that." Drew didn't want her to worry about what he might think. This wasn't about him. It was about her.

She turned to face him. It was dark inside the tent and he couldn't see her expression, but he heard the emotion behind her words and he was pretty sure she was either crying or close to it. "I wish I could say it back. I just . . . I can't."

Unable to resist, he reached out for her, and folded her into his embrace.

Beth tucked her head into his shoulder and shuddered. She put on a good front most of the time. Whether she realized it or not, letting him see her this vulnerable said more about her feelings for him than any words.

Drew held her until he heard her breathing change. Kissing her temple, he shifted them both so that he could lie on his back yet still hold her against him. Beth loved him. He knew it in the very core of his being. She might not be able to admit it to herself yet, but he knew she'd get there eventually.

Closing his eyes, he let the warmth of her body seep into his muscles and take everything negative that had happened that day away. He'd told the absolute truth when he'd said he wanted to spend the rest of his life with her. Beth was the first person Drew thought about when he woke up every morning and she starred in his dreams every night. He couldn't think of anything better than spending the rest of his days worshiping her in every way possible.

THE RISE AND FALL OF DREW'S CHEST WAS THE FIRST THING TO ENTER INTO Beth's awareness as she awoke early the next morning. She had no recollection of moving into this position with her head resting over his heart. The last thing she did remember was feeling confused about everything except for how good it felt to be wrapped up in his arms. Crazy, considering that the whole reason for her distress in the first place was that she couldn't tell him that she loved him back. Knowing that she needed some space before she had to face him again, she carefully extracted herself from his warmth and crawled out of the tent.

It was a brisk morning. The wind blew just enough to make her shiver. Beth knew she could rebuild the fire he'd started the night before—there was still a small pile of wood to her right. If she did that, however, Drew would wake up and she'd be right back where she started. The day ahead would be stressful enough as it was. She didn't want to add to it.

With that in mind, she hugged herself and headed toward the house. Hopefully, Nancy would be up getting things ready for the party and Beth could help. Baking always relaxed her and she was counting on it to provide some much-needed balance before people started to arrive.

Drew found her almost an hour later rolling out piecrust. He walked up to her and gave her a kiss on the cheek. It was completely innocent, but it still made her pulse quicken.

"I woke up and you were gone." A simple statement full of meaning. He'd thought she'd left.

She looked up at him and lowered her voice so that only he would hear. "I needed some space. And I figured your mom might need some help getting things ready."

He scanned her face as if he could see into the inner workings of her soul. Instead of making her uncomfortable, it had her fighting to hold onto coherent thought. What was it about him that twisted her insides into knots?

Seth stumbled into the kitchen looking for coffee, pulling them both out of the bubble that they had created. Beth wasn't sure if she was happy with the interruption or not. She knew things weren't settled with Drew—not by a long shot—but she couldn't deal with her feelings right now. Not with his family around and everything else that went with it.

The morning flew by as they all worked together, even Seth, to set things up for the big party. There were two long tables placed in the side yard along with ten smaller tables surrounded by as many chairs as would fit around them. She'd thought for sure that the setup was more than enough for any barbecue, but she was wrong. A little before noon people began arriving. By twelve thirty, cars lined both sides of the long driveway and there were people everywhere.

"You doing all right?" Drew asked, coming to stand beside her.

"Yeah. I didn't think there'd be this many people, though." If she had to guess, there were at least fifty people present.

He shrugged. "In a rural area like this, a barbecue is a big deal and my parents invite all the neighbors and local farmers. There'll probably be a few more late arrivals before it's all said and done."

"More?" He couldn't be serious.

Drew chuckled. "Most likely. The Clarks are notorious for being late to stuff like this."

She felt like a fish out of water. Other than Drew and to some extent his family, Beth didn't know anyone here.

What she was feeling must have shown on her face because Drew laced his fingers through hers and squeezed. Beth was grateful for the support—especially after this morning. He could have easily left her to her own devices.

It turned out Drew was right. Three more families showed up with covered dishes and lawn chairs in tow. His dad fired up two separate grills and filled them with hamburgers, hot dogs, and brats. The smell of cooking meat filled the yard and seemed to animate the already lively conversations that were taking place among the neighbors.

By the time the last car backed out of the drive, Beth was exhausted. Over the previous eight hours, she'd met more people than she could ever hope to keep track of. Drew introduced her to everyone in attendance. He knew them all by name with the exception of two little girls that were new additions to their families. Beth didn't even think she knew that many people, and certainly not with the ease of familiarity everyone at the barbecue displayed.

"I wish you both didn't have to head back tonight," Nancy said as she and Drew walked toward where Beth was standing.

He gave his mother a kiss on the cheek. "Unfortunately, we both have to work tomorrow."

Nancy sighed as her husband came up to stand beside her. "Are you sure you have everything?"

"Yep. I loaded all our stuff from the campsite into the car this morning."

Seeming not to want to say goodbye, Nancy pulled her son in for a hug. "You take care of yourself, you hear?"

When she released him, Bill moved in to embrace his son. "Stay safe."

Drew's parents might both support their son's decision to become a firefighter, but that didn't mean they didn't worry about him. Then again, Beth knew her parents worried about her, too. It wasn't the same, but she figured all parents who loved their children worried about them to some degree.

Seth jogged down the front steps to join them. He'd been pleasant to her during the barbecue, but he still wasn't overly friendly. She had no idea why and wondered if maybe Drew did. They'd gotten sidetracked and she'd forgotten to ask him about it.

"Are you heading back to the city tonight?" Drew asked his brother.

"Nah. I'll get up early and drive back in the morning. These things always wear me out. I need a good night's sleep first." It was the most Beth had heard Seth say since she'd met him.

"I wish we could as well, but work beckons."

"You'll call me when you get home? Let me know you made it back in one piece?" Nancy asked.

Drew grinned. "Don't I always?"

It was getting late and they needed to get on the road. With that in mind, she addressed Nancy and Bill. "It was very nice to meet you. Thank you for having me."

The next thing Beth knew, Drew's mom once again had her locked in a tight, albeit brief, embrace. "You're welcome any time."

When Nancy stepped back, Bill surprised Beth with a hearty hug as well. "Make sure my boy treats you right, now. If not, you let me know. I'll set him straight."

Drew's father winked at her, and she laughed. She liked Bill and Nancy. Not only because they were her boyfriend's parents, but also because they were good people.

Bill stepped closer to Drew and she discovered Seth standing in front of her. Beth really hoped he wasn't going to hug her, too. Although from Drew's parents it was a little awkward, from his brother it would have seemed less than genuine.

"Beth." He said it as if her name held some sort of hidden meaning.

Two could play at that game. "Seth."

Amusement lit his face and one side of his mouth pulled up in the closest thing she'd seen to a smile from him. "Have a safe trip."

Not what she'd been expecting, but she'd take it. "Thank you."

"You ready?" Drew asked.

She turned her attention away from Seth and nodded.

It took them another five minutes to make it down the driveway and head home as there was another full round of goodbyes from Drew's parents. He only made the drive home a few times a year and according to his mother, that wasn't enough. She got the impression that Nancy was hoping Beth could persuade her son to come see them more often.

The back roads were dark and there was even less to see than there had been the day before. Drew was quiet behind the wheel. It wasn't until they reached the highway that he spoke. "Did you enjoy the barbecue?"

"Yes. Everyone was very nice and welcoming."

He nodded. "That's a small town for you. I've known most of them all my life."

"Sounds nice." Growing up in the suburbs, most neighbors kept to themselves. Sure, you might see them outside mowing their lawn or tending to flowerbeds and you would wave, but it wasn't as if you invited them to dinner. Even if you did, it was nothing like what Drew's parents had put on.

Silence filled the car again for several more miles before Drew cleared his throat. "Did my brother . . . did Seth say anything to you?"

She shrugged. "Not really. In fact, I'm not sure he said more than ten words to me."

"Don't let him get to you. He knows how to push people's buttons. It's what he does for a living." Drew sighed. "And for some godforsaken reason, he thinks he has to look out for me or something."

"He's your brother."

Drew glanced over at her. "I'm twenty-eight years old. If I needed a big brother to look out for me, it was when I was growing up. Not now."

"I'm sure he has his reasons." Why she was siding with Seth—whom she hadn't really been all that impressed with—she had no idea.

"He does. Or at least, he thinks he does." Drew pressed his lips together. "Yesterday after you walked off, he was grilling me about you. Or about your financials anyway."

"Me? Why?" That made no sense. Beth had never met Drew's brother before he'd strolled into the kitchen.

"No idea. I got the impression that he thought you may be trying to take advantage of me or something."

Beth furrowed her brow.

"I wouldn't worry about it. It's probably just Seth being Seth. He's always been a numbers guy. Maybe he's only being like this because I brought you home. He knows if I did that you have to be pretty important to me." And they were back to the one subject she really didn't want to talk about.

But Drew didn't go there. Instead he reached for her hand and tangled their fingers together. It was a simple gesture, but it was exactly what she needed. How was she not to fall in love with him?"

It took them a little over an hour to get home. He drove up to her house and parked the vehicle along the curb. "Do you want me to come in?"

Did she? For all her insistence that she wanted space, the thought of him not being in her bed caused a lump in her throat. She should send him home. If for no other reason but to prove to herself that she didn't need him as much as it felt like she did.

She couldn't do it, though. "Yes."

He retrieved their bags from the trunk and followed her up the walkway to her front door. It wasn't too late. She could still tell him to go home.

Then she felt his breath on the back of her neck. Desire shot through her, settling at the junction between her legs. Last night was the first time they'd slept next to each other and not fooled around. She wanted him. And whether she liked it or not, she needed him.

Turning the lock, she opened the door and stepped over the threshold. As soon as they were both inside with the door closed firmly behind them, she faced him and brought his mouth down to hers.

Drew dropped their bags and circled his arms around her, resting one hand on her ass.

Beth drew back enough to look into his eyes. He'd rejected her last night. She was hoping he understood her need and wouldn't do it again tonight.

When she didn't see any hesitation from him, she reached behind her and took hold of the hand he had groping his favorite body part. As much as she wanted to fuck him and forget the swirl of emotions, she needed to make love to him. Everything else—all the analyzing of what it all meant—would have to wait until tomorrow.

Chapter Twenty-Nine

Things returned to normal over the next week . . . or as normal as they were going to get until Beth could figure out her feelings. Drew was trying to give her time. He hadn't brought up the subject of their future again, but she could tell he was frustrated. The stalemate they were locked in was entirely her fault.

Although he'd spent the night with her on Monday, he'd told her he had some things to do on his day off on Wednesday and might be out late so he didn't come over. With him working on Thursday, she didn't get to see him again until Friday. He picked her up for dinner and then they made their way to Serpent's Kiss.

It felt as if it had been more than a week since they'd been inside the club. She took a look around to see who was there. Jeff had some sort of work function, so she knew he and Nicole wouldn't be making an appearance. Drew's friends Allison and John were across the room and Daniel was at one of the bar tables chatting with a small group of Doms.

When Beth's gaze landed on Katrina, Beth blew out a breath and turned to Drew. "Why don't you go get us something to drink and see if you can find Allison and John? I'll join you in a few minutes. I need to talk to Katrina about something first."

He raised his eyebrows slightly, but after a moment, he nodded. "Do you want your usual?"

Beth nodded. "Yes, please."

She watched his retreating back and knew she had to figure this out soon.

Drew was a great guy and she knew she could trust him. But knowing it and believing it were two different things.

Katrina was finishing up a conversation with a man Beth didn't recognize. She guessed he was a new member. He looked to be not much older than Beth, but he had a cane. Considering he appeared to be in fairly good shape, the cane seemed out of place.

"Beth," Katrina greeted. "I'd like you to meet Alexander. He just moved to St. Louis last week."

He shifted his weight to offer her his hand and Beth realized he must be recovering from some sort of injury. "It's very nice to meet you, Beth."

"You, too." Although she really did want to talk to Katrina, Beth was curious about this new arrival. It wasn't often that someone moved into town one week and joined a private kink club the next. "What brings you to St. Louis?"

Something passed across his face before he answered. "It's a long story, but I made a promise to a buddy of mine."

"And that promise was moving to St. Louis?" She knew she was being nosy, but considering his cryptic response how could she not be?

He chuckled. "Not exactly. It's more that he wanted me to give something to someone and I'm here trying to find them."

"Does that mean you're just passing through?" If that was the case, it still didn't make sense as to why he'd joined Serpent's Kiss.

"I haven't decided. So far, I'm enjoying the city. I might decide to stay and open a practice here."

"Lawyer?" she asked.

"No. I'm a doctor. Spent nearly ten years in the army before this"—he tapped his leg with his cane—"forced me out."

Beth supposed that explained the cane. And his age. "I'm sorry to hear that. Hopefully you'll like it here and decide to stick around."

"That is a very real possibility." He shifted his weight again as if his leg was bothering him. "Now, if you'll excuse me ladies. I need to sit down for a while and get off my leg. It's been a long day and I'm afraid I've pushed myself more than I should."

She watched him walk toward the bar and noticed a small limp. "Dom?"

Katrina nodded. "He'll be a good addition to the club, I think."

"If he sticks around."

"We'll see." Katrina shrugged as if it was no big deal either way. "And how are you and your new sub doing?"

"Good."

Beth drew out the word and Katrina picked up on it. "You don't seem too confident."

When she'd decided to talk to Katrina, Beth hadn't considered how she'd broach the subject with the club mistress. Nicole may have been her best friend, but she and Katrina had always had a good relationship. In the beginning, when Beth had no clue what she was doing, Katrina had helped her with Ben. Beth trusted Katrina's advice. "I wanted to ask you something . . . personal."

Katrina cocked her head to the side. "And what would that be?"

The more she thought about it, the more Beth thought this wasn't such a good idea. "Never mind."

"Beth. It isn't as if we just met. If you want to ask me something, ask me. I can always tell you it's none of your business." She smiled to soften the impact of her words.

"And you may very well do just that."

"Never know if you don't ask," Katrina said.

"Okay. Well . . . how did you know your husband was 'the one'?" Saying it out loud made her feel silly.

Katrina's eyes went wide and flashed in Drew's direction. "Really? That's wonderful, Beth."

"Is it? I don't know." Beth chewed on the inside of her cheek. "That's why I wanted to know how you *knew*."

It took Katrina a moment to answer. "I'm not sure I can really help you. My relationship with my late husband was complicated, especially during the last few years. But to answer your question, it was more a feeling that I didn't want to be without him. For all of our issues, he had a way of making me feel as if I were the only woman in the room."

Beth nodded.

Katrina placed a comforting hand on Beth's arm. "Are things not going well with Drew?"

"No. I like him. A lot."

"But?"

"But nothing, really. I want to be with him all the time even though I know that's probably not healthy." She smirked. "So what you're saying is that you're in love."

Beth frowned.

"That isn't a good thing?" Katrina looked confused.

"It's just so fast. Everything with us seems to be going at lightning speed."

"Love takes as long as it takes." Katrina shrugged. "It isn't always practical. I learned that the hard way."

It was a lot to think about. As much as she hated to admit it, Beth was pretty sure she was in love with Drew. That didn't mean confronting it didn't scare her half to death.

"Look, don't stress too much about it. Things will work out the way they're meant to."

Katrina's gaze flickered to the right and Beth turned her head to see what had caught her attention. Nothing immediately stood out until she realized that Ryan was dancing with Madi, another one of the club's Femdoms. Normally this wouldn't be a big deal—Madi danced with a lot of the single guys, Dom or sub. The look on Katrina's face, though, made Beth think she was missing something.

Then she remembered the wax play demonstration Katrina had and her thinking it was odd that Ryan hasn't been involved. Something had obviously happened between Ryan and Katrina. Beth just had no idea what. She got the impression no one else at the club did either.

"Something wrong?" Beth asked. Since she'd been dumping her problems on Katrina, she figured it was only right to give her the opening to do the same.

She shook her head and smiled. "Not at all."

"Well, if you ever want to talk, I'm willing to listen. Heaven knows you've been privy to more than your share from me."

"Thank you. I appreciate the offer and will keep that in mind." Beth could tell the chances of Katrina reaching out to her were slim.

"I should probably get back to Drew. He's going to think I deserted him."

She started to walk away when Katrina's voice stopped her. "If it makes any difference, I like him. He's much better for you than Ben ever was."

Beth nodded and continued across the room to where Drew sat with his friends. His face was full of questions. She sat down beside him and leaned in to whisper in his ear. "I want you kneeling at my feet."

This was one of those gray areas in their arrangement. He could refuse, but he didn't.

Getting up, he moved to her other side, placed one of the pillows on the floor, and lowered himself onto it. He looked up at her, his eyes still questioning but trusting as well. As Beth combed her fingers through his hair, she felt him relax. Their connection was strong. She could feel the stress of the week melting away as he knelt at her feet.

⊛

AFTER THEIR CONVERSATION ON MONDAY, DREW HAD HAD MIXED FEELINGS as to what to do. Beth said she needed some space and had shown that by hightailing it into the house to help his mom instead of waking him up. Then she had completely contradicted herself by asking him to stay over that same night.

Throughout his shift on Tuesday, he'd weighed his options. Things could go on as they were and he could pretend nothing had changed, or he could actually give Beth a little space and hope she figured out what she wanted. Neither option appealed to him. He didn't want them hanging in limbo for the rest of their lives, but that warred with his desire to be with her at every possible opportunity.

His crew helped to distract him most of the day, but it was at night when he was lying in his cot that this dilemma hit him full force. He needed to give Beth some time to figure out what exactly she wanted. If that meant putting a little distance between them, he would have to do it. Even if it wasn't what he really wanted.

With all his good intentions, Drew was only able to stay away from her for three days. Honestly, he wasn't sure he would have made it more than two had work not kept him from hopping into his vehicle and going over to see her. It wasn't the sex—although he missed that, too. No, it was Beth herself. He missed the feel of her hands in his hair and that mischievous smile of hers. It only reinforced that she was the one. Drew had never missed a woman like that before.

Beth played with the hair at the base of his neck while she talked with Allison. He was only half paying attention to what they were saying.

He felt something poke him in the leg and he shifted his attention in that direction. John had joined him on the floor and was grinning back at him. Drew could only guess that his friend was mentally saying 'I told you so.' The first night he attended the club the hardest thing for him was seeing the male subs kneeling at their mistress' feet. It felt wrong somehow.

During the course of the night, he watched John do the same thing. His friend had explained the best he could how freeing it was, but Drew wasn't convinced. Of course, then he met Beth and the draw to her had been difficult to explain, even to himself. He wanted to worship her in every way possible.

Drew rolled his eyes at John, letting him know where he could stick his smugness.

His friend chuckled.

"You should talk to Michael," Allison said. "He's a good teacher."

Drew knew who Michael was—everyone in the club did. He was one of the dungeon monitors. What Drew didn't understand was why Beth would want to talk to him. Then again, if he'd been paying attention to their conversation from the start, he would have had his answer.

"I probably should. Drew likes being bound and my experience with rope is limited."

He guessed that answered his question.

Allison lifted her drink to her lips with one hand and ran her nails down John's back with the other. He closed his eyes and let out a hum of contentment. "Haven't you ever seen one of Michael's demonstrations? The man is a true artist."

"No. My . . ." Beth paused. "My previous sub wasn't into rope bondage."

Unease seem to hang in the air for a moment before Allison spoke again. "That's too bad. John has come to enjoy it immensely, haven't you?"

"Yes, Mistress." There was almost a longing in his friend's voice, and Drew wondered if Allison and John would be heading upstairs before the night was over.

The topic of conversation soon shifted from bondage to some television show. Drew lost interest, closed his eyes again, and went back to enjoying the moment. Beth's fingers were hypnotic. It had been a long week, and he felt himself drifting.

"Drew?"

He glanced up. Beth looked worried about something. "What's wrong?"

"I was going to ask you the same thing."

Drew grinned. "I'm fine. More than fine."

She caressed the side of his face, and he leaned into her touch. "I take it you like sitting on the floor at my feet?"

"Yes. John was right. It's liberating." Speaking of John, he was no longer on the floor beside Drew. Allison was gone as well. When had that happened?

Beth bent down and brushed her mouth over his. "I quite like you there myself." She held his gaze and ran the tip of her tongue along the seam of his lips. He opened willingly.

By the time she broke the kiss, the position Drew was in was becoming uncomfortable. His erection was stretching his jeans to the limit.

She lowered her gaze, and he knew she could see how painfully hard he was. "Stay with me tonight."

Although it hadn't been phrased as a question, he knew he had the option. He could always say no. Even if he said yes, there was no guarantee they would have sex. Granted, since this wasn't one of his four days off, he could jack off, but that wasn't even close to what he wanted. It had been four days since he'd felt his cock inside her pussy. If there was the slightest chance that he would get to make love to her, he would take it. "I'll have to stop by my apartment to get some clothes for tomorrow."

Beth kicked off her shoe and brought her foot to rest on top of the bulge in his pants. He sucked in a breath as she started moving her foot in a back and forth motion.

"I'm sorry I ran away."

What? What was she . . .

"I should have stayed in the tent until you woke up."

Drew closed his eyes and tried to concentrate on what she was saying and not what she was doing to his appendage. "It's okay. I-I understand."

She increased the pressure slightly and he opened his eyes. "That's no excuse and I want you to know that I'm sorry."

"B—" He caught himself, but just barely. "Mistress? Please?"

Her breath tickled his ear, only adding to his arousal. "Please what?"

"You're . . . if you keep it up, I'm going to come." He hated to admit it, but it was the truth.

"And would you like that? To come here in front of all these people?"

He took a deep breath, trying to clear his head enough to give her an honest answer. "I don't know."

Beth licked his ear and removed her foot.

Drew stared up at her, not sure if he should be grateful or not that she'd stopped.

She grinned down at him and grazed the side of his face with her fingertips. "Think about it and let me know."

Swallowing, he nodded. It was like with the kneeling. Drew knew what she had done should embarrass the hell out of him. If they'd been anywhere else it would have, he was sure of it. But this wasn't just anywhere. This was a kink club and it wasn't as if he hadn't witnessed subs being made to come before. It didn't happen often on the main floor but Drew had seen it. On his third visit, he observed a female submissive who had been made to wear a chastity device with vibrating dildos filling both her pussy and her ass. Her Dom was able to control it remotely and had spent the entire night turning it off and on.

"And what are you thinking about?" Beth asked.

There was no reason to lie. At the time he'd felt kind of bad for the woman, but now, seeing it from the other side, he wasn't sure if he should have. "I was remembering seeing a sub being made to come here at the club."

Beth's smile grew wider, but she didn't comment.

They didn't stay long after that. It was already after ten and they both had to be up early the next morning. As they walked out of the club, Drew tried to ignore the fact that he was still hard as a rock. Following Beth out and watching her backside swaying side to side in that tight skirt of hers wasn't helping.

Somehow he made it to his apartment, ran inside to grab what he'd need for work the next day, and got back out to his car in under two minutes. Beth knew what was on his mind. She had to. The evidence was front and center for anyone to see.

When they turned onto her street, Beth instructed him to pull his car into her driveway. Normally he parked on the street at the curb, but he wasn't going to argue.

She reached into her purse, and the next thing he knew her garage door was opening. "You can park alongside me."

He shot her a quick glance, and then maneuvered his vehicle in beside hers.

Before he could put the car in park, Beth removed her seat belt and pushed the button to close the garage door. She waited until he shifted gears and turned off the engine before turning in her seat. "Take your seat belt off and push your seat back as far as it will go."

Chapter Thirty

Drew hesitated and Beth wasn't sure if he was going to do as instructed. Then he reached down and released the lever allowing him to push his seat all the way back. Smiling, she hiked her skirt up around her waist and climbed on top of his lap, straddling him. He placed his hand on her hips to stabilize her when she began sucking on his neck and moving her hips.

"Maybe . . . maybe we should go inside."

"No." She snaked her hand down the front of his shirt until she reached his waistband. "I want you, and I want you now."

He leaned his head back, giving her better access to his neck. "I want you, too, but . . ."

She scraped her teeth over his earlobe as she began working him free of his jeans. "But?"

He groaned and moved his hands down to her legs. Slowly, he started working his way higher until the tips of his fingers were brushing her inner thighs. It was getting hard to concentrate, but there was something she needed him to know first before they went any further. As much as it scared her, Beth knew she needed to own up to her feelings. He'd been nothing but honest and he deserved the same from her.

Taking a deep breath, she grazed the tips of her fingers over the head of his cock and went for it. "I love you."

It took a minute, but she knew exactly when what she'd said registered.

Drew froze. The hands that had, moments before, been close to touching the part of her that was wet and throbbing for him were now motionless.

Beth's heart skipped a beat as she waited for his reaction.

Drew turned his head so he could see her. He searched her face and then looked into her eyes. "Say it again."

It wasn't a command. More of a pleading request.

She swallowed nervously, but held his gaze. "I love you."

Doubt flickered across his face. "Beth, please don't say it unless you really mean it. I don't want you to feel . . ."

Beth placed her index finger over his lips and he stopped talking. "I was talking to Katrina tonight and I realized something. When I overheard you telling your dad that you loved me and wanted to spend the rest of your life with me, I was overcome with fear. Fear that it was too soon. That if we admitted how important we were to each other after such a short time then the heartbreak would be even worse when it fell apart." She paused. "But she reminded me that love takes as long as it takes. It doesn't always follow the timetable we think it should."

Removing her finger from over his mouth, she caressed the side of his face. "I'm still scared out of my wits, but you deserve to know how I feel. That I'm emotionally invested in this relationship, too."

His lips curled up in a smile. "I never doubted your commitment, Beth. Never."

She smiled. "Thank you for that."

They sat grinning at each other, enjoying the moment, until he shifted beneath her, drawing her attention back to their current position. Beth's hand was still tucked down the front of his pants and she was still straddling him with her skirt up around her waist.

With a mischievous glint in her eye, she used her free hand to reach between them and push her panties out of the way. "Push your jeans down. I want your cock inside me and I don't want to wait until we get inside."

He swiftly moved to obey. Even in the confines of his vehicle, it didn't take him more than a few seconds to push his pants down around his thighs. His erection popped free and Beth's mouth watered. If they had more space, she would have gone down on him first. As it was, there just wasn't room. Plus, after opening herself up to him like she had, she really needed to feel him inside her.

Drew scooted down some to help with the angle as she positioned herself over his cock. She lowered herself down a little at a time, holding her breath as he filled her. When he was finally in all the way, they stared at each other. This was different. It felt different. Yet it was familiar at the same time. She recognized it for what it was, and also that never once had she felt this way with Ben.

Moisture pooled in her eyes and tumbled down her cheeks. Drew wiped the tears away as they fell. It was such a loving gesture and it only made her flood of emotion worse.

"What is it? Am I hurting you? Is the angle wrong?"

His voice was full of anxiety. She knew she had to do something, so she pressed her mouth against his. He kissed her back even though she knew he was bewildered.

Beth opened her eyes and met his gaze, her lips hovering a breath away from his. "Nothing's wrong. In fact, right now I'm pretty close to perfect."

A lightbulb seemed to go off in his head and he captured her mouth once more in a kiss—this one more passionate than the last—and pulled her against him. Beth could have chastised him or pushed him away, but instead she went with it, kissing him back with an equal amount of enthusiasm.

Gradually, their lower bodies seemed to get with the program and they began grinding against each other. Beth moved her hands under his shirt as she rocked her hips. She felt as if she couldn't get close enough.

Drew seemed to feel the same way. His hands were constantly in motion along her back, ass, and legs. It only drove the flames higher. She was quickly racing toward her climax. Part of her yearned to reach that peak, but there were other parts that didn't want it to end. Beth wanted to stay like this for as long as possible.

They kept kissing and touching. She had no idea how long it went on, but eventually the orgasm knocking at her door was impossible to ignore. Tilting her hips forward slightly, she increased the pressure against her clit with every downward movement. Drew caught on to what she was after and splayed one of his hands on her hip, helping to guide her movements.

As she got closer, she stared into his eyes, doing her best to match her breathing with his. "Breath with me. Come with me."

It was something Beth had read about, synchronizing your breathing with your partner's. She'd tried it once before—with Ben—but he'd never quite gotten it. Drew, however, followed her instructions perfectly. When she inhaled, he did. And when she exhaled, Beth felt his warm breath blow across her moist lips.

Everything else fell away as they moved. She'd always felt a connection with Drew, but this seemed to amplify it. Slowly they climbed, inching toward the finish. When she felt that tightening in her belly, she gasped and his breathing stuttered as well. It was coming, and Beth could tell it was going to be intense. She anchored herself, digging her fingers into his shoulders.

"Beth."

Her name came out as little more than a whisper, but there was so much emotion behind it. Her legs began to shake. Then her arms. It was as if the energy could no longer be contained and was leaking out through her limbs.

Beth's orgasm hit her with a force she'd never imagined to be possible. She screamed, needing to let it out and unable to keep it inside even if she'd tried.

Somewhere in the mental chaos, Beth felt a spasm work its way through Drew's body, but it was only when she floated back to earth that she realized they'd done it. They'd climaxed together, or pretty close to it anyway, and it had been better than she imagined.

Her heart was still pounding in her chest, so she buried her face in the curve of his neck until she was fairly sure she could speak normally again. "Wow."

"Yeah. *Wow.*"

His hands roamed up and down her back, making her feel completely safe and content. It was too bad they would have to go inside soon.

❧

IF NOT FOR THE CRAMPED POSITION, DREW COULD HAVE STAYED THERE IN his car with Beth on his lap all night. That and the fact that he could feel the evidence of their activities leaking down the inside of his leg.

"We should go inside, but I don't want to move," she said.

Instinctively, he held her closer. "I don't either."

Beth was quiet for several moments. "I meant what I said earlier."

He knew what she was referring to and he grinned. "I know."

After a few more minutes, Beth sighed, and climbed back over to her side of the vehicle. He looked down at his lap and, even in the dim light, he knew that he was going to need a shower.

She rearranged her clothes enough to be decent, and leaned over to kiss him. "Now every time you get into your car for the next few days you're going to be reminded of what we just did."

Tangling his fingers in her hair at the base of her neck, he gazed into her eyes. "I'm not sure I'll ever be able to forget that."

She smiled. "Good."

He waited until she exited the car before reaching into the back to get his bag. By the time he got out of the car, she was already inside. Drew waited at the bottom of the stairs while she walked through the downstairs, making sure the house was locked up for the night, and then followed her to the second floor.

As much as he wanted to ask her to join him in the shower, he didn't. It was edging closer and closer to midnight. Her alarm would go off at five. While he couldn't seem to get enough of Beth, Drew also knew that they both needed their sleep.

After toweling off, he didn't bother to put any clothes on as he made his way back into Beth's bedroom. She was turned on her side, facing away from him. The only part of her he could see clearly was the back of her head and the tops of her shoulders.

It wasn't until he was about to get into bed that he realized she was already asleep. He pulled back the covers and slipped under the blanket. Beth must have felt the movement because she rolled over.

Trying not to wake her, Drew positioned himself as carefully as possible. He thought he'd been successful until he felt her move again—this time she migrated closer to him. Her hand grazed his abdomen before sliding back down on the bed.

Drew lifted her hand—her left hand—and kissed her ring finger. After tonight, he was hoping that one day in the not too distant future she'd agree to marry him. Hearing her say that she loved him had warmed him down to his toes. He just needed to be patient.

He brushed the hair away from her face, and she released a contented sigh. Drew laid his head on his pillow and gently rubbed his thumb along her cheek. "I love you, Beth Davenport. I will burn for you for the rest of my days. All you have to do is say the word and I'm yours forever."

Lowering his hand, he closed his eyes and let sleep claim him.

When the alarm woke him the next morning, he felt the mattress shift under her weight as she reached up to the nightstand to turn it off. Blinking, he opened his eyes and was greeted with the most amazing view of her backside. "Now, that's something I could get used to seeing every morning."

Beth glanced over her shoulder and quirked an eyebrow at him.

He circled his arm around her waist and tugged her down on top of him. Palming her ass, Drew pressed his morning wood against her stomach. She looked so beautiful with her hair all mussed from sleep, which did nothing to help the state he found himself in.

"What do you think you're doing?" There was laughter in her eyes so he knew he wasn't in too much trouble.

"Getting my hands on your delectable ass." He gave her derriere a squeeze.

"Yes, well, this is the only way you're going to be getting your hands on this ass for the next twenty-four hours if we don't get a move on."

Drew groaned.

Beth laughed and extracted herself from his greedy hands. "Think you could use another shower this morning?"

It took only a second for him to realize what she was offering, and less time than that for him to jump out of bed.

She chuckled.

"Did you really think I'd pass up a chance to see you naked and wet?" he asked.

Lifting her tank top over her head, she tossed it into the hamper. His gaze immediately went to her tits. She knew what she was doing, of course, and smirked as she pushed the shorts she'd worn to bed down her legs.

He swallowed. His cock was standing at full attention.

She bent down to pick the clothing up from the floor, making sure she turned enough for him to get a good view of her backside. His erection pulsed and he clenched his fists together. If she kept this up, he wasn't sure he would be able to control himself.

Luckily, she must have realized he was hanging on by a thread because she strolled over to stand in front of him. "Do you like?"

"Very much."

She took hold of his cock and he closed his eyes. "If we had more time, I'd make you earn your release."

Why did the thought of that turn him on so much? "Yes, Mistress."

Beth ran the pad of her thumb over the head of his penis until it began leaking pre-cum. His breathing was already starting to become labored. He was so turned on. It wouldn't take much to send him over the edge. He closed his eyes, enjoying the feel of her hand on him . . . and then she was gone.

Drew opened his eyes and saw she was halfway across the room.

"Are you coming?" she asked.

He moved as fast as his feet would carry him into the bathroom behind her. Whether he came or not would be up to Beth. As they stepped into the enclosure, Drew realized that he hadn't masturbated since that first night with her. He hadn't had any desire to do so.

That wasn't entirely true. Pretty much every time he thought about Beth he ended up aroused. It was a given. The difference was that on some level, he didn't feel it was his right anymore. His body belonged to her as much as his heart did.

Water cascaded down on them and he reached for her loofah and body wash. It had become an unspoken rule between them that when they showered together, he would wash her. Only once had that not happened due to a lack of time and afterward, he'd longed for another opportunity so he could worship her body the way she deserved.

"A penny for your thoughts?" she asked as he ran the sponge up the inside of her thigh.

Drew grinned. "I was thinking about how much I enjoy this. Washing you."

She stepped closer, trapping his hand between them. "So do you like getting dirty or clean better?" Her mouth hovered over the pulse in his neck and he willed her to use her teeth.

"Both."

Beth hummed and sucked the beating flesh into her mouth. He groaned and dropped the sponge in favor of grasping her hips. She wrapped her leg around his waist and he moved his left hand to support her leg.

"Do you want me?" she asked, her teeth worrying his skin.

She raked her nails down his back and he gasped. "Yes."

The next thing he knew, she was anchoring her arms around his neck and pulling herself up. Instinct kicked in and Drew cupped her ass, bringing her in line with his erection.

"Put your cock inside me and show me what it is you want."

He didn't need to be told twice. Turning them, he used the shower wall as support and lined himself up with her entrance. Feeling her muscles contract around him as he pushed inside made him feel as if he'd died and gone to heaven. It was truly a spiritual experience.

Doing as she'd asked, he dug his fingers into her ass and thrust his hips upward. Beth clung to him as he pounded into her against the wall. Soon he was sweating and it had nothing to do with the steam coming off the shower.

Beth must have been as primed as he was because it didn't take long before she reached between them and began rubbing her clit.

"I love it when you do that."

She gripped the back of his neck hard. "You like knowing I'm pleasuring myself?"

"Yes." It was all he could do to hold on to his sanity knowing he was fucking her up against a wall while she was trying to make herself come.

Drew thought he felt her grin, but he wasn't sure. Her fingers were forked so that with each thrust, she rubbed him and her clit at the same time. He could feel his balls tightening.

Then, without warning, she threw her head back and released a loud moan as she reached her climax. He felt her muscles hug his cock and watched her face turn a bright shade of red.

He clenched his jaw, waiting, hoping she would give him permission to come. As he waited, he kept up a steady movement, not sure if he should stop or keep going. Finally, she met his gaze. There was something in her expression that he didn't like.

"Let me down."

Drew guessed that was his answer. He shouldn't be surprised. She'd let him orgasm every time they'd had sex so far. He knew sooner or later, she'd decide otherwise.

Once her feet were back on the ground, Drew tried his best to calm himself down. That was until she shocked the hell out of him with her next command. "Use your hand. I want to see you make yourself come for me."

She was serious, so after a moment, he reached down and took his cock in his right hand. Beth picked up the loofah, giving him another stellar view of her butt. He groaned and increased his pace. At this rate, it wouldn't take him long. He'd been on the edge when he'd been inside her.

With the sponge in hand, Beth began washing the evidence of their morning activities from her body. She made a show of it, teasing him. Man, he loved her.

When she reached between her legs, that was it for him. He came with a grunt, spilling his cum on the tile below his feet.

Getting out of the shower several minutes later, Beth handed him a towel. "Next time maybe you'll rethink molesting me first thing in the morning."

He was confused. Then again, he wasn't sure all the blood had made it back to his head yet. "Why?"

Beth wound a towel around her head and used another on her body. "Cocky boys don't get to come inside their mistresses. Remember that," she said as she strolled out of the bathroom.

Drew was left speechless for a moment, and then he laughed. He doubted life with Beth would ever be predictable, and he was perfectly okay with that.

Chapter Thirty-One

Beth managed to make it to work on time. How, she didn't know. Sex in the shower had taken longer than anticipated, but she and Drew had worked together to make breakfast and she was able to get out the door in record time. That was good because she had plans for her evening and she didn't want to be stuck at work any later than she needed to be.

Granted, that was happening less and less since Beth had hired Grace. She was a good worker. A little shy, but polite and more than competent. In her short time at the café, Beth had learned that Grace had lost her husband about six months ago. He was a soldier killed overseas. Beth hadn't gotten any details. She wasn't sure Grace could have held it together long enough to give them to her.

The woman in question walked into the kitchen with an empty tray. "We ran out of blueberry muffins."

Nodding, Beth motioned toward the sink. "It's too late in the day to make any more. That's the second time this week, though. I might have to reconsider how many we're making each day."

Grace did as instructed and then joined Beth at the counter. "Tommy says things are slowing down out there so he doesn't need me."

"Okay. Well, why don't you go check on the customers and then you can start getting things cleaned up back here. Maybe we can all get out of here a little early today."

Things worked in their favor, and they were able to get everything cleaned and closed down before three o'clock. Having a third person made a huge difference.

As Beth was leaving the cafe, her cell phone rang. She looked at the caller ID, but didn't recognize the number. It was local, though, and just in case it was Drew, she answered. "Hello?"

"Hello, Beth. It's Seth Parker. Drew's brother. I was hoping I could speak with you."

Beth wasn't sure she wanted to talk to Drew's brother after the way he'd been the weekend before, but she had to admit she was curious. "Okay. Go ahead."

"I'd rather talk in person."

Her defenses went up. "Your brother's working today, but I'm sure we could arrange—"

"I'd prefer it be just the two of us, if you didn't mind. I'm out in front of your business now if you have time."

He was here? Now? She glanced over her shoulder expecting him to magically appear, but no one was there. "All right. Give me ten minutes and I'll meet you out front."

She hung up the phone and turned around to find Tommy standing there. "Everything, okay?"

"Yeah. Everything's fine. You ready to go?" she asked.

They walked out the back door and she locked it behind her. Tommy climbed in his car, and she waved goodbye to him as he drove off. Grace had an appointment at three she couldn't reschedule, so Beth had sent her home as soon as they'd closed since they were caught up.

Beth waited until Tommy's car was out of sight before getting into her vehicle and driving around to the front of the building. Seth was there, leaning up against the ledge of one of the café's large windows. She parked along the curb and climbed out to see what he wanted.

"I was hoping I'd catch you before you closed but I had a meeting that ran late," he said, pushing away from the building.

He looked like an older version of Drew, but the way he carried himself was quite different. Drew could act full of himself sometimes, but he was also very approachable. Beth imagined Seth went after what he wanted and didn't take no for an answer. A profitable skill for a lawyer, no doubt, but completely undesirable in a mate as far as Beth was concerned.

"What can I do for you?" Beth figured it was better to cut to the chase.

"I'm told I owe you an apology."

That surprised her.

Clearly, her shock showed on her face because he continued. "After you left, both my parents laid into me about how rude I'd been to you. And then my brother called to harass me as well."

Drew had called him? When?

"I guess he didn't tell you that."

"No. He didn't." Beth wasn't sure if that was a good thing or not, but she wasn't going to let that sidetrack her. "So you came to apologize because your parents and your brother told you to?"

Seth grinned. "No. But I think you already know that."

She did. Seth didn't strike her as someone who bowed to pressure from anyone, even his family.

"I'm here because I wanted to see for myself if you were who you said you were."

"What's that supposed to mean? Who exactly did you think I was?"

He put his hands in his pockets. "I didn't know. That was the point. I didn't even know you'd be there until I walked into the kitchen and found you sitting at my mom's table."

"So what you're trying to tell me is that because my presence surprised you, you decided to be a jerk."

"You don't pull any punches, do you?" Seth chuckled. "I can see why Drew likes you."

Beth wasn't sure if she should be flattered or not.

"I do apologize if I acted like a jerk. Drew hasn't had the best history with women and it worried me when he'd suddenly brought one home to meet us. I wanted to make sure you weren't taking advantage of him."

As good as that sounded, Beth wasn't sure she believed him. "You were trying to protect your brother? Don't you think he's old enough to do that on his own?"

"You'd think so, wouldn't you, but my baby brother tends to see the best in people."

Beth knew there had to be a story there, but quite frankly, she didn't care. Her relationship with Drew was none of Seth's business. "If you have an issue with your brother being with me then you need to talk to him."

"Oh, I have. As a matter of fact, I just came from there. He wouldn't hear any of it. Told me to mind my own damn business." Beth sensed a level of pride there. She wasn't sure she would ever understand Seth Parker.

"Maybe you should listen to him."

Seth opened his mouth to comment, but someone came around the corner and cut him off. "Having an afternoon rendezvous? Is this your new boy-toy, then?"

She spun around to find Ben striding toward them. He looked determined, and Beth knew there was little chance she'd be able to get rid of him this time without allowing him to say his piece. "What are you doing here, Ben?"

"I came to talk to you." He looked Seth up and down. "Is this him? I heard you were with someone new."

Drew's brother didn't flinch. He stared Ben down with a level of contempt that had been missing from her first encounter with Seth. "And you are?"

"I'm her ex."

Seth crossed his arms over his chest and she had to admit it made him much more intimidating. "If you're her ex, then why are you here demanding to know who she's having a conversation with outside of her own restaurant?"

"That's none of your business," Ben snapped.

"Since you've barged into our discussion, you've made it my business." Seth never raised his voice. He was chillingly calm.

Ben continued to stare at Seth until he realized it wasn't going to get him anywhere and refocused his attention on Beth. "This is a waste of time. I need to talk to you."

"So you said." She sighed. "Go ahead. I'm listening."

He glanced over at Seth. "Alone."

She opened her mouth, but Seth interrupted her. "No. If you have something to say to her, then you can say it here in front of me. Otherwise, be on your way."

Ben got a smug look on his face. "Fine. Amy decided that I needed to see a sex therapist. It was the only way I could keep her from walking out on me after she found out about you and me."

Beth felt Seth stiffen beside her, but otherwise he didn't react.

"I'm supposed to confront my addiction and that included tracking you down and telling you that . . ." He glanced over at Seth and then back to her. "That letting you do those things to me was a way for me to get back at my wife. That was all it ever was."

She blinked. "Anything else?"

Ben looked to be considering his next words.

Seth must have picked up on the same thing she did. Ben was out to hurt her, embarrass her, or maybe a little of both. "I think you've said enough. You can leave now."

"Pfft." Ben rolled his eyes and took a step back toward the alley. "Good riddance. I did what I said I'd do. I hope you have fun with your new plaything while I'm having a *real relationship* with my wife."

With those parting words, he was gone. He disappeared around the corner, presumably to the back of the building where she'd been not long ago. Beth wondered if he'd planned to ambush her when she left the café or if he was planning to follow her home. Neither sat well with her.

"So that was your ex?" Seth asked.

"Yes. Unfortunately." At that moment, Beth realized that any feelings she'd had for Ben were long gone. She'd been able to view his words for what they were—an attack. He was angry he was being made to jump through hoops to save his marriage and he was lashing out. It didn't look like therapy was working. Then again, it only worked if the person committed to the process. Ben had proven that commitment wasn't one of his strong suits.

"Want to explain?" Seth asked.

"No." Explaining the meaning behind what Ben had said to Seth, someone who already didn't seem to care for her, was the last thing she wanted. Beth was starting to think that she and Drew had a real future together and she didn't want to create any more bumps in the road with his family than she had to. "If there isn't anything else, I have things to do tonight."

She began heading toward her car.

"Hot date?"

"No. I'm meeting a friend at a club. The only hot dates I have these days are with your brother and you already know he's working." She waited until she was at her car before addressing him again. "In case you didn't pick up on it, my ex is a vindictive, manipulative bastard. I think that is all you need to know."

Not giving Seth a chance to respond, she climbed into her car and drove away.

Beth was pulling onto her street when her phone rang. Not wanting to deal with Ben or Seth again, she made sure to check the caller ID. When she saw Drew's name on the screen, the stress of the last half hour disappeared. "Hello, handsome."

He laughed. "Hello. You sound like you're in a good mood."

Pulling into the driveway, she maneuvered her car into the garage. "I am now."

She heard some noise in the background and then movement. "Sorry. I'm upstairs trying to get some privacy, but that doesn't seem to have worked out very well."

"Don't worry about it."

"Anyway, I called to let you know that you might be getting a visit from my brother. He stopped by earlier today."

"I know," she said. "He's already been to see me."

A muffled sound came through the phone that almost sounded like a grunt. "I'm sorry. I was going to call you as soon as he left but a call came in and I couldn't."

Beth shook her head even though he couldn't see. "Don't worry about it. I can handle your brother."

"I have no doubt. Even so, I know he can be a pain in the ass when he has a bug up his butt about something."

She loved that Drew was feeling protective of her, but in this case, he didn't need to be. "Your brother may never approve of us, and I'm okay with that as long as you are."

"Seth's opinion doesn't matter to me."

"He's your brother." Beth felt the need to point that out. Especially considering that Seth was there to hear Ben's rant.

"And you're the woman I love." There it was. Right there. Her chest clenched and she felt moisture fill her eyes. When Drew said he loved her, she knew he meant it. The words weren't just window dressing or said because he thought it was what she wanted to hear.

"I love you, too."

This time she did hear an unmistakable groan come through the phone. "I wish I could hold you right now."

"Will you come over tomorrow morning? We can sleep in. Maybe even spend the entire day in bed."

"You're on."

Beth grinned, but then she remembered that there was something else she needed to tell him. "Drew, something else happened today you should know about. While I was talking to your brother, Ben showed up."

Drew didn't comment for a few moments and she wondered if he was working to control his temper. Ben wasn't one of his favorite subjects—nor hers—for obvious reasons. "What did he have to say?"

She was surprised that Drew sounded rational. If she didn't know any better, she would have thought they were having a conversation about where to meet for coffee. "His wife is making him go to therapy and part of that was him confronting the people in his past. I'm guessing he was supposed to apologize and explain why he did what he did, but of course it didn't come out that way."

"He upset you." Beth could hear the anger in his voice. He was controlling it, but just barely.

"Not as much as you'd think. Honestly, I'm more concerned with Seth's reaction. Ben thought your brother was my new 'boy-toy.' Seth now knows that I dated a married man and that he let me 'do things to him'. Ben wasn't specific, luckily, but I'm sure your brother can use his imagination."

Drew didn't respond.

"You still there?" she asked.

"Yes." She imagined he was counting to ten. "Don't worry about Seth. If he says anything else, just tell him to come talk to me."

"I already did."

"Good." Drew sighed. "This is so hard. I want to be there right now to comfort you."

"I'm fine. Really. Regarding Ben? Well, seeing him again made me realize that he no longer has any hold over me. I've moved on and I've found a much better man to spend my time with."

"Yeah?" She was almost positive he was smiling.

"Yeah."

"Parker!"

"Coming!" Drew yelled back to whoever had called his name. "Sorry. I've got to go."

"I'll see you in the morning. I love you."

"I love you, too."

Then he was gone and something she'd been tossing around in her mind came to the forefront once again. Deciding to go with it, she dialed Nicole's number.

"Need something to keep you busy while your man's working?"

"Hello to you, too."

Nicole laughed.

"Do you have some time this afternoon? I could use your help with something," Beth said.

"Sure. What do you need?"

"I'd like your help picking out a collar for Drew. I want it to be something he can wear at all times." Nicole would know what he was allowed to wear and what he wasn't. Beth didn't want to buy something that he would have to take off whenever he went to work.

"I need to finish what I'm working on, and then I can come over. Say about an hour from now?"

"See you then."

Beth hung up the phone and headed into the house. She spent the next hour straightening the upstairs and making sure her bedroom was in order. Sunday began another four days off for Drew and she planned to make them memorable.

A little before five there was a knock on her front door. She went to greet Nicole. If they were going to get both a collar for Drew and make it to the club that night, they needed to get going.

Two hours later, Beth was in possession of Drew's new collar. To the casual observer it looked like a regular watch. Nicole had informed Beth that the only two pieces of jewelry he would be allowed to wear were a wedding ring and a watch. That narrowed down her choices considerably. In the end, however, she'd found the perfect watch and had the back plate engraved. A symbol of their relationship would be pressed against his wrist whenever he wore it.

With that objective accomplished, Beth and Nicole went their separate ways agreeing to meet back up at the club. Beth ran upstairs and tucked the watch in her top drawer before getting ready for a night at the club. Since Drew wasn't going to be there with her, she opted for a pair of black jeans and a nice top. She wasn't out to impress anyone and she needed to be comfortable.

Nicole and Jeff were already there when Beth arrived. She stopped to say hi to the two of them and then excused herself to go find Michael. He was a master at rope work and she wanted to see if he'd teach her something. Drew loved to be bound and she wanted the night she collared him to be special.

She found Michael, who also happened to be one of the club's dungeon monitors, upstairs outside room number four. He was watching Daniel flog someone. She thought she recognized the sub, but she couldn't be sure since her head was down.

Michael acknowledged her arrival. He also noticed she was alone. "Flying solo tonight?"

"Drew's working."

"Ah." He turned his attention back to the scene in front of him. Considering Daniel was one of the more experienced Doms in the club, Beth knew Michael wasn't watching for safety reasons. "So what brings you upstairs without a sub in tow? You never were much of a voyeur."

It was true. The only time she came upstairs to watch was when she wanted to learn something new. "No. I was looking for you, actually."

He turned to face her. "I'm flattered. What can I do for you?"

"I was hoping you could help me with some rope bondage. Drew likes to be bound and while I can do some simple wrist ties, I was hoping maybe you could show me something a little more involved."

A huge grin spread across Michael's face. "Sure. Let's see if we can find an open room."

Chapter Thirty-Two

Drew worked alongside his crew to clean the truck and make sure everything was stocked and ready to go for the next run. It had been a busy shift. Both lunch and dinner had been interrupted by calls. It was a good thing it was Sunday, otherwise they'd be scrambling to get the daily maintenance finished.

His brother's appearance that afternoon had been unexpected. Why he was so concerned about Drew's relationship with Beth was a mystery. It wasn't as if Seth had ever taken a great interest in the women Drew dated before.

Although his conversation with Seth, and his brother's subsequent visit with Beth, irritated Drew, it had nothing on what he was feeling toward Beth's ex. Fury ran through his limbs as he washed the windshield of the fire truck.

"I don't know what the windshield did to you, but I'm sure it didn't mean it."

He looked down to find Shawn standing there with his hands on his hips. Drew sighed and wiped off the last of the solution he'd applied before hopping down. "Stressful day."

"I can see that. Want to talk about it?" Shawn asked.

"Not really." Talking about it wasn't going to help. What he really wanted to do was punch something—preferably Ben's face. Since that wasn't an option . . .

Shawn was quiet for a moment. "You almost done here? I was thinking of trying to get a workout in if you wanted to join me."

Rolling his shoulders, Drew thought that might be the best idea he'd heard all day. He needed to release some of his pent-up energy. "Give me ten minutes."

Nodding, Shawn left Drew to finish his work. Luckily, most everything was done. His crew had finished washing down the truck and all their gear was cleaned and in place. The only thing he had left to do was check in with them and make sure there were no issues from the previous run to go over. Irwin had some problems getting the hose hooked up and Drew wanted to see if there was a way to keep it from happening in the future. In a fire, seconds counted.

He found all the members of his crew huddled together at the back of the truck. "Hey, Cap."

Something was going on. "What are you knuckleheads up to?"

"Not a thing," Romeo said.

Yeah. Drew didn't buy that for a minute, but he decided to ignore their strange behavior. "I wanted to talk about what happened with the hose connection today."

Irwin spoke up. "Not much to tell. Looked like some kids had been messing with it or something. I had a hard time getting the cap off."

"What do you mean? What was wrong with it?" Drew asked.

"Someone must have been trying to pry it open with something and whatever it was got wedged in there. The only way to get the cap off was to dig it out." Irwin shrugged.

Drew nodded. "I'll brief Chief Franks on the issue. I think I remember one of the other crews saying they had a problem with a hydrant recently as well. In the future, if you can't get whatever it is out after a few seconds use the sledgehammer. Anything else?"

Baily cleared his throat. "Just one more thing."

"Yes?" Drew asked when Baily didn't automatically spit it out.

"We." Baily pointed to Romeo and Irwin. "We're wondering if your girlfriend was going to be stopping by tonight. You know. To say hi."

Drew guessed that answered his question on what they'd had their heads together about. Figures it was about his personal life and not work. "No. Beth isn't stopping by."

"Well, you know, if you needed to work off a little tension, we'd cover for you," Romeo said.

"Good to know you all would go through such a sacrifice for me." Drew strolled over to the cabinet and replaced the cleaning supplies he'd been using.

"See if you three can keep out of trouble for the next hour. I'll be in the gym if you need me."

He could hear them laughing as he left. They were good guys and a great crew. In all honesty, they probably didn't understand why he wasn't sharing details. He had in the past. Then again, his relationship with Beth was different. It had been from the start.

As promised, Shawn was waiting for him in the gym. They were alone. Apparently, no one else had felt the need to burn off any excess energy.

For the next forty-five minutes, Drew lifted weights, did leg presses, and spent some time on the treadmill. He was still angry, but at least he had it under control.

"Feel any better?" Shawn asked.

"Yeah. I do." His friend handed him a bottle of water and Drew downed most of it in one go. "How's the new apartment?"

"Quiet."

Drew nodded and followed Shawn into the showers. It was almost nine and things would be winding down. Considering the day they'd all had, Drew was guessing most of the guys would be crashing early tonight.

Freshly showered, he went to his desk and finished the paperwork on the small house fire they'd responded to earlier that day. Once that was completed, he placed the file on Chief Franks' desk and went to find a spot to read before going to bed.

By eleven o'clock, the station was quiet. Most of the guys were upstairs asleep or heading in that direction. Drew closed his book, tucked it under his arm, and began climbing the stairs.

He was halfway to the top floor when the intercom came to life. Drew froze and waited. You never knew if it was going to be an EMT-only call or if the trucks would be needed.

It wasn't meant to be. The dispatcher announced that a fire had been reported. Drew turned on his heels and made a beeline for the fire engine. He was still putting on his gear when the rest of the guys began filing into the bay. Less than a minute later, they were climbing into their trucks and driving away from the station.

Drew's crew pulled up to the building first, so he jumped out and began assessing the situation. Taking his radio with him, he jogged around the side of the building to get a look at the back. It was much the same as the front, unfortunately. The third floor appeared to be completely engulfed in flames.

Bringing his radio up, he relayed the information. "There's evidence of fire on sides A, B, C, and D. Request second alarm."

"Copy that. Dispatching additional trucks to your location."

By the time Drew made it back to the front of the building, everyone was in position and ready to go.

"Do we know if anyone is in the building?" Romeo asked as he came up beside Drew.

"No idea." He said it loud enough for everyone around him to hear. They all knew what that meant. They were going to have to go in and find out.

Shawn and his crew took the lead. When they first entered the building there was very little smoke. It wasn't until they came to the top of the second level that they began to encounter serious evidence of the fire. Drew and Romeo stayed on the second floor to look for anyone who might be inside while Shawn and Kelly continued on to the third floor.

As Drew began checking each of the rooms, an eerie feeling settled into his bones. The building was under construction. It was being renovated and it looked like apartments were going in. That meant the chances of there being people inside were slim, which was good. It also meant that it had the potential of being a target for the arsonist.

A shout came from up top and Drew and Romeo took off toward the noise. They ran up the stairs. As soon as Shawn saw them, he tilted his head toward the standpipe. "It's not working. We're going to have to get one of the ladders to feed us hose from the outside."

"On it," a voice came across the radio.

"Bring it to the second floor. I don't think we can get close enough to any of these windows on the third," Drew said.

The four of them hightailed it back downstairs and made it to the windows as the ladder was maneuvering up to the window. They pulled in two hoses. Shawn and Kelly took one, Drew and Romeo the other.

Out in the hallway, they met with the crew who'd searched the first floor. "All clear on one."

All six of them began their journey back up to the third floor. They could hear the water hitting the building from the outside. The aerial trucks must have arrived. That was good because this fire was a hot one. It only reinforced Drew's thoughts that this might be another fire courtesy of the arsonist.

It took a while to get the fire under control. Every time they thought they'd managed to get everything, they'd find another hot spot. It was a big building and unlike the others the arsonist had hit, this one was probably only a month or so from taking on tenants. Once the main fire was out, they had to go room to room to make sure there were no live embers.

Finally, they got the last of it and made their way back downstairs. When they reached the first floor, something caught their attention and they all turned. They couldn't see anything, but something or someone had made that noise. The first floor had been checked, so no one should have been down there.

"Hello?" Drew shouted into the darkness.

There was no answer, but they did hear what sounded like metal.

"We'll check it out," Shawn said. "You guys stay here."

Shawn and Kelly were halfway down the hall when the figure of a man appeared and bolted into one of the far rooms. Kelly took off after him.

"Kelly wait," Shawn yelled.

The rookie didn't listen. He took off after the guy and Shawn had no choice but to follow.

Drew clicked the switch on his radio. "We've got a civilian inside the building. Shawn and Kelly—"

The sound of an explosion ended the transmission. Drew and the other guys automatically ducked in reaction.

"Is everyone all right? What the hell happened in there?" came across the radio.

"No idea. We're gonna check it out. Shawn and Kelly are unaccounted for," Drew said.

"Were they anywhere near that explosion?"

Drew swallowed, trying not to think the worst. "Yes."

"I'm sending in the rapid intervention team."

By the time the RIT got there, Drew was already on his knees next to Shawn. His friend was unconscious. Drew checked for any major injuries, but couldn't find anything beyond some superficial wounds on his face from where his helmet had been knocked off. Chances were he had a concussion.

Romeo was beside him. The other team was checking on Kelly. It looked like the door had been rigged. When Kelly tried to follow the guy out, it had gone off. From what he could tell, Kelly's injuries were much worse than Shawn's were. Part of his jacket was torn and Drew could see and smell burnt flesh. Shawn had been collateral damage. Kelly had taken the bulk of the blast. The force of the explosion seemed to be concentrated near the door.

When he walked out of the building a few minutes later, the sun was coming over the horizon. They'd been at it all night.

Drew waited for the EMTs to load Shawn and Kelly into the ambulance and drive away with the sirens blaring before heading back to his truck and his crew. They had a couple of hours left in their shift and then he'd head over to the hospital to see how Shawn and Kelly were doing. It was a far cry from how he'd planned to spend his morning.

❧

SOMETHING FELT OFF. IT TOOK BETH A MOMENT TO REALIZE IT WAS BECAUSE she was alone in her bed. Drew had to work last night. The only saving grace was that he was coming over this morning.

Sighing, she turned her head to look at the clock beside her bed. Beth was shocked to see that it was almost nine o'clock. She sat up and glanced around the room. There was no sign of Drew or the duffel bag he always brought with him.

Beth flung the covers off her and went downstairs to check her cell. Maybe he'd gotten held up at work or something—at least, that's what she was hoping. She didn't want to consider it might be something else.

The first floor was as empty as the upstairs. She went to the kitchen and removed her phone from the charger. There was one text message.

Went to the hospital. Call you later.

Her heart began pounding in her chest and all the air from her lungs seemed to disappear. Was he hurt? Of course he was. Why else would he have gone to the hospital? She hit the call button and tried not to hyperventilate while she waited for him to pick up.

But he didn't pick up. The phone went straight to voice mail.

She hung up, not bothering to leave a message, and then berated herself for even trying to call. If he was being treated for an injury in the hospital, then he probably wouldn't be able to answer his phone.

Beth knew she needed to calm down and think rationally. If he'd sent the text message, then he couldn't have been that badly hurt, right? Then the thought crossed her mind that maybe he hadn't sent the message. Maybe he'd asked one of the guys he worked with to send it for him. Before she could talk herself into a panic attack, Beth called the only person she knew could help her.

"Isn't this supposed to be your day off?" Nicole yawned in her ear.

"I need your help."

Her friend must have picked up on how desperate Beth sounded. "What's wrong? What do you need?"

She took a deep breath and explained. "Drew was supposed to come over this morning, but instead I got a text saying he went to the hospital. I tried to call him back but he isn't answering. I need to know what's going on and I know if I call the station they won't tell me anything."

"Okay. Hold tight. I'll see what I can find out and call you back, okay?"

"Okay."

Beth paced while she waited. Nothing could happen to him. It couldn't. She'd just told him she loved him. They had so much more to experience together.

When the phone rang, she jumped. "Hello?"

"Drew's fine. He's not hurt." Nicole must have known those were the words Beth needed to hear most.

"Then why did he go to the hospital?"

"They were responding to a fire last night and two other guys were hurt. One was Drew's former captain."

Beth swallowed. "Shawn."

"Yeah." Nicole gave her a moment. "I didn't get all the details, but apparently something happened as they were exiting the building and two of the responding firefighters were injured. I got the impression that Drew, along with most of the other guys from that station, headed over to the hospital as soon as their shift was over."

"What hospital?" Although Nicole had assured her that he was all right, Beth needed to see it for herself.

It took her almost a half hour to get dressed and drive to the hospital where Shawn was being treated. She was still trying to convince herself that Drew wasn't the one hurt as she parked her car and headed into the emergency room waiting area.

If there had been any doubt that she had the right place, it disappeared as soon as she walked through the sliding doors. There had to be a dozen firefighters taking up various positions around the large room. All of them were still wearing their dark blue pants and polo shirts with the St. Louis Fire Department logo.

"Beth?"

Beth turned to her left and saw Drew striding toward her. She released a cleansing breath when she saw he was perfectly fine. "Drew."

He pulled her into his arms and held on tight. "Not that I'm not happy to see you, but what are you doing here? Didn't you get my text?"

She still hadn't let go of him. "Yes. I got your text. Your text that said you'd gone to the hospital."

Drew leaned back and searched her face. Then his gaze softened as he realized how she'd taken the message. "You thought it was me? That I'd been taken to the hospital?"

"Yes, you insufferable man." Beth wiped the moisture from her cheeks. "I've never been so scared in my life."

"Aw, Beth, I'm so sorry. I never meant to make you worry. It didn't occur to me that you'd take it to mean I'd gotten hurt."

She tried to pull herself together—everyone was watching them. "How's Shawn?"

"How did you . . ." He paused. "Nicole."

"Yeah. I didn't know what else to do when you didn't answer your phone, so I called her."

He rubbed his hands up and down her arms, still trying to comfort her. "The last we heard he was still unconscious, but stable. I think they're trying to get him a room now. Kelly, though . . . they took him upstairs for emergency surgery. He got beat up pretty bad by the explosion."

Drew guided her over to a set of chairs in the corner. The other firefighters left them alone, but she knew they were paying attention. She took hold of both his hands and gathered them into her lap. "I was scared. I thought . . ."

"I know. And I'm sorry. I promise next time to give a little more information when I text you."

Next time. Beth knew there would be a next time. With his line of work, it was inevitable.

"What are you thinking?" he asked.

"I'm thinking how hard this is going to be going through this for the rest of my life." He grew really still, and Beth looked up to see what was wrong. "What is it?"

"You said the rest of your life."

She hesitated. "I did, didn't I?"

"Yes. You did."

Beth flipped over one of his hands and traced the lines in his palm. "I'm not ready to get married yet, but I want you in my life, Drew Parker. And one day, hopefully not too long from now, I will be ready to walk down the aisle with you, and have a family with you . . . the whole nine yards."

A huge smile spread across his face, and before she knew what was happening he was kissing her—right there in the waiting room. It was only when a couple of the guys whistled that Drew pulled back. They were both breathing heavily. She never thought she would get a kiss like that in a hospital waiting room.

"I love you. I meant it. I'll wait as long as it takes for you to be ready," he vowed.

She caressed the side of his face. "I don't think it will take that long. You seem to have a way of breaking through all my defenses."

He kissed her again. "Good. I'll keep chiseling away."

Beth grinned. "But you have to promise me something."

"Anything."

"You have to do everything in your power to keep yourself safe. I don't think I could handle it if something ever happened to you."

Drew brushed his lips against hers. "You got it."

Chapter Thirty-Three

Beth pulled into her driveway and smiled when she saw Drew's car was already there. It had been ten days since she'd sat across from him in the emergency room and admitted that she wanted a future with him. She'd imagined going home after that and celebrating their new commitment with a long bout of kinky lovemaking. What actually happened was about as far removed as it could get.

Shawn didn't regain consciousness right away and Drew refused to leave his side until he did. She stayed with him as long as she could, but eventually he asked her to go home and get some rest. There really wasn't anything she could do there. All he was doing was sitting alongside his friend's bed waiting for him to wake up.

It took more than twenty-four hours, but eventually Shawn did open his eyes and start talking again. He had a concussion, of course. On top of that, they also found out that he'd dislocated his shoulder. Drew stayed with him at the hospital until he was released and then took him home. Since Shawn didn't have anyone else, Drew effectively moved in with his friend until he had to return to work. Even then, Drew checked on Shawn as much as he could, making sure he had everything he needed.

Needless to say, while he was watching over his friend, Drew and Beth hadn't spent much time together. They talked on the phone and sent text messages, but it wasn't enough. Not for him and certainly not for her. It scared her how much she needed him.

Parking her car and turning off the engine, she made her way toward the door that led into the house. Drew was staying with her for the next four days and she planned to make the most of every minute.

As she reached for the doorknob, she paused. Beth had a lot to be thankful for. Drew was safe and they were ready to start their future together—whatever that might be. Shawn was going to recover. He'd be on desk duty for a while, but from everything Drew had told her, that wouldn't keep him down for long.

Things hadn't gone so well for the other firefighter, James Kelly. He ended up having complications from his injuries and died in the hospital four days later. They'd attended the funeral. Drew had to work, but that hadn't mattered. All the guys from the station were there. The ones who were on duty showed up in their uniforms alongside their trucks. Beth met Drew at the gravesite, wanting to be there with him.

Taking a deep breath and pushing back the wave of emotion that was threatening, she opened the door and stepped inside. If all went right, she was planning to give Drew the watch she'd bought him tonight. She needed to feel that connection with him now more than ever. "Honey, I'm home."

Drew strolled out of the kitchen in nothing but one of her aprons. "You're early."

Beth chuckled and wrapped her arms around his waist, making sure to grab two handfuls of his bare behind. "And what do we have here?"

He smiled. "I wanted to surprise you. I'm making dinner."

"Hmm." She rose up on her tiptoes and gave him a lingering kiss.

"Do you like it?" he asked, glancing down at his attire. "I'm not sure it's much of a fashion statement."

She dropped her arms and motioned for him to turn around. When he did, he gave his tush a shake. Beth responded with a solid smack on the rounded flesh.

Drew reached for her hand and twisted them both around so that she was pressed flush against his front. She felt his arousal growing with every touch.

Raising an eyebrow, she ran a single finger down the side of his face. "Later."

His pupils dilated and darkened.

Beth grinned. "Dinner first."

He sighed dramatically and led her toward the kitchen. "I suppose it's only fitting. Me slaving away in the kitchen, serving you before I serve you in other ways."

Deciding to go with it, she strolled over to the kitchen table and made a show of sitting down in one of the chairs. "And what are you making your mistress this evening?"

Drew glanced over his shoulder before going back to chopping the vegetables. "Chicken enchiladas."

She sat and watched him for a few minutes. "Is it going to be a while before it's ready?"

He nodded. "At least another thirty minutes."

"I'm gonna go grab a shower, then." She waited until he'd laid the knife down before coming up behind him and reaching between his legs. He jerked and a few of the onions missed the skillet. "After dinner you're mine."

Beth could see the muscles in his throat move as he swallowed. "Yes, Mistress."

Leaving him alone, she climbed the stairs and ambled into her bedroom. Drew's duffel bag was near the door and she knew that was something else they needed to discuss. Beth wasn't ready for marriage yet, but she knew she wanted him with her. They would have to figure it out. Having him move in brought with it a whole other level of uncertainty, but whenever he wasn't around, her house felt empty. It hadn't been like that before.

She walked over to her dresser and opened the top drawer. Her gaze fell on the black case that held Drew's watch. Beth picked it up and placed it on the nightstand beside her bed. Then she stripped out of her work clothes and headed in to take a shower.

❧

Forty-five minutes later, Drew sat across from Beth at the kitchen table. When he'd placed the dish in front of her, Beth had told him to remove the apron and have a seat. Although Drew could have said no, he didn't want to. He'd ached for her this past week. He craved her companionship and her domination. If she told him to sit at her feet rather than at the table, he probably wouldn't bat an eye before complying.

"How was your day?" she asked as if he weren't sitting a few feet away from her in nothing but his birthday suit.

He shrugged. "I spent most of the day cleaning my apartment and doing laundry. Nothing terribly exciting. It made for a long day."

Beth shifted in her seat. She seemed suddenly nervous. "I wanted to ask you something."

Laying his fork down, he gave her his full attention.

When she didn't come out with it, he reached across the table and covered her hand with his. "It can't be all that bad."

He'd been trying to lighten the mood, and it seemed to have worked. She glanced up at him and gave him the smallest hint of a smile.

"No. It's not. But . . ." Beth sat up and took a deep breath. "I'd like you to move in with me."

Drew opened his mouth in shock. Whatever he'd been expecting her to say, it wasn't that. He'd thought it would be months before she was ready to consider them living together. Even still, he had to know what had prompted such a leap. "Are you sure? I told you that I'm willing to wait until you feel comfortable—"

"Yes. I'm sure." She met his gaze and although he could still tell she was nervous, there was something else there as well. "This house felt empty last week when you were gone. It feels like something is missing every time I come home and you're not here. I don't like not having you there beside me in bed at night. I want . . ." Beth took another cleansing breath and laced her fingers with his. "I want you here. With me."

Wow. He was flabbergasted and happier than he could put into words.

Obviously his stunned silence left her with the wrong impression. "You can say no. I know it's soon, but—"

"Yes."

She blinked. "What?"

He grinned and squeezed her hand. "I said yes. I'll move in with you."

"Are you sure?"

Drew chuckled. "Wasn't that my line?"

Her eyes twinkled with amusement. "Are you contradicting your mistress?"

Picking up her hand, he kissed the inside of her wrist. "Only when needed."

They both laughed before turning serious again. "So you're really going to move in?"

He nodded. "Only if you want me to."

"I do."

"Then I guess I'm moving in." He released her hand and they both went back to eating their dinner.

The rest of their meal was much of the same. She told him about her day at the café. Her new employee, Grace, was turning out to be a godsend. Beth was actually considering taking a day off during the week.

Once they were both finished, Beth told him to go upstairs and shower while she cleaned up. He was to meet her in her room in fifteen minutes wearing only a pair of jeans. The jeans threw him, but he did as she requested.

When he stepped into the room, the first thing he noticed was that the blanket chest that was normally at the end of her bed had been pushed against the wall. The next thing that caught his attention was that Beth was standing beside her nightstand. That might not seem all that unusual, but typically when they were about to play, she was at her dresser where she would have laid out the implements and toys she planned to use. He debated asking if something was wrong, but he held his tongue and waited. They were in her bedroom and it was during their agreed upon playtime. She called the shots. He'd have to be patient.

She turned around and pointed to a kneeling pad on the floor. He'd seen them at the club plenty of times, but he'd never used one. Whenever he'd knelt before Beth, he'd always done so with his knees directly on the floor. It made him wonder if he'd be kneeling for an extended period of time tonight.

He lowered himself onto the floor and placed his knees on the pad. His jeans strained a little as anticipation of what was to come began to build. That was one of the nice things about being naked—you never had to worry if there would be enough room to comfortably contain your erection.

Once he was kneeling, Beth walked behind him. He could hear her moving around, but couldn't tell what she was doing. Several minutes later, she touched his back with one hand and dragged it across his shoulders and chest as she made her way back around to his front. When she removed her hand, he had to bite back a whimper. He wanted more, but knew it was not his place to ask.

Beth lifted his chin with her index finger until he was looking up at her. It was only then that he realized what she'd been doing when he'd heard her moving around. She had stripped down to a red corset and a short black leather skirt.

"Are you happy with our arrangement?" she asked.

"Yes, Mistress."

"You wish it to continue?"

"Yes, Mistress. Very much." He had no idea where she was going with this, but he was excited to find out.

Turning on her heel, she walked back over to the nightstand and retrieved something from a black box. When she returned to stand in front of him, he could see it was a silver watch. "I found out from Nicole that you're only allowed to wear a wedding ring and a watch while you're working. That limited me as to what type of collar I could get you since I wanted you to be able to wear—to have a piece of me with you—at all times. Even while you're working."

His heart started pounding in his chest as what was happening hit him. Beth might not be quite ready for marriage, but she was making a commitment to him nonetheless. While there was an urge to blurt out yes as swiftly as possible, he didn't want to ruin the moment. Drew knew how important this was for both of them.

She turned the watch over and showed him the engraving. It was a fireman's axe with a rose wrapped around the handle. The rose had thorns, of course, and they were embedding themselves into the axe handle. It was such a perfect symbol for them.

"I had no idea what to make of you that first night when you came over to sit beside me at Serpent's Kiss. The last thing I wanted was another man in my life. Another submissive." Beth brushed the back of her fingers along the side of his face. It was a loving gesture and he leaned into it, enjoying both her touch and the love she was expressing. "You changed my mind. You changed everything."

There was so much emotion behind her words. His chest ached knowing how much of her soul she was revealing to him.

"I love you, Drew Parker. I want you to be my submissive as well as my partner in life. Will you give me your submission? Will you accept my collar and wear it as a symbol of our relationship and all that comes with it?"

Drew held up his right arm and presented her with his wrist. "Yes. I will proudly wear your collar, Mistress."

The cool metal touched his skin as she put the watch on his wrist. He normally wore a watch—most of the guys he worked with did. The only reason he didn't have his on now was because he knew they were going to play and Beth often had him in cuffs or sometimes even rope. Watches tended to get in the way.

With the watch secured, Beth took a step back. "Stand up."

He rocked back on his heels and did as he was told.

Beth strolled over to her dresser and picked up a length of rope. She was going to bind him. He was salivating already.

Folding the rope in half, she ran the cotton over his skin. He knew what was coming, and the feeling of the softness against his chest and back was almost hypnotic.

"We're going to try something new," she whispered in his ear as she moved behind him. Drew waited, holding his breath to see what it was that she had in mind.

Luckily, he didn't have to wait long. She took him by the hand and guided him to the foot of the bed. Once he'd sat down, she knelt and had him cross his ankles. As she began wrapping the rope around his feet and ankles, he felt his balance shift. It didn't take him long to realize that he wouldn't be able to walk. He knew for some that would cause a rise in anxiety, but instead he felt a calm overtake him as more of the rope encased his legs.

"How does that feel?" she asked, glancing up at him.

"Good. I can't move my legs, though."

"That would be the point." She smirked. "Scoot that cute ass of yours up further onto the bed. I don't want your legs hanging off."

It took some effort, but he was able to get his entire body onto the bed. Beth stood patiently by, watching as he moved. She seemed to be in no hurry at all. He didn't know if that should worry him or not.

When his head rested on the pillows below her headboard, Beth hiked up her skirt and climbed onto the bed. She straddled his legs and bent her head over his denim-clad crotch to scrap her teeth along his erection. He clenched his fist to keep from reaching for her.

"Do you like that?" The glint in her eyes told him she already knew the answer.

"You have no idea."

"Oh, I think I do." She did it again. Then she wrapped her lips around his length and began licking and sucking and using her teeth. By the time she sat up, his crotch was wet and his cock was painfully pulsing against his jeans.

Drew had no idea what she would do next. All he knew was that he wanted her and he was hoping she'd let him come. The how wasn't as important.

She crawled her way up his body, making sure to brush her tits seductively against his chest until his nipples hardened in response. Not touching her was becoming more of a challenge with every minute. It had been too long since he'd had his hands on her.

"Your turn," Beth whispered in his ear moments before she positioned her knees on either side of his head. He had a clear view up her skirt. She wasn't wearing panties.

Pushing her skirt up so that it was completely out of the way, she gripped the headboard and lowered her pussy down onto his face.

Drew didn't need any further instruction. He dove into the moisture that was already coating the outside of her labia. As he probed and licked, Beth began moving her hips. The more he flicked his tongue in and out of her, the faster she rode his face. He had to concentrate on his breathing, but it didn't matter. Drew was still in heaven. With every intake of breath, her musky scent filled his nostrils and he knew her juices covered his mouth and chin.

There was a hiccup in her movements as her legs began to tremble.

"More," she demanded.

He brought his arms up, hooked them around her legs, and started eating her out as if she were his last meal. Her clit brushed against the tip of his nose with every thrust of her hips. She was getting close. Drew knew she wouldn't last much longer.

Seconds after the thought crossed his mind, she threw her head back and gasped as a fresh flood of liquid seeped onto his tongue. He lapped it up greedily.

She let him continue to lavish attention on her swollen flesh while she floated back down to earth. When she did look at him from her perch above, he could still see desire in her eyes. Beth wasn't done.

All at once, she pushed herself away from the headboard and began working her way back down his torso. When she reached the top of his jeans, Beth popped the button and then lowered the zipper. "Lift your hips."

It wasn't a request. He lifted his hips as best he could with his limited range of movement. She worked them down his legs until she reached his knees. Then she abandoned them completely and straddled his hips.

Between what she'd done with her mouth and then having had her come on his face, Drew was more than primed. Beth, however, didn't appear to be in any rush. She placed one hand at the base of his cock, lining it up with her entrance. But instead of lowering herself down onto his erection, she stroked him against her clit.

Watching her was one of the most amazing sights. She was completely focused on making herself feel good. Knowing she was using him like that did nothing to calm his desire. By the time she lowered herself down on his cock, he was on the edge.

"Give me your hands."

He raised his hands and she laced their fingers together in a firm grip. Beth used his arms as leverage just as she'd used the headboard earlier. It didn't take long for her muscles to start quivering.

"Come for me." The words were soft and strained, but he heard them. His entire body heard them and began racing toward the finish line.

Drew tried to hold off until she came again, but it wasn't possible. Her permission had triggered a reaction that he couldn't keep a lid on. He closed his eyes and groaned as cum shot out of his cock and up inside her.

By the time he came to his senses again, Beth was still sitting astride him, but she had a shit-eating grin on her face.

"Did you?" he asked. The thought that she hadn't finished bothered him.

She leaned down and propped her head up on his chest. "Oh yeah."

He smiled and brushed a damp strand of hair away from her face. "I love you."

Her expression changed. The lighthearted air of moments before was gone. In its place was a look that warmed him down to the tips of his toes. "I know."

Epilogue

One Month Later

Drew made sure the back door was locked before heading into the foyer. They would be leaving for Serpent's Kiss as soon as Beth came downstairs. She'd wanted to take a shower before changing into her club wear. He had no idea what outfit she was going to put on. She said she wanted to surprise him, so he'd ducked downstairs to watch some television while she finished getting ready.

Living together had presented a few challenges that neither one of them had foreseen. He hadn't lived with anyone since his parents. And while Beth had technically shared a living space with Ben, he was often gone on 'business trips.' Drew's twenty-four-hour shifts were a lot different than Ben's two- to three-week jaunts.

They were working it out, but it was taking some major communication. In a way, their obstacles were a good thing. When something came up, they both had to figure out what it was about the particular issue that was causing the problem and then find a solution. It was ultimately bringing them closer and building more trust.

Hearing her heels on the stairs, Drew turned toward the sound. When he got his first glimpse of her, his mouth dropped open. Beth was wearing that blood-red top that he'd loved so much—the one that dipped down low in the front—and a pair of fitted black pants with heels. She looked downright sinful.

He reached out a hand and helped her down the last few steps. "You look amazing."

"Thank you," she said, slipping into his arms.

Drew took the opportunity to cup her ass.

She chuckled. "So predictable."

"What can I say? I adore your ass."

Beth kissed him. "I don't think anyone would argue with you."

He squeezed her backside, pulling her flush against his body as he relished the feel of her lips on his.

"Hmm. Are you ready to go?" she asked.

"More than ready. It's been a long week." Drew released her, and they made their way to the garage. What he needed was to get out of his head for a while. Nothing did that better than kneeling at Beth's feet. He was looking forward to a night of light conversation with friends and serving his mistress.

They walked into the club holding hands. It was the middle of July and even at nearly eight at night, the heat from earlier in the day was still making itself known. He'd spent some time earlier, while Beth was at work, helping to deliver fans to the elderly. They were expecting to see temperatures near one hundred in the next two weeks. He wasn't looking forward to fighting fires in that kind of heat. He'd rather deal with the snow.

Beth stopped right inside the door. They were alone in the small foyer. She didn't say anything, just simply ran her thumb back and forth over the inside of his wrist below the watch she'd given him. He needed to focus.

Nodding, he lowered his eyes getting himself into the right mindset. As they'd gotten closer as a couple, Drew found that he embraced his submission to her more and more. He didn't think he'd ever be able to submit twenty-four-seven like some, but there were times, even outside the bedroom, when he wanted and needed to let go of himself and just be.

Seeming satisfied, Beth swiped her card and led them into the main lobby. Ali was there reading a book. Given the rising temperatures outside, there wasn't much call for a coat check.

Ali waved at them. "Good evening, Lady Beth. Drew."

"How are you, Ali?" Beth asked. While Drew didn't have any speech restrictions while they were at the club other than being polite and respectful, he tried to remember his place and defer to her whenever possible.

"Glad to be in the air conditioning. Mine's out."

Beth strolled over to the small alcove that surrounded Ali. "I hope you're getting it fixed. It's supposed to be pretty unbearable next week."

"I told my landlord. He's supposed to come over tomorrow and try to fix it. We'll see. He doesn't always do what he says he will." She shrugged as if it was no big deal, but Drew knew it was. When temperatures got this high, their EMT calls went through the roof with everything from heat exhaustion to dehydration.

"That's horrible." Beth sounded disgusted, and honestly, he was, too. "Hopefully your landlord will do the right thing."

"I hope so, too."

There wasn't much more to be said, so Beth wished the woman a good night, and they walked into the club.

As soon as they were away from Ali, Drew squeezed Beth's hand to get her attention. She met his gaze. "I might be able to get Baily to help Ali. He's a whiz at stuff like that."

Beth nodded. "That's a good idea. We'll ask her tomorrow night if her landlord was able to get it fixed. If not, then we can make the suggestion. Do you think he'd be willing?"

"I do. He loves working on appliances. His dad used to own an appliance repair shop years ago and Baily used to help his dad growing up. I honestly think if his dad still had that shop, joining the fire department wouldn't have even crossed Baily's mind."

She smiled and gave him a peck on the lips. "Come on. Let's get a drink. Then, I'm thinking a foot rub would be nice."

"Of course, Mistress."

Chad was behind the bar. "What can I get you tonight?" he asked Beth. Chad had been working at Serpent's Kiss long enough to know the protocol.

"One of my usuals and a beer." Drew was a little surprised to hear she was ordering him alcohol. Then again, it was early. It wasn't as if one beer was going to leave him intoxicated and unable to function.

"Coming right up." Chad quickly filled Beth's glass with half Coke and half Sprite before grabbing a beer out of the refrigerator and popping the top off it. The whole process took less than a minute. "Here you go."

Beth handed him her membership card to swipe, and then they were off to find their friends. Over the last month, there had been some rearranging. Allison and John had joined Nicole, Jeff, Daniel, and a few others, including the club's newest member, Alexander. Drew followed Beth over to their group. He waited for her to sit before tossing a pillow down on the floor and kneeling beside her.

"How's everyone been? I feel like this week went on forever," Beth said, getting comfortable and kicking off her shoes. Drew took a swig of his beer and then placed it on the coffee table in front of him so he could get to work on that foot massage.

Nicole apparently liked Beth's idea and kicked off her shoes as well. "It's the heat. Makes the minutes feel like hours." She paused and then sat up suddenly looking directly at him. "Oh. I almost forgot. I got a call this afternoon. They caught the arsonist."

Despite his desire to please his mistress, Drew halted his movement and gave Nicole his full attention.

"That's great news."

Beth bumped his hand with her foot, letting him know she wanted him to continue. He mumbled his apology and went back to work.

Nicole, however, didn't miss a beat. "Yes, it is. He's caused enough damage over the last few months. But they caught him red-handed. Someone saw him entering an abandoned building and the police found him in the process of starting another fire. He even had burn marks on his hands and arms. Although signature-wise they can tie him to the other fires, they are going to see if Madison can identify him as the man he and Kelly saw running from that building. If so, the DA will likely add murder to the charges as well."

Beth scratched her fingers along Drew's scalp in an affectionate gesture. He knew she was offering him comfort. He might not have been all that close to Kelly, but it didn't matter. Kelly was a firefighter who had been killed on the job.

❧

THERE WERE SOME THINGS BETH KNEW SHE WOULD NEVER FULLY understand. The connection between Drew and his fellow firefighters was one of them. She didn't know what it was like to walk into a burning building and put your life and your trust into the hands of the men and women who were in there with you.

They'd talked a lot over the last month about what had happened to Kelly and even Shawn. The fear that something like that could one day happen to Drew was still there—it probably always would be—but she was learning to accept it and to trust in his training.

As they sat there with their friends, she tried to offer him what comfort she could. Gradually, she felt his tension ease. He rested his head against her leg as he continued to massage the muscles in her tired feet.

Alexander cleared his throat. He was the newest member of the club and had struck up an almost instant friendship with Daniel. They were both ex-military. Although Daniel had only served for four years back in his twenties, it was a connection they both seemed to be embracing. "Since we're sharing good news . . . I think I've finally located my buddy's wife."

A couple of weeks ago, Alexander had shared more information with them as to what had brought him to St. Louis. The same incident that had caused his own injuries had killed his best friend. When he got back Stateside, he started his search for his friend's wife. The only problem was that she'd moved —to St. Louis, apparently. He wouldn't go into detail, but from what Beth gathered, Alexander had a message of some sort to pass on to her.

"That's great news," Daniel said.

"It is." Alexander cupped his glass with both hands. Beth couldn't see what was in it, but she would bet it was something strong.

"Are you nervous? I mean you've been here looking for almost two months." Maybe it wasn't Beth's place, but there was an underlying anxiety in the way he held himself.

He snorted. "Terrified."

Daniel raised his glass of amber liquid. "To the end of Alexander's search. May all go well."

They all raised their glasses and toasted.

Katrina strolled over to the group and propped herself up on the edge of one of the couches. "Are we having a party over here?"

"Something like that," Alexander said, tilting his glass toward her. "The PI you recommended, Peter Monroe, found her. He found Grace."

Beth nearly choked on her drink. Grace? Surely he couldn't mean . . .

But the more she sat and thought about it, the more things added up. She debated whether or not to say anything, but decided to keep her mouth shut. It wasn't as if Alexander hadn't already found her. Any information she would provide wouldn't assist him in accomplishing whatever it was he meant to do. Besides, maybe it wasn't the same Grace he was looking for. There had to be more than one Grace in St. Louis, right? And who could have also lost their husband in combat. Even as she thought it, she knew the chances that there were two Graces in St. Louis with the same circumstances were unlikely.

She felt as if someone was staring at her. When she looked down Drew was gazing up at her with a concerned look in his eyes. "Are you okay, Mistress?"

The last thing she wanted was for Drew to think something was wrong. If anything, everything was right. She and Drew were living together. They had even begun to talk about marriage. Work was good. Her friends were happy. What more could she ask for?

Beth caressed the side of his face before tangling her fingers in his hair.

"I'm not sure I could be any more perfect. I was just thinking about how far we've come in the last few months."

That brought a smile to his face. "Does that mean you're ready to say yes and marry me?"

She played with the hairs at the base of his neck. The words were there on the tip of her tongue. "What would you do if I said yes?"

His eyes went wide. "Are you serious? Are you really saying yes?"

All conversation around them stopped. She knew their friends had picked up on the fact that something big was happening. They might not know what it was yet, but she knew that would change in the next moment.

Beth worried the side of her cheek and nodded.

All sense of decorum left Drew as he all but tackled her, kissing every inch of her skin that he could reach. Perhaps she should have been upset—they were in the club, after all—but she was too happy. Surrounded by their friends, she kissed him back with just as much excitement.

"I'll make you happy for the rest of our lives. I promise," Drew declared.

She looked him in the eyes and ran the pad of her thumb over his bottom lip. "I'll hold you to that."

"Promise?"

"Oh yeah," she said as she brought him in for another kiss. Life might not always be a bed of roses, but as long as Drew was with her, she was more than willing to embrace the thorns that came along with it.

LONGING FOR HIS KISS

SERPENT'S KISS, BOOK 2

LONGING FOR HIS KISS

SERPENT'S KISS SERIES BOOK 2

SHERRI HAYES

This book is dedicated to all the men and women who serve, and have served, in the armed forces. Thank you for all you do and for the sacrifices you and your families make every day to protect the freedoms we hold dear.

Chapter One

Lieutenant Colonel Alexander Greco sat in his vehicle, staring down at the envelope in his hand. Captain Kurt Martin had given it to him eight months ago. It was a letter to Kurt's wife, Grace. Life in a combat zone was unpredictable, which Kurt knew all too well. They'd both watched too many soldiers shipped home in a body bag. Because of this, it wasn't uncommon for a soldier to make a video or write a final letter to their loved ones back home. Just in case.

Most of the time, the letter was in the soldier's personal effects. Their next of kin would discover it upon going through their loved one's things. Kurt didn't want that. He'd made Alexander promise that if anything should happen to him, Alexander would deliver the letter to Grace in person.

A chill raced down Alexander's spine as he recalled the morning that had taken Kurt's life and left Alexander with an injury that would end his military career. There had been an incident in a nearby village. They'd needed a doctor, so Alexander had loaded up his gear and joined the convoy heading out.

Everything was going as planned until they were packing up to leave. Someone yelled and then all hell broke loose. An IED exploded, sending him and several others flying. He hadn't been hurt bad from that first explosion, but it had knocked the wind out of him. Before he could get up and move, however, another explosion hit. Debris began falling from all directions. He couldn't move fast enough to get out of the way.

When the dust settled and the area secured, Alexander was pulled out of the rubble, his left leg crushed. A doctor who couldn't stand for more than an hour at a time was of no use to the Army.

Kurt hadn't been so lucky. One of the IEDs exploded right in front of him. He hadn't stood a chance.

For ten years Alexander had been an army doctor. Over that time he'd lost soldiers—men and women he considered friends. It was par for the course in a war zone. But nothing had prepared him for losing Kurt, a man he considered his brother.

Alexander closed his eyes and pinched the bridge of his nose to keep the tears at bay. Kurt was gone, along with six others in their squad.

An SUV drove past, the driver sending him a curious look. He'd been sitting in the same spot for twenty minutes with the windows rolled down letting in the breeze. Even so, the sun was beating down on his car.

Releasing a loud breath, he folded the envelope and tucked it into his shirt pocket before rolling up the windows and climbing out of the vehicle. His leg throbbed a little as he stood. He waited for it to subside as his body adjusted to the new position.

A car door slammed down the street followed by the sound of a kid laughing. Alexander shook his head, trying to clear his thoughts. After locking up the car, he crossed the street to the address he'd been given. He needed to keep his wits about him and not get distracted. He had a promise to keep.

Alexander ascended the steps of the beige two-story house. It had taken him over a month to locate Grace. By the time Alexander was released from the hospital and gotten his discharge papers, she was no longer living at the address Kurt had given him. She'd happened to mention to one of her neighbors that she was going home to be close to family. From his conversations with Kurt, he knew Grace was from St. Louis. That narrowed it down, but St. Louis was a big city. It had taken time and the help of a private investigator to finally locate her.

A wide porch ran the width of the house, but aside from an empty clay pot, it was bare. And although the yard was neat and well kept, it didn't look as if she spent much time outside. There were no flowers planted, no chairs or lawn ornaments.

He took in every detail, memorizing it. Alexander knew he was stalling. He also knew it wasn't going to get any easier the longer he put it off, and he owed it to Kurt. He'd given his word.

The sound of his knuckles against the old wood door bounced off the semi-enclosed space. He shifted his weight even though he knew it would do nothing to ebb the discomfort he was feeling. Or prepare him for facing his brother's widow.

Several minutes went by and no one came to the door. He was about to give up when he heard the sound of the deadbolt being unlocked. The door creaked open a few inches, and the small chain made a clinking sound as it moved and stretched. It was dark inside the house compared to the brightness outside, so the only thing he could see was a stray lock of blond hair.

"Can I help you?" a timid voice asked.

"Hello. I'm looking for Grace Martin. I was told she lived here." He used his most soothing doctor voice—the one he employed when he had to deliver bad news to a patient.

The woman on the other side of the door didn't respond. Maybe the private investigator had been wrong. Maybe Kurt's widow didn't live there.

"My name is Alexander Greco. I served with her husband and I was hoping to speak with her. I can come back if she's not home." His words trailed off as he heard the chain being released and the door opened wider.

"What did you say your name was again?" The woman's voice was a little stronger this time.

"Alexander Greco, ma'am. I was a doctor at the forward operating base where Grace's husband, Kurt, was stationed." He paused, his memories pulling him in a direction he didn't want to go. "We used to go on our morning runs together."

The woman opened the door wide, letting him get his first real glimpse of her. She was dressed in jeans and a faded Army T-shirt. He'd seen a picture of Kurt's wife. She was beautiful. The woman in front of him wore no makeup and had her hair pulled up in a messy ponytail. It didn't matter. Grace Martin was still stunning.

She tugged at the bottom of her shirt. "You served with Kurt." This time it wasn't a question.

"Yes, ma'am." Alexander wondered if Kurt had mentioned him to her. From the change in her features, he was assuming he had.

Grace glanced over his shoulder and furrowed her brow as though she were deep in thought. "Would you like to come in?"

"If it wouldn't be any trouble."

She stepped back, allowing him to enter.

The inside of the house was much as he imagined. She was probably renting, which explained the stark white walls and lack of pictures.

He followed her down the hallway past what looked to be a modest living room to the kitchen. It was old with laminate countertops and cabinets that looked to have been painted several times over. Along one wall was a small table with three chairs. It wasn't overly stylish, but it had a homey feel to it.

"Can I get you something to drink?" she asked.

"I'm good. Thank you."

She glanced around before lowering herself into one of the wooden chairs.

Alexander pulled out a chair and sat down, making sure not to crowd her. The last thing he wanted to do was make her feel uncomfortable. "My apologies for not calling ahead of time, but I didn't have a working phone number for you."

Grace averted her eyes and swallowed. "That's because I don't have one."

He leaned closer out of pure instinct. "You don't have a phone?"

She looked down. "Not a landline. I have a cell phone for emergencies."

Alexander relaxed a little. He knew her family was from here, but a woman living alone should at least have a phone, some way to call for help should she need it. Maybe that sounded old-fashioned, but he didn't much care. He was who he was.

A heavy silence filled the air for several moments as he searched for how to start. While Kurt had talked about his wife, Alexander didn't really know her and she didn't know him. He and Kurt had gotten to know each other during their time overseas when Kurt had been injured a few days after Alexander's arrival at the base. They'd bonded over their love of baseball and good pizza. Of course, they'd had differing opinions on both.

She met Alexander's gaze for a second, and then looked away again. "I'm okay."

The corners of his mouth lifted despite the seriousness of the situation. She obviously knew her husband well. Kurt had been a protector, just as Alexander was. It was probably another reason why they'd gotten along so well. "Kurt talked about you a lot."

Grace nodded. "He mentioned you in a couple of his emails. He said . . . he said you were a good friend."

"He was a good friend to me as well." Alexander paused. "He asked me to come see you. To find you should anything happen to him."

Alexander saw the moisture well up in her eyes and his heart broke. The urge to reach out to her was strong, but he held back. He didn't want her to be in pain, but he also knew it was inevitable. The letter Kurt asked him to deliver most likely contained his last goodbyes. Alexander didn't know how he'd handle seeing her break down in front of him, but he would do it for his friend. He owed Kurt that much.

"Were you there?" she asked, her voice barely loud enough for him to hear even sitting so close.

He felt the muscles in his throat constrict. "Yes."

She gripped the edge of the table, her fingers turning white under the pressure. "The men who came . . . they wouldn't tell me anything. Just that he . . . that he died in combat." She glanced up at him then, her eyes pleading.

As much as he didn't want to talk about that day, he would. He'd answer whatever questions she had. For Kurt. For her.

৩৯৫

GRACE'S HEART FELT AS IF IT WOULD BEAT OUT OF HER CHEST AS SHE WAITED for her guest to answer. Once his name had registered, she recalled Kurt talking about Lieutenant Colonel Alexander Greco several times. Her husband trusted him, which was what had led her to inviting him inside. If Kurt had trusted him, then she knew she could, too.

"We were in a village when we came under fire. There were explosions all around us." He paused and she held her breath waiting for him to go on. "It all happened very quickly."

Quickly. She closed her eyes as her chest constricted. It had happened quickly. He hadn't lain there and suffered. "Thank you."

The pressure of a hand on hers caused her to open her eyes. "I have something for you."

She looked at him, confused. The men who'd come to tell her that her husband had died in combat had given her Kurt's personal effects.

"Your husband gave me a letter. He asked that I deliver it personally."

Grace resisted the urge to touch her collar—the one Kurt had placed around her neck before his last deployment. It had been her only comfort the day the soldiers had knocked on her door in full dress uniform to inform her that her husband was dead. She'd lain in bed for two days before a neighbor and fellow Army wife had come to check on her. It would be so easy to sink back into that black hole. She'd been tempted several times since that day. It was only her family that had stopped her.

She'd been so lost in her thoughts, her memories, that she almost missed the envelope Alexander held in his hand. He seemed to hesitate and then held it out to her.

Reluctantly, Grace took it and placed it in her lap. With a single finger, she outlined her name written in her husband's chicken scratch. A smile tugged at her lips but was swiftly followed by a gut-wrenching ache deep in her chest. She'd always teased him about his handwriting. She'd never . . .

"Kurt asked me to make sure you weren't alone when you read it, but I can go in the other room if you'd like some privacy." His words were soft, comforting.

She shook her head, or at least she thought she did. So many emotions were rolling through her she couldn't be certain. He didn't move, though, so maybe she had.

Grace had no idea how much time had passed before she garnered the courage to pick the envelope back up and turn it over. She carefully broke the seal and removed the two sheets of paper inside. Once they were in her hands, the words staring back at her, she froze. "I can't do this."

Alexander reached out again. He grasped her free hand in his and held on tight. It was as if he could sense how much she needed his strength.

She wiped the tears from her cheeks with the back of one hand and held Alexander's fingers in a death grip with the other. He was the only thing keeping her grounded.

Her hand shook as she began to read.

My Grace,

I had dreams for us. Big dreams. We were going to go on a road trip across the country and stop at all the interesting towns along the way. We were going to go on that Alaskan cruise and watch the whales playing in the bay. Hike the Grand Canyon and make love under the stars. So many things we wanted to do together once my tour was up.

But if you're reading this, it means we aren't going to get to do those things together and I'm sorry about that. Something has happened to prevent me from returning to you and you know that only death would keep me away. You are my heart, my soul. You are everything good and beautiful in this world, my Grace.

When I sat down to write this letter, I knew in my mind what I wanted to say, but now the words won't come. I don't want to say goodbye to you, Grace. I don't want you to have to say goodbye to me, but you have to. I know it will be difficult at first, but you are strong, Grace. You always have been.

You have to move on. You have to live.

With that in mind, I am giving you my last orders, my sweet submissive.

I want you to move back home to St. Louis. Your family is there and you will need their support. Let them love and comfort you.

I know you will need time to grieve. I want you to take that time, but I also don't want you to hide inside yourself. You have to live, remember? Make new friends, travel. Do all the things that you and I talked about doing together.

And lastly, I want you to find a new Master. I know you'll most likely go home to St. Louis, so before my deployment I did some digging and found out about a local club there called Serpent's Kiss. It's run by a woman named Katrina Mayer. I think it will be a good place for you and she can help you and make sure you find a good Dom who will take care of your needs.

I know what you're thinking, Grace, but I'm asking this of you. I'm asking you to move on. To let me go. I will always love you. Never forget that. Never doubt that. But as much as I wish it weren't so, I can't be there to care for you anymore.

Alexander is a good man. If you need anything, ask him. I have no idea if he is in the lifestyle or not, but I trust him.

Please do not mourn for me too long, my Grace. You have a lot of life left to live.

Kurt

HE COULDN'T MEAN IT. HE COULDN'T.

"Grace?"

She heard someone call her name, but it sounded far away.

"Grace."

This time the voice sounded louder. Closer.

"Grace!"

A hand shook her arm, causing the letter to fall to the floor. She reached for it without checking her balance. Only a set of strong arms wrapping around her torso kept her from face-planting onto the floor.

Those same arms helped her to right herself, but all she cared about was the letter. She had to read it again. Surely she had misunderstood. She couldn't . . .

Grace scanned over the words again, but they were the same as they had been the first time. Kurt wanted her to find another Master. The rest she could do, she was already trying to do as best she could, but that? How?

Something made her look up. Alexander Greco knelt beside her on the floor, deep concern etched into his features. He must have been the one who'd called her name.

"Are you all right?" he asked.

Chapter Two

Once he was fairly sure she wasn't going to faint, Alexander pried himself off the floor and went to get her some water. He found a handful of glasses in the cabinet to the left of the sink, grabbed one off the shelf, and filled it with water from the tap.

Grace hadn't moved. She was still sitting on the floor with a look of grief and what seemed to be an edge of panic on her face. The crying he'd been expecting, but not the other. What could have been in the letter that would cause such a reaction?

He bent down, careful not to change positions too quickly to allow his leg time to adjust, and handed her the glass.

It took her a moment, but she reached out and accepted the offering. "Thank you."

Alexander grinned. "You're welcome."

She took a sip of the water, and then eased herself back into the chair. Alexander followed her lead and retook his seat. He wanted to comfort her— the desire was almost overwhelming—but didn't want to crowd her either. They'd only just met and she didn't know him.

Several long moments passed before she cleared her throat. "Did my husband tell you what was in the letter?"

Her question made him more curious. "No. He only made me promise to deliver it to you and asked that I stay while you read it. He said he didn't want you to be alone."

Moisture filled her eyes once more, although he had no idea why. She was clearly upset. He needed to do something. "When was the last time you ate?"

Grace glanced up. She blinked several times before answering. "Um, I had a muffin this morning for breakfast and some soup for lunch."

It was after three in the afternoon. "Just soup?"

"I wasn't all that hungry." She averted her eyes, looking almost ashamed of her response. "I know I should be taking better care of myself. Kurt would be disappointed in me."

Her choice of words had him shifting his gaze to the necklace she was wearing. It was a silver chain with a heart that rested right above her collarbone. The heart had a keyhole in the center. Alexander had been practicing BDSM for close to fifteen years. Being a Dom was something that came naturally to him. He thought back to the conversations he'd had with Kurt. His friend had never said anything, but that didn't mean he and his wife hadn't been in a Dominant/submissive relationship.

"Grace." Alexander waited until she was looking at him. "Is there food in your refrigerator?"

She stared at him for a heartbeat, as if what he'd said hadn't registered. "Yes."

Alexander nodded, stood, and walked over to her refrigerator.

"I'm not—"

"You need to eat," he said as he went to open the door and take a look inside. He wasn't going to back down on this. She needed to take better care of herself. "Nothing's going to jump out at me, right?"

That brought a small smile to her face, which was what he'd intended. "No. At least I don't think so."

The inside of her refrigerator looked a lot like the one in his apartment, which wasn't saying much. It had the staples: milk, eggs, juice, some yogurt, and some leftover pizza. He pulled out the pizza since that would be quicker and less messy than the eggs. "You need to go grocery shopping."

"I know. I don't eat much at home."

He paused to give her a questioning look before putting some of the pizza in the microwave. Alexander knew he was probably charging through a bunch of boundaries he shouldn't, but if what he suspected was true, Grace hadn't only lost her husband. She'd lost her Dom. And since she was in a new city, chances were she didn't have anyone local she could share that loss with. She needed to be taken care of, and until she chose someone else for the job . . .

Grace looked sheepish again. "I work a café and I eat while I'm there most of the time."

"Good." At least she was eating. That made him feel a little better. "Your family is from St. Louis, right? Do they visit often?"

The microwave chimed and he took the pizza over to her at the table.

"Thank you." She gave him a grateful smile and picked up a piece. Apparently she'd decided not to fight him on the food.

"You're welcome." He sat down across from her, a little closer than before.

"I feel like I'm being a bad host," she said after swallowing her first bite.

He chose to ignore her comment. "Your family?"

"My sister stops by a few times a week to check on me, and I usually see my mom on the weekends." Grace took another bite, and then hesitated. "I feel like I'm being rude, eating in front of you like this."

"Are you forgetting who insisted you eat in the first place?" He quirked one eyebrow up in question, which made her grin again. It was good to see some of the sadness in her eyes fade, even if only for a moment.

"I can see why you and Kurt got along. You're a lot alike."

"I'll take that as a compliment."

She picked off a slice of pepperoni, seeming to examine it closely, and then whispered, "He was the best man I'd ever known."

This time Alexander didn't hesitate to comfort her when he saw the tears threaten again. He placed a gentle hand on her arm, letting her warmth seep through the tips of his fingers. "If I could have traded places with him, I would have. He talked about coming home to you all the time."

The next thing he knew, Grace leaned toward him and he pulled her into his embrace. He tucked her head into the crook of his neck and held her while she let go. Her entire body shook as she cried, and each time it was like a punch to his gut.

He let her weep, offering what comfort he could, and eventually her sobs quieted. "I'm sorry," she said, trying to pull herself together. "I shouldn't have—"

"No apologies needed." Without thinking, he reached up and brushed a tear from her cheek. "I'm more than willing to lend you my shoulder to cry on anytime you need it."

Her gaze met his and held for a moment before pulling away. "Excuse me for moment. I need to . . ."

"I'll wait."

Grace nodded and rushed out of the room. When she returned to the table, the only sign of her recent crying jag was the redness around her eyes.

He sat quietly across from Grace while she ate another two pieces of the pizza he'd warmed up for her. As much as he would have loved to continue talking to her, he wanted her to eat her food more. Everything else could wait.

"Did you want the rest?" she asked. "I can't eat anymore."

"Thank you for offering, but I had a big lunch. And besides, you might get hungry later." He smiled and went to put her leftover pizza away. "Is there anything I can do for you? Anything you need?"

He'd expected her to respond, but she didn't. She was looking back down at the letter, which was lying on the table.

Alexander was getting ready to ask again when she spoke. "Are you married, Mr. Greco?"

Her question threw him for a moment. "No, I'm not. And please call me Alexander."

"So you didn't have someone back home waiting for you?"

He had no idea where she was going with this. "No. I haven't had much time for relationships since I joined the Army, and even less since I was discharged."

Grace brushed her fingertips over the paper. She appeared deep in thought. "Thank you for bringing my husband's letter to me."

It very much sounded as if he was being dismissed. Alexander fished his wallet out of his back pocket and retrieved a business card with his cell phone number on it. One day he hoped it would also include information about his private practice, but until then it was an easy way to pass along his information when needed. "Take my number. If you need anything, call me. Day or night. I'm planning to stay in St. Louis . . . at least for a while."

For a second he thought she was going to refuse, but instead she took the card and nodded. "Thank you. For everything."

He climbed into his vehicle a few minutes later. With his errand accomplished, he should have felt a weight lifted off his shoulders, but he didn't. If anything, he felt more of an obligation now than he had before he'd met Grace Martin.

Pulling away from the curb, Alexander wondered if she'd use the number he'd given her. It would be easier for him if she didn't, but he'd never been one to take the easy road. If he had, he wouldn't have spent ten years serving in the Army. He would have put in his time and gotten out. But if he'd done that, he wouldn't have met Kurt Martin, and now Grace.

Alexander was reminded again of the necklace she wore. The necklace he was almost positive was a collar. Had that been the reason Kurt insisted Alexander be the one to deliver Grace the letter? Had he known Alexander was a Dom?

There was no way to know the answer to that question, but Alexander did know one thing. This wasn't going to be the last time he saw Grace Martin.

❧

GRACE STOOD BY THE WINDOW, BEHIND THE COVER OF THE CURTAINS, AS Alexander drove away. He'd been reluctant to leave. Given the way she'd broken down, she really couldn't blame him. He probably thought she would fall apart again the moment he left.

He wasn't far off the mark. Once his car was out of sight, she made sure all the doors were locked before traipsing upstairs to her bedroom.

Her bed took up most of the space, but there was a small nightstand on one side with a lamp and a stack of books. She strolled over and turned on the light before kicking off her shoes and crawling onto the bed. Over the last month or so she'd started reading again. Her boss, Beth, had even lent her some of her favorite novels.

But tonight the only thing on Grace's mind was her husband's words. Sure, she could ignore her master's last command, but Grace had never been good at that. She'd always been a good little sub, and disregarding her Dom's last order wasn't in her.

Without much thought, Grace kicked the sheets down until she was able to burrow beneath them. Fall had arrived and the weather was starting to cool. She hadn't needed to turn on the air-conditioning for the last week. Still, most people probably wouldn't have wanted more than a sheet, let alone the comforter she kept on her bed, but she liked the weight.

She unfolded the letter and read it for the third time, hoping somehow that the words would have changed. They hadn't. It had taken years for her and Kurt to build the trust they'd had together, years to form the bond that gave her so much joy and pleasure. Even when he'd been thousands of miles away she could feel their connection.

He'd given her no timetable for finding another master. She could put it off, but in her heart she'd know she was disobeying.

Sliding farther down onto the mattress, she brought the sheet up until it was tucked beneath her chin, and rolled onto her side. Was she ready to start dating again? Find another master?

She had no idea how to answer that.

Somewhere along the line, Grace must have fallen asleep. It was dark out when she opened her eyes. She went to use the bathroom and get a drink of water before returning to her bed. There were so many decisions she needed to make and she'd never been good at that.

Grace lay there contemplating her options until her alarm went off at five thirty. It was Tuesday and she had to get ready for work. At least there she knew her place, what she needed to do.

Tommy was the first person Grace saw when she walked through the back door of the café. He was putting some of Beth's blueberry muffins into the oven. The thought alone made her mouth start to water.

"Morning, Grace."

She gave a small wave and went to put her purse on the shelf and grab her apron.

"How was your weekend?" he asked.

"It was good. How was yours?" It was the same way she answered every time he asked.

"Tommy had a date this weekend," Beth chimed in as she came around the corner and placed a large bag of flour on the counter. "Morning, Grace."

Grace went to the sink to wash her hands so she could help with the baking. "Morning."

They fell into what had become their normal routine. Beth and Tommy had known each other for years, since before Beth had opened the café, and you could tell by the way they teased each other. Grace never felt left out, though. They tried to include her as much as possible in their conversations and she appreciated it. The café was the one place Grace felt like she belonged these days.

The buzzer went off and Tommy went to get the muffins out of the oven to cool while Grace and Beth loaded the front counter with all the goodies they'd made that morning. Once everything was in place and ready to go, they each pulled a stool up to one of the prep tables and grabbed a muffin. It had become a morning ritual of theirs.

Beth said it was because she rarely was able to grab breakfast before she left for work anymore since her fiancé, Drew, had moved in with her. She said they tended to get distracted and food wasn't high on their list of priorities. While Grace could see where Drew could be a distraction, their morning muffin break hadn't started until after Beth had found out that Grace didn't always eat breakfast before coming to work.

"So have you and Drew set a date?" Tommy asked Beth as he polished off his muffin.

"We're still discussing it."

Tommy shook his head. "I don't know what you're waiting for."

"We've only been engaged for a month." Beth looked to Grace. "That's not long, right?"

Their discussion was cut short when the oven timer went off, letting them know that not only were the scones ready, but it was time to open the doors. Tommy hopped off his stool and took his plate over to the large stainless steel sink along the wall then he disappeared through the swinging doors that separated the front of the restaurant from the kitchen area.

"I guess that means it's showtime," Beth said, scraping some crumbs off the counter.

Grace tied a clean apron around her waist. "I'll get the soup started."

The day flew by and before Grace knew it, they were putting food away and wiping down tables. In the two months she'd been working for Beth, she'd gotten to know a lot of the regulars. They greeted her with a smile and always brightened her day. She felt like she'd found an extended family at Beth's Café. She owed her sister, Gabby, a huge thank you for pushing her to apply for the job.

"Any big plans for tonight, Grace?" Tommy asked as he cleaned the display case.

The first thing she thought of was her husband's letter. Of course, she couldn't say anything about that to Tommy. "I might swing by my sister's." It was a lie, but he didn't need to know that. Grace was planning to do the same thing she did most nights after work—go home to her lonely house and find a way to pass the time.

He poked his head up over the display case. "You should come out to dinner with us."

It took her a second to realize she must have missed something. "Dinner?"

Tommy chuckled. "Yeah. Dinner. Me. Beth. Drew. Nicole and Jeff. You could invite your sister, too. I'm sure Beth wouldn't mind."

"What wouldn't I mind?" Beth strolled into the dining room, carrying the vacuum.

He didn't miss a beat. "If Grace and her sister joined us for dinner tonight."

A smile lit up Beth's face. "Of course I wouldn't mind. Grace, we'd love for you and your sister to join us."

Grace felt backed into a corner. She wanted to make an excuse, to say no, but it wasn't in her. There was something about her that wanted to please. She'd always been that way. "I'll ask her."

"I can use my charm on her if you want," Tommy said. "I can be very persuasive when I need to be."

She'd seen it firsthand with their customers. All the regulars loved Tommy.

He knew all of them by name and made each one of them feel special. It was something Grace envied, but she'd never have his outgoing personality.

Before she could think of something to say, Beth did. "I think she can handle it all on her own, can't you, Grace?"

A wave of gratitude for her boss washed over her. Beth seemed to understand her shyness even if Tommy didn't. "Yes."

Because she'd said she would, Grace called her sister and asked if she wanted to go out to dinner with Grace's coworkers and some of their friends. She'd no sooner gotten the question out when her sister told her she'd call their mom about watching Taylor and asked what time they needed to be there, which was how Grace found herself sitting at a table with her sister, Beth, Tommy, and a bunch of people Grace didn't really know all that well.

She knew Drew. Kind of. He'd stopped into the café a few times to see Beth, but given her timid nature, Grace hadn't said much more than hi to the guy.

The lack of knowing anyone didn't deter her sister. Gabby jumped right into the conversation. "Grace said you two recently got engaged. Congratulations."

"Thank you," Drew said, taking Beth's left hand in his. He kissed the ring on her finger. "It took me a while, but eventually I wore her down."

Beth rolled her eyes. "Maybe I just wanted to see how far you'd chase me."

He leaned in, his lips a breath away from hers. "To the moon and back."

Grace's chest constricted watching the exchange. The love Beth and Drew had for each other rolled off them in waves. It was a precious gift, one that had been taken away from Grace all too soon. She hoped they both knew how blessed they were and didn't take what they had for granted.

When their food came, the conversation turned to some outreach work Drew and his friend Shawn, who'd also joined them for dinner, were doing at a local school.

By the time she and her sister headed home, Grace was ready to drop. It had been almost a year since she'd socialized so much and it was exhausting.

"Are you okay over there?" her sister asked as they drove toward Grace's house.

"Yeah, I'm fine."

"You did well tonight. I'm proud of you."

Grace glanced over at her sister, her voice dripping with sarcasm. "Thanks."

Gabby laughed. "I didn't mean it that way. It's just . . . it was good seeing you get out of the house and enjoying yourself a little. You've been a bit of a recluse since you've been back."

"I get out of the house. I work five days a week."

Instead of responding to what Grace had said, Gabby went a different route. "I know it was hard on you, losing Kurt. I can't say I know how you feel, but I know he wouldn't want you to be miserable for the rest of your life. He'd want you to be happy."

"I know," Grace said, looking out the window at the passing houses. If only her sister knew exactly what it was Kurt wanted her to do—how he wanted her to get on with her life. But that wasn't something she could share with Gabby. "I'm working on it."

Chapter Three

Alexander had plenty to keep him busy for the rest of the week. An Army buddy of his had made a call and got him an interview with a company that might be interested in having him do some consulting work. If he was going to stay in St. Louis long term then he was going to need a job.

Eventually he wanted to get back to seeing patients of his own, which meant filing all the paperwork through the state of Missouri for a medical license. It would take time—probably a year—before he'd be able to begin looking at opening a practice of his own or joining an already established one in town. Until then, he would be stuck reading through files and offering opinions.

But did he want to permanently move to St. Louis? It was the question he'd asked himself multiple times throughout the week. He could go anywhere. There wasn't anything holding him there anymore.

Except there was. He'd been in town for less than two months but he'd begun to feel settled in a way he hadn't in a long time. Growing up a military brat, and then joining the Army right out of med school, he hadn't put down many roots outside his years in college. The only time he'd ever felt he had a place was when he'd visited his grandparents. And it was thanks to them that he had some wiggle room financially to figure out exactly what he wanted now his military career was over.

On Friday evening Alexander hurried into the old brick building that housed Serpent's Kiss, trying to get out of the rain as swiftly as his legs would carry him.

Ali smiled when she saw him step into what they all referred to as the coatroom. He grinned as he ran a hand over the top of his head to brush away any water droplets. "How are you this evening, Ali?"

"I'm good, Sir. How about you?" Ali was always polite. She was a good sub. Why she didn't have a Dom he didn't know.

"Glad it's the weekend."

She smiled wider. "Long week?"

"You could say that." Long was one way of putting it.

"Well, I hope you enjoy your evening," she said.

Alexander nodded and headed into the main room of the club.

He'd been in his share of kink clubs over the years. They all were a little different. Some bordered on gentlemen's clubs but with a kinky theme. Others were wall-to-wall play areas. Serpent's Kiss was neither. The main floor was set up much like any other club. There was a bar, a dance floor, and sitting areas where people could gather and socialize. Although, that didn't mean things were kept vanilla. Not by a long shot. All around the room, subs—some more clothed than others—knelt at their Dom's feet.

As he made his way across the room toward the bar, he passed a Dom leading a female sub by a leash. They were headed upstairs to where the play areas were. The woman had a smirk on her face, which caused Alexander to chuckle. It looked as if someone was going to have some fun tonight.

"What can I get you?" Brandon asked from behind the bar. The man was in his mid-thirties, same as Alexander was, but Alexander could have passed for being ten years his senior. That was what war did to a person.

"Scotch on the rocks." He wasn't playing tonight, but it wouldn't matter. The club owner, Katrina Mayer, was a stickler for rules. Club members were only allowed one drink of hard liquor or two beers per night. It was a good rule and it ensured everyone came for the right reasons. This wasn't somewhere a person went to drown their sorrows.

With his drink in hand, Alexander scanned the room while Brandon moved down the bar to wait on someone else. Alexander had gotten to know many of the club members since he'd joined. Some he'd clicked with more than others. One of the Doms he'd gotten to know spotted him from halfway across the room.

"Rough week?" Daniel asked as he came up beside Alexander, tilting his head toward the glass in Alexander's hand.

"The longest." Alexander took a drink of his scotch before resting it on the bar. Between the interview and filling out all the paperwork required for his licensing, the week had seemed as if it would never end.

The other reason his week had seemed so incredibly long was because his thoughts kept drifting to Grace Martin. He'd done his duty: delivered the letter. He should be able to move on, but he couldn't. Something kept bringing her to the forefront of his mind.

A mischievous glint in his friend's eye gave Alexander fair warning of what was coming next. "I'm sure you could persuade one of the subs to play. Maybe even more than one. I've seen some of the looks a few of them have sent your way. Speaking of which . . ." Daniel nodded in the direction of the dance floor where a group of subs were dancing.

As if sensing Daniel and Alexander's gaze, two members of the group looked their way. One of them, Bridget he thought her name was, quickly lowered her gaze and blushed. Her reaction amused him, but did nothing to spark his interest. "I think I'm good."

"Suit yourself." Daniel ordered a bottle of water from Brandon, downed half of it, and then pushed away from the bar. "Missy asked if I would test out the newest addition to her toy bag. I'll find you later?"

"I'll be around."

Alexander finished his scotch, grabbed a bottle of water for himself, and went to find a seat. It had been a good day for him physically. So far his leg wasn't bothering him, but there was no sense in pushing his luck.

An hour later, Daniel had joined him and several others in one of the larger seating areas with Missy, who looked completely content after their scene. She sat quietly beside him wrapped in a blanket, sipping her water. The two weren't a couple, but they did play together from time to time. Then again, Daniel played with a lot of subs. He was a master flogger and the club's subs loved him for it.

"Did you ever track down the woman you were looking for?" Beth, one of the club's Femdoms, asked him.

Alexander hadn't been paying much attention to the conversation, so it took him a little longer than it should to answer. "Yes, I did."

"Does that mean you'll be leaving town soon?"

The question came from Beth's fiancé and sub, Drew. "No. I'm thinking of sticking around for a while. See what my options are."

Katrina chose that moment to walk by. She stopped when she heard what they were talking about. "Did I hear that right? Are you staying in St. Louis?"

"It looks that way."

She rested her hip against the side of the couch and stretched one arm along the back. The position was casual, but the men in the area turned to look. Katrina had a body on her and every male in the room, Dom or sub, could appreciate it. "Good. I was kind of hoping I could talk to you about doing a medical scene demonstration. I know there are members who would appreciate exploring that area of play."

"Maybe you could get Bridget to help you," Daniel said.

Alexander ignored him. "Let me think about it."

"Just let me know. The invitation is there." Katrina's gaze went to the stairs. She stood and straightened the corset she was wearing. "If you'll excuse me, it looks as if I'm needed upstairs."

The rest of the evening dissolved into ideas for the scene Alexander had been asked to consider doing. It seemed Katrina wasn't exaggerating when she said members were interested. Role playing was the easy part. Knowing how to use the instruments properly and to maximum effect was where it could get tricky.

At eleven o'clock he said farewell to his new friends and drove back to the one-bedroom apartment he was renting. It was small but adequate. The space had come furnished, which had made things easier.

After tossing his keys onto the long kitchen counter that separated his living room from his kitchen, he strolled into his bedroom and stripped out of his clothes. The steam from the shower filled the bathroom as he stepped under the spray. He tilted his head forward, letting the water trail down his back and shoulders before reaching for the soap.

A jolt of pain streaked down his leg when he moved to rinse, and he knew he needed to hurry. Dealing with his physical limitations was part of his reality now. But he'd take it considering the alternative.

Of course his train of thought, as was so often the case this week, had led him to Grace. How was she holding up? Was she eating enough? Taking care of herself? He'd hoped she would call, but she hadn't.

❧

GRACE CRAWLED OUT OF BED SATURDAY MORNING AND GOT READY FOR work. Her sister had come over the night before for a girls' night while their mom watched Gabby's daughter, Taylor, for a few hours. They'd watched a movie, eaten pizza, and downed about a dozen cookies. Gabby really was trying to pull Grace out of her shell, and in some ways it was working. For the first time since she'd gotten the news that Kurt had been killed, she hadn't needed to leave the room when the two people in the movie had kissed. The scene had still made her chest clench and caused moisture to well up in her eyes, but she'd held it together. Barely.

That didn't mean she hadn't shed more than her share of tears this week. She'd read her husband's letter over and over again and each time she ended up an emotional mess. Grace still had no idea how she was going to fulfill her Master's last command, but she would try.

The roads were practically empty as she headed downtown toward the café. During the week, people were already on their way to work at this hour, but on a Saturday most of them were still at home in bed. She appreciated the solitude.

After pulling up to what had become her spot behind the café, Grace made her way inside. She waved to Beth and Tommy and donned her apron before getting to work.

"The DJ was awesome," Tommy said as he helped her take the chairs off the tables and get them ready for customers. "We're going back tonight. You could come with us."

She flipped another chair and placed it on the floor before responding. "Thanks, but I think I'll pass."

He shook his head but didn't say anything more.

When Kurt was home, they would go out on dates, to munches, or to play parties, but that was different than going out to a dance club. It was either only the two of them, or people in the lifestyle who understood her tendency to let her husband take the lead.

Beth strolled into the front room with a tray of fresh cherry Danishes. "Everything almost ready up here?"

"Yep. We're good," Tommy said, already making a beeline toward the back. He'd fully embraced the preopening muffin break.

Beth chuckled. "You'd think he didn't eat breakfast before he came."

Grace grinned at her boss. "Typical man."

This earned an even bigger laugh. "So true."

The breakfast and lunch rush came and went with them all rushing around trying to fill orders as quickly as possible. By the time things started to slow down, Grace was feeling it. So when Beth nodded toward a stool and pushed a sandwich her way, it didn't even cross her mind to object. "Thanks."

Normally, they all tried to take a break before lunch, but there hadn't been time for more than downing a slice of bread with a little butter on it. And even then, Beth had to run an order out to a table for her. Saturdays weren't typically so busy.

Beth moved a few things around before pulling up a chair across from

Grace and picking up her own sandwich. Tommy could handle the customers, and if not he'd come get them.

"Any plans for tonight?" Beth asked between bites.

"Not really. I'll probably finish reading this book I've been working on." Grace didn't mind Beth asking about her plans. She wasn't as pushy as Tommy and there was something about her boss that made Grace think she kind of understood, at least maybe a little.

"Is it any good?"

"Yeah. It's pretty good." Grace really hoped Beth didn't ask her what the name of it was. She wasn't sure she could handle that. Given Kurt's wishes for her to move on, to find a new Dom, she'd been attempting to get herself into the correct mindset. In order to do that, she'd dug out some of her old novels, the ones that had made her interested in the lifestyle to begin with, and began reading them again.

"I might be interested in borrowing it. I'm always looking for a good read."

Grace swallowed. What would Beth say if she found out Grace was a submissive? Or would Beth just think Grace enjoyed reading kinky romance novels? She had no way to know and Grace didn't want to lose this job.

The doors that led to the front counter pushed open and Tommy poked his head in. "I'm gonna go ahead and flip the sign."

Beth stood. "How many customers are still out there?"

"Just two tables. I've got it, B. You two finish eating."

Instead of sitting back down, Beth started filling the sink with water. One of the downsides to working in a restaurant of any kind was the dishes. Grace finished the rest of her sandwich, rolled her sleeves up, and went to help.

It was a little after three when she said goodbye to Beth and Tommy behind the café. Grace was ready to go home, but first she had to stop at the store. She was completely out of milk and she'd had to throw out the bread she had this morning because it had molded.

Everything was going fine—well, maybe not fine, but okay—until she was leaving the grocery store and her car wouldn't start. She tried to crank the engine but nothing happened.

Her first instinct was to call for roadside assistance, something Kurt had insisted upon since he was overseas, but then Grace remembered that she'd let the coverage lapse. It hadn't seemed important with everything else she was dealing with. Besides, she never went anywhere anyway. Why would she need it?

Fate was laughing at her now.

The only person she knew to call was her sister, although she had no idea what Gabby would do. Call a tow truck probably. And that was assuming her sister wasn't working today, which she often did on Saturdays. If not, Grace could be sitting there, milk spoiling in the back seat, for a couple of hours. Her mother was another option, but again all she would be able to do was call someone.

Alexander's words came back to Grace. *If you need anything, call me. Day or night.*

She hesitated for only a minute before digging his card out of her purse and dialing his number.

"Alexander Greco." His voice was strong and confident as he answered.

"Hi. It's Grace. Grace Martin." She felt silly calling him, but did she really have another option?

"Grace. I'm glad you called." He sounded genuinely pleased, which eased some of her tension.

"I'm sorry to bother you, but my car won't start and both my sister and my mom—"

"Where are you?"

Grace gave him her location and he said he'd be there in fifteen minutes. Knowing he was coming allowed her to relax. She rolled down the windows to let the breeze keep the inside of the car from getting too warm.

She spotted him first and got out of the car to get his attention. He grinned when he saw her and pulled his vehicle in a few spaces down from hers.

"Thank you for coming," she said when he approached.

"I told you to call me anytime. I meant it." He motioned toward her car. "Do you mind?"

"No, no. Of course not." She moved so he could get behind the wheel.

Alexander tried to turn the engine over twice but it did the same thing for him as it did for her—nothing. "Sounds like your battery's dead. How long have you had this one?"

She had to think. "I don't know. Four or five years, maybe."

"They usually only last about five years." He exited her vehicle, pulled out his phone, and started searching. "Surely there has to be a place nearby that sells batteries. We'll go get you a new one and get it put in. That should take care of the problem."

They loaded the few groceries she'd bought into his car, and then drove a few miles away to a place he found on his phone that said they sold car batteries. She followed him inside and waited while he told the woman behind the counter what they needed. It took them less than an hour to get the battery and for Alexander to switch the old one out with the new one. While he was replacing her battery, he even turned on his car's air conditioner to keep her groceries from spoiling.

"Thank you again," she said, sliding into the driver's seat, unable to convey how grateful she really was for his help. Her engine was running, good as new, once he'd replaced the battery.

"You're very welcome, Grace." She'd expected him to go, but he didn't. "Would you like to have dinner with me tonight?"

Grace knew she had to look as if she'd seen a ghost, but she hadn't been expecting his question. "Dinner?"

"I haven't had good Italian food since before I left on my last tour, and a friend told me about a restaurant here in town I've wanted to try. I'd be honored if you'd come with me."

It was on the tip of her tongue to say no, but her husband's insistence that she move on was there in the back of her mind. Going to dinner with Alexander would be a good test run to see if she could do this. "I need to take my groceries home first."

His answering smile had nervous butterflies dancing in her belly. "That's perfect. How about I pick you up at six? That will give me time to make the reservations and change."

"Sure," she said. The butterflies were fluttering away with no sign of stopping. "Six."

Picking her up at her house? Reservations? Whether it was supposed to be or not, it was sounding very much like a date.

Chapter Four

Grace checked her reflection in the mirror for the sixth time. She had no idea what to wear so she'd stuck with a dark blue skirt she'd had for a while and a simple white shirt. They were going to dinner and she wanted to look halfway put together on the outside even if she was feeling like a jumbled mess on the inside.

The thought of putting herself out there again scared the hell out of her. She'd only dated a few guys before she'd met Kurt in her freshman year of college. Even if she found a Dom who would meet her submissive needs and forget about the rest, she'd still have to open herself up to someone new and that wasn't something she'd done, at least not on such an intimate level, for over a decade. She also knew that wasn't what her husband had asked of her. He wanted her to move on, and she knew that meant more than just finding a new Dom.

But first things first. She'd go out to dinner with Alexander, talk, and try to have a good time. Baby steps.

The sound of her doorbell sent her heart racing. *Not a date,* she reminded herself.

After looking through the peephole to confirm it was Alexander, she unlatched the chain and opened the door. He was dressed in a suit and tie, freshly shaved—and in one hand he held a black cane.

"I'm a little early," he said, bringing her attention to his face once more. "I wasn't sure if you'd be ready, but I didn't want to sit out in my car like some crazy stalker."

She knew it was meant as a joke, but she was too anxious to laugh. "Let me grab my purse, and then I'll be ready to go."

Before he was able to respond, Grace hurried inside and snatched her purse from where she'd left it in the kitchen. He was still standing in the same spot when she returned, patiently waiting for her. She locked up and they headed out.

He held the car door open for her and waited while she slid into the passenger seat. "You look nice this evening."

Heat flooded her cheeks at the compliment. "Thank you."

Grace took several deep breaths as he made his way around the vehicle and climbed behind the wheel. It would make her look like a crazy person if she started to hyperventilate. This was not a date. They were . . . friends? Acquaintances? Two *people* having dinner together.

Alexander pulled away from the curb and headed toward downtown. "This is supposed to be the best Italian restaurant in St. Louis. Being of Italian heritage, it's hard to find places that live up to my standards." He glanced over at her, humor in his eyes.

"It's been a while since I've had anything besides spaghetti with sauce that came from a jar."

He gasped in mock horror. His gaze flashed in her direction, his eyes wide, before turning back to the road. "Blasphemy!"

A bubble of laugher built in her chest and escaped her lips before she could stop it. It felt good. But there was a little voice in her head that told her she should feel guilty about that.

When her laughter abruptly cut short, he noticed. "Feeling guilty?"

She had no idea how he'd known that. "How did you—"

"I'm a doctor, remember? And I was in the Army for ten years. I've seen survivor's guilt many times." He paused. "Too many times."

Survivor's guilt. That pretty much summed it up. Why should she be happy and enjoy life when Kurt couldn't?

She already knew the answer to that, too.

"You were happy and you felt guilty about it, right?" He didn't wait for an answer. "Like you shouldn't get to go on and be happy because he can't."

She pinched the fabric of her skirt with her fingertips and released it several times before answering. "Something like that."

Exactly like that.

"I've experienced it myself." He swallowed hard and she watched as he increased his grip on the steering wheel. "Sometimes it's difficult to rationalize why you're still here, living and breathing, and someone who has a family back home waiting for them isn't."

Grace could hear the underlying pain in his voice and it was strangely comforting. This man she didn't know very well understood, at least on some level, what she was feeling.

"How do you deal . . . get past it?" It was the unknown that had been lingering all around her.

"You don't."

That hadn't been the answer she was expecting.

He shot her a quick look before pulling up in front of the restaurant. She could already see a valet walking toward them. "It's one of those things you have to take one day at a time, Grace. I'm not sure it's something you ever really get over. It's just something you learn to deal with."

Alexander opened his door, and then a second later her door opened as well. Another valet was there to help her from the vehicle. When Alexander joined her he had the cane with him again. She tried not to be obvious, but he must have noticed her staring at it as they were going into the restaurant.

"You're wondering about my cane," he said once they were seated.

She averted her gaze, unable to look him in the eye. For some reason his observation embarrassed her.

"Grace." His voice was soft but firm, and she couldn't help but look up. "It's fine. I was wounded. My left leg was crushed, so sometimes I overdo it and have to use a cane." He paused. "All in all, I was very lucky."

"I'm sorry."

"There's no reason to be sorry. It is what it is. As I said, I was one of the lucky ones."

She didn't get the chance to respond as their server came up to their table to get their drink orders. "Do you like wine?" Alexander asked her.

"Yes, but it's been a while." The last time she had some was with Kurt. It was right before his last deployment. He'd taken her to her favorite restaurant, and then they'd come home, curled up by the fire, drunk an entire bottle of wine, and ended up making love on the couch.

The memory had tears prickling her eyes and she had to blink them away. When she had control of herself again, the waiter was gone and Alexander was staring at her. She reached for the water the waiter had brought and took a sip.

Grace was sure he would say something about her emotional state, but instead he said, "I ordered us some burrata to get us started."

"Thanks." She was grateful he didn't bring up her extreme reaction to his question about the last time she'd had wine.

"You're welcome." He smiled and picked up his menu. "Have you ever been to a restaurant like this before?"

She shook her head. The restaurant itself was fancy. White linens covered the tables and the waiters and waitresses were all in black and white tux-like uniforms. A single candle sat in the center of their table, creating a romantic ambiance. Grace could safely say she'd never been to a restaurant like this before.

"Traditionally there are five courses." He pointed to the sections on her menu.

It was then she noticed the prices. All the breath seemed to leave her lungs and she tried to find the right words so as not to offend him.

Once again, he seemed to know what was going through her mind. "Ignore the prices, Grace. I asked you to join me tonight." When she didn't comment, he added, "Would you prefer if I ordered for the both of us?"

Unable to get the words out, Grace met his gaze and nodded.

A few moments later their waiter returned with the wine Alexander had ordered. He presented the bottle for Alexander's approval, and then opened it and poured a sample for Alexander to taste. Once he approved the sample, the waiter poured them both a glass. Grace was almost afraid to drink it. She hadn't looked at the wine prices, but if it was anything like the cost of the food she didn't want to.

"Did you need a few more minutes with the menu?" their waiter asked.

"No, we're ready," Alexander said with what looked like a slight smirk on his face when he met her gaze. "For our second course we'll have penne filetto di pomodoro and spaghetti aglio e olio. Followed by chicken bruschetta and —" He turned his attention to Grace. "Do you like veal?"

"I don't know. I've never had it," she answered honestly.

He switched his focus back to the waiter. "Veal Sorrentino. Then a bronzini and gamberi fra diavolo."

"And for dessert, sir?" The waiter seemed unfazed by the long list Alexander had given him.

"Your tiramisu and your ricotta cheesecake with espresso con grappa."

"Very good, sir. I'll get this in for you right away and your burrata should be out shortly." The waiter took their menus and disappeared.

"Something wrong?" he asked.

Grace must have had a bewildered look on her face. "That's a lot of food."

He reached for his wine and held it up as if he were about to give a toast. "Didn't you know? Italians like to eat."

ALEXANDER TOOK A DRINK OF HIS WINE, NEVER TAKING HIS GAZE OFF HER. He was enjoying the look on her face too much. She'd seemed genuinely horrified by the price of the food earlier. He was positive she'd been doing calculations in her head. He wasn't rich by any means, but he could afford to splurge on a good meal once in a while.

Gradually, a grin began to pull at her lips. "I guess I didn't realize how true that was."

"I promise all your doubts will be gone by the end of the evening."

She started to say something, but then stopped when their waiter approached the table with their burrata and bread. Once he stepped away again, Grace seemed in no hurry to continue with whatever had been on her mind.

He cut open the burrata and motioned for her to help herself. "You said you worked in a café."

"Yes." After several long moments, she seemed to realize he wanted her to elaborate. "It's not far from here, actually. The woman who owns it, Beth, she's really nice." Grace paused. "Working there has really helped me, with . . . you know."

The wheels were turning in Alexander's head as the pieces began slipping into place. He pushed them out of the way for the moment and reached out to lightly touch the back of her hand. "I do."

A moment passed between them, one that those around them wouldn't understand. It was one of understanding, grief, and of picking up the pieces when life threw you a curveball that knocked you flat on your ass.

She caught him slightly off guard when she flipped her hand over and rested her palm against his. "Thank you."

Alexander gave her hand a slight squeeze and grabbed the bread, offering her some more. "I meant what I said the other day. If you need me, all you have to do is ask."

Grace nodded.

For the rest of their dinner he tried to keep things light, although he was dying to ask more about Beth and the café where Grace worked. Surely it couldn't be a coincidence? Beth was a common name and St. Louis was a big city, but how many Beths could there be in St. Louis who also owned cafés? And if it was the same Beth, did she know that *his* Grace was her employee?

Calling her *his Grace* seemed wrong somehow. She wasn't his. She was Kurt's. And even though Kurt was gone, it still felt like she belonged to him.

His gaze traveled to the necklace she wore. Maybe that was it. If it was in fact a collar and she still wore it, then she still belonged to him.

Which was completely irrelevant when it came down to it because Alexander wasn't looking to start anything with Grace Martin. He was there to watch over her—to be her friend. That was it.

At least that's what he kept telling himself.

Hours later, with their bellies full, they pulled up in front of her house, the last rays of the sun casting an almost orange glow on everything it touched. He turned off the engine and made his way to the passenger side of the vehicle to open her door. His leg was throbbing and he was having to lean on his cane, but he'd been taught you always walked a woman to the door and that's what he was going to do.

"Thanks," she said, pulling her skirt down as she stood.

"It's me who should be thanking you." Alexander closed the door. "I quite enjoyed the company. It gets boring having dinner with just yourself every night."

She chuckled and there was a slight redness in her cheeks. He felt that pull to her again he couldn't explain and he didn't want to examine too closely.

As the evening wore on, Grace had begun to relax. He wasn't sure if it was solely that she felt more comfortable with him or if the wine had something to do with it. Since he was driving, he'd limited himself to two glasses with dinner. Grace had polished off the rest of the bottle, but she wasn't unsteady on her feet. That could have had something to do with the amount of food she'd eaten. He was sure it had been a while since she'd consumed that much in one sitting.

Alexander began walking toward the house and, as he'd hoped, Grace followed him. He noticed she kept glancing at his leg again, which made him realize how much he must be leaning on his cane.

"I'm fine." She didn't respond, so when they reached her door he stopped to face her. Her brow was furrowed and the edges of her mouth were turned down into a slight frown. He didn't like it. Especially since only moments before she'd been in such a good mood. "Really, I'm fine. I worked out this morning, that's all, and I'm paying the price for it now."

Grace met his gaze as if searching to see if he was really telling her the truth or only saying that to make her feel better. Whatever she saw, it must have satisfied her. "You should take better care of yourself."

Her reprimand was so out of character with the shy woman he'd known up to this point that he could barely contain his amusement. "I'll keep that in mind."

They stood there, unmoving, as if waiting for something. If this had been a date then this was when Alexander would have either been kissing her good night or seeing if she wanted to invite him in.

But it wasn't a date and this was Kurt's widow. "Good night, Grace."

"Good night."

Alexander waited until she unlocked the door and went inside before heading back to his vehicle. He debated for about two seconds before deciding to drive to Serpent's Kiss. It was still early—only nine thirty—and even though his leg needed rest, something more important drove him. He needed to talk to Beth, and going to her place of business wasn't an option at this point.

He barely acknowledged Bridget sitting at the coat check as he passed by her to enter the club's main room. If he was being honest, he barely noticed her. The pain in his leg was getting worse the more he stood on it. He knew he should have gone home and waited to talk to Beth, but he wasn't willing to wait a week to find out if what he suspected was true.

As he scanned the room looking for Beth, he grew more irritated, both that he didn't see her and because of his leg. He limped over to the bar, feeling like a man twice his age, and took a seat.

"What can I get you tonight?" Brandon asked.

He wasn't looking for a drink, but the bartender might be able to help him anyway. "I'm looking for Beth. Is she here tonight?"

"Yeah." He looked over Alexander's shoulder. "They were here a few minutes ago to get some waters. I think . . . there they are," he said.

Alexander turned. Beth was in a midnight blue corset, a matching thong, and a pair of boots that came halfway up her thigh.

"I think they are heading upstairs to play."

By the looks of it, Alexander would have to agree. "Thanks."

Forcing his legs to move, he crossed the room to where she was waiting at the bottom of the staircase. She was facing away from him as he approached, so she didn't see him until he was almost on top of her.

"I didn't realize you were here tonight." She was relaxed and smiling, ready to have some fun with her sub.

"I need to speak to you about something." His tone must have alerted her something was off because he saw some of her good mood disappear.

Drew chose that moment to come out of the locker room. His feet were bare and all he was wearing was a pair of jeans. He walked up to them and stood beside his mistress.

Beth placed a hand on Drew's naked chest and met his gaze. "Go upstairs and get into position. I'll be up in a minute."

He didn't move right away, and she gave him a look that let him know it hadn't been a request.

"Yes, Mistress."

Once they were alone again, she was all business. "What did you need to talk to me about?"

Alexander needed to sit down, so without saying anything he made his way over to a chair a few feet away.

She followed and took the seat opposite him.

"It's been a long day and I'm not going to beat around the bush. Does Grace Martin work for you?"

Beth didn't blink. It was almost as if she'd expected his question. "Yes."

"You knew she was the woman I was looking for." He hadn't meant it to come out as an accusation exactly, but he knew that was the way it sounded.

She nodded. "A few weeks ago you mentioned her name was Grace. And before you'd said she was the widow of an Army friend of yours who'd been killed."

He took some time for that to sink in, not wanting to lash out at her because of his pain. Besides, if she'd said something to him earlier, would it have really made a difference? If he recalled correctly, Alexander had mentioned Grace's name to their group of friends at the club only days before he'd gone to see her that first time.

"Grace told me you make sure she eats while she's at work."

Beth relaxed the set of her shoulders, but didn't sit back in her chair. Alexander knew he needed to let her go so she could join her sub.

"She tried to brush off lunch one day. When I asked her what she'd had for breakfast that morning she told me she'd had half a banana and a few bites of toast," Beth said.

He thought back to the huge meal he and Grace had eaten earlier and, despite the pain he was in, he instantly felt better. "Thank you for looking after her."

Beth hesitated. "She needs someone to look after her."

Did Beth know?

Of course, as soon as the thought crossed his mind, Alexander pushed it away. He didn't even know. Not for certain.

Still, it seemed Beth had picked up on some of the same things he had. "Yes, she does."

They shared a look before Beth stood, her boots making her taller than she usually was. "Let me know if I can do anything to help."

"Have fun with your sub," Alexander said.

The twinkle in Beth's eyes was back. "Oh, I plan to."

Chapter Five

"Could you hand me that glass, Grace?"

It was Sunday morning and she was over at her mom's, helping her go through some boxes. Caroline Lewis was a force to be reckoned with when she got something in her head. She was convinced some papers she needed were stashed in the attic, so she'd asked Grace to come over and help her find them. Two hours into the search and they hadn't turned up much besides some old receipts and a lot of dust.

"Are you sure you remember putting them in one of these boxes and not in the filing cabinet?" Grace asked.

The sound of the back door opening was swiftly followed by her sister's voice. "Knock, knock. Anyone home?"

"In here," their mother yelled.

Gabby strolled into the living room, her three-year-old daughter, Taylor, in tow, dragging a stuffed animal. "What's all this?"

"Mom has a meeting with a guy to talk about her retirement this week—"

"Yes, and I need to find the paper that has all the information about your father's pension." Her mother scowled and reached for another box. "Otherwise I'll just have to go back again."

Her sister shot her a look and Grace shrugged. Their dad had been a meticulous record keeper. Their mother . . . not so much. She tended to throw things in boxes and worry about it later.

Gabby sat down next to Grace and settled Taylor on the couch beside her. "I thought maybe we could all go out for lunch."

She hadn't even finished her sentence and their mother was shaking her head. "I can't go anywhere until I find this." Licking the tip of her index finger, she began riffling through the stack of papers she had resting on her lap. "You three should go, though. Grace never eats enough these days."

Grace's cheeks heated with embarrassment. "Mom!"

"You know it's true," her mother said without looking up from her task.

"We can bring you something back," Gabby said as she gathered her daughter onto her lap.

"That's all right. I have leftovers I can warm up when I get hungry."

Gabby stood. "Grace, you ready?"

Instead of answering her sister, Grace addressed her mother. "Mom, are you sure you don't want me to stay and help?"

"Go with your sister. I'll be fine."

Ten minutes later they were sitting at a booth in a chain restaurant she'd frequented a lot growing up. It was one of those places that pretty much stayed the same no matter how much time had passed. They'd changed the carpet to a slightly darker shade of gray and the walls looked as if they'd received a new coat of paint recently, but other than that it hadn't changed.

Grace reached for a menu and was surprised to find she was actually hungry. Considering the amount of food she'd consumed the night before, she figured she'd be good for most of the day.

"So I swung by your place last night," her sister commented as she perused the menu.

Grace hummed, hoping her sister would move on to other things.

She should have known better. Once they'd given their order to the server, Gabby made sure Taylor was occupied with the placemat and crayons the restaurant had provided, and then leaned in toward her sister. "It was after seven and you usually don't go out that late."

If she made a big deal of hiding her evening out, it would only make things worse. "I was invited to dinner."

Gabby's eyes lit up. "With?"

"An Army buddy of Kurt's stopped by the other day. He gave me his number and told me to call him if I needed anything. I had some car trouble yesterday, so I called him. Afterward, he invited me to have dinner with him."

Her sister's eyes looked as if they were about ready to bug out of her head. "What?"

"What, she asks. What?" Gabby shook her head in disbelief. "You got asked out on a date and you didn't tell me?"

"It wasn't a date."

Gabby sat up straight and folded her hands in front of her on the table. "Did he pick you up?"

"Yes."

"Did he pay for dinner?"

"Yes." Grace didn't like where this was going.

"Did he walk you to the door afterward?"

"What does that matter?" She was deflecting and she knew it.

"I guess that answers my question." Her sister leaned forward again, lowering her voice as if she were sharing some big secret. "I know you're a little rusty at this, sis, but that's what we in the modern world call a date."

"He's new in town," Grace said, trying to convince her sister. "He just wanted some company."

"Uh-huh."

"Fine, don't believe me. But it wasn't a date."

Her sister chuckled, but let it go. Their server brought their lunches a few minutes later and conversation turned to their mother's impending retirement. "She's going to go stir-crazy."

"Maybe she's looking forward to slowing down," Grace said without much conviction.

Gabby snorted. "Yeah, right."

Although the thought had crossed Grace's mind as well, she'd chosen not to dwell on it. "Maybe she could babysit Taylor more. Free you up to, you know, do other . . . stuff."

A wicked smile bloomed across Gabby's face. "Are you suggesting I need to get laid?"

"No," Grace barely managed to spit out through her shock. Her sister had always been blunter than she was. "I just meant you'd have time to . . . to go out. That's all."

The gleam in her sister's eyes hadn't lessened. She was enjoying Grace's discomfort. "Date."

"Sure," Grace said, looking anywhere but at her sister. "If that's what you want."

Her sister opened her mouth to say something that would no doubt embarrass Grace more, but she stopped short when Grace's phone rang.

There weren't very many people who had Grace's cell phone number and one of them was sitting across from her. As she opened her purse to retrieve the phone, her first thought was that it was her mother ringing to say she'd changed her mind and to ask if they'd bring her something back. But when she looked at the screen she knew it wasn't her mother.

Grace hesitated for a second, debating whether or not to answer. She recognized the number from when she'd called it yesterday. It was Alexander, but she had no idea why he was calling.

"Aren't you going to answer it?" her sister asked. If she didn't answer it, her sister would have more evidence that her dinner with Alexander last night had been more than simply two people sharing a meal.

"Hello." Her voice sounded shaky to her own ears as she answered the call.

"Grace, it's Alexander Greco."

That brought a small smile to her lips. "I know. I recognized your number."

There was a slight pause before he said, "I hope I'm not interrupting anything. I wanted to make sure you weren't having any more issues with your car."

"I drove it to my mom's this morning and it started right up." Grace could feel her sister's stare from across the table, but she was trying her best to ignore it.

"Good." She heard a door opening in the background. "Remember that battery has a warranty on it, so if it gives you any trouble we'll take it back."

"All's good so far."

There was a prolonged silence. "Sorry. I was trying to do two things at once." He laughed. "Probably not the best move. I'm not as agile as I used to be."

"Is your leg bothering you today?" Grace had a feeling he'd been downplaying how much it was hurting last night.

"No. It's much better today. Thank you for asking." She heard another noise in the background, but this time she couldn't tell what it was. "The other reason I called was that I wanted to see if you'd like to join me for dinner again sometime this week. I was thinking maybe Tuesday or Wednesday? I'm flexible." He paused. "In some ways at least."

A giggle escaped before she could stop it. She knew her sister was sitting there listening to every word and that once she ended the call the gloves would come off. Still, she owed Alexander an answer. "Sure. I don't have any plans."

"Tuesday, then?"

"Okay."

"I'll pick you up. Say, around six?" he asked.

Once the time was agreed upon, she told Alexander she needed to go. He didn't keep her, but reminded her to call if she needed anything before Tuesday.

She avoided looking in her sister's direction until her phone was safely tucked back into her purse. When she did finally chance a glance, Gabby had a knowing smirk on her face. "Want to try telling me again it wasn't a date?"

Grace swallowed. There would be no deterring her sister now. If Grace had thought Gabby's questions had been bad before, they were nothing compared to what was coming. All Grace could do was brace for impact.

❧

ALEXANDER ARRIVED AT GRACE'S HOUSE WITH FIVE MINUTES TO SPARE. He'd made sure to take it easy that day so there wasn't a repeat of the discomfort he'd been in on Saturday evening, even using his cane when he'd swung by what was to be his new office to sign some paperwork. Sitting behind a desk wasn't how he wanted to spend his days, but it would have to suffice for the time being.

He was halfway up the walkway when Grace stepped out onto her front porch. She must have been watching for him.

The dress she wore teased her legs as the wind whipped around the hem and she held tight to the shawl draped over her shoulders as she came toward him.

"Hungry?"

A blank look crossed her face momentarily before it changed to a look of shy embarrassment. "I wanted to save you from having to walk up the steps."

While he was touched by her gesture, it was unnecessary. He had limitations, but nothing that would keep him from picking a lady up at her door. "You didn't have to do that."

She must have heard something in his tone because her expression shifted again. "I didn't mean to offend you."

Alexander didn't want her to feel bad about what she'd meant as a courteous gesture. "You didn't." He turned. "Shall we?"

Grace hesitated for a second before nodding.

He decided to keep things more casual this time around, so he chose a barbecue restaurant he'd heard a few people talking about. When they pulled up in front he noticed her eyes light up. "I take it you've been here before?"

"Pappy's? Of course. They have the best barbecue in town."

Alexander chuckled as he turned off the engine. "That's what I've been told."

The restaurant was busy when they made their way inside. He had to move to one side more than once to allow someone to pass. It was a good sign. Between the amount of people there on a Tuesday night and Grace's endorsement, he was hoping the food would be good. It had been years since he'd had good barbecue.

A petite woman stood behind the register. She smiled as they approached. The time they'd had to wait in line had given him the opportunity to decide what he wanted.

After placing their order, they went to find a seat. He spotted an empty booth along the far wall and pointed it out to Grace. She followed his line of sight and maneuvered her way across the room. Alexander followed close behind.

"Has the place changed much since the last time you were here?" he asked when he noticed her looking around.

She grinned and shook her head. "Not at all."

He smiled back.

Their food arrived and he had to admit it was good. Really good.

"I'll definitely be back," Alexander said as he finished the full rack of ribs he'd ordered. "That was amazing."

"Everything here is so good."

"Maybe we can make this a weekly stop." He'd said it as a joke, but she didn't laugh. "What's wrong?"

She picked up her fork, not looking at him. "Nothing."

"Grace."

He saw her swallow. "It's just something my sister said, that's all."

"What did your sister say?"

Grace pressed her lips together and met his gaze. "She said I shouldn't be going out to dinner with you because you're going to get the wrong idea."

"I see."

Shifting in her seat, Grace set her fork down. "I don't—" She sighed. "I don't think I'm ready to . . . date yet."

"Is that what we're doing?" he asked, not taking his gaze off her.

"I don't know. Is it?"

He chose his words carefully. "I'm new in town and I don't know many people I would like to spend an evening out with, and I enjoy your company."

She was quiet for a long minute. "Okay."

They finished up and headed back to his vehicle. There was still some unease floating in the air around them and he knew he needed to defuse it. He didn't want Grace to feel awkward about going out to dinner with him.

Although, he didn't quite understand his desire to hang out with her either. Maybe it was only because she was a connection to Kurt. Maybe it was because he felt an obligation to look after her, having seen her reaction to reading her husband's letter. "Do you know anywhere around here we could get some ice cream?"

Grace clicked her seat belt in place before looking in his direction. "There used to be a place down by the Arch."

He pulled out into traffic and made his way across town, the Arch already poking out through the buildings. She sat beside him, looking out the window, not saying anything. For some reason he still felt as if something was bothering her. Alexander had no idea if it was her fear that she was misleading him or something else.

"Kurt told me you were from St. Louis. Did you grow up here?"

It took her a few moments to answer. "My parents moved here when I was three. Dad got a job offer he couldn't pass up." She paused. "The ice cream shop is right there."

Alexander nodded and parked behind a black SUV. As he climbed out he recognized a few of the nearby buildings. He'd driven down this way when he was looking for Serpent's Kiss.

By the time he made it to the sidewalk Grace was already there waiting for him.

The shop was small. It only had a handful of tables, so after getting their ice creams they took them outside so they could people watch.

"Can I ask you something?"

He scooped up some of the chocolate fudge ice cream he'd ordered and nodded. "Grace, you can ask me anything."

"If we're not on a date, why is it that you always insist on paying?"

Alexander smiled. "Habit, I suppose." He paused while he took a bite of his ice cream. "Or I guess you could just say I'm old-fashioned."

She didn't say anything.

He waited for several minutes, hoping maybe she'd ask another question. When she didn't, he turned to look at the Arch figuring that would be a safe topic. "Have you ever been up?"

"What?" she asked, distracted.

"The Arch. Have you ever been up to the top?"

"Oh. Yeah, once. When I was little. Ten, I think. Everything down below looks really tiny."

Her gaze was on anything but him. Not in a way to make him think she was engrossed in what was going on around them, but more as if she was avoiding eye contact with him. So much so he felt he needed to ask, "Do you want me to take you home?"

That made her look at him.

"You seem uncomfortable tonight and I don't want you to be uncomfortable. This was meant to be fun. For both of us."

A look of guilt crossed her face and it made him regret his words.

"It's not you," she said. "I have a lot on my mind."

"If you need someone to listen, I'm here. I know we don't know each other all that well, but—"

"Kurt wants me to move on."

Her statement caused his mind to go completely blank.

Before he could recover himself, she continued. "The letter you brought me. Kurt said he wanted me to move on, find someone else, and . . . well, I'm trying to figure out how to do that. I'm not sure that I can."

Things were beginning to fall into place. "Is that why you asked me about this being a date?"

Grace nodded.

Alexander set his ice cream aside and turned to face her. He was still trying to process what she'd told him with what he knew about his friend. "If you don't feel you're ready, then you're not ready."

"But what if I'm never ready?" she asked, pleading in her eyes.

"I think you will be. Eventually." She opened her mouth to say something, but he went on anyway, cutting her off. "I know it may not feel that way now, but you even told me yourself that you've gotten better since you started your job at the café."

She started to say something else but then seemed to change her mind. Instead, she nodded.

They went back to eating their ice cream in silence, watching the cars go by. Hearing the anguish in her voice reinforced Alexander's determination to be there for her and help her in any way he could.

Chapter Six

Grace ran her hands over her hair in a nervous gesture. As she reached her neck, she felt her collar still around it. She went to the mirror and took a long look at herself.

Again, her gaze zeroed in on her collar. If she was going to do this, Grace knew she needed to take it off. She couldn't truly move on if she was still wearing another man's collar.

Her hands shook as she eased them beneath her hair at the nape of her neck and her fingers grazed the clasp. It took her several attempts, but finally it came free. She held it in both her hands, staring at it for what felt like forever before closing her eyes and forcing herself to breathe.

Once she was fairly sure she wouldn't lose it, Grace crossed the room to her closet. She lifted a small cardboard box from the shelf and placed it on the bed. Inside were several of Kurt's things, things she wasn't willing to part with, including a dried flower from their first date.

Grace opened the box and was immediately assaulted by memories. It took everything in her not to say fuck it, put her collar back on, and stay home. But that wasn't what Kurt wanted for her.

Before she could talk herself out of it, she placed her collar inside the box along with her wedding ring, closed it, and put the box back in the closet. She ran out of the house, needing to get away before she changed her mind.

GRACE TOOK A SHAKY BREATH, OPENED HER CAR DOOR, AND PLACED HER feet on the pavement. Each step she took toward the brick building felt heavier than the one before. She felt naked. Exposed. And utterly terrified. It was the first time she'd been without her collar for almost ten years.

It had been over a month since Alexander had delivered her husband's letter to her. A month that she'd spent preparing for today—the first step in fulfilling her master's last command.

When she reached the door, a little voice in the back of her head told her she still had time to turn around and leave. Seconds before she followed that voice, the door opened and a woman appeared. "You must be Grace."

"Yes." Her voice sounded shaky to her own ears, but maybe Katrina Mayer, the owner of Serpent's Kiss, couldn't hear it. At least that's what she was hoping.

"Come. We'll go to my office."

Grace followed Katrina inside. They walked through a small foyer, then a larger one. Then they stepped into what had to be the club itself. It was empty, of course—it was the middle of the day, after all—but Grace could still picture what it would be like full of people. She swallowed and clutched her purse tighter to her chest.

They went down a short hallway before reaching Katrina's office. There was a large wooden desk in the center of the room, two chairs, a love seat, and some filing cabinets. It looked like any other office.

"Please, have a seat."

"Thank you," Grace whispered, lowering herself down into one of the chairs.

Katrina leaned back in her chair and Grace tried not to fidget. She hadn't known what to expect from the club mistress. Katrina had been nice enough on the phone when she'd called and explained who she was and why she was calling, but people weren't always the same in person as they were on the phone. When Grace had spoken with her, she would have guessed Katrina to be around Grace's age, but if Grace had to guess, she'd say the club's mistress was closer to fifty.

"Are you sure you're ready for this, Grace? You said it's been less than a year?" She was surprised at the level of sympathy she heard in the woman's voice.

The best thing to do was be honest. "I don't know if I'm ready. I don't think I'm going to until I try."

Over the last two weeks, she'd been out to dinner with Alexander several more times and each time it had gotten a little easier. They'd formed a friendship of sorts. He didn't know many people in St. Louis and she needed to start living again, something she hadn't done much of since moving back home. Alexander seemed to understand that. He'd helped her get ready for this next step even though he didn't fully understand what that next step was.

Katrina stared at her from across the desk for a long minute before speaking. "Did you bring your paperwork with you?"

"Yes." Grace pulled the papers from her purse and handed them to Katrina. One was an explanation of the club's rules, which Grace had to sign. The rest were her test results. All club members had to be tested for STIs every six months.

The club mistress took her time scanning over the documents, making sure everything was in order. She laid the papers on the desk. "Do you have any questions for me before we take a tour of the club?"

Grace shook her head. "I don't think so."

They headed down the hall back to the large room. "The club is open Friday and Saturday from six in the evening until two in the morning. There's no attendance requirement, however, the more often you come the more comfortable you'll get with the club and its members." She stopped and held Grace's gaze. "I know this is a big step for you."

"It is." Grace started to reach for her collar, but then remembered it was no longer there. If she was going to find a new Dom, she couldn't be wearing her husband's collar.

Another wave of sadness and anxiety rolled through her.

Katrina gave her a minute, and then they continued on. The first floor had plenty of seating, a bar, a dance floor and a stage. Katrina explained that the stage was used for demonstrations.

"Would you like a water before we head upstairs?" Katrina asked, moving behind the bar.

"Yes, please." Grace felt parched and she had no idea why. Probably nerves.

After handing Grace a bottle of water, Katrina led the way over to the staircase up to the second floor. "Over there," she said, pointing to a hallway behind the stairs, "are the locker rooms. We don't have a dress code here. You can dress how you feel comfortable." Katrina's eyes lit up. "Or however your Master or Mistress desires."

It was strange, but listening to Katrina talk about things eased some of Grace's fears. What she was seeking was normal in this place. No one would think it odd or crazy for her to be there looking for a Dom. In fact, it would be expected.

The second floor was a long hallway with a series of rooms. Each had a large window giving those in the hallway a front seat view to whatever was going on inside. She'd seen most of it before. These were the playrooms and whether her mind was ready or not, her body was. It had been almost two years since she'd felt the sting of a crop on her backside.

But was she ready for a man who wasn't her husband to wield it? That was the question. A question she wasn't sure she had the answer to.

After taking a look at each of the rooms and explaining how they handled the use and care of the toys, Katrina led Grace back to her office. "Do you still wish to join Serpent's Kiss, Grace?"

She knew she could say no, walk out that door, and go on with her life as she had been, but she trusted her master. He knew better than anyone what she needed. "Yes. I still want to join."

Katrina nodded. "Wait here. I'll go get your membership card ready. You'll need it to get into the club."

The time passed slowly, even though Katrina was only gone for a few minutes. During that time Grace wondered how she was going to go about finding a new Dom. She'd been to clubs before, but never on her own.

"Here you are."

The suddenness of Katrina's reappearance startled Grace.

Katrina chuckled. "Sorry. I didn't mean to sneak up on you. Here is your membership card."

"Thanks." The card was a dark gray with a red *S* and a black *K*. She tucked it into her purse.

"The main door out front is always unlocked if the club is open, however, you'll need to swipe it to get into the main lobby, and then again to enter the club. If you have any trouble, call me. I'm always here if the club's open."

Grace nodded.

"Before you go," Katrina said, moving back to the other side of her desk, "I've been thinking. Given your situation, I'd like to assign you a protector."

"A protector?"

"Yes. One of our Doms would stay with you, show you around, introduce you to some of our club members. Answer any questions you have. At least for your first night."

To be honest, that sounded wonderful. If she was on her own, she'd probably sit in a corner all night and not interact with anyone. "Thank you. I think that would help."

Katrina grinned. "Did you have any other questions I can answer?"

"Do I need to bring my limits list with me?"

"You can, if you'd like, but it's not necessary. I'm assuming you've negotiated a scene before?"

She had, but it had been a while. "Yes."

"If you decide you'd like to play, just let your protector know what kind of play you're looking for and he can help guide you to a Dom who might be able to meet your needs. But that's up to you. If all you want to do is observe and meet a few people, that is fine, too."

The more she talked to Katrina the better Grace felt. Some kink clubs were all about play, but that didn't seem to be the case with Serpent's Kiss.

"The goal is to enjoy yourself. There's no pressure."

She thanked Katrina again as she walked Grace to the door.

"We're glad to have you. I think you'll make a great addition to the club."

Grace said goodbye, promising she'd be there Friday night around six thirty. Katrina thought it would be best if Grace arrived before the club got busy. She couldn't disagree and to Grace's surprise, as she pulled away from the club and drove home, she wasn't filled with dread about Friday night. Maybe this wouldn't be so bad after all.

❧

ON FRIDAY DURING HER SHIFT AT THE CAFÉ GRACE WAS A MESS. SHE ALMOST dropped a handful of orders and managed to spill soup on her shirt. Luckily, Beth had a change of clothes in her car. The shirt was a little big on her, but considering the alternative of wearing one with a huge tomato soup stain down the front, she'd taken it.

She'd been nervous all week, so much so that she'd bowed out of her dinner plans with Alexander on Thursday night saying she wasn't feeling all that great. He'd offered to bring her something instead, insisting she needed to eat. Grace hadn't been able to say no, so he'd brought her chicken soup and a large baguette. His generosity made her feel guilty for lying.

"Any plans for the weekend?"

It took her a moment to realize Beth had been talking to her. "Um, I don't know yet."

"Drew and I are thinking about driving to Chicago after we close on Saturday. He's never been."

Grace grinned. Even talking to Beth had become easier over the last month. "It's been years since I've been to Chicago. I'm sure it's changed."

Beth threw a dirty towel into the laundry bin and removed her apron. "I haven't been there in about five years myself, but he surprised me last week with tickets to a show." Her eyes lit up as they both grabbed purses and walked to the back door. "I'm excited about getting away more than anything. Just the two of us. Alone in Chicago."

As happy as Grace was for her boss, she couldn't shake the sadness she felt. But it was slightly different this time. Before when she'd listened or watched the obvious signs of another couple in love, she'd felt such a pang of loss for her husband that it was almost debilitating. Grace still felt the loss to an extent, but she also felt a longing as well. She missed that feeling. Maybe that meant she really was ready.

She was on her way home when her phone rang. Since she was driving, she let it go to voice mail. It could only be one of three people. Her sister. Her mother. Or Alexander, which was most likely. They were the only three people to ever call her besides Beth, and considering Grace had seen her less than ten minutes ago, it was highly unlikely it was her.

Once she made her way into the house and took off her coat—the weather had finally begun to turn two days ago—Grace checked her phone. She'd been right. It had been Alexander. She'd call him back, but not before she took a shower. Even with the fresh shirt, Grace could still feel the remnants of soup on her.

Twenty-five minutes later, Grace headed downstairs in her robe to heat up dinner. As her food was warming in the microwave, she called Alexander back.

"I was starting to get worried." His obvious concern made her feel bad for not returning his call as soon as she'd gotten home.

"Sorry. I was driving home when you called and I really needed to take a shower. I was a bit clumsy today and managed to spill a full ladle of soup on myself." She still couldn't believe she'd done that.

"Did you burn yourself?"

"No, but my shirt didn't fare so well. Beth had a spare in her car that she let me borrow." Speaking of which, Grace made a note to get Beth's shirt washed this weekend so she could return it to her on Tuesday. She'd do it tonight, but there wasn't time before she needed to be at Serpent's Kiss and she didn't want to be late.

"Maybe you should have stayed home and rested." She knew he was referring to her not feeling well the night before, which only made her feel worse since it had been a lie.

"It wasn't that. I was just distracted and not paying attention to what I was doing." The microwave beeped, letting her know her food was ready. Grace tucked the phone between her ear and her shoulder as she retrieved her dinner. She took extra special care not to spill anything on her way to the table. Taking another shower before getting ready would only put her in a crunch for time.

"What's for dinner?" he asked, and she knew he must have heard the microwave.

"The rest of the chicken soup you brought over." She paused before taking another bite. "Thank you again. You didn't have to."

"That's what friends are for, right?"

They talked until she was finished eating her soup, making plans to go out to dinner the following week. Twice, he said, in order to make up for her canceling on him on Thursday.

By the time she trekked back upstairs to get ready, she was feeling more relaxed. That was until she went to her closet and pulled out her outfit for the evening. Katrina had said there wasn't really a dress code, but Grace had been in the lifestyle long enough to know what was expected and what wasn't. Especially if the goal was for her to find a new Dom.

The black corset showed off her curves, as did the tight black skirt she was wearing. Grace chose a black thong to go with the outfit. She wasn't planning to play with anyone tonight, but she still needed to look the part. That was the whole point of going, right?

Her anxiety increased as she drove toward downtown St. Louis, and skyrocketed when she pulled into the small parking lot alongside the club.

Sitting alone in her car, engine off, she tried to give herself a pep talk. Grace had never searched for a Dom before. She and Kurt had discovered the lifestyle together. It had been fun and revealing. They'd learned so much about each other.

Was she ready for that with someone else?

Grace turned to look at herself in the rearview mirror. "You can do this," she muttered to herself.

Before she could talk herself out of it, Grace got out of the car. She clutched her coat tighter to her body as she hurried across the parking lot— or hurried as much as she could in heels. The wind had kicked up, blowing from the north. It was going to be a chilly night.

She stepped into the small foyer, out of the wind, and removed the membership card Katrina had given Grace from the small purse she'd brought with her. With shaky hands she swiped the card. There was a soft clicking noise, letting her know the door was unlocked. She turned the knob and stepped inside.

The room she walked into was exactly as she remembered it with one exception. Tonight there was a woman sitting in the alcove at the far end of the room. She looked up when she heard Grace enter.

"Are you Grace?" she asked.

Grace nodded.

"Katrina told me you'd be coming tonight. Welcome to Serpent's Kiss."

"Thanks."

The woman smiled. "I can take your coat and purse if you'd like. You won't need it in the club."

It was only then that Grace realized she had a death grip on her coat and purse. The woman probably thought she was crazy.

Crossing the room, Grace removed her coat. She handed it to the woman, followed by her purse.

"Do you need something to keep your membership card in while you're inside? We have little ID holders with wristbands if you need one."

"No, thank you. I have a pocket in my skirt."

"Perfect." She grinned and turned to hang up Grace's coat and purse. "I'm Ali, by the way."

"Nice to meet you." Ali was dressed similar to Grace except she wore tight leather pants instead of a skirt.

"Katrina should be here any minute."

"Oh. Okay." Was that normal or had she done something wrong already?

Ali chuckled. "Don't look so worried. Katrina does this with every new member. I think she likes to see their first reactions, but in your case she also wants to introduce you to Justin."

Grace didn't get a chance to contemplate that before the door to their right opened. Katrina strolled into the room in a midnight blue corset and black pants that looked as if they'd been painted on. She finished off the outfit with black boots that came up to her knees. She looked every bit the Domme she was.

"Good evening, Grace."

Without conscious thought, Grace's gaze lowered. "Good evening, Mistress Katrina."

There was a pause before Katrina responded. "I think you're going to do just fine here, Grace. Come on in. I want to introduce you to your protector, Justin. He'll be sticking with you tonight while you get used to things."

Grace followed Katrina over to the door where she'd entered.

"Make sure you keep your membership card with you. You'll need to swipe it here." She pointed to the card reader on the wall next to the door. "And you'll also need it for any drink purchases at the bar." When she didn't move, Katrina tilted her head toward the card reader. "Go ahead and swipe your card and we'll get started on finding you a Dom."

Swallowing, Grace took her membership card and swiped it through the reader. Just like with the other door, she heard a click. It was time.

Chapter Seven

The music was the first thing that caught Grace's attention when she followed Katrina into the club. It wasn't as loud as she'd thought it would be. While its beat did fill the room, the volume was at a level where it didn't impede conversation.

"Doing all right?" Katrina asked.

Grace hadn't realized she'd stopped moving until Katrina said something. "Yeah. Just . . . taking it all in."

Katrina chuckled. "You haven't seen anything yet."

They walked farther into the large room. There weren't a lot of people there, but it was early. Even so, there was already a sub sitting in her Dom's lap while he talked with another club member. The sub looked on edge, but then again that could be because she wasn't wearing much and her Dom was playing with her breast with no sign of stopping or taking things further anytime soon. Her legs were also clenched together more so than was natural. If Grace had to guess, the sub had a vibrator somewhere.

Seeing the scene made Grace's internal muscles pulse. It had been so long since she and Kurt played. Sure, he'd given her commands to follow via email and through their random phone calls, but it wasn't the same as him being there—being the one who slipped the vibrator in her pussy or in her ass.

Grace was so distracted by her memories that she almost ran into Katrina, not realizing she'd stopped. Luckily, she'd caught herself in time before she embarrassed herself by tumbling into the club mistress.

A tall man with broad shoulders stood a few feet in front of them, looking down at Grace. "Grace, I'd like you to meet Justin. Justin, this is Grace."

The man nodded in her direction. "It's nice to meet you, Grace."

"You, too, Sir," Grace said, wanting to be polite and respectful. Still, it felt strange. She hadn't called anyone *sir* besides Kurt for years.

Katrina ignored any awkwardness. "Justin will answer any questions you have. If you'd like him to introduce you to some of our members, he can. If you'd rather strictly observe, that's fine, too. It's entirely up to you."

"Thank you, Mistress Katrina."

Katrina grinned and glanced over her shoulder. "If you'll excuse me, there are some things that need my attention. Come find me if you need anything."

Justin wasted no time once they were alone. "The club will get quite busy in an hour or so. Would you prefer to be on a leash or are you good staying at my side without one?"

The look on his face was one she knew well. He appeared indifferent, but he was fully expecting an answer to his question.

"I think I'm good without the leash," Grace said. "I'll stay by your side, Sir."

He nodded. "Very well, then. Let's get you something to drink."

Grace didn't object. In fact, she realized she was quite parched. She'd been too full of nerves before to notice.

Moments after approaching the bar, the bartender was there in front of them. "What can I get you two this evening?"

Justin turned to her. "What would you like?"

While alcohol sounded really good right about now, she didn't really know Justin or Katrina or any of them. She needed to keep her wits about her tonight. "Water, please."

"Just two waters for now, Brandon."

Brandon opened a small refrigerator behind the counter, retrieved two bottles of water, and placed them both on the bar in front of Justin. "Here you go."

Justin picked them up and handed one to her. It was kind of crazy, but something as simple as that eased some of her tension.

"Brandon, this is Grace. Grace, Brandon. He tends the bar most nights, but occasionally Katrina lets him have an evening off."

Brandon shook his head as he wiped the counter in front of him, removing two water rings from the bottles he'd set down. She hadn't even noticed. "Welcome, Grace."

"Thank you." She was tempted to add *sir* to the end, but she had no idea if Brandon was a Dom or a sub. Sometimes it was hard to tell.

"Did Katrina explain to you how the bar works?" Justin asked.

"Yes." It was one of the first things Katrina had told her during their tour.

Brandon tossed the towel behind him and turned his attention back to them. "Justin showing you around tonight?"

"Yes." Grace swallowed. She was still thirsty and yet she hadn't taken a drink of her water.

Justin must have realized because he looked down at her water and then at her. "There's no limit on water, or soft drinks."

Without a word, she twisted the cap off her water and took a sip. The cool liquid coated her throat. When she glanced over at Justin, he had a smirk on his face. She wished she understood how Doms knew stuff like that.

"You're lucky you have Justin here showing you around tonight. He'll make sure you're taken care of. It can be a little overwhelming for newbies," Brandon said.

Grace looked around the room. In the time they'd been at the bar at least ten more people had entered. She could only imagine what it would be like in another hour or so.

One of those new people stepped up to the bar, needing a drink, and Brandon excused himself to help them.

Justin turned to her. "Let's take a walk upstairs before things get crazy."

He didn't wait for her to agree, but she followed anyway.

When she'd been upstairs with Katrina the place had been empty, of course. As soon as they reached the top of the stairs, it was clear that was no longer the case. The sound of someone moaning was impossible to ignore. A man stood, arms crossed, in front of a large window. She remembered it from her tour. He was staring into one of the playrooms. The same room the moaning was coming from.

Justin didn't appear to be fazed by whatever was going on in the room. "Grace, I'd like you to meet Cooper. He's one of the club's dungeon monitors." To Cooper he said, "Grace is a new member."

The man had half turned as they approached to give her a once-over before returning his attention back to the room.

Justin looked into the playroom and she followed his gaze. A woman was lying spread-eagled on a bed. She had a dildo between her legs while the man stood above her, a flogger in one hand and a magic wand in the other. The woman's eyes were closed, her head thrown back in what looked to be pleasure. Again, Grace's body reacted.

"He's brought her to the edge a half dozen times." Cooper's voice was even, businesslike, but Grace didn't miss the bulge in his jeans.

"I wonder how long she'll last."

It was more of a rhetorical question, but Cooper answered Justin anyway. "If the sounds coming out of her are any indication, not long."

Another loud moan tore from the woman's throat as the man pressed the magic wand against her clit. She arched her back off the bed, her breath coming in rapid pants. It was completely mesmerizing and Grace found that she couldn't look away.

The man bent down, not removing the magic wand, and whispered something in the woman's ear. Every muscle in Grace's body clenched a split second before a long cry erupted from the woman as finally she was allowed to orgasm. Grace remembered that feeling. The feeling of finally being granted release.

A mixture of longing and sadness rushed over her. She missed that. She wanted that. But at the same time, Grace knew she'd no longer be able to experience it with her husband, the man she'd loved and served for most of her adult life.

When she finally tore her gaze away from the scene, Grace realized both Justin and Cooper were staring at her. She couldn't read the expression on Justin's face, but there was no mistaking the one on Cooper's. He knew what watching the end of that scene had done to her.

Grace felt the heat rise to her cheeks and lowered her gaze to the floor. As much as she craved to submit again, she didn't think she could handle a scene as intense as the one she'd just witnessed. She wasn't even sure she was ready to submit to another Dom at all.

Movement inside the room caught her attention again. The man had released the woman and climbed up on the bed with her. He held her against his side while he stroked and kissed her. The sight caused a knot to form in the pit of her stomach. Would she ever experience that deep connection with a man again?

She barely noticed as another couple walked past the three of them down the hall. Or when Cooper excused himself to go help the other couple.

Justin was patient with Grace. He let her stand there immersed in what was going on in her head without comment. It made her wonder how much Katrina had told him.

She had no idea how much time had ticked by before she met Justin's gaze.

"We should head back downstairs. Give them some privacy." Justin didn't wait for her agreement. He placed a hand on her lower back and guided her toward the staircase.

They were halfway down the stairs when Grace gasped.

Justin noticed right away and turned to see if she was okay. "Do you need to sit down?"

No. She didn't need to sit down. She didn't know what she needed.

All the air left her lungs as she saw Alexander lower himself onto a couch about thirty feet away.

She needed to get out of there. She needed to leave. Now. Before he . . .

It was as if some cruel turn of fate caused Alexander to look in her direction. His gaze settled on her and his eyes went wide. So much for running away.

❧

ALEXANDER COULDN'T BELIEVE HIS EYES. ALL AFTERNOON HE'D WANTED TO go check on her, but he'd stopped himself, opting for a phone call instead. Grace had come out of her shell quite a bit since their first meeting, but he hadn't wanted to crowd her. There were times he still saw the sadness in her eyes. He hated seeing it, but he also knew she needed the time to grieve.

It was because of that he was sitting there staring at her in shock. The expression on her face said she was as surprised to see him as he was to see her.

The urge to cross the room was almost overwhelming, but he resisted. She was with Justin. Alexander didn't know him well, but he was one of the club's Doms and often acted as a protector to new subs. He didn't have a sub of his own and he'd been in the lifestyle for several years, from what Alexander had heard. The subs at Serpent's Kiss, and more importantly, Katrina, trusted him. That didn't, however, change the irritation Alexander felt seeing him hovering over Grace.

"Everything all right?" Daniel's question jarred Alexander back to the present, but he didn't take his gaze off Grace. She'd frozen in place halfway down the staircase. Justin was saying something to her and she shook her head.

"Not sure," Alexander said to his friend.

Grace tore her gaze from Alexander's and turned to Justin. She said something, lowered her head, and rushed the rest of the way down the stairs, Justin keeping pace with her as she made a beeline for the door.

Alexander stood and took an automatic step to intercept her. Then stopped. If he pushed himself, he'd be able to catch her, but to what end? They needed to talk and this wasn't the place for it.

"Do you know her?" Daniel asked, obviously figuring out who had captured Alexander's attention.

Grace almost collided with another couple as she rushed out the door. Only Justin's quick reflexes prevented the impending disaster. She mumbled something, probably an apology, and then disappeared into the coatroom.

Alexander sat back down. "Yes. I know her."

His friend looked confused by his tone. "I take it that's not a good thing?"

"I don't know yet."

After Grace left, the night seemed to drag on. He couldn't relax and enjoy himself. Daniel had tried to engage him in conversation a couple of times before giving up and leaving Alexander to his thoughts.

The temptation to swing by her house nagged at him during his drive home. It wasn't that late and he was almost certain she'd be awake. But he forced himself to go to his apartment instead.

As he crawled into bed that night, Alexander replayed that handful of minutes when they'd locked gazes across the room. She hadn't been wearing her necklace, the one he'd never seen her without. It only reinforced his notion that it was her collar. The collar Kurt had given her.

He ran a hand over his face in frustration and released a deep sigh. While he'd suspected she was a sub, that didn't explain what she was doing at Serpent's Kiss. Grace had told him more than once she didn't think she was ready to move on. Yet, if she'd joined the club, surely that would mean she was ready. Didn't it? And if so, what had changed?

There was also the question of what he was to do with this new nugget of information. Over the last month he'd come to care about Grace. Their friendship meant something to him. Aside from Daniel, she was his only real friend in St. Louis. If she needed a Dom, Alexander could be that for her.

But did he want to be? That was the real issue. Did he want to cross that line? Could he? Even if it meant she really wasn't ready to fully move on and only wanted to relinquish control?

That, of course, didn't even take into consideration the guilt he was experiencing for what he was already feeling when it came to Grace. She was his brother's widow. He was supposed to look out for her, not take her into his bed. And yet as the thought took hold in his mind that's exactly what he wanted to do.

Grace was sexy, smart, kind, and now he knew for certain she was submissive. All of that together had his lower half waking up. He hadn't been

with a woman since before his last deployment. Until then, that had been
perfectly fine with him.

Shaking his head, he tried to push the thoughts out of his brain.
Fantasizing about something that might never—and maybe shouldn't ever—
come to be was only going to add to his frustration. As much as he didn't like
it, the ball was in her court now. She was the one who'd changed the game by
showing up at the club. The next move was hers.

Chapter Eight

Grace didn't sleep that night. Or the next. She kept seeing Alexander's face every time she closed her eyes, that look of shock and disbelief. What was he doing at Serpent's Kiss?

Okay, she knew that was a stupid question. If he was there that meant he was in the lifestyle. And instinctively, Grace knew he was a Dom. She remembered Alexander bringing her water that first day after she'd read Kurt's letter. He'd taken charge and made sure she was all right, or as all right as she was going to be given the circumstances.

She'd thought for sure he'd call on Saturday, or show up at the café, but he hadn't. The silence from him was worse than if he'd confronted her.

As she gathered up her dirty laundry on Sunday morning, she moved about in an almost robotic fashion, unable to turn off her mind. Friday night was supposed to have been a chance for her to feel things out—to see if she could fulfill her master's last request. And if so, to take those first steps in trying to find a man she was comfortable enough with to submit to. Everyone she'd met had eased her nerves about this new mission she was on, and Grace had begun to believe that maybe she could do this.

Then she'd spotted Alexander and her instinct to flee had taken over.

Grace groaned as she tossed her clothes into the washer. Although Alexander hadn't called her on Saturday, Katrina had. She wanted to make sure Grace was okay given her quick exit the night before. Justin was worried something had happened, but had no idea what.

It occurred to her that she should probably apologize to Justin. When she'd frantically told him that she had to leave—now—he must have seen the crazed look in her eyes because all he did was nod and offer to walk her out. If not for him, she would have bowled over a couple while attempting to leave as quickly as her feet would carry her.

In retrospect her reaction seemed over the top and irrational. She'd apologized to Katrina for her rash behavior even though the club mistress had been understanding about it. At the time it felt as if running had been Grace's only option.

All it had done, however, was delay the inevitable. There was no way she'd be able to avoid Alexander forever. Sure, she could try, but somehow she knew he'd only tolerate that for so long. Sooner or later he was going to want answers and she felt she owed them to him. Kurt might have asked Alexander to deliver the letter to her, but after that, he could have left her alone. He'd done his duty.

Thinking about the time Grace and Alexander had spent together in the last month had her feeling nauseous. Not because it was bad in any way. On the contrary. If not for him, she might never have called Katrina. The reason her breakfast was disagreeing with her was because on some level she felt as if she'd betrayed him somehow.

She owned him an explanation. No more running. The next time she came face-to-face with him she needed to be prepared. Grace knew he would have questions. After the way she'd insisted she wasn't ready to move on, he had to.

Grace was still trying to figure out what she was going to say to Alexander when she arrived at her mom's. Before she could turn the car off, her sister was striding toward her. "You're late."

Grace glanced at her watch. It was five minutes past twelve. "Not that late."

Her sister linked her arm with Grace's as they made their way into the house. "Tell me it was because you were doing something fun—preferably with that doctor you've been hanging out with—and not something mundane like doing laundry."

Embarrassment at how well her sister knew her had heat rising in her cheeks. "I had to put a load in the washer before I left. It took longer than I expected." She didn't mention that the reason it took her so long was because she'd been distracted.

Gabby wrenched open the door and shook her head. "What am I going to do with you?"

It wasn't as if her sister hadn't made her thoughts on the subject crystal clear. If Gabby had her way, Grace would be spending her nights being ravished by Alexander.

She opened her mouth to tell her sister she just wasn't ready, like she had in the past, but the words died in her throat. A thought began to form, one she really needed to think through and not when her sister and mother were close by, so she put on the best smile she could manage and headed inside. Her sister followed, not appearing to be bothered at all by Grace's lack of acknowledgement.

"There you are," her mother said the moment they crossed the threshold into the kitchen. "I was beginning to think we'd have to send out a search party."

Grace crossed the room and gave her mom a hug, making sure to sidestep the spoon in her hand. "Sorry I'm late."

"Why don't you grab some glasses from the sink and take them to the table? Everything's almost ready," Caroline said.

While Grace gathered the glasses, her sister began carrying food to the table.

"Taylor with her dad this weekend?" Grace asked when she didn't see her niece.

"Yeah." Gabby twisted to the side, getting out of the way of the hot plate their mother was carrying. "Jax called Friday night. His folks came down for the weekend and wanted to spend some time with her." She shrugged. "I couldn't say no."

Grace filled their glasses with the iced tea their mom had made, and then sat down. "I'm sure they appreciate it."

"I have no doubt she'll come home with at least a half dozen new toys."

"Less you have to buy," their mother pointed out. "Besides, it's a grandparent's right to spoil their grandchildren."

Both Grace and Gabby rolled their eyes. Most of the toys Taylor owned had come from Caroline.

After that the conversation turned to Caroline's impending retirement. She'd found the paperwork she needed. All that was left was for the date that was circled on her calendar to get there.

"Any idea what you're going to do with all your new free time?" Gabby asked.

"I was thinking of doing some volunteering."

The conversation took off from there with Gabby and her mother sharing different ideas on where Caroline could volunteer. Grace was only half listening. Every now and then she'd contribute to the conversation, but for the most part, she sat quietly and let Gabby and her mom talk. Grace had too many other things on her mind. Besides, the last thing she wanted was for her sister to bring up Alexander in front of their mother. As far as Grace knew, Caroline didn't know about him, and at the moment Grace wasn't up to answering questions.

After spending most of the afternoon with her mom and sister, Grace drove home. She glanced at the clock when she walked into the kitchen. It was still early. Plenty of time to follow through with what had been rattling around in her mind the entire time she was at her mom's.

But could she do it? Should she?

Grace chewed on the end of her thumb as she stared at her purse like it held some sort of great wisdom. It didn't, of course. This was a decision she had to make for herself.

"What should I do?" she asked the empty room.

As she stood there, Grace realized she really did want an answer and the person she wanted the answer from was Alexander. She was in a place where she didn't know which way to turn.

More than anything, the way she was feeling in that moment, the desire for his guidance, was what compelled her to move her feet. She found her cell and scrolled until she saw his name pop up on her screen.

Seconds ticked by as Grace waited for him to pick up.

"Grace?"

"Hi. I was wondering—" She swallowed. "I was wondering if you'd like to come over for dinner tonight."

There was a long pause. "What time?"

Her mind went blank for a second. "Seven?"

"I'll see you at seven, then."

Grace hung up the phone and clutched it to her chest. Even though she was nervous, she was also certain she was doing the right thing. All she could do was hope that Alexander agreed.

❧

ALEXANDER PULLED UP IN FRONT OF GRACE'S HOUSE AT SIX FIFTY-SIX. THE porch light was on, welcoming him, even though sunset was still almost an hour away. He took his time getting out of his vehicle, even though his leg wasn't bothering him tonight, and made his way up the walkway. It had been almost forty-eight hours since he'd watched Grace scurry out of Serpent's Kiss. To say he was anxious to hear what she had to say was a vast understatement.

He rang the doorbell and within seconds she was there, framed in the doorway. She looked small and unsure of herself. Over the last month he'd seen her begin to come out of her shell, some of her shyness melting away. However, the more lighthearted Grace he'd gotten to know was nowhere to be seen.

"Good evening, Grace."

"Hi." She tucked a lock of hair behind her ear and took a step back, inviting him inside. "Dinner's almost ready."

Alexander stood off to the side as she closed and locked the door, before following her into the kitchen. This was her show, and as tempting as it was for him to demand answers, he was going to wait her out.

She busied herself with finishing dinner but every now and then he caught her shooting glances in his direction. When she finally did join him at the table, she kept her gaze on her plate. She didn't make a move to start eating, so neither did he.

"Aren't you hungry?" she asked in a shaky voice.

"I am." He paused before reaching for the serving spoon she'd placed on the table and handing it to her.

"I'm not sure if I can eat."

He didn't budge. "You invited me to dinner."

There was a moment's hesitation before she took the spoon and scooped some of the casserole onto her plate. He waited until she was done before getting his. The meal was awkward. She picked at her food more than she ate it. The temptation to order her to eat was strong, but he bit back the urge.

Her fork slipping from her fingers and clattering onto her plate drew his attention.

"I'm sorry," she whispered.

Alexander wiped his mouth with his napkin and placed it next to his plate before speaking. "What are you sorry for?"

She released a loud breath and for a second he thought maybe she was crying, but then she looked up to meet his gaze. "I told you I wasn't ready, and then I went to the club."

He waited for her to continue.

"I didn't lie. I still wasn't sure I was ready, but . . ." She looked down at her lap. "I told you about Kurt's letter. About how he wants me to move on." When he didn't respond, she glanced up. "You've probably guessed that Kurt and I . . . we . . . he was my Master."

Alexander had suspected as much after seeing the necklace she wore the first time they met, but hearing her say it out loud had him putting what she hadn't said into perspective. "When he said he wanted you to move on, he didn't just mean for you to start dating again, did he?"

She shook her head. "No."

It made sense. Kurt would want his sub's needs to be taken care of. "So you were at Serpent's Kiss to find a Dom."

"Yes."

He was still digesting this new information when she slid to the floor, kneeling next to his chair. She placed her hands on her thighs, palms up. He knew that pose. Knew what it meant.

Placing a finger under her chin, Alexander made her look at him. He raised an eyebrow, silently asking her to explain herself.

"I would like for you to be my Dom, Sir." Her gaze didn't waver.

As the moments ticked by, Alexander couldn't resist the opportunity to tease her. "How do you know I'm a Dom? Maybe I'm a submissive."

Grace's eyes widened for a second before the look of panic in them faded. "I don't think so, Sir."

"Why's that?"

She took her time thinking about her answer. "I guess it's a lot of things. The way you carry yourself. The way you've looked after me, even when you didn't have to."

He dropped his hand and seriously considered her assertion. She wanted him to be her Dom. And if she'd gone to Serpent's Kiss then she was probably looking for someone to play with. A part of him was screaming, "*Yes!*" But the more logical side of his brain wondered if that would be altogether smart. He was beginning to have feelings for her, and adding a power exchange relationship to the equation was only bound to enhance those feelings. He was opening himself up to heartache.

"Take a seat." Seeing her kneeling before him wasn't helping his brain function properly.

Grace stood and retook her seat next to him at the table.

The look on her face made him want to say fuck it and to hell with the consequences. He had to keep his wits about him, however. This wasn't a time for being impulsive.

"Tell me what it is you want, Grace." She opened her mouth to speak, but he cut her off. "Not what Kurt wanted. What *you* want."

She didn't answer right away. "When I read that Kurt wanted me to find a new Dom, I didn't think I could do it. I wasn't in a place mentally where I felt I could give that much of myself to anyone. I know what it takes to be a sub. Letting go and trusting. Giving up control."

Her voice shook slightly, but there was determination behind it as well. She was braver than she was giving herself credit for.

"Then you started coaxing me out of my shell . . . getting me out of the house and back into the world." The edges of her mouth rose in a small smile. "You gave me the confidence to believe that maybe I could do it. Contacting Mistress Katrina and going to Serpent's Kiss was a test."

"And what did you find out?" he asked.

"It made me realize Kurt was right. Being submissive is part of who I am and I can't pretend it's not just because he's not here anymore."

Alexander had to ask. "When you saw me you couldn't get out of there fast enough."

"I hadn't expected to see anyone there I knew. And when I did, I panicked." She met his gaze. "I didn't know what to do, so I ran."

What she said swirled around in his head. If he said no to being her Dom, there was a good chance she'd go back to Serpent's Kiss and find another Dom who'd be more than willing to take her on. Grace was beautiful and she was an experienced submissive. He had no doubt someone would be happy to step up and fill that role. The thought turned his stomach.

"Are you sure, Grace? There's no rush. You have time."

"You don't want to be my Dom?" An air of sadness came over her.

He placed his hand over hers, unable to resist touching her. "I didn't say that."

She looked down at their hands then back up at him. "I trust you, Alexander. If I'm going to do this, I want it to be with you."

That simple assertion was what broke him. How could he say no? "We'll need to go over your limits and what your expectations are."

A look of pure, unadulterated relief crossed her face. He still had no idea how he was going to deal with his developing feelings for her, but he'd cross that bridge when he came to it.

Chapter Nine

Grace couldn't articulate how grateful she felt that he'd agreed. "Thank you."

One side of Alexander's mouth quirked up in a half smile. "Maybe you should wait until we compare lists before you thank me."

She chuckled.

"You never know. I might be a wicked sadist." He wasn't even trying to hide his grin.

This was the Alexander she'd gotten to know over the last month. The one that made her laugh and feel as if there was still life to be lived. "Maybe I'm a masochist."

"Are you?" he asked, amusement lighting his eyes.

Grace considered fibbing for the sake of drawing out their back and forth, but thought better of it. Even if a spanking wouldn't be an altogether bad thing. "Not really."

He released her hand and sat back in his chair. "Had to think about that for a minute, did you?"

"No. But . . ."

When she didn't continue, he leaned forward again. This time he didn't touch her, but that didn't mean she wasn't highly aware of him. She felt the dynamic shift even though they were still sitting at her kitchen table. "But what?"

She glanced down at her lap again, unable to look him in the eye as she admitted her thoughts. "It's been a long time, and I considered fibbing a little so that maybe you'd realize I wasn't being completely truthful and think I deserved a spanking."

Alexander was quiet for so long that she tilted her head up to see his face. He appeared to be studying her.

"But I decided against it." Her words died in her throat as he stood.

Without saying anything, Alexander held out his hand. She only hesitated for a second before placing her palm in his.

He led her into the living room, walked over to the couch, and sat down. After releasing her hand, he patted his leg twice.

Grace's heart rate kicked up a notch. She knew what he wanted her to do. Knew what he wanted and she was unable to deny she wanted it, too.

On less than stable legs, she closed the distance between them and lowered herself so she was lying stomach down across his lap, her ass on display for him.

The feel of his hand on the curve of her back made her tense. Grace took a deep breath and tried to relax.

He gave her some time to settle in, not rushing anything. It gave her even more confidence that she was making the right decision.

"What's your safeword?" he asked.

She hadn't even thought about safewords. That's how much she wasn't thinking at the moment. This was a man she'd never played with. Of course there needed to be a safeword. Even for something as basic as an over-the-knee spanking. "Mushroom."

His hand twitched and she wondered if he was grinning. "Mushroom?"

She nodded, or at least tried to, considering her position. "Kurt hated mushrooms."

Alexander's entire body vibrated before he ran his hand down over her backside. "Mushroom it is."

Even though she was wearing pants she still felt the heat of his hand as he rubbed his palms over her ass. With every caress she relaxed more, giving herself up to the moment. Then with a quick flick of his wrist she felt the sting she'd been waiting for . . . longing for.

He landed another smack to her other cheek, then another and another. Heat spread from where his hand was making contact up her spine and throughout the rest of her body. It was almost as if something in her let go a little more with each blow he landed to her flesh. She felt settled. Grounded. As if things that hadn't made sense for so long did in that moment.

It wasn't until Alexander began stroking her back and whispering, "It's okay. Let it out," that Grace realized she was crying. And not quiet tears. No, these were loud, gut-wrenching sobs that seemed to come out of nowhere. Everything she'd been holding in was spilling out. She couldn't have stopped it if she tried.

At some point she rolled over on her side, curling in toward him. Alexander helped her to sit up but didn't let her go. He held her on his lap, continuing to comfort her as her tears subsided.

"Feel better?" he asked, brushing the hair away from her face.

Grace nodded. "I don't know what that was."

"Endorphins."

She didn't argue. She didn't have the energy. All of a suddenly she felt very tired. Her lack of sleep over the past two days was catching up with her.

"Tired?"

"Yeah. I didn't sleep very well the last couple of nights."

He helped her to sit up and wiped the moisture from her cheeks with his thumbs. "Why don't you go upstairs and get ready for bed? I'll clean up down here."

Grace didn't want to move, but she knew he was right. As appealing as the thought was, she couldn't stay in his lap all night.

Alexander stayed on the couch as she made her way out of the room and up the stairs to her bedroom. As she changed her clothes, Grace could hear him moving around downstairs. It should be her doing the dishes and putting things away, but when he'd suggested she get ready for bed it hadn't even crossed her mind to protest. She was too tired. Just keeping her eyes open was a challenge.

Once she was changed, she debated whether or not to go downstairs or crawl into bed. The latter was tempting, but somehow she knew Alexander wouldn't leave without saying goodbye.

He was waiting for her at the bottom of the stairs. When she reached the last step, some of the awkwardness from before returned. Grace started to look down, but his finger caught her chin. "There's no need to be embarrassed with me, Grace. Not ever."

"Thank you. For earlier, I mean."

Alexander traced the line of her jaw back and forth several times. "I imagine I enjoyed it as much as you did."

His comment brought a different kind of embarrassment flooding through her.

This only seemed to amuse him. "I already checked to make sure the back door was locked and everything is turned off. All you have to do is lock up behind me. Then I want you to head to bed and get some rest. I'll call you tomorrow and we'll set up a time when we can go over everything."

She knew by *everything* that he meant their lists and what kind of arrangement they would have. It was something she hadn't given much thought to. It hadn't seemed real. Until then.

He held her gaze for a moment longer before dropping his hand and backing toward the door.

Grace locked the door behind him and watched through the window as he climbed into his vehicle and drove away. Once she could no longer see the lights of his car, she slowly headed back upstairs. Like a good little sub, she made a pit stop in the bathroom, and then slid into bed.

Her ass still tingled a little from the spanking she'd received. If she closed her eyes she could almost feel the impression of his hand lingering. It was comforting.

She released a contented sigh, turned on her side, and wrapped her arms around her pillow. There was a lot she needed to think about, but it was going to have to wait until tomorrow. Sleep was slowly pulling her under and she didn't want to fight it.

❦

ON MONDAY MORNING ALEXANDER WOKE UP WITH GRACE AT THE forefront of his mind. Granted, this wasn't the first time she'd dominated his thoughts. He often found himself remembering something she'd said or done when he'd least expect it. This morning, however, his mind was more focused. He'd agreed to be her Dom without knowing anything about her limits or what she wanted from him. It wasn't the smartest decision of his life, but he couldn't bring himself to regret it. This was Grace. He'd be what she needed him to be.

Yeah, he knew that made him a sucker or a sap or whatever, but at least he was man enough to admit it. If only to himself. She was special and he planned on doing everything he could to help her realize it.

His workday dragged. It wasn't that he hated his job exactly, but he'd be lying if he said he loved sitting behind a desk all day looking over various malpractice complaints. On the plus side, he was learning what not to do with his future patients. Most of the things that crossed his desk were simple cases of lack of communication. Many doctors, it seemed, took for granted how much their patients knew and understood. He'd read over the patient's issue, and then the doctor's response. He could see the disconnect.

At five o'clock, he rubbed his eyes with the heels of his hands. He'd never been happier to be done with a day's work.

"Long day?" Jewel, one of the paralegals, stood in front of his desk, clutching a stack of folders.

He set the folder he'd been working through off to the side and pushed away from his desk. "Little bit."

"Some of us are going to BJ's for drinks. You're welcome to join us."

"Thanks," he said, grabbing his jacket. "But I have some things to do tonight."

She didn't seem upset by his declining the invitation. "Maybe next time."

"Sure."

Jewel wished him a good night and strolled into the file room.

The first thing Alexander did when he got in his car was check his cell to see if he had any messages from Grace. He'd been half expecting her to call or text him at some point saying she'd changed her mind, but there was no such message. That meant she either hadn't changed her mind or she was too scared or nervous to say she had.

While her changing her mind might make things easier for him, it wasn't what he wanted. After having her sprawled across his lap the night before, that had been painfully obvious to him. *Painful* being the operative word. He'd played with a sub once since being discharged from the Army. It had been a very basic scene at Serpent's Kiss about two weeks after he joined. A way to get his feet wet again, as it were.

He hadn't, however, had sex for close to two years. Between his deployment, and then his recovery, there hadn't been all that many opportunities. And grabbing a quickie, locked in a latrine in the middle of the desert hadn't really been an option. At least not for him. Seeing Grace like that, touching her—spanking her—had sent all his blood rushing to his groin.

Remembering had his problem rising to the surface again. Alexander groaned and tried to focus on the task at hand. He needed to call Grace like he promised.

The phone rang three times before she answered. "Hello."

"Hi." Hearing her voice brought a smile to his face. "How was your day off?"

"Good. I slept in, and then did some reading." She paused. "I also spent some time updating my limits list."

He hadn't known if she'd bring it up first or not, but he was glad she had. "I did that about two months ago after I joined Serpent's Kiss."

"Mistress Katrina mentioned it when I met with her." She let her words hang in the air.

Alexander understood. Grace wasn't the type to jump into playing with someone she didn't know, and if she wasn't playing then there was no reason to update her limits list. "Are you having any second thoughts?"

She responded quicker than he thought she would. "No."

Someone walked in front of his vehicle, but he barely noticed. He was entirely focused on his conversation with Grace. "I'd like to take you out to dinner tonight."

"All right." She paused. "Should I bring my list?"

"I think that would be a good idea."

They made arrangements for him to pick her up in an hour before hanging up. He needed to get home, shower, change, and figure out where they would go. While he wanted to keep things casual, he also wanted them to have at least some privacy. That would be difficult if they were seated in the middle of a busy restaurant. Plus, he wanted the night to feel important because it was. This was a big step for Grace, and Alexander understood that.

She was ready and waiting for him when he arrived. Her blond hair was loose and it made him wonder what it would feel like to run his fingers through it. He resisted the urge. It wasn't his right. Yet.

"I like your hair down like that," he said as he opened the passenger-side door for her to get into the car.

Grace lowered her gaze, but she didn't comment. He was pretty sure he saw the telltale signs of a blush creeping up her neck.

As they drove to the restaurant, she sat with her purse in her lap and her hands folded on top. She looked at the road ahead, her shoulders back. It was very proper and very non-Grace-like.

"There's no need to be nervous."

He saw her glance over at him out of the corner of his eye. "I know. It's . . . been a long time since I've done this."

"Had dinner?"

Her soft giggle was exactly the reaction he'd hoped for.

Reaching for her hand, he gave it a gentle squeeze. "It's just dinner, Grace. The same thing we've done twice a week for the last month. The rest? We'll figure it out. There's no pressure."

Out of the corner of his eye he saw her nod. She didn't say anything more and he didn't push.

They pulled into the restaurant parking lot and he went to open the door for her. She took his arm as she had many times before and they headed inside.

The place was small. There were maybe ten tables in the whole place, which in Alexander's opinion was perfect. That, coupled with the fact that it was a Monday night, meant there were only a few other customers.

Once they were seated at a booth in the back corner and the server had taken their order, Alexander figured maybe it was time to get down to business. She wasn't going to relax until things were out in the open. "Did you bring your list?"

Grace nodded and reached into her purse. She held it out to him.

There were several pages. He recognized it as the template Katrina had on the Serpent's Kiss website. One of the nice things about it was that it was detailed. There were even obscure kinks listed, some of which he hoped to never witness. He understood and supported the *my kink is not your kink* assertion, but as a doctor there were some things he couldn't get behind.

Alexander scanned what Grace had marked and was pleased to see that most of their kinks lined up. There were a few exceptions, there always were, but nothing they couldn't work with. What did give him a little pause was that she had marked oral, vaginal, and anal sex as 'love.' Not that he'd expected her to hate it, but he figured there'd be a note or that they would be listed as soft limits. Did that mean she was ready to jump into a sexual relationship?

He turned the papers over and placed them on the table off to the side. Their server had brought their drinks and their appetizer while he'd been reading over her list. It didn't escape his notice that Grace had yet to touch any of it. "Help yourself."

With a little reluctance, she picked up some bread, tore off a piece, and dipped it into the hummus. He followed suit, watching as she placed the pita into her mouth and swallowed. After reading her limits list, he couldn't help that his mind went in the direction it did. He grabbed his water and downed half of it.

She picked at her napkin a few times. "Was there something wrong with my list?"

"Not at all. Why would you think that?"

Grace shrugged. "You look uncomfortable."

He couldn't help but snort. She wasn't far off, but not for the reasons she was thinking. He leaned in and lowered his voice. "I just read a breakdown of all the things you'd like me to do to you." Alexander stopped to let that sink in. "Let's hope I don't have to get up from the table anytime soon."

Her eyes widened with shock, and then with what he thought might be interest. He held her gaze until their server came with their food. The spell was broken, but that was okay. Interest he could work with. He was determined to make sure Grace didn't regret asking him to be her Dom.

Chapter Ten

Grace concentrated on her food and attempted to ignore the way her body reacted to his words. Her lower half pulsed with anticipation. It had no issue jumping headfirst into this arrangement with Alexander.

And that's what it was: an arrangement. He was agreeing to be her Dom, not her boyfriend. It wouldn't be the same type of relationship she'd had with Kurt. She knew that. Which was why there was a little voice in the back of her brain asking if she was really sure she wanted to do this. That voice, however, wasn't very loud and it was easily overtaken by her need to open up and let go of everything she'd been dealing with for the last nine months.

Her thoughts drifted back to the night before when she'd been draped across his lap, feeling his hand make contact with her backside. The sting had been gone when she'd woken up that morning and she'd missed it. Grace wondered how long she'd have to wait before he would do it again. Or she could ask. Maybe . . .

"How's your dinner?"

She looked up to find him staring at her. "It's good." As if to prove her point, she took a bite and grinned.

He waited for several seconds. "Grace, if something's bothering you, you need to tell me."

"No. It's . . . I was thinking about last night." She felt the blush start to rise on her cheeks. "On the couch."

"Ah." Alexander chuckled. "Yes. I can see why that would have you distracted."

His response in no way helped with her blush. She tucked her head down and dug back into her food.

Of course, he wouldn't change the subject to something more mundane like the weather. She should have known better. He was a Dom after all. "I'd like to take you to the club with me this weekend."

She swallowed and met his gaze. Wasn't it too soon for that? "You do?"

He nodded. "I think it will be an excellent way for me to gauge where we should begin. Plus, I think it will be good for you to be around other subs."

That made sense. She and Kurt had known each other for over a year before they'd started playing and they'd done a lot of experimenting at first to see what they both liked. This was a different situation entirely. "I guess that's probably a good idea. I need to apologize to Justin anyway."

"Yes, you do." He took another bite. "Running away isn't the answer. What's going to happen the next time you see someone at the club you know?"

Grace had a hard time swallowing down the food she'd been chewing. She hadn't thought about that. "I don't know."

"You should know that as your Dom, I won't let you run away again. Being a sub isn't something you should ever be ashamed of."

"I know." She laid her fork down on her plate. "I just don't know how to react. Kurt and I mainly played in our house, and the few times we did go to clubs, we didn't know anyone else there."

Alexander seemed to take that in but didn't comment. At least not right away. He waited until their server cleared their plates and brought dessert. "Did you have any questions for me?"

She thought about all the things she could ask him. "How long have you been in the lifestyle?"

He appeared pleased. "I started experimenting in med school."

A part of her didn't want to ask the next question for some reason. The answer didn't really matter, but something compelled her to ask it anyway. "How many subs have you had?"

"How many have I played with or how many have I had a relationship or agreement with?" he asked.

"Um . . . both?" She knew how unsure she sounded.

He picked up a piece of baklava before answering. "I've played with twelve women over the years, only two of whom I've had any sort of formal arrangement with."

That wasn't so many. Not if he'd been in the lifestyle for ten years and was single. Of course, he'd also been in the military, which meant deployments.

Her silence must have been a lot louder than she thought. "Does that seem like a lot?"

Grace shook her head. "No, I suppose not."

He moved on. "I want to talk to you a little about my expectations."

"Okay." All of a sudden the baklava tasted very dry in her throat as she tried to swallow.

"I don't know how things worked with Kurt, but when we're playing I expect you to obey me. You'll have your safeword, but unless you choose to use it, I expect compliance."

She nodded. "Yes, Sir."

"Good." He retrieved the papers she'd given him at the start of their meal, looked them over again, and then met her gaze across the table. "Now, we have just a few more details to go over."

They stayed at the restaurant for almost another hour going over specifics on her list. Nothing too graphic. They kept their language vague in case someone was listening, but still there were times she wanted a hole to open up beneath her and suck her in.

As he drove her home, Grace tried not to read too much into Alexander's insistence that they continue their dinner dates during the week. They wouldn't be playing then. He'd said he wanted them to have some downtime where the rules didn't apply.

He'd also asked her about sex, which had been the most embarrassing topic of conversation to have in the middle of a restaurant. They were alone and most of the other customers had cleared out. Neither of those facts mattered as she turned beet red.

She'd known the subject would come up given what she'd marked on her list, but she hadn't expected him to bring it up then. Mortified, she'd told him that she wasn't sure. That her body was more than ready, but she didn't know if she was actually ready to have sex with someone who wasn't her husband.

To her relief, Alexander understood. He assured her that they would take things slow in that regard and figure it out along the way. It was the perfect response, and yet it wasn't. She should have been grateful he wouldn't push her into jumping into bed with him, but she couldn't deny that she was a little disappointed.

He parked in front of her house and walked her to her front door.

"Did you want to come in?" she asked. He'd come in sometimes after their dinners, and to be honest, she wasn't sure she wanted to say good night to him yet even though it was already after nine.

"I don't think that's such a good idea."

She was a little confused until she saw the look in his eyes. Their conversation earlier had had an effect on him, too.

Before she could think of anything to say, he reached up to brush the back of his fingers against her cheek. "It's not that I don't want to, Grace."

The air around them felt heavy and she felt herself leaning into his touch.

He placed his hand under her chin and tilted it up until she was looking at him. "I'll email you a list of rules and requirements tomorrow."

That had been the last thing she'd thought he'd say.

Alexander released his hold on her and dropped his hand down to his side. "How about I take you to dinner Thursday evening and you can let me know if you'd like to make any changes before Friday?"

Friday. The club. She'd almost forgotten.

"Grace?" He had one eyebrow raised and was waiting on an answer.

"Sounds good," she managed to choke out.

"We'll go as slow as you need. I promise."

A sort of peace came over her. She released a deep breath and smiled. "I know. I trust you."

He held her gaze for a long moment and she saw something in them change. She knew that look. It made her insides flutter. "Go inside, Grace."

She took out her keys and opened the door, sending one last look at Alexander. "Good night."

"Good night."

❧

As promised, Alexander emailed an outline of their arrangement along with his limits list to Grace first thing Tuesday morning. He knew she was at work, so she most likely wouldn't get a chance to look it over until later that night, but that didn't help the bit of anxiety he felt. She'd never played with anyone but her husband, whom she'd known for a decade. It was going to be different for her, an adjustment. He could only hope she would embrace it.

Her assertion the night before that she trusted him had almost sent common sense out the window. He wanted to take her up on her offer to come inside, but he knew that wasn't wise. They needed to do this right. He wanted to do it right for her. And even she had admitted she didn't know if she was ready for sex yet.

Scrubbing a hand over his face, Alexander ignored the growing discomfort in his groin. He'd taken care of things when he'd gotten home the night before, but it didn't feel like it. Thinking about Grace and all the things he wanted to do to her, with her, was enough to have his libido soaring out of control. He really did need to get laid. The only problem with that was the only woman he had any interest in taking to his bed was Grace.

He had a meeting over lunch that ran well into the afternoon. Over his ten-year military career he'd had a few commanders that liked to chatter on instead of getting to the point, but the man who was currently standing at the far end of the conference room took the cake. He'd been rambling on about medical billing procedures for almost forty minutes. It might not have been so bad had he been sharing some sort of new way of doing things, but he wasn't and Alexander wasn't the only one in the room who looked as if he were about to fall asleep.

The man finally sat down and another man took over. There was a collective sigh of relief in the room when the new speaker began talking about an upcoming case involving an experimental drug.

By the time the meeting let out, it was nearly three thirty. Almost everyone went to their desks to check their email and voice mail. They'd been in that dreaded meeting for close to four hours with only one bathroom break. He would rather have run ten miles.

Given his job, he doubted he had any important emails waiting for him at his desk, so after making a quick stop at the bathroom he headed downstairs to the patio for a little air. He took a seat on one of the benches and scrolled through his phone. There was no way to know if Grace had opened his email or not. She was most likely home by then, but that didn't mean anything.

Alexander hated that he was so anxious. It wasn't like him at all. But this was Grace and there was so much that could go wrong.

His thumb hovered over the screen as he debated whether or not to send her a text. He was still debating when his phone dinged.

Got your email. – Grace

It was crazy how something so simple could bring a smile to his face.

Have you opened it yet? – Alexander

It took a minute for her to answer.

Yes. Just now. – Grace

Okay. Let me know if you have any questions. – Alexander

He waited for another few minutes to see if she would send him another message before he went back inside, but she didn't. Tucking his phone back into his jacket pocket, he stood and made his way back inside. As much as he didn't want to, he needed to get back to his desk. There was a stack of papers that needed his attention.

Grace didn't contact him again that night or the next day. If he was being honest, it worried him a little. Had she read something that put her off? Had she changed her mind? The rational part of his brain told him that he'd sent her a lot of information to go over and that she still had work. It wasn't as if she could sit in front of her computer all day dissecting what he'd sent her.

On Wednesday morning he'd been tempted to swing by the café and see her, but he hadn't wanted to seem like a stalker. Instead, he'd gone to work as usual and kept his phone close by.

He was sitting at his desk that afternoon when he got a text from her.

Can you come over tonight? – Grace

His heart sank.

Sure. What time? – Alexander

Six? I'll make dinner. – Grace

I'll be there. – Alexander

He set his phone aside and tried not to jump to conclusions. It was entirely possible that she wanted to go over some things and either didn't want to wait or didn't want to talk about whatever it was out in public. He hadn't missed how uncomfortable she'd gotten during various parts of their conversation on Monday evening.

With as much optimism as he could muster, Alexander rang the doorbell at exactly six o'clock. A gust of wind whipped around the corner, reminding him that he needed to get a heavier jacket before winter. Although it didn't get as cold in St. Louis as it did in DC, he would still need something more substantial than the windbreaker he was sporting.

Grace answered the door with a smile on her face. It gave him hope that she hadn't changed her mind and decided she didn't want him as her Dom. "I'm glad you came."

"Of course," he said as he stepped over the threshold into her home.

"Can I take your jacket?"

He shrugged out of his coat and handed it to her. "Thanks."

Grace had the table already set and there was a bowl of salad at each spot. She stood by her chair and waited. It took him a moment to realize she was waiting for him.

Pulling out her chair for her, he gestured that she should sit. She'd obviously read over his rules.

Alexander joined her at the table, picked up his napkin, and placed it over his lap. "I see you've read over what I sent you."

"Yes, Sir. I have."

"Is that why you asked me to come over tonight?" While he was always happy to see her, it did concern him that she hadn't wanted to wait until tomorrow night.

"Yes. I wanted to talk to you about some things and . . . well, I didn't want to talk about them at the restaurant."

He put some dressing on his salad, picked up his fork, and gestured for her to go ahead.

"I would like for us to play tonight."

His fork stopped halfway to his mouth.

"If it's all right with you, Sir."

Alexander laid his fork down, wiped his mouth, and placed his napkin on the table before giving Grace his full attention. While he had no issue with them playing tonight, he needed to understand her reasoning. "Why?"

She worried the bottom of her lip with her teeth before glancing up at him with those wide eyes of hers. "I've been thinking about it and thinking about it, and when I do I get more and more nervous."

"Maybe you're not ready." He reached out to touch the back of her hand. "It's okay if you're not."

Grace shook her head. "That's not it. I just keep thinking of all the what-ifs. I mean, I've never played with anyone but Kurt. What if it's different with someone else? What if I can't . . ."

"What if you can't what?"

"What if I can't submit to someone else?" she whispered.

This was a real fear. He could see it in her eyes.

Resituating his napkin, he picked his fork back up. "Eat," he said, motioning toward her salad.

She hunched her shoulders in what looked to be defeat and reached for her fork. "I'm sorry. I didn't mean—"

"If you want us to play tonight, you'll need your energy. Eat."

Grace froze, and then a sly smile tugged at her lips.

"That's right. You're getting what you want, *gattina*. Don't get too used to it." He winked at her, letting her know he wasn't upset.

If truth be told, she'd probably get away with more than she should in this relationship—arrangement—or whatever it was you wanted to call what they were about to embark upon. He was hard-pressed to deny her much of anything. There was something about Grace that called to him whether she wanted it or not. Somehow he doubted it would take long for her to steal his heart. He only hoped she didn't rip it out and stomp on it.

Alexander knew she wouldn't do it on purpose, but he wasn't naive. He knew she was still in love with her husband. Knew that the only reason she was doing this was because Kurt had asked it of her. But that didn't change how he felt. Grace needed someone to take care of her—love her—and he was more than up for the job as long as she would let him.

Maybe that made him a sucker, but he could live with that.

Chapter Eleven

He worked beside her to clean up after their meal before saying they should head up to her bedroom. It was really going to happen. They were going to play.

Grace tried to control her breathing as they climbed the stairs. With each step she took she counted her blessings that Alexander had agreed to be her Dom. As nervous as she was about tonight, she knew it would have been ten times worse with someone else.

When they reached her room, she paused outside the door. This was it.

Grace took a deep breath in and let it out slowly before crossing the threshold. She stood off to the side as Alexander strolled into the room and took a look around. He ran his fingers over the comforter on the bed before glancing at the items on top of her nightstand. She saw his brief hesitation before he picked up one of her books.

During one of their dinners, she'd mentioned how much she liked to read. What she hadn't told him was the type of books she preferred. Grace stood by helplessly as he flipped the book over and read the back.

After several moments, he placed the book down and moved on without comment. A small part of her was disappointed. At least if they talked about her books she could focus on something other than the scene they were going to do tonight.

"Do you have a toy bag?" His voice came out of nowhere and startled her.

When she met his gaze across the room he had a smirk on his face. He'd known what he was doing.

"It's a chest," she said. "It's in the closet. It's locked."

When she didn't move, he raised an eyebrow.

"Oh. Yes. Sorry." Feeling a bit silly she hadn't realized he was asking her to get the toys out in the first place, she rushed to her nightstand to get the key.

She and Kurt had picked up the chest years ago at a town market. At the time it had been overkill for what they had, which wasn't much outside a small crop, a flogger, and a few vibrators. Grace pulled the chest from the closet, unlocked it, and lifted the lid. Their toy collection had grown over the years.

With a little extra care than what was normal for someone of Alexander's age, he knelt down in front of the chest.

"I can get you a chair, Sir."

He looked up, meeting her gaze. "Thank you, but I'm fine. Is everything in here clean?"

"Yes, Sir."

Without saying anything more, he went back to inspecting her toys.

They stood there for several minutes as he looked things over. Every now and then he'd pick something up to move it, but for the most part he seemed to be taking an inventory of what she had. With each passing second she grew less sure of herself.

Without selecting any of the toys, Alexander stood. He looked her up and down before staring her in the eye. "There is no shame if you need to use your safeword tonight."

"Yes, Sir."

He held her gaze for a moment longer before speaking. "Remove your shirt and pants."

Grace swallowed and reached for the hem of her shirt. She could do this.

Cool air hit her skin as she lifted the shirt over her head. It wasn't that cold in the room, so she imagined it was the situation itself that had her so sensitive.

She reached for the button of her jeans, pushing it through the material, and then lowered the zipper. Grace had stripped many times for her husband, but this was different. Alexander had never seen her naked. What if he didn't like what he saw?

Her nerves started to get the best of her and she froze.

"Is there a problem?"

Grace shook her head. No, there wasn't a problem. Only her own insecurities. "No, Sir."

Before she could overthink it anymore, she wiggled the jeans lower, letting them drop to the floor. She bent down to pick them up, but Alexander's voice stopped her. "Leave them."

She felt incredibly exposed standing there in nothing but her bra and panties, but she knew from experience that this was only the beginning. It was what she'd asked for and on some level needed. Already, despite her nerves, she felt her body responding.

Alexander took a step forward, closing the distance between them. She could feel the heat from his body even though he wasn't touching her. It felt as if he were six inches taller all of a sudden.

He moved to stand behind her, still close. The hairs on the back of her neck stood at attention, anticipating. He leaned in, his breath ghosting over her ear. "You're a beautiful woman, Grace."

"Thank you, Sir." She wasn't sure what to think about the way the muscles in her belly clenched at the sound, the feel of his voice vibrating against her skin. It had been so long since she'd felt anything like this.

"Remove your bra, Grace." The command was spoken as softly as his compliment regarding her body, but she knew it was a command nonetheless.

With shaky hands, she reached behind her back and unclipped her bra. The straps slid down her shoulders and she let them fall, pulling the cups away and exposing her flesh. She knew without looking that her nipples were hard.

She heard him hum behind her and knew he'd seen the state of her nipples. The sound sent another wave of anticipation through her.

"Cup your tits with your hands."

What? Why wasn't he—

"I won't ask again. Do it, or use your safeword."

Using her safeword hadn't even crossed her mind. It was only not understanding the reasons behind what he was asking that had her hesitating. But it wasn't her job to understand. She trusted Alexander and she knew he'd take care of her.

Grace cupped her breasts, holding their weight in her hands. It wasn't as if she'd never touched herself before. She had. A lot, actually.

As if he could read her mind, Alexander's breath brushed her ear again. "Take your thumb and forefinger and pinch your nipples."

This time she didn't think about it. She just did what he asked.

"You know I'd do it harder than that, Grace."

She pinched harder and felt a zing race down her spine.

"Harder."

A gasp left her lips and warmth rushed between her legs.

"That's better." She could hear the smile in his voice. "Do you pinch your nipples like this when you masturbate?"

"Sometimes." Questions like this shouldn't bother her. Especially since she fully expected Alexander to not only pinch her nipples himself at some point but have sex with her as well.

"Does that embarrass you?" he asked, still not touching her. Was that his plan? To tease her all night?

"Yes." She paused. "A little."

"Then you might turn as red as a beet before we're finished."

The shock of his statement caused her to lose concentration and release her hold on her nipples for a second.

He chuckled. "Oh, *gattina*, I'm going to have so much fun with your shy nature."

She didn't respond. What was she supposed to say to that? Besides, it hadn't been a question.

Her nipples were growing more sensitive the longer she stood there pinching them. The feel of him standing behind her, towering over her, watching was also making it very hard to concentrate on anything outside the two of them. She wanted him to touch her, but didn't know if she should ask him to.

"What are you thinking, *gattina?*"

Grace didn't want to lie and knew she shouldn't. "I was thinking how much I want you to touch me, Sir."

"We have plenty of time for that." He moved a strand of her hair out of the way so he could see better. "Take your right hand and slide it inside the front of your panties. I want you to touch yourself."

Her nipple throbbed when she released it, sending pulses down to her sex. Of course, part of that could have been anticipation as well. It had been almost two years since she'd masturbated in front of a man. She was equal parts nervous and excited. And completely turned on.

The feel of her damp flesh hit her fingers, showcasing how aroused she truly was. Grace was never able to get this wet when she was by herself. Even though Alexander hadn't touched her, he was there, and every cell in her body knew it.

"Are you wet, Grace?"

"Yes, Sir."

"Is your clit swollen?" Every word he said sent tingles down her spine and seemed to have a direct line to her sex.

Without thinking about it, Grace ran her middle finger over her clit and gasped. "Yes."

"That's good." She heard the smile in his voice again. "Now take your panties off and go lie on the bed."

⊗

ALEXANDER WOULD HAVE GIVEN ABOUT ANYTHING TO READ GRACE'S MIND when he'd ordered her to remove her panties and get onto the bed. The look on her face had been enough to let him know he'd caught her completely off guard, which was what he wanted. If she didn't have time to think too much about things, she wouldn't have the chance to second-guess herself. He knew what this meant to her and that it needed to go well.

Throughout dinner, he'd been contemplating their scene. While he'd put a scene together on the fly before, it had never been with a sub such as Grace. She wasn't new to the lifestyle, which had its advantages. He wasn't worried about her not saying her safeword should she need to use it. There also wasn't the issue with her not knowing her hard and soft limits.

No, with Grace the problem was a lot more complicated. He needed something that would test the waters, get them used to each other in these new roles yet allow her to set the pace without having her top from the bottom. It was a delicate balance and one that was sure to leave him needing a long cold shower when he got home.

Grace pushed her panties over her hips and down her legs, revealing her amazing ass. It had taken considerable effort for him to keep his hands to himself. Alexander knew what it felt like against his hand when he'd spanked her, but that had been with her clothes on. He wanted to feel her soft skin against his palm as it turned a lovely shade of pink.

A groan nearly escaped his throat when she climbed onto the bed, ass in the air. Luckily, he stifled it. Tonight wasn't about him. He'd get his needs taken care of another time. Tonight was about what she needed.

He waited until she was lying face up on the bed. She'd spread her legs without being asked, a sure sign this wasn't the first time she'd been told to do something similar. The tips of her nipples were dark pink from where she'd been pinching them. It really was a beautiful sight.

Once she was in position, Alexander went to the toy chest. When he'd looked it over earlier he saw a few things he felt would be perfect for their scene.

There were a few crops in the chest, but one looked to be more worn than the others. He removed that, along with a small flogger, a lifelike dildo, and a bullet vibrator.

When he turned around, he found Grace was watching him. Her brow was furrowed a bit and she was breathing a little harder than normal. Other than that, she remained still. Her legs were still spread and her hands were flat on the bed.

Alexander placed the toys on her nightstand next to her books. When Grace had told him she liked to read romance novels, he hadn't given it much thought. Being in the military for ten years he'd known there were kinky romance novels out there, but for some reason he hadn't pictured Grace reading them. Maybe it was because she was so shy. Then again, before Friday he hadn't known she was a submissive.

He stood next to the bed, looking down at her. "How are you doing?"

"Good, Sir."

"Are you ready to continue?" he asked.

There was still a bit of uncertainty behind her eyes, but she answered anyway. "Yes, Sir."

"Place your hands above your head and press your palms against the headboard. I want those gorgeous tits of yours up in the air."

Grace had to use her feet to scoot herself higher onto the bed in order to reach the headboard, which made him grin. The position naturally arched her back slightly, thrusting her breasts up.

He picked up the crop and used it first to nudge her legs apart. When she'd moved, she'd closed her legs a little more than he liked. She opened up, giving him a great view of her pussy. He took the time to really look at it for the first time. As of tonight that pussy belonged to him.

That thought did nothing to help the growing problem in his pants, but he had no desire to stop the train of his thoughts. He trailed the crop up the inside of one of her thighs, across her belly button, and then down the inside of the other thigh. Like a good little sub, she held perfectly still.

Alexander flicked his wrist twice, landing a single sting to each of her inner thighs. She closed her eyes and pressed her lips together.

He did it again, higher up. This time he saw the muscles of her sex clench. She liked that. He also noticed that most of the tension in her body had disappeared. Grace was in the moment and he wanted her to stay that way.

Running the tip of the crop over her clit caused a whimper to leave her throat. It wasn't a sound of distress in the least. She was turned on and she wanted more.

All in good time.

Alexander took his time exploring her body with the crop. Everywhere he wanted to touch with his hands, his lips, he kissed with the crop instead, lingering where he wanted to linger. Grace had an amazing body. When he'd first met her she'd been too skinny, most likely from not eating the way she should. Between Beth's efforts and his own, they'd managed to put some meat back on her bones, and he was enjoying the results.

When he got to her breasts, he circled them several times making sure to cover every inch before zeroing in on her nipples. She arched her back, silently begging for more as he teased her. When he lifted the crop and snapped it back against the tip, she moaned. The sound went straight to his cock.

Before he threw all common sense out the window and starting sucking on those pretty tits of hers, he returned the crop to the nightstand and reached for the dildo. He held it up at an angle she could see. "When was the last time you used this?"

Her eyes fluttered open and she blinked several times as if she were coming out of a fog. She probably was. He saw the muscles in her throat move as she swallowed. "It's been a while, Sir."

He nodded. "Open your mouth."

She did as instructed and he placed the dildo between her lips. Grace didn't need to be told what was expected of her. She began sucking and licking the dildo as if it were a real cock. If she kept it up, he was liable to come in his pants.

When he couldn't take it anymore, Alexander removed the dildo from her mouth and placed it between her legs. He sat on the edge of the bed and pressed the head against the entrance of her pussy. With shallow movements, he began working it deeper. He was entranced by the way her body swallowed up the fake cock.

His plan had been to insert the dildo into her pussy, and then leave it there while he used the flogger and vibrator on her, but plans changed. He pulled the dildo halfway out before pushing it back in with a little more force. Grace's reaction made him want to do it again, and again. She was doing her best not to move, but she wasn't completely succeeding.

Her breathing became more labored and her fingers pressed against the headboard. He could tell she was close.

He teased her for several more minutes, alternating between deep hard thrusts and faster, shallower ones. She seemed to like the deeper, harder ones best, which was good to know. He looked forward to testing her reactions when it was him instead of a flexible piece of silicone.

Stretching, Alexander grabbed the bullet from the nightstand and turned it on. He placed it against her clit.

Grace's mouth fell open and she tilted her head back. He thrust the dildo into her hard and fast several times and her hips came up off the bed. It was obvious she wasn't thinking straight anymore. He was honestly surprised her hands were still on the headboard. It was no doubt the result of her previous training.

He turned the speed up on the bullet and that was all it took. An almost strangled sound erupted from deep within her throat as she came.

Alexander removed the bullet and the dildo, putting both on her nightstand before taking the blanket at the end of the bed and placing it over her. Forgetting about everything else, he lay down on the bed beside her and pulled her into his arms. He wanted to kiss her, but settled for brushing his lips against the top of her hair.

"You did good, *gattina*. You did good."

Chapter Twelve

It took Grace a moment to realize she wasn't alone and why. Her eyes had drifted closed after their scene and before she knew it, she was asleep. She'd felt safe, relaxed, and a little pleased with herself. Despite her fears, she'd done it. But more than that, she'd enjoyed it.

As soon as that realization popped into her head, guilt began to creep in. She knew it wasn't logical. Kurt had told her to move on, to find another Dom, and she'd done that. He'd want her to be happy and she was. Mostly.

Grace couldn't ask for a better man than Alexander to help her with this. The way he'd handled the scene was exactly what she'd needed.

Thinking about their scene had her blushing. He'd seen every inch of her, made her come. She could still smell a hint of sex in the air.

His arms tightened around her as he shifted his weight. The blanket covering her naked body slipped lower on one side, exposing one of her breasts.

She went to pulled it back into place, but he beat her to it. "Are you cold?"

The sound of his voice, the feel of his body next to hers, had her temperature rising again. She was far from cold. "No."

"How are you feeling?" he asked as he ran a gentle finger from her elbow to her wrist. It was distracting.

She tried to ignore her body's response. "A little sleepy, but good."

"I wasn't expecting you to conk out on me." Grace could tell he was smiling. It helped lighten the mood.

"Sorry."

"It's fine. Just don't make a habit of it." He gave her a gentle squeeze, letting her know he was only giving her a hard time.

Neither of them moved as several minutes ticked by. It wasn't awkward or uncomfortable. In fact, Grace felt more at ease than she had in a really long time. "Thank you."

"You're welcome." He brushed his thumb along the inside of her wrist. "Although, I should probably be the one thanking you."

Grace didn't agree, but decided to let it go. Alexander was happy. The scene had gone well. Great, even. She was now relatively sure she could accompany him to Serpent's Kiss and not embarrass him or herself.

"We need to talk about the scene," he said a while later. She'd been close to drifting off to sleep again. Being in his arms felt more right than anything had since her world fell apart.

"Okay."

He seemed to sense she was waiting on him to start. "Was there anything you didn't like?"

"No, not really."

"That doesn't sound definitive."

He shifted again and she wondered if his leg was bothering him. She began to pull away.

"Where do you think you're going?" His Dom voice was back, slightly deeper than his normal voice. It made her heart rate kick up a notch.

"You keep shifting your weight. I thought maybe your leg was hurting. I wanted to give you some space." She saw his frown and knew he wasn't pleased.

"Let me worry about my leg." He tugged her back against his side. "You're avoiding the question. Was there something about the scene you didn't care for?"

"No. There wasn't anything you did I didn't like." That was the truth. She'd loved it all. And she'd wanted more. That's the part that had her feeling the guiltiest. If he'd wanted to have sex with her tonight she would have let him.

Alexander knew there was something she wasn't telling him. "But?"

She glanced down at her hands where they rested in her lap. Honesty. "You didn't touch me."

When he didn't respond, she looked up. He appeared to be amused.

"What?" she asked, confused.

"I used a crop on you and shoved a dildo inside your pussy."

At that moment, she wanted to crawl under the covers. She'd never been good at talking about this stuff and Alexander wasn't mincing words. "I know."

He placed a finger under her chin and forced her to meet his gaze. "But you wanted my hands on you."

She nodded.

Alexander cupped the side of her face, his fingers tickling the hairs at the base of her neck. He leaned in closer. She could feel his breath on her face. Was he going to kiss her?

"There are so many things I want to do to you, Grace. So many ways I want to touch you. But tonight wasn't about that. Tonight was about you letting go of your fears and realizing that you are still a woman who has needs, wants, and desires. A woman that needed to see that she could let go again and trust that I would catch her."

Grace felt the moisture prick her eyes and tried to hold back the tears. He'd seen her cry enough already.

He pressed his soft lips against hers for a brief moment before pulling back. "You need a bath, and then bed. You have work tomorrow."

Without waiting for her to reply, he eased himself out of her bed. He held out his hand for her and she took it. The blanket fell away, leaving her naked in front of him.

Alexander didn't even pretend he wasn't looking. His gaze lingered on her breasts before he headed lower. If she'd ever wondered if he was attracted to her, she now had her answer. The look in his eyes told her everything she needed to know.

For a second, she thought he was going to kiss her again, but then he turned and led her into her bathroom. Grace had to admit she was disappointed. She'd wanted him to kiss her.

He drew her a bath and helped her into the tub. "Relax and enjoy your bath then get some sleep. I'll make sure the house is locked up when I leave."

She wasn't sure why, but she'd been hoping he'd stay. It was silly. They both had work tomorrow and he had no clothes there. Plus, it wasn't as if he was her boyfriend or anything. They weren't dating. He was her Dom. It was an arrangement.

"What's wrong?"

"Nothing." She tried to smile, but it must have fallen flat because his frown was back.

"This doesn't work if you lie to me."

"I'm not." His skeptical look had her backtracking. "I'm just not used to this kind of . . . arrangement."

He leaned back again the doorframe and crossed his arms over his chest. "What kind of arrangement is that?"

"You being my Dom. Me being your submissive."

"You've had a Dom before," he said, obviously not understanding what she was getting at.

"Yes, but I was married to him." She sighed, frustrated that she was having trouble explaining herself. "We were . . . I mean . . . it was just different, I guess."

Alexander took a moment before answering. "Grace, I'm not sure what you think this arrangement is or isn't, but maybe I need to spell it out for you. As my submissive, you belong to me. And as your Dom, I belong to you."

Grace nodded. She knew that.

But he didn't stop there. "I won't be playing with anyone else while we're together. I won't be dating anyone else either."

She felt her mouth fall open.

He pushed off the doorframe and turned to go. "Finish your bath and get some rest. I'll text you in the morning and I expect you to text me back as soon as you're able. Do you understand?"

"Yes, Sir."

Alexander exited the bathroom, leaving her pondering what he'd said. Did that mean they were dating? Exclusive? She had no idea, and to be honest, she didn't know how she felt about it. Not that she was planning on going out and dating anyone else, but dating implied there was an emotional element to their relationship.

Grace could hear him moving around downstairs, making sure her doors and windows were locked. The sound of the front door opening and then closing had her sliding down lower into her bath. Did Alexander want their arrangement to be more? It certainly sounded like that. The question became could she give him that if it was in fact what he wanted?

She didn't know the answer and that frightened her even more than the thought of going to Serpent's Kiss again, this time as Alexander's submissive.

The water began to cool, so Grace got out and reached for a towel. She'd do her best—try to be the best sub she could be for him. Hopefully, that was enough.

ALEXANDER SENT GRACE A TEXT BEFORE HE LEFT FOR WORK ASKING IF SHE'D slept well last night. He knew she was most likely busy at the café, but he expected her to get back to him before lunch. They'd texted back and forth during the day before and it never took her more than an hour or so to get back to him. He hoped what had happened last night between them didn't change that.

To his surprise, his phone dinged as he was getting into his car.

Yes. – Grace

There was a pause.

I hit the snooze three times this morning. – Grace

He chuckled. Grace wasn't exactly a morning person, but she was used to her schedule and she enjoyed her job. They'd talked about how she always had to hit snooze once in the mornings before she could drag herself out of bed. Three times meant she really hadn't wanted to get up.

I'm glad you got some rest. – Alexander

Have a good day at work. I'll pick you up at 6. – Alexander

When she didn't respond right away, he went ahead and drove to work. Halfway there he heard her message come in. Unfortunately, he had to wait until he arrived at work to check it.

Okay. I'll be ready. – Grace

His day went by quickly. There'd been a mountain of new folders on his desk that required his attention and at lunch he'd had to run to the post office. The state licensing board had sent him another form they needed to be filled out and sent in. He wanted the process of getting his license to practice in Missouri completed as soon as possible. That meant staying on top of whatever the licensing board required. He sure as hell didn't want to be sitting at a desk for the rest of his days going over malpractice suits.

Jewel asked if he wanted to join her and some others for drinks again. He felt bad that he had to keep turning her down, but there was no way he was giving up the evening with Grace. He also didn't think she'd feel comfortable tagging along with him while he hung out with his coworkers. The new terms of their relationship alone had her leery.

He hadn't missed the look on her face when he'd told her there would be no one else as long as he was with her. She'd lost a little color in her face and her jaw had dropped. Alexander had thought he'd been clear before about exactly what he expected, but apparently he'd not been clear enough. He didn't want to scare her, but she needed to know he wasn't going to be playing, or dating, anyone else as long as they were together.

Thinking about seeing Grace again had him whistling on his way to his vehicle. He got a few strange looks, but he didn't care. In less than an hour he'd see Grace again and tonight he planned on pushing her boundaries a little more.

As promised, Grace was ready and waiting when he showed up at her house. She had her hair pulled back and a little makeup on. The makeup was new. And while she looked nice, he preferred her natural beauty.

"Shall we?" he said, offering her his arm.

She locked the door and hooked her arm through his.

It didn't take long to get to the restaurant. They'd been there before and had both enjoyed the food. That was good since he was starving. He'd skipped lunch in favor of going to the post office.

"Good evening. Two?" the hostess asked.

Alexander nodded. "Yes, and a booth please, if you have it."

She grinned and picked up two menus. "Right this way."

The booth was along the wall in the center of the room. Not as private as he'd like, but he could work with it.

He motioned for Grace to have a seat. Instead of taking the seat opposite, he slid in beside her.

Grace scooted closer to the wall, making room for him. One they were both settled and the hostess had left them alone, he rested his hand on her knee as he picked up his menu. He was very glad she'd chosen to wear a skirt tonight.

She sucked in a breath.

"Problem?" he asked.

"No, Sir."

"Good." He smiled. "Hopefully you know what you want because I could eat a horse."

Careful not to move her lower half, Grace picked up her menu.

When their server stopped by their table, he ordered their drinks and an appetizer, giving Grace a few more minutes to decide what she wanted. He was being good, keeping his hand still while she looked.

Their server returned with their drinks and a basket of bread. She jotted down their orders and told them she'd return shortly with their appetizer.

Once they were alone again, he decided it was time to have some fun. He pushed the hem of her skirt up a little and began tracing small circles on the inside of her leg a few inches above her knee. Grace tensed.

He turned and whispered in her ear. "Relax. No one is going to know I'm doing anything unless you act as if something's wrong."

He saw her swallow.

"If I'm doing something you don't want me to do, all you have to do is say the word." Grace knew exactly what word he was talking about.

She remained silent.

He picked up a piece of bread and handed it to her. "Did you eat lunch today?"

"Yes." She was trying hard to keep still. "A sandwich and some soup."

Alexander was glad to hear Beth was still taking care of her. "Good. I expect you to eat three full meals a day, no exceptions."

When she didn't answer, he gave her leg a light pinch. "Yes, Sir."

"I'm going to make sure you take care of yourself, *gattina*." He inched his fingers a little higher. "That's part of my job."

Grace nodded.

He removed his hand and reached for a piece of bread for himself, leaving her on edge. That was good.

Their appetizer came, a fondue. The interactive nature of the food lightened the mood a bit and he was pleased to see her release some of her tension. He dipped some of the bread into the melted cheese and held it to her lips.

She opened her mouth and he watched as her lips sucked the food inside. It was almost as bad as watching her give that fake cock a blow job the night before. He wanted to feel those lips around him, sucking him into oblivion.

Shaking the thought from his mind, he skewered another piece of bread and dipped it into the cheese. Pushing Grace was one thing, but jumping into bed with her was another. He wanted her to feel completely comfortable with him and what they were doing before he went there. This wasn't just about him getting laid or getting her off. At least not for him. He didn't want her to regret anything they did together. Ever.

Their meal came and he steered things to safer topics, all the while continuing to touch and caress her beneath the table. He asked about her mom and how things were going with her upcoming retirement. By the time they finished their meal, it almost felt like it had before he'd seen her at the club. She'd giggled at his jokes and even snorted when he'd suggested maybe her mom could take up juggling as a hobby.

Grace was smiling as he drove her home. A real, genuine smile. Throughout dinner she'd gotten more and more used to his touch. His heart felt lighter and heavier all at the same time.

She hugged her jacket against her as they stepped onto her front porch. Fall had definitely arrived in St. Louis. "Do you want to come in?"

Want had nothing to do with it.

He walked forward, backing her up against the door. Grace looked up at him, her eyes sparkling in the evening light.

"I don't think that's a good idea," he whispered, his lips hovering an inch above hers.

Grace licked her bottom lip. "Why?"

He stifled a groan. She didn't make this easy.

Instead of answering with words, he closed the distance between them, wrapped his arm around her waist, and pulled her against him. She let out a tiny squeak before his mouth covered hers.

It was the first time he'd kissed her. Really kissed her. Sure, he'd brushed his lips against hers a few times in the past, but this was different.

Her lips gave under the gentle pressure of his mouth. He sucked her bottom lip into his mouth, remembering how her tongue had moistened it moments before. She was so soft in his arms, molding her body to his.

Alexander dug his fingers into her hip, needing her closer. He slipped his tongue into her mouth, exploring, tasting. It wasn't enough, and yet he knew it had to be. For now.

Breaking the kiss, he rested his forehead against hers as he met her gaze. She was breathing hard, her chest rising and falling, making it that much more difficult to do what he knew he needed to.

"Good night, Grace."

She blinked as if she were waking from a daze. His male pride soared at having been the one responsible.

Even though he knew she'd heard him, Grace didn't move.

"Grace?"

"Hmm?"

"You need to unlock the door and go inside." He released her and took a step back—the cool air helping to bring some sanity back to the situation.

It seemed to do the same for her. Grace dug her keys out of her purse and turned to unlock the door. She looked over her shoulder before going inside. Several strands of her hair were loose and her lipstick was almost completely gone, even though she'd gone to the bathroom before they'd left the restaurant and reapplied it. Alexander was most likely wearing the other half of it himself. He couldn't care less.

"Good night, Grace."

A light pink tinted her cheeks. "Good night."

Chapter Thirteen

Friday morning dawned and Grace had to drag herself out of bed. It had taken her a while to get to sleep the night before. Her mind and body had been too worked up from the kiss she'd shared with Alexander. He'd kissed her before. A few times. But even she knew last night had been different. His kisses before had been innocent. Chaste. There'd been nothing innocent about what happened on her porch.

She went to work, happy for the distraction. That was until Alexander texted her at noon to remind her he'd be picking her up at six. After that, she hadn't been able to think of anything else. They were going to the club and this time around he would be her Dom and she would be his submissive.

Beth noticed she was distracted. "Any big plans this weekend?"

Grace debated how to answer her boss. "I sort of have a date."

It was the easiest way to explain her and Alexander's plans for the evening. Especially to someone who didn't know anything about BDSM. She could only imagine Beth's reaction if Grace told her she was going to a kink club with her Dom.

"That's great." Beth paused. "Right? I mean I'm assuming you like the guy. You agreed to go out with him."

"Do you remember me telling you about Kurt's friend, the Army doctor?" Grace asked as she put the food Beth had prepared onto a tray.

Her boss' eyes lit up. "Really? That's great." She put the finishing touches on another sandwich and handed it to Grace. "But haven't you been out with the guy before? I mean maybe not on an official date or anything, but out to dinner and stuff?"

"Yeah." Grace didn't know exactly how to explain it without going into detail. "I guess it's just that things are changing."

Beth studied her face. "Is that not what you want?"

"No. I do." Grace released a frustrated sigh. She wasn't doing a very going job explaining. Then again, how could she? The only one who knew the whole story was Alexander. "It's just . . . new."

"Now, that I can relate to." Beth laughed. "My advice? Don't worry so much. Things will work out the way they're meant to."

Grace picked up the tray full of food feeling a little better after talking to Beth. She still had no idea what to expect from tonight, but her boss was right. Things would work out the way they were meant to, good or bad.

At three thirty Grace said goodbye to Beth and Tommy and made her way to the store before heading home. She had a lot to do before Alexander picked her up. After showering and shaving, she went to her closet to find something to wear. She didn't want to disappoint her new Dom.

Grace tried on a handful of outfits before settling on the same fitted leather skirt she'd worn the week before and a white top that dipped low in both the front and the back. Because of how it was made, Grace wouldn't be able to wear a bra. If Alexander was anything like her husband had been, he would like that.

The doorbell rang a little before six and she raced downstairs as fast as her three-inch heels would carry her. Figuring it was Alexander, she opened the door without looking, only to find her sister staring back at her with her eyes about to bug out of her head, holding her niece. The look on her sister's face had her wanting to cover up.

"What are you doing here?"

It took Gabby a moment to answer. "I tried to call, but you didn't answer." She gave Grace a long once-over. "Now I know why."

This wasn't a conversation Grace wanted to have standing in her doorway, so she took a step back and let her sister inside. "Sorry. I was probably in the shower."

Her sister scanned her surroundings, and then met Grace's gaze with a smirk on her face. "Are you waiting on your doctor?"

She started to say he wasn't hers, but stopped herself. He was hers. At least for the time being. "He's taking me to a club."

"Oooo. Dancing. Fun." Her sister placed a single finger in the center of her top and pushed down, revealing more of Grace's skin. "No bra. Nice. Someone's hoping to get lucky tonight."

Grace batted Gabby's hand away. She could already feel her blush starting. "You said you called?" She really needed to get her sister's attention away from what she was wearing and how she was going to be spending her evening.

Gabby repositioned her daughter on her hip. "When I picked Taylor up tonight, her babysitter told me she had a death in the family and won't be able to watch her tomorrow or Monday. Mom said she can watch her tomorrow while I'm at work, but I was hoping you could cover Monday." A sly grin appeared. "That is if you're not spending your day off with your new man."

"I can watch her Monday." Grace chose to ignore the rest of what her sister said.

"Great! We'll talk more Sunday." Gabby gave her a swift kiss on the cheek before heading toward the door. "I'll get out of your hair so you can finish getting ready, but I'll expect details."

Grace tried not to groan, and waved goodbye to her sister. Every time Gabby had asked her about Alexander in the past, Grace kept insisting there was nothing going on between them, that they were just friends. It wasn't as if she could claim that anymore. They were definitely more than friends now. He was her Dom. Everything else? Grace wasn't sure about that herself. She had no idea how she was going to explain it to her sister.

With Beth it had been easier. Beth wasn't going to ask for a blow-by-blow, as it were. Gabby would want to know when things changed and why Grace had been holding out on her. It made her want to call her mom and tell her she wasn't going to make it over this week. Of course, that would only put off the inevitable.

She heard Alexander's footfalls on the porch and opened the door before he had a chance to ring the bell. He was dressed in black slacks and a greenish-blue shirt that buttoned down the front. Her heart rate picked up at the sight of him.

It wasn't until he came inside that she realized he had his cane with him. "Is your leg bothering you?"

He raised an eyebrow and she realized her mistake. Not a great way to start the evening.

"Sorry, Sir." She lowered her gaze to the floor as he closed the door.

Grace wasn't sure what she was expecting his reaction to be, but she nearly jumped out of her skin when she felt his hand on the back of her thigh. "Easy, *gattina.*"

She bit down on the inside of her cheek and told herself to breathe.

He gave her a moment, and then eased his hand up under her skirt and ran his fingers along the seam of her thong. "Very nice."

"Thank you, Sir."

His hand remained on her ass as he moved to stand in front of her. He lifted her chin with his free hand, his cane dangling only an inch from her breast. "I approve of your top as well."

She swallowed, not saying anything as he ran the back of his hand down her neck to the hollow between her breasts where the material of her shirt pooled. But unlike her sister, he didn't tug at her shirt to confirm she wasn't wearing a bra. Then again, he didn't have to. Grace could feel her nipples pressing against the silky fabric, trying to get free.

Grace was so focused on her body's reactions she almost missed his next words. "It's going to be a big night for you, and as I said before, there will be no running. You will be by my side as my submissive and you will conduct yourself as such. If there is a problem, you will tell me immediately."

"Yes, Sir."

They stopped to have dinner. He'd sat beside her again, but this time he kept his hands to himself. She didn't know if that was due to the fact that the restaurant was crowded or if it was because he could tell how nervous she was.

When they arrived at the club, he helped her out of her coat and handed it to the woman behind the desk in the lobby. "Thank you, Ali."

"You're welcome, Sir," the woman said. "Have a fun time tonight."

He placed a hand on Grace's lower back and guided her into the club.

❧

Alexander paid close attention to Grace's reaction as they walked into the main room of the club. He kept his hand on her lower back as he guided her through the crowd and over to the seating area. Daniel was already there chatting with Nicole and Jeff.

Daniel saw them first. His gaze fell on Grace, and then back to Alexander. "And who do we have here?"

It was then he saw Nicole's expression change. She recognized Grace. And from the looks of it, so did her sub, Jeff.

A moment later, he knew Grace had recognized them, too. Alexander had been so concerned about her reaction to seeing Beth that he hadn't considered she'd also know Nicole and Jeff. He knew Nicole and Beth were best friends, but he wasn't aware Nicole and Grace had ever met.

Alexander circled his arm around Grace's waist and pulled her closer to his side before answering Daniel's question. He wasn't about to have her take off on him. "This is my submissive, Grace."

His friend raised one eyebrow in silent question, but didn't comment.

Turning to Nicole, Alexander said, "I think you may already know each other?"

"Yes. Grace works at the café with Beth."

He edged Grace closer to the couch, sat down, and tugged her onto his lap. "I didn't realize you frequented the café."

Nicole shrugged. "I drop by every now and then."

Alexander also heard her unasked question lingering behind her words. Did Beth know Grace would be at the club tonight? He subtly shook his head and saw her frown. While he could understand her concern for her friend, it wasn't Beth he was worried about. Grace had been in the lifestyle with her husband for years. She wouldn't out her boss. She might, however, try to run again.

"Well, clearly I'm the odd one out here," Daniel said. The two Doms had hit it off right away due to them both having a military background even though Daniel was almost twenty years older than Alexander. Then again, there were days when Alexander felt twenty years older than he actually was. Daniel leaned toward Grace. "It's nice to meet you."

Nicole appeared mildly irritated at the casual way Alexander was handling the situation. Jeff, on the other hand, looked somewhat bored. This new development didn't seem to bother him. Daniel took another long look at Grace. Alexander could only imagine what his friend was thinking.

But the reaction he was most focused on was Grace's. Her breathing had picked up and her fingers were white from pressing them as hard as she could into her legs. He pried her fingers up and laced them with his.

"How did you two meet?" Nicole asked.

Alexander slipped his thumb under the hem of Grace's shirt and began rubbing back and forth. He needed her to relax. "Her husband and I served together."

It was as if a light bulb went off in everyone's head.

"So this is the woman you spent so much time searching for," Daniel said.

Alexander grinned, not breaking the rhythm of his touch against her skin. "She made herself difficult to find."

Grace let her shoulders sag a little. She was paying attention to the conversation even though she hadn't said a word. He hadn't given her any speaking restrictions for tonight other than letting her know that she owed both Justin and Katrina an apology for running out last Friday. Her silence thus far, however, didn't surprise him. His Grace was shy.

Daniel chuckled, either unaware or ignoring Grace's reaction. "I remember."

Conversation turned to a new piece of equipment Katrina had acquired for the club. Alexander was only half paying attention. Grace was still stiff in his arms.

Several more minutes passed and the topic of conversation shifted again, but Grace's posture hadn't changed. He lifted their linked hands and brought them to his lips. She met his gaze. "Would you like something to drink?"

"No, thank you, Sir."

Alexander released her hand and cupped the side of her face. "Tell me what's bothering you."

Her bottom lip trembled. "What if Nicole tells Beth and I lose my job? I don't want to lose my job."

"You're not going to lose your job."

"You don't know that," she whispered.

He stared back at her, both eyebrows raised.

She lowered her gaze. "Sorry, Sir. I didn't mean—"

He tipped her chin up so she was looking at him again. "I'm not upset with you, *gattina*. I do, however, want to understand why you think your boss would fire you for being a member of a kink club when her best friend is one."

That, at least, had her thinking. "I just don't want Beth to think less of me."

"Why would I think less of you?" They hadn't heard the couple approach, but it was obvious at least part of their conversation had been overheard.

Grace stiffened once again in his arms.

"Good evening, Beth. Drew," Alexander said to the new arrivals.

The look on Grace's face was priceless. Her eyes were as big as saucers and her mouth was parted in an *O* shape. He could see the wheels turning in her head. If Beth was here, that meant she was a member as well.

"Alexander." Beth took a seat beside Nicole and tossed a pillow onto the floor near her feet. Without any further instruction, Drew lowered himself down onto the pillow.

A few seconds passed before Alexander brushed his thumb over Grace's lips, drawing her out of her thoughts and back to the present. "I do believe Beth is still waiting on an answer."

Grace swallowed before twisting slightly so she didn't have her back to Beth. "I don't know. I just . . . you never know how people will react." She paused and glanced down at her lap. "I didn't know you were . . ."

"A Domme?" Beth looked mildly amused.

Grace looked at Beth and he saw the beginnings of a smile. "Yeah."

"I was wondering if you were a submissive," Drew said from Beth's feet. It had been interesting watching their relationship evolve over the last two months. "It's good to have another sub to balance things out."

Beth ran a single nail along the back of Drew's neck. Alexander was grateful for Drew's levity. He'd made Grace feel as if she was part of the group.

"Were you and your husband in the lifestyle?" Beth asked Grace.

Grace nodded. "For about ten years."

"That's impressive," Nicole said.

Alexander had to agree. Keeping up any relationship while overseas came with challenges. He couldn't fathom the difficulties of balancing a D/s relationship when one partner was in a war zone.

"It just worked for us." He felt Grace shrink against him and knew she was ready for the spotlight to be off her.

Patting her leg, he indicated he wanted her to stand. "Excuse us. We're going to get something to drink, and then we need to find Katrina and Justin." He used his cane to help him to stand even though he really didn't need it tonight. He'd only brought it as a precaution.

They made their way across the room to the bar. There were several people waiting on drinks, so it was a few minutes before Brandon got around to serving them. "What can I get you?"

Alexander looked at Grace. She was nervous, but he didn't think she was about ready to bolt so that was progress. "What would you like?"

"White wine, please."

He nodded. "One white wine and a water."

Brandon grinned and headed toward the opposite end of the bar.

Once he returned with their drinks, Alexander surveyed the crowd until he located Katrina coming out of the back rooms, most likely from her office.

Alexander placed a hand on Grace's back and began heading in Katrina's direction.

Chapter Fourteen

Grace felt as if everyone was staring at her. They weren't, of course. Most of the club members were engrossed in their own conversations and play. The only person who was focusing on her was Alexander as he eased her across the room toward Katrina.

The club mistress stopped to talk to a couple as they strolled by. She smiled and seemed to be in a good mood.

As the other couple walked away, Alexander picked up their pace and closed the distance. Katrina noticed. She acknowledged Grace, but posed her question to Alexander. "How are you this evening?"

"We're good. You?"

"I can't complain." She chuckled. Then her gaze landed once again on Grace. "I wasn't aware the two of you had been introduced."

"Grace is the one who brought me to St. Louis."

Katrina looked Grace over again as if seeing her with new eyes. "I see."

Did everyone at Serpent's Kiss know about him searching for her? It was beginning to sound like it. And did they know about the letter, too?

Grace didn't get a lot of time to ponder the questions running through her head before Alexander spoke up again. "We've been getting to know each other for the last month, but until I saw her at the club last week, I didn't know she had any interest in BDSM."

The club mistress' mood shifted and she was all business. "I'm guessing you two have come to some sort of an agreement?"

Alexander nodded. "Yes."

He didn't go into any details and Katrina didn't ask. Grace tried to recall if the club had any specific policies when it came to couples who had a negotiated contract but her mind was completely blank.

Pressure against her back had her meeting Alexander's gaze. He looked down at her as if he was waiting for something.

It only took her a few seconds to realize what exactly he was waiting on. She turned to Katrina and lowered her gaze to the floor. "I wanted to apologize again for running out last Friday. It was rude of me."

After a brief interval, Katrina responded. "I accept your apology, Grace." She paused. "I assume the reason for your swift departure had to do with Alexander?"

Grace nodded. "Yes, Mistress. I saw him and panicked."

"Seeing people we know from the outside world inside the club can be jarring. We are making ourselves vulnerable."

"Yes, Ma'am." Grace shifted her weight. "I need to apologize to Justin as well."

"I'm sure he would appreciate that. I do believe he's upstairs helping Cooper tonight."

"Thanks."

Less than a minute later they were heading up to the second floor. A few steps from the top she began to hear sounds of play. They were all muffled, but unmistakable.

Alexander took her hand and led her down the hallway. "We'll kill two birds with one stone while we're up here. After you apologize to Justin, we're going to watch some scenes."

She knew that was part of the plan for tonight, for him to see firsthand what she liked, but being there surrounded by the sounds and the smells of the dungeon had her pulse racing. It didn't mean she wasn't still nervous, but her nerves were being overshadowed by an energy that had her excited to see what the rest of the evening had in store. She just had to get through her apology to Justin first.

The man in question stepped out of one of the rooms with a toy bag in his hand. He walked in the opposite direction, opened a door at the end of the hall, and placed the bag inside. Grace didn't think the door went to a playroom.

Justin saw them when he spun around. He seemed to breathe a sigh of relief at seeing Grace. "I'm glad you came back."

She decided to jump in with both feet. That was why they'd sought him out, after all. "Sir, I wanted to apologize for running off last week. I know I caused you worry and that was not my intention. I saw Alexander and I didn't know what to do, so I ran."

The two Doms exchanged a look. "Thank you for explaining, Grace. And I am glad you're back. I would hate for you to miss out on the fun because of your fear."

"Somehow I don't think that will be permitted anymore, Sir."

"No, *gattina*. It won't," Alexander said.

Justin glanced over his shoulder. "Did you two want a room? There's one down the hall that's available."

"Thank you," Alexander said. "But we'll just be observing tonight."

"Let me or Cooper know if you need anything," Justin said before going to assist someone in room number five.

Alexander didn't give her any time to let her mind wander. He headed in the opposite direction Justin had gone and stopped in front of the large viewing window of room number one. The couple inside looked to be finishing up a scene. She lay curled up on her side with him holding her from behind. It was such a tender moment. Grace felt as if they were intruding.

After a few moments, they moved on to room three. A man was chained to the ceiling, his cock and balls covered in clothespins. She'd had clothespins attached to various parts of her body before and she could see the tension in the man's arms as the woman placed weights through tiny holes in the clothespins that were attached to his balls.

They didn't stay in front of that room for long. Although watching a scene like that didn't really bother her, it didn't do anything for her sexually either. Alexander seemed to realize that.

It took them two more tries before they came across a scene that had the muscles in her abdomen clenching. The woman was on her knees, clamps with a long chain attached dangling from her nipples, while she sucked on the man's cock. He had her hair gathered into a ponytail and used it to guide her movements. It was so erotic that Grace felt herself getting wet.

Alexander moved to stand behind her, but Grace barely noticed until he reached up under her skirt and ran his thumb over her clit through the thin material of her panties. She couldn't help the moan that escaped her throat. "You like that, don't you? Seeing her suck his cock?"

There was no point in denying it. "Yes."

He brushed his thumb against her clit again. And again. Her breathing began to pick up and she almost spilled her wine.

Alexander removed it from her grasp and placed it on the window ledge before returning his attention to her. "This is what you wanted, wasn't it? For me to touch you?" he whispered in her ear as she continued to watch the scene in front of her.

Before she knew it, she could feel her orgasm approaching. Alexander had the front of her skirt pulled up and wasn't doing anything to hide what he was doing to her. Something inside her said she should be embarrassed, but it did nothing to curb her arousal.

"Come for me, *gattina*. Let go and come."

She closed her eyes and imagined that it was her in there on her knees with Alexander's cock in her mouth. A fresh wave of arousal leaked out and her breath hitched. She wanted to know what he tasted like—what he felt like—between her lips.

He moved her panties out of the way and stroked her clit without any barrier. Between that and her imagination, she was a goner. Her orgasm rippled through her, causing her knees to buckle.

Alexander steadied her, his arm wrapped tight around her waist.

It took her a few minutes to recover and when she did, she realized they had an audience. Justin, Cooper, and two other couples were watching. The embarrassment took up residence in her cheeks and she buried her head in Alexander's chest.

He kissed the top of her head and removed his fingers from her panties, ignoring the onlookers. "That was beautiful, *gattina*. You have no reason to be embarrassed. In fact, you should be quite proud of yourself. Every man who witnessed that is having to adjust himself to make more room in his pants."

His statement did nothing to curb her discomfort. In the moment, it hadn't mattered, but now that her arousal had faded, she couldn't believe she had done that. "Are they gone?"

Alexander chuckled. "Everyone except Justin and Cooper, yes."

Grace groaned. She was not an exhibitionist.

Then she remembered how hard she'd come.

Maybe she was an exhibitionist. Or maybe it was Alexander. He brought things out in her, had her thinking of things she hadn't before.

He reached for her wineglass and handed it to her. "Let's head back downstairs. I want to talk to Daniel before we call it a night."

❧❧❧

GRACE SPENT THE REST OF THEIR TIME AT SERPENT'S KISS SITTING ON HIS lap. He kept his hand on her leg, tracing little circles with his fingers. Every now and then she would squirm when he would inch his way a little higher. He wasn't sure if she was trying to get away or urge him to move his hand farther up her leg.

He'd told Grace he wanted to talk to Daniel, which was true, but he'd also hoped to talk to Beth again. Unfortunately, Beth and Drew were nowhere in sight. When he'd asked about them, Nicole said they'd cut out early because they both had to work in the morning. Considering they couldn't have been there more than an hour, Alexander wondered if it had more to do with Drew's comment than them having to work the next day.

Nicole and Jeff excused themselves and headed upstairs to play, leaving Alexander, Grace, and Daniel alone. Daniel was in real estate and Alexander wanted to get a feel for what was out there in respects to office buildings he could use to set up a practice. Even though it could take up to a year for his license to come through, he didn't want to wait until the last minute to start looking for a space to rent.

"I was wondering if you could put together some numbers for me for commercial buildings."

"Did your license come through already?" Daniel asked before taking a sip of his drink.

Alexander shook his head. "I just want to stay on top of things and see what's out there. Besides, it will take a while to get things up and running before I can start seeing patients. I can get all the back end stuff out of the way in the meantime."

"You're thinking ahead." Daniel grinned. "I wish more of my clients thought like you did. You'd be amazed how many come in needing something yesterday."

"I prefer to have a game plan. I can improvise when I have to, but things go much smoother when there's a plan in place."

Daniel lifted his glass in a mock salute. "I couldn't agree more." He took another sip of his drink. "Did you want to stop by tomorrow and take a look at the listings?"

"Sure. What time?"

"Around noon? We could make it a working lunch."

With plans made, Alexander decided it was time to get Grace home. She had to be at work early tomorrow and she needed her rest.

When they arrived at her house, he got out and walked her to her door. Unlike the night before, he followed her inside.

Grace placed her keys on the side table and removed her coat. She barely got it off before he backed her against the wall and covered her mouth with his.

Her response was immediate. She circled her arms around his neck and kissed him back for all she was worth. His little kitten was worked up.

Alexander pushed her skirt up and tugged her panties down, letting them fall to the floor. He wasted no time touching her pussy. All his teasing earlier had him hard as a rock, but what he wanted more than anything was to touch her, and lucky for him that seemed to be what Grace wanted as well.

She bucked her hips, pushing against his hand, and he slipped two fingers inside. They slid easily in and out as he mimicked the rhythm with his tongue. It felt so good to finally be able to touch her like this after he'd been dreaming about it for weeks.

He cupped her breast with his free hand and felt her pebbled nipple press against his palm. As much as he loved her shirt, it needed to go. "Take your shirt off. It's in my way."

Grace grabbed the hem of her top—no hesitation at all in her movements —and wiggled it up her torso and over her head. He wasted no time palming her tits and teasing them with his fingers. In the not too distant future, he imagined spending hours paying homage to them.

For now, though, he contented himself with being able to touch her freely. He squeezed one of her tits, lifting it, and brought his lips down, sucking it into his mouth. Feeling her flesh on his tongue had him groaning. He felt as if his cock were going to explode out of his pants.

She rode his fingers while he licked and sucked on her lovely tits. It seriously didn't get much better than this. He could feel her arousal coating his fingers as he continued to pump in and out of her. Grace's head was thrown back, her mouth open slightly, and her chest rose and fell with her rapid breathing. He wanted to take a picture so he could keep the sight of her like this with him forever.

"Sir?" Her voice was breathy.

He eased his fingers in and out of her a few more times before answering. "Yes?"

"Sir, may I come?" He could hear the pleading in her voice. She was close.

Alexander took her nipple between his teeth and tugged slightly. "Not quite yet, *gattina*."

She dug her nails into his shoulders as if she were trying to hold onto something to keep herself from coming.

He licked her nipple, easing the pain he'd inflicted, before lowering himself down to his knees. It wasn't as easy a position for him as it used to be, but for her it was worth it. He placed his free hand over her abdomen and used his fingers to spread her open. Without preamble, he went in.

A whimper left her lips as he circled her clit with his tongue. Grace fisted her fingers in his hair, looking for purchase but couldn't seem to find it. Her legs began to tremble, and then a shudder went through her entire body. He knew she wasn't going to be able to hold on much longer no matter how hard she tried.

Alexander gazed up at her from his perch between her legs. Her eyes were unfocused, glassy, and her skin was flushed, not from embarrassment as it so often was, but from how turned on she was. "You may come, *gattina*."

Unlike before at the club where it had still taken her several minutes to fall over that peak, this time it was as if he'd flipped a switch. A scream came from deep in her throat and a shockwave rippled through her body until she slid down the wall onto the floor beside him.

He twisted around and positioned her onto his lap. The floor wasn't the most comfortable place in the world to sit, but he couldn't carry her with his leg and he didn't think she would be able to walk at the moment.

She burrowed against his chest, her fingers outlining the buttons on his shirt as her breathing returned to normal. His erection pressed against her thigh, demanding attention, but he did his best to ignore it. Tonight was about her. He'd get his pleasure, just not now.

"How are you feeling?" he asked once he was sure she was fully aware of her surroundings again.

She snorted, which made him smile. "Spent."

Alexander laughed. "That's good. It means you should sleep tonight."

"Yeah." Then she looked up at him through hooded lashes. "But what about you?"

"Don't you worry about me. I'm fine."

"But—"

He placed a finger over her lips. "I'm fine. Nothing a cold shower won't cure."

The look on her face told him she didn't understand. In a way, he didn't either, but something was holding him back. He kept telling himself it was her that he was waiting on, but was it really? He didn't know the answer and that bothered him.

Instead of delving into the whys, he lowered his head and captured her lips with his once more. This time the kiss was soft and deep, and he hoped conveyed a fraction of what he felt for her. Something might be holding him back but it had nothing to do with his feelings for Grace.

She sank into the kiss, holding tight to his shirt as they let their tongues explore.

As much as he didn't want to, eventually he had to break the kiss. "You need to get to bed. You have work tomorrow."

"I know." She looked up at him and worried her bottom lip with her teeth.

"What is it?" he asked.

Grace averted her gaze, choosing to look at the hardwood floor instead of at him. He was about to demand she tell him what was wrong when she asked, "Will you stay?"

It took him a moment to process what she said. "You want me to spend the night?"

She nodded and met his gaze.

"Grace, I don't—"

"Please?"

He looked into her eyes and knew he couldn't say no even though he wasn't sure it was the best idea, not when his cock was straining against his pants as it was. Would he be able to keep his hands to himself if he was lying beside her all night? He didn't know the answer to that. And more importantly, did he want to?

Alexander took her face in his hands and placed a chaste kiss on her lips. "Okay. I'll stay."

Chapter Fifteen

Grace grabbed her shirt and panties from where they'd been discarded on the floor, and they headed upstairs to her bedroom. Inviting him to spend the night wasn't something she'd thought through. She hadn't wanted him to go. That was all she knew.

As they walked up the stairs, she could tell his leg was beginning to bother him but she didn't say anything. Every time she did he shrugged it off and told her not to worry about it. But wasn't it her responsibility as his sub to take care of him? She wanted to care for his needs and that included easing his physical pain if she could.

"You take the bathroom first," he said when they entered her room.

She nodded and padded into the bathroom. As she readied herself for bed, Grace couldn't help but wonder if the reason Alexander was holding back was because he thought she wasn't ready. And while she could understand that given the conversations they'd had in the past, after tonight she realized she was. More than ready. Even after two orgasms her body was humming.

When she reentered her bedroom she was naked. Alexander was sitting on the end of her bed. She saw how his gaze roamed over her curves and how his pants were still tented with his very obvious erection. He stood, but he didn't approach her. Instead, he made his way into the bathroom.

He seemed to be attracted to her. So what was the problem?

The thought occurred to her that maybe she needed to make the first move, but that didn't sit well with her. She didn't like to be the aggressor in the bedroom. That was the whole point of being submissive. She wanted her partner to take the lead, to take control.

Images of Alexander hovering over her had her blood pressure spiking again. What was she going to do if he didn't take her soon?

"Do you want to put some pajamas on?" She jumped a little, not realizing he'd walked back into the room.

Grace figured this was a good time to push things without actually doing anything. The decision would still be his. "Do you want me to?"

He seemed to contemplate it for a moment, and then said, "I think that might be best."

Disappointment filled her as she went to her dresser and pulled out a T-shirt and some shorts. If she had any lingerie she would have worn that, but Kurt hadn't liked her in anything when he was home, and since he'd been gone she'd reverted back to her old standby.

Alexander waited for her to climb into bed before stripping down to his boxer briefs and joining her. He wrapped his arm around her waist and pulled her close.

Grace lay there for several minutes listening to their breathing. He was still awake. She could tell. And even though she could no longer see his erection, she imagined he was still worked up. He hadn't been in the bathroom long enough to take that cold shower he'd mentioned.

"Sir?"

"Yes?"

She scraped her teeth along her bottom lip, anxiety gnawing at her stomach. "I want you to know that I'm ready for us to have sex." Grace blew out a shaky breath. "I didn't . . . I didn't want you to be holding back because you thought I wasn't."

He combed his fingers through her hair. "I'll take that under advisement. Now get some sleep."

Grace frowned, but knew it wouldn't do any good to try and change his mind. At least not tonight. She closed her eyes and tried to enjoy the fact that she'd won one battle tonight. He was there, in her bed.

The next morning she woke up alone. After glancing around the room, she noticed Alexander's shirt was still folded neatly on the dresser. Grace didn't think he would leave without saying goodbye, but for a moment doubt had crept in. She immediately felt guilty.

Alexander came strolling into the room, carrying a tray of food. He'd put his pants back on from last night. "You're awake."

"Yeah." Grace looked toward the window. It was still dark out. At least she hadn't overslept. "What time is it?"

"Five thirty. I was just coming to wake you up." He placed the tray on the nightstand beside her bed.

She sat up, resting her back against the headboard. "You made me breakfast?"

He grinned and his eyes lit up, pulling her in as they so often did. "Did you miss the part about me insisting you eat three meals a day?"

"No, Sir."

His gaze softened and he brushed the tips of his fingers along the side of her face. "As much as I love hearing you call me *Sir*, you don't have to when we're not playing. Alexander is fine."

She picked up the half a bagel he'd brought her. "Sorry. I guess it's habit. I always called Kurt *Sir* or *Master* unless we were around others who weren't in the lifestyle."

"We're still feeling things out. It takes time. But I wanted you to know I don't expect it or require it unless we're playing."

Grace nodded and took a bite of her bagel. "Thank you for breakfast."

He kissed her forehead and stood. "Anytime."

She watched him put on his shirt, socks, and shoes. "Are you leaving?"

"You need to finish getting ready for work and I want to get a workout in before I meet Daniel," he said as he finished tying his shoes.

"Okay."

Alexander walked back to her side and tipped her chin up until she was looking at him. "I'll see you tonight." He ran his thumb over her bottom lip then turned and left, leaving her to finish her breakfast alone.

Tommy was his usual perky self when Grace arrived at the café. He prattled on about the club he and his girlfriend went to the night before, going on and on about how great the DJ was. Grace was only half listening. Beth had smiled at her when Grace first got there, but other than that she'd been fairly quiet. Then again, Tommy hadn't really stopped talking.

It wasn't until several hours later when Tommy was busy manning the front register that she found herself alone in the back with Beth. The morning rush was over and they still had some time before people began coming in for lunch. Beth poured herself a cup of coffee. "Want some?"

"No, thanks." Grace bit the inside of her cheek to keep from adding *ma'am*.

Beth nodded, brought her coffee over, and sat down. She tilted her chin in the direction of a nearby stool. "Might as well take a load off while you can."

Grace took a seat.

"You know, there's no need to be nervous or uncomfortable. I'm still the same person I was two days ago and so are you," Beth said.

Grace thought she should be honest. "I feel like I should start calling you *ma'am*."

Beth snorted. "I wonder what Tommy would think of that."

"Does Tommy know?"

"About our lifestyle?" Beth kept her wording vague in case they were overheard. "No. And to my knowledge he and his girlfriend lead a very vanilla life."

Grace hadn't met Tommy's girlfriend, so she'd have to take Beth's word for it.

Beth placed her coffee mug on the counter and met Grace's gaze. "Nothing has to change. At least while we're at the café. I'm still Beth, your boss, and you're still Grace, my employee."

"I guess I wasn't sure if . . . how . . ."

"We're just two people sitting here having coffee." Beth smirked. "Or one person having coffee and the other keeping her company."

Grace grinned. "It's not weird for you at all?"

"Not really," Beth said, picking her mug back up and taking a sip. "And it shouldn't be for you either. You have nothing to be ashamed about. It's part of who you are just like it's part of who I am."

"You don't think any less of me?" Grace felt guilty asking it, but she needed to know.

"Do you think I think less of Drew?" Beth asked instead.

"No."

"Then why would I think less of you?" Her boss leaned forward and placed a comforting hand on Grace's arm. "I've known you had submissive tendencies since the day I met you. It didn't bother me then and it doesn't bother me now. In fact, I'm glad to see you embracing who you are."

Grace never got the chance to respond since Tommy burst through the doors, holding up a piece of paper. "We've got a large order and they need it ASAP."

Without a word, she and Beth hopped off their stools and got to work.

❧❧

DANIEL'S OFFICE WAS DOWNTOWN NEAR THE ARCH, WHICH WOULD HAVE made it easy to find even if Alexander hadn't had GPS. When he walked in, all the desks were empty and there was not a person in sight. He checked his watch. It was eleven fifty-six. "Hello?"

A few seconds later a young man who looked to be right out of college popped his head out of a room on the left. "Hello. Can I help you?"

"I'm looking for Daniel."

The young man opened his mouth, but at the sound of someone else entering the room, he turned, leaving his words unsaid.

Daniel strolled into the main room with a folder tucked into the crook of his arm. "Right on time."

"Years of being made to run miles for being even a minute late is a hard habit to break."

His friend chuckled. "One of the many things I don't miss about the military." Then he addressed the young man. "I'll be gone for a couple of hours. If the Robinsons call, let them know I still haven't heard anything back."

"Will do."

Daniel plucked his jacket from the coatrack near the entrance and they headed out. "There's a nice bistro around the corner that recently opened up."

"Sounds good."

The bistro was close enough to walk to, so Alexander left his car in front of Daniel's office. It was a little windy, but at least the sun was shining. Considering the amount of times he'd been deployed in the desert, the change in temperature was still a bit of a shock to his system.

Once they took their seats, Daniel handed Alexander the folder he'd brought with him. "I spent the morning putting together some listings I thought might interest you. All of them have easy access to the highway. I figured accessibility would be important."

"Yes. Very." Alexander took his time going over the locations Daniel had put together. There were close to a dozen, but only two piqued his interest. They were both the right size, in great locations, and the prices were reasonable.

Their server brought their food, and Alexander set the paperwork aside to dig in.

"What do you think? Is there anything in there you think could work?" Daniel asked.

Alexander wiped his hands, flipped the folder around, and pushed it across the table toward Daniel. "I think these two might work."

Daniel gave the listings a casual glance. "Would you like me to see if I can set up a time where you could take a look at them in person?" he asked before going back to his food.

"That would be great."

The two of them concentrated on their meal for several minutes. Alexander had to admit that the food was good. He was going to have to bring Grace.

"How did Grace like the club last night?" Daniel asked. "She seemed a bit unnerved around Beth."

"Beth's her boss and she wasn't expecting to see her there." Alexander shrugged. "You know how it is."

"I do. And I also know it's usually a much harder transition for subs than it is for us."

Alexander nodded, but didn't say anything more. All things considered, Grace had done extremely well. She hadn't run, so that was a plus. He also had confidence that Beth would try and smooth things over with Grace. The conversation he and Beth had in regards to Grace reassured him that Beth felt almost as protective of Grace as he did.

"This isn't only an arrangement for you, is it?" The question came out of the blue and when Alexander looked at his friend he realized that he must have let his mind wander for longer than he thought.

There was no reason for him to lie, but for some reason he didn't want to talk about his feelings for Grace. Not even with Daniel. "Grace and I are still feeling things out. In many ways she's still mourning her husband."

Daniel studied him for a long moment, and then dropped the subject. They spent the rest of their meal talking about the two listings Alexander indicated he wanted to take a look at. It was a nice way to pass the time on a Saturday afternoon.

After leaving Daniel's office, Alexander went back to his apartment. The temptation to drop by the café to see Grace had been great, but he'd resisted. He didn't want to crowd her. Especially since he had his own shit to figure out. Like why he hadn't made love to her last night.

Thinking about lying in bed with her—her soft body curled next to his— had the muscles in his groin tightening. He wanted her. There was no doubt about that.

He kicked off his shoes and tossed his keys onto the counter. Desire was not what was stopping him. That much he knew.

For a month he'd contented himself with being her friend. Now he had the green light for more and he was getting cold feet. It made no logical sense, but as a doctor Alexander knew that often emotions weren't logical. In fact, most of the time they were downright illogical. He'd told Grace as much on more than one occasion.

Alexander sat on his couch and turned on the television. Some woman came on the screen. She was talking, but his mind was elsewhere.

Without even thinking about it, he pulled his phone out of his pocket and checked it to see if Grace had texted him. She hadn't. He could only hope that meant things had gone well and she hadn't run out on Beth and her job.

Unable to sit still, Alexander turned off the television, shoved his phone back in his pocket, stood, and scooped up his keys before heading toward the door. If he had time to kill, he was going to use it for something productive. Even if he couldn't wrap his head around what exactly was stopping him from claiming what was now by all rights his, he could at least be her Dom.

With the help of his phone, he found a store nearby that carried lingerie and club attire. The place was full of leather, lace, and satin, as well as a wide variety of sex toys. As tempting as the toys were, he steered clear of that section for the moment and focused on what he'd come there for: an outfit for Grace.

"Can I help you find something?" a woman in her twenties asked from behind the counter.

"I wanted to see what kind of club wear you carry."

She walked around the counter. "Our club line is back here."

Alexander followed her to the back of the store. There were skirts, tops, and even high heels that would make Grace almost as tall as he was. "Thanks."

"Anytime. Let me know if you need any help." She gave him a long look that made him think she was talking about more than help with clothing choices, and then made her way to the front of the store again.

He found a few items he thought looked interesting. One was a red dress that had a similar neckline to the top Grace had worn the night before only it dipped even lower. Alexander was already fantasizing about pushing the draping fabric out of the way to free her tits so he could play with them.

Slinging the dress over his arm, he continued looking. Although he had every intention to see her in that dress, it wasn't exactly what he wanted her to wear tonight.

It took him a while longer before he came across the outfit he wanted. He ran his fingers along the barely there hem and imagined Grace's ass poking out from beneath.

Taking the outfits he'd chosen to the front, he swiftly paid for them and was on his way. He needed to get home, shower, and change before picking up Grace. Thinking about Grace in the clothes had Alexander needing to adjust himself several times during the drive home. He couldn't wait to see her in the little skirt and top he'd picked out. The question was how long would she stay in them.

Chapter Sixteen

Grace had to admit she was feeling a little better about things by the time she said goodbye to Beth and Tommy in the parking lot. She figured she'd most likely see Beth at the club later. Their talk had helped ease a lot of Grace's fears.

As soon as she arrived home, Grace raced upstairs to her bathroom and stripped. Last night she'd been full of nervous energy, still afraid on some level that she'd embarrass her new Dom. Tonight she was thinking more along the lines of seduction.

She reached for a towel as she stepped out of the shower and began mentally cataloguing what she had in her closet. There was a midnight blue dress that was kind of sexy, and a green and black skirt she could pair with a corset. The skirt wasn't overly short, but it did hug her curves.

Wrapping the towel around her torso, she headed into her bedroom. It would be so much easier if Alexander was there. He'd tell her exactly what she should wear and she wouldn't have to be worrying about it.

Thinking about Alexander had her picking up her cell to see how much time she had before he was due to arrive. It ended up being a good thing she checked her phone because he'd sent her a text fifteen minutes ago.

Wear something comfortable tonight. You will be changing at the club. – Alexander

Well, she guessed that solved that problem. She quickly typed back to let him know she'd gotten his message.

Yes, Sir. – Grace

So instead of worrying so much about finding the right club outfit, Grace spent a little extra time making sure everything else was perfect. She shaved and trimmed her pubic hair, did a swift pass over her legs with a razor, and plucked some unruly hairs from her eyebrows.

When she was satisfied with her grooming, she went back to her closet and selected her favorite jeans. They fit her like a glove and made her backside look really good. She hoped he liked them.

At six she opened her door to Alexander and let him inside. He closed the door behind him, and then raked his gaze over her figure before making eye contact. "Have I seen you in those jeans before?"

"Once, I think."

He motioned with his finger that she should turn around.

Grace obediently faced away from him, secretly pleased at his reaction. She sucked in a breath when she felt his hand cup her ass. He massaged the soft flesh before going lower. With gentle pressure that only made her want more, he ran two fingers up and down the seam between her legs.

His breath ghosted over her ear as he leaned in. "I like these jeans a lot. You should wear them more often."

She swallowed as the ache inside began to build. "Yes, Sir."

Then his hands and his breath were gone. "We need to get going. I want to get to Serpent's Kiss by seven."

He removed her coat from the closet and held it out for her while she put it on. Kurt used to do that for her as well. It was something so small and she hadn't realized she'd missed that part of being taken care of, but she did. He even pulled her hair out from the collar for her. "Thank you, Sir."

Alexander grinned and opened the door.

They ended up having dinner at a Mexican restaurant. Neither one of them had ever been there before, but it was good. Nothing out of this world amazing, but it had the usual standard fare.

Dinner did, however, take them longer than anticipated and they didn't pull into the parking lot outside Serpent's Kiss until almost seven thirty. She knew he had wanted to be there earlier, but she saw no sign of agitation. He seemed to just accept it.

He came around to help her out of the car before reaching into the back seat to retrieve his cane and a bag. She guessed the bag contained whatever she was to wear.

There was a different girl manning the coatroom tonight. She greeted them when they entered and took their coats. "Enjoy your evening."

The first thing Grace noticed when they walked into the club was that there were a lot more people there tonight than there had been last night. She wondered if it was like that everywhere—where Saturday nights were busier than Friday nights—or if this was an anomaly.

Grace didn't get a lot of time to contemplate that before Alexander handed her the bag. "You know where the locker rooms are?"

She nodded. "Katrina . . . Mistress Katrina showed me during my tour."

He didn't seem overly bothered by her slip. It was playtime. Titles mattered. "I'll be at the bar getting us some waters. Come find me when you've changed."

"Yes, Sir."

The locker rooms were at the back of the club, which meant she had to maneuver her way through the main floor of the club in order to get to them. A few people nodded in her direction as she weaved her way through the crowd, but no one spoke to her. In any other setting that might seem odd, but here it didn't. Especially if they'd seen her come in with Alexander.

She passed through the bathroom to the women's locker room. Metal lockers lined one wall. Grace placed her bag on a bench in front of one of the empty lockers and began removing her clothes.

"You're Grace, right?"

Grace had already removed her shirt and bra, leaving her standing there topless, but she didn't want to be impolite and ignore the woman. "Yeah." Grace cleared her throat, resisting the urge to cover up. "Yes. I'm Grace."

The woman held out her hand. "I'm Ali. We met last night." At Grace's confused look, the woman added, "I was in the lobby. I took your coat."

At that, it clicked. "Oh yes. Yes. I remember."

"Anyway, I just wanted to say hi and welcome you to the club. I know it can be somewhat overwhelming at first, but it really is a great place. Mistress Katrina makes sure of it."

"Thanks."

"I'll let you get back to changing. I wouldn't want to get you in trouble with your Dom." Ali winked.

Her reference to Alexander had her wondering. "Does everyone already know I have a Dom, then?" Not that she minded, but they'd only been there one night.

Ali chuckled. "Pretty much. You'll find that word travels fast around here." With that, Ali was off.

Grace shook her head and went back to what she was doing. She finished removing her clothes and went to see what was inside the bag.

There was a blue skirt—if it could be called that. Grace held it up against her waist. It barely teased her thighs. There was no way it could cover her butt, at least not completely. The top wasn't much better. It was a lace corset. She already knew her nipples would be visible.

Trying not to think about it, she put on the outfit. It was what Alexander wanted and she would be a good sub and do as he asked. Besides, she had said she wanted to seduce him.

Taking a look in the mirror, she figured this might do it. She'd been right about the skirt. The bottom curve of her ass was exposed. He hadn't given her any panties and knew better than to put on the ones she'd been wearing. That meant anytime she bent over her pussy would be on display.

Thinking about that did the opposite of what she'd expected. She could already feel herself getting wet.

Grace pressed her thighs together, giving herself a little friction, but it did nothing to ease the ache she was experiencing. She knew better than to do more than that. Her Dom would not be pleased if she made herself orgasm.

Placing her things, along with the now empty bag, into the locker, Grace took the key and headed out into the club to find Alexander. She tried to ignore the looks she got as she made her way over to the bar. It made her want to pull her skirt down, but then she remembered there was nothing to pull down.

Alexander sat at one end of the bar, chatting with someone. Their backs were turned, so she was a few feet away when he spotted her. A smile that was full of pride graced his features. As uncomfortable as she was, Grace was happy she'd pleased him.

The man turned and she realized it was Justin. He gave her a once-over and she didn't miss the male appreciation in his eyes.

"Grace." Alexander held out his hand, beckoning her to his side.

She took his hand and he nudged her between his thighs, her ass pressed against his groin, as he resumed his conversation with Justin. They were talking about cars. From the sound of it, Justin ran or owned his own mechanics shop. Grace knew nothing about cars, as was evident in her having to call Alexander when her battery died.

As time went on, Alexander's hands began to creep. At first it was a brush of her leg. Then it was more deliberate as he dipped his fingers up under her skirt and began playing with her right there in front of Justin.

GRACE HAD MARKED EXHIBITIONISM AS A SOFT LIMIT ON HER PAPERWORK, but after getting her off the night before, Alexander had a feeling she was more into other people watching than she thought she was. He'd been teasing her for the last twenty minutes as he talked to Justin, priming her, and Justin was enjoying the show.

She let out a soft purr when he finally touched her and tilted her hips up toward his fingers. Alexander used his other hand to steady her hips. He wasn't ready for her to come quite yet.

"How long have you had your shop?" Alexander asked, acting as if he wasn't fingering his girl's wet pussy.

"It'll be eight years in March." Justin kept glancing down. "I'm thinking about opening up a new location about an hour outside of the city, but I haven't found the perfect location."

"I understand. I've recently started looking for an office building. Once my license processes through the state I want to get a practice up and running. Pushing papers all day isn't my idea of fun."

Justin lifted his glass. "I hear that. I detest paperwork, but unfortunately it's a necessary evil of being a business owner."

Alexander curled his fingers upward, grazing Grace's G-spot. She dug her nails into his thigh, causing him to harden more than he already was. "Why don't you hire an office manager? Help take some of the pressure off." At the word pressure, he shifted his hand again so with each stroke he was applying pressure to her clit. He heard her suck in a breath and her chest began to rise and fall rapidly. She was getting close.

"I may have to look into that, but for now I'm focused on expanding."

"Daniel's in real estate. Have you spoken to him?" Alexander asked as he continued to torture the woman in his arms. The sounds coming out of her were making it difficult to concentrate on anything but her.

"No, but that's a good idea."

Grace's nails were digging holes in Alexander's jeans and her nipples looked as if they were hard against their lace confines. He wanted to take them between his lips and suck on them until he heard her scream.

He ran the tip of his tongue along the rim of her ear, and then gave it a playful bite. "Would you like to come, *gattina*?"

"Yes. Yes, Sir," she said, her chest heaving.

Alexander inched her skirt up a little more, exposing her completely to Justin before continuing his assault on her clit. "Justin's going to watch your pretty pussy come for me, so don't hold back. Show him how much you like it when I fuck you with my fingers."

Grace sucked in a harsh breath as he gave up any pretense of teasing. She bucked her hips and threw her head back against Alexander's shoulder. He felt her inner muscles clench and release several times before a whine rose from her throat as she came.

Justin wasn't the only one to witness Grace's orgasm, but other than a smirk or two from a few Doms and an envious look from a couple of nearby subs, everyone else in the club continued with what they were doing. It wasn't as if a sub being made to come on the main floor of the club was unusual. Serpent's Kiss was a kink club after all.

Alexander removed his fingers and reached for a napkin from the bar. As he was wiping the evidence of Grace's orgasm from his hands, Brandon placed a fresh bottle of water in front of him. "I figured the lady might be thirsty."

Grace heard Brandon and opened her eyes. It was clear by the look on his face that he'd enjoyed the show. Alexander saw the blush begin to rise on her cheeks.

"There's no reason to be embarrassed, Grace," Justin said. "That was lovely to watch."

"He's right," Brandon assured her. "There isn't anything better than watching a woman truly lose herself in pleasure."

Alexander twisted the lid off the water bottle and handed it to Grace. She took it and brought it to her lips, not responding to Justin or Brandon's comments. He could tell they were both highly amused by her shyness. He had to admit it was extremely appealing. Even more so since minutes ago she'd been coming on his hand, not caring who was watching. It was only when the haze of her arousal faded that her timid nature took hold again.

Eventually Brandon got called away and Justin excused himself, leaving them alone. She continued to sip her water, her eyes downcast.

"Talk to me."

"You like making me come when others are watching." She spoke the words so softly he barely heard them.

He made her stand up and turned her to face him. "Yes, I do. And you like it, too." Alexander dared her to deny it.

She picked at the label on her water bottle. "I've never . . . before."

"You've never been made to orgasm in front of other people before or you've never wanted to?" he asked.

It took her a moment to answer. "Both."

Alexander took the bottle of water from her hand and placed it on the bar before pulling her against him. He slipped his hand under her skirt and palmed her ass. "I've never made a sub come before an audience either before last night."

Her eyes widened. He'd shocked her. Well, there were a lot of things she didn't know about him just as there were many things he didn't know about her. They had time to figure it out. He didn't plan on going anywhere.

"Then why . . ."

"Last night was an experiment of sorts. You'd put it on your list as a soft limit and it was something I was curious about. Seeing you so worked up watching that couple made me want to test the waters. I'd half expected you to use your safeword." He'd been almost certain of it. How wrong he'd been.

"It didn't even cross my mind." He could tell how hard it was for her to admit that.

He grinned and rubbed his thumb along the side of her face. "I know."

Her blush, which had been fading, bloomed once again.

Alexander chuckled. She was too adorable when she was like this. "Go to the locker room and get your things. I'm taking you home."

He released her and she took a step backward. "Do you want me to change?"

"No. Leave your outfit on. I'll remove it later."

She nodded and hurried off to the locker room. It was only a little after nine. The night was still young. He'd thought about staying, taking her upstairs and getting a room, but he figured he'd pushed her enough for one night. Besides, he was ready to have some alone time with her. He had some boundaries of his own that needed pushing.

Chapter Seventeen

Grace still couldn't believe she'd done that. And even more amazing was that she'd enjoyed it. The embarrassment had only kicked in later. It hadn't even occurred to her to use her safeword. Not once.

That didn't, however, make it any easier exiting the club and knowing everyone had been watching her. Even Ali, the woman who'd introduced herself to Grace in the locker room, waved goodbye to her from across the room with a knowing smile.

Alexander helped her into his car, making sure she was covered. Not only would it be indecent exposure, but it was also quite chilly. She huddled in her coat as he drove through the downtown streets toward her house. A few miles from their destination, he turned the heat on full blast.

"Thanks." She held her hands up to the vents, trying to warm up.

He reached over and squeezed her knee in response. The gesture had her body beginning to warm in a complete different way. It didn't matter that there had been nothing sexual about it. Her body reacted to his touch.

Like the night before, Alexander waited for her to unlock the door and then followed her into her house. It didn't feel odd at all for him to be there, and the way he casually hung up both their coats spoke to how comfortable he was as well. Realizing that brought her up a little short.

"What is it?" he asked when he noticed her staring.

"Sorry. I was just thinking how comfortable it feels having you here."

He closed the small distance between them and ran his hands up and down the outsides of her arms. "Does that upset you?"

"It should," she whispered. Then she met his gaze and asked, "Shouldn't it?"

Alexander brought his hands up to cup her face. "There's no wrong answer here, Grace. You feel how you feel."

They didn't appear to be playing now. This wasn't a Dom talking to his sub. This was Alexander being there for her and helping her deal with the complicated emotions that kept bubbling up inside like he had from that first day. She had no idea why he put up with her. Without thinking about anything else except what she wanted in that moment, Grace rose on her tiptoes and pressed her lips to his.

Her eyes fluttered open to meet his gaze as she pulled back. Alexander eased his palms up her arms, following the curve of her neck until he bracketed her face with his hands. He rubbed his thumbs along her cheeks several times before bringing his mouth down to cover hers.

Unlike her chaste peck on the lips, his kiss was firm and demanding. Her Dom was back. He held her face in the exact position he desired as he took what he wanted. Grace forgot about everything else and allowed herself to get lost in his kiss.

It ended as abruptly as it had started it. He released his hold on her so quickly she struggled to keep herself upright. "Upstairs. Now."

Grace only paused for a moment to catch her breath before scurrying up the stairs. She didn't waste any time upon entering her bedroom before taking up position on the floor, making sure her legs were spread wide so he would know she was ready and willing for whatever he had in store.

Several minutes passed. She heard him moving around downstairs, most likely making sure everything was locked up tight. Grace hoped that meant he planned on spending the night again. When she finally heard him on the stairs, her heart began pounding in her ears. She focused on taking deep, calming breaths, trying to get herself in the correct mindset.

The sound of his footfalls stopped when he reached her bedroom. She knew he could see her kneeling there, waiting for him, but he didn't approach her. Not right away.

Right when she thought she wouldn't be able to take it anymore, he walked up to her, gathered her hair into one of his large hands, and tilted her head back, forcing her to look up at him. The sensation sent tingles all the way down to her toes.

He traced the outline of her lips with his free hand before reaching for the snap on his jeans. Within seconds his pants were down around his ankles and he was stepping out of them. Something flashed through his eyes for a split second, and then it was gone. He didn't give her time to contemplate it before moving forward and pressing his cock to her lips.

Grace relaxed her jaw. Her mouth fell open, inviting him in.

As he pushed inside, Alexander closed his eyes as if what he was doing took great concentration. She ran her tongue along the underside of his head and she heard a sound she didn't quite understand come out of him. She looked up to find him staring down at her.

He brought his hand up to her mouth, cupping her face. It was a very loving gesture—in contrast to the emotions she saw racing across his face.

Then he spoke, his voice raspy. "Tap on my wrist if you need me to slow down."

It was all the warning she got before he thrust his hips, sending him deeper. His cock bumped the back of her throat before retreating. She had to remember to relax her throat and breathe. It had been a long time since she'd done this for a man. He repeated the motion over and over again as she massaged her tongue along his salty flesh, wanting to increase his pleasure.

The closer he got, the more his fingers flexed in her hair. He was watching her with an intensity that had every muscle in her lower half pulsing with anticipation and satisfaction. In that moment her only focus was on serving him, and that brought her a peace she hadn't known for a long time. It was absolutely freeing.

He stopped moving and for a second she thought maybe she'd done something he didn't like, but he was still buried inside her mouth. Thoughts were swirling around in her head as he just stood there, his cock filling her mouth. She could taste the saltiness of his pre-cum as it gathered on his tip, but he remained where he was, in some sort of holding pattern.

"You look breathtaking like this," he said out of the blue.

She didn't know what to say—couldn't say anything given their position— so she gave his cock a long slow lick instead.

Alexander closed his eyes once again as if savoring the sensation. Then he looked down at her with a fire in his eyes. "You are too tempting for your own good, *gattina*." He removed himself from her mouth and dropped his hand from her hair. "Get on the bed with your ass in the air."

Hurrying to her feet, she crawled onto the bed facing away from him on all fours, her ass in the air as instructed. Given how short her skirt was and that she wasn't wearing any panties, she knew her pussy was on full display for him.

Grace didn't get a chance to think much about it or anything else before he was sliding his hand between her legs, his fingers going straight for her clit. She couldn't stop the moan that escaped. It felt so good to have him touch her like this.

"Do you like that?" he asked.

Before she could answer, he landed a solid blow with his free hand to her backside. She let out a little yelp. "Yes, Sir."

He switched to the other side. The sound of his hand meeting her flesh bounced off the walls of her tiny bedroom. The sting left behind only added to the heat between her legs, driving her closer and closer to orgasm.

The assault on her bottom continued, warming it and sending her into an almost floaty state. His hands left her body, and then she heard the sound of a wrapper being opened. Only vaguely did it register that he must be putting on a condom.

Before she knew it, his hands were back. This time his thumbs spread her wide before she felt the head of his cock nudging her entrance.

"Please," she begged. "Please . . ."

Grace gasped as he plunged forward until his balls pressed against her.

"You all right?" he asked, his voice sounding as if he was in pain.

She nodded. "Yes. Yes, Sir. I'm more than all right."

With her enthusiastic reply, Alexander placed one hand on her hip as he began to move. She closed her eyes, letting the sensations racing through her body take over. This was what she'd wanted. Everything else in the world fell away until there was only him.

❧

ALEXANDER GRITTED HIS TEETH AS HE PUMPED IN AND OUT OF GRACE. SHE felt better than he could ever have imagined. Her walls hugged his cock and welcomed him as if he belonged. It was both pure pleasure and absolute torture all in one.

Right before she'd taken him into the warm recess of her mouth it had occurred to him that guilt was what had been holding him back. It was one thing to give her pleasure, to provide her what she needed. To take from her was an entirely different animal. Kurt had been his friend—the best friend he'd had since joining the Army. A part of him felt as if he was somehow betraying him by being with her like this, but heaven help him, Alexander couldn't resist anymore.

The sound of their bodies coming together echoed in his ears and the smell of sex invaded his senses. Then there were the sounds coming out of Grace herself. It was intoxicating. He wanted more.

He reached forward to cup her breast, but it was still covered by the corset she wore. With more hatred for the material in that moment than he should have, he tugged at the hooks until he felt them release. It wasn't pretty, but pretty wasn't what he was going for.

Once her tits were free, he found her nipple and placed it between two of his fingers, twisted, and pulled. A cry erupted from Grace's lips that had him increasing his pace. He dug his fingers into her hip, slamming her back against him with every forward thrust of his pelvis.

A pain shot down his leg and Alexander knew whether he wanted to or not he was going to have to change their position. This time when he retreated, he slipped out of her completely. He thought he heard a soft whimper from Grace.

"Don't worry, *gattina*. I'm not nearly done with you yet." He smacked the right cheek of her ass. "Take that corset off and turn over."

Grace rose up, removed the corset, tossing it onto the floor as if she wanted to be rid of it as much as he did, and lay down on the bed facing him this time. Her hair was in disarray from him having his hands in it, and her skin had a beautiful pink hue from their activities.

Alexander shed the rest of his clothing and crawled onto the bed to hover over her. He wasted no time capturing her lips in a searing kiss. This woman made him burn in the best possible way.

Taking his time, he kissed and touched what was his. Grace ran her hands along his back and shoulders. It had been years since anyone had touched him like this and it was almost his undoing. He wasn't even inside her and he felt as if he was on the verge of coming. Alexander needed to slow things down.

He licked his way down her neck and collarbone until he was staring at her tits. Her nipples were hard and asking to be sucked on. Who was he to deny them?

Grace arched her back and tangled her fingers in his hair as he took one of her breasts into his mouth and sucked as if his life depended on it. Her nails scraped against his scalp when he added his teeth to the torture, alternating between pain and pleasure, hard and soft. He remembered thinking how he could spend hours worshiping her tits. It wasn't far from the truth.

She began squirming beneath him, looking for friction, but he didn't give her any. Instead, he held her hip down with one hand while he moved to torture her other breast.

"Sir?"

"Yes?"

"May I come?" He felt her still trying to move beneath his hand, but he held her still, not giving her what she wanted.

He took a moment to meet her gaze. Her eyes were hooded and darker than usual from her arousal. "Can you come from me playing with your tits?"

Grace blinked. "I don't . . . I don't know."

A sly smile crossed Alexander's face. "Let's find out, shall we?"

With that, he went back to what he'd been doing, sucking and licking and biting her very delectable tits. He'd heard of women who could come solely from breast stimulation, but he'd never witnessed it. Grace was very worked up, however, and the way she was straining for friction made him think she was close.

Alexander readjusted their position so he could use his lower half to keep her hips still, freeing one of his hands. He cupped her other breast and began kneading it in his hand. Every now and then he'd bring his fingers together to pinch her nipple or tease it with the tip of his finger. Then he'd switch breasts and start the torture all over again.

He had no idea how long he spent playing with her breasts, but the little mewling sounds coming from Grace told him she was both enjoying it and hating it at the same time. Her breathing had become increasingly labored and with more and more frequency she dug her nails into his shoulders. He'd probably have marks. The thought only drove him on.

Grace bent her leg, and then let it drop back down onto the bed. She did this several times before she began thrashing her head back and forth. A gasping sound came out of her moments before she arched her back and clung to his head, holding him in place. A ripple went through her body as more moans and pants released from deep inside her.

With a final lick of her now very abused nipples, he pushed himself up until he was face-to-face with her. He didn't even try to hide the satisfied smirk on his face. "I guess we answered that question."

She tried to bury her head in his shoulder. "I can't believe that just happened."

Alexander chuckled, making him even more aware that his cock was inches away from her pussy. It wiped the smile from his face as his own need took over. "I'm going to fuck you now. You're not to come again until I say. Understand?"

"Yes, Sir."

With a slight adjustment of his hips, the tip of his cock was once again at her entrance. "Bend your legs."

As soon as she was spread open for him, he tilted his hips forward and let himself sink into her warmth once more. She was so wet he slipped inside easily.

He leaned down and captured her mouth with his. Grace parted her lips, allowing him to take whatever he wanted, and he took. She wrapped her arms around his neck and held on as he moved in and out of her, steadily increasing his pace. He felt her body begin to tighten, her fingers begin to flex against his skin, but she didn't ask for permission to come. She bit down on her bottom lip and rode it out like the good little sub that she was. His sub.

The memory of her on her knees, sucking his cock, had Alexander barely holding on. He could feel the surge of energy getting stronger. He wasn't going to last much longer.

Propping himself up on one elbow, he took her hand and brought it down between them. "Touch yourself."

She didn't hesitate. He could feel her rubbing circles over her clit, driving her closer to orgasm. Still she didn't ask to come.

He placed his hand over her neck possessively and looked into her eyes. "You're mine and your orgasms are mine. You only touch yourself if I tell you that you can."

Her internal muscles spasmed and released around his cock, telling him more than her words. She tried to nod, but his hold on her neck prevented that. "I'm yours and my orgasms belong to you. Only you."

He barely let her get the words out before he kissed her again. "Come for me, *gattina*."

Grace moved her fingers faster over her clit as he continued to drive in and out of her. She clung to his shoulders, digging, scraping her nails. Her pussy clamped down on his cock a split second before a strangled cry left her lips and her body began to shake.

Knowing she'd reached her climax, Alexander let go and it didn't take him long before he felt his orgasm roll over him. All the pent-up passion he'd kept inside for this woman exploded all at once, leaving him completely spent.

He tumbled to the side, making sure not to crush her, and gathered her into his arms. The emotions that had been scratching the surface for over a month were there in front of him, plain to see and unable to be pushed back into the box he'd had them stuffed in.

He was in love with Grace.

It was too bad he didn't know if she would ever be able to love him back.

Chapter Eighteen

Grace wasn't sure she could get more relaxed. Every bone in her body felt as if it had been turned into flexible rubber. She sighed and cuddled closer to Alexander, enjoying the moment and not thinking about much of anything.

He sat up a little to pull the edge of the blanket over her, flexing his stomach muscles. She recalled him mentioning working out, but somehow she thought his injury would make it difficult for him to maintain the same level of fitness that had been required when he was on active duty. Granted, he might not be able to run or climb, or do all the things he used to that required the full use of his legs, but his upper body was beyond impressive. Unable to resist, she traced the outline of his abs with her index finger.

Alexander seemed unaffected by her exploration of his body until he noticed her gaze had lowered to his legs. There were scars along both legs, but one had a long angry one that ran almost the entire length of his limb. She could only imagine the kind of pain he must have been in to have that type of damage.

"I wasn't awake for most of it." He seemed to sense the direction of her thoughts.

"But after? When you woke up?" Grace tilted her head up to look at him.

He shrugged. "I'm told I briefly regained consciousness during the transfer in Germany, but I don't remember it. The first conscious memory I have is waking up stateside and by then I was being pumped full of morphine."

The tough guy act wasn't going to work with her. She knew better. "Still, eventually they had to take you off the morphine."

Again, he downplayed it. "It wasn't anything I couldn't handle."

He wasn't looking at her, but she could see the muscles in his jaw clenching. She thought back to the look on his face earlier. Things began clicking into place. They'd talked about it before, at least her side of things, the guilt, the confusion. But all that had been before they'd begun their agreement. Before they'd begun to have a physical relationship.

Grace rested her head on his shoulder, her gaze once again going to the scars on his legs. She worried her bottom lip and debated whether or not to say anything about the thoughts going through her head. She'd always been able to talk to him about things . . . things she couldn't talk to anyone else about because he understood. But they were lying in her bed, naked, after having sex. Could she really ask him if he was feeling guilty about sleeping with her?

"You're tensing up. Something's bothering you." It wasn't a question.

"Just thinking." She was hoping he wouldn't press her, but of course she knew better.

"What are you thinking about?"

She hesitated a little too long.

"Are you having second thoughts about our arrangement?" He kept his tone even, but that only told her there was more emotion behind his question than he was letting on.

"No. I'm not having second thoughts."

"Then what is it?" he asked. "And don't tell me it's nothing."

Grace couldn't help but grin. She hugged him tighter, some part of her fearing his reaction to what she was about to say. "I was thinking about the look on your face earlier when I was kneeling. You looked as if you were in pain."

He didn't bother trying to contradict her.

"And I was thinking about how I'd told you I was ready and still you waited for us to have sex."

Again, he remained quiet.

Grace wasn't sure how she felt about having a one-sided conversation, but she pressed on. "I was wondering if you were feeling guilty. About being with me. Physically, I mean."

His body beneath her turned to stone. She'd obviously hit a nerve.

"This is what Kurt wanted. You shouldn't feel guilty." She paused. "Neither of us should."

Grace lay listening to his breathing, letting what she'd said sink in. She had no idea if it would make any difference in his mind. Guilt was a funny thing. She knew that well.

Time dragged on with neither of them saying anything. The stiff set of his body hadn't eased and she was beginning to regret saying anything. She should have let it go and changed the subject. That was if he would have let her.

"You're right," he said out of the blue. "A part of me does feel guilty, like I'm betraying him somehow."

She squeezed her eyes shut as a wave of emotion hit her. "You're not."

He didn't answer.

Grace was torn. They needed to have this conversation, get it out in the open, but everything was so raw. She pressed her lips against his throat. "I'm glad if I was going to do this that it was with you."

With that he relaxed a little and circled his arms around her, holding her tighter. His lips grazed the top of her head, lingering. "You should get some sleep."

"Will you stay?"

There was a long pause before he spoke. "Sure."

They each took a turn in the bathroom before climbing into her bed, this time under the covers. She wondered if Alexander would put his boxer briefs back on, but he left them on the floor.

Grace rolled over on her side to face him. He noticed. "Do I need to order you to go to sleep?" It was meant to be teasing, but she knew he was doing it to deflect. Why did men always have to run away from feelings?

"No, Sir. I'll go to sleep."

When she didn't move or close her eyes, he raised an eyebrow at her in question. "But?"

"But I wanted to ask you something first."

He looked wary. "And what's that?"

"Do you regret our arrangement? Having sex with me?"

"No," he said. "I don't regret our arrangement."

She didn't miss that he'd only really answered half her question. "And sex?"

Alexander sighed and turned toward her. "It's complicated. But no, I don't regret that either."

"Why is it complicated?" She knew she was pushing and it shocked even her. Normally she wasn't so brave.

He looked down the length of the bed, and then at Grace. "Do you really want to have this conversation here? Now?"

While she understood the awkwardness of their current position given the topic, she needed to know. "Yes." She pressed her lips together and met his gaze. "I think we need to. Don't you?"

Alexander searched her face for a long moment and then nodded. "Maybe we do."

She fumbled beneath the covers until she found his hand and laced their fingers together. He'd been there for her so many times and it seemed as if he was struggling.

"It didn't feel right to take pleasure in your body," he admitted.

Thinking back to their first scene, and then the club, things began to make more sense. "It was okay to give me pleasure but taking it for yourself . . ."

"I felt guilty as hell." He paused. "Still do."

"Why?" He gave her a look that said he couldn't believe she was asking that question, so she clarified. "I mean we talked about it and you knew me moving on, finding another Dom, was what Kurt wanted. He may not have envisioned it would be you who would be my Dom, but I have to assume he'd be okay with it. You were his friend. He respected you. Trusted you enough to deliver that letter to me."

"Don't you see that's why I feel so guilty?" He must have seen her confusion written plainly on her face. "Kurt trusted me. He trusted me to find you and give you his letter. He didn't expect me to start fucking his wife."

If she hadn't been so used to Kurt's cursing, Alexander's words would have bothered her. As it was, Grace realized them for what they were. "Is that what you're doing? Fucking me?" Using that word felt strange. She could only imagine what it sounded like to him. She never cursed.

He looked at her as if maybe she'd lost her mind, giving they were currently lying in her bed, naked after doing exactly that. "Did you forget about the last two hours?"

"That's not what I mean." She brought their hands up and studied the way they were entwined together. "I know what we have isn't normal or traditional, or whatever, but it's more than just sex. You're my Dom and my friend."

There was something else that flashed in his eyes, and then it was gone. It wasn't quite the same as before and it was gone before she could analyze it. He scooted closer, drawing their linked hands up to his mouth. "It doesn't change the fact that what I want to do to you is anything but friendly."

As he kissed a line down her arm, Grace's eyes rolled back in her head and she forgot what she was going to say. "Alexander?"

He lunged forward, pushing her onto her back, and pinned her to the mattress. The look in his eyes was heated and her body reacted. "What do you call me while we're in this bed?"

Grace moistened her lips. "Sir."

Alexander grinned. "Much better." Then he kissed her. Everything Grace had been about to say was thrown out the window as he reached between them and began making her body sing again.

◈

HE STARED AT THE POPCORN CEILING IN GRACE'S BEDROOM. IT WAS AROUND three in the morning and Grace was sound asleep beside him. After he'd ravished her again she'd barely been able to keep her eyes open. That, of course, had been the plan.

Tossing the covers to the side, Alexander got out of Grace's bed and walked into the bathroom, making sure to wait until the door was closed before turning on the light. He didn't want to wake her. Grace needed her sleep.

There was a little bear sitting on the back of the toilet, holding an American flag, which seemed to be watching him as he relieved himself. Alexander had noticed several bears positioned around her house and wondered if she collected them. He'd have to ask. It wasn't something he'd thought about before.

He flushed and went to the sink to wash his hands. His leg was aching, but considering he could hear the rain outside hitting the windows, he wasn't surprised. It was par for the course with an injury like his.

Opening Grace's medicine cabinet, he found some ibuprofen and tossed two in his mouth, chasing them down with a handful of water from the tap. He was reaching to turn off the water when there was a soft knock on the bathroom door.

"You can come in. I'm decent." Which was a total lie. He was standing there in his birthday suit, but it wasn't as if she hadn't seen all of him earlier that evening.

She slowly pushed open the door and edged her way inside as if she wasn't sure of herself. Maybe she wasn't. After their talk, he wasn't sure about much of anything.

"Everything okay?" she asked.

He turned off the water and dried his hands. "Yeah. My leg was bothering me, so I swiped a couple of your ibuprofen."

Grace frowned. "Is there anything I can do?"

"I'll be fine." His limp as he moved toward her only deepened the creases in her forehead.

"I used to give Kurt massages. Would that help?"

The thought of her hands on him had his cock twitching. "I don't—"

"Please, Sir. Let me help you."

It was the pleading look in her eyes that broke him. "All right."

At his agreement, she jumped into action. Grace opened one of the drawers beside the sink and removed a dark blue bottle of what he assumed was lotion. Then she took hold of his hand and led him back into the bedroom. "Lie down."

He gave her a hard look.

She lowered her gaze to the floor, looking utterly submissive and adorable. "Sorry. Sir, would you please lie down on the bed so I can massage your leg for you?"

As tempting as it was, he resisted the urge to touch her. Alexander knew if he did, they'd end up having sex again, his leg be damned. Instead, he stretched out on the bed and placed his hands behind his head. That was the only way he could be sure he'd keep them to himself.

Grace squeezed some of the lotion into her hands, and placed the tube on the nightstand before rubbing her hands together. With the gentlest pressure, she began massaging the lotion into his leg. As she grew more confident she wasn't hurting him, Grace used her fingers more, pressing against his muscles. She glided over his scars as if they didn't bother her at all.

Alexander closed his eyes as the ache in his leg began to fade. He didn't know if it was the ibuprofen kicking in or what Grace was doing or both. Either way, he wasn't going to complain. Besides, even if it was the pills, Grace's fingers were heavenly.

The more she worked her magic, the more his mind began to move in a different direction. He was less focused on the discomfort and more on how Grace's hands felt pushing and pulling on his skin—and how they would feel gliding along another part of his anatomy. He groaned as the picture formed in his head.

Grace heard him and halted her movements.

He looked down, meeting her gaze. "Don't stop."

"I don't want to hurt you," she said.

Alexander shook his head. "You're not. It feels amazing. Thank you."

It took her a minute to resume what she'd been doing.

Once she was finished with one leg, she moved on to the other. That leg didn't pain him like his left one did, so his mind was much more aware of her touch. Especially as she inched higher toward the top of his thighs. The closer she got to his groin, the more his cock began to sit up and take notice.

Grace noticed, too. She grazed her fingers along the inside of his thigh and his cock jerked in response. He'd already come twice tonight, but apparently a certain part of his anatomy hadn't gotten the message.

She lifted her hand then lowered it before meeting his gaze. "May I, Sir?"

The part of him that was still riddled with guilt about taking pleasure from her screamed at him that he should refuse—that he should thank her for the massage and order her back to bed—but there was something in her eyes that told him this was what she wanted. As usual, he couldn't tell her no. He nodded his agreement.

Instead of touching him right away, she reached for the lotion again. After coating her hands, she gripped his length. Her slick hands glided along his flesh, drawing a delicious moan deep from within his chest. He gritted his teeth as she used one hand to pump his cock and the other to caress his balls.

She ran her thumb along his head, circling the tip, before sliding back down to the base, and then returning to do it all over again. He pressed his head farther into the pillow to keep himself from reaching for her. Who knew a hand job could be this good? It sure wasn't when it was his own hand, and he couldn't recall it ever being like this. Even thinking back to when he was younger, the last time a woman had given him a hand job that hadn't only been a prelude to her going down on him, he couldn't remember it ever being like this.

Grace didn't let up, and soon he was doing his best to control his breathing. He was going to come and it was going to happen sooner rather than later if she kept it up. There was no way he was going to make her stop, though. Not now.

She seemed to know he was getting close. "May I swallow your cum, Sir?"

The innocent look on her face belied what she was asking. It was beyond hot. "Yes, *gattina*. Swallow my cum. Swallow every last drop."

Given the look on her face, one would have thought he'd offered her a prize. Then again, maybe he had. It was considered an honor for a sub to take her Dom's cum into her body.

Most of the lotion she'd used had long been worked into his skin, making it easy for her to wrap her lips around the head of his cock and suck as she continued to work his length with her hand. She used her tongue to coax him on almost as if she were licking the most delicious lollipop.

At the last minute, moments before he came, Alexander reached down, grabbed the back of her head, and pushed himself deeper into her mouth. He felt his cock hit the back of her throat. It was the final straw. He emptied his cum down her throat and, good girl that she was, Grace didn't miss a beat. She breathed through her nose and swallowed several times, making sure she got it all. Every last drop. Exactly as he'd instructed.

When she lifted her head, she had a satisfied look on her face, which helped with the still-present guilt he felt.

Alexander sat up, took her by the arms, and brought her so she was lying on top of him. He raked his fingers through her hair and kissed her, plunging his tongue inside her mouth.

When he released her, they were both breathing hard. "Thank you, *gattina*."

She smiled back at him. "Anytime, Sir."

Chapter Nineteen

The next morning Grace didn't wake up alone. Alexander was still in bed beside her, his back propped up against the headboard, reading. It took her a few moments to realize that he had the romance novel she'd been reading in his hands.

Before the anxiety could really take hold, he looked over and met her gaze. The expression on his face was unreadable. "You're awake."

She sat up, holding the blankets to her chest, which was kind of silly considering what they'd done the night before. "Morning."

Alexander closed the book and placed it on the nightstand before facing her again. He moved closer, bringing one hand up to cup her face. "How did you sleep?"

"Good." In truth, she'd slept better than she had in a long time, most likely due to the multitude of orgasms he'd given her. "How about you?"

"Very well, thank you." He grinned, although there was still something there in his eyes she couldn't put her finger on, and brushed his thumb along her cheekbone. His touch had all her nerve endings coming alive. "Do you have plans with your mom and sister today?"

Grace swallowed. Her mouth was really dry all of a sudden and it had nothing to do with his question. "Yes. Dinner."

He hummed. "What time is that?"

"Noon." She was whispering, but she had no idea why. It wasn't as if anyone could hear them.

"Anything you need to do before then?" His voice had this sensual tone to it that had her pressing her legs together under the covers, seeking friction.

"No."

The smile on his face got bigger. "Good."

Her breath hitched as he began to move. But instead of coming toward her, he went in the opposite direction and placed his feet on the floor before easing himself into a standing position. She hadn't missed how he'd favored his leg, making sure he was steady on his feet before turning to her and holding out his hand.

Grace blinked several times then took his offering and let him help her up. He led her into the bathroom, stopping right inside the door. "Do you need me to give you a minute?"

Grace was grateful he'd asked. She didn't think she could go to the bathroom in front of him. "Yes, please."

"Open the door when you're done." He stepped out of the room, pulling the door closed behind him.

She swiftly did her business, and after washing her hands, she gave her teeth a once-over with her toothbrush. A glance in the mirror told her that her hair was standing on end, but she let it go for now.

Alexander was waiting right outside the door when she cracked it open. He strolled inside and wrapped his arm around her waist, giving her a hard kiss. "I figure we both need a shower after last night."

A blush stained her cheeks at the reminder. She'd had no shame last night, begging him to come in her mouth.

Without a word, Alexander turned on the shower and adjusted the temperature. Once he was satisfied, he helped her step into the tub and followed after her.

The water was warm, filling the room with steam. He took his time washing her hair for her before grabbing her body wash and working his way down her body, making sure every inch of her was clean. Nothing he did was overly sexual, but her body didn't seem to get the message. By the time he turned her so she could rinse off, she was primed and ready.

He didn't touch her, though. Not the way she wanted him to. He grabbed the body wash and went to work cleaning himself from head to toe. She was left standing there vibrating with pent-up sexual energy while he washed away the evidence of their night together.

Grace was caught a bit off guard when the water shut off. She'd been so focused on watching the movements of his body that she hadn't realized he was done.

They both stepped out, drying their feet on the mat she kept on the floor.

"Towels in here?" he asked, tilting his head toward the linen closet.

She nodded, words seeming to leave her as she watched the muscles in his thighs flex as he moved. He really was in great shape considering he'd spent six months in a VA hospital recovering from his injuries.

He removed two large towels, placed one on the counter, and unfolded the other. She went to reach for the one he'd set on the counter, but before she could, he began drying her off with the towel in his hands. It was a caring gesture, but all it did was make her want him more. Since when had she become such a horny mess?

When he was done, he wrapped the towel around her torso.

"Thanks."

He sent her a panty-dropping grin that had her clenching her thighs together again, and picked up the towel he'd laid on the counter. She thought about asking if she could dry him off as he'd done for her, but before she could, he was done. He secured the towel around his waist and they headed back to the bedroom.

"Would you like to go out to breakfast?" He gathered his clothes from where he'd discarded them on the floor. Considering he had nothing else with him, he was going to have to put his dirty clothes back on. She wished she had something else to offer him, but she didn't think the few things she had left of Kurt's world fit Alexander.

Much to her surprise, thinking about her husband didn't have her feeling as if she were going to fall into some sort of abyss as it had in the past. Grace still missed him and she probably always would, but the prospect of going on without him wasn't as scary as it had been. She was moving on exactly how he wanted her to.

She slipped on a pair of pink panties and some jeans. "I can cook."

They ended up sitting at her kitchen table twenty minutes later eating bacon and eggs. It felt comfortable, natural, to have Alexander sitting there beside her, eating his breakfast. She liked having him here even though there were still those moments of guilt that would pop up. Grace kept having to remind herself that this was what Kurt wanted.

The thought had her pausing mid-bite. Had it been what Kurt wanted? Not the moving on part, but Alexander. Was it Kurt's plan all along for Alexander to become her Dom? Was that why he'd asked Alexander to deliver the letter to her in person? Had he known about Alexander's lifestyle? These were questions she would probably never know the answers to.

"Everything okay?" Alexander had noticed she'd stopped eating.

She tried to smile. "Yeah. Just thinking."

He gave her his full attention. "Anything you want to talk about?"

While she knew she could tell him her thoughts, they were too fresh. Instead, she told him the other worry on her mind. "Gabby stopped by Friday night. She saw me all dressed up and wanted to know if I had a date. I told her you were taking me to a club." Grace paused. "I didn't tell her what club, of course."

"Of course." Alexander wiped his mouth and took hold of her hand. "And you don't know what to tell her about us."

Grace nodded.

He turned her hand over and pressed his lips to her open palm. It sent tingles up her arm in the most delicious way. "Would it be easier if you told her we were dating?"

"I don't know," Grace admitted. "She's going to question me either way."

"True. But I'm sure she'd have a lot more questions if you told her I was your Dom." He winked at her, trying to lighten the mood.

It worked. A tiny giggle escaped her lips. "You'd be okay with that?"

Alexander didn't answer right away. He seemed to be debating how to respond to her question. Unease began to fill her gut.

The look on her face must have tipped him off to her thoughts because he moved closer and placed both hands on her face, drawing her in. She could smell her soap on his skin from their shower. He searched her eyes before pressing his forehead against hers. "You are more than my sub, Grace. Much more. I . . ." He swallowed. "I don't have a problem with you telling your sister we're dating."

"You're sure you don't mind?"

He kissed her forehead, and then leaned back in his chair and resumed eating. "I'm sure." He motioned toward her plate. "Your food's going to get cold."

Still somewhat concerned over what he obviously wasn't saying, Grace picked up her fork and began to eat.

Several minutes passed before he spoke again. "How would you feel if we were dating?"

She had to force the food in her mouth down her throat. "I don't know. I mean . . . we're friends . . ."

"Grace, what I feel for you is much more than friendship." There was no misinterpreting his words. He wasn't talking about their play arrangement.

"Besides, it only seems right if I'm going to defile my best friend's widow that I at least be dating her."

"So you want to date me because of some sort of sense of honor?" She wasn't sure how she felt about that.

"No." The look in his eyes gave her no reason to doubt him. "I want to date you because you deserve more than just me coming over every weekend to fuck you."

Blunt. But she wouldn't have expected less. "So what would that mean? Us dating?"

Alexander pushed his chair back and reached for her, pulling her into his lap. He nipped his teeth along the side of her neck and ran a hand up her leg. Her heart beat faster, anticipation coiling in her belly. "It would mean you'd be my girlfriend."

"Your girlfriend?" She was only half paying attention to his words. Most of the blood in her brain was going south. "That sounds kind of cheesy, doesn't it?"

"Hmm." He nuzzled his nose along her collarbone. "Lovers?"

Grace sighed and tangled her fingers in his hair. "Better."

"I'm not sure I like that. *Lovers* still implies our relationship is limited to the bedroom."

"Relationship?" The words were barely out of her mouth before he pressed his lips to hers, cutting off anything she was going to say. It was the last word either of them spoke for a while.

At a little after eleven Alexander said goodbye, promising to call her later. He gave her a kiss that left her breathless and wanting more, even after their intense make-out session in her kitchen. The man could kiss. It took her a full ten minutes after he walked out her front door before her heart rate returned to normal.

The drive to her mom's felt as if it took no time at all. She made every traffic light between her house and her mom's, which in and of itself was some sort of miracle, or maybe it was a curse. She hadn't decided which. Grace had kind of hoped she'd get stuck in traffic or something, anything to postpone the inquisition from her sister. If only Gabby hadn't stopped by Friday night. Or if Grace hadn't opened the door.

Grace groaned. If she'd thought it'd been bad before . . .

Luckily, Grace got a small reprieve. Her sister didn't come out to greet her when she pulled up. That was probably in part due to the fact that they were experiencing a cold snap. St. Louis didn't get as chilly as places farther north, but it wasn't uncommon for it to get down into the thirties at night in November. Unfortunately, they hadn't been above forty-five for the last three days. She, and almost everyone else in the city, was ready for it to warm up a little.

A high-pitched shriek greeted her as she opened the door to her mom's house, followed by the sound of a little girl giggling. Taylor.

Hanging up her jacket, Grace followed the sound into the kitchen. The sight tugged at her heartstrings. Gabby had Taylor in her arms, half upside down, a huge smile on her face. Grace and Kurt had been talking about starting a family, but they'd wanted to wait until his deployment was over. He didn't want to miss the doctor's appointments and the birth because he was stationed half a world away.

"Hey," her sister said when she noticed her standing there.

Grace buried her melancholy feelings and headed into the room. At least she had her niece. "Hey."

Their mother strolled into the room. "It's about time."

"I'm on time." Grace even double-checked with the clock hanging on her mother's wall.

"Barely." Caroline stirred something on the stove and then removed two dishes from the oven. "Grab some extra napkins, and let's eat."

Dinner conversation mainly centered around the upcoming holiday. Taylor's father had asked if he could have his daughter for Thanksgiving. "I told him I'd think about it, but I don't know how I can say no. I mean he finally seems to be taking an interest and wants to spend time with his daughter."

"What's changed?" their mother asked, although the same question had been on the tip of Grace's tongue.

"I have no idea. I just hope it lasts. I'd hate for Taylor to get attached and then he takes off again."

Both Grace and Caroline nodded. It was a real concern. He'd been involved in the beginning, but shortly after Taylor was born he said he got a job out of state and took off for over a year. To his credit, he'd sent Gabby money every month to help with bills, but he'd never called or come to see Taylor. The only way her sister had known he was back in town was because of the postmark on the envelopes.

"I gots a new toy, Aunt Grace."

"Did you?" All talk of Taylor's father ceased and they gave their attention to the little girl.

"Uh-huh. Mommy says we have to eat first and then I can show you."

Grace smiled. "I can't wait."

The toy ended up being a stuffed animal. Apparently the dog was from a cartoon. Grace stood there grinning and nodding her head as Taylor went on and on. It had been years since she'd watched a cartoon and this wasn't one she'd ever heard of.

Gabby came into the room and made a beeline for her daughter. "Did you want Skye to take a nap with you?"

Taylor held on to the toy in a death grip and nodded.

Grace watched as the two disappeared down the hallway in the direction of the bedrooms.

"It's too bad you and Kurt couldn't have had any little ones." Her mother went to the couch and sat down.

This wasn't something Grace wanted to talk about. "Do you want anything to drink?"

Her mom shook her head and patted the spot next to her.

Reluctantly, Grace took a seat.

Caroline placed an arm around Grace's shoulders and gave her a one-armed hug. "I know this is hard for you, but things will get better. You'll find someone else. He may not be the same as Kurt was, but that's okay. You deserve to be happy, sweetie."

Moisture formed in Grace's eyes, but she willed it away. She didn't want to cry. She'd cried enough for a lifetime already.

But her mother's words brought back the conversation she'd had with Alexander. "I've started seeing someone."

Her mom sat up and turned to face her. "Really, Grace? That's wonderful. Who is he?"

Gabby walked into the room and took a seat a few feet away, the smile on her face saying it all. "He's a doctor. Right, Grace?"

"You knew about this?" their mother asked, the hurt in her voice evident. Grace could already feel the blush starting.

"I stopped by Friday night and she was all dressed up for a night on the town. He was taking her dancing."

Caroline turned her attention back to Grace. "That sounds like fun."

"Yeah." Grace tried not to think about Friday night. It wasn't the type of thing one wanted to relive when sitting in front of your mother.

"So tell us about him. What's he like? Where did you meet him?"

Grace spent the next half hour answering questions about Alexander. When she told them he'd served with Kurt, her mother had admonished her for not inviting him to join them for dinner. And then her mother had floored her with her next suggestion. "You should invite him to Thanksgiving. If he's new in town he probably doesn't have any family here. It's not right for him to spend it alone."

She also heard what her mom didn't say. Bringing him to Thanksgiving dinner would mean they'd get to meet him. Was she ready for that? "I'll ask."

Chapter Twenty

Gabby had kept her questions about Alexander fairly tame while they their mother was present, letting their mom set the tone of the conversation. But when Caroline excused herself, saying she needed to make a phone call, Gabby got up and plopped herself down on the couch beside Grace. "Okay, out with it."

"Out with what?" Grace wasn't going to make this easy. Why should she?

Her sister rolled her eyes. "Your date, silly. And why didn't you tell me? This is big news."

"It's not."

Gabby snorted. "For months I tried to get you out of your house. All you did was go to work and come home. You kept telling me that you had no desire to put yourself out there again. Now here you are dating a doctor no less." Her sister gave her a once-over. "And you're obviously sleeping with him."

Grace ducked her head, trying to hide the red in her cheeks.

It was no use, of course. Her sister knew her too well and she wasn't going to let it go. "I knew it!"

"Gabby, I—"

"Oh, no you don't. You don't get to tell me you don't want to talk about it." Gabby grabbed hold of both Grace's hands and waited until she looked up. "I'm so happy for you."

"Thanks," Grace said. "I think?"

Gabby chuckled. "So how is he in bed?"

Grace wanted a hole to open up in the floor and swallow her. "Can we please change the subject?"

Her sister released an overexaggerated sigh. "Fine."

"Thank you."

Gabby squeezed Grace's hands, causing her to glance up again. "You look happy."

That surprised her a little, although sitting there thinking about it, Grace had to admit she'd been doing a lot better over the last month or so. That was due in no small part to Alexander. He'd made her feel as if there was still hope. Hope for a life—a real, meaningful life—after losing Kurt.

Their mother ambled back into the room with a sleepy-looking Taylor. The little girl was leaning her head against her grandmother's shoulder, clutching her toy in one hand and rubbing her eyes with the other. "This little one wanted to see her mommy."

Gabby abandoned their conversation and stood to take her daughter. "Did you have a good nap with Skye?"

Taylor nodded. "She was really tired, Mommy."

Gabby brushed some damp hair away from her daughter's face. "Are you thirsty?"

The little girl nodded.

Again, the scene between mother and daughter tugged at Grace's heart. Her mother sat down beside her, taking up the spot Gabby had vacated moments before. They watched as Gabby carried Taylor into the kitchen.

"You know it's not too late," Caroline said.

Grace looked at her mother a bit confused.

"To have kids of your own, I mean."

"I don't think—"

"How about this doctor? Does he want kids?" her mother asked.

"Um. I don't know. We haven't talked about it." Other than their play arrangement and their brief conversation that morning about telling her family they were dating, they hadn't talked about the future at all. He was her Dom. And maybe her boyfriend? Even that was unclear. They'd kind of gotten sidetracked.

"Might be something to think about. You aren't getting any younger." Her mother's words hit their mark. She was going to be thirty-four next month. Her biological clock was ticking.

Shortly after Gabby and Taylor reentered the room, Grace said she needed to go, making some excuse about needing to get things situated before Taylor's visit the next day. She didn't think her mother or her sister were fooled.

Once she was back home, Grace worked mindlessly to tidy up, not wanting to have lied. She made sure anything that was breakable or potentially dangerous was either put away or moved high enough Taylor wouldn't be able to reach them. It didn't take her long. There wasn't much on her first floor outside of her kitchen anyway.

Next she headed upstairs to change the sheets. The moment she stepped foot in her bedroom the reminders of her and Alexander's night together were everywhere. The sheets were still twisted from their bodies and the air had a heavy musky scent. With every breath she relived the memory, her body already wanting more.

She held the sheets up to her face, inhaling as she stripped the bed. Alexander didn't wear cologne, so his scent was more subtle. It was still there, though, and she found even that comforted her. She almost didn't want to change the sheets.

An hour or so later her phone rang. She set the basket full of clean clothes on the table before she answered. She knew from the caller ID it was Alexander. "Hi."

"Hi." There was a pause. "How did things go with your sister?"

Grace pulled out a chair and sat down. "She asked if we'd had sex."

He laughed. "Direct and to the point."

"Yeah. That's Gabby." Her sister did not know the meaning of tact. At least not when it came to Grace. Gabby was always pushing Grace's buttons. But maybe that was a sister thing.

"I'm assuming she doesn't know about your lifestyle choice?"

"No." Grace knew her eyes were probably bugging out of her head at his suggestion even though there was no one there to see. "I'm pretty sure she thinks I've only ever had sex in the missionary position."

His amusement came through the phone. "If she only knew."

The color in her cheeks was back. "Yeah."

"You're blushing, aren't you?"

She touched her face, as if doing so would somehow stop her reaction. "I can't help it."

"That's okay. I think it's rather cute." He lowered his voice an octave. "Especially when I'm doing things to your delectable body."

That certainly didn't help cool her down. She needed to change the subject. "Um. My mom wants me to ask you if you'd like to join us for Thanksgiving dinner. You don't have to, but when Mom found out you were new in town and most likely didn't have any other family, she—"

"Grace, I'd be honored to have Thanksgiving dinner with your family."

She swallowed. "You would?"

"Of course." He paused. "Unless you don't want me there."

"No. It's not—" She blew out a breath. "I just don't want you to be uncomfortable. My family . . . they think we're, you know, together. A couple."

He didn't answer right away. "I thought we covered that this morning."

"That we would tell my family that we're dating." So did that mean . . .

"Not only your family."

"Oh." She guessed that answered her question.

Alexander gave her a minute. "Does that scare you?"

She couldn't lie. "A little."

"Grace, nothing has to change. We can let things happen naturally. We can go as slow as you want."

She didn't respond.

"Stop worrying about what you might not be able to give, or have, or whatever is going through that head of yours."

That had the corners of her mouth tipping up. "Habit."

"Do I need to come over there and spank you again?" She could hear the smile in his voice.

"Maybe." She was being sassy, which wasn't like her at all.

There was a rumble through the line. "I'm tempted to take you up on that, but if I come over there right now I won't just be spanking your ass."

Her body heated and this time it had nothing to do with embarrassment.

"But we both need to be up early in the morning and I want you to get some sleep. If I'm there, I'll most likely wake you up again."

"I didn't mind," she whispered into the phone.

Alexander groaned. "Not helping, Grace."

She giggled. "Sorry."

"No, you're not, *gattina*, but that's okay. I'm sure I can think of several ways you can make it up to me."

"I'm sure you can, Sir." Her words sounded breathy and faint.

"I want you to do something for me tonight." There was something in his voice that did nothing to calm her desire.

"Yes?"

"I want you to plug yourself for me."

Her ass clenched as if it already knew where he was going with this.

"I saw several butt plugs in your toy chest. Use the smallest one since it's been a while. I want you to start preparing yourself for me, which means every night before you go to bed I want you to plug yourself."

"I don't think I have any lube."

He paused. "It's getting late. I'll stop by the store tomorrow on the way home and drop it off to you. You can start tomorrow."

"Yes, Sir."

"And Grace?"

"Yes?"

He made her wait. "I'm very much looking forward to fucking your ass in the near future."

She sucked in a breath, her body tingling.

"Good night, Grace," he said. "Sweet dreams."

Lowering the phone, she pressed her hand to her forehead and tried to breathe. Something told her any dreams she would be having tonight wouldn't qualify as sweet.

❧

ALEXANDER CHUCKLED AS HE HUNG UP THE PHONE. BY THE END OF THEIR conversation, he doubted she even remembered talking about where their relationship was going. He had so much fun playing with her, which was a definite plus in his book. So far, they seemed to be very well matched in the bedroom.

Of course, they were a good fit in other ways as well. She was easy to talk to once she got past her shyness. And because she'd been an Army wife for so long there were things she understood about him many civilians didn't. She was a great companion as well as a lovely sub.

The issue was to get her to see that. Sometime Grace concentrated so much on where she was lacking that she missed all the things she was good at.

He'd spent a good portion of his day catching up on some reading. There were years' worth of medical journals full of new technology he needed to brush up on. In the Army everything was about triage—patch 'em up and send 'em on. From time to time he would have the opportunity to sit down and go over the latest and greatest in the world of medicine, but for the most part if it didn't have to do with how to stop someone from bleeding out, removing shrapnel from wounds, or amputation, he skimmed over it.

Things were different now. When he'd finished medical school, Alexander had every intention of serving his six years and then starting his own practice, but he hadn't been able to abandon his comrades. That, and by the time his six years were up, his parents had both passed away. There was nothing calling him back home. At least in the Army he had a place.

It was the hardest part of the transition—the being alone. There wasn't much alone time in the Army, especially when you were deployed. If you wanted to be alone, you pretty much had to lock yourself in one of the latrines.

When he'd woken up in the VA hospital it was late at night. One of the first things he noticed was how quiet it was. Oh, there were noises, lots of little beeps and clicks, but nothing compared to what he'd been used to. It had frightened him at first, the lack of noise, until he'd realized he was in a hospital and he was stateside.

The microwave dinged and he removed his bowl of soup, carrying it into the living room where he could continue his reading. Before he knew it, the sun had gone down and it was time to get ready for bed.

He removed his clothes and tossed them into the basket he kept beside the door in his bedroom. Grace had never been to his place, a problem he thought maybe he should solve in the not too distant future. He wanted her to warm to the idea of them being a couple, and maybe being in his space would help with that. It wasn't much, but for now it was home.

His bathroom wasn't as nice as hers. It was pretty basic. But considering he used to share a shower with a hundred or so guys, it could have been a pipe sticking out of the wall for all he cared.

After washing up and taking care of business, Alexander made his way over to his bed. He'd spent the last two nights with Grace, her warm body pressed against him. His bed felt cold in comparison and he questioned his wisdom to stay there tonight instead of with her.

He hadn't wanted to crowd her, though. That and he needed a little perspective as well. He was still dealing with the guilt of pursuing his best friend's widow even though he knew that in some ways they were doing it with Kurt's blessing. Or at least that's what Alexander was telling himself. Kurt wanted Grace to be taken care of and he could do that. He would do that if she would let him.

Rolling onto his side, he ran a hand over the cool sheets and imagined her lying there beside him. He knew she was okay with their D/s relationship. She'd embraced that part. It was the rest that had her wavering and he wasn't sure exactly what it was that kept her holding back. She said it was because she didn't know if she could give him what he needed, but that didn't make sense to him. Not really. He didn't know how to help her get past it. All he could do was hope and pray that time would get her to see they could be good together, and not only as Dom and sub.

The next morning dawned way too soon. He stretched before lowering himself to the floor to do his morning sit-ups. Before his injury he was able to do one hundred easy, but lying in a bed for months had destroyed that.

He'd had to work his way from doing tiny crunches in his hospital bed to finally being able to do sit-ups again. After seven months, he could manage fifty before his muscles began to protest. Still, it was good to feel his strength returning, even if he had little hope of ever recovering the full function of his leg again.

Sweat rolled off him as he made his way to the shower. He placed his hands against the wall, leaning forward, letting the water trail down his back. It felt good, but not as good as Grace's hands.

Alexander tipped his head back, letting the water hit his face. He couldn't stop thinking about her. Even the simplest things brought her to his mind.

His cock began to harden, and he knew he needed to change the direction of his thoughts. Alexander reached for the soap and began to lather his body, ignoring the ache in his groin. He would see her tonight when he dropped off the lube and maybe she could relieve his growing problem.

As he was getting dressed for work, his gaze drifted back to the bed, then to his closet. Before he could overthink it, Alexander stuffed a change of clothes in a black bag, and went to find some breakfast. He knew it probably wasn't the best idea for him to stay overnight during the week, given they both had to work, but last night he had missed having her beside him. It was insane considering he'd slept alone his entire life with very few exceptions, but there it was and he wasn't going to fight it.

His day went by faster than he expected. He'd been sure it would drag since he was anxious to see Grace again, but the two meetings he'd had to attend had helped. There hadn't been time to do much of anything beyond answer question after question regarding various medical procedures, their uses, and their effectiveness. It was a good thing he'd been reading up on all the latest techniques and trials.

By the time he stopped by the grocery store to pick up some coconut oil and the adult store for a few other things, he was desperate for some stress relief. Alexander pulled up outside Grace's house, grabbed his black bag, his recent purchases, and his cane. He walked up the stairs to her front porch and rang the doorbell.

Several minutes passed and no one answered.

He'd told her he would be stopping by. Had something come up and she'd forgotten to call him?

Alexander tried again.

Before he was able to remove his finger, the door swung open to a very harried looking Grace. "Alexander."

"Grace? Is something wrong?"

"No. No. I—"

"Grace, who is it?" The sound of a woman's voice floated in from the other room.

"Umm."

"If you need me to tell them to go away—" The woman appeared behind Grace. She was a little taller with a few more curves, but there was no mistaking these two had to be related.

Grace met his gaze. She looked almost apologetic. Then she half turned to her sister. "Gabby, this is Alexander. Alexander, this is my sister, Gabby."

Gabby stepped forward, thrusting her hand out for him to take. "It's good to finally meet you, Alexander."

He took her hand and gave it a firm shake. Grace's sister was a lot more outgoing than Grace, that was for sure. "Very nice to meet you, Gabby. I've heard a lot about you."

"Well, that makes one of us." She dropped her hand and backed farther into the house. "Are you going to invite him in? Or are you going to make him stand out in the cold?"

Grace mouthed the word 'sorry', and opened the door more to allow him to step inside. He wanted to say more, to tell Grace it was all right, but Gabby was right there, not taking her gaze off him. He'd have to wait until later. When they were alone. For the time being, he tried to let her know as best he could that it was fine. He was going to have to meet her family sooner or later.

Chapter Twenty-One

Grace waited for Alexander to remove his coat and hung it up for him. Her hand was still on the hanger when she felt his hand on her lower back. He bent to place his bag on the floor inside the closet. It was only then she realized he'd been carrying three bags. One looked to be an overnight bag. The other two were plastic—one of which looked like the kind they gave you at a novelty store. Given their conversation the night before, Grace had to assume somewhere in one of them was the lube he promised to pick up. She only hoped her sister hadn't seen it.

She met his gaze.

He grinned and gave her back a gentle rub. "Relax."

The sound of something falling on the floor caught their attention and they all turned in the direction the sound came from. Without missing a beat, Gabby headed toward the noise. "Taylor, what are you doing that you're not supposed to?"

As soon as her sister was out of earshot, Grace faced Alexander. "I'm so sorry. I thought she'd be gone by the time you got here."

He turned her to face him and pressed his lips against her forehead. "It's fine. I was going to meet her eventually."

This was true. Still, she hadn't meant to spring it on him. Gabby could be a little . . . much.

They made their way into the kitchen, not wanting Gabby to come looking for them. When they walked in, her sister was on the floor cleaning up the yogurt Taylor had managed to drop. It had gone everywhere. Gabby looked up. "Yogurt, anyone?"

Alexander chuckled beside her. "No, thanks. I think I'll pass."

Gabby shrugged. "Suit yourself." She threw the paper towels she'd been using to clean up the mess into the trash, and went to the refrigerator to grab another yogurt. Within seconds, she'd removed the foil lid and placed the new container in front of Taylor along with a spoon. "Eat your yogurt. You can play with your toy after."

It was almost six o'clock, so Grace wasn't surprised her niece was hungry. They'd had lunch hours ago.

"So tell me about yourself," Gabby said to Alexander as she took a seat beside her daughter, not seeming to be in any hurry to leave.

Grace cringed at what she knew was coming, but there wasn't much she could do other than kick her sister out, and she knew how well that would go.

Alexander seemed unfazed. He pulled out a chair, offered it to Grace, and sat down beside her. "What is it you'd like to know?"

Gabby wiped some yogurt from her daughter's mouth. "How old are you? Where are you from? Are you planning to stay in St. Louis?"

"I'm thirty-five. A lot of places. And yes."

Her sister leaned back in her chair, crossing her arms. "Define a lot of places."

Alexander placed his hand on Grace's leg before responding. She hadn't even realized she'd been bouncing it. "My father was an Army officer, so we moved around a lot."

"I see," Gabby said. "Did you have a favorite?"

"Probably Alaska. Although, I'm not sure I could take the winters anymore." Grace had known he'd lived all over the place. He'd told her how hard it had been to make friends growing up.

Her sister shifted gears. "Grace told us you're a doctor."

It wasn't exactly a question, but Alexander answered anyway. "Yes, that's right."

"What kind of doctor?"

"My specialty is in pediatric medicine," he said.

That surprised Grace. She wasn't sure why. Doctors with all sorts of specialties went into the military for various reasons. It also struck her that she'd never thought to ask him. What a great girlfriend she was turning out to be.

"So you like kids?" Her sister probed deeper. Grace thought about saying something, trying to change the subject, but didn't figure it would do any good.

Even if Gabby went with the flow and dropped her current line of questioning, she'd find a way to bring it up again—today, or heaven forbid at Thanksgiving.

Alexander didn't seem to mind her question. "I love kids. One of these days I'd like to have several of my own." This was also news to Grace. In all their conversations, they'd never discussed children. But why would they have? It wasn't as if they were a couple.

But now they were. Sort of. The reality of what they were was still a bit fuzzy.

Her sister's eyes sparkled at Alexander's assertion. "That's good to know. Isn't it, Grace?"

Grace couldn't believe her sister was doing this. "Yeah."

Alexander squeezed her leg, offering comfort. It was Grace who should be comforting him. She couldn't believe her sister.

He tilted his head toward Taylor. "If I remember correctly, Grace told me your little one was three, correct?"

This seemed to please her sister. "Yes. She'll be four in March." Her sister ran a hand over the top of Taylor's head. "She's growing up so fast."

"They do that," he said.

Taylor was almost finished with her yogurt, so Grace thought this was as good a time as any to try and get her sister out the door. "Did you need me to help you take any of Taylor's things out to the car?"

"Trying to get rid of me?"

"I—"

Her sister waved her hand in front of her face in a dismissive gesture and stood. "No, it's fine. I'll get out of your hair. I'm sure you want to spend some quality time with your man." She scooped her daughter up and walked to the sink to wipe her face and hands before addressing Alexander. "It was nice to finally meet you."

"Likewise."

"Walk me to my car?" Gabby asked Grace.

Grace nodded, and then to Alexander she said, "I'll be right back."

Gabby didn't say much on their way outside. She waited until Taylor was secured into her booster seat before drawing Grace in for a hug. "I like him."

"Thanks." What else was she supposed to say?

Her sister looked her in the eye, her face serious. "I know this last year has been hard, but you seem to have found a good man. Don't push him away because you feel some sort of obligation to Kurt. He's not coming back. And you've got a living, breathing"—she grinned—"hunk of a man in there who seems to adore you. Don't mess it up."

Grace's throat constricted as a flood of emotions washed over her. She couldn't speak even if she wanted to.

Gabby gave her another hug and left her standing on the sidewalk as she got in her car and drove away. Her sister's words were fresh in her mind. *Don't mess it up.* Grace looked back to the house knowing Alexander was inside. He wanted them to be a real couple. At least she was fairly sure he did.

Could she do it? Could she let go of her doubts and just let things happen naturally, as he'd suggested?

A cool breeze came from the north and she pulled her coat tighter around her as she headed back inside. She didn't know if she could be what Alexander needed, but she knew one thing: she was going to try. Gabby was right—Alexander was a good man, and for good or bad she wasn't willing to let him go.

❧

ALEXANDER MADE HIS WAY INTO THE LIVING ROOM WHEN HE HEARD THE door open. From what Grace had shared with him about her sister, he'd known Gabby was direct and she hadn't disappointed. Gabby's line of questioning had made Grace uncomfortable, but it hadn't bothered him. She had a right to know about the man who was dating her sister.

He'd been reluctant to talk about the future when it came to him and Grace, but it wasn't as if he was hiding it either. Alexander just didn't think it was something Grace was ready for. She seemed content to live in the moment for now and he was okay with that. He could wait.

Grace stopped when she saw him standing there. It was as if she didn't know what she should do or say. He had to wonder what her sister had told her because he had no doubt, given what little he knew of Gabby, that she would have given her opinion, good or bad.

He crossed to where she was standing a few feet from the door. She still had her coat on, so he reached for the zipper and helped her remove it.

"Thanks," she muttered as he hung her coat up for her.

"Do you want to talk about it?"

Grace took a step closer to him and placed her hands palm down on his chest. It was a bold move for her. "I didn't mean to ambush you."

Placing his hands on her hips, he pulled her against him. "I know you didn't."

"She doesn't have a filter sometimes." Grace gazed up at him through her lashes. It was such a submissive look.

"I didn't mind her questions." He wanted to ease her mind. "She was feeling me out to see if we're a good match."

Her jaw flexed as if she was going to say something then thought better of it.

He brushed his thumb against the side of her face. "What is it?"

She averted her gaze, staring at his chest. "She told me not to mess it up."

Alexander couldn't help but chuckle, which brought Grace's head up. She was surprised by his reaction. "How exactly does she think you'll mess it up?"

"By pushing you away." It sounded as if she were admitting to some heinous crime.

He brought her closer, letting his lips linger an inch away from hers. "Is that what you want? For me to go away?"

The muscles in her throat moved beneath his hand as she swallowed. "No."

"Good." He smiled and figured this was as good a time as any to bring up their sleeping arrangements for the night. "I brought a change of clothes with me."

She had no problem following the shift in conversation. "You're spending the night?"

"If that's okay with you."

Grace licked her lips, drawing his attention back to her mouth. "I'd like that."

He hummed as he closed the distance between them. As much as he wished otherwise, Alexander tempered his kiss and kept it fairly chaste. "Have you eaten dinner yet?"

"No. Not yet."

"Me either." He kissed her again.

"I could make something," she suggested.

Alexander didn't release her. "Or we could just order in."

She circled her arms around his neck and pulled him closer, letting him know she was in the moment as much as he was. "Sounds good."

It would have made more sense for them to put things on the back burner until after they ate, but he couldn't seem to stop kissing her. Alexander began walking backward toward the kitchen. She followed him step for step, not allowing any space to come between them.

When they reached the table, he used one hand to push the napkins that were lying in the way onto the floor. He'd worry about picking them up later. All he could think about at the moment was Grace and getting inside her.

He lifted her until she was sitting on the table and spread her legs so he could position himself between them. She was warm and inviting, and the little moans coming out of her were going straight to his cock.

"Lift your arms," he muttered between kisses.

She didn't hesitate and neither did he. Alexander reached for the hem of her shirt, worked it up her torso, and threw it on the floor, not caring where it landed. He went for her bra next and it soon joined her shirt on the floor.

"I love your tits," he said, cupping one of her breasts, feeling the weight of it against his palm. "They fit perfectly in my hand."

Her fingers pressed into his scalp when he brought his fingers together and pinched her nipple. He loved playing with her breasts, but that wasn't what was at the forefront of his mind. The need to feel her surrounding him was too strong to deny.

He removed his tie, letting it fall to the floor, before unbuttoning his dress shirt. She met his gaze and held it. This felt different. At least it did to him. He hoped she felt it, too. There was no playing, no protocol. It was just the two of them. Being together. Connecting.

Grace helped him push the shirt off his shoulders, running her hands back up his arms. Her fingers left a trail of heat in their wake. He picked up one of her hands and pressed his lips to the inside of her wrist. "You are so beautiful."

Almost immediately he saw the color rise in her cheeks. "Thank you." Then she surprised him by using her free hand to draw a line from his collarbone to the top of his slacks. "You're not so bad yourself."

Something passed between them, a moment that had him thinking that maybe his feelings for her weren't all one-sided. That maybe, just maybe, she might be able to feel the same way about him someday.

"My bed was rather cold last night." It was a way to say he'd missed having her in his bed. He was afraid if he came out and said it that it might scare her, which was the opposite of what he wanted.

She pressed her lips together and looked down, her gaze on the hand with which she was fingering the top of his pants. "I'm glad you're staying tonight."

It wasn't exactly as good as saying she'd missed him, but he'd take it. He released her wrist and went for the button on her jeans. She watched as he popped the button and eased the zipper down. "Lean back a little."

Grace placed her hands behind her on the table, leaned back, and lifted her hips. He worked the material down her legs, removing her shoes in the process. She stared at him with such trust in her eyes that he couldn't help but react. His heart beat hard in his chest and his erection pressed impatiently against the seam of his thin dress slacks.

Alexander placed his hand on her chest, letting her know he wanted her to lie back. He hooked his fingers into the sides of her panties and got rid of them as well, leaving her completely naked before him.

Taking his time, he knelt down and spread her open with his fingers. He leaned in, allowing her musky scent to fill his senses, before taking a long leisurely lick. There was something about going down on a woman that Alexander loved.

He did it again and again, circling her clit, sucking her labia into his mouth, and dipping his tongue inside every now and then to taste even more of what she had to offer. Grace's hand came off the table as if she wanted to reach for him, but then she let it fall again. He realized she wasn't sure if that's what he wanted or not.

Shifting a little, he took hold of her hand and placed it on top of his head, giving her permission. Grace laced her fingers through his hair. He loved when she touched him. She didn't try to control his movements. It was more tactile—another point of connection, grounding.

He felt the trembling of her limbs and knew she was close. But suddenly he didn't want her to come this way. He wanted to be inside her when she fell off that cliff.

When he stood, her hand fell away and she opened her eyes, worry in them. He swiftly put to rest any concerns she had that she'd done something wrong by removing his pants and rolling a condom down his length.

Alexander didn't waste any time once he was sheathed. He nestled himself between her legs once more and pressed his cock against her entrance.

Holding her gaze, he pressed himself home, feeling her walls contract around him. It took everything he had not to close his eyes to savor the sensation, but he hadn't wanted to break eye contact.

He reached for her and she came willingly, sitting up and wrapping her legs around his waist. While he had no issues making love to her spread out on the table, she was too far away.

They kissed and touched while they moved. There was no hurry, nothing that required their attention outside the two of them. He'd never felt anything like it before and he knew why.

I love you was on the tip of his tongue, but he bit it back. She wasn't ready. He knew that. Instead, he chose different words. Words that expressed how he felt, but that she could take in a number of different ways. He grasped the back of her head, forcing her to look at him as he reached between them and began massaging her clit. "Mine."

Grace gasped as her orgasm approached and he gripped her head tighter.

She dug her nails into his biceps as he pumped in and out of her, driving her higher. His signs of dominance were making her hot.

"Say it," he demanded.

Her breath hitched and he felt her muscles contract around his cock in response. "Yours."

"Damn right," he muttered before crushing his lips against hers. "Now come for me."

He thrust into her harder, faster, not relenting until he heard her muffled screams into his mouth.

Only then did he let go and join her, allowing his release to flow through him as he held her.

Chapter Twenty-Two

Grace pulled her ponytail tight and took a final look at herself in the mirror before leaving the house. She was running a little later than usual but she couldn't bring herself to be sorry. Alexander had woken her up in the most delicious way. She could still feel his hands ghosting over her body . . . his teeth nipping at her skin. He seemed to know exactly how to touch her.

"You look happy this morning," Beth said when she and Grace were alone a few hours later.

She had no reason to deny it. Besides, if Beth hadn't already heard about what had happened at the club Saturday night, she probably would. Especially since she was part of Alexander's circle of friends. Grace grabbed several bottles off the shelf next to her and began filling them. "I am."

"I'm glad. You deserve it."

Grace didn't respond.

Unfortunately, Beth picked up on her silence. "Something wrong?"

"No. Everything's good. Great, even."

"Why do I sense a *but* coming?"

"It's nothing." She focused on what she was doing and Beth didn't pry. Thing was, Grace wanted to talk to someone about what she was feeling and her options were limited. There was no way she could tell her sister, and Alexander wasn't an option either. Not about this. She needed someone that was unbiased but who understood. At least in part. "Do you think it's too soon?"

Beth carried on as if there hadn't been a break in the conversation. "Too soon for what?"

This was the hard part. Finding the words to explain. "Alexander. He's . . . he's more than—" She searched for the right words. "What I feel . . ."

Beth placed a bowl in the large industrial sink and selected two clean ones from the shelf. "You're falling for him."

Direct and to the point. In some ways Beth was a lot like Grace's sister. But Beth seemed to pick her words a little more carefully.

"Shouldn't it be too soon?" It was an honest question and one she'd been struggling with for a while. With every passing day her feelings for Alexander grew. He'd become important to her.

Beth eyes softened as she met Grace's gaze. "Only you can answer that. Do you think it's too soon?"

"My sister doesn't think so."

"That's not what I asked." The Domme in Beth was coming out a little and hit its mark.

"I don't know. A part of me says it is, but then when I'm with him I just . . ."

"Forget about everything else but him?"

Grace nodded. "Yeah."

Beth grinned. "Then I think you have your answer."

"I know Kurt wants me to move on."

It was said more to herself than to Beth, but her boss heard it nonetheless. "He wants you to move on?"

"What?" Grace asked, confused.

"You said Kurt wants you to move on. Not that you know he'd want you to move on." Beth paused. "You can tell me to butt out if it's none of my business."

Right then Grace made a decision. If it was anyone else, she would probably have made something up or said she'd said it wrong, but she didn't think Beth would judge her. Or Kurt.

She took a deep breath and released it. "Kurt wrote me a letter. Before he died. He asked Alexander to deliver it to me if anything happened to him."

"I see." Beth said, wiping her hands on a nearby towel. "So this letter . . ."

"Kurt said he wanted me to move on. To find another Dom."

Beth took Grace's hand and squeezed, offering her a bit of comfort. She knew this wasn't easy for Grace to talk about. "That's why you came to the club."

"Yes." Grace used the back of her free hand to wipe the moisture from her eyes. "Kurt had done some research and found out about the club and Katrina. He'd . . . he'd known I would come back to St. Louis to be near my mom and sister."

"Sounds like he was a good husband and master. Very prepared."

Grace smiled despite the heaviness in her heart. "He was."

"And now you seem to have found another man who wants that place in your life." It wasn't a question and Grace had to wonder how much Beth had picked up on in the little time she'd seen Alexander and her together.

"He wants a relationship. Outside of play." They were slow at the moment, the morning rush over. Otherwise there was no way they'd be able to have so much uninterrupted time to talk. Grace was actually surprised Tommy hadn't burst through the double doors yet.

Beth propped her hip against the counter. "And that's not what you want?"

The way she said it gave Grace the impression that Beth didn't believe that for a second. Considering the smile she'd strolled in with that morning, it was the obvious conclusion. "I do."

It only took a moment for Beth to connect the dots. "So what's the problem?"

"I guess it's insecurity. I mean I was with Kurt for ten years. I don't know how to be someone's girlfriend anymore." Grace lowered herself onto one of the stools. "Stupid, right?"

Her boss' eyebrow rose and she gave Grace a look she was all too familiar with. Did all Dominants get pulled into a room and shown how to give a sub that look of disapproval?

"Sorry. Poor choice of words."

"Yes." Beth went to the big walk-in refrigerator and retrieved a bag of lettuce. She placed it on the counter and tore it open. "I won't tell you I know what you're going through because I don't, but your husband went out of his way to let you know he wanted you to find someone else who could meet your needs. If Alexander is that man, why not embrace it and let things happen naturally?"

"You sound like Alexander."

Beth grinned. "Wise man." She pointed to the counter a few feet away from Grace. "Can you hand me those cucumbers over there?"

Grace hopped off her stool and brought the cucumbers to Beth. "It's easier to do when I'm with him. It's only when I'm alone that I can't get my brain to shut off."

"Give it time. If it's meant to be, it will all work out. Look at what happened with me and Drew. I wasn't exactly looking for a relationship when we met, but he was persistent. Eventually, I had to give in." She said the last part with affection.

Every time she'd seen the two of them together, the love between them was there plain as day. Then Grace had seen them together at the club. They had a connection, a bond. She'd had that once with Kurt. She wanted it again.

That afternoon as they were leaving, Beth pulled her aside. "If you ever need to talk, call me. It doesn't matter what time."

"I couldn't—"

"Yes, you can." Beth took hold of both her hands this time. "I may be your boss, but I'm also your friend. I know you have Alexander, but sometimes it's good to have another female to talk to. Especially one that understands the lifestyle you've chosen."

She hesitated and Beth raised her eyebrow again.

"All right. Okay," Grace said.

"Good. Now that we have that settled, do you have any plans tonight or would you like to grab some dinner with me? Drew's working, so I'm going to be stuck at home by myself unless I can convince you to join me."

Grace was tempted to roll her eyes, but she didn't. Dominant types didn't tend to like that. And even though Beth wasn't her Dom, it still felt as if doing so would be very bratty behavior. "I don't have any plans."

"Great. I need to swing by my house to shower and change. How about we meet at Imo's in an hour?"

"Sounds good."

As soon as Grace walked through the front door of her house, she hung up her coat, kicked off her shoes, and reached for her phone to text Alexander. She had no idea if he was planning to come by tonight, but she didn't want to worry him if he did stop by and she wasn't home.

Beth invited me to dinner. Drew is working. – Grace

While she was waiting for his response, she trotted up the stairs to take a shower. Working in a restaurant, no matter what, at the end of the day you smelled like food. It was inevitable.

By the time she stepped out of the shower ten minutes later, she felt much cleaner and she had a message from Alexander.

I'm still stuck at work. Have fun with Beth. – Alexander

Grace bit her lower lip as she considered her response. Should she ask him to come over tonight? That was an acceptable thing for a girlfriend to do, right?

Would you like to come over later? – Grace

Several more minutes passed that had her second-guessing herself. Given he'd be coming over after dinner, it was clear she was asking him to spend the night. Again.

It might be something a girlfriend would ask, but she wasn't only his girlfriend. She was his sub. Had she overstepped some sort of boundary?

I'll have to stop by my house for some clothes. Around 8? – Alexander

She breathed a sigh of relief. It had been years since she'd had to navigate the dating waters, even if it was with Alexander.

I'll see you then. – Grace

Several more minutes went by and she wondered if maybe it was taking him so long to respond because he was in a meeting. That would make sense.

I'm very much looking forward to it. – Alexander

And Grace, make sure you eat well. You'll be burning off a lot of energy tonight. – Alexander

Two sentences and her body temperature rose by at least ten degrees. She blew out a loud breath and glanced over at her bed—the bed she and Alexander had shared several times now. A smile pulled at her lips. She was sure the guilt would keep cropping up now and then, but she wasn't going to try and pretend this wasn't what she wanted anymore.

She sent him a quick text back before she headed out to meet Beth.

I'm looking forward to it, Sir. – Grace

⚜

FUCKING LAWYERS. THEY WERE THE THORN IN HIS SIDE THESE DAYS. WHY they didn't get medical degrees of their own if they were going to try cases involving malpractice he didn't understand. They certainly thought they knew better than everyone else, including those who actually had a medical degree.

He'd been stuck in that conference room for six hours. Six fucking hours, attempting to explain to that pompous jackass of a lawyer that the scenario he was proposing was not only absurd but downright impossible. But the idiot had been convinced he was right. Even Alexander's boss agreed, but still the man persisted. In fact, after a while Alexander began to think the man dug in his heels *because* of Alexander's boss backing him up. Janet might not be a doctor, but she'd been in this business for close to twenty years. She wasn't stupid.

Alexander tried to shake it off. What he needed was something to get his mind off the idiot he'd left up on the fourth floor. What he needed was Grace.

After climbing into his car, he drove home. He had some time to kill since it was still early. When Grace had texted him to say she was having dinner with Beth, it had given him a moment to catch his breath and not strangle a certain lawyer. He was glad she and Beth were forming a deeper relationship. Grace didn't have many friends. Any, that he knew of actually. Hopefully going to the club would change that. She could connect with other subs and not have to worry about them judging her.

After showering and changing out of his suit into something a bit more comfortable, Alexander swung through a drive-thru before making his way to Grace's. He was a little early, but he had no problem waiting.

Grace pulled into her driveway around seven forty-five. The sun had already set, but the lights from the streetlamps bounced off her blond hair, drawing the eye of anyone who was watching.

She turned toward the noise when she heard him get out of the car. The look on her face morphed from concern to joy as she realized it was him. He would never get tired of seeing that look. It had been appearing more often the last few days. Alexander hoped that meant she was getting used to the idea of them being a couple. Based on the conversation they'd had the night before, he was hopeful.

"Have you been waiting long?" she asked as she came toward him.

He grabbed his overnight bag and his cane and locked up his vehicle. "Not too long." In truth, he'd been there since a little after seven. It didn't matter. He pulled her against him and gave her a swift kiss before they went inside. "How was dinner?"

"Nice." She removed her coat and hung it in the closet before taking his and doing the same. "Did you know Beth grew up in Ohio?"

"Can't say that I did."

"She moved here to go to school—"

He crushed her against him and cut off her words with a bruising kiss. When they came up for air a few minutes later, her breathing was labored and her lips were swollen. "As much as I want to hear all about your evening, there are more pressing matters I want to attend to first." Alexander took her hand and placed it over his erection.

She cupped him and rubbed her palm up and down, causing him to groan. It felt good, but it wasn't exactly what he wanted.

Before all thought went out the window, he removed her hand. The cooler air hitting his groin brought back a little sanity. "I want you in your room, kneeling on the floor, waiting for me when I come upstairs."

Her pupils dilated a little more. "Yes, Sir."

Alexander dropped his hands, releasing her. He waited at the base of the stairs while she ascended and turned the corner toward her bedroom.

The time it took him to check the downstairs and make sure everything was locked up for the night gave him the opportunity to settle himself. After the day he'd had, what he needed more than anything was to let it all go and sink into the dynamic he and Grace had. The thought of seeing her gazing up at him with those expressive eyes of hers while she waited for his command had him hurrying up the stairs as fast as his bum leg would take him.

When he walked into her bedroom, he found Grace exactly as he'd requested. She was naked, kneeling by the end of her bed, her knees spread wide. Her breathing told him she was as excited as he was for what was to come. She was such a beautiful submissive, and she was his. The internal voice inside his head telling him he should feel guilty for the thoughts running through his head was almost nonexistent. He wanted Grace and she wanted him. They weren't betraying anyone.

He closed the distance between them, using his cane to steady himself. It had been a long day. She kept her gaze on the ground as he approached, but that wasn't what he wanted. He wanted to see her eyes, to see the emotion in them staring back at him.

Reaching out with his left hand, he threaded his fingers through her hair, letting the silky strands run through his fingers. Even such a simple gesture brought him some much needed peace. He heard her sigh and knew she felt it, too.

Alexander gathered her hair together and tilted her head back so she was looking up at him. There was complete trust in her eyes, and he decided to take a chance. He lifted his other hand, his cane dangling from his fingers, and rubbed his thumb and index finger along the line of her jaw. "I missed you today. I had a horribly long meeting and all I could think about was how much I would rather be here with you." He paused. "Or anywhere with you."

There was a slight shift in her eyes and he could tell she wanted to avert her gaze, but she didn't—her years of training evident. He waited for several minutes to see if she would bolt or use her safeword, but she didn't.

When he was satisfied she wasn't going to abruptly end their scene, he continued. "We're going to enjoy some impact play tonight. I want you to lie on the bed facedown, legs spread. I'm going to have some fun."

Chapter Twenty-Three

Grace could feel the warmth from her shoulders to her knees. Alexander had worked her over good with several different floggers. She'd forgotten how good it felt to drift into subspace as the flogger kissed her skin.

A contented sigh left her lips as she snuggled closer to Alexander. He tightened his hold, giving her breast he held in his palm a little squeeze. "All right?"

"Hmm. More than all right. I think I'm still in subspace."

His chest vibrated beneath her cheek. "You did seem to enjoy your flogging quite a bit."

"Yes, I did." She placed a kiss on his chest and skimmed her hand down the length of his torso. "Are you feeling better?"

It hadn't taken her long to realize he'd had a bad day and had needed to work through some of his frustrations. He hadn't been rough with her, not really. But as the scene went on, she felt his mood shift as he let go of whatever it was that had been bothering him. She'd been pleased she was able to help.

"Much better. Thank you, *gattina*." His lips brushed against the top of her head.

They fell into a contented silence as they lay there touching. Everything felt right. Peaceful. She thought about what her sister and Beth had said. She knew they were right. It was time she fully embraced whatever this was between her and Alexander and stopped living in the past.

Making that decision took a huge weight off her shoulders. "Are you staying?"

She felt his lips turn up into a grin. "Unless you're kicking me out."

"Nope. No kicking."

He continued to play with her breast as they talked, and her lady parts were starting to wake up again even though he'd already given her three orgasms tonight. She knew she needed a distraction. "Can I ask you a question?"

"Anything."

"What does *gattina* mean? I'm assuming it's Italian?" She absentmindedly traced a circle around his nipple, memorizing the dips and bumps.

"It is." He lowered his hands to her waist and shifted her so she was lying on top of him. "It means kitten."

She could feel his erection growing against her belly and wondered if her playing with his nipple had a similar effect on Alexander as his massaging her breast had on her. Still, she tried to focus on the conversation at hand. "Do you call all your submissives *kitten*?"

An amused smirk appeared on his face. "No."

So it was only her. For some reason she liked that he'd reserved that name for her alone.

Alexander cupped the side of her face with one hand and reached between them with the other, finding her clit. He circled it slowly as he held her gaze and whispered, "My sweet *gattina*."

She heard his words, but more than that she felt the emotion behind them.

He increased the pressure on her clit, driving her higher, yet he made no move to change their position or reach for a condom. Instead, he cradled her face in one hand with the gentlest pressure while he drove her toward another orgasm.

Her body was still buzzing from earlier, so it didn't take long before she was teetering on the edge. "Sir?"

"Yes, *gattina*?"

"Sir, I'm so close. May I come? Please?"

He pulled her face down to his. "Let go. Come for me."

His words were barely audible, but she'd heard them. More importantly, her body heard them and responded. He caught her gasp with his lips, plunging his tongue inside her mouth to devour every moan she had to give while she rode out her fourth orgasm of the night.

As she was coming back down to earth, she heard him rip open a condom.

Moments later, he lifted her hips and placed his cock at her entrance. There was no talking, no sounds other than their kisses as he lowered her down onto his erection.

He held onto her hips, guiding her movements. Time slowed and all her nerve endings felt as if they were right below the surface of her skin. She could feel the air around them brushing against her flesh. It was so much cooler than the heat, the fire, she felt inside.

She had no idea how long they rocked back and forth, grinding against one another. He kept her on the brink without allowing her to fall over the cliff for what felt like forever, but she didn't mind. He seemed to need this as much as he'd needed to flog her earlier. And to be honest, she needed it as well. Things were shifting between them. It had been happening for a while, since the beginning really, but she'd been resisting it. But this. Here. Now. There was no way to pretend. Somehow, Alexander had pushed past all her walls.

Eventually, he flipped them over so he was pressing her into the mattress, but he refused to pick up the pace. He hiked her leg up over his hip, changing the angle. The new position had her digging her nails into his shoulders. She wasn't going to be able to hold on much longer.

He must have been able to read her mind because he reached between them and pinched her nipple. Hard. "Don't you dare come. Not yet."

A whimper escaped her. Grace gritted her teeth, hoping she could stave off her orgasm. She didn't want to disappoint him.

The exquisite torture went on until she saw sweat beading on Alexander's temples. It was obvious he was trying to hold his own climax at bay. "Sir, are you okay?"

He met her gaze, took hold of the side of her head, and kissed her. "I'm fine. Just enjoying fucking my submissive. I can't seem to get enough of her no matter how many times I'm inside her. Or for how long."

Her pussy liked that and responded by tightening around him, trying its best to hold him deep.

Alexander propped himself up on one elbow, but didn't stop the gentle torture as he continued to move his hips in and out. He ran his index finger along the curve of her neck and her mind immediately went to what was missing. His gaze locked with hers. "I want you to wear my collar. The next time we go to Serpent's Kiss, I want my collar around your neck, letting everyone there know you're mine."

She swallowed, a flood of emotions surging through her body. He watched her face and waited for her answer. The answer was easy. Despite her back and forth, her uncertainty that whether or not what she felt for him was right, this thing between them was real. She felt it every time he touched her—every time she thought about him. "I would be honored to wear your collar, Sir."

He took hold of the side of her face, tilted her head back, and kissed her hard. "I will make sure you don't regret it, *gattina*. I promise."

Alexander didn't give her a chance to answer as he continued to kiss her with abandon. As his tongue danced in her mouth, his hips increased their rhythm. She held on, lifting her hips to meet each of his thrusts.

Snaking his hand down over her breast and along her side, he splayed his hand on her hip. He eased his thumb between them, placing it over her clit. The sensation was too much to bear. Her head fell back and her muscles contracted around him in a vise grip. She was panting, desperate to come. Her heart felt as if it would beat out of her chest.

"Do you wish to come, *gattina*?"

She could barely get the words out. "Yes, Sir."

"I do like seeing you like this, so close and trying not to come without permission."

He brushed his thumb over her clit again and she jerked. Not because she didn't want him to touch her, but because he was right. She was about ready to blow whether she wanted to or not.

Alexander scraped his teeth against her neck as he placed gentle pressure against her clit once more. "Come for me."

As he offered his permission, he bit down on her neck, sucking the skin into his mouth. At the same time, he picked up his assault on her clit and began pistoning in and out of her deeper, harder. It was too much. She screamed as her climax hit her like a freight train.

Seconds later, while she was still riding out her own orgasm, she heard Alexander grunt as he reached his own climax. His entire body shook as he emptied himself inside her, letting her know that his reaction to their extended joining had been as powerful for him as it had been for her.

He peeked up at her through his lashes, a satisfied smile on his face. "We will definitely be doing that again."

Maybe it was the look on his face or maybe it was the fact that her emotions were still so close to the surface after what they'd done, but she started laughing. A concerned look crossed his face for a moment before he decided to join her.

ALEXANDER WOKE UP DRENCHED IN SWEAT. AFTER HE'D REGAINED consciousness in the hospital, he'd suffered from frequent nightmares. They were vivid and terrifying. It was always the same. He was trapped, his leg pinned down, preventing him from moving more than a few inches, while he watched his buddies get picked off one by one. He could see all their faces—the look in their eyes the moment they realized their fate—and there was nothing he could do to stop it.

As his body recovered, he'd also worked on healing his mind as well. He'd talked to one of the VA shrinks a few times and wrote down everything he could remember in a journal. It had been one of the most difficult things he'd ever done in his life, but he knew that if he didn't face it head on that it would slowly destroy him. But dealing with the realities of PTSD was a lot different than reading about it in a medical journal.

He took several deep breaths, trying to calm his heart. It had been months since he'd had one this bad. And usually he could take a few moments to center himself and he'd be okay. For some reason, that wasn't happening this time.

Careful not to wake Grace, he climbed out of bed and made his way into the bathroom. He felt hot and cold at the same time. It was unsettling, but rationally he knew it was most likely the difference in his internal temperature and the cooler air hitting his sweat-covered body.

The logical part of his brain forced him to turn on the shower and get under the spray. As the warm water fell against his skin and the steam filled his lungs, he began to breathe a bit easier. He reached for the soap and began working the latter between his hands, taking his time washing his body.

By the time he turned off the water and reached for one of Grace's towels, he was feeling somewhat normal again. Or as normal as he ever felt these days.

Alexander threw his wet towel into the hamper and turned off the light before heading back into the bedroom where Grace was still sleeping. She was lying on her side, her arms tucked up under her chin. A light from outside streamed in through the windows, landing on her hair. It almost looked as if it had flecks of gold in it the way the light was hitting it.

His chest clenched with a surge of emotion. It was so powerful it nearly sucked the air out of his lungs. It was a combination of overwhelming love mixed with the weight of responsibility he felt to do right by her.

A sigh escaped her lips as she rolled over. The movement caused the sheet to pull away from her chest, leaving most of her upper body exposed. Although his libido wouldn't balk at going another round, he knew she needed her sleep. They both did.

With that in mind, he slipped back into bed as gently as he could. Alexander closed his eyes and tried to relax back into sleep. He listened to Grace breathing beside him, the soft inhale and exhale relaxing him.

The feel of her fingers against his arm made him open his eyes. He looked over at her, but her eyes were still closed. She sucked in a breath and scooted a couple of inches closer to him. "You okay?" Her words were mumbled, barely audible.

He gathered her in his arms and turned them so her back was against his chest. "I'm fine. Go back to sleep."

A sleepy grin appeared on her face. "Yes, Sir."

Alexander smiled and placed a kiss on the back of her head before closing his eyes again.

It took a while, but he did eventually fall asleep again. Holding Grace had helped ward off the nightmares.

Her alarm went off at five thirty. Neither one of them seemed all that anxious to get up, but they both had work. He pulled her to him and gave her a lingering kiss. "Why don't you grab a shower while I go downstairs and make the coffee?"

She stretched. "Okay."

He waited until she was out of sight before he got out of bed. Last night his adrenaline had been pumping, so he hadn't paid much attention to his leg. This morning he was paying for the neglect. It took him several minutes until he felt comfortable putting his full weight on it.

The sound of the shower turning on told Alexander he needed to get a move on. He'd brought his cane upstairs the night before and he reached for it without hesitation. Last night was amazing, but it had taken a toll on his body.

Alexander was pouring their coffee into mugs when Grace strolled into the kitchen. He handed her one before taking a seat at the kitchen table.

"Thanks." She took a sip and set the mug down on the table. "We had some muffins left over yesterday."

"Sounds good." He wasn't picky. At this point he probably would have eaten just about anything she put in front of him. They'd both burned off a lot of calories last night.

Grace brought a plate of five muffins to the table. "There's cranberry, banana nut, and one blueberry, I think."

They spent the next several minutes devouring the muffins. To be honest, he probably could have eaten all five himself.

As they were cleaning up, Alexander felt he needed to broach the subject of her collar again. Although he was fairly sure she did want to wear his collar, it was always better to address these things when hormones were not in play. This was a serious commitment for both of them.

He wrapped one arm around her waist and tugged her flush against him. Grace came willingly, circling her arms around his neck. She looked almost angelic as she smiled up at him.

"I thought we could go shopping tonight."

The look on her face told him she hadn't been expecting that.

Alexander pressed on. "I know some Doms like more traditional collars for their submissives, but I want something you can wear everyday as well."

He felt her muscles tense, but she didn't comment.

"Have you changed your mind?"

Grace stared back at him with wide eyes. "No." She swallowed. "I just . . . Kurt picked out my collar himself. I figured . . ."

"I can pick something out on my own if you'd prefer, but I'd rather have your input." He cupped her ass and pressed her pelvis against him in a suggestive way. "The final decision will be mine, of course."

She smiled up at him. "Of course."

He placed a kiss on her lips and released her. "I'm hoping to get out of work on time today. How about I pick you up at five thirty? We can get something to eat and then go look for your collar."

Alexander's day went much smoother than the previous one. The idiot lawyer was nowhere in sight.

After lunch his boss stopped by his desk. "I was wondering if you have a minute."

He glanced at the stack of folders to his left. It wasn't as if they were going anywhere. "Sure."

Once they were inside Janet's office, she walked behind her large wooden desk, sat down, and invited him to take a seat. "I wanted to talk to you about the meeting yesterday."

His good mood went out the window. "What about it?"

"I wanted to let you know I was impressed by how you handled yourself. Gregg is an ass and more than once I've wanted to drop-kick him into next week."

Alexander chuckled. "You won't get any argument from me."

Janet grinned. "He likes to goad people. It's how he's made his reputation. You didn't bite."

"After having drill sergeants shouting in your face, Gregg Bowers isn't all that scary."

"I imagine not." She laughed. "Anyway, I wanted to talk to you about your future here. You're a great asset and I'd hate to lose you. I know when we first talked you were hoping to start your own practice."

She left the sentence unfinished, giving him an opportunity to take it wherever he wished. "At the moment, that's still the plan."

Janet leaned back in her chair. "What can I do to change that?"

Chapter Twenty-Four

Grace was surprised to find her sister sitting on her front steps when she got home from the café. It was the middle of the day, which meant Gabby should have been working. "Hey."

Gabby looked up as Grace approached. "Hey."

She took a seat on the steps next to her sister. "Shouldn't you still be at work?"

"I took the day off." Her sister shrugged like it wasn't a big deal, but she could tell something was off. Especially since Gabby wasn't asking Grace the latest details regarding her relationship with Alexander.

"Want to talk about it?" Grace asked when Gabby didn't say anything more.

It took a moment for her sister to respond. Gabby stared down at her hands, twisting them nervously in front of her. "I did something stupid. Really, *really* stupid."

Grace was almost afraid to ask. "What did you do?"

"I slept with Jax."

"When?"

Grace tried to keep the shock out of her voice, but she didn't know how well she succeeded. Her sister looked as if she wanted to crawl into a cave and disappear. "Last night."

When Grace remained silent, her sister continued. "He wanted to take Taylor to the park after work, so I arranged for him to pick her up at the babysitter. By the time I got to his place to pick her up at seven thirty, she was already passed out on his couch."

"How exactly does that translate into you two . . ."

Gabby cracked a bit of a smile at Grace's reluctance to go on. "Having sex?"

"Yeah." It was stupid. Grace had no trouble talking about all sorts of kinky things with Alexander, but with her sister she felt like she was a bumbling teenager again discussing her first kiss.

"I don't know exactly. One minute we were talking about how he wanted to see Taylor more, and the next we were kissing." Gabby dropped her head into her hands. "Before I knew it, our clothes were on the floor and we were in his bedroom. We didn't even make it to the bed."

"Was it good?"

Gabby snapped her head up to meet Grace's gaze. "What?"

"The sex. Was it good?"

Her sister looked at Grace as if she's lost her mind. Maybe she had. This wasn't the type of thing Grace normally talked about. "That's not the point. It shouldn't have happened."

"Maybe not. But it did."

"I know." Her sister lowered her head into her hands again. "What am I going to do?"

"What do you want to do?"

"Hide."

Her sister's honest answer made Grace laugh. "I'm serious."

"So am I. All I want to do is curl into a ball and hope no one finds me."

Grace could see this conversation wasn't going anywhere fast. It was warm out by November standards, but there was still a nip in the air. "Do you want to come inside?"

"Do you have anything harder than pop in your fridge?"

"I think I may have some wine." She was pretty sure she still had an unopened bottle in the back of one of her cabinets.

Gabby pushed her hair away from her face. "Unless you have a whole vineyard in there, I don't think it's going to be enough."

"Come on, it can't be that bad." Grace rubbed a hand up and down her sister's back.

"Yeah, it can."

Grace felt as if she was missing something. Sure, Gabby sleeping with her ex wasn't ideal, but this seemed like overkill.

They sat there for a while, not speaking, the cool concrete they were sitting on slowly seeping through her jeans. Her sister seemed to be thinking about something and Grace didn't want to interrupt her thought process.

Eventually, her sister sighed. "I think I'm falling for him again."

Grace waited.

"He's been so nice lately—wanting to spend time with Taylor, asking if I need help with anything." Gabby glanced in Grace's direction. "The last time he took off he broke my heart and left me trying to raise a newborn on my own."

"I know." Grace pulled her sister in for a hug.

After a few minutes, Gabby pulled back. "I should go. I need to pick Taylor up soon."

"Do you need someone to watch her tonight?" Grace wasn't sure how Alexander would feel about it, but her sister needed her. If it cost her a sore bottom, she'd take it.

"No. That's all right. I've had all day to wallow. Besides, I don't want to mess up your evening."

Her sister stood, brushing the dirt off her jeans, so Grace did the same. "You wouldn't."

Gabby ignored her. She gave Grace a peck on the cheek and turned toward her car. "Thanks for listening."

Her sister was halfway to her vehicle before Grace could respond. "Call me if you need me."

"I will." Her sister opened her car door and slid inside.

Grace stood at the base of her front steps and watched as Gabby drove away.

Once her sister was out of sight, Grace ascended the stairs, unlocked her door, and went inside. Gabby had always been more spontaneous than Grace. Which, all things considered, was a little ironic. As far as Grace knew, her sister wasn't into kinky sex.

After hanging up her jacket and kicking off her shoes, Grace checked her watch. It was a little after four, which meant she had about an hour and a half before Alexander came to pick her up. More than enough time to shower and put in a load of laundry.

Alexander knocked on her door at five twenty-seven. She snatched her coat from the closet and opened the door, ready to leave. But before she could cross the threshold, he stepped forward, pushing her back into the foyer, and shut the door behind him. He gripped her waist with both hands and jerked her closer. Her heart pounded in her chest as his lips found hers and she melted against him, letting her tongue tangle with his.

Alexander rested his forehead against hers, but didn't let her go. "That's better."

She hummed. "Did you have a bad day again today?"

"No. Actually, it went well." He didn't seem surprised that she'd picked up on his mood the day before. "I even got a job offer."

"Really? Where?" Maybe it should have seemed odd that they were standing in her foyer, foreheads still pressed together, having this conversation, but it didn't feel awkward.

"Same company I work for now." He brushed his mouth against her forehead and let his arms fall down to his sides. She didn't miss that he still had his cane. Nor had she missed how much he'd leaned on it that morning. "But my position was always meant to be temporary, until my license came through and I could open my own practice."

She knew how important starting his own practice was to him. They'd talked about it a lot over the last two months. "What are you going to do?"

He picked her coat up off the floor and helped her into it. "I don't know. The money's good. Benefits. Vacation. 401K."

"But it isn't what you want." She could hear it in his voice.

"Shuffling papers around isn't exactly how I saw my future." He opened the door for her and followed her outside. "Then again, up until a year ago I figured I'd be spending at least another ten years in the military."

She nodded, not feeling as if words were needed. Plans changed. Circumstances changed. They both knew that.

Over dinner Grace told him about her sister's visit. "If you needed to take care of your sister tonight, all you had to do was let me know."

"Thanks." Knowing that made her feel a bit better. They were still feeling things out, especially the relationship part. "Her relationship with Jax has always been complicated. The chemistry was always there, but I think she was looking for something more permanent than he was."

"And now?" he asked, swiping a fry from her plate and popping it into his mouth.

Grace shrugged. "I don't know. He seems to be more invested in Taylor, wanting to spend time with her . . . be her dad. But I'm not sure Gabby's willing to open herself up again. He really broke her heart when he took off the first time."

"Hopefully they'll be able to figure it out. It's never easy when kids are involved. Too often they get stuck in the middle." The way he said it made her think he was speaking from personal experience, but as far as she knew his parents had a happy marriage. He seemed to know where her thoughts were going. "My best friend in junior high. In the two years I was there, his parents had split, gotten back together, and then split again. Last I heard, he was living with his mom and spending weekends with his dad. It was hard on him."

"I'm sorry."

Alexander stole another fry. "It was a long time ago."

They finished their dinner and walked hand in hand down the block to a jewelry store. Grace had passed by it several times, but she'd never been inside. She'd never had reason to.

He held the door open and gestured for her to go first. "After you."

❦

A WOMAN BEHIND THE COUNTER LOOKED UP AS THEY ENTERED. SHE SMILED. "Welcome. Anything particular I can help you find today?"

Alexander placed a hand on the small of Grace's back and guided her forward. "We'd like to look at your selection of necklaces."

"Right over here."

She directed them to a long glass case full of necklaces. Most of them he immediately discarded. They were too flashy. He wanted something she could wear every day and to the club.

"I'll give you a few minutes to look. Just holler if you need anything," the woman said before walking to the other side of the store to help another customer.

He moved closer to Grace, his chest pressed against her back as he peered over her shoulder. "See anything you like?" Alexander could feel her hesitation. "I want it to be something you're comfortable wearing."

She glanced up at him, and then back to the case. "I like these two."

The two necklaces she pointed out were in line with what he was looking for, but neither was quite right. One had two circles, one inside the other. The other had a single circle with a small jewel hanging from the center.

Then he spotted something a little farther down. It was almost hidden because it was at the end of the row, next to the bracelets. He moved them closer to get a better look.

"What do you think?" he asked once they were standing in front of the necklace.

"It's pretty."

He brushed her hair back away from her neck with the tips of his fingers and leaned in to whisper in her ear. "Do you like it?"

She sucked in a breath. "Yes, S—"

"Did you find something?" the sales woman asked, reappearing with a flourish from around the corner.

Alexander pointed to the necklace. "We'd like to see that one."

"Of course." The woman removed the necklace from the case and placed it on top of the counter. "It has a simple elegance to it."

"That it does." He picked it up, letting it drape over his fingers. "You'd be able to put a small charm on at the back?"

The saleswoman leaned in slightly, taking a look at the clasp. "That shouldn't be a problem. What did you have in mind?"

"A heart. And I'd want it engraved." He turned to face Grace. "Turn around and lift up your hair. I want to see what it looks like on you."

Obediently, she turned so her back was to him and lifted her hair away from her neck. It only took a few seconds to secure the necklace. As soon as it was in place, she faced him, letting her hair fall. The three linked circles rested just above her collarbone.

He ran a single finger along the black chain down to the gold circles. Seeing it around her neck confirmed it was the one.

Grace's gaze met his. The look in her eyes matched what he was feeling inside: pride, joy—and, he dared to hope—love. "We'll take it."

The sales woman said something, but he didn't catch it. His focus was on Grace.

"Sir?"

Alexander tore his gaze away from Grace and turned to address the sales woman. He had no idea what she'd said, but it didn't matter. "How long to get the charm and have it engraved?"

"As long as we have the charm in stock, we should be able to have it to you in a few days. A week at most."

It took them another half hour to finish things up. He'd looked over the charm options carefully, trying to find one that would work with the necklace and be big enough for what he wanted to have written on it. In the end, he'd settled on a gold heart about the size of Grace's thumb. He filled out the form for the engraving, making sure every letter was legible.

As they were leaving, a sharp pain shot up his leg and he stumbled. Grace reached out to steady him. "Do you want to stay here while I get the car?"

He breathed through the pain and waited for it to subside. "No. It's not that far."

Grace didn't argue, but she did stay close to his side. He hated having to lean on his cane so much, but it was that or he was going to fall flat on his face.

It took a bit longer, but they made it back to the vehicle. He sat down behind the wheel and breathed a sigh of relief as the aching in his legs eased some. Grace watched him, her brow furrowed. He reached for her hand and brought it up to his lips for a kiss. "I'm all right. My leg just gets a little testy when I've been standing on it for too long."

"Can you take anything to help with the pain?" she asked.

"I have some pills at home, but I try not to take them."

"Why not? If they help—"

"Because it's not that bad. Really." He kissed the inside of her wrist and released her hand. "I just need to stay off it for a while and rest."

She didn't comment as he maneuvered into traffic and began heading toward her house. It wasn't until they turned onto her road that she shifted in her seat. "Are you staying tonight?"

He'd been debating that the entire drive. As much as he wanted to stay, having her lying beside him and not being able to have her would be torture. Still, if he had to lie there and do nothing, he'd rather be with her than alone in his apartment. "If that's all right with you."

"Of course." She smiled. "I can massage your leg like I did before, if you'd like."

Memories of the last time she'd massaged his leg, as well as other parts of his anatomy, had a whole new type of ache beginning. He put the car in park in front of her house, unbuckled his seat belt, and turned to face her. Tucking a strand of her hair behind her ear, he leaned in and brushed his lips against hers. "Now, that's an offer I can't refuse."

She grinned.

The walk inside was full of discomfort. Getting up the stairs was the worst and he knew he had an entire flight of them to conquer in order to reach Grace's bedroom. He didn't object when she took his coat and hung it up for him. The only thing he could think about was sitting down and getting the pressure off his leg.

"I think I have some wine in the kitchen."

"That sounds great."

She nodded and hurried down the hall, leaving him alone.

He made his way into the living room, albeit slowly, and lowered himself onto the couch. Grace appeared a few moments later with two glasses of wine.

"Thanks," he said, taking one.

"You're welcome." Grace sat down beside him, folding her legs up beside her.

Alexander placed an arm around her shoulders and hugged her against his side as he took a sip of his wine. It wasn't his preferred drink, but it would do well enough to take the edge off the pain. Hopefully enough that he'd be able to get up the stairs and into her bed.

They sat there quietly, drinking the wine and talking until Grace started to yawn. "We should probably get you up to bed."

She smiled up at him. "And I still owe you a massage."

He drew her face closer, bringing her in for a kiss. "Why don't you go and get things ready? I'll be up in a few minutes."

For a moment, he thought she was going to protest, but then she nodded and stood. "I'll be waiting for you, Sir."

Chapter Twenty-Five

As it turned out, the exact charm Alexander wanted for Grace's collar wasn't in stock, which meant it wasn't ready by the weekend. She wondered if he would forgo going to the club, but in the end they went. For the most part, they socialized. Alexander thought it was important for Grace to get comfortable with the club. She began to understand why when Katrina stopped by their group Saturday night.

"Were you still interested in me doing the demonstration we talked about?" Alexander asked during a lull in the conversation.

"Of course." Katrina glanced over at Grace, an amused glint in her eye that Grace immediately recognized. It was the look Dominants got when they were about to push their sub's limits "Just let me know when and what you'll need. I'll make sure everything's set up and ready to go."

"I was thinking sometime next month. Maybe a week or so before Christmas."

"Perfect."

The rest of the conversation consisted of somewhat vague talk of tables and toys, along with an exchange of emails. Grace had no idea what type of demonstration they were taking about, but she had a feeling she was going to find out. All the demonstrations she'd ever witnessed, which granted weren't many, included a submissive. Since she was Alexander's sub, Grace imagined she'd be filling that spot. He didn't say anything for the rest of the evening and the conversation shifted to more mundane topics.

On the drive home, Grace expected him to bring up the subject again, but he didn't. He didn't bring it up the next day either. So Sunday night as they were lying in bed, she broached the subject. "Last night you were talking to Katrina about a demonstration."

"Yes." She could hear the smile in his voice even though she couldn't see his face.

"What kind of demonstration does she want you to do?"

He rolled them both over so he was looking down at her. "She's asked me to do a demonstration on medical play."

It only took a moment for Grace to realize what that meant for her. As anxious as she was about it, she could already feel herself getting wet at the thought of him doing things to her while everyone watched. She really was an exhibitionist. "What will I have to do?"

A smirk appeared on his face. "You're going to be my patient." He paused. "My very naughty patient."

She felt her body temperature rise a few degrees.

Alexander skimmed his lips along her jaw to her ear. "Do you trust me?"

That was easy. "Yes."

He reached down between them and glided his fingers over her pussy. "I'm going to have a fun making you come in front of all those people."

Grace moaned as he slid two fingers inside her. She wrapped her arms around his neck, bit her lower lip, and held on tight as he moved his fingers in and out of her in a steady rhythm.

It was so easy to get lost in the sensations as he touched and teased her, keeping her on edge for as long as possible before allowing her to fall. Her body knew what it wanted, what it longed for. She wasn't going to fight it anymore.

The next couple of days flew by. Grace had talked to her sister several times, including at their mom's on Sunday afternoon. Gabby was still beating herself up over sleeping with Jax. To make matters worse, when Gabby had picked Taylor up at the babysitter's Tuesday night, her daughter had asked if Daddy was coming to Thanksgiving. Her sister had danced around the subject and eventually redirected her daughter's attention. "What am I supposed to say if she brings it up again? She's only three. It's not like she's going to understand."

Grace felt sorry for Gabby. She was doing her best. It couldn't be easy. Especially when her own feelings for Jax were all over the place. "Probably not. I hate to say this, but maybe you and Jax need to talk . . . figure out what you're going to tell her. Chances are she's going to ask more questions the older she gets."

A frustrated sigh came through the line. "Not exactly what I want to do at the moment, but you're right. We do need to talk. About a lot of things."

That was probably the understatement of the year.

"Enough about me, though. Let's talk about something happy. How are things going with you and your doctor? Are you still bringing him with you Thursday?"

Thinking about Alexander brought a smile to Grace's face. "Yes, he's still coming."

"I bet." The way her sister said it made it clear she wasn't talking about Thanksgiving dinner anymore.

Grace felt her cheeks heat. "Can we please talk about something other than my sex life?"

Her sister laughed. "I don't understand why you get so embarrassed about it. I mean you were married for almost ten years and I know you tapped that as often as humanly possible."

If her sister only knew. Whenever Kurt had been away, whether on deployment or for training, as soon as he got back they would lock themselves in the house for two or three days. He'd taken her in every way humanly possible and she'd loved it. She'd be sore for several days after.

Recalling that time left her with a sense of loss. She waited for the feeling of a weight pressing down on her chest and the nausea to settle in as it always did whenever she thought back on those times—on Kurt and their life together—but it didn't come.

"Grace? Are you there?"

"Yeah, I'm still here." Grace forced herself to refocus on the conversation. "Sorry."

Her sister grew serious. "I didn't mean to make you sad. I know thinking about Kurt—"

"No, it's fine. I'm fine."

"Are you sure?" Gabby didn't seem convinced.

"Yes." A change in subject was needed. "Now, what are you bringing to Mom's? I was thinking about making some pasta salad."

They talked for a while about food and work, both avoiding the subject of their relationships, past and present. At nine thirty, she said good night to her sister, made sure the house was locked up, and headed upstairs to get ready for bed. Alexander had to drive to Kansas City for work and wouldn't be back until the next day. It was the first time she'd slept alone in almost two weeks and her house felt incredibly empty. It was strange given she'd spent months alone at a time when Kurt was deployed, not to mention the months after his death. She was trying not to dwell on it, though.

Grace burrowed under the covers and reached for Alexander's pillow. The smell of him mixed with sex had her grinning as she recalled how she'd woken up that morning—with his head between her legs. She could still see the satisfied smirk on his face as he'd crawled up her body like a cat on the prowl.

As she was lying there remembering, her phone dinged, letting her know she had a message.

This bed is awfully lonely without you in it. – Alexander

I was just thinking the same thing. - Grace

A few seconds passed before he replied.

I'd call, but I know you have to be up early tomorrow and if I get you on the phone I doubt either of us will be falling asleep anytime soon. - Alexander

He was probably right. As much as she'd love to hear his voice, chances were good that if he called they'd either be up talking until midnight or they'd end up fooling around. Neither of those options sounded terrible to her, but he was right. They both needed their sleep. She wasn't so worried about herself, but she didn't want him groggy driving home.

What time will you be home tomorrow? - Grace

Hopefully by 2:30 or 3. I have a nine o'clock meeting that shouldn't last more than an hour. - Alexander

Grace bit her bottom lip as she contemplated how to respond.

Call me when you get back? - Grace

I will. - Alexander

There was a long pause.

Good night, *gattina*. Sweet dreams. - Alexander

❧

TO GIVE ALEXANDER A TASTE OF WHAT HIS JOB WOULD ENTAIL SHOULD HE decide to stay, his boss had asked him to join her in Kansas City for several meetings. He'd been introduced to the company executives and a handful of lawyers the company worked with on a regular basis. It wasn't as bad as he'd feared, but he still wasn't sure this was something he wanted to do long term.

Their final meeting ended and he began gathering his things. Alexander wanted to get on the road home as soon as possible. He'd received a voice mail this morning from the jewelry store saying the necklace was ready to be picked up. As they had no plans tonight and neither had to be up early tomorrow for work given the holiday, he wanted to go all out and make this special for Grace. That meant he had some planning to do.

"Heading back?" Janet asked.

"Want to beat the traffic."

His boss wasn't fooled. "Sure you do." She shook her head and chuckled. "Enjoy your long weekend."

"Thanks. You, too."

The drive between Kansas City and St. Louis seemed to take longer than it did the first time around. Maybe that was because he was anxious to get home. He turned on some music, hoping that would make the time go faster.

He ran into some traffic about a half hour outside St. Louis. It took him almost thirty minutes to travel less than five miles. Luckily, once he got past the accident, things got moving again. Still, it was later than he'd hoped. So instead of going home and changing first as he would have liked, he drove straight to the jewelry store.

There weren't any other customers in the store when he arrived, so he was able to get in and out quickly. He made a quick pit stop at his apartment to shower, change, and grab enough clothes for the weekend since he didn't plan on sleeping at his place for the next few days.

Alexander didn't even have to ring the doorbell. She was there waiting for him with a shy smile on her face. He scooped her into his arms and gave her a thorough kiss. "Hi."

"Hi."

They separated so he could close the door, remove his coat, and set his bags down.

"Are you hungry?" she asked.

He reached for her again, crushing her against him. "Starving."

Grace giggled. "I meant for food."

"Oh." He leaned down to kiss her neck. "Yeah. That, too."

She tilted her head to the side to give him better access. "I made lasagna and some garlic bread. I figured you'd be hun—"

His lips covered hers as he backed them into the living room toward the couch. He reached between them and began working her sweater up her torso. "Do you have anything in the kitchen that will burn or catch on fire if it isn't attended to in the next fifteen minutes?"

Grace shook her head. "No."

"Good," he said, working his own shirt over his head and letting it drop to the floor. "There's something that needs my attention first."

An hour later, their bellies full of pasta and bread, they curled up on the couch to watch a movie. He ran his fingers through her hair as she rested her head in his lap. It was one of the most relaxing things he'd done in a long time —just the two of them, lounging on the couch. There was nothing requiring their attention. No reason to rush to bed since they didn't have to be up early the next day.

The movie ended, but neither moved. He glanced down to find her looking up at him. There was something in her eyes that had him concerned. "What is it?"

She smiled and reached up to cup the back of his head, drawing his face down to hers. He allowed the distraction, mainly because he didn't want to push her. This thing between them was still so new and they both had baggage.

"I saw you brought a bag," she whispered.

He hummed and lifted her so she was straddling his lap. "I figured I'd need clothes for tomorrow."

Grace averted her gaze and he wondered if this was what had been on her mind a few minutes ago. He wasn't overly concerned with meeting her mother, but maybe she was having second thoughts about it. Meeting her family was a big step. "Do you not want me to go?"

Her eyes widened as she looked at him again. "No. I mean, yes, I still want you to go. If you want." She paused. "I'm sorry. This isn't coming out right."

Alexander took her face in his hands and waited for her to gather her thoughts.

She closed her eyes and sighed. "I just don't want you to feel you have to."

He pressed his lips to hers with the gentlest of pressure, but it was enough to get her to open her eyes. "Grace, you're important to me and if we're going to continue our relationship, I'd like to get to know your family."

"Even after all Gabby's questions?"

"I had commanders barking orders at me for ten years. I think I can handle your sister."

He'd meant to lighten the mood, but Grace wasn't having it. "Just remember you said that."

Deciding it was best to let it go for now, Alexander gave her another brief kiss before letting her go. "Why don't you head on up to bed and I'll be up in a few?"

Something changed in her eyes. She stood and shot him a look through lowered lashes that spoke volumes.

Almost instantly, with that one look, there was less room in his pants.

When he'd suggested they turn in, he hadn't been talking about sex, but now it was at the forefront of his mind. "Get undressed and wait for me."

"Yes, Sir." He caught sight of her grin as she turned to make her way upstairs. She was rather pleased with herself since she thought she was getting what she wanted.

Alexander took his time making his rounds downstairs, making sure every window and door was locked. With casualness he didn't feel, he retrieved his bag from where he'd left it by the door and headed up the stairs. His heart rate rose with each step as his anticipation grew. He knew what he'd find when he walked into her bedroom, but even so the sight had his cock begging to be let out of its confines.

Strolling into the room, he set his overnight bag on the end of the bed, removed her collar, and placed his bag in the corner. He wasn't going to need clothing tonight.

The entire time Grace remained in position, waiting. He palmed her collar in one hand and went to stand behind her. One of the advantages of his long drive from Kansas City was that he'd been off his leg for most of the day. Alexander didn't need his cane, which meant that both his hands were free.

He rested the palm of his hand on her head, allowing both of them to take in the moment. Everything was quiet. It was just the two of them, completely at peace.

With a featherlight touch, he petted her hair, letting them both sink deeper into their roles. She released a noise from deep in her throat that sounded almost like a purr.

"Are you relaxed, *gattina?*"

"Yes, Sir." The words came out on a sigh.

Alexander continued to pet her hair. "The jewelry store called me this morning to let me know your collar was ready. I picked it up this afternoon."

She remained silent, but it seemed more as if she was in the moment rather than any sort of discontent.

He moved to stand in front of her. "Look at me."

Grace tilted her head up, meeting his gaze. There was no hesitation in her eyes, no uncertainty.

"Will you accept my collar, Grace?"

"Yes, Sir."

He held the necklace so she could see the charm on the back next to the clasp. On the underside of the heart it said *La Sua Gattina—His Kitten.* "Lift your hair for me."

The love he felt for her filled him as he unclasped the necklace and secured it around her neck. Alexander gathered her hair in both his hands and she released her hold, giving over control. He tilted her head back, admiring his collar around her neck.

Of course it didn't hurt that at this angle he had an amazing view of her breasts as well. He bent to kiss her while reaching down with one hand to toy with her nipple. The sound she made had him wanting to throw her onto the bed and lose himself in her warmth. It was only years of experience that allowed him to remain in control of his baser instincts.

That didn't mean he wasn't going to get what he wanted. Fucking her senseless had its advantages, but so did indulging.

He gave her nipple one final tweak before releasing her and stepping back. "On the bed and spread your legs. I want to taste my pussy."

Chapter Twenty-Six

Grace was a nervous wreck by the time they arrived at her mother's house. Alexander kept sneaking glances at her as he drove, the frown on his face deepening the closer they came to their destination. He parked along the street, put the car in park, and reached for her hand. "Why are you so jittery?"

"Sorry." She shot him a feeble grin. "It's just been a really long time since I brought a boy home to meet my mom."

Alexander chuckled. "It's been a while since anyone's called me a boy."

He was right, of course. No one in their right mind would call Alexander a boy. "I meant—"

"I know what you meant, *gattina*, but I promise you it will be fine. I can handle whatever your mother—or your sister—throw at me. They aren't going to scare me off." He cradled the side of her face in his hand and brushed his lips against hers. "Relax." The pad of his thumb grazed her bottom lip. "That's an order."

She closed her eyes, leaned into his hand, and concentrated on the feeling of his skin against hers. This wasn't wrong. She had every right to move on, to find happiness again. It's what Kurt had wanted.

This time when Grace looked at him, she was more at peace. The anxiety was still there, but if he wasn't going to worry about it then she would try not to as well. "Yes, Sir. I will try my best."

He smiled. "That's all I ask."

Alexander balanced two casserole dishes in one hand while Grace brought in the pasta salad and a pumpkin pie. If he hadn't needed his cane, she knew he most likely would have insisted on carrying everything. They'd been up late the night before. He'd brought her to the edge time and time again, not allowing her to go over until he was inside her. Her nipples were still a little sensitive from where he'd clamped them and sucked on them to the point she was begging him to allow her to come.

"Everything all right?" he asked as they approached the door.

Grace didn't get a chance to answer before the door swung open, revealing her sister. "I thought I heard voices."

After Alexander and Grace removed their coats and said a brief hello to Taylor as she ran past them, the three headed into the kitchen where Caroline was taking the turkey out of the oven. She looked up when they strolled into the room. Her gaze rested on Alexander for a long moment, allowing herself to get a good look at him.

Grace placed what she was carrying on the counter, and then took the dishes Alexander had and set them down as well. "Mom, this is Alexander Greco. Alexander, my mom . . . Caroline."

Alexander didn't miss a beat. He stepped forward and extended his hand. "It's great to finally meet you, ma'am."

Her mom stared at his offering for a long moment before wiping her hands and accepting his handshake. "Grace says you served with her husband, Kurt."

"Yes, ma'am. We were both deployed at the same base overseas."

Before things could get awkward, Grace decided to act. "Does anything need to be done?"

Caroline picked up a pair of potholders and dumped a pot full of boiling water and cubed potatoes into a strainer she had sitting in the sink. "Just take what you brought to the table. Once I get these potatoes mashed and the turkey carved, we'll be ready to dig in."

Less than fifteen minutes later, they were all seated around the table, filling their plates with food. Even though they were at her mother's, Grace waited for Alexander to start eating before she took her first bite. The simple gesture brought some balance, which turned out to be a very good thing since the questions from her mother started a few minutes later.

"How long were you in the Army?"

Alexander finished chewing and swallowing his food before he answered Caroline. "Ten years."

"Did you like it?" she asked. Grace had no idea where her mother was going with this line of questioning, but considering the alternative, she'd take it.

"I enjoyed the discipline, the order, knowing what was expected of me and of the men I served with."

Caroline grabbed a roll from the basket. "Grace said you were hurt."

"Yes, ma'am. My leg was crushed in an explosion."

"I'm sorry."

He shrugged. "I was lucky."

They all heard what he didn't say, that Kurt hadn't been so fortunate. What her family didn't realize was that the incident that had caused Alexander's injury was the same one that had killed Kurt. It wasn't something she wanted to get into. Especially not at the dining room table.

After several moments of silence, her mother switched to another line of questioning. "Do you plan on staying in St. Louis?" Grace cringed a little. It was almost as bad as her mother asking what Alexander's intentions were.

"Yes. I'm in the process of getting my medical license here in Missouri, but for the time being I'm working as a consultant." It was his way of saying he was putting down roots. Nothing he said was news to her, but for some reason hearing him tell her mother made it sound more definite. As if he really was declaring his intentions.

Her mother kept pressing. "Grace has been through a lot this last year."

He met her mother's gaze across the table. "Yes, she has."

It was as if something unspoken passed between them. Grace waited for her mother to comment, but she only nodded then went back to her food and a new line of questioning. "Do you have any hobbies?"

The first thing that popped into Grace's mind was the feel of his hand on her backside as he'd spanked her the night before. Of course, Alexander didn't mention BDSM. He chose something more mundane to share with her mother. "I enjoy reading when I have the time."

"Grace likes to read, too." Gabby inserted herself into the conversation for the first time.

Alexander looked at Grace with a knowing glint in his eye. "Yes. She's shared some of them with me."

"Wow. You must be special. Every time I ask her about her books she just tells me I wouldn't like them." Her sister narrowed her eyes at her in mock irritation.

Grace stared at her plate, avoiding eye contact.

"Are you an avid reader yourself?" Alexander asked Gabby, redirecting the attention away from Grace. She wanted to kiss him.

"I've been known to pick up a romance novel when I have some downtime." As if on cue, Taylor dropped her fork on the floor. Gabby scooted her chair away from the table so she could pick it up. She placed the dirty spoon out of Taylor's reach, and then took her own spoon and handed it to her daughter. "But I don't have much of that these days."

Alexander nodded. "Children do tend to require a lot of one's attention, but in the end it's worth it. Time is one thing you can't replace."

Caroline took the opening and ran with it. "Do you have any children, Alexander?"

"No, ma'am."

"Ever been married?"

"Mom!" Grace felt her cheeks heat in embarrassment. She was thirty-four years old. She didn't need her mother vetting her boyfriends anymore.

"It's a perfectly reasonable question," her mother insisted.

Alexander didn't seem fazed. "No. I haven't been married. I do, however, hope to remedy that someday soon."

Grace turned to look at him. She could only imagine the look on her face. Was he talking about her? Surely, he couldn't be—they'd only been seeing each other for a few weeks. Granted, they'd been talking and going out to dinner together for longer, but still.

It was too soon.

The conversation continued, although Grace wasn't really paying attention to what was being said. All she could think about was how casually he'd said he hoped to get married soon. He wasn't seeing anyone else. That was part of their agreement. So if he wasn't talking about her, then who?

"Grace, do you want any pie?"

She blinked and looked up at where her mother was standing not two feet away from her, plate in her hand. "What?"

Caroline raised her eyebrows, clearly wondering where her daughter's mind had gone. "I asked if you wanted pie. Gabby's slicing it up."

"Oh. Yes, please."

Her mother walked away chuckling and shaking her head. Grace was sure her mother thought she was daydreaming or something. It was easier to let her mother think that than tell her that what Alexander said had her head spinning. Was she ready to get married again?

ALEXANDER HAD BEEN WATCHING GRACE FOR A WHILE, BUT AS SOON AS they were alone he placed a hand on her leg, drawing her attention. "Everything okay?"

She nodded, but he didn't miss how she pressed her lips together, a sure sign she was nervous about something. He didn't get a chance to examine it any further, though, since her mom and sister reentered the room.

They weren't alone again until they said their goodbyes and headed home several hours later. Grace's mom and sister had been full of questions, wanting to know about his childhood, his parents, and even if he'd had any pets growing up. For the most part, Grace had remained quiet throughout the conversation, only commenting when someone asked her a question.

"Tell me what's wrong," he demanded as they made their way back to her house.

It took her too long to answer.

He glanced over and saw her fidgeting, pulling at her fingers. "Grace?"

"You said you want to get married." She paused. "Soon."

The wheels started turning in his head, rushing to catch up to what she'd obviously been mulling over for hours already. "Yes. I would like to get married someday."

Alexander waited to see if she would continue. He figured he'd give her until they reached their destination before he took more drastic measures to get whatever it was out of her. Luckily, she didn't make him wait that long. "Is there someone else?"

They were at a stoplight, which turned out to be a very good thing seeing as how her question had caught him completely off guard. "No. Why would you even think that? Have I given you any reason to think—"

"No," she hurried to explain. "It's just that . . . when you told my mom you wanted to get married soon, at first I thought you were talking about us, but then I thought you couldn't possibly. I mean we haven't known each other for that long and . . ."

The light turned green and as there was a vehicle behind them he had to drive. As soon as he saw an opening, however, he maneuvered his car off the road and put it in park. He gathered her hands in his, needing to touch her. His heart was pounding in his chest. He'd known her mother and sister would ask questions, vet him to make sure he was good enough for Grace, and when she'd asked about marriage he wasn't going to lie. And even though he'd known Caroline's questioning could go down this road, he'd been hoping to put off this conversation with Grace for a little while longer. "I was talking about us."

Grace swallowed.

Her lack of verbal response worried him. "Do you not want to get married again?"

"I hadn't really thought about it."

Time ticked by as they sat in the warmth of the vehicle. He held tight to her hands, not letting go. "I know what we have is new and we're still feeling things out, but if war taught me one thing it's that life is fleeting. And if you want something, you need to go after it, because tomorrow isn't a guarantee."

Alexander cupped her face with one hand, massaging her cheek with his thumb. "I want to fall asleep beside you every night for the rest of my life. And when I wake up every morning, the first thing I want to see is you." He let that hang in the air for a moment before he continued. "I love you, Grace."

He could feel her pulse race beneath his palm. For weeks he'd been biting his tongue, knowing she wasn't ready to hear how he felt. Finally putting it out there was one of the most terrifying things he'd ever done. He had no idea how she'd react.

The only thing he could hear was their breathing and the blood pumping through his eardrums as he waited. Although it was no more than a minute, it felt like an eternity. "What about our agreement?"

There was such vulnerability in her eyes as she stared back at him. He wanted to gather her into his arms and never let her go. "There isn't anything in our agreement that says I can't fall in love with my submissive."

"Yes, I know." She looked down at where he was still holding one of her hands. "I'm not saying this right."

He tilted her chin up, meeting her gaze. "There's no pressure here, Grace. When I told your mother I wanted to get married soon, I didn't mean next week or even next month." One side of his mouth tilted up a little. "Although, I wouldn't say no if that's what you wanted."

Her eyes opened wide at his admission.

"What I meant was that one day, hopefully in the not too distant future, you will agree to become my wife. If that's months from now, or years . . ." He shrugged.

"We've only known each other for two months."

"So?" He released her fingers and cradled her face in his hands as if she were the most precious thing in the world to him. "I've been falling in love with you since that moment in your kitchen when you cried in my arms."

"I don't know what to say," she whispered.

"You don't have to say anything." He brushed his lips against hers. "Let's get you home, and then we can talk some more if you want."

"All right."

He couldn't get back to her house fast enough. As the miles passed, he felt her withdrawing again. It made no sense and because he had to keep his focus on the road, there wasn't much he could do about it at the moment.

When they arrived at her house, he waited until they'd brought everything inside and put it away before leaning against the counter and drawing her into his arms. "Talk to me."

"I don't know what you want me to say."

He pressed a kiss to her temple as he held her against him. "Tell me how you're feeling."

"Nervous. Confused."

Alexander wished Grace's mother had never asked him that stupid question or that he had answered it differently somehow. He'd known what she was doing—they both had—but he was positive Caroline wouldn't have anticipated Grace's reaction. At most, Alexander had figured she'd be shocked or maybe even a little uneasy given they had known each other for such a short time. Originally, he'd planned on waiting another month or two before telling Grace he loved her. Then, when the time was right, he was going to ask her to marry him. Her mother's question and his subsequent answer had thrown that plan out the window. Or the first part of it, at least.

He opened his mouth to ask her what she was confused about when she stepped out of his arms and met his gaze. "I think I'd like to be alone tonight."

The urge to make her talk to him was strong, but he decided to give her some space. He wouldn't let her push him away for long. "If that's what you want."

Grace let her shoulders drop as if a huge weight had been lifted. It was obvious she'd expected him to protest. "Thank you."

He pushed himself away from the counter and closed the distance between them once more. Taking hold of her forearms, he placed a kiss on her forehead. "Call me if you need anything."

She gave him a brief smile, which gave him hope. "I will."

Reluctantly, he dropped his arms, retrieved his cane, and headed toward the door.

When he reached for the knob, her hand covered his, stopping him.

"I just need some time to think."

Without giving it too much thought, Alexander turned to face her. He took hold of her face and kissed her.

They were both breathing hard when he let her go. The air around them was charged and heavy. He didn't think it would take much to convince her to change her mind, to let him stay, but he knew that wasn't what she needed. Sex wouldn't fix whatever was going on in her head. If anything, it would only complicate it more.

He backed away. "Good night, Grace."

"Good night."

Before he could talk himself out of it, Alexander walked out the door.

Chapter Twenty-Seven

It was the Friday after Thanksgiving—Black Friday—the first official shopping day of the Christmas season. People were out trying to scoop up all the deals stores were advertising, and all those people needed to eat. Beth had anticipated they would be busy, but even Grace didn't think she'd understood just how many people would come through their doors that day. From the time Tommy opened up there was a steady stream of people.

With all the running around, Grace didn't have much time to think. She smiled and did her job making sure the customers had what they needed.

Her feet were killing her by the time the last customer walked out the door. She gingerly lowered herself into a chair at the back of the dining room. Seconds later, Tommy joined her, two glasses of water in his hands. He pushed one her way.

"Thanks," she said, gratefully taking it and drinking until half the contents were gone.

Tommy sagged in his chair. "I don't think I've ever seen that many people in my life."

Beth pulled out a chair and sat down without finesse. She looked as tired as Grace felt. "I'll have to crunch the numbers, but I'm willing to bet today was our best to date. I must have made five hundred sandwiches during the lunch rush."

Tommy raised his glass before taking another long drink. "And just think, tomorrow we get to do it all again."

"Maybe it won't be as bad," Grace said, sounding hopeful.

Beth shook her head. "Don't bet on it. Tomorrow is small business Saturday. All the shops downtown will be open, trying to entice shoppers. Chances are good that we'll be just as busy as we were today."

Both Tommy and Grace groaned.

They all sat there for several more minutes, sipping their waters and enjoying doing absolutely nothing.

The reprieve was short-lived, however. Beth finished her water, placed her palms on top of the table, and stood. "I hate to say it, but we need to get this place cleaned and set up for tomorrow. Then I'm going home for a nice long soak in the bathtub."

Cleaning up took longer than usual. Some of that had to do with the fact that they were low on everything. Salt and pepper shakers had to be filled. Coffee restocked. Napkins. The list went on and on. It also didn't help that they were all dead tired.

Grace pulled into her driveway at quarter to five, starving, but having no desire to cook. Instead, she called for pizza. She'd barely made it through her second piece before her eyes started closing and she knew she needed to call it a night.

Stripping out of her clothes, Grace slipped under the covers. She didn't bother putting on any pajamas. Her Dom didn't like when she wore clothes to bed. He preferred her naked and easily accessible.

She reached up to touch her collar. The feel of the metal against her fingertips—it symbolized the connection she felt to her Dom and he felt to her. Despite her jumbled thoughts and feelings, she missed him.

Without thinking about it, she grabbed her phone and dialed his number. He picked up on the second ring. "Grace?"

"Hi." Just hearing his voice soothed her. "I wanted to let you know that I'm all right."

There was a long pause. "Thank you. I've been worried about you."

"I'm fine. Just tired. The café was slammed today." Grace knew she was changing the subject, but she wasn't ready to talk about them yet.

At first, she didn't think he was going to follow her lead, but finally he seemed to sense she didn't want to go there. "I should let you get to bed, then."

For whatever reason, she felt a little feisty and she was too exhausted to fight it. She lowered her voice a little, giving it a seductive tone. "I'm already in bed."

"Are you wearing anything?" His husky tone did all kinds of wonderful things to her body. He didn't even have to touch her and already she was getting ready for him.

"No."

The groan that came through the line had her thinking of other needs besides sleep, like feeling him sucking on her nipples while he held her hands above her head. Or him hovering over her while he filled her with every inch of his cock.

Heaven help her, but her body and heart ached for him and it had only been a day.

"You'd better not be touching yourself, *gattina*." Alexander knew exactly where her mind had gone.

"No, Sir." While it was tempting and she could definitely use the release, she would not defy her Dom. Not in this. Her body was his. If nothing else, she knew that to be true beyond a doubt. And she suspected that despite all the confusion going on in her brain, he owned her heart as well.

Alexander cleared his throat, breaking some of the spell. "I'd like to see you tomorrow."

"I have to work." It was a weak excuse.

"After work," he said, refusing to be deterred. "We can go to dinner."

There was a part of her that was disappointed. Of course, that was the horny part and not the rational part. He was right. They did need to talk—sort this out—and figure out where to go from here. She couldn't let him go. That much she knew. "I'd like that."

"I'll pick you up at six."

"Alexander?"

"Yes?"

Grace worried her bottom lip with her teeth. "Thank you for being so understanding."

There was a lengthy silence on the other end. When he spoke again, she could hear the affection he had for her coming through his words. "Good night, *gattina*. I'll see you tomorrow."

"Good night, Sir."

She placed her phone on her nightstand and burrowed under the covers. As tired as her body was, Grace had some decisions to make. Alexander said he wasn't pushing her into anything, and that, while he wanted to get married, he wasn't expecting her to do it tomorrow.

After throwing off the covers, she went to the closet and dug out the box of Kurt's things she'd saved. Most of it was from his childhood. She kept meaning to ask his mom and dad if they wanted them, but kept putting it off.

There were also pictures, pictures of her and Kurt, along with her wedding ring and her collar.

Grace brought the box over to the bed and opened it. Everything was exactly how she'd left it, her collar and ring sitting on top being the newest additions to the box. She grazed her fingertips over the silver heart and closed her eyes. A peace fell over her and the weight she'd been feeling lifted from her chest.

She'd always felt as if Kurt was watching over her, even when he was deployed. The connection they had was strong, even from the beginning. It was then she realized that there was a part of her that had resisted truly letting go and moving on. Having an agreement with Alexander was different than giving him her whole self. It would mean that she no longer belonged to Kurt. She would truly and completely be letting him go. Saying goodbye.

The collar felt heavier than she remembered as she lifted it to her lips. The cool metal against her skin brought with it memories of when Kurt had placed it around her neck. Even then he'd known what she needed. He'd been a wonderful Master. Not perfect, but he always made sure her needs were taken care of.

Tears streaked down her cheeks as she returned the collar she'd worn for almost ten years back to the box and closed the lid. It was time for her to truly and with her whole heart obey her Master's last command and move on.

❦

SINCE ALEXANDER HAD LEFT GRACE'S HOUSE ON THURSDAY EVENING HE'D been worried about her. He was glad she called him Friday night, if only to let him know she was okay. The more they'd gotten to know each other, both in and out of the bedroom, the more intense his feelings for her became.

On his way to pick her up Saturday evening, he stopped to buy her some flowers. Their relationship might not be conventional, but he was treating tonight as a date. This wasn't about their arrangement. This was about them. As a couple. A couple that hopefully had a future together.

It seemed Grace felt the same way about their upcoming evening. She answered the door wearing a fitted red dress that came down to her knees. It was more conservative than what she would wear to the club, but it still made his mouth water. There were strips of lace that gave hints of the skin underneath, skin he wanted to touch and kiss and lick . . .

He had to focus. They needed to talk. Fucking her senseless wouldn't solve anything in the long term and that's what he wanted. Forever. With her.

Alexander held the flowers in front of him, presenting them to Grace. "You look lovely tonight."

"Thank you." Grace blushed and took the bouquet from him. She brought the flowers up to her face and inhaled. "They're beautiful."

She took a few steps back, allowing him to come in. "I should put these in some water."

"I'll wait."

Grace nodded and disappeared into the kitchen. As she walked away, his gaze was transfixed on her ass. He could have followed her, but he didn't want to test his self-control. Last night had proven that even though Grace's mind was confused, her body didn't seem to have the same issue. He didn't want to tempt fate.

By the time she returned, he'd regained control of his libido—or as much control as he was able to manage in her presence. He helped her into her coat and they made their way to his car.

Instead of going to one of their usual places, he decided to head farther out of town. After a little research, he'd found a restaurant about an hour west of the city that overlooked a small stream. The pictures online had made it look cozy and romantic.

"Was the café as busy today as yesterday?"

"No." Grace turned to face him, resting her head on the back of the seat. She seemed more relaxed than she had when he'd left her Thursday night. Or maybe she was just tired. "Things started a bit slower and we had a short break between breakfast and lunch. Beth was still happy, though. She's pretty sure this week will be her best since opening the café."

"That's great."

"It is."

He turned off the highway and continued down a two-lane road that would lead them to their destination. They still had quite a way to go and he wanted to keep the conversation light. "Have you ever been out this way?"

"I think so, but it's been years. Dad used to like to go for long drives in the country sometimes. We'd get in the car and head out with no destination in mind. We found some really cool places. A lot of small towns and parks that we had no idea existed."

"You don't talk much about your dad," Alexander said, leaving it open for her to say as little or as much as she wanted on the subject.

"He died about five years ago. Parkinson's. Kurt was stationed in Texas at the time, so Gabby and Mom had their hands full. One day Gabby called to tell me that I should come home if I could, that they didn't expect Dad to make it more than another month or two."

"I'm sorry." Alexander hadn't meant to go down such a sad path. He'd figured she'd maybe share childhood stories of her dad, not reminisce about his death.

It was almost as if he hadn't said a word. "When I got there, I realized my dad was already gone. His body was still there, but his mind wasn't. He didn't recognize me. He didn't recognize anyone . . . not even my mom. We were all strangers to him."

Alexander knew what Parkinson's disease could do, both to the person and to their family. Hearing about it from Grace's perspective, however, was a lot different than reading about it in a textbook or seeing it in a clinical setting. This wasn't some random person he had no connection with. This was Grace's father.

Purely on instinct, he covered her hand with his.

She laced their fingers together and squeezed. "Kurt and I had gone to see him the year before. We'd talked about going to Hawaii, but changed our minds. I'm glad we did. Dad was still in his right mind then."

Alexander remained quiet, holding her hand and letting her talk. Grace had stayed in Missouri with her mother and sister for the last month and a half of her father's life. She'd helped her mom with the funeral arrangements and helped her get all the legal stuff in order before she'd returned to Texas.

"Was Kurt able to get leave to come to the funeral?" Alexander asked. He really hoped she hadn't had to deal with that alone.

"Yes. It was lucky he was stateside at the time. It wasn't a month after we returned that he was shipped out."

They talked a bit more about her family throughout the remainder of the drive. It wasn't the lightest of conversations, but since it appeared to be the direction Grace wanted to go, he went with it.

"Oh wow," she said when they pulled up in front of the restaurant. There were white lights everywhere—along the roofline, draped over bushes, woven through the trees. They were clearly going for a winter wonderland theme. All it lacked was the snow.

He rounded the vehicle and opened her door, offering her his hand. "Ready?"

Grace placed her palm in his and exited the car, a look of awe on her face. "This is amazing."

"Wait until you see the inside."

As promised, the inside of the restaurant was as spectacular as the outside.

Alexander gave the host his name and they were led past the large fireplace in the center over to a bank of windows. The host held out Grace's chair for her while she sat down. "Thank you."

He handed them both a menu. "Your server will be right with you. Enjoy your dinner."

Alexander knew the moment Grace looked outside. The lights lit up a scene that looked to be out of a painting. "How did you find this place?"

"You can find just about anything on the internet these days."

She seemed a bit flabbergasted, which made him smile. It was the exact reaction he'd been hoping for.

"Good evening. My name is John. I'll be taking care of you this evening. Can I get you started with some wine?"

Alexander ordered them each a glass of wine and an appetizer while Grace continued to gaze out the window. He let her drink in the scenery while he scanned over the menu, every now and then glancing her way.

John returned with their wine. "Do you still need a few more minutes?"

That seemed to jar Grace out of her fixation. "Oh." She turned her attention to her menu and began scanning over the items.

Alexander chuckled. "Yes, please."

Nodding, their server left them alone again.

Then Grace surprised him. She looked up, meeting his gaze, and placed her menu facedown on the table. "Will you order for me, Sir?"

He was trying not to read too much into her request. "If that's what you want."

"It is." Her voice was full of conviction.

When their server returned with their appetizer, Alexander ordered for both of them, making sure to get something he knew she'd like. "I'll get this put in for you right away. Is there anything else you need at the moment?"

"No. I think we're fine. Thank you," Alexander said.

John nodded. "Enjoy your appetizer."

Alone once more, Alexander speared one of the stuffed mushrooms and held it up for her. "Mushroom?"

She giggled, leaned forward, and opened her mouth. Her lips closed around the food and he felt a reaction below his waist. Grace was flirting with him. That had to be a good sign.

He ate one of the mushrooms himself, and then stabbed another one and offered it to her. "I want to talk about Thursday."

There was a slight hesitation as she took the mushroom. Grace finished chewing and swallowing before she responded. "I know." She glanced down at her empty plate, and then back at him. "I'm sorry I freaked out. I just . . . I needed time to think about some things . . . to come to terms with how I feel."

Alexander swallowed and it felt as if he had a lump stuck in his throat.

"When Kurt died, I didn't imagine I'd find anyone else that would make me feel the way he did. I thought I'd be alone for the rest of my life and I was okay with that. Or, I'd accepted it, at least. Then, you showed up with his letter. I didn't know what to think, but I trusted Kurt. He knew me better than anyone."

The noise around them faded into the background as he waited for whatever would come next.

Grace lifted her right hand and placed it flat at the base of her neck over her collar. She met his gaze and held it as she spoke. "I'm ready, Master. Ready to be yours."

Chapter Twenty-Eight

Alexander took his time responding. Hearing her call him Master had him wanting to take her right then and there, to hell with all the people around them. That, however, would most likely get them both arrested. Not exactly how he foresaw the evening ending.

He studied Grace, trying to get a feel for exactly what she'd meant by saying she was ready. She toyed with her napkin as she waited for his response.

Picking up his wineglass, he took a sip. "I'm going to need a bit more than that. What, exactly, are you ready for, *gattina?*" He'd added the term of endearment to let her know he wasn't upset by her declaration.

Grace looked out the window, and then to him. Her eyes held something in them he'd never seen before. "I realized I've been holding back. Emotionally." She paused. "I'm sorry."

He'd known that, but he'd been willing to give her time to work through it. "You were still grieving."

She nodded. "Yes."

Several minutes passed as he waited for her to continue. It would have been so easy to brush this conversation under the rug and go on with their evening, but they needed to talk this through.

"When we started"—she glanced around the room before going on— "seeing each other, I hadn't thought of sharing my life with another man. My heart still belonged to Kurt, and as far as I was concerned that was how it would always be."

He'd known this as well. The love Grace had for her husband wasn't in doubt. Neither was Kurt's love and devotion to his wife. He'd been an attractive man and had numerous opportunities to cheat while they were deployed, but he never had. It had made Alexander long for that type of connection with someone.

Grace gingerly placed her hand over the top of Alexander's where it rested at the base of his wineglass. He twisted his wrist so he could grasp her fingers.

"When you told my mom that you wanted to get married, I panicked. Not because I couldn't see myself marrying you, but because I could. The more I thought about it, the more real it became." She hesitated. "And then you said you loved me."

Grace closed her eyes and shook her head, trying to keep it together. He gave her hand a gentle squeeze, encouraging her to take her time.

"I wanted to say it back," she admitted, "but I couldn't. It felt like, if I did, that I would be betraying Kurt. Giving you my body was one thing. Giving you my heart . . ."

Alexander's own heart felt as if it was going to beat out of his chest, but he waited until she looked at him again. "And now?"

"Now I realize that what I felt for Kurt doesn't mean I can't feel that way for someone else. I don't have to choose. Kurt was my past." Her shoulders rose and fell as she took a deep breath in and let it out. "You are my future."

They stared at each other across the table, holding hands. This was how their server found them when he brought their food. Alexander thanked him, not breaking eye contract with Grace, and sent him on his way.

After brushing his thumb along the inside of Grace's wrist, Alexander let go of her hand so they could eat. She followed his lead and picked up her fork.

They concentrated on their dinners for a while, letting everything that had been said sink in. Alexander was the first one to break the silence. "I never want you to feel as if you have to forget Kurt. His memory lives on as it should. In both of us."

Moisture pooled in her eyes, but she fought to keep the tears at bay.

Nothing more was said as they finished their meals. Alexander paid the check, and then whisked Grace out the door.

Outside, he steered them away from the parking lot to a walking path that led down to the stream. It was lit with the same holiday lights that surrounded the restaurant. He wrapped his arm around Grace's shoulders and she snuggled close.

The sound of the stream became louder as they rounded the corner. It was chilly and there were no other people in sight, which suited him just fine.

Alexander led her over to a wooden bench a few feet from the path, sat down, and pulled her into his lap.

Grace leaned against him, her eyes focused on the rambling water in front of them. "Thank you for bringing me here."

He held her close and buried his face in the crook of her neck. "You're welcome."

The sounds of the night surrounded them as they sat. He took the edges of his trench coat and tried to cover some of her legs so she wouldn't get cold.

"You know, I've never been to your apartment."

Alexander grinned against her shoulder. "Is that your way of trying to wheedle an invitation out of me?"

She shrugged. "Maybe."

"Well, since neither of us has work tomorrow, why don't you stay over at my place? It will, however, mean you'll have to take the walk of shame tomorrow since you don't have any clothes there." He hugged her closer.

"I'm okay with that, if you are."

He ran his nose up the length of her neck to her ear. "Anything that has you in my bed is all right by me."

A shiver rippled through her. "Master?"

His cock was already sitting up to take notice. "Yes, *gattina?*"

"I think I'd like to go home now."

Alexander took a deep breath in and released it, letting hot hair blow against her cooled skin. "Your home or mine?" He didn't want there to be any miscommunication.

She turned to face him, circled her arms around his neck, and rested her forehead against his. "Yours. I want to see where you live."

The drive back to St. Louis seemed to take forever. It didn't take any longer than the drive *to* the restaurant, of course. The only reason it felt that way was because he wanted to get her naked. And in order to do that, he first had to get them to his apartment. He'd thought, briefly, about pulling off the side of the road and having some fun, but dismissed it. Not only would it be awkward in the small space, but what he wanted to do to her wouldn't be easy to accomplish in a vehicle.

With every mile they drew closer to the city, the room in his pants decreased. It was a good thing he'd worn slacks otherwise he would have been in quite a bit of discomfort by the time they pulled up in front of his apartment.

He took her hand in his and led her inside. After turning on the lights, he motioned for her to have a look around. "I'll get us something to drink."

Grace appeared torn, as if her want to get on with their evening warred with her curiosity. In the end, however, her curiosity won out. Or maybe it was her submissive nature letting him set the pace. She strolled through his small apartment as he grabbed some glasses out of the cabinet and filled them with water and ice.

Alexander found her in his bedroom, looking out the window. He handed her one of the glasses.

"Thanks," she said, bringing the glass to her lips.

He took a drink of his water and set the glass on the nearby table before moving to stand behind her. "What are you thinking about?"

"I was wondering where we'll live. Did you want to stay in the city?"

Her train of thought surprised him. He spun her around to face him. "Grace, there's no rush. I know I said I want to get married, but I wasn't exaggerating. We can take this as slow as you want to."

She shook her head. "No. You were right. Life's too short. Kurt and I missed out on so much when he was deployed and I can never get that time back. I don't want to do that again."

Alexander held her face in his hands and pressed his lips to hers with the gentlest pressure. "Maybe we should try living together first." She opened her mouth to argue, but he pressed a finger to her lips, cutting her off. "See if you can put up with me."

Grace hesitated before nodding.

He smiled, and leaned in to kiss her again. "See, that wasn't so hard."

As their lips mingled together, thinking became more difficult. He crushed her against him and ran his hands up and down her back, cupping her ass. Her breathy moans only fueled the fire he'd been trying to bank for the last hour.

"I want you," he mumbled as he kissed his way down her neck.

"Take me, Master. I'm yours."

That was all he needed to hear. Alexander removed the glass from her hand, placing it next to his on the table. He flipped her around and pushed her against the wall, facing away from him. Reaching for the zipper of her dress, he yanked it down. The dress parted, revealing her skin beneath. He pushed it off her shoulders and watched as it fell to the floor at her feet, leaving her in her bra and a pair of stockings.

Pressing himself flush against her back, he ran a hand down her side and over the curve of her hip. "Are you wet for me?"

Without waiting for her response, he slid his hand between her legs.

GRACE GASPED AT THE FEEL OF HIS FINGERS SLIDING OVER HER PUSSY, AND then plunging inside her. The weight of him against her, pressing her against the wall, keeping her there, only added to her arousal. She could feel his erection pressing into her backside, begging to be let out of its confines.

"It's too bad we didn't go to Serpent's Kiss tonight. I would have made sure to make you come so everyone could watch."

Thinking about it had heat rushing between her legs.

He must have been able to feel her body's reaction because she felt a satisfied rumble erupt from his chest. "You like that, don't you? No worries, *gattina*. Soon I'm going to have you coming in front of the entire club. They're all going to be watching as I make your pretty pussy sing."

His words were barely able to sink in before his hand was gone and he was turning her around. He took hold of her forearms and held her still while he kissed her, his lips hard and demanding. She loved every minute of it. Now that she'd made her decision, she wanted to feel him filling her, surrounding her, making her his.

Before she knew what was happening, he was lifting her into his arms and carrying her to the bed. "What—"

"Hush."

"But your leg—"

Alexander tossed her onto his bed and swiftly removed his clothes. "I will probably never be able to carry you up a flight of stairs, but a few feet to the bed I can manage. Now, where was I? Oh, yes."

She propped herself up on her elbows and watched as he went to his dresser, knelt down, and opened the bottom drawer. When he turned around, he had a rope in one hand and something she couldn't see in the other. Whatever it was, it was small.

"Give me your wrists," he ordered.

Grace held her wrists out to him, palms up.

He flipped them over and began binding them together. By the time he was finished, she felt the beginnings of subspace coming on, that calm, floaty feeling she loved.

After checking to make sure the ropes weren't too tight, he used the loose end to tug her toward him. He leaned down, pressing a kiss to her lips. It wasn't nearly as aggressive as the last one, but still possessive. "I love you."

The look in his eyes left her no doubt that was true. How had she gotten so lucky to find not one but two men in her lifetime that could love her so deeply? She hadn't stood a chance. There was no way she couldn't have fallen for Alexander. "I love you, too."

He cupped the side of her face and brought their foreheads together. "I promise I will make you happy, Grace. I will do everything in my power to make sure you are safe and loved."

"I know you will."

One side of his mouth quirked up as he lowered his hand from her face and ran it down the length of her arm. "I'm also going to make sure you're fucked senseless on a regular basis."

And just like that, the air in the room was charged once more.

"Lie back and scoot yourself toward the pillows."

She followed his instructions, using her legs to wiggle her body up toward the headboard.

"That's good."

Once she stopped moving, he reached above her head and secured the rope to the headboard. He checked her wrists again, and walked to the other side of the room. When he returned, he had a metal wheel with spikes on it in his hand. Grace tensed.

"Have you ever had one of these used on you before?" he asked.

She shook her head. "No."

He spun the spikes around the wheel with his finger. "I figure since we're going to be doing a demonstration, we should probably practice ahead of time with some of the toys."

"Will it hurt, Master?" It wasn't that she didn't trust him. She did. Completely. But she'd never seen one of those things before and it looked painful.

"That depends on its user."

Grace swallowed.

"Ready?"

"Yes, Master."

He started by running it along her abdomen. She could definitely feel the spikes, but she wouldn't say they were painful.

Changing direction, he moved upward, making a circle around her breast before drawing a line down the center and over her nipple. "For those who enjoy edgier play, they can increase the pressure and draw blood." He repeated the process over her other breast. "But I know that's not something you're into and neither am I."

He continued to run the spiked wheel over her body, trailing it down each of her legs and back up again. Each time he got dangerously close to her sex, but at the last minute would change direction. The longer it went on, the more relaxed she became and the more she enjoyed the sensation.

"Spread your legs for me."

It wasn't until he spoke that Grace realized he'd stopped. She did as he asked, spreading her legs wide.

Alexander knelt between her parted thighs and ran his finger from her clit to her ass. "Did you plug yourself the last two nights, *gattina?*"

"I didn't Thursday, Master." She wondered if he would punish her for disobeying.

"Given the circumstances, I will let it slide this time." He brushed his thumb against her clit several times. "Next time, though, your ass will be paying the price."

She heard a noise and looked down. Alexander had put on a latex glove. Given his previous question, she knew something was going to be going up her ass.

He lubed up his fingers and used his other hand to spread her open before inserting his fingers. Grace blew out a breath and tried to relax. She used to enjoy anal play. It had just been a while.

"That's it." He eased two fingers in and out, gradually stretching her. Once he was satisfied she was prepped enough, she felt him remove his hand. Within seconds, it was replaced by something that felt rubbery. The feel of it reminded her of a dildo, which it very well could have been. She wasn't at an angle where she could see exactly what it was.

As the object was inserted into her ass, she took several deep breaths, giving her body time to adjust.

"I would love to fuck your ass tonight, but you're not quite ready for that yet." He gave the butt plug, or whatever it was, a little twist, causing another gasp to escape from Grace's lips. "Soon, though."

Then whatever he'd placed in her ass started buzzing. The vibrations lit up her nerves and had her sex throbbing in no time.

He wasn't finished, though. Something touched her clit, and then it started humming as well. She realized immediately what it was—a bullet vibe. Small, but effective. And it was about to send her spiraling over the edge.

The feel of his cock nudging the entrance to her pussy only added to everything else she was experiencing. "Please, Master. I want to feel you inside me."

Alexander grasped her hip with his free hand and, with a jerk of his pelvis, he plunged inside until his balls were pressing against her sex. She was full, utterly and completely, and she'd never felt better.

He rode her relentlessly, living up to his promise of fucking her senseless. As usual, he drew out her pleasure for as long as possible, until she couldn't stand it any longer. She really hoped his neighbors weren't home, because if they were they'd undoubtedly heard her scream as she'd been overcome with her orgasm.

Afterward, they made their way to the shower, taking their time washing each other, and then curled up together in his bed. As she was drifting off to sleep, she couldn't help but wonder how different her life would have been if Alexander hadn't delivered her that letter. Would she have ever put herself out there again, or would she have spent the rest of her life alone, clinging to her husband's memory?

Luckily, she would never know the answer to that question. Alexander was now part of her life. She looked forward to what the future had in store for them. Whatever it might be.

Epilogue

Alexander came up behind Grace and pulled her against his chest. "Ready for tonight?"

Grace chuckled. "No. Not even a little bit." She leaned in to him, taking comfort in his arms.

"You'll do fine." He rubbed his hand along her backside. "Did you have any problems with the prep?"

The prep. Cleaning herself out for tonight's play. It wasn't horrible, but it wasn't the most pleasant thing she'd ever done. "I managed."

He ran the tip of his nose along her neck, sending shivers down her spine. "I promise I will make it worth it."

Of that she had no doubt. Almost three weeks had passed since that night in his bedroom where she'd told him she loved him for the first time. It had been a turning point for them. He'd stopped holding back and so had she.

They still hit a few bumps in the road every now and then. Like two nights ago when she'd been putting some of Alexander's things in the closet. He'd been slowly transferring his things to her house, both having agreed that, given the size of his apartment, him moving was the better option. She'd pushed some of her clothes aside and came across one of Kurt's dress uniforms. She hadn't been able to get rid of it when she'd packed up and come to St. Louis, but she'd completely forgotten it was there. Alexander had found her sitting on the floor of her bedroom, holding the uniform in a death grip. She'd been out of it for the rest of the evening.

As usual, Alexander was nothing but understanding. He'd lowered himself onto the floor beside her even though she knew getting down there had to be a challenge because of his injury. No words were spoken as he held her in his arms.

But tonight wasn't about Kurt, or her past, or his. Tonight was about the two of them performing a scene in front of the entire club. She was scared out of her wits, but she was also incredibly excited. He'd been getting her ready by introducing her to all the toys he was going to use on her, letting her ask questions as they went. It had eased many of her concerns.

"We need to get going. I want to look over all the equipment before too many people get there."

It was almost seven by the time they arrived at Serpent's Kiss. They'd barely walked in the door before Ali noticed them. She waved to Grace from across the room where she was standing with a woman Grace didn't recognize.

"Go on over and say hello. I'll be busy for a bit," Alexander said.

"Yes, Master."

Ali smiled as Grace approached. The two had gotten to know each other much better over the last few weeks. It was nice having another sub she could talk to. Beth was great, but there were some things only another sub would understand, and Grace wasn't sure she would ever be that comfortable talking about that kind of stuff with Drew, sub or not.

"Are you ready for tonight?" Ali asked, unable to contain her enthusiasm.

Grace blew out a breath. "As ready as I'll ever be."

"I'm sure you'll have fun. Your Master knows what he's doing."

Yes, he did. He'd proven it time and time again.

The woman she didn't know elbowed Ali.

"Oh. Sorry. Grace, I'd like for you to meet my best friend, Kim. She came here a couple of months ago to check out the club and now she's decided to join. Isn't that great?" Maybe Ali's enthusiasm wasn't all about tonight's demonstration.

Kim started to offer her hand, and then pulled it back. "It's nice to meet you. Ali was telling me that you're fairly new to the club, too."

"I joined a little over a month ago."

"Oh wow. And you're doing the demonstration tonight? I'm not sure I could be that brave," Kim said.

Ali giggled. "Grace is an exhibitionist. We've gotten to see that firsthand a number of times."

Grace felt her cheeks heat. "I didn't used to be."

Kim nodded toward the platform along the back wall. "Is that your Dom?"

Turning to look in the direction Kim was, Grace saw Alexander bent over a small metal tray, examining its contents. "Yes. That's my Master."

"Isn't that a bit unusual?" she asked.

Grace tore her gaze away from Alexander and back to Grace. "Unusual?"

"To find a master so quickly. You said you'd only been a member of the club for about a month."

Ali looked to be about to say something to her friend, but Grace didn't mind the questions. If Kim was new to the lifestyle then it was understandable that she'd want to know as much as possible. "We met before, but didn't realize we were both into BDSM until we saw each other here."

"That had to be awkward."

Grace snorted. "I ran away."

Kim furrowed her brow in confusion.

"When I saw him across the room, I freaked out and left as quickly as my feet would carry me." She frowned. "It was a rash decision, but at the time I didn't see any other option."

"I probably would have done the same thing."

This time Ali was the one who snorted. "No, you wouldn't. Knowing you, you would have marched up to him, your head held high, and demanded to know what he was doing here."

That didn't sound all that submissive to Grace, but then again maybe Kim wasn't a sub. Ali hadn't really said.

Kim laughed. "Maybe."

"There's no maybe about it," Ali said. "I know you."

Katrina made her way over to them. "How are you ladies this evening?"

"Good, Mistress," Grace and Ali said in unison.

Kim's response showed how new to the lifestyle she really was. "Good." Then she seemed to realize her mistake and added, "Mistress."

Katrina didn't seem fazed by the slip. Subs had the choice, or their Doms did, of whether or not to attach an honorific to a Dominant's name at the club. The only exception to this was Mistress Katrina. She was the club mistress and every sub used her title without exception. It wasn't written in the rules or anything, but it was what was accepted and expected. "All ready for tonight, Grace?"

"Yes, Mistress Katrina." Grace glanced once more in Alexander's direction. This time he appeared to be examining the table itself. "Master is making sure everything is the way he wants it."

She followed Grace's gaze and grinned. "I should probably make sure he has everything he needs."

Katrina excused herself, leaving the three alone again.

"Have you been in the lifestyle long?" Grace asked Kim, curiosity getting the better of her.

"Um. Well . . ." Kim shifted her weight several times, hemming and hawing as if she were unsure how to answer. "I've only done it once."

Grace's eyes widened. She'd only had kinky sex once and she'd joined a kink club? Wow. That was . . . wow. Grace couldn't imagine. Maybe Kim really was a Domme.

While Grace was still trying to figure out how to respond, Kim's attention shifted to something across the room. Grace looked to see what had caught her eye. Justin, the Dom who'd shown her around that first night—the one Alexander had made her come in front of—was striding toward the bar. He wasn't looking their way. As far as Grace could tell, he hadn't noticed them yet.

The look on Kim's face appeared to be more than casual interest. "Do you know Sir Justin?"

Ali was the one who spoke up. "He's her brother's best friend. They've known each other for years. Right, Kim?"

It took Kim longer than it should to answer. "Yeah. We've um . . . we've known each other since high school."

As if he knew they were talking about him, his gaze landed on the three of them. Only a second passed before shock crossed his face followed by what appeared to be extreme displeasure. Given there was no reason for him to be upset or even surprised by Grace or Ali's presence at the club, she could only assume that his reaction was for Kim. He clearly wasn't happy she was at Serpent's Kiss.

"I . . . I need to use the bathroom," Kim muttered before making a beeline for the locker rooms.

"What was that all about?" Grace asked.

Ali shook her head, looking in the direction her friend had gone. "I have no idea. Maybe she's afraid he'll tell her brother."

Maybe. But that wasn't the vibe she was getting.

Unfortunately, she wasn't able examine it any further. Alexander came up beside her and placed a hand on her lower back. "Ali."

"Good evening, Sir."

He looked down at Grace. "Meet me on the platform in fifteen minutes. I'm going to get us some waters."

"Yes, Master."

Ali fanned herself as Alexander walked away. "You are so lucky."

Grace couldn't disagree. "I know."

Not wanting to linger, she told Ali she'd catch her later and headed to the restroom. She had no idea how long their scene would last and it was better to be prepared.

She walked into the bathroom, finding an empty stall. At first, she thought she heard a humming sound, as if someone was singing. But then she realized it wasn't singing. It was talking. And considering the low volume, whoever it was had to be talking to themselves.

Grace finished up and exited the stall. Once she'd washed her hands, she waited, but no one came out. She debated whether or not she should go and get someone, but what would she tell them? That she thought someone was mumbling to themselves in the bathroom?

Realizing she had to make a decision, Grace went back to the stalls and found the one the sound was coming from. She tapped on the door of the stall and the noise stopped.

"Are you okay?" Grace asked.

No one answered. Then then door opened to reveal Kim. She looked somewhat embarrassed. "Sorry. I didn't realize anyone could hear me."

Grace frowned.

Kim stepped out of the stall and Grace moved out of the way. She went to the sink and turned on the water. "Justin has been my brother's best friend since high school. I guess I wasn't as ready to see him as I thought I was."

This surprised Grace. "So you knew he was a member here?"

"Yeah. When I came with Ali a few months ago, I saw him then."

Grace thought about what Ali had told her. "Are you afraid he'll say something to your brother?" She highly doubted it. From what she knew of Justin, he was a well-respected Dom at the club. To betray another member's privacy, friend of the family or not, would be a huge violation and would probably get his membership revoked.

"No. I don't think so." Kim smiled, but it didn't reach her eyes. "Don't you have to go? I thought you were doing a demonstration or something tonight."

All the color drained from Grace's face. She'd been so worried about Kim, she hadn't been thinking about the time. The last thing she wanted was to start the scene off on the wrong foot. "I—"

"Go. I'll be fine. Promise."

Grace had no choice but to believe her. She hurried out of the bathroom and went straight to the stage. When she realized Alexander wasn't there yet, she breathed a sigh of relief.

"Cutting it close, aren't you, *gattina*?" Alexander's voice came from behind her.

She lowered her gaze to the floor. "Yes, Sir." Later, when they were alone, she'd explain why she'd almost been late, but given their audience, she decided not to go into detail.

He studied her face for a moment, and then nodded before reaching for a white lab coat that was draped across a round stool.

As he put the coat on, Grace saw Kim emerge from the restroom. She stayed along the edge of the crowd.

Alexander moved to stand in front of her, blocking her view of everyone but him. He tilted her chin up, making her look at him. He rubbed his thumb along her jaw as he gazed into her eyes. "Ready?"

For him, she would always be ready. "Yes, Master."

HIS FORBIDDEN KISS

SERPENT'S KISS SERIES BOOK 3

His Forbidden Kiss

Serpent's Kiss Series Book 3

Sherri Hayes

About This Book

She's the one woman he can't have.

Kim Langley is beautiful, sexy, and confident. She makes Justin's heart skip a beat every time he sees her. There's only one problem. She's his best friend's little sister. Off-limits. Then, she shows up on his doorstep, offering herself to him.

Justin McKay has been starring in Kim's fantasies since she was a teenager. When she finds out he's an experienced Dominant, she knows he's the one she wants to explore her sexuality with. One night with no strings.

But what if one night isn't enough for either of them? Is he willing to risk betraying his friendship to be with her?

Chapter One

"Are you sure this is all right?"

Kim Langley halted right outside the door to Serpent's Kiss. There were no signs on the outside of the building. If she didn't know any better, she would have thought it was a warehouse used for storage. She knew better, however. Inside was a private club where those who were into BDSM could indulge in all their kinky fantasies.

Two weeks ago, she'd been hanging out with her best friend, Ali. They were in Ali's apartment eating rocky road ice cream and commiserating about Kim's latest bad date. It was that night, by accident when she'd been searching for a shirt in Ali's closet that Kim had stumbled on a bag full of her friend's 'toys'. It had led to a discussion about Ali being a submissive and what all that meant. Kim wasn't sure what to make of it, and she'd left with more questions than answers.

Throughout the next week, Kim couldn't forget what Ali had told her, so when they'd gotten together the following weekend Kim brought up the subject again. By the end of the night, Kim was wondering if that was what she'd been missing in the guys she'd been dating. They were all too...nice.

Not that she didn't want a nice guy—she did—but she also wanted someone who wasn't afraid to push her up against a wall and kiss her until she was breathless. She wanted a man who went after what he wanted, including her. And all the other things Ali told her about—being held down or tied up— didn't sound half bad either.

Which brought her back to tonight.

"Of course it's okay," Ali said. "I talked to Mistress Katrina. She said it was fine as long as you stayed with me the whole time and that you agreed to keep what you see, and who, confidential."

"Are they going to know I'm not..." Kim tried to get a hold on her nerves. She had no idea what was behind that door.

Ali turned toward her friend, placed both hands on her upper arms, and looked her in the eye. "We don't have to do this if you're not sure. We can go back to my place and gorge on ice cream again."

Kim grinned. "If we keep doing that neither one of us is going to be able to fit into any of our clothes."

Her friend shrugged. "It's a sacrifice I'm willing to make."

As tempting as it was to take Ali up on her offer and forget about the thoughts she'd been having, she didn't want to. If she could find the answers she'd been seeking inside the club, then she needed to face her fears and go for it. It wasn't like her to run and hide. She'd learned long ago that if she wanted something she had to make it happen. "I love you for offering, but I want to do this. I need to do this."

Ali nodded and dropped her arms. "Let's get this party started, then."

Kim took a deep breath and followed Ali through the front door. She was a little shocked, however, to find they were now in a small foyer no bigger than the bathroom in her apartment. Her friend shot her a smile before swiping a card through a reader beside another door directly opposite the one they'd entered. A light turned green and then there was the sound of the door unlocking. Ali took hold of the knob and opened it.

Again, the room they entered wasn't what she'd been expecting. They were in another foyer, but this one was much larger. It was long, and on one end there was what looked to be a coat check. There was a woman standing inside and she greeted them as they approached. "Hi, Ali. Who's your friend?"

"Bridget, I'd like you to meet my best friend, Kim. Kim, this is Bridget."

"Nice to meet you." Kim didn't miss the curious look the woman gave her. It made her wonder how often nonmembers were allowed into the club and just how many strings Ali had to pull in order to allow Kim to come with her. It was a private club, after all. She knew there were background checks and membership fees. Ali had explained it all to her the previous weekend.

"Thanks." Kim felt as if there were a big sign on her forehead that said *newbie* on it.

"Bridget, could you buzz Katrina for us?" Ali asked. "She wanted to meet Kim before we go inside."

"Sure."

The woman reached below the counter and smiled.

"Thanks." Ali grinned back at Bridget.

There seemed to be something going on that Kim didn't understand. Then again, she was sure that would happen a lot tonight. She knew very little about BDSM outside of what Ali had told her.

A minute or two later, a blond woman who looked to be in her forties strolled into the room from a door Kim hadn't even noticed only a few feet away. Kim thought she heard some noise on the other side and wondered if that was the club.

The new arrival approached them with a warm smile. "Good evening."

Ali cleared her throat. "Mistress Katrina, I'd like you to meet my best friend, Kim Langley."

Unlike before, there was no introduction of Mistress Katrina to Kim. She wondered if that was intentional.

"It's nice to meet you, Kim," Mistress Katrina said. "Ali here tells me you're curious about our lifestyle."

"Y-yes. I am." Why was she so nervous? Oh yeah. She was about to enter a club where who knew what happened and she was standing there talking to the owner of said club. Nothing at all to be anxious about.

The club mistress chuckled. "Relax. I'm not planning to use my whip on you. You're perfectly safe here."

"Sorry."

"It's fine. Everyone's first time is nerve-racking. It's to be expected."

That made her feel a little better. "Thank you."

Mistress Katrina nodded. "Ali went over the rules with you?"

"Yes. I won't say anything to anyone and I'm pretty sure I'll be plastered to Ali's side the whole night."

"Very well." Mistress Katrina seemed amused by her answer. "Relax. Have fun. If you want to try anything, let Ali know and I'm sure we can find someone willing to give you a demonstration."

Kim swallowed. "Um. Thanks."

The older woman shot Ali a look before extending her hand to Kim. "It was nice to meet you. I need to get back inside. Please take whatever time you need."

Once they were alone again, or sort of alone—Bridget was still there but she was typing away on her laptop—Kim leaned over to whisper in her friend's ear. "She was intimidating."

"She can be." Ali turned to face Kim. "You ready to go inside?"

"Now?"

Her friend laughed. "Were you wanting to stand out in the lobby all night? I thought you were curious?"

"No. I mean, yes. I am. Curious, I mean." Kim took a deep breath to calm herself. "Okay. I'm ready."

Ali looked doubtful, but began walking toward the door Mistress Katrina had disappeared behind a few moments before. Kim followed. It was now or never, right? Better to jump in with both feet and get it over with.

She wasn't really sure what she'd expected to find on the other side of the door, people chained to walls maybe? Instead it looked a lot like any other club she'd gone to. There was a bar, a dance floor, and places for people to sit and talk. The room had a small stage even though there wasn't any sign of a band.

"Doing all right?" Ali asked.

"Yeah. Fine." She was just trying to take it all in and reconcile it with her preconceived notions.

"Good. Let's get something to drink and I'll introduce you to Brandon."

As they made their way toward the bar, Kim continued to look around. While at first this looked like a regular club, she was beginning to see some differences. The main one was that there were quite a few people sitting on the floor, even some with their heads in another person's lap. That certainly wasn't something one would normally see at a nightclub.

The other thing she observed was the clothes, or lack thereof. She blinked as she saw a guy being led up the stairs by a leash attached to his penis. That wasn't something you saw every day.

"Good evening, ladies. What can I get for you tonight?" The man behind the bar grinned at them. He was cute. Maybe five to ten years older than they were, but Kim had always liked her men to be a little older. At thirty-two, she had no desire to mess around with some twenty-year-old who didn't know what he wanted or what to do with a woman. The guys her age were bad enough in that respect. She was ready for different, which was why she was here.

"Brandon, I'd like you to meet my friend Kim."

The smile Brandon shot her made her belly do a little flip-flop. Oh yeah. She could get used to that. "Nice to meet you, Kim. Is this your first time in a kink club?"

"Yes. I mean, yes, sir." That was right, wasn't it? Or was he not a Dom?

His eyes twinkled with amusement as he leaned forward, resting his forearms on the bar in front of him. "No need for formalities. At least, not yet. But I'm sure we could arrange something if you'd like."

Kim's eyes went wide.

"Maybe another time, then." He smirked, and turned his attention back to Ali.

She ordered them both sodas and while he went to fill their order, Kim took a few moments to catch her breath.

"You okay?" Ali whispered.

"I think so." Kim paused as she tried to organize her thoughts. "He's a... a..."

"Yes, Brandon's a Dom."

Kim nodded.

"Remember you don't have to do anything you don't want to. Brandon's a good guy, though, and he seems interested."

"I just think—"

They were interrupted when Brandon returned with their drinks. "Here you go. Oh. And Kim?"

"Yes?" The question didn't come out as confident as she would have liked.

"Come see me if you change your mind." He winked at her, and then moved down the bar to help someone else.

When she looked over at Ali, her friend was trying to suppress a giggle.

Kim felt off balance after her exchange with the bartender and maybe even a little annoyed, although she couldn't say if she was more annoyed with herself or Ali. Why hadn't her friend warned her? Given her a heads-up? Something. Was the entire night going to be like this?

"Come on," Ali said, bumping Kim's shoulder. "I want to introduce you to some people."

"Oh joy," Kim muttered as she followed her friend across the room.

They walked up to a group of people who smiled as Kim and Ali drew closer. An older man stood and repositioned himself farther down on the couch to make room for them.

After they'd taken their seats, Ali made the introductions. The older man's name was Daniel. There were two couples in the group, Beth and Drew, and Nicole and Jeff. Kim learned that both were female dominants and the men were the submissives in the relationships. Kim had to admit it was a foreign concept to her. Then again, so was BDSM really. But as she watched the couples interact throughout the night, the appeal began to resonate. It was in the subtle body movements and the way they touched. Watching them created an ache inside Kim she didn't understand.

"Would you ladies like something more to drink?" Daniel asked.

He was talking to Ali and Kim. She thought she saw her friend blush slightly as she said 'yes, please' and handed Daniel her glass.

Kim did the same, minus the blush, and stared at her friend. Was something going on between the two of them? Surely not. Ali was thirty-two, the same as her. Daniel had to be at least fifty.

As she was contemplating that, her attention shifted to the sound of someone behind her. The voice sounded familiar. When she turned, Kim got the shock of her life. Justin, her brother's best friend, was standing five feet away. He had his back to Kim so she was able to get a closer look. Justin was talking to a man and a woman and in his hand was a leash—a leash that was attached to a young woman wearing a barely there dress.

Kim quickly turned back around. What was he doing here? Was he into this?

Of course Kim already knew the answer. He had to be. What else would he be doing at a kink club?

"Kim?"

She glanced over at Ali. Her friend looked worried. The impact of seeing Justin must have been written all over her face. Kim couldn't help it, though. He was the last person she'd expected to see here.

During her teenage years, she'd had an ongoing fantasy that Justin would sneak into her room during one of his many sleepovers with her brother and make mad passionate love to her. That never happened, of course. He'd shown no interest in her that way. Then her brother had left for college and the next time she saw Justin was when he'd brought his girlfriend home with him when Mark had returned for spring break. At the time, she'd been crushed.

Seeing him with his girlfriend had been the kick in the pants Kim needed to wake up to reality. Justin was never going to see her as anything but Mark's little sister. She had to move on and she did. Sort of.

Two months after coming face-to-face with Justin's girlfriend, Kim lost her virginity to Kyle Zimmerman in a cheap motel room. It had been her way of saying goodbye to Justin.

As it turned out, Kyle wasn't the best of choices. He'd shown his interest in her the entire year leading up to prom, the night she'd finally relented and gave it up. She liked him, she really did, but he wasn't Justin. Afterward he'd rolled off her, gone to the bathroom to get rid of the condom, and then began gathering his clothes. Maybe it was just her, but she'd expected there to be more...to feel something different. Instead, she felt sore and a little empty.

Ali wrapped her hand around Kim's upper arm and shook her. She blinked and refocused on her friend. Kim must have been lost in her thoughts longer than she thought.

"I'm fine," she said.

Her friend looked doubtful.

She knew she was going to have to say something. It only took her a split second to come up with a topic that would turn the tables on her best friend and put Ali in the hot seat. Leaning in so no one around could hear them, Kim asked the question that had been on her mind moments before she'd spotted Justin. "Is there something going on between you and Daniel?"

Ali flushed. "No."

Kim gave her a skeptical look.

"He's nice. He watches out for me."

"And?" Kim knew there had to be more to it than that given her friend's reaction before.

"And nothing."

"Riiiight."

Speaking of Daniel, he walked over with their drinks in hand. "Here you go, ladies."

They both thanked him, although Kim still thought there was more behind Ali's 'thank you' than simple politeness.

Daniel leaned back, resting his arm along the back of the couch. Kim didn't miss how her friend stiffened for a moment before relaxing again. Even if there wasn't anything there, she was pretty sure Ali would be open to it if he was.

"What do you think of Serpent's Kiss? Do you have any questions?" Daniel's inquiry was directed to Kim, of course.

"It's different."

He smirked. "Yes, it is. And you haven't even seen the second floor yet."

Kim froze. "The second floor?"

"That's where the fun stuff is." Nicole winked at her.

Not sure how to react, Kim swallowed nervously.

"Would you like to see?" Daniel asked. "I'd be more than happy to accompany you ladies if you'd like."

"I don't know..." Kim looked to Ali for help.

Instead, her friend shrugged. "It's up to you, but you did come here to see what it was all about."

Like it or not, Ali was right. If she was going to do this, she needed to suck it up and do it. "All right."

She stayed close to Ali while shooting discreet glances in Justin's direction.

Kim had no idea who the woman was. As far as she knew, he wasn't dating anyone. But if that was the case, then who was she and why was he leading her around by a leash?

Justin was still talking to the couple as she passed within ten feet of where he was standing. Another man joined them. As she continued to spy on him, the new man took hold of the woman's leash and kissed her. Did that mean the woman didn't 'belong' to Justin? Just thinking that left her with a bad taste in her mouth, but she shook it off and looked again at the small group. Justin didn't seem upset by the other man stepping in and staking a claim.

Kim averted her gaze. So far he hadn't noticed her. That was good. She had no idea what she'd say to him if he did.

As they reached the top of the stairs, Kim could feel a change in the atmosphere. At first it didn't make sense because, while there were a few people milling about in the hallway, none of them were doing anything more than standing or talking. Then they came to the first window and Kim glanced inside.

On the other side of the glass was a woman kneeling. She was completely naked and on display for whoever chose to look. Her head was bent so Kim couldn't tell if her eyes were open or not.

A man she hadn't seen walked up behind the woman, wrapped his hand around her ponytail, and jerked her head back. He said something to her and she responded. The next thing Kim knew, the woman was being led over to some sort of padded chair-type thing. Instead of sitting, however, she placed her knees on what Kim had assumed was the seat and rested her chest on the flat upper part. When she was in position, the man placed a hand between her legs. She opened them as wide as the bench/chair would allow.

What he did next stunned Kim and had heat rushing to her core. The man ran two fingers along the woman's slit and then inserted them into her pussy. After pumping them in and out a few times, he removed his fingers. Kim had expected him to wipe them off on a towel or even lick the moisture off as she'd seen done in porn, but that didn't happen. Instead, he walked to the side and placed his fingers in front of the woman's mouth. He said something, and a second later she opened her mouth and began sucking on his fingers.

Suddenly there was a loud smacking sound as a leather paddle made contact with the woman's ass. Kim had been so focused on the woman's mouth that she hadn't noticed what the man was doing with his other hand. She felt the moisture leak out of her body. With each smack she got wetter and wetter. Did that mean she was submissive? Kim didn't know, but she was pretty sure she wanted to find out. And she knew exactly who she wanted to enlist to help her explore these new fantasies.

Chapter Two

Justin McKay loved owning his own business. Usually. It was days like today when he seriously questioned his decision to open his own mechanic's shop two years ago. Shaking his head, he strolled into the small utility room that contained his washer and dryer. He removed his grease-soaked clothes and tossed them into the washer with a generous amount of soap. Why couldn't he go back to the night before when he'd been hanging out with his friends at the club without the worries of employees and everything that came with them?

The morning had been a nightmare. Normally Saturdays weren't that bad. They were only open half a day and the guys spent most of their time doing simple oil changes. It all came down to Jax. He'd hired the kid about a month ago, and he was about as bright as a box of rocks. Even after hearing the explanation, Justin still wasn't sure what the kid had done exactly. All Justin knew was that one minute he was working underneath the car and the next he was being covered in dirty oil. Once he got the leak plugged, Justin had sent Jax home and spent the next two hours cleaning the oil off everything and throwing sawdust on the floor of his garage so it could soak up some of the mess. He'd have to go in early on Monday and sweep it up.

As much as Justin didn't want to fire the kid, he was only nineteen and seemed excited by the idea of being able to work on and restore vintage cars. The problem was that Justin couldn't trust Jax on his own. Every task he was given he screwed up somehow. It wasn't on purpose, but it still cost time and money. Justin had been hoping to have Mr. Smith's car back to him early next week. After today, that wasn't likely to happen.

Sighing, Justin padded naked to the bathroom. He needed a shower. While he was used to working in grease and grime, he wasn't used to wearing it.

Ten minutes later, Justin was feeling better. He'd scrubbed himself down—twice—and put on a comfortable pair of jeans. He had nowhere to be until later that night.

Thinking about Serpent's Kiss, the kink club he'd been a member of for the last year and a half, brought a smile to his face. He hadn't been sure it was a great idea with him being single and all, but it had ended up being a very good thing. There was a nice mix of singles and couples at the club and everyone was friendly. Of course, a lot of that had to do with the club mistress and owner, Katrina Mayer. She made sure things worked the way she wanted them to. If you created too much drama, then she politely asked you to leave.

He rolled his shoulders as he headed toward the kitchen for some lunch. Maybe he could find a play partner tonight. It had been a while since he'd done more than socialize at the club or keep an eye on Kate when her husband had to work late and wasn't able to accompany her to the club.

Grabbing the leftover Chinese food from the refrigerator, he dumped the contents of the container onto a plate and popped it into the microwave. Quick, easy, and ready in minutes. Considering he was starving, those were all pluses in his book.

The microwave dinged, letting him know his meal was ready. He removed the plate of beef lo mein and took it into the living room. Surely there was a game on he could watch while he scarfed down his food.

Justin had just swallowed his last bite when there was a knock on his door. He glanced up at the clock. It was half past two. Since he wasn't expecting anyone, he had no idea who it could be. A delivery, maybe? But even then, he was left scratching his head. He hadn't ordered anything recently.

Setting his empty plate on the coffee table, he walked over to the door and looked through the peephole. He jerked back and swiftly opened the door. Standing on his threshold was his best friend's little sister. Justin and Mark had been best friends since they were sixteen. In high school they'd done everything together—even went on a few double dates. Now that they were both adults, they got together at least once a month to catch up and shoot the bull while downing a few beers and yelling at whatever game happened to be on the big screen of their local sports bar.

Kim stood there staring at him with wide eyes.

"Hi," he said.

"Hi." She looked nervous.

"Did something happen?"

She shook her head. "No. Nothing...no. May I come in?"

He took a step back and motion for her to enter. Kim walked inside and he closed the door behind her. "Are you sure you're all right?"

"Yeah. I'm fine. Promise." She flashed him one of those sweet smiles of hers. It caused his chest to clench every time. He didn't see her as often anymore as he used to, but they still ran into each other on occasion. Justin had been such a fixture at their house during the last two years of high school that he was often invited to family gatherings. Whether he wanted to admit it or not, seeing Kim at those times had been a definite highlight.

He reached for the remote and turned off the television. She was obviously here to talk to him about something. "Would you like something to drink?"

"Sure."

She was acting really strange. "What would you like? I have water, soda, beer, wine...pick your poison."

His joke fell flat.

"Water. Thank you."

He nodded and ducked into the kitchen.

Justin took his time getting Kim's water. Standing in his living room fidgeting with the belt of her coat, she looked almost fragile. It threw him because he knew she wasn't any such thing. Kim had graduated at the top of her class in college and landed a job almost immediately thanks to one of her professors. She'd excelled in her position and quickly rose within the company. Last he'd heard, she was being considered for a promotion. The woman knew what she wanted and went after it. That was one of the things he admired about her—one of the things he'd always admired about her.

As he headed back into the living room where Kim was waiting, he racked his brain trying to figure out why she was here. All thoughts went out the window, however, when his gaze fell on Kim kneeling on the floor, naked. Her head was bowed, her knees parted, and her forearms rested on her thighs, palms up.

He froze. It had been seventeen years since he'd seen this much of her. And even though he'd seen dozens of women sans clothing since then, it didn't lessen the effect she had on him. Seeing her bare flesh flushed and her chest heaving with every breath had him instantly hard and his cock straining against his jeans.

The last time he'd been seventeen and he'd walked by her bedroom one night on his way to brush his teeth. She'd left the door open a crack and when he'd glanced inside, unable to resist, he'd watched her change into her pajamas. Kim was the first live woman he'd ever seen naked.

"What are you doing?" He somehow managed to choke out the question even though it felt as if he had no air left in his lungs.

She didn't look at him, which bothered Justin a great deal, but at least she answered. Sort of. "I want to submit to you."

Placing the glass he was holding down on the side table, Justin closed the distance between them. When he was in front of her, he extended his hand.

At first, she hesitated, but then she took it, and he helped her up. Once Kim was on her feet, he left her long enough to retrieve a blanket from his room, and then wrapped it around her shoulders. It didn't completely cover her, but it made things a little less distracting. He'd wanted Kim Langley from that first time he'd seen her dressing in her bedroom. The only thing that had kept him from making a move on her was her brother. Mark would kill him. Or castrate him. Maybe both.

Trying to keep a level head, Justin led her over to his couch. He sat down facing her, their knees within inches of each other. It would be so much easier if he weren't so aware of her. "Now, tell me what this is about."

Kim glanced up at him and then back down at her lap. Her cheeks were flushed and she looked embarrassed. "I saw you."

He furrowed his brow in confusion. "Saw me?"

"Yes. At Serpent's Kiss. You're into BDSM. You're a Dom, right?"

Justin's heart skipped a beat. She was at the club? Why? How?

"Anyway, I want you to be the one to show me. I want to submit to you." The words were spoken in not much more than a whisper.

It wasn't often Justin was at a loss for words, but this was one of those times. Needing some space, he stood and walked to the other side of the room.

His mind was racing and his cock was throbbing. How many times had he fantasized about her over the years? How many times had it been the memory of her face and body that had brought him to orgasm? Now here she was offering herself to him and he couldn't do it. He couldn't. If Mark ever found out he would view it as a betrayal. And as much as he wanted her, he couldn't do that to his best friend. Or to her.

The sound of sobs had him whipping his head back around in her direction. She was clutching the blanket around her and tears were streaming down her face.

Justin's heart broke. "Please, don't cry."

She shook her head and wiped at the moisture on her cheeks. "You don't want me."

"It's not that," he said as he strolled back over to her side.

"It's okay. I understand."

He lowered himself back down onto the couch and rubbed a hand over his face in frustration. "No you don't."

This time she met his gaze. He tilted his head downward toward the physical evidence that contradicted her assumption. When she looked up again, there was a clear question in her eyes.

"Kim, I can't do that to you. You deserve more than one night of kinky sex."

She straightened her shoulders and gave him a look he was far more familiar with. This wasn't the timid Kim who'd walked through his door. "What if that's all I want?"

"What about your brother?"

"Mark has nothing to do with this." Kim folded her hands in her lap. "I want to know if I'm really submissive. I think I am, but..." She took a deep breath. "Ali said that BDSM is about trust. I trust you."

He heard the tremble in her voice. "Do you?"

"Yes."

Deciding to test the waters, he ran his index finger over her collarbone and down to the valley between her breasts. Kim sucked in a deep breath.

"What did you think of Serpent's Kiss?" he asked while he continued to move his finger along her skin. His touch was innocent for the most part, but he couldn't deny how good it felt to touch her like this.

"I-I liked it."

He raised an eyebrow at her. She'd have to do better than that.

"Ali took me up to the second floor."

So she'd seen some play. "And?"

"I watched a woman get spanked."

Justin didn't miss how her breathing changed. "Did you wish it was you?"

"What?"

"Did you want to be the one who was getting spanked?" he asked.

When she didn't answer, he tried again. "Have you ever been spanked before, Kim?"

She swallowed. "No."

"Have you ever been tied up? Held down?"

"No. I..." A new rush of blood warmed Kim's cheeks. "I've only had regular sex before."

"And did you enjoy it?"

She seemed startled by his question. "The sex?"

"Yes." He skimmed the top of her breast with his fingertip. "I want to know if you enjoyed your vanilla sex."

"Yeah. I mean, of course I did. Sex is supposed to be enjoyable, right?"

Justin grinned. "It is. But I was more trying to figure out what it was that led you to your exploration of kink."

"Oh. Well, I sort of...I found Ali's toy bag. Or I guess you could say I tripped over it."

That made him chuckle. "What did you find in there? Anything intriguing?"

The blush was back. He was enjoying this. Probably too much, but how often did he have a beautiful woman sitting naked in his living room?

Kim shrugged and it brought his finger in contact with more of her breast. "She had a lot of dildos and vibrators."

He grinned and dropped his hand. His erection wasn't going away. "Where are your clothes?"

She seemed confused by the change in topic. "I didn't wear any. Just the coat."

Well, that explained her wearing a coat when it was seventy degrees outside. "You came over here in nothing but your coat?"

"Yes. I wanted you to know that I was serious. I want you to show me. I want to see if I can do this. If this is what's been missing from my relationships." She looked as if she was ready to cry again.

He took her face in his hands and brought his mouth down to hers.

It took her only a moment before she was kissing him back and, oh, it felt good. More than good. Her lips were soft and luscious and she tasted like peppermint—no doubt from a mint she'd been sucking on in the car on the way over to his house.

When he broke the kiss, Justin rested his forehead on hers and looked her in the eye. He had a decision to make. He could make her put her coat back on and send her packing, or he could take her up on her offer. They were both adults. He knew that. But could he betray his best friend by defiling his little sister?

Kim seemed to know what he was thinking. "Mark doesn't have to know. I won't tell him if you won't."

"He would never forgive me." It was the truth and they both knew it.

"Please."

Her plea did something to him. Right then he didn't care about Mark or any other member of her family. He'd wanted her for almost twenty years and here she was sitting in his living room offering herself to him.

"It can only be tonight." He had to put that out there.

"I know."

Grabbing hold of her hair at the base of her neck, he tilted her head back and kissed her hard. She gasped, but then met his aggressive tongue with an enthusiasm he knew was genuine.

When he pulled back several minutes later, he was out of breath. So was she. "The club requires we get tested for STIs every six months."

As usual, the change in subject didn't affect her in the slightest. "I got tested after I broke up with my last boyfriend."

Justin didn't need to ask her how long ago that was. He remembered Mark ranting about how the scumbag had stood his sister up one time too many and she'd finally thrown him to the curb. She'd been single for three months. How sad was it that he'd been keeping track?

He could see the hope in Kim's eyes as he sat there weighing his options. Sure, he could tell her no and send her home, but heaven help him, he didn't want to.

"Your safeword tonight will be teddy bear," he said. "If at any time I do something you don't want me to do, say it and I'll stop."

She smiled and nodded. He knew she understood the significance of the safeword he'd chosen. When she'd graduated from high school he'd gotten her one of those little graduation teddy bears.

He stood and motioned for her to follow him.

Justin led her down the hall to the room across from his bedroom. It had a bed like any other spare bedroom, but it also had several other things that he'd adapted for play.

Kim stood there eyeing everything. It wasn't anything close to the setup at Serpent's Kiss, but it fit his needs whenever he brought a sub home.

He ambled over to the spanking bench in the corner of the room and ran his hand along the leather. "Tonight you'll be my submissive."

She watched his every move.

"You will call me Sir at all times and when I give you an instruction you are to follow through without hesitation. Is that understood?"

"Yes."

He walked over to stand in front of her. "Yes, what?"

"Yes, Sir," she whispered.

"I'm sorry, I didn't get that."

Her eyes widened again at his tone, but this time she answered with more confidence. "Yes, Sir."

"Good." Justin brushed his thumb along her jaw. He would have to remember that this was her first time. "What's your safeword?"

"Teddy bear, Sir."

He smiled and trailed his fingers down her neck to where she was clutching the blanket. She loosed her grip as he began separating the fabric. The blanket slid off her shoulders, revealing her tits. Earlier he'd been in such a hurry to get her covered up that he hadn't taken the time to appreciate them, but they were truly magnificent.

Pulling the blanket completely away from her body, Justin lowered his gaze. His cock strained against his jeans as he took her in. Tonight she would be his to do with whatever he wished. Tonight he would fulfill his fantasies.

Throwing the blanket on the back of the chair, he never took his eyes off her as he extended his hand for her to take.

Chapter Three

Kim shook as she placed her hand in his. Justin hadn't taken his eyes off her since he removed the blanket and she felt incredibly naked. Of course, that was probably because she was. But it was different. She'd slept with a handful of guys over the years and they'd all seen her without clothing. With Justin, though, it felt more intimate, like he was seeing even the parts of her that she was trying to hide from the world.

He led her over to the edge of the bed and sat down. When he released her hand, he patted his leg twice. "I want you over my lap with your ass in the air."

Was he serious?

One look at his face told her that he was.

She took a shaking breath and did what he'd instructed. It took her a minute or so to get into position with her stomach resting on his thighs and her legs and chest on the mattress on either side of him. Kim was pretty sure what was going to happen next, but she still flinched when his hand came down sharply on her backside.

"You've been a very bad girl, haven't you?" As he said the words, he landed another solid blow to her other butt cheek. "Visiting kink clubs and driving across town in nothing but a thin trench coat."

Another two hits and her behind was beginning to warm. The crazy thing was that wasn't the only thing she noticed heating up. Kim was becoming aroused. She could feel the wetness growing between her legs.

Smack.

Smack.

"A very bad girl, indeed."

Why was this turning her on? She didn't understand it at all, but the evidence didn't lie. With every swat on her ass she was getting wetter and wetter.

Then he took both her cheeks in his hands and began massaging them. It felt so good and a moan escaped from deep in her throat.

"Mmm. Something tells me you like being spanked, Miss Langley."

To her horror, he dipped his hand between her legs and ran his fingers over her pussy. She knew what he'd find. If she could feel how wet she was, Kim knew he'd be able to as well.

"Just as I thought."

Before she could form any sort of response, he moved his fingers lower and began tapping out a rhythm on her clit. Holy shit, why did that feel so good?

As he continued, she felt the energy coiling in her belly, driving her toward her climax. Her breathing picked up and soon she was rocking her hips back toward his hand, silently begging him for more. What he was doing felt good, but she needed more pressure. She needed faster. She needed...more.

Kim opened her mouth to tell him that when suddenly his hand was gone. She almost cried.

"Not yet, sweetheart, and not until I say. Tonight your orgasms belong to me. I decide when you find release."

Before she knew what was happening, he'd turned her over onto her back. The rough material of his jeans brushed against her abused backside, making it impossible to forget that she'd been spanked moments before like a misbehaving child. It should have made her furious to be treated like that. She was a grown woman and a successful one at that. None of this should be appealing to her on any level. So why was it that her entire body felt as if it were more alive than it had ever been?

All thoughts fled as Justin lowered his mouth to her breast and began sucking it into his mouth. He swirled his tongue around her nipple before scraping his teeth along the moist flesh.

When he began to pull back, she instinctively reached to hold him in place. Justin wasn't having that, however. He took hold of both her wrists, placed them on the bed above her head, and held them there.

"I want to touch you," she said though her labored breathing.

"No," Justin mumbled around the breast he was currently paying homage to.

She opened her mouth to protest and he bit down on her nipple. "Ouch!"

He chuckled and met her gaze. "Have you changed your mind? Do you want me to stop, let you get dressed and send you on your way?"

Of course she didn't want that. Was he joking?

Kim shook her head. "No, Sir. I don't want to go home."

With her answer, he took her other nipple between his teeth, worried it until it was almost painful, and then released it. She'd felt it all the way down to her pussy. It was as if all the nerve endings in her body were connected to the space between her legs. That had never happened before.

Cool air fanned over her damp breast, causing goose bumps. Then he switched sides, sucking her other nipple into his mouth, licking around her areola, and then working it between his teeth before releasing it and blowing on it. She felt cold and hot at the same time.

Kim could honestly say that foreplay had never been like this before. Most guys would have dived in as soon as they realized she was wet and ready. Not Justin. He seemed content to take his time and explore her body. Maybe it was because they were only giving themselves this one night. Maybe that was what made the difference.

He shifted his hold on her wrists, freeing one of his hands. "I'm going to make you feel good tonight, Kim. How many times would you like to come?"

"What?" She'd been lost in her thoughts and the feel of his mouth as he peppered kisses on her chest and collarbone.

She felt his lips curl up into a smile against her skin.

"I asked you how many times you wished to come tonight." Justin punctuated his statement by tracing a line up her collarbone to the curve of her neck with his tongue.

"I thought that wasn't my decision." It was difficult to concentrate with his lips so close to her neck.

"Oh, it's not, but I still want to hear your answer." He drew some of her flesh into his mouth and began sucking on it gently. Was he going to give her a hicky? Normally that would annoy the hell out of her, but she found she didn't care.

It was hard to concentrate while he was doing that, but she tried to focus. How many should she say? The most she'd ever had during a sexual encounter was two and that was only because the guy had gone down on her first. Usually one was a stretch for her. Then again, this was Justin and if he hadn't stopped earlier she would have come.

He released the skin he'd been sucking on and ran the tip of his nose up to the base of her ear. "I'm waiting."

"Two?"

Justin whispered in her ear, "Try again."

She swallowed. How many should she say? "Four."

Lifting his head, he met her gaze and shot her a mischievous grin. "I think five sounds like a nice round number, don't you?"

"Five," she said. Never had she experienced five orgasms in one night, not even when she'd helped herself.

He chuckled at her expression. "Are you doubting my abilities, Miss Langley?"

While he was talking, his free hand kneaded her breast. Kim had to keep reminding herself that she wasn't dreaming this. She was really here with Justin's hands and lips on her. And hopefully by the end of the night she'd know what it felt like to have him inside her as well.

"I've never had five before." She swallowed. "In one night, I mean."

Why did she feel shy admitting something like that to him? She was spread out naked across his lap, for crying out loud.

"There's a first time for everything."

Justin pulled her earlobe into his mouth as he lowered his hand down her abdomen to the junction of her legs. He didn't rush and the anticipation was killing her. She wanted him to touch her—to make her come.

When he reached his destination, she spread her legs for him, desperate for his touch. He cupped her pussy and used the flat of his palm to press slow circles on her clit. Her eyes rolled back in her head because it felt so good.

"Please."

"Please, what?" he asked, releasing her earlobe.

"I need to come. Please, Sir, a little harder." Kim knew she was begging but she needed this.

He shifted his hand and curled his fingers so that he had one on each side of her clit. What he did next caused her back to arch and a very unladylike sound to escape her lips. Every nerve ending in the lower half of her body went on high alert as he rolled and pinched her clit. He seemed to know how to make her body sing better than she did.

In no time at all, the energy built to the point where it had nowhere to go. With one final pinch between his fingers, Kim was flying.

❧

JUSTIN HAD TO KEEP REMINDING HIMSELF THIS WAS REAL. OF COURSE, THE fact that his cock felt as if it were about to rip a hole in his jeans helped to drive the point home. So did seeing the look on Kim's face as her orgasm overtook her. It was absolutely beautiful how her brow furrowed and her lips pursed as if she were about to whistle. It was cute and endearing. And he wanted to see her doing it over and over again.

The heat radiating from between her legs had him wanting to dive in and taste what she had to offer. If this was their one and only night together, then he wasn't going to hold back. Everything he'd been dreaming of doing since she began starring in his fantasies was now going to become a reality. Justin was going to make sure of it.

Releasing his hold on her wrists, Justin helped her to sit up. He ran one hand up along the curve of her hip. The other hand cupped the back of her head. "That's one."

Kim was still trying to catch her breath, but she laughed anyway.

"Ready to get started on number two?"

Before she could answer, he pulled her against him and kissed her. It took her only a moment to catch up and then her hands were in his hair and she was kissing him back. She met every stroke of his tongue with one of her own. Blood was pumping through his veins and he wanted nothing more than to plunge his cock deep inside her and make her forget her own name.

If he'd been ten years younger that would have been exactly what he would have done. But he was older now. Wiser. He'd promised her five orgasms and that was exactly what he intended to give her.

Ripping his mouth away from hers, he stood and flipped her over onto the bed. The look of surprise on her face told him that he'd caught her off guard. She'd been so dazed by the kiss that she hadn't been paying attention to how he'd shifted her on his lap or moved both his hands to her hips for leverage.

He didn't let her get her bearings before falling on top of her and starting to ravish her mouth again. It felt incredible to kiss her—to have her under him. Kim wasn't a stick of a woman. She had gentle curves and a nice set of tits that demanded to be touched and played with.

With that thought, Justin shifted his weight and rolled over to reach inside the nightstand. He kept a variety of toys in there, most of which were new since it wasn't often he brought a woman home. That was one of the great things about being a member of Serpent's Kiss. Most of the women he played with were members. Given the wide variety of implements and furniture the club offered, it didn't make sense to bring them back here when playing there was more convenient for both of them.

Justin felt Kim watching him as he rifled through the drawer. It didn't take long, but by the time he returned his attention to her she was breathing normally again. He brushed the back of his hand along the side of her face, and held up the item he'd retrieved from the drawer. Her eyes widened a little when she saw the nipple clamps he had in his hand. They were a simple pair of tweezer clamps, but they had a chain linking them together. Perfect for what he had in mind.

"Have you ever worn nipple clamps before?" he asked.

She shook her head and kept eyeing them with trepidation.

A thrill rushed through him as he thought of what her reactions to the clamps might be. Every woman was different. Depending on her sensitivity and her pain tolerance, she may love them or hate them.

Not allowing her to spend too much time worrying about how the clamps might feel, he leaned down and took one of her nipples into his mouth again. It had softened, but it didn't take long to get it hard. He took his time licking and touching—bringing her level of arousal back to where it had been before.

Kim's fingers tangled in his hair as he continued to worship her tits. He took his time memorizing the texture of them, knowing he needed to store up memories of tonight to last him a lifetime.

By the time he pinched her nipple between his fingers and situated the clamp on either side, Kim was completely focused on what she was feeling. She was paying attention to what his mouth was doing, not his hands. That was until he pushed the clamp closed around her nipple. She gasped and pulled at his hair.

Justin took her other nipple between his teeth and smiled up at her. She was shaking her head. "Justin."

His only response was to dig his teeth into her nipple a little more, causing her to suck in another sharp breath. He followed that up with a soothing brush of his tongue and then he attached the clamp. If she was interested in being someone's submissive, she was going to have to learn that her Dom called the shots during a scene, not her.

He held her gaze as he moved down her torso and settled himself between her legs. She looked uncertain, but as soon as he lowered his mouth to her pussy he heard a soft moan escape her lips. Kim tilted her head back and dug her fingers into the mattress as he ran his tongue over her lips and up to circle her clit. She was still slick with evidence of her previous orgasm. He took his time devouring every ounce of it.

Needing better access, he pushed her thighs farther apart and wrapped his arms around the tops, locking them in place. It also brought the chain that was attached to the nipple clamps within easy reach. He wrapped his fingers around the center of the chain and gave it a gentle tug as he ran the tip of his tongue over her clit.

She cried out. "Justin? Sir?"

He eased up on the chain, but continued his mission between her legs. "Yes?"

"I don't...it's too much." She was breathing hard and, given how wet she was, Justin was fairly sure it wasn't going to take much to get her to that second orgasm.

His only answer was to redouble his efforts. He buried his face in her pussy and used his lips and tongue to drive her closer and closer to the edge of reason.

When he felt her legs begin to shake, he focused his efforts solely on her clit and timed each swipe of his tongue with a tug of the chain. Before long she was bucking her hips. He held her firm and steadily increased the pressure on her clit.

Less than a minute later, she opened her mouth and released a silent scream. It was one of the most beautiful things Justin had ever seen. Watching a woman orgasm never got old, but even he had to admit that with Kim it was even more special. He would give her the five orgasms he'd promised her and then he would let her go. It would kill him never to be with her like this again, but he would do it because he had to. Tonight, however, she was his and he was going to make sure she never forgot their amazing night together because he knew he never would.

Chapter Four

Kim couldn't remember the last time she'd had two powerful orgasms within such a short period of time. She'd known her night with Justin would be full of new experiences. What she'd witnessed at Serpent's Kiss had told her that much. She had known very little about dominance and submission before her discovery at Ali's apartment. All Kim knew was that what her friend had shared had appealed on a level she didn't understand.

She was still trying to catch her breath when Justin released her legs and began moving up her body. Without thinking, she reached for him. If she'd been thinking properly, she might have second-guessed her actions considering he was supposed to be in charge this evening but it didn't cross her mind until her hands were already massaging his shoulders.

He placed a single kiss on each of her nipples. It was only then that she realized the clamps were still attached. How had she missed that? When he'd first put them on they had hurt. The pain was still there but her body was still singing from her climax. Everything else was secondary.

"That was two."

Justin grinned up at her and she felt her belly do a somersault. She pushed the feeling aside. Tonight was about sex. That was all it was—all it could be. They both knew that.

His face grew serious. "I need to take the clamps off. When I tell you, I want you to take a deep breath and hold it. Understand?"

She nodded and braced herself, hoping the pain wouldn't be as bad as when he'd first put them on.

"Deep breath."

Kim did as he said but she still felt the pain zip through her.

Then his warm mouth was there. The soft lapping of his tongue eased the pain considerably and then took it away completely. She sighed and cupped the back of his head, holding him to her chest.

He chuckled and shifted to the other breast. "One more to go."

"No," she whined.

She felt his lips curl up into a smile against her skin. "Deep breath."

A split second later the pain hit her. Even though she'd known what to expect, it still caught her off guard. But then he was there easing her pain and making her melt all over again.

"Better?" he asked.

She combed her fingers through his hair. "Yes. Thank you."

If given the chance, Kim could have fallen asleep right there. She was completely relaxed. Her bones felt as if they were disconnected from her body. She couldn't ever remember that having happened before.

"Uh-uh. No falling asleep on me. We aren't nearly done yet."

His voice sent a pleasant tingling to the pit of her stomach even though her mind was ready to shut off. Apparently her body still wanted to fool around, not that she could blame it. Justin was by far the sexiest man she'd ever encountered.

She felt his breath on her face and opened her eyes. He was hovering above her, his lips an inch from her own. Justin had the most amazing eyes. They were a vivid green framed with the longest lashes she'd ever seen on a man. Every time she looked into his eyes she was lost.

He lowered his mouth onto hers and began kissing her as if he had all the time in the world. At first it was all gentle suction, then he traced the outline of her lips with his tongue. She opened to him, wanting nothing more than to taste him. Kim could smell herself...taste herself on his tongue. It mixed with Justin's own flavor creating something altogether new and highly intoxicating.

As he continued to kiss her, Justin lifted her right leg up over his shoulder, spreading her open. She felt exposed. With anyone else Kim would have protested, but this was Justin. This was their night. If that was how he wanted her, then she wasn't going to protest. Besides, so far she'd had two of the most powerful orgasms in her life. She would have to be crazy to not want more.

The feel of his fingers drawing circles along the inside of her thigh tickled. It caused her to tense up.

"You're thinking too much," he whispered as he brushed his lips along her neck.

Then he was tugging her hands away from where they'd been buried in his hair. Before she could protest, Kim felt something wrap around her wrists. When she looked up, Justin was using a thin red rope to secure her wrists together. He let her leg fall to the bed as he positioned himself higher to concentrate on his work.

There was a part of her that wanted to resist. This was different than when he'd been holding her down earlier and she wasn't sure she liked it.

Justin must have noticed her uncertainty because he paused and met her gaze. "Do you trust me?"

"Yes, Sir." There was no doubt about that. Kim trusted Justin more than any other man besides maybe her brother and her father. She knew he wouldn't do anything to hurt her. But that didn't mean she wasn't nervous. This was new, different…and just a little scary.

He held her gaze for a moment longer, and then went back to what he was doing. A few seconds later, he gave the rope a jerk, and ran his finger along the edge. Justin flashed her a devious smile and hopped off the bed. He knelt down beside her head, and then she felt a pull on the rope. Instinctively, Kim knew he'd tied it to the side of the bed. Even without testing the rope, she knew it was secure. Justin had been a Boy Scout the same as her brother. He knew how to tie a rope and secure it.

She breathed through her nerves and focused on the fact that this wasn't some random guy. It was Justin. And if what she'd experienced so far was anything to go by, she still had three more earth-shattering orgasms to go.

Movement had her looking up. Justin was standing over her, this time with a scarf. He held it in both his hands.

"What are you going to do with that?" She was pretty sure she already knew the answer.

The side of his mouth pulled up into an amused smirk. "I'm going to blindfold you."

In the next second, the silky fabric was being pressed against her eyes, plunging her into darkness. He lifted her head and tilted it to the side to secure the scarf behind her head. Then he placed a soft kiss on her lips. For some reason, even that simple kiss felt different. Not only could she feel his lips, but she could feel his breath against her cheek—smell the musky scent of her and him. She even caught a whiff of the soap he used.

Kim arched her back as he backed away, hoping to prolong the connection.

She heard Justin chuckle. "Not yet, sweetheart. I have plans for you first."

Maybe that statement should have made her nervous, but it didn't. If anything, she was excited for the possibilities.

There were sounds of drawers opening and closing, and then his hands were on her legs. One by one, he wound something around her ankles and attached them to the edge of the bed. She wondered if it was the same red rope that he'd used for her wrists. Either way, Kim was now lying sideways on Justin's bed, blindfolded, with her wrists secured above her head and her legs spread wide. She was completely helpless and exposed. The logical part of her brain told her that she should be upset. This wasn't normal. She shouldn't find this arousing.

But whether it made sense or not, the evidence of her excitement was right there between her legs. Her heart was racing and blood was pumping through her veins. Not because she was terrified, but because she couldn't wait to see what Justin would do to her next.

෴

JUSTIN HAD KIM EXACTLY WHERE HE WANTED HER. HER WRISTS WERE TIED together and attached to the bedframe. Her legs were spread as far apart as was comfortable. His mind was racing with all the things he wanted to do to her. It was taking considerable effort on his part to stay focused. If this was their only night together, he wanted to give her the full experience. But this was new to her and Justin wanted her to enjoy it. He wanted tonight to be what filled her fantasies.

It was stupid and completely irrational. Logically Justin knew that. But logic had nothing to do with this. He'd wanted her almost from the first moment he'd laid eyes on her after moving to St. Louis his junior year. The selfish part of him wanted to ruin her for any other man.

Shaking his head, he banished the thoughts from his mind. Thinking like that wouldn't change the situation. Justin knew he wasn't Kim's first lover and he knew he wouldn't be her last. She was a beautiful woman. Any man with half a brain would be thrilled to have her warming his bed every night. Justin knew he would. If things were different.

He watched the rise and fall of her chest as she lay there waiting for what would come next. To the casual observer, she looked as if she wasn't bothered by the pause in activities but he knew Kim well. Whenever she was nervous or unsure about something she would scrape her teeth along her bottom lip in the cutest way—just like she was doing now.

Grinning, Justin rested his knee on the bed between her spread legs. He placed his hands on either side of her arms, bracing himself above her. She seemed to relax some knowing that he was close. Did she really think he would leave her alone tied up like this?

"You look so beautiful tied to my bed," he whispered against her lips before moving down to the curve of her neck.

She tilted her head to the side to give him better access. "I do?"

He hummed in answer, too busy kissing her sensitive skin to break the connection long enough for words.

For the next few minutes, he nuzzled and kissed every inch of flesh from her ear down to her collarbone. There was something about a woman's neck that made him crazy. Lucky for him, most of the women he'd been with loved when he paid extra close attention to that part of their body. Going by Kim's responses, she enjoyed it as well. Her chest rose and fell more rapidly as he explored and memorized the scent of her—the feel.

Shifting his weight, he lifted one of his hands and began touching her. He started with her arms and slowly worked his way down. By the time he got to the small patch of hair that covered her pussy, she was arching her back trying to prolong the contact with his fingers as they skimmed her flesh.

"Does my bad girl want me to touch her pussy?" he asked.

"Yes."

His lips brushed her ear. "Yes, what?"

"Yes, Sir. Please touch me."

He scraped his teeth along the outline of her ear. "I am touching you. Is there somewhere specific you want me to touch? If there is, you need to tell me."

Kim swallowed. "Please touch my pussy, Sir."

Justin smiled and cupped her heat with his hand. "So hot."

Raising her hips, she tried to get him to move faster. But that wasn't how this worked. Obviously, she needed a reminder.

He retracted his hand slightly and brought it down with a firm smack against her swollen flesh.

She let out a squeak.

"We do this on my time." He hit her pussy again with the palm of his hand. "Not yours." Again he spanked her, this time landing the blow more on her clit. "Understand?"

"Yes. Yes, Sir." The words came out somewhere between a gasp and a moan. It was incredibly sexy.

He ran a finger through her slit and then spanked her again. "Looks like my bad girl likes to have her pussy whipped as much as her ass."

As he switched between smacking and stroking, Justin noticed the telltale signs that she was getting close to another orgasm. Tugging a nipple into his mouth, he worked it between his teeth while continuing to spank her pussy.

It didn't take long for her to start tugging on her restraints and her legs to begin trembling. He picked up the pace, slapping her clit in quick succession. She threw her head back and let out a high-pitched scream as yet another orgasm ripped through her.

Justin suddenly had the need to taste her. He could feel how wet she was and he wanted it on his tongue.

Giving the top of her breast a quick kiss that was in complete contradiction to the spanking he'd just given her most sensitive area, he worked his way down her body until he was kneeling between her legs. Running his hands from her calves up the inside of her thighs and back down, he breathed in the musky scent of her sex.

His gaze narrowed on her clit poking out of its hood surrounded by her dark pubic hair. Her legs were smooth as silk and the patch on her mound neatly trimmed. He wondered if she'd shaved before she'd come to his house or if she preferred waxing.

Again, he shook off his wayward thoughts. It didn't matter. After tonight, he'd never be in a position to see or know what she did or didn't do to her lady parts.

Before he could get sidetracked again, he used his thumbs to part her lips and licked a long line from the base of her pussy all the way up to her clit. Kim's mouth fell open and she released a near-silent sigh. He didn't even want to think about how many times he'd fantasized about this.

He made sure to take his time massaging everywhere he could reach with his tongue both inside and out. Her lips had a darker hue to them after his spanking, as did the skin around them. He worshipped it all, soothing the sting of the spanking.

Before he'd even reached her clit, she was panting. He knew it wouldn't take much.

"Ready for number four?" he asked a moment before his lips engulfed her clit.

Kim sucked in a ragged breath and came on his tongue.

While she was catching her breath, Justin stood and stripped off his clothing. His erection was painful at this point. He needed to be inside her and feel her tight and wet surrounding his cock.

Rolling on a condom, he leaned over her outstretched body, his lips hovering a breath away from hers and his left hand pressed against the side of her face. The need to possess her was overwhelming. And suddenly he was filled with a longing to see her eyes staring back at him. For her to see just how much he desired her.

Pushing the fabric he'd used to blindfold her out of the way, he watched as she blinked up at him, her eyes readjusting to the light in the room. Justin waited until she was staring up at him—her eyes were still glassy and dilated. That was good since she had one more orgasm to go.

Giving her a hard kiss, he didn't hold back as he took what he wanted. When he broke their connection, he pressed his thumb into the side of her face, commanding her attention. "I'm going to fuck you now. And I'm going to make sure you'll feel it with every step you take tomorrow."

"Please," she begged.

His heart clenched. He loved hearing her all hot and needy for him. If only they had more time...more than just this one night.

But they didn't.

Reaching between them, he wrapped his hand around the base of his penis and lined it up with her entrance. He thrust his hips forward, sinking deep into her warmth. The feeling was incredible and he knew without a doubt that one night with her would never be enough.

But it was all he had, so he was going to make it an experience neither one of them would ever forget.

Chapter Five

Kim's entire body was vibrating. And that was before he pushed his way past her now sensitive labia and stretched her more than she could ever remember being stretched before.

The heat from his body burned her as he pressed her into the mattress, his hips slapping against her thighs. This wasn't making love. This was fucking. With every thrust she could feel him claiming what he wanted. He'd promised she'd feel it in the morning and Kim had no doubt that was true. But the last thing she wanted him to do was stop. She'd never been this aroused before. Never felt as if the only thing holding her to the earth was him.

She tilted her head back and closed her eyes. Every time he surged forward he brushed against her already sensitive clit. After four orgasms, Kim would have thought she would have had enough. Her body, however, disagreed. It wanted more—more of whatever Justin had to give.

"Open your eyes."

His breathless instruction had her opening her eyes and gazing up at him. Sweat glistened on his naked chest. She wished her hands were free so she could run her fingers over the muscles she saw flexing as he pounded into her pussy.

As if he could read her mind, Justin reached up over her head and released her bindings. With her arms free, she stretched, needing to feel him almost as much as she needed her next breath.

Justin fell forward, bracing himself on either side of her body with stiff arms. Even with the movement he never stopped his assault. Every time his pelvic bone made contact with her clit she felt herself climbing farther and farther up that magical peak that would give her another mind-blowing orgasm. She couldn't believe how close she was...again. How was it possible to want someone so much?

His hands were everywhere. So were hers. Now that Kim could touch him, she wanted to touch him everywhere all at once.

Justin shifted his weight, released one of her legs, and then wrapped it around his waist. He repeated the process with the other leg until both were bracketing his hips and hugging him tightly.

"You feel amazing." The words were said in between thrusts which only added fuel to the fire. He was completely focused on her. It was as if nothing outside the two of them mattered.

Her orgasm was building. She knew it wasn't going to take much more before she was falling over the edge into oblivion.

Then, out of the blue, he circled his arms around her, picked her up, and brought her back down on the bed with her head on the pillows. He never lost their connection while repositioning them.

Bringing his mouth down to meet hers, he kissed her with unrestrained passion. His tongue mimicked what his body was doing. Her heart felt as if it would beat out of her chest and as she ran her hands over his torso she could feel his own heart pounding out a quick and hard rhythm against her fingers.

The need to come became too much to take. He had her so primed and ready yet she couldn't get over that final hurdle. Kim knew what she needed, so she snaked her hand between them.

She was inches from her goal when Justin's fingers wrapped around her wrist. He broke the kiss and stared into her eyes. "What do you think you're doing?"

"Umm..."

He quirked an eyebrow at her, letting her know he expected an answer. To accentuate his point, he pushed into her hard.

"I need to come."

He brought her hand up to his lips and kissed her fingers before placing her hand back over his heart. "You don't get to come until I say, sweetheart."

"But—"

He cut off her protest by kissing her again. This was another one of those no-holds-barred kisses that had her toes tingling.

"No buts. I promised you one more orgasm tonight, but it will be on my terms, not yours. Are we clear?"

Why did that make her even hotter?

"Yes, Sir."

He thrust his hips again, rotating them in a way that had her eyes rolling into the back of her head.

When she gazed up at him again, he had fire in his eyes.

"Kiss me," he demanded.

Unable to deny him and not wanting to, Kim brought his head down and captured his lips with her own. She kissed him for all she was worth.

After that, thinking became difficult. He picked up his pace and quicker than she thought possible she was burning. She needed to come. Never in her life had she needed a release the way she needed it now. Kim felt as if she would combust right there in his arms if she didn't get some relief soon.

"Please," she mumbled as best she could around his kisses. "Please, Sir, I need...I need to come."

"Not. Quite. Yet."

Justin punctuated each word by plunging his cock deep inside her. He moved his mouth down to her neck and began attacking the skin there. Everything he was doing only added to the sensations pulsing through her body and culminating right between her legs.

Just when she thought she couldn't take any more, he took her legs and spread them wide, stretching her open as far as she could go. It drove him deeper and made her feel as if she would split in two.

Kim had no idea how long he kept pounding away at her pussy. She'd passed the point of anything but feeling.

Then he released one of her legs and brushed a single finger over her clit. She went off like a rocket. A scream tore from her throat and filled the room. Her orgasm seemed to go on and on, leaving her feeling as if she were floating.

⊗

SOMEWHERE IN THE MIDDLE OF KIM'S ORGASM JUSTIN FOUND HIS OWN release. He'd drawn it out for as long as he could, torturing them both in the process, but he hadn't wanted it to end. It was stupid and probably not the wisest decision he'd ever made, but the whole situation—them sleeping together—wasn't exactly smart either. Even so, Justin couldn't bring himself to regret it.

Climbing off the bed, he quickly cleaned himself up before grabbing a blanket and rejoining her. She was shaking, which, given the circumstances, was to be expected. He'd worked her hard.

Justin covered her with the blanket and pulled her into his arms. She felt soft and warm and perfect. Like she belonged there.

He closed his eyes and tried to push the image out of his mind. She wasn't his and she never would be.

"I can't seem to stop shaking," she said, huddling farther into the blanket.

"It'll pass. You need to drink some water as soon as you think you're ready." She nodded and cuddled closer to him.

Circling his arm around her waist, he pressed his body against hers hoping to transfer his warmth.

As he lay there with her he tried to take in every detail—the texture of her hair as he tucked her head under his chin, the way every one of her curves fit perfectly against him. Even though it would be painful to remember and never be able to experience the perfection that was being able to possess Kim again, Justin never wanted to forget. He'd known when he agreed to this that once he had her he'd want more and that not being able to have it would haunt him for the rest of his life. But it was worth it. If only Mark wouldn't be so opposed…

But it was a fool's hope. Justin knew his best friend. Mark wouldn't approve of Justin pursuing his little sister no matter how honorable his intentions.

"What are you thinking?" she asked.

He noticed that she'd finally stopped shaking. "Are you ready for some water?"

It took her a second too long to answer. He knew she hadn't missed the fact that he hadn't answered her question. "Sure."

Reluctantly, Justin rolled away from her and got up to get some water from the small fridge he kept in the room. He also swiped a chocolate bar from his stash before returning to her side.

Kim stared up at him as he lowered himself back down onto the mattress. He situated himself with his back against the headboard, and then helped her into a sitting position. Before he handed her the water and chocolate, he gathered her against him once more. If this was all they got, he wasn't letting go of her until he absolutely had to.

"Thanks," she said, and took a bite of the chocolate.

"The sugar will help." He ran his fingers through her hair and down the side of her face. She was the most beautiful woman he'd ever met.

Kim was quiet for several minutes. She looked down and then back up at him. "You don't have to, you know."

"I don't have to what?" he asked.

"Take care of me like this. That wasn't part of the deal."

She'd lowered her gaze again and that just wouldn't do. Gripping her chin, he turned her to face him. "It most certainly is part of the deal. Aftercare is part of BDSM and any Dom who doesn't think so isn't worth his salt, in my opinion."

Kim swallowed and nodded.

"You're staying here tonight so I can watch you. I worked you hard and I want to make sure you're okay." The thought of her going home and experiencing subdrop alone had him feeling sick to his stomach.

"I don't—"

Justin placed his index finger over her lips, silencing her. "This isn't up for discussion. You're staying."

She turned away from him again and he hated it. There wasn't anything he could say, however. Both of them knew that when the morning came everything had to go back to the way it was before.

When she finished both her chocolate and her water, he took the empty bottle and stood. Extending his hand to her, he helped her up. Without words, he led her out of the room and across the hall to his bedroom. Normally if he let a submissive stay over he'd have them sleep in the other room. Kim was different. But then again, she always had been.

Once in his bedroom, he flipped on the light and went to his dresser to get her a T-shirt. As much as he would love to sleep naked next to her, he needed to begin the separation process or he'd never be able to let her go come daylight.

"Here," he said, handing her the dark blue shirt with his shop's logo on it and pointing to the door that led to the master bathroom. "You can wear this to sleep in. I'll wait here while you get changed. There's an extra toothbrush in the linen closet you can use."

Kim took the shirt and hugged it to her chest. It only accented her tits, which had his cock twitching.

"Go on. We both need to get some sleep." He hadn't meant the words to sound as harsh as they'd sounded, so he took a step forward and touched her cheek. Kim leaned into his touch. When he dropped his hand, he winked at her and she smiled.

"I'll be right back." She brushed past him.

"Hurry."

Running a hand through his hair, Justin grabbed a pair of underwear out of his top drawer and put them on. He knew he'd need more than just the T-shirt she'd be wearing to keep him from sinking his cock into her again. Not that clothing of any kind would completely prevent that. Kim brought temptation to a whole new level.

Justin strolled over to the bed and turned down the covers. It had been years since a woman had slept in his bed. Not since his last long-term girlfriend.

Before he could take a trip too far down memory lane, Kim walked back into the room. When he saw her he blinked several times. How was it possible she looked sexier in his shirt than she had out of it?

He crossed the short distance separating them and gathered her into his arms. Massaging his thumb along the side of her face, he looked deep into her eyes. She was too desirable for her own good.

"What's wrong?" she asked, gazing up at him.

Instead of answering her question, he refocused on the task at hand. "Climb into bed. I'll be right back."

Justin didn't wait to see if she followed his instructions. He couldn't.

Once he was inside the confines of his bathroom, he did his business and then took a moment to catch his breath. When Justin was fairly sure he could get into bed with her and not jump her again, he headed back into his bedroom. When he crossed the threshold, his gaze was immediately drawn to the woman lying in his bed. She was staring back at him with those soulful brown eyes of hers.

He tried to ignore the stirring in his groin as he got into the bed beside her. Kim pulled the covers higher as if she was shielding herself. That wouldn't do. He reached out and tucked her head into the curve of his shoulder.

"How are you feeling?" he asked as he ran a gentle hand over her head and down the smooth slope of her back.

"Fine." Her answer was quiet.

Tipping her chin up, he gave her a stern look. "I need the truth."

She tried to avert her gaze, so he tightened his hold.

"Why?" she asked. "Why do you want to know?"

"I told you. It's part of being a Dom." He cupped the side of her face. "Are you sore?"

Kim nodded. "A little."

He smiled. "Roll over. I'll massage your shoulders."

"You don't—"

"It wasn't a request." The look he gave her let her know he wasn't taking no for an answer.

Sighing, she turned away from him. Justin positioned his hands on either side of her shoulders and began to massage the tension out of her muscles. As he rubbed and kneaded her flesh, Kim began to moan. It went straight to his cock. What was wrong with him? He hadn't reacted like this to a woman in...

well, ever. Even with his first girlfriend he was usually good after one hard session.

Kim moved her hips and bumped against his erection. When she felt it, she froze and turned her head to look at him. "Really?"

He'd expected exasperation or something like it but instead she seemed genuinely shocked that he'd want her again so soon. In truth, he was having a difficult time believing it as well. But it wasn't like he could deny it. The evidence was right there.

As if his hand had a mind of its own, he slipped it around her and palmed her breast. This time when she moaned it had nothing to do with the easing of sore muscles. Kim arched into his hand, seeking more. Who was he to deny her?

Releasing her long enough to sheath himself with a new condom, he returned and repositioned them so he could slide into her from behind. He'd worked her over good earlier. This time he'd take it nice and slow. Justin loved kinky sex, but as he moved in and out of Kim...as he felt her pussy pulse around him...he realized that with her slow and easy was satisfying in its own way.

Justin kept up a gentle pace until he felt her legs begin to quiver. Snaking a hand between her legs, he circled her clit with his fingers. Kim gasped and shuddered around him as she reached her climax. Feeling her come apart in his arms was almost spiritual.

Placing a kiss at the base of her neck, Justin closed his eyes and let his orgasm take him. It wasn't as explosive as their joining earlier, but it was more powerful if that was possible.

He pulled out of her and she twisted so that she was facing him. Her face was flushed. Gorgeous.

"I need to clean up," he said, kissing the tip of her nose. "I'll be right back."

When he returned, she was exactly where he'd left her. Gathering her into his arms, he held her close to his chest. They had eight hours until morning. Eight hours until he had to let her go.

Chapter Six

Kim awoke to a warm body lying beside her. It only took her a second to replay their night together. Trying not to make any sudden moves, she looked to see if he was awake. His eyes were still closed and he had the most adorable look on his face. She could have stared at him for hours and not gotten tired of looking at him. That, however, wasn't an option.

As quietly as she could, she snuck out of his bed and into the bathroom. Glancing in the mirror, her lips were a little swollen and there were a few red marks on her neck from his whiskers. That's all that was visible, but she had the most delicious ache all over her body. Never had she had sex like that. Not the kinky stuff or what had transpired later in his bed. Before she would have said that the sex she'd experienced in the past was good. What transpired with Justin last night changed her definition.

Splashing some cold water on her face, she took the toothbrush she'd used last night and brushed her teeth, then used the bathroom. As much as she wanted to get out of there before things got weird between them, Kim knew she couldn't. It wasn't as if she'd never see him again. Justin was Mark's best friend. He came to all their family functions, as well as the occasional family dinner. If things were weird, her family—and especially her brother—would notice.

Squaring her shoulders, she marched back out into Justin's bedroom with nothing on but his shirt. As promised, she was feeling the residual effects of the night before with every step she took.

He was awake when she walked into the room. "Hi."

Justin propped himself up on one arm. "Morning."

Neither said a word for several charged moments.

"I should go," she said.

He continued to look her over for what felt like forever, and then nodded. "Would you like some breakfast?"

She shook her head even though her stomach protested. They hadn't stopped to eat dinner last night, but it had been worth the sacrifice. "No. I think I should go."

Not sure what to do since her coat was still out in the living room where she'd left it, she debated whether or not to take his shirt off here or wait until she had something to cover up with. Even though he'd seen all of her there was to see last night, in the light of day things were different.

Justin must have sensed her indecision. "Keep the shirt. And grab a pair of my boxers out of the top drawer. You can wear those home under your coat."

A part of her wanted to protest, but when she thought that maybe she'd get to take home something to remember him and their night by, she couldn't say no. Doing as he'd instructed, she selected a pair of dark blue boxers to match the shirt she was wearing, and stepped into them. He never took his eyes off her the entire time.

Once she was dressed—or as dressed as she was going to be—she crossed her arms over her chest and took one last long look at him. "Thank you. For last night."

"It was entirely my pleasure."

"Well. I should go." She moved toward the door. Before she stepped through, she met his gaze once more. Everything she felt was right there reflected in his eyes. If only things were different.

But they weren't, so she took a deep breath and walked away from him. Back to her boring life. At least she'd have her memories of their night together. It was enough. It would have to be.

For now.

Chapter Seven

Kim's heels clicked on the concrete floor of the parking garage as she rushed to her car. She tugged her coat tighter around her as the cold air sent a shiver down her spine. The sun had set over St. Louis and the temperature had dropped. It was New Year's Eve and while there was no snow in sight, the wind had picked up, leaving a bite in the air.

She hurried the final steps to her vehicle and slid behind the wheel. No sooner had she started the car than the sound of her phone ringing filled the small space. Her best friend's name popped up on the screen in big letters.

"Hey, Ali."

"Hey, yourself. Are you on your way to your parents' house?"

"Yeah. I'm just leaving work. Got stuck on a call. You already there?"

Silence met her question.

Every second that passed where her friend didn't answer had Kim's heart rate kicking up a notch. "Ali?"

"Don't kill me, okay, but I won't be able to make it."

"What? Why?" Kim's voice vibrated in the small confines of the car.

"I'm sorry. You know I was planning to be there, but my mom called about an hour ago. She and her current boyfriend had a huge fight, so I told her she could stay with me for the night. She's curled up on my couch with a huge glass of wine and a box of tissues. I'm sorry."

Kim's anxiety ratcheted up another notch. She'd been counting on Ali being there…being her buffer. But it wasn't as if she could fault her friend. Ali was supporting her mom. How could she be mad about that?

"It's okay," Kim said. "I forgive you." Ali and her mom didn't have the best relationship. It was kind of messed up, actually. Ali tended to act like the parent while her mom hopped from boyfriend to boyfriend, looking for someone to fix all that was wrong in her life.

"Thanks." Ali paused. "I am sorry, though. I hate leaving you hanging like this."

"I'm a big girl. I'll be okay." Maybe if Kim said it enough times, she'd believe it.

The long pause on the other end of the line told Kim that Ali wasn't convinced. "Call me later if you need me. And give your mom and dad a hug for me."

"I will."

Kim released a loud breath as she disconnected the call and headed out of the city toward her parents' home in the suburbs. It was already after six, which meant she would most likely be the last to arrive. Not that her parents' New Year's Eve party was a major social event. It wasn't. But it was a big deal for them.

Every year, her mom and dad opened up their home to their nearest neighbors and to a few close friends. Her mom would bake dozens of cookies, make her famous punch, enough food to feed an army, and decorate her house from top to bottom. It was a big affair. As far as her family was concerned, anyway.

Normally, it was something Kim looked forward to. Her brother's best friend—the man Kim had spent the last seventeen years fantasizing about—Justin McKay, would be there. Unfortunately, he was also the reason she was dreading tonight.

Maybe dreading was too strong a word. It wasn't as if she didn't want to see him. She did. The man still starred in her fantasies. The problem was that now she didn't have to dream about what it would be like to have him touch her, kiss her. Kim knew what it was like and she got to relive their one night together in vivid detail every time she closed her eyes.

It had been three months and she'd been avoiding him since. Well, sort of. If avoiding him meant that she'd joined the private BDSM club, Serpent's Kiss, where he was a member and watched from afar as he flirted with various submissives every night.

It was torture, but she'd brought it on herself. She'd thought she could handle it. Thought she could find a connection with one of the other Doms like the one she'd felt with Justin when he'd draped her over his lap and spanked her. But so far, all being at the club had done was make her ache even more to have Justin's hands on her again.

At the club, they kept their distance. She hung out with Ali and her friends, while Justin mingled or sat at the bar talking to Brandon, one of the bartenders.

Tonight, however, avoiding him wouldn't be so easy. Her family would notice if she gave him the cold shoulder or left the room every time he entered. No, she was going to have to suck it up and face him. They were both adults. They could do this. Adults had one-night stands all the time. Right?

As she pulled up in front of her parents' house, she was still trying to convince herself. Maybe she should call and say she was stuck at work or that Ali needed her to help with her mother's latest boyfriend disaster. While Kim didn't want to put her friend in that position, she knew Ali would back her up.

The decision was made for her, however, when the door opened, and her brother peeked his head outside. He was looking straight at her. So much for ducking out before being noticed.

Turning off the engine, Kim scooped her purse from the seat and stepped out of the vehicle. As she neared the house, her brother crossed his arms to ward off the chill. "Hurry up, Sis. It's cold out here."

"No one told you to stand there with the door open. I'm an adult, you know. I can walk from my car to the door by myself."

He moved to the side to let her pass. "Gotta do my chivalrous duty to protect the womenfolk."

Kim turned and stuck her tongue out at her big brother before hanging her coat up in the hall closet. She'd barely got her coat on the hanger when she was lifted a foot off the floor. "Mark! Put me down."

Her brother laughed.

"Mark Jacob Langley, put your sister down." Belinda Langley's voice boomed from the kitchen.

"Yes, ma'am." Her brother was still chuckling when he set her feet back on the floor. "Saved by Mom."

Kim rolled her eyes and straightened her clothes. "Don't you have someone else to annoy?"

"Of course," Mark said. "But picking on you is so much fun."

"I thought you said you were looking to protect me," she said as she headed toward the kitchen, leaving him behind.

"I can do both," he called from behind her.

Ignoring him, she stepped into the kitchen to find her mother stirring a pot on the stove. Kim walked over and gave her a kiss on the cheek. "Happy New Year."

Her mom smiled and wrapped one arm around her daughter's waist, pulling Kim against her side. "How's my baby girl? Work going okay?"

"Work's good. Busy as always. Sorry, I'm late."

With a peck on the cheek, her mom released her. "I know you work hard. I'm just glad you made it." Her mom removed the sauce she'd been stirring from the stove and poured it into a bowl. "Is Ali coming?"

Kim snatched an olive from a nearby tray and popped it into her mouth. "Something came up with her mom, so she can't make it."

"That's too bad. Her mom needs to find a nice man to settle down with instead of chasing these bad boys."

Kim didn't say anything because she knew what was coming next.

Sure enough, with barely a pause, her mother continued. "Speaking of men, do you have a new fella in your life these days?"

To give herself a minute, she ate another olive, taking time to suck the pimiento out of the center before devouring the rest of the olive. She was about to answer her mother when her brother and Justin strolled into the room. They were both smiling from ear to ear, laughing at some joke, no doubt.

Justin's gaze zeroed in on her and her heart rate kicked up. The juicy olive lost all its flavor as she stared into Justin's vivid green eyes. He only held her gaze for a few seconds, but it was enough to raise her body temperature and have her clenching her thighs together. The memory of those eyes staring back at her in a much more intimate moment had her wishing for things that would never be.

Completely oblivious of the tension in the room, her brother removed two beers from the refrigerator, handing one to Justin, and before she knew it, they were gone.

"Are you okay, honey?" her mom asked, reaching up to check her forehead to see if she had a temperature. "You look flushed."

Kim gave her mom what she hoped was a reassuring smile. "Yeah, I'm fine. Did you need me to carry anything into the dining room?"

Her mom frowned but let it go. "If you could carry these two trays in, that would be wonderful."

Without giving her mom a chance to say anything else, Kim picked up the trays and headed into the formal dining room where all the food would be arranged buffet style for their guests. She breathed a sigh of relief when there was no sign of Justin or her brother. Kim knew she wouldn't be able to avoid him forever, but she was going to try and delay the inevitable.

⁂

JUSTIN STOOD IN THE LANGLEY'S DEN WITH MARK, MARK'S DAD, DAVIS, and two of their neighbors. Music played in the background as they chatted about who they thought would make it to the Super Bowl this year. Justin liked sports, but it wasn't something he obsessed about. He'd much rather talk about cars.

Unfortunately, not even that would have been able to keep his attention tonight. His mind was still upstairs in the kitchen with Kim. She'd been sucking on an olive when he'd walked into the room and the only thing he could think of was what it would feel like to have those lips wrapped around his cock.

He stifled a groan and tried to pay more attention to the conversation happening right in front of him. Kim was thirty-two years old. Hardly a child. And sexy as hell. But that didn't change the fact that the man standing beside him, his best friend of seventeen years, was her older brother. Her very protective older brother.

The group laughed and Justin realized he'd missed something. He smiled and chuckled, trying not to draw attention to himself. He'd thought it worked until Davis excused himself to go check on his wife and their little group broke up, leaving him and Mark by themselves.

"Car or woman?" Mark asked before taking a swig of his beer.

It took a moment for it to register what his friend was asking. Justin's brain was too muddled with thoughts of Kim. Thoughts he shouldn't be thinking with her brother standing right in front of him.

"Car," Justin said, forcing his mind away from the woman he'd spent way too much time thinking about lately. "A 1970 Road Runner to be exact."

Mark released a slow whistle. "Nice."

"It needs a lot of work, but it's gonna be sweet once I get finished with it." All that was true, but he hadn't thought about the car all day. He'd known Kim would be at the party and, as much as he shouldn't, he wanted to see her.

"Man, I envy you. I wish I had your talent for cars."

"Hey, I tried to get you to take shop with me in high school, but you wanted to go the college route." Justin took a sip of his beer and waited for what he knew was coming.

"And pass up the college girls? Nah."

Justin laughed and shook his head. Mark had gone to college for a traditional four-year degree, while Justin spent that same time at a local garage doing tune-ups and oil changes. His best friend liked to think going to college somehow granted him some magic with females, especially now that he had a good job and made a decent living. In reality, Justin's sex life saw a lot more action than Mark's, but it wasn't something Justin discussed often with his friend. At least, not in recent years. Their sexual tastes had veered off in very different directions. Mark tended to stick to what people in the lifestyle liked to call vanilla sex, whereas Justin preferred a little more...variety.

Before the two could continue that line of conversation, Davis bounded down the stairs and announced that the food was ready. Everyone stopped what they were doing and made a beeline for the stairs as if none of them had eaten for days. Justin included. Belinda Langley was an amazing cook and she went all out for her annual New Year's Eve party. Justin could hold his own in the kitchen, but on his best day, he didn't hold a candle to Belinda.

There wasn't a horizontal surface in the formal dining room that didn't have some type of food or drink on it. She had everything from typical party meats and cheeses to more elaborate options like roast with the most delicious sauce known to man. His mouth watered thinking about it.

As he filled his plate, he was keenly aware of where Kim was in the room. Justin told himself it was so he could make sure he was keeping his distance, but that wasn't entirely true. He was honest enough with himself to admit that. Not that it mattered. She was off-limits and always would be. No matter how difficult it was, he was going to have to forget about their night together. It wasn't going to happen again. Hell, it shouldn't have happened in the first place.

To remove the temptation, he headed back downstairs once he'd gotten his food. Most people remained in the dining room, keeping close to the food, talking while they ate. Normally, he'd be right there with them, but he couldn't this year. He should have known he'd want more after he'd gotten a taste of her.

It was bad enough that she'd joined Serpent's Kiss. The one place where he could relax and indulge. With her there, it was becoming a place of torment.

The thing was, he couldn't even be upset about it. She was a submissive...at least in the bedroom...and she deserved the opportunity to explore her newfound sexuality. She deserved to find a Dom who could give her what she needed. It wasn't her fault that every time a Dom looked her way, Justin wanted to land a solid punch to the guy's face.

Justin was sitting near the fireplace, his plate almost empty, when Mark found him. "There you are. I was wondering where you'd disappeared to." He plopped down on the chair beside Justin. "I thought maybe you'd sweet-talked Jackie into giving you a pre-New Year's blow job and snuck off to my old bedroom."

Mark thought he was being funny. Jackie had been trying to get Justin's attention since she and her family moved into the neighborhood ten years ago. Justin was twenty-four at the time. She was seventeen. He hadn't been interested then and he wasn't now. That didn't stop her from flirting with him every chance she got. "Nope," Justin said. "She's all yours."

His friend chuckled and took another drink of his beer. Justin had no idea how many that was for Mark, but Justin could already tell his friend was getting tipsy.

To keep the subject from continuing down the path of women and sex, Justin changed the topic. "You should swing by sometime and see the Road Runner. I should have it down to barebones in a few weeks. Maybe you could get your hands dirty for once."

"I don't know," Mark said. "Women seem to like my baby soft hands. Don't want to mar their skin with any rough calluses."

Justin snorted. "I've never had any complaints."

"Well, of course you don't. The women you're with like that sort of thing."

A retort was on the tip of Justin's tongue, but he bit it back. He'd been trying to avoid talking about women and sex. How did they end up right back on the same subject again?

Oh yeah. Mark. When he was drinking, it was hard to get him to talk about anything else.

Justin stood. "I'm gonna grab a cold one from the fridge. You want another?" It wasn't like his friend was driving tonight.

Mark drained his current bottle and handed it to Justin. "Sure."

At the top of the stairs, Justin tossed his and Mark's beer bottles into the trash can. Instead of heading straight for the kitchen, Justin changed direction and walked down the hall toward the bathroom. Sounds of laughter and talking filled the house, and it was almost a relief to duck into the bathroom and shut the door.

Normally, he was a social person. He enjoyed hanging out with friends. But he was swiftly learning that anything that involved Kim became a struggle in restraint. As a Dom, he was used to drawing things out...delaying gratification...but this was more than that. There wouldn't be a reward at the end for his patience. He wouldn't be able to lose himself in the release of all that built-up tension.

Closing his eyes, Justin willed his feelings away—the ones that had him longing for more with the one woman on the planet he couldn't have.

It didn't work.

The image of Kim tucked into him as he drove into her from behind had his cock hardening despite his need to piss. A low moan left his throat as he forced his eyes open and focused on the one thing that would kill his erection faster than anything. Mark. And the betrayal his friend would feel if he ever found out that Justin fucked his sister.

It worked. At least, enough that he could relieve himself.

Zipping up his jeans, Justin flushed the toilet and washed his hands before reaching for the doorknob. He pulled the door open and took a step forward without looking where he was going...and came face-to-face with the one woman he'd been trying to avoid.

Chapter Eight

Kim's heart felt as if it were going to pound out of her chest. She hadn't realized Justin had come upstairs. He'd disappeared downstairs as soon as he'd filled his plate with food over an hour ago and she hadn't seen him since. After her brother headed down as well, she thought she could breathe a sigh of relief. Apparently, she'd been wrong. Now she was standing in the hallway outside the bathroom with less than two feet between them.

Their gazes met for a long moment before he stepped out into the hallway. His broad shoulders seemed to take up too much space and her body reacted to the proximity. He was wearing one of those long-sleeved T-shirts that molded to every one of his muscles.

His gaze dipped down to linger on her mouth and her lips began to tingle at the memory of him kissing her. When he looked at her again, there was a heat in his eyes that told her he was remembering, too.

The air around them felt charged as they stood staring at each other. She wanted to touch him, but that was dangerous. Anyone could see them...especially her brother...and she didn't want to cause a rift between Mark and Justin. Mark wasn't exactly known for being accepting of Kim's boyfriends.

Not that Justin was her boyfriend. They'd had one night together. A night she'd begged him to give her, to show her what it would be like to submit to a Dom. He'd given her that. He'd opened her up to the world of Dominance and submission and made her realize what she'd been missing in her past relationships.

Justin cleared his throat. "Bathroom's all yours."

Kim swallowed. "Thanks."

Neither of them moved.

She had no idea how long they stood there. Eventually, their bubble burst when her brother's voice filled the hallway less than five feet from them. "There you are," he said, his words slurred. "I thought you were bringing me another beer."

Justin shoved his hands in his pockets and turned to face Mark. "Had to take a leak."

Kim watched as Justin and Mark turned and walked away, leaving her standing in the hallway alone. Justin didn't look back. Not that she'd expected him to. They weren't a couple. It was just sex. She was going to have to figure out a way to forget about it.

There were plenty of fish in the sea, right? She could find another Dom who made her feel like Justin did. One who sent her heart racing with one heated look. She just had to keep looking.

Even as she tried to convince herself, she feared it wasn't true. She'd been a member of the club for almost three months now and the closest she'd come to feeling anything like what Justin sparked inside her was when she'd watched a scene between one of the female dominants, Beth, and her submissive, Drew. It was as if Kim could feel the connection between them...feel the pull they had toward one another.

Kim finished up in the bathroom, then ducked into her old room. She needed a minute...or two.

Her old room hadn't changed much since she'd moved out. Her bed was still there and so were some of her old posters. The only addition were some boxes stacked by the closet.

Kicking off her shoes, Kim climbed onto her bed and closed her eyes, trying to focus her breathing like her yoga instructor was always telling her to. Slow breath in. Slow breath out. Slow breath in...

Five minutes later and she didn't feel any better, so she did the only other thing she could think of. She called Ali.

Her friend didn't bother with a standard greeting. "What happened?"

"Hello to you, too."

"Hi," Ali said. "And you didn't answer my question. What happened? Did you and Justin end up having crazy monkey sex on your old bed?"

Kim snorted. "No, we didn't have crazy monkey sex."

"Plain old vanilla sex, then."

Kim rolled her eyes. "No sex." At least, not tonight anyway. Ali didn't know about the night Kim and Justin had spent together. One of the few secrets Kim had ever kept from her best friend.

"Bummer." Ali sounded disappointed.

Deciding it was a good time to change the subject, Kim directed the conversation to less dangerous territory. "How's your mom doing?"

"She drank two bottles of wine and passed out on the couch." Ali sighed. "Not exactly the fun-filled New Year's celebration I'd been hoping for."

"Sorry."

"It's okay. I'm used to it."

Unfortunately, Kim knew that was true. "So does that mean she's crashing at your place until she finds the next guy?"

"Probably. It's not like she has anywhere else to go."

Ali's mom didn't have friends she could turn to because she tended to burn any friendships she developed at the whim of whatever guy she was dating. On the flip side, Ali was overly cautious when it came to relationships. Kim and Ali had been friends since their freshman year of college and Kim could count on one hand the number of guys Ali had dated in that time.

The two talked until a knock on her bedroom door brought Kim's attention away from the phone. It was her mom. "Everyone's gathering downstairs for the countdown."

Kim glanced at the clock. Sure enough, it was almost midnight. "Thanks," she said to her mom as she began scooting off the bed.

"I'll let you go," Ali said.

"I'll call you tomorrow."

"Happy New Year."

"Happy New Year."

Kim disconnected the call and tucked the phone into her pocket. The call had worked. She was feeling more like herself again.

By the time she made it downstairs, everyone was facing the television, watching the host as the clock counted down the last seconds of the year. Her dad came up beside her and handed her a glass of champagne as everyone in the room joined in with the countdown.

Ten...nine...eight...seven...six...five...four...three...two...one!

Fireworks filled the skyline on the big screen television as everyone screamed Happy New Year before taking a drink of their champagne.

"Happy New Year, sweetheart." Her dad placed a kiss on her cheek.

"Happy New Year, Dad."

The room joined in as the host led everyone in Auld Lang Syne. By this point in the night, almost everyone was tipsy. People were signing at the top of their lungs, hugging and kissing each other to celebrate the start of a new year.

Several people pulled her into their embrace and most kissed her on the cheek before moving on to the next person. The atmosphere was full of joy and hope.

She saw her mom and went to go wish her a Happy New Year, but before she could get across the room, someone bumped into her. The man turned around, brushing his arm against her breasts. With the way her body reacted, she knew who it was before their eyes met.

It was the hallway all over again. Time seemed to stop as they stared at each other before someone else bumped into Justin, seeming to break whatever trance they were in. He bent down and placed a soft kiss on her cheek, the same as at least a dozen other people in the room, but unlike those other kisses, when Justin's lips touched her skin, she felt it all the way in her belly.

"Happy New Year," he whispered before turning on his heel and walking away.

Taking a deep breath, Kim forced her feet to move. She found her mom and pulled her into a tight hug, needing the comfort of her mother's embrace. "Happy New Year, Mom."

"Happy New Year, honey."

Her mom didn't say anything about the extra-long hug, of course that could have had something to do with her brother. As soon as she'd released her mom, Mark came up behind her and lifted her off the ground again. "Happy New Year, Sis."

He was talking way too loud and she could smell the beer on his breath. "Happy New Year to you, too. Now put me down."

Mark laughed but lowered her feet to the floor again.

❧

JUSTIN STOOD IN THE CORNER, WATCHING KIM, MARK, AND BELINDA. THE Langleys had been good to him. He'd lost count of how many nights he'd stayed over during the last two years of high school. And when his parents had moved out of state when he was eighteen, Davis and Belinda had gone out of their way to make sure Justin was doing all right on his own.

He and Mark had met on the first day of football practice and they'd hit it off right away. Before long, Justin was spending more time at the Langleys' than he was at his own home. He ate meals with them and even tagged along on a vacation to Florida the summer before their senior year. They treated him like family.

Mark was the brother Justin never had, but the feelings Kim evoked in Justin were anything but sisterly. She was only fourteen when they first met and shy. He'd thought she was cute, but to be honest, he'd been more focused on sports at the time. Sports and cars.

But as time went on, the way he looked at her began to change, and by her sixteenth birthday, Justin was reminding himself daily why he couldn't make a move on her. That didn't mean he didn't notice everything about her down to how her glasses would slip down to the tip of her nose while she was reading and she wouldn't notice until they were on the verge of falling off. He'd wanted to be the one to push them back up or take them off altogether so he could look into her eyes, but he'd been a good boy and kept his hands to himself.

It had been easier once Kim graduated from high school and left for college. He didn't see her as much and threw himself into achieving his own goals for the future. Sure, he saw her when she came home to visit, but she'd often bring a friend with her and it was easy enough to keep his distance.

For seventeen years, he'd been a downright saint when it came to Kim Langley. A saint until she'd shown up at his home and knelt naked on his living room floor, offering herself to him on a silver platter. He should have said no, but years of attraction and longing had convinced him to give in just once.

It had been a huge mistake. Before, he'd only imagined what it would be like to sink his cock deep inside her and hear her moan and gasp as he pumped into her sweet pussy. He'd thought that was torture enough, but he'd been wrong. His body knew what being with her felt like and it wanted more. He wanted more.

An hour later, people began to head off for the night. Many lived in the neighborhood and were able to walk home. Some called for rides as they'd drunk a little too much to get behind the wheel. Except for a few sips of champagne at midnight, Justin had stopped drinking over three hours earlier. He lived too far to walk and there was no way he was crashing at Davis and Belinda's. Having Kim sleeping under the same roof was too much of a temptation.

Justin pulled into his driveway a little before two in the morning. The street was quiet other than some dogs barking. In his twenties, he'd lived in a loft downtown and he'd loved it. He could walk to bars, restaurants, and clubs. It was great.

But he wasn't twenty anymore and his life had changed quite a bit from that of a randy twenty-year-old who was out looking to get laid. He'd learned that quality was more important and quantity when it came to sex. That's not to say he was a monk or anything, because that wasn't the case, but he was more discerning with his partners than he used to be.

Of course, thinking about his sex life brought his thoughts back to Kim. He could still feel her there. Still smell her perfume wafting in the air if he closed his eyes.

Justin needed to get over her and move on with his life, but he had no idea how. Two weeks ago, he'd taken a sub upstairs at the club to play, something he hadn't done since being with Kim. The scene went all right. He'd taken care of his sub, but there had been a disconnect for him. He couldn't get into the right headspace no matter how hard he'd tried and he knew why.

Stripping off his clothes, Justin headed into the shower. He was hoping the warm water would help to relax him and make him sleep.

The spray cascaded over his broad shoulders and down his torso. He tipped his head back into the water before reaching for the shampoo.

As he lathered his head, Justin tried to figure out what he was going to do about the one woman he couldn't have but couldn't stop thinking about. There was no easy answer he could come up with and her being at Serpent's Kiss complicated things.

The way he saw it, he had three options, and none of them were great. He could keep ignoring her as he had been, which didn't seem to be working all that well if the hard-on he'd been sporting for most of the night was any indication.

Option number two was that he could help her find a Dom. It was what she wanted. Or, at least, it was what she said she wanted.

He rolled that option around in his brain even though thinking about it made him sick to his stomach. It was a logical option. Once she belonged to another Dom, maybe his libido would get with the program and realize she was off-limits.

The third option brought back all the guilt he'd felt since that night. He could forget about his friendship with Mark—forget about all that the Langleys had done for him—and give in to what he wanted. It would be the easy solution. At least, in the short term.

Justin already knew what Mark's reaction to that option would be, but he had no idea how Davis or Belinda would feel about it. They thought of him as a son. They'd told him that many times. But that didn't mean they'd be thrilled about him dating their daughter.

Was the risk worth it?

He didn't know, and it was so hard to think around his desire to feel her in his arms again. His body knew what option it wanted.

Letting his head fall forward, he watched as the suds ran down his body into the drain before disappearing. Was he willing to flush his friendship down the drain for a woman? Not just any woman, grant you, but a woman nonetheless.

Could he break the trust of the family who'd been there for him at every turn? He was closer to Davis than he was to his own dad. Hell, it had been Davis who'd sat him down before Justin's first date with Monica Jenkins and talked to him about responsibility and being safe. All his own father had done was toss him a box of condoms and tell him not to be stupid.

And it was Belinda who'd sat with Justin for hours on the porch steps after he found out his grandmother had died.

Turning off the water, Justin reached for a towel. As much as he hated it, there was only one real option. He had to find Kim a Dom. A Dom who was worthy of her and would take care of her like she deserved. As much as the idea turned Justin's stomach, he couldn't betray Davis, Belinda, or Mark any more than he already had.

As he slipped into bed, Justin noticed a side effect of his decision. Thinking of Kim with another Dom had successfully killed his erection.

Chapter Nine

As her eyes fluttered open the next morning, it took Kim a few moments to remember where she was. She'd had every intention of driving home last night, but the last guest had lingered until almost two and by the time everything was cleaned and put away, it was pushing three-thirty. All she'd wanted to do was kick off her shoes and climb into her old bed.

Thankfully, she'd done a little more than that. Before crawling into bed the night before, she'd stripped off her work clothes and slipped on an old nightshirt she kept in the closet for the rare occasions when she slept over. Her mom always washed it for her, so it was ready to wear any time she needed it.

Thinking about Belinda Langley brought a smile to Kim's face. Her mom was the perfect balance of career woman and housewife. She'd stayed home with Mark and Kim until Kim was off to school, and then spent her days working as a mortgage loan officer up until two years ago when she retired. It was what Kim had always hoped to become. She wanted a husband, a family, and she wanted that balance in her life. The problem was she was now in her thirties and didn't even have a boyfriend.

She dressed in her work clothes from the night before and ran a brush through her hair before piling it on top of her head with a clip from her old nightstand. Seeing Justin last night had caused everything womanly in her to sit up and take notice. She'd read countless books where women found that connection with a man, but she'd yet to find it with anyone else but Justin.

There was something about him that sparked inside her every time they were in the same room.

Closing her eyes, she tried to push thoughts of Justin McKay out of her head. Dwelling on what couldn't be wouldn't do anything but make her miserable. It wasn't going to change anything.

Grabbing her jacket from the back of the chair, she followed the smell of food to the kitchen where she found her mom and brother already sitting around the table. Belinda looked as if she'd had hours of restful sleep. Her brother, on the other hand, wore wrinkled clothes and his hair was standing up all over the place. Had he even brushed it?

"Morning." Kim went straight to the coffeemaker.

"Good morning, honey. I made cinnamon rolls for everyone, or there's bread on the counter for toast."

Kim brought her coffee over to the table, sat down, and reached for one of the cinnamon rolls. She hummed as the sugar hit her tongue. "Thanks, Mom."

"You're welcome." Belinda smiled. "How did you sleep?"

"Good." And she had. It was one of the blessings of being so tired. She'd been able to fall asleep, for perhaps the first time in three months, without dreaming about Justin.

She was halfway through her cinnamon roll when the back door opened and her dad strolled inside. He looked even more chipper than her mom. How was that possible? They hadn't gone to bed any earlier than Kim and Mark had.

"You two sleepyheads are up, I see." He gave his wife a kiss on the head before making his way to the coffeemaker. He took a loud sip of the hot liquid before joining the rest of them at the table. "Do either of you have any plans this afternoon?"

"Sleep," Mark murmured. "Lots and lots of sleep." He turned to look at his dad. "How are you not dragging this morning?"

Davis chuckled. "Well, for starters, I drank water instead of beer last night. And I always get a good night's sleep when I'm next to your mother." He winked at his wife.

Mark groaned. "TMI, Dad. TMI."

Their father grinned into his coffee as he took another sip, but otherwise ignored his son's reaction. "Think you can help me move the tables and chairs back into the garage before you catch up on that sleep?"

Her brother ran a hand through his already messy hair, then stretched his arms high above his head. "Sure."

Belinda turned her attention to Kim. "Are you going to see Ali today?"

Her mom's question wasn't unexpected. Kim polished off the cinnamon roll she'd been eating and reached for another one. "I thought I'd stop by on the way home and see how she and her mom are doing. When I talked to her last night, her mom had passed out on the couch."

Kim didn't need to fill in the blanks. Ali's mother had a pattern with men and that included showing up on her daughter's doorstep, then drowning her sorrows in alcohol until she passed out. It also meant that by noon today, she'd be taking over Ali's kitchen, cooking every sweet known to man, while going on about how men are the scum of the earth. In the thirteen years Kim and Ali had known each other, it had happened at least a dozen times and the pattern never changed.

Belinda stood. "I put some leftovers aside for her last night. To help balance out the sugar."

"Thanks, Mom. I know she'll appreciate it."

One by one, Belinda removed enough food from the refrigerator to feed ten people and placed it on the counter.

Ali rarely asked for help, but Kim knew the toll it took on her every time Ali's mom showed up on her doorstep after another breakup.

After devouring two cinnamon rolls, Kim kissed her parents goodbye and drove to Ali's apartment. She desperately needed a shower and a change of clothes, but her best friend wouldn't care what she looked like.

Kim stood outside Ali's door with two grocery bags full of leftovers. She could hear lots of movement inside and knew that Zelda, Ali's mom, must already be in the kitchen. A few moments later, the door swung open, revealing a weary-looking Ali.

Stepping inside, Kim dropped the bags on the floor and pulled her friend in for a hug. She held her there for a good minute before releasing her. "That bad, huh?"

"I should be used to it."

"Who is it?" Zelda yelled from the other room.

"Kim stopped by with some food from her mom's party last night." Even though Kim hadn't told her friend what was in the bags, Ali knew Belinda would send leftovers.

"Oh, good," Zelda said, appearing in the archway between the kitchen and the living room. "I have cupcakes in the oven and I'm almost done with the no bake cookies."

"Hello, Zelda." Kim picked the bags up off the floor and headed into the kitchen to put the food away. When she'd first met Ali's mom, she'd called her

Ms. Foster out of respect, but Zelda wasn't having any of that. She insisted Kim call her by her first name.

Ali took the bags from Kim and began unloading them.

"Do you have any plans today, Kim?" Zelda asked.

"Beyond a shower and a change of clothes? Not really. I was kinda hoping to veg out on my couch and catch up on my shows."

Zelda waved her hand in the air before going back to her cookie mix. "Boring. You need to come shopping with us. We're going to have a girls' day out, right, Ali? No boys allowed."

Kim looked at Ali, but her friend was avoiding all eye contact. Ali hated shopping. Not that she didn't do it, but more that she was one of those people that if she needed something, she'd go to the store, get it, and then get out. She hated marathon shopping trips, which Kim knew was more along the lines of what Zelda had in mind.

But she also knew Ali wouldn't tell her mom no. So what was a best friend to do? "I'll need to stop by my apartment first."

"Yay! This is going to be so much fun." The look of excitement on Zelda's face was a complete contrast to the dread on Ali's. Unfortunately, there wasn't much more Kim could do until her friend stood up to her mom and Kim didn't see that happening anytime soon.

Four hours later, they were in their fifth store, Zelda combing through racks of clothes while Kim and Ali hovered around the cart that was full of clothes Ali's mom would never wear. In fact, two or three days from now, Zelda would conclude that she didn't need the new clothes and return them. This would usually come the day after Zelda had met a new man.

Something caught Zelda's eye in another aisle, leaving Ali and Kim blissfully alone for a few seconds. "Are you ready for tonight?"

Ali frowned. "No. I know *Thelma and Louise* is supposed to be a great movie about female empowerment, but just thinking about watching it again makes me want to hide."

"Maybe you could suggest another movie."

Her friend snorted. "I've tried that before. It never works. She says there's nothing that says girl power more than *Thelma and Louise*."

"Girls, you've got to see this," Zelda said from two aisles away.

Kim put an arm around her friend and squeezed. "Two more days at most."

Ali sighed. "I know. That's what I keep telling myself."

IT HAD BEEN TWO DAYS SINCE KIM HAD SEEN JUSTIN. SHE WOULD LOVE TO say she hadn't thought about him since, but the truth was that she couldn't stop thinking about him...about their encounter in the hallway.

She'd done her best to avoid him since their night together. It was a matter of self-preservation. He'd only promised her the one night and she'd eagerly accepted thinking it would be enough.

What a fool she'd been. It hadn't been enough. Not even close. And a part of her dreaded the possibility that their night together hadn't had the same effect on him.

But he didn't look unaffected when they'd come face-to-face on New Year's Eve. If anything, the opposite was true. He'd looked at her as though it was taking every effort he had not to push her up against the wall and kiss her.

Which was why she was currently standing outside his mechanic's shop dressed in a knee-length pencil skirt and a red blouse that dipped low enough to give a hint of the cleavage beneath. It wasn't the sexiest outfit she owned, but in order to get here before he closed, she'd had to come straight from work.

Taking a deep breath, she hiked her purse a little higher on her shoulder and strode inside.

Sandi, the receptionist slash office manager, looked up as Kim walked through the door. Her smile was instantaneous. Sandi had been working for Justin since he opened his shop five years ago and she knew all the Langleys well as they were frequent customers. "Kim. How have you been? It's been a while since I've seen you."

"I'm good, Sandi. Work's been crazy. What about you?" Sandi was two years older than Kim. She'd gone to school with Mark and Justin. In fact, at one time, Kim thought there might be something between Sandi and her brother, but nothing had ever come of it. At least, not that she knew about, anyway.

"The same." Sandi chuckled. "There's always something to do around here. Justin's reputation for fixing older cars has started to grow and business has been booming lately."

"That's great."

Sandi stood and walked around the desk to stand in front of Kim. "So, what brings you by today? Everything okay with your car?"

Kim shifted her weight from one foot to the other. Why was she so nervous? Oh yeah. Because she was there to talk to Justin. "Nothing major. It just needs an oil change. I was hoping maybe Justin could squeeze me in."

"Let me check," Sandi said. "Chuck and Zach were still working on a transmission last I checked, but I'll see if Justin's free."

Before Kim could say any more, Sandi disappeared through the door that led out to the shop area. The sound of a tool being used filtered through for the few seconds the door was open before it swung shut behind her. Kim was tempted to follow Sandi, but she kept her feet planted firmly on the floor. She wanted to talk to Justin, but not with an audience. If she'd played her cards right, Justin would agree to do the oil change and by the time he was finished, it would only be the two of them left in the shop. She didn't want to have this conversation with anyone else around on the off chance she'd read him wrong the other night.

A few minutes later, the door opened again. But instead of Sandi, it was Justin. He was dressed in overalls that had a patch with his name on it over his heart. There was a smudge of grease on his cheek and his hair was sticking up in several places.

His gaze raked over her from head to toe before coming back to her face. "Sandi says you're here for an oil change."

"Yes." Her response came out less confident than she wanted, so she tried again. "Yes. I was hoping you could fit me in before you close."

Justin glanced at the clock. "We close at six."

"Yes."

"It's five-forty."

She swallowed. "Yes."

"An oil change takes at least thirty minutes."

These were all things she already knew. "Does that mean you can't do it?"

He looked at her so long it took everything in her to stay still. Kim wished she could know what he was thinking, but he was giving nothing away.

"Give me your keys." Justin held out his hand and waited for her to drop them into his palm. "Take a seat. I'll come get you when I'm finished."

With that, he turned on his heels and strolled into the shop, leaving her alone.

Kim blew out a breath and sat down on the faux leather couch that had seen better days. She pulled out her phone and began scrolling through her emails. Eventually, Sandi returned to the desk and began closing everything down for the night. "I can go ahead and get you checked out."

Nodding, Kim tucked her phone back in her purse and dug out her credit card. Once all the paperwork was done, Kim returned to her place on the couch and reached for her phone again.

At six o'clock, Sandi turned off the lights on her desk, made sure the coffeemaker was ready to go for the morning, and strolled over to where Kim sat. "Did you need anything before I go? I hate leaving you here."

"No, I'm good. Enjoy your evening," Kim said with a smile.

Sandi gave one last glance into the shop before heading to the door. "It shouldn't be too much longer. Good night."

"Good night."

Kim watched as Sandi locked the door behind her, essentially securing Kim inside. Once Sandi pulled out of the parking lot, Kim watched as the other two mechanics who worked for Justin got into their vehicles and did the same. Kim and Justin were the only two left in the shop.

It was now or never. She stood, walked over to the door that led to the shop, and turned the knob.

Her car was at the far end of the room, its hood up. At first, she didn't see Justin, but then he appeared from behind a large toolbox that was as tall as him. He leaned over the front of her car, pulling the overalls tight over his ass. Her muscles clenched in appreciation.

Justin's head whipped around as soon as he heard her heels clicking on the concrete floor. His brow furrowed and his lips turned down in a frown before going back to whatever he was doing. "I told you to wait in the lobby."

"No, you told me to take a seat, which I did."

The scowl on his face didn't go away. "I also told you I'd come get you when I was done."

She ignored him. "Sandi ran my credit card already and locked everything up."

"I know." He stood to his full height, grabbed the top of the hood, and lowered it back into place. Without a word or a look in her direction, Justin strolled over to the sink and washed the grease from his hands. "What are you doing here?" he asked as he turned off the water.

No beating around the bush. Now or never, right? Why did this seem harder than showing up at his place and kneeling naked in his living room? Oh yeah, because a relationship was worlds different than one night of kinky fun.

She took a step forward, then stopped herself. "I wanted to talk to you."

He reached for a towel to dry his hands. "I wanted to talk to you as well."

That surprised her. "You did?"

"Yes. I know you joined Serpent's Kiss to explore your submissive nature. The best way to do that is to find a Dom, one you're comfortable with and can experiment with to find out what you like and don't like."

Justin unzipped his overalls and stripped them off, tossing them into a nearby bin and leaving him in jeans and a T-shirt that had her wanting to investigate the muscles beneath. She was so transfixed by his body that she almost missed what he said next.

"You need to find a good Dom and I've decided to help you."

Kim blinked. Surely, she hadn't heard him right. "What?"

He handed her the keys to her car before walking over to the far side of the room and turning off several lights. "Finding a good Dom can be difficult, especially given your strong-willed personality and the fact that you're new to the lifestyle. We need to find you someone who's willing to deal with your somewhat bratty nature."

"I'm not a brat," she said, somewhat offended. Over the last three months, she'd been learning more about the lifestyle and the terminology. Strong-willed? Yes. A brat? No. She didn't act out or object to be contrary or to get attention.

Justin gave her another long look. "No. You're right. You're not. But you're also not a trained submissive."

She took a few moments to digest what he was saying. "So you want to help find me a Dom."

"Yes," he said, lifting the bay door, then opening the driver's door of Kim's car for her, motioning for her to get inside. "I think that's the best solution."

Had she really misread the other night so wrong? And what about their night together? Had the sparks she felt only been on her side?

Lowering herself behind the wheel, she looked up at Justin. He seemed perfectly at ease with the conversation.

Before she could put words to her feelings at what he was suggesting, he continued. "We can start tomorrow. Meet me at the club around seven-thirty and we'll begin weeding through the prospects."

Chapter Ten

Justin spent the next twenty-four hours running through the available Doms at the club in his head. He'd tried to go over all the options with an open mind, attempting to keep his own feelings in check. The thought of Kim with someone else had every muscle in his body tightening and not in a good way. It was something he was going to have to get over, though. She was off-limits and always would be. Nothing was going to change that.

By the time he arrived at Serpent's Kiss on Friday night, he'd narrowed it down to three possible Doms for Kim. The first was Daniel. He was a little old for Kim, but he had a lot of experience in the lifestyle and the patience that would be needed to train a new submissive. Plus, Kim was already comfortable with him as he was friends with her friend, Ali. The second was Brandon. He acted as the lead bartender at the club, but he'd been in the lifestyle for over ten years and had an even temperament. The third option was a newer member of the club, younger than the other two. Gabe was only twenty-eight, but he carried himself well. Justin had been asked to observe Gabe's first play session two weeks ago, and despite the sub trying to push her weight around a few times, he'd handled the scene like someone who'd been playing for years.

Straightening his shoulders, Justin stepped inside the main room of the club and surveyed his surroundings. It was early. Most members didn't arrive until after seven.

Katrina caught his gaze and motioned for him to join her. Justin often helped her with new members, introducing them around, answering their questions, and making sure they understood how things worked. He was hoping that wasn't the case tonight as he was on a mission of his own.

"Good evening, Mistress Katrina." She was in her signature corset and leather pants that showed off her boobs and ass to perfection. Even though he had no interest in Katrina, that didn't mean he was blind. The woman had a body on her that would make a man drool.

Katrina smiled in greeting. "You're here early tonight."

"I managed to close up the shop a little early." While that was true, it was intentional. He'd wanted some time to get his bearings before Kim arrived.

"I see." She signaled for him to walk with her as she began making her way around the perimeter of the club's main floor. "How's Kim settling in? I haven't seen her play with anyone yet."

He hadn't expected Katrina to bring Kim up, but he shouldn't have been surprised. Kim had listed both him and Ali on her application. "We're hoping to rectify that soon. I'm going to help her find a suitable Dom."

Katrina stopped walking. She turned and gave him a hard look...one that said she wasn't liking what she was hearing.

"As a family friend, I want to make sure she finds someone who can handle her. She's new and she's quite strong-willed." The look she was giving him didn't change. "I have it narrowed down to three possibilities."

She raised one eyebrow, but still she said nothing.

He gave her the name of the three Doms he felt might be a good fit for Kim and waited to see what she'd have to say.

Instead of answering right away, Katrina began moving again. She made him wait until they were halfway up the stairs that led to the playrooms. "I don't think Daniel would be a good idea."

"You don't think he'd be willing to take on an untrained sub?" Daniel had played with inexperienced subs in the past, so Justin wasn't understanding Katrina's reasoning.

"That isn't the issue."

They were on the second floor now. He followed Katrina as she entered each of the playrooms, one by one. About an hour from now, they would be full.

"How do you think Ali would feel if Kim began playing with Daniel?" Katrina asked when they entered the fifth room. "I don't need that kind of drama at the club."

"You think Ali would have a problem with Kim being Daniel's sub?"

Katrina shook her head. "Men. You can be so clueless sometimes."

It took him a moment to understand what she was getting at. Daniel and Ali?

Justin took some time to think it over as they finished inspecting the rooms. He'd never seen them play together. Daniel did play with other subs on occasion, but that was usually because a sub would approach him, asking for a scene. The older Dom had a reputation for being a master at flogging.

Racking his brain, he tried to recall the last time Ali had gone upstairs with a Dom and he had to admit it had been a while. Granted, he wasn't keeping an eye on her all the time, but when she was at the club she was either working the front lobby or hanging out with her friends...which included Daniel.

Interesting.

"I'll mark Daniel off the list, then."

"Smart decision."

After they were finished with the rooms, they headed downstairs again and Katrina was pulled away to help with something in the women's locker room. The club was filling up fast and he knew it wouldn't be long before Kim got there. That is, if she showed up at all. It would be like her to stay home solely because he told her to meet him there.

A part of him wanted her to defy him so he could remind her she was the submissive and he was the Dominant. But then he had to remind himself that he wasn't *her* Dom. She wasn't his and he wouldn't be the one to punish her for her willful behavior. That would fall to someone else.

The thought caused his chest to tighten and the muscles in his neck to tense. He was going to have to get past these irrational feelings of possessiveness. Kim needed him as a friend. She needed his experience in the lifestyle to help her find a good Dom. One who would treat her right. One who would care for her.

Brad and his wife, Kate, saw him from across the room and began making their way over. Brad was a surgeon and often had to work late. On the nights when Kate would come alone, Justin would watch over her for Brad. Their relationship was stricter than most of the other couples that frequented the club, but it seemed to work for them.

Tonight, Kate wore a black dress that went down to her ankles, but it was anything but modest. Both sides of the skirt had slits that came all the way to her waist. And the top was almost as revealing. Cloth stretched over her ample breasts, highlighting her pierced nipples. Those two were not shy about their sexuality. Especially not while inside the club. Justin knew that because of Brad's position, they had to keep up appearances out in public.

"You're here early tonight," Justin said in way of greeting.

"No surgery today. It's rare I get a full day at the office anymore. I wanted to take advantage of it."

As they continued to talk, Brad moved his wife to stand in front of him. He slipped his hand beneath her top, plucking her nipple as the conversation moved from work to the scene Alexander and Grace, two of the club's newer members, had done a few weeks ago.

It was impossible not to be drawn to the interaction between Brad and his wife, especially as she moaned against him. But that only lasted until Kim walked through the door. Justin felt her before he saw her, drawing his attention in her direction.

The moment he saw her, he knew something was wrong. To someone who hadn't known her so well, they probably wouldn't notice, but after all these years, he knew her tells. She had her hands balled into fists at her side, a sure sign that she was upset about something.

Justin scanned the area for Ali, but he didn't see her. She was most likely working the lobby. That meant Kim was on her own tonight.

While that could be the source of Kim's tension, he didn't think so. Ali worked the front at least three times a month. This wasn't the first time Kim was on her own in the club.

His suspicions were confirmed when she noticed him staring. Her eyes narrowed and she swiftly turned on her heel and marched in the opposite direction.

Brad had noticed his distraction. "One of the new subs caught your eye?"

Justin never took his gaze off Kim. "She's my best friend's little sister."

The sound of Brad's suppressed laughter brought Justin's attention back to the other Dom. "Well, that could get interesting."

"Yeah," was all Justin said as his gaze returned to the woman in question.

An hour later, he was sitting on a barstool, watching Kim from across the room as she chatted with one of the youngest Doms at the club. The man had little to no experience and was the opposite of what she needed.

"Are you going to drink that or wear it?"

Justin McKay looked over at the bartender, Brandon, then followed Brandon's gaze to the bottle of water Justin was holding in a death grip.

Releasing the bottle, Justin turned his back on the woman he'd been watching as she leaned in to say something to the other Dom. He needed to stop. It wasn't doing anyone any good, let alone himself or his mental well-being.

"You know," Brandon said, "you could do yourself a favor and ask her to go upstairs with you. Maybe if you two released some of that sexual tension that's floating around, you wouldn't be trying to kill your water bottle."

"It's not that simple."

Brandon reached behind him and grabbed Justin a beer he hadn't asked for. He wasn't playing tonight, so having a drink wouldn't matter. Not that it would anyway as the club had strict rules on alcohol consumption whether you were playing or not.

"Thanks," Justin said when Brandon set the open beer bottle in front of him. He took a swig and let the cool liquid slide down his throat.

Someone signaled for Brandon and he walked to the other end of the bar to see what they needed. Justin was so fucked.

He tried not to watch the exchange between Kim and the other Dom, but it was impossible. It was as if she were a beacon he couldn't look away from. His gaze was drawn to her tongue as she took a drink, then licked her lips. The memory of her tongue sliding against his in a sensual dance of give and take as he'd thrust into her had his cock straining against his pants.

He couldn't take his gaze away from Kim and deep down he knew it wasn't because the Dom she was talking to was young and inexperienced. What the hell was he going to do?

Finishing his beer, Justin continued to watch the exchange and forced himself to remain firmly planted in his seat. Every time the other Dom's fingers brushed her hand, the beer Justin drank churned sour in his gut. Kim didn't pull away or send the man packing when he ran a single finger down her arm, and for a moment, Justin thought that was it. That was the night when she was going to say yes to one of the Doms at the club, maybe just to spite him, and there wasn't a damn thing he could do about it.

Squeezing his eyes shut, he tried to remember all the reasons why he couldn't...shouldn't intervene. Why, despite the other Dom being young and inexperienced, Kim finally accepting and exploring her submissive nature was a good thing.

"Looks like you dodged another bullet," Brandon said as he wiped down the bar a couple of feet away.

"What?"

Brandon nodded for Justin to look behind him.

Justin turned to see Kim rejoining her group of friends, the other Dom moving on to another unattached sub. His shoulders sagged in relief.

Brandon shook his head. "What are you going to do when she takes one of them up on their offer to play? You know Mistress Katrina isn't going to be happy if you punch one of the other Doms for laying a hand on a girl you haven't claimed."

He wasn't wrong.

Maybe Justin should stop coming to the club for a while.

But even as that thought formed in his head, he knew he couldn't...wouldn't do that. What if something happened and she needed him?

Then...what if something happened and she didn't? In theory, helping her find a Dom was the right thing to do. It was logical. But what he was feeling at that moment wasn't logical. He wasn't even sure it was sane.

Brandon rested his elbows on the bar. It was the middle of January and the club wasn't as busy as it usually was. Normally, Brandon wouldn't have time to question him, but as luck would have it, no one was currently in need of his services.

"I'm not going to punch anyone," Justin said.

The bartender raised an eyebrow. The look of doubt clear on his face.

"I haven't punched any of them yet," Justin mumbled and downed the rest of his water.

"Yet being the operative word in that sentence." Brandon stepped away for a second to hand one of the other Doms a bottle of water for their sub, then returned to stand in front of Justin. Brandon looked him over and sighed. "If you're not gonna play with Kim, then how about one of the other subs? Bridget's here tonight."

Bridget was one of the submissives Justin regularly played with. Or had been before Kim joined the club.

Justin snorted. He'd attempted to play with one sub since that night he'd spent with Kim, and it had been lacking, to say the least. It was pathetic and even he knew it. He couldn't remain celibate for the rest of his life.

As rational as Brandon's advice was, the thought of playing with Bridget or anyone else held no appeal for him. He really was screwed.

"I'll take another," Justin said, lifting the empty beer bottle in front of him. It would be his last given the club rules. Mistress Katrina didn't bend the rules for anyone.

"You know," Brandon said, "if all you're going to do is drink beer, you could do that at a regular bar. Or at home." He paused. "Of course, at home the view isn't quite as nice."

Kim was making her way to the dance floor with Lady Beth. Justin watched as Kim swayed her hips to the music, making his fingers itch to touch her. By the time they stopped dancing, he'd finished his beer and had switched back to water.

Kim headed to the bathroom, but before she went inside, she glanced toward the bar. Her gaze met his and he felt that spark all over again. The smile that had been gracing her face for the last half hour disappeared. Their gazes locked for a long moment, then her attention was pulled away when someone exited the bathroom. Justin's chest clinched as he watched her walk away. He had to do something.

Before he knew what he was doing, Justin slid off the barstool and made a beeline for the bathrooms. He took up a position right outside, waiting for Kim to come out.

Justin got several curious glances as he stood, not so patiently, against the wall. He wasn't even sure what he was doing. All he knew was that he needed to talk to her.

Her eyes went wide the moment she saw him hovering outside the bathroom entrance. Then he saw her stubbornness kick in. She straightened her shoulders and closed the distance between them.

The crazy thing was, he had no idea what he was going to say. Waiting for her to come out had been impulsive, which wasn't like him at all. He'd learned long ago that it was much better to go into things with a plan.

"Dance with me." He didn't know where that had come from, but now that it was out there, he was craving the opportunity to get his hands on her.

"I don't think that's a good idea."

"Why's that?" he asked.

She pressed her lips together like she did when she was trying not to lose her temper. For some reason, that excited him more. It was an irrational reaction, but that seemed to be the norm for him when it came to Kim.

"Aren't you worried that might give the other Doms the wrong impression?"

He took a step toward her without thinking about it. "What do you mean?"

Kim lifted her chin, not backing down despite their closeness. "I'm supposed to be finding a Dom, aren't I? If they see me dancing with you, they might think we're a couple, and we wouldn't want that, would we?"

A shot of jealously surged through him and he took another step forward, bringing her close enough to touch. He saw the muscles in her throat contract as she swallowed, and her chest rose and fell more rapidly at his proximity. She was as affected by him as he was by her, which was the problem. "Dance with me."

This time when he said it, the words were barely above a whisper. It wasn't a demand, but a plea.

Justin held his breath until she nodded, giving him the permission he was seeking. He wasted no time taking her hand and leading her onto the dance floor. Pulling her into his arms, he closed his eyes and savored the feel of her body against him. She wrapped her arms around his neck and moved with him to the slow beat pulsing out of the speakers. Mark was going to kill him.

Chapter Eleven

Kim would like to say it was the music that was responsible for the warmth radiating through her body as she danced with Justin, but that would be a lie. When he'd pulled her into his arms, she'd wanted to get as close to him as possible. Every womanly cell in her body was calling out to her, ready and willing to be close to him again, to feel that connection. Her fingers itched to play with the hair at the base of his neck, but she resisted. Barely.

While her body was ready, willing, and able, she was still upset. She'd gone to his shop wanting to talk to him about what had happened on New Year's Eve. To confirm that what she was feeling wasn't one-sided. But instead, he'd announced he'd be helping her to find a Dom.

She was still mad at herself for not saying anything then, but his suggestion had completely thrown her off guard. It wasn't until she was halfway home that the anger started boiling up inside her.

Kim had almost turned around and driven back to the shop to confront him, but she'd thought better of it. She had a temper. She knew that. And over the years, she'd gotten better at controlling it. Even still, as the night wore on, she'd decided that if he didn't want her, then she would take matters into her own hands. She didn't need his help. She'd find her own Dom.

While she'd spoken to several Dominants at the club since she'd joined, she hadn't taken any of their advances seriously. Not even the ones who'd asked if she'd like to go upstairs and play. She hadn't been interested.

When she'd arrived at the club tonight, she'd made a point of seeking out one of the Doms who'd been especially attentive to her recently. He was nice enough. Younger than her, but did that really matter? Age didn't necessarily dictate whether a person was a good Dominant or not.

But the entire time she'd been talking to Kurt, she could feel Justin's gaze on her. She knew he was watching, and it made it difficult to focus on what Kurt was saying. Eventually, she found an excuse to end the conversation and rejoin Ali's friends.

They didn't quite feel like her friends yet, even though they had welcomed her into their group. She was still trying to get used to all the different dynamics and how the lifestyle worked.

Outside of Ali, the one she felt most comfortable with, was Lady Beth. She wasn't sure why, but there was something about her that put Kim at ease. So when Beth had asked her if she wanted to join her on the dance floor, Kim had jumped at the chance. She needed to get out of her own head and thought maybe if she wasn't talking to another man, Justin would find someone, or something, else to focus on.

That didn't happen. She'd tried not to look in his direction as she danced next to Beth, to ignore him, but it was impossible. Kim could feel him watching her.

What she hadn't anticipated was that when she came out of the bathroom, he'd be there waiting for her. Her plan had been to avoid him, but all that went out the window when she saw him standing there.

"I'm mad at you," she said.

He opened his eyes but didn't meet her gaze. "I know."

When he didn't continue, she figured she'd have to be the one to say something. "Do you think I'm that incapable that I can't find a Dom on my own? I know I'm new here, but Ali's been helping me, and—"

"It's not that." His hands flexed on her hips and the muscles in his jaw tightened.

"What then?"

It took him a few moments to answer. "I thought that maybe if you found a Dom, belonged to someone else, this thing between us would somehow go away."

So she wasn't imagining it. He was feeling it, too.

"That was really stupid."

Justin tugged her closer, bringing their lower halves together. She could feel the hard length of him against her stomach. "Stupid doesn't begin to cover it."

Kim didn't think he was talking about his asinine suggestion of helping her find a Dom anymore. She decided to take a leap of faith and put it out there. "I want you to be my Dom."

He pinched his eyes closed again and leaned forward to rest his forehead on hers. She could feel the tension radiating off him.

Kim knew what was going through his head. "Mark doesn't have to know."

Justin's eyes popped open.

"No one outside the club has to know."

He lifted his right hand and cupped her jaw. His touch was firm, possessive. She loved it.

"You're not going to be my dirty little secret. I won't hide you away like I'm ashamed of you."

She thought he'd be pleased with her suggestion to keep their relationship hidden, but he seemed offended by the notion. Still, she wasn't ready to let go of her suggestion. "Not forever. And I know you're not ashamed of me. But maybe this thing with us will fizzle out if we stop trying to put the brakes on. Is it really worth upsetting Mark if we're not going to last?"

Justin tilted her face up, bringing them nose to nose. "I've wanted you for seventeen years. The only thing getting a taste of you has done is make me want you more."

Her chest clenched at his declaration. She licked her lips and swallowed. Her heart felt as if it were going to pound out of her body. He'd wanted her for seventeen years? "Why didn't you say anything seventeen years ago?"

"You know why."

His gaze was on her lips now and she knew he wanted to kiss her. She wanted that, too. She wanted to lose herself in the only man who'd ever made her feel this way. "I used to lie in bed after football games and think of you in those tight pants while I touched myself."

Justin groaned. She couldn't tell if it was a good groan, or if he was upset by her confession. "When?" he choked out.

"The first time?"

He nodded.

"It was the first game of your senior year. I was wiggling in my seat the entire evening. Mom scolded me because I wouldn't sit still." Kim slid her fingers up into his hair, bringing their bodies more in line. Normally, even at a dance club, being this entwined with a guy on the dance floor would have her self-conscious. But they were at Serpent's Kiss, and what they were doing was considered tame given they both still had all their clothes on. "As soon as we got home, I shut myself in my room and...relieved the tension."

His left hand, which had been on her hip, moved lower to cup her ass. "Why does that make me horny as hell?"

Normally, she'd laugh, but the vibe pulsing through the air was thick with suppressed sexual tension. "Did you ever..."

He knew what she was asking. "Frequently."

The song they were dancing to changed, and the pulse of it beat in her veins. Justin adjusted their bodies, positioning his leg between hers. His thigh was against the heart of her need and instinctively, she pressed herself against him.

A smirk formed on his lips, and she realized he'd done it on purpose. For some reason, that only made her hotter.

The hand that was gripping her ass ground her against him with the rhythm pounding out of the speakers. It was hypnotic and sensual. Kim felt her arousal building. She was dry humping him right there on the dance floor in front of everyone and she didn't care.

She closed her eyes, letting the sensations build. He knew what he was doing and she felt his breath on her lips as she inched closer to that elusive peak.

"Are you going to come for me?"

Her breath hitched and she nodded.

His thumb grazed the side of her neck. "Open your eyes and look at me. I want to look into your eyes as you come."

Kim did as he asked and met his heated gaze. She knew he was as turned on as she was. His erection was pressing hard against her belly, only adding to the fire burning inside her. She'd never been one for exhibitionism, but in that moment if he'd asked her to drop to her knees and suck him off, she would have done it in a heartbeat.

All thought left her as he placed both of his hands on her hips and used all his efforts to grind her against his leg. "Come for me, baby," he whispered in her ear.

His words seemed to have a direct connection to her clit. She tightened her hold on him. She was so close. All she needed was a little more...

Justin gripped her ass again, this time with both hands, and began moving her with a purpose. There was no hiding what they were doing, but that didn't matter. The only thing that mattered was what she was feeling in that moment.

Her orgasm hit her fast and hard. A squeak left her lips before she could contain it. She buried her head in Justin's chest as her body trembled with her release.

As her heart rate returned to normal, their surroundings came into focus. She glanced over at some of the people nearby and knew that what they'd done hadn't been missed. Embarrassment trumped her orgasmic high and she tried to step away.

Justin held firm. "Where do you think you're going?"

She couldn't look at him. "I can't believe I did that."

Her words were mumbled into his chest, but she knew he'd heard her.

He chuckled.

"It's not funny."

That only made his chest vibrate more. "No one cares that you dry humped me on the dance floor. Did you forget where we are?"

"No." She hadn't forgotten where they were, but that didn't change the fact that she'd never done anything like that in public before.

When she didn't say anything else, he tilted her chin up so he could see her face. "There's no need to be embarrassed."

"I know, but..."

They'd stopped dancing. "But?"

Silence fell between them as she thought about what she was feeling. In the moment, she hadn't cared. Wanted more, in fact. But now her levelheaded nature was kicking in.

Justin dropped his hand. "Have you changed your mind about me being your Dom?"

Despite her embarrassment over what they'd just done, that hadn't changed. She wanted him. The night they'd spent together had altered something in her. And not only the realization that she was submissive. She felt a connection with Justin that she'd felt with no other man.

At first, she'd thought it was because he was a Dominant. The way he'd taken control that night had set her body on fire. She'd convinced herself she could feel that with another Dom, but after months of interacting with other Doms, she learned that wasn't the case. She didn't just want a Dom. She wanted the one standing in front of her. "No. I haven't changed my mind."

Justin didn't answer right away and she hadn't missed that his left hand was still firmly on her ass. He didn't seem inclined to remove it anytime soon. "Is Ali's mom still living with her?"

She hadn't been expecting the drastic subject change. "As far as I know, but I haven't spoken to her today."

He nodded, and to her dismay, he took a step back, separating them. Before she could ask what he was doing, Justin took her hand and led her off the dance floor.

Kim followed. Not that he gave her much choice.

Stopping a few feet away, he released her. "Katrina can print out a limits sheet for you to fill out. I believe Ali is in the lobby tonight. I'm sure she can help you if you have any questions." The tone of his voice had become more serious, his demeanor more businesslike.

"Okay."

"Are you free tomorrow morning?" he asked.

Again, she was somewhat thrown by his question. "I think so."

He raised a single eyebrow.

Why did such a simple gesture from him make her want to squirm? "Yes. I'll be free."

Justin nodded. "Be at my house at ten. I'll make us brunch and we can discuss our lists."

"Can't we just play like we did before?" she asked.

"No." He ran his index finger along her jaw. His touch had the muscles in her stomach tightening again. "Before it was about you. Giving you a taste of submission."

"And now?" Her question came out in not much more than a whisper.

"We will be testing your limits. Exploring. There will also be expectations. For both of us. It's best to be on the same page before we begin."

She was happy to hear he wasn't fighting this thing between them any longer.

Justin brushed his hand down her arm as he stepped closer, invading her space once more. "I'll give it one month."

She blinked, not understanding what he was talking about. One month?

Her confusion must have been clear on her face. "If after a month we both decide we want to continue, then we'll sit down with Mark and your parents."

Kim swallowed, her nerves returning, but she nodded. This was what she wanted. Them. Together. She met his gaze. "Yes, Sir."

He lowered his head, covering her mouth with his.

The kiss was chaste. Especially after what they'd done on the dance floor. But still, her body reacted. She wanted more. She always wanted more with him.

But before she could do more than release a quiet moan, he ended it. "Get the form from Mistress Katrina. Fill it out. Talk to Ali." Justin lifted her hand to his lips, turned it over, and kissed her palm, sending a spark of heat up her arm. "I'll see you tomorrow at ten and we'll go over everything."

He didn't give her a chance to comment before he strolled over to the bar, returning to the seat he'd occupied most of the night before their dance.

Kim blew out a breath, trying to regain her bearings. Justin always made her feel off-kilter but centered at the same time. It was a strange feeling.

"Everything all right?"

The worried look on Daniel's face pulled her attention from Justin. "Yes. I'm fine."

"You're sure? You appear worried about something." The older Dom's concern touched her.

She decided to be honest. "I am. A little. I need to get a limits list from Mistress Katrina."

"Ah." The side of Daniel's mouth quirked up into a half smile. "I was wondering when you two would stop tiptoeing around each other."

"You knew?" She and Justin had barely spoken since she'd joined Serpent's Kiss.

"For those who were paying attention, it was hard to miss."

Kim wasn't sure how she felt about that.

"But if you're looking for Katrina, she's over there." He pointed to the far side of the room.

Sure enough, Mistress Katrina was talking to a couple she'd seen several times before at the club. "Thanks."

Daniel chuckled. "Don't be nervous. We were all new at one point."

He was right. And it wasn't like Justin didn't know her.

Kim shot him a grateful smile and made her way over to Mistress Katrina. She hung back, waiting for the conversation to wrap up.

When the couple walked away, Katrina turned her attention to Kim. "How can I help you this evening?"

For some reason, the woman was intimidating, but Kim stood her ground. She could do this. She dealt with intimidating people all the time at work. "I need a limits list."

Katrina nodded, not seeming to be bothered that Kim's request hadn't been filled with confidence. "Follow me to my office."

The club owner didn't wait for Kim to agree. She turned on her heel and expected Kim to follow.

They made their way down a hallway off the main room to Katrina's office. Kim had been there once before, and it still felt as imposing as it had that first time.

A large wooden desk that sat in the center of the room dominated the office. There were no windows, and on the one wall hung a variety of whips, floggers, and other implements. The first time she'd been in the room, she'd been so nervous she hadn't paid much attention, but outside the items hanging on the wall, the room could have been any office in countless buildings across the city.

"Here you are," Katrina removed several papers from the printer and handed them to Kim.

"Thank you."

Katrina grinned. "I know you have Ali, but if you need help, or have any questions, let me know."

"Thank you, again, Mistress Katrina."

With the papers in hand, Kim left Katrina's office and headed back to the main floor of the club. Almost immediately, she spotted Justin at the bar talking to Brandon. She thought about going to him but changed her mind. He'd told her to fill out her list and come to his place tomorrow morning. If she was going to be his submissive, then that meant learning to follow instructions. That wasn't going to be easy for her, but this she could do. Clutching the papers to her chest, she exited the club and found her friend sitting behind the coat check reading a book.

Ali's face lit up when she saw Kim, but then she must have seen how anxious Kim was and her excitement dimmed. "What's wrong?"

Kim shook her head. "Nothing's wrong. I-I need your help with something."

"Did something happen?"

Instead of answering her friend's question, Kim handed over the paperwork.

Ali's happy expression returned the moment she realized what Kim had given her. She knew what it meant. Her friend had been a member of the club for a few years. A limit list wasn't required if people wanted to do a scene together. That could be negotiated before the scene began. The limit list, however, was for those who wanted to enter a longer-term arrangement.

Before Ali could start asking questions, Kim decided to get it all out in the open. "And I need to tell you something else."

Her friend's delighted expression wavered. "You can tell me anything. You know that."

Kim knew that and keeping this secret from her best friend had been eating at her.

She took a deep breath and went for it. "I slept with Justin."

Chapter Twelve

Ali's eyes looked as if they were going to pop out of her head, then she jumped off her chair and engulfed Kim in a tight embrace. Kim wasn't sure what kind of reaction she'd get from her friend, but she'd been unprepared to be squeezed to within an inch of her life.

Eventually, Ali released her. She pulled another chair from the closet and placed it a foot from the one she'd been occupying before Kim's announcement. "Okay, tell me everything. Did you two go upstairs tonight?"

Kim shook her head, and then lowered herself into the offered chair. Taking a deep breath, she prepared to spill her guts. "Do you remember the first time I came to Serpent's Kiss with you?"

"Of course. You were so nervous, I wasn't sure if I was going to be able to get you through the door."

"Well..." Kim hesitated, knowing what she would say next was going to hurt. Not because Ali would be upset she slept with Justin, obviously, but because Kim didn't tell her right after it happened. "I saw Justin here that night and figured if I wanted to explore my submissive side, he'd be the perfect one to do it with." Kim didn't look at her friend, afraid that if she did, she wouldn't get through this next part. "So, I showed up at his house the next day and..." She paused. "Offered myself to him."

Her confession was met with silence.

Kim peeked at her friend. She had a look on her face Kim didn't know how to interpret. "I'm sorry I didn't say anything earlier, but it was supposed to be a one-time thing. An experiment."

Again, nothing.

"Well?" Kim prompted. The silence was killing her.

"It explains a lot," Ali said. Then she sighed. "I can't believe you didn't tell me."

"I know. I'm sorry." Kim paused. "And what do you mean it explains a lot?"

Ali shrugged. "I don't know how to explain it. You've just seemed a little distant." She frowned. "Now I know why."

"I'm sorry."

Waving her off, Ali squared her shoulders. "It's okay. It's not like I've never kept anything from you. I mean, I was a member here for over two years before you found my toy bag in the closet."

"Still. It's not the same. I understand why you didn't tell me about this. To be honest, I'm not sure if I would have been ready to know sooner." Kim took hold of Ali's hands. "You've known about my crush for years, almost since the beginning of our friendship. This was a big deal, and I should have told you."

A tiny smile tugged at Ali's lips and the vise around Kim's chest eased. "But you've told me now, and you need my help."

Kim smiled back and nodded. "I do. He wants me to fill out this limit list. I'm supposed to bring it to his house tomorrow so we can go over it."

Grabbing a pen from the desk in front of her, Ali placed the papers on the flat surface and handed the pen to Kim. "We'd better get started then."

JUSTIN LINGERED AT THE BAR FOR THE REST OF THE NIGHT, EVEN THOUGH IT meant giving Brandon the opportunity to razz him about finally getting his head out of his ass. He didn't explain to Brandon this was only a trial run. A month to see if they worked as a couple.

He still wasn't crazy about the idea, but he understood where Kim was coming from. And to be honest, he wasn't looking forward to Mark's reaction. His best friend was as vanilla as they came. Mark didn't understand Justin's need to dominate. Once he'd commented how he felt sorry for the women Justin dated, that Justin insisted they perform like trained animals.

Justin had let the comment slide. Mark had been drunk at the time and he had no filter when he was like that.

But Justin knew Mark wasn't comfortable with his lifestyle. The one and only time Justin had brought a sub around, someone he'd been dating for a few months and felt it was time to introduce them to his best friend, Mark had acted as if he were waiting for Justin to order her to her knees at any given moment.

If Justin and Kim made their relationship public, he had no idea how Mark would react. He could almost deal with any disappointment from Belinda and Davis. Ultimately, they wanted their daughter to be happy and well cared for. Over time, he could prove to them that he could do that. Mark, on the other hand, would know or suspect what was going on behind closed doors.

Mark's possible reaction plagued Justin for the rest of the night.

When Justin's alarm went off the next morning, he knew he needed to get his head in the game. He had lots to do to prepare for Kim's arrival.

Working out helped to clear his head. He pushed himself harder than he usually did, needing to feel the burn and push the concern from his mind. Today was about him and Kim. No one else. They had to be the ones to figure this out. Time had already proven whatever pull they felt toward each other wasn't going away. They needed to deal with this.

After a shower, he put on some comfortable clothes and powered up his computer. He pulled up his limits list, gave it a quick run-through to make sure everything was up to date, and then hit print. Justin knew what he liked and what he didn't. He'd been in the lifestyle for over ten years and had played with a multitude of submissives. But in all that time, he'd never been as anxious to see his partner's list of desires as he was to see Kim's. Given her inexperience, he didn't know what it would look like.

Bringing his list with him into the kitchen, he placed it on the counter and began prepping for brunch. He had one hour before Kim was set to arrive and lots to do.

At nine-fifty-eight, his doorbell rang. Justin turned off the stove and went to answer the door.

Kim stood on his front porch, clutching her purse to her chest. Unlike last time she showed up on his doorstep, she was wearing more than a trench coat.

"Come in," he said, motioning for her to come inside.

"Thanks."

He helped her remove her coat and placed it on the coat rack by the door. She wore a lovely burnt orange sweater and a snug pair of jeans that showed off her curves. His hands were itching to touch her, but first things first. "I hope you're hungry."

She gave him a shy smile. "Starving."

Justin knew she was nervous. He would normally keep things platonic between himself and a potential sub until limits were discussed, but he wanted to help put her at ease. Cupping the side of her face with his right hand, he brought their lips together for a chaste kiss. "We'll eat first, then talk. All right?"

Kim nodded and followed him into the kitchen.

He had her take a seat at the table while he brought everything over.

"Were you planning to feed an army?" she asked.

Justin laughed. "Nope. Just us."

"I know you eat a lot, but this could feed us for the entire week."

Once everything was on the table, he sat down next to her. "It probably will. Or me, at least."

She scrunched up her nose in confusion.

Handing her a plate and encouraging her to help herself, he explained, "I usually do the bulk of my weekly cooking, or at least prepping on Sundays. Since I don't always know how late I'll be at the shop during the week, it's easier to have the food ready for me no matter what time I get home."

"Oh," she said. "That makes sense."

They ate in silence for several minutes before Justin turned the conversation back to last night. "Was Ali able to help you?"

Kim swallowed her bite of food and nodded. "Yes. It was a good thing, too, because I didn't know what some of the stuff was." She lowered her voice and asked, "Do people really like to pee on each other?"

He chuckled. "Yes, there are people who like all sorts of things, including that."

"I guess I've been living under a rock, then, because I've never heard of that."

"You've never heard of golden showers?" he asked. While she might not have the variety of sexual experience he did, she wasn't exactly a virgin.

Her eyes widened for a moment before going back to normal. "That's what that means? I never knew that."

Smiling, he reached for another piece of bacon. "What else did you and Ali talk about last night?"

She glanced up at him through her lashes. "I told her we slept together."

"We did more than sleep," Justin said with a pointed look.

Kim blushed, averting her eyes. "Yes, well, I told her that, too. She tried to downplay it, but I know she was hurt that I didn't tell her. She knows I've had a crush on you for years."

He placed a finger under her chin and guided her gaze to his. "I didn't tell my best friend either."

Silence fell between them as the reason for that hung in the air.

"How bad do you think it will be?" Kim asked.

Justin frowned. "I don't know. Your brother knows about my lifestyle. Even if he doesn't know the details of our bedroom activities, he's going to at least have a clue as to what's going on." Dropping his hand, Justin picked up his plate and carried it over to the sink. "While Mark's never said anything directly to me, I've always gotten the impression that he doesn't approve. Or at least he doesn't understand my need to dominate my partner. Nor their desire to submit."

"And me being his sister..."

Her words lingered in the air as she joined him at the sink, putting her plate down next to his.

This was a strange situation they found themselves in. Normally, he wouldn't give a rat's ass what Mark thought of the women he dated, but this was different. She was Mark's sister, and he didn't want his friend thinking any less of her or their relationship.

That is, if this month-long trial went well.

Without overthinking it, Justin pulled her into his arms, resting his lips against her forehead. "If anything, he'll take his frustration out on me, not you."

"That doesn't make me feel any better," Kim said, leaning into his embrace.

Her words pulled a smile from him. Taking a step back, Justin put a little distance between them. As much as he wanted to skip to the good stuff, they needed to take care of business first. "Are you ready to go over our lists?"

"Not really."

Justin took another step back. Maybe she wasn't ready for this. One night of kinky sex was different than entering into a D/s relationship. "Have you changed your mind?"

Her eyes widened and she shook her head. "No, I haven't changed my mind. I'm just..." She leaned back against the counter, putting more space between them. "I'm worried our lists won't...mesh."

At his look of confusion, she continued. "You've been doing this for a long time."

"And you're worried I'll want something you aren't willing to do?" he asked.

"Yes." She pushed off the counter and began pacing. "I mean, I've watched stuff at the club, but my one and only experience was with you and I know now that was pretty tame."

He could see she was beginning to panic. Taking hold of her hand, he forced her to stop and face him. "Do you trust me?"

"Yes." Her answer came swift and sure.

"That's the most important thing in these types of relationships. That and communication. Everything else can be figured out and negotiated." He paused. "I think we've already figured out we're compatible in the bedroom."

The smirk on his face aimed to lighten the mood and it worked. A small grin pulled at the side of Kim's lips. "Very compatible."

Figuring it was time to get down to business, Justin led her back to the table. "Do you have your list?"

Kim retrieved her purse from the floor and removed several sheets of paper. Carefully, she unfolded them and laid them on the table in front of her. She placed her palms flat over the papers and looked up at him. "What happens now?"

Normally, they would exchange lists, read them over, and then discuss, but he wasn't sure that was the best option in this case. She was clearly nervous, and she was right. He had been doing this for a long time and he had a wide variety of interests. The last thing he wanted to do was increase her anxiety.

But he also wanted to do this right. If this thing between them didn't work out. If, and even thinking about it made him sick to his stomach...if she did this with another Dom someday, he wanted her to know what was normal. Red flags, like not going over lists and negotiating the relationship expectations first before any play began, were important to spot early.

"We exchange lists. You read over mine and I read over yours, and then we talk about it."

Kim took a deep breath in, her chest rising with the action, and he couldn't stop his gaze from drifting to that part of her body. He hadn't spent nearly enough time worshiping them. A problem he aimed to remedy soon.

She slid her papers toward him and he did the same, forcing himself to concentrate on the task at hand. There would be time later for indulging.

For the next fifteen minutes, they read over each other's lists in silence. It didn't take him that long to get through hers. A lot of items were marked as *don't know*. She'd marked all the things they'd done during their one night together as *like*, which brought a smile to his face. The only things she had marked as *hard limit* were the more extreme items on the list, which were fine. He had no interest in hard-core S&M.

As he sat waiting for her to finish going over his list, he wondered what she'd think of his likes and dislikes when it came to play. She was correct when she said what they'd done before had been tame. He'd wanted to give her a good experience, so he'd gone easy on her. A little spanking, a blindfold, and a little bondage can go a long way with someone who's new to kink.

When she met his gaze from across the table, she looked...apprehensive. He grabbed her hand and held it between both of his. "Talk to me."

"Can I have some water?" she asked.

Not what he'd been expecting, but...

"Sure."

Returning to the table a few moments later, Justin handed her the glass of water she'd requested. She brought it to her lips and took a sip. "Thanks."

He sat back down and waited, his own anxiety creeping up the longer she remained silent. Was there something on his list that had frightened her? He wouldn't think so, but he couldn't be sure.

Finally, she met his gaze. "Does it always feel this overwhelming?"

"What do you mean?"

Kim sat her glass on the table in front of her and blew out a breath. "I mean, I knew how much there was, but seeing it all in front of me and how many things you have checked that you've tried."

She didn't continue and he felt compelled to respond. "I've been doing this for a long time."

"I know. And part of me is glad because it means you know what you're doing." She ran her hands over the papers in front of her. "Ali said if both of us were new to the lifestyle, it would be harder."

"Yes, that's usually true."

Then he noticed a tear leak from her eye and roll down her cheek. "I want to be a good sub for you but look at my list and look at yours."

Seeing her cry nearly broke him. He didn't like seeing her this distressed, and especially not over something that could be remedied with time.

Justin used the pad of his thumb to wipe the tear from her cheek. "Experience isn't everything." He didn't usually talk about past subs when negotiating a new arrangement, but this was different. Kim was different. They both knew they weren't going into this to get their rocks off. "I've played with subs who've had as much experience in the lifestyle as I do."

She groaned.

"And while they were good subs, there was no connection. Not like the one we have."

"What if you tell me to do something and I screw it up? I don't want to embarrass you at the club."

A light bulb went off in his head. "Everyone at the club knows you're new, so no one is going to expect you to be perfect out of the gate. Not even me." He paused. "But if you disobey me while we're playing, at the club or not, your ass will be feeling it."

She squirmed a little in her chair, so she knew exactly what he was talking about.

Justin grinned. "Let's get through our lists, and then we have some business to take care of before tonight."

"Tonight?"

"Yes. Tonight, you make your debut at the club as my submissive."

Chapter Thirteen

Kim swallowed and tried not to let her nerves get the best of her. He was right. Everyone at the club knew she was a newbie. And if she did screw up, it wouldn't be the first time. She still remembered the night Ali had brought her to visit Serpent's Kiss. She'd stumbled over herself when she'd met Brandon, calling him Sir and blushing like a schoolgirl. Kim had survived that. She could this too. And she would have Justin there guiding her. She only had to let him.

"Let's start with the easy stuff," he said. "Tell me about the blow jobs you've given?"

Her eyes went wide. "What?"

Justin smirked. "You've marked love to give on your list, but I want to know your level of experience with them."

"Um..." She had to look like a deer caught in the headlights. She felt like one. Kim had no clue what to say. No guy had ever asked her something like that before. "I don't know. Average, I guess."

When she didn't elaborate, he pressed further. "Do you prefer soft and gentle or rough and deep? Have you ever deep throated?"

Her level of embarrassment hiked up another notch. She could feel the heat radiating from her face. Did he really need to know this? She'd never talked about her prior sexual encounters with anyone besides Ali, and her best friend hadn't ever asked her if she'd sucked her boyfriend's cock down her throat. "Um...medium, I guess."

"So not too rough, but not too gentle either." He refocused on the papers in front of them, but she thought that was more for her benefit than his. "What about deep throating?"

"I tried once, but I gagged."

He nodded, then moved on to the next subject. "What about hair pulling? You marked I don't know. A guy's never pulled your hair during sex?"

"I don't think so." She blew out a loud breath. "Do we really need to go over this in such...detail?"

Justin met her gaze. "Yes. I need to know what you like, what you don't like, and what you're willing to explore. I can't do that if I don't have all the information."

While that made sense, it didn't make it any less embarrassing. "What about you?"

The smirk was back. "Which one? The hair pulling or the blow jobs?"

His eyes were dancing with amusement, but it didn't make her feel self-conscious...or at least any more self-conscious than she already was. "Both."

Reaching out, he cupped the back of her head and twisted a fistful of hair around his hand. "I love to pull my partner's hair. And as for blow jobs, I love receiving them in any form, but I would enjoy feeling my cock hit the back of your throat." He leaned in and, with a gentle tug on her hair, whispered in her ear, "We can always work on your gag reflex."

Heat surged between her legs. "Okay."

Then, to her disappointment, he released her and turned his attention back to their lists. For the next hour, he had her explain, in detail, her level of experience on everything she'd marked *love, like, dislike,* and *soft limit.*

It was strange to sit down and talk about her preferences in the bedroom and what she'd done in the past with other partners, but the more they talked, the more comfortable she felt. Kim wasn't sure what she'd expected a relationship with Justin to be like, but this much discussion about sex and preferences didn't come close to anything she'd ever done with a boyfriend.

In fact, the only conversation she'd ever really had with a guy regarding sex was with her first college boyfriend. They'd each only been with one other person before and had both been awkward and unsure of what they were doing. The whole thing had lasted no more than five minutes and consisted of whether she was on birth control and if they should wait or not since they'd only been going out for a month. It was nothing like sitting across a table with Justin and talking about what her favorite positions had been, or her level of experience when it came to blow jobs.

She'd got to ask him a few questions as well, although he didn't seem bothered by any of them. Most of them came up when they were talking about the things she marked as dislike. He had a lot of questions about those and after he asked her why she disliked anal sex, she turned the question around on him. "Why, you like it?"

Justin smirked. "Well, for one, it feels amazing. The visual isn't bad either." Then he got serious again. "Now explain to me what it is you don't like about it. Did you have a bad experience?"

Just thinking about it made her sore and not in the good morning after type of way. "You could say that."

"Tell me."

It really wasn't something she wanted to talk about or remember, for that matter, but they'd talked about every other embarrassing sexual encounter she'd had, so why not. "He was behind me and, well, you know." She blew out a breath. "It hurt. A lot. I screamed. He stopped. End of story."

Unfortunately, that wasn't enough for Justin. "Where were you when it happened? Did he prepare you? Use any type of lubrication?"

She could feel her cheeks warming again. "We were in a bathroom. It was a party and we were a little buzzed. We were both horny, so we snuck into his friend's master bathroom, locked the door, and started moving clothes out of the way."

Kim was hoping she could leave it at that, but of course, Justin wanted more. "Go on."

"There isn't much more." She shrugged. "He bent me over the counter and somewhere in the middle of it, he pulled out. When he"—she cleared her throat and looked down—"well, it tried to enter a different hole."

"So no preparation and no lube."

"I don't know what you mean by preparation, and we'd been having sex, so he was...you know...wet from..."

Justin shook his head. "That isn't enough. Anal sex requires the muscles to be stretched beforehand." He frowned. "It also takes more lubrication than the human body can naturally produce. At least not unless inducing pain is the goal."

Again, she cringed, remembering.

He took her hand in his and gave it a comforting squeeze. "We'll leave it off the table for now, but just know that when done right, anal sex can be pleasurable for both parties and I'd love it if you'd give me a chance to show you one day."

A flutter began in the pit of her stomach. The tender look in his eyes made her think that maybe with him it would be different. Their one night together had been worlds apart from her previous sexual experiences. Why wouldn't other things she'd experienced?

Once they'd gone through both their lists, Justin stood. "Do you have any other questions for me regarding the lists?"

Kim shook her head. "I don't think so. But..."

"But?"

"How? I mean, what do I do as your submissive? Even though I've watched the subs at the club, I've never done this before."

Justin helped her from the chair and led her down the hallway to the bedroom where they'd spent the first part of their night together. She was immediately flooded with memories. Heat began pooling between her thighs in preparation.

He turned to face her, cupping her cheek with his hand. "We need to talk about protocol."

"Protocol?"

"What I expect of you." His thumb rubbed along her bottom lip. "As my submissive."

"Okay." She wanted to lean into him, to forget about everything else. Hadn't they waited long enough? It had been over three months. She wanted to feel him inside her again.

"First, you will call me *Sir* whenever we are playing."

"How will I know when that is?"

He slid his hand down to grip the back of her neck. "If we're at the club, or in this room, then we're playing. Outside of that...you'll learn how to read my signals." One side of his mouth tilted up into a half smile. "If I tell you to get to your knees, that's a good indication."

Kim tried to concentrate on what he was saying. This was important. "But what if I don't want to play?"

"Did Ali talk to you about safewords?" he asked.

"Yes." Kim recalled the first time she'd heard a submissive at the club use their safeword. She and Ali had been hanging out with Daniel when another couple had stopped by to speak with him. She'd seen Alexander and Grace around Serpent's Kiss, she'd even watched them do a scene on her first night as an official member, but she'd never met them directly before that night. As Daniel and Alexander talked, the conversation turned to their time in the military. Kim had begun to space out, not overly interested in their conversation, when she'd heard Grace say *mushroom*. All conversation had stopped and Alexander had taken Grace to one of the quieter areas of the club.

As soon as she'd been alone with Ali, she'd questioned her friend. Ali had explained that *mushroom* was Grace's safeword.

"Do you remember your safeword?"

"Yes. My safeword is teddybear." Then she recalled what he'd said moments before about being in this room. "Sir."

He grinned, seeming to be pleased that she'd remembered and corrected herself.

"Because you're new to this, I'd also like to use elements of the stoplight system." Her confused look must have given away her lack of understanding because he continued. "If something isn't right, say the ropes I bind you with are too tight or your leg is beginning to cramp, say the word yellow. That tells me that while you don't want to stop playing, I need to assess the situation before continuing."

She'd heard *yellow* used before when she'd ventured upstairs at the club. "What if you do something I don't like?"

"You're asking very good questions." His fingers began massaging her scalp and she let her eyes drift closed, sinking into the feel of his hands finally being on her again. "Submission is about giving up control, which means letting me guide the scene where I want it to go. If you don't like the position I've placed you in, you can say yellow, wait for me to ask you to explain, and then I will decide if I want to adjust the scene or not. Safewords, however, are to be used in situations where something isn't right and the situation needs to be assessed, not because you'd rather something different be happening. When we talk about the scene after, you can tell me what you liked and didn't like."

Kim knew that would be hard for her. Sure, she'd given up control to him once before, and she'd enjoyed every minute of it, but they weren't only talking about one night. Could she give him complete control of their sex life?

"Tell me what you're thinking?" he asked.

"I just hope I can do it. Not tell you what I want while we're...playing. Or if I don't like something."

That sly smile pulled at Justin's lips again. "I seem to remember you giving off some pretty clear signals of your enjoyment the last time."

The blush was back, but she was less bothered by it this time. Maybe it was because they were in this room and not at his kitchen table. "I just want this to work," she whispered.

Justin stepped forward, closing the gap between them, bringing their bodies flush. He tilted her head back so her mouth was a breath away from his. Her hands went to his sides. "If we talk things over with each other, the rest can be figured out."

Her heart was pounding, and she felt hot all over. "All right."

He backed her up against the wall, pressing his body into hers. She could feel his erection pressing against her belly. All she wanted to do was lose herself in Justin. Couldn't the talk of safewords and whatever else wait?

Seeming to read her mind, he brought their noses together and locked his gaze with hers. "If something isn't right and you want the scene to stop, say teadybear and I'll stop the scene."

"Are we going to play now?" Why she spoke, she had no idea. All she wanted him to do was kiss her. She didn't want to talk anymore.

His only answer was a hard kiss that pressed her body flush against the hard surface at her back.

Her eyes fluttered closed as she held on, desperate to be as close to him as she could. As his tongue played with hers, darting in and out of her mouth, she reached for the button on his jeans. She wanted to feel his cock in her hands.

Fingers wrapped around her wrist, stopping her movement. She opened her eyes and gazed up at him, not sure why he'd stopped.

"What do you think you're doing?"

JUSTIN HAD LOST HIS HEAD FOR A MOMENT, THE DESIRE TO KISS HER overwhelming him. That hadn't happened to him for over a decade. Normally, when he was with a submissive, he was in complete control. But his need for her was clouding his better judgment. They should have talked about safewords and protocol in the kitchen.

But it was too late now. His cock was rock-hard and he could feel the heat of her breath on his face from her labored breathing. A little voice in the back of his head screamed at him that he shouldn't be doing this with her, but it was being drowned out by a larger voice that said she was his and always had been.

He brought her hand to rest on his chest while he tried to get his own breathing under control. It was so easy to let go with her. And he wanted to let go, to lose himself in her, but they needed to finish what they'd started. Even if it killed him.

Raising an eyebrow, he waited for an answer to his question.

She blinked, her brown eyes rich with her arousal. "I want to touch you."

"When we're in this room, I'm in control. If you want to touch, you need to ask."

"I can't touch you?"

Justin moved her hand back down, this time to cup his erection. "I didn't say that. But in here, when we're playing, I call the shots. You obey." He could see her mind working. Even though Kim was the baby of her family, she was extremely independent. He knew this was going to be a challenge for her. "I'm a very agreeable Dom, though, so if you ask me nicely, I'll likely grant you permission."

"Only in here?" she asked.

"And at the club." He paused. "For now."

Her eyes opened wide. "For now?"

"Relationships evolve over time, even D/s ones. You may find you like asking my permission."

Kim looked doubtful. "I don't know about that."

Justin took her wrist and guided her hand back to the top of his jeans. He didn't say more, just waited to see what she'd do. His cock was aching, but he'd been doing this for a long time. He knew how to control himself. Usually.

Several very long moments passed before she spoke. "May I touch you?"

"Are you forgetting something?" She looked confused. "How do you address me when we're in this room?"

"May I touch you, Sir?"

He released her wrist. "You may."

Kim wasted no time slipping her hand beneath the fabric of his jeans. His cock pulsed at the first brush of her fingers. The zipper gave way when she wrapped her fingers around him.

It was still too constricting for his liking, so he pushed the jeans down his hips, freeing him the rest of the way. He rarely wore underwear when he was hanging around the house, and today he was grateful. It was one less thing between them.

She didn't miss a beat and began pumping her hand from base to tip. It felt so good to have her touching him freely like this. For so long he'd dreamed of her hands, her mouth, her tits...

He sank his fingers into her hair and captured her mouth with his, angling her head the way he wanted it. Her eager response only encouraged him. He deepened the kiss, pressing their bodies together, trapping her hand between them.

His cock pulsed in her hand, driving him mad. He wanted everything at once...her hands...her mouth...

Tilting her head back, Justin kissed down her jaw to her neck. As he neared the base of her neck near her collarbone, she released the most delicious moan. Her hand squeezed his cock and he knew in that moment what he wanted.

He released her and took a step back, waiting until she met his gaze. "Get on your knees. I want to feel your mouth around my cock."

This time, she didn't hesitate. Kim knelt before him and brought her lips a breath away from his erection. She looked up at him with a level of sweet innocence that mocked what she was about to do. "May I suck your cock, Sir?"

Instead of answering her with words, he took hold of the back of her head and guided her mouth the rest of the way home.

Chapter Fourteen

Justin closed his eyes as her warm lips encircled his length. He let her set the pace, wanting to see what she would do.

She was tentative at first, gently licking and sucking his length. It was torture when all he wanted was to sink deeper into her mouth, but he forced himself to remain still. At least, for now.

After a few minutes of exploring, she picked up the pace, seeming to gain confidence. It felt amazing having her hot mouth engulf him, but it wasn't enough. He tightened his hold on her head and pressed forward with his hips, taking control.

Slowly, so she could get used to him, he increased the speed of his thrusts, going a little deeper each time until he was hitting the back of her throat. Justin both felt and heard her gag a little, so he eased up to allow her to adjust. He gazed down at her. "Relax and breathe through your nose."

He waited for her to take a couple of breaths.

"Are you all right?"

She nodded, not releasing her hold on his cock.

"Good girl. I'm not going to push you too hard today, but I am going to fuck your face and come down your throat."

She stared up at him, her eyes telling him she was as into this as he was. He wondered how wet her panties were and knew he wanted to find out, but not before he'd found release. Having her suck him off was something he'd been dreaming about for longer than he cared to think about.

"Since your mouth is otherwise engaged, if you need to use your safeword, tap on my wrist three times. Otherwise, you will take what I give you." Increasing his hold on her hair, he didn't wait for a response before surging deep into her mouth again.

She gagged again but then focused on breathing each time he pulled out. Soon, she was able to adapt to his rhythm. "That's it. Take what I give you. You look so beautiful on your knees sucking my cock, baby."

He noticed her breathing slowed even more and her eyes dilated to nearly black at his words. His girl liked it when he talked dirty. He was going to have to remember that and use it to his advantage.

With two hands fisted in her hair, he focused on watching his hard length move between her lips. Her tongue massaged the underside of his cock, coaxing his orgasm closer and closer. He could feel it building in his balls and knew it wouldn't be long.

As the surge built at the base of his cock, Justin began thrusting harder. "Swallow every drop."

It was the only warning he gave. Seconds later, he was coming—shooting streams of cum into her mouth and down her throat.

Justin felt her swallow around him and eased his grip on her hair. He took a steadying breath before stepping back. Extending his hand, he helped her to stand. Then, without warning, he crushed her to him and kissed her.

Kim didn't miss a beat. She threaded her fingers into his hair and wrapped one leg around his waist. His jeans were still around his ankles, throwing him off balance with the force of her movement.

He fell against the wall, taking her with him, but he didn't stop kissing her. Instead, Justin hiked her leg higher on his hip. The position opened her legs wider, making him wish she wasn't wearing jeans. "From now on, when you enter this room, you will either be wearing a skirt or nothing. Do you understand?"

"Yes, Sir."

Her breathing was labored, drawing attention to her breasts, but they would have to wait until later. He had other priorities.

Setting her legs back on the ground, he took a step back and pulled his own jeans back into place. "Strip."

She blinked. "Now?"

He folded his arms and waited.

After only a moment's hesitation, she began removing her clothes. Her sweater went first, revealing a brown lacey bra that clasped in the front. Next to go were her jeans. She shimmied them down her hips and kicked them over to join her sweater. Her panties matched her bra, the lace giving hints of the silky skin beneath.

She removed the bra first, tossing it onto the floor with the rest of her clothes. Her nipples were hard and begging for him to suck them as she bent to remove her panties. His mouth watered as she lowered the fabric down her legs and stepped out of them.

Before she could throw them in the pile with the others, he held out his hand. "Give them to me."

Kim froze. "You want my panties? Why?"

"Did you forget where we are?" he asked.

She glanced around the room, then back at him. He could see the wheels turning in her head as if she were trying to decide whether to hand over her underwear. After seeming to consider her options, she stepped forward and handed him her panties.

Justin took them and tucked them into his front pocket. He'd planned to get her off before they began preparing for tonight, but it seemed she needed a reminder that she was the submissive in the relationship.

He walked over to the bed and sat down. "Lie across my lap, your ass in the air."

Kim looked uncertain as she crossed the room and lay across his lap.

He waited for her to get settled. "What did I tell you would happen if you disobeyed me?"

She lowered her forehead to the mattress. "That my ass would be feeling it, Sir."

"That's correct." Justin rubbed his hand along her bottom. "And was I unclear when I told you to hand me your panties?"

"No, Sir."

Learning to give up control was going to be the hardest part for Kim and we both knew it. But if this was the type of relationship she wanted, then she was going to have to learn to obey her Dom. "You'll receive ten swats for your disobedience."

He didn't wait for a response before landing the first blow to her ass.

"Ow!" She reached back a hand to shield her ass.

"Remove your hand and keep them on the bed or I'll get rope to secure them."

Kim brought her arm to rest over her head. "I'm sorry. I didn't mean to—"

He landed two more smacks to her ass in quick succession. This wasn't a playful spanking like before. This was discipline.

"Please." Despite her pleading, she kept her hands flat on the bed.

Justin didn't want to draw this out any more than he needed to, so he ignored her protests and the tears sliding down her cheeks and finished what he was doing. After the final hit landed on her now rosy ass, he massaged the warm flesh several times before helping her to sit up.

He went to wipe the moisture from her face, but she brushed his hands away. As much as that irked him, he let it go. She was new to this and he knew that once she realized having a D/s dynamic involved more than kinky fun, she might decide this lifestyle wasn't for her.

"Are you all right?" he asked.

"I'm fine." She shifted on his lap. "May I get up now, Sir?"

"Not yet."

Her eyes flashed to his and he saw the anger boiling beneath the surface. Kim had always had a temper. He'd seen it a lot when she was a teenager, but he'd been lucky enough to steer clear of it for the most part. "Do you understand why I punished you?"

"Yes. Sir."

She was definitely angry.

Justin wondered whether he should push the issue or let her calm down first. He decided to let it go. For the time being anyway. "Get dressed, and then we have some shopping to do before we head to the club tonight."

Kim stood and marched over to retrieve her clothes. She kept her back to him while she dressed.

"I'll be in the living room. Come out when you're done."

"Is that an order, Sir?"

He sighed. "A request."

Not waiting for a reply, Justin left her to finish.

He ducked into his room and threw on a shirt, socks, and shoes before heading into the living room. Scraping a hand over his face, he fell back against the couch. That hadn't gone the way he'd hoped. Then again, he knew embarking on this with her wouldn't be easy. But he thought they'd make it past the first few hours before hitting their first hurdle. For all he knew, she would walk into the living room and tell him off.

Maybe that would be for the best. At least, they'd know they'd tried and that it didn't work. It wasn't as if they hadn't gone over everything beforehand. She'd known what she was getting into. In theory, anyway.

Kim had finished dressing and began to pace. How dare he spank her like that. Her ass was still burning.

Her gaze drifted over to the bed where he'd dulled out his punishment. This hadn't been like the spanking he'd given her the last time. Their night together had been about pleasure. There was no pleasure in what she'd just experienced.

She'd given him her stupid underwear. Granted, she hadn't given them to him right away. And she'd question him why he'd wanted them. But did that mean she deserved to be humiliated?

Kim blew out a breath. She needed to calm down. He was out there waiting for her and whether she felt like it or not, she was going to have to face him sooner or later.

Squaring her shoulders, she stepped out of the room, closing the door behind her. He was waiting for her in the living room, exactly where he'd said he'd be.

As soon as he saw her, he stood. She'd expected him to look smug, but instead he appeared worried. That took some of the wind out of her sails.

Neither said anything for the longest time. He was the first one to break the silence. "Did you want to sit down?"

"No," she snapped, unable to help herself. "My butt is a little sore at the moment."

He sighed. "We need to talk about what happened."

"There's nothing to talk about."

"Of course there is." He started to take a step toward her, then thought better of it. "Have you changed your mind?"

"Why do you keep asking me that?" That was beginning to irritate her more than her tender backside.

Justin rubbed his hand along the back of his neck, then dropped it back down to his side. "I know how strong-willed you are. Being submissive is about giving up control."

"I know that." She closed her eyes and took a deep breath before meeting his gaze again. "Look, I know I should have given you my panties when you asked. I just wasn't expecting you..."

"To spank you?"

"Yes." She crossed her arms. "I'm not sure what I expected. At the time, I just didn't understand why you wanted my underwear. I still don't."

This time, he came to stand in front of her. He must have realized the biggest part of the storm was over. "It doesn't matter why I wanted them. I'm your Dom. As my submissive, you need to do what I ask you to do or use your safeword. That's how this works."

"I'm not sure I can do that."

He chuckled. "Then you'd better get used to having a sore ass."

She narrowed her eyes at him.

Justin held his ground and waited to see what she'd do.

As much as she hated to admit it, he was right. She could either suck it up and follow the rules, not follow the rules and deal with the consequences, or throw in the towel. Walking away wasn't an option. Not after less than a day. Which meant she either needed to learn how to follow his instructions or, as he put it, get used to having a sore ass.

She decided to change the subject. "You said we had shopping to do?"

He hesitated for a moment, then answered her question. "Yes. I want to get you something to wear for tonight."

"I have clothes I wear to the club at home."

"Are you disagreeing with your Dom again?" he asked.

"We're not playing. I'm allowed to disagree as much as I want."

Justin laughed. "True." He ran the back of his hand down the side of her face and along her collarbone. "But this has to do with playing, so it falls under my domain."

She huffed, but there wasn't any heat in it. "Fine. Can I at least get my underwear back?"

"No."

Thirty minutes later, they pulled up in front of a store called Leather and Lace. She'd never been there before, but given the name, she had an inkling of what type of clothing they'd have inside.

He rounded the car and opened her door. Kim stepped out, making sure there wasn't anyone watching, then waited for him to lock up the car. Even though she was wearing jeans, she felt naked without her panties. She couldn't believe he hadn't given them back.

Justin reached for her hand and laced their fingers together like it was the most natural thing in the world. And besides her discomfort going commando in public, it kind of was. She felt...safe with him. Not that she didn't feel safe before, but it was different. "Your brother doesn't venture to this side of town often. We're safe."

He thought she was worried about her brother seeing them. Well, she was. Kind of. But in truth, it was the clothes situation that had her uncomfortable more than anything else.

Inside wasn't exactly what she'd expected. The store was bright and open with lots of clothes. As the title suggested, most of the clothing had either leather or lace.

He guided them through the racks, stopping to look closer at a few items. Kim kept her comments to herself. This was play-related and she needed to remember that he was in charge.

At one point, he held up a bodysuit that revealed more than it covered. She wasn't sure she'd be comfortable walking about the club in something like that. Some subs did. Hell, some of the subs didn't wear any clothing at all. But that wasn't her. She didn't get off on other people seeing her naked.

"Excuse me," he said to the woman behind the counter. "Do you have a fitting room?"

"Of course. Right this way."

Justin handed Kim a black leather skirt and a tiny white top. He nodded for her to follow the woman. "I want to see what it looks like on you."

Kim froze and leaned in to whisper so only he would hear. "But I'm not wearing underwear, remember?"

A grin stretched across his face. "There's nothing wrong with my memory."

When she realized he was serious, Kim debated her options. In the end, she took the clothes from him and headed toward the fitting room.

"Let me know if you need a different size," the woman said before leaving her to try on her items.

For the second time that day, Kim stripped. She took her time, folding her clothes and laying them on the bench inside the small room before reaching for the skirt and top.

To her surprise, the skirt wasn't bad. Not something she would have chosen for herself, but at least it covered everything. It hugged her curves and had the right amount of detail to be flattering. The top, however, was a different story. Not that it wasn't flattering, exactly, but it left little to the imagination. It barely covered her breasts, dipping low to show off as much cleavage as possible.

Her belly was on full display as well. Normally, she wasn't self-conscious about her body, but this outfit was definitely out of her comfort zone.

Knowing she couldn't stay in there forever, she gathered her courage and opened the door. He was right outside, waiting.

When she stopped in the doorway, he motioned her out. "I want to see the whole picture. Come closer and turn so I can see the back."

She did as she was told, turning in a slow circle.

He was smiling when she faced him again.

"It doesn't cover much," she said, even though she knew it was useless. He obviously liked the outfit and she was ninety-nine percent sure she would be wearing it tonight.

"I can always have you try on the bodysuit instead."

She should have known he'd say that. "I like this better."

"So do I." He cupped her face and gave her a hard kiss. "Get changed and we'll head back."

Without another word, she returned to the dressing room and changed back into her jeans and sweater.

She found him at the register. He already had a bag in his hand but didn't seem keen on sharing with her whatever was in it. At least not yet. Kim had a feeling she'd know exactly what was in the bag before the night was over.

"Everything fit all right?" the woman asked.

"Yes. Everything fit. Thank you."

The woman finished ringing up the items and Justin paid. Kim waited for him to finish, then followed him outside. After placing the bags in the trunk, they both climbed into the car and headed back home.

"Do you have any shoes that will go with that outfit or do we need to stop and get shoes, too?" he asked.

"I have some black boots that will work, I think."

He took her hand and brought her fingers to his lips. "Thank you for trusting me."

Trust wasn't the issue. Not the trusting him part, anyway. She trusted him with her life. Justin wouldn't hurt her. She knew that.

Her problem was she didn't know how to get her brain to shut off. But she knew if this was going to work, she was going to have to figure it out. She only hoped he didn't give up on her first.

Chapter Fifteen

The drive to Kim's apartment didn't take long. Since it was the weekend, traffic wasn't too bad and her place wasn't near any major shopping areas. Justin parked in front of her townhouse and followed her inside.

The last time he was there was the day she moved in. He'd helped Mark and Davis move her furniture. It looked a lot different now that there were pictures on the walls and a nice area rug in the center of the living room.

"Is there anything else you want me to get while we're here?"

Justin had debated on the drive here whether to have her bring an overnight bag. He wanted her in his bed, but he also knew she might need some space after her first real venture into D/s. The selfish part of him, however, didn't want to give her space. He'd given her seventeen years of space. "You might want to pack an overnight bag."

"Am I staying at your place tonight?" she asked, sounding more unsure than he was used to from Kim. The last time he'd heard that tremble in her voice was the day she'd showed up on his doorstep three months ago. He didn't want her to be uncertain about their relationship. He was all in. For this one month at least.

He pulled her into him and covered her mouth with his. The kiss was long and deep, and he felt her body give against him.

When Justin broke the kiss, he waited until she was looking at him. "I want to wake up with you beside me. It's the one thing I missed out on the first time."

Thinking about that morning brought all his mixed emotions to the surface. He'd woken up to an empty bed and for a second he thought she'd left without waking him. And maybe she would have if given the chance. They'd never know.

"I wanted to stay."

He kissed her again. This time, keeping things light. "Get your things. We still need to swing by my house."

Kim nodded and disappeared into her bedroom.

Justin strolled over to the window and attempted to get himself in check. He was hoping for a good night, but after this afternoon, he wasn't sure. She had a lot to learn, and he was hoping in time she'd be able to fully trust him with her submission. Only time would tell.

After stopping by his house so he could change, they headed to the club. It was early, but he knew Ali would most likely already be there. Kim's best friend often helped to set things up before the club opened on Saturdays on top of her coat check rotation.

He swiped his membership card to allow them entrance, hung up both their coats in the coat check, and then guided Kim into the main part of the club. Katrina was making her way down the stairs. She spotted them right away and he was positive he saw a smile tug at her lips.

The sound of Katrina's heels echoed in the space with the lack of people and no music to drown out the sound. She walked toward them. "You two are here early this evening."

"We were hoping to catch Ali before everyone else got here," Justin said.

Katrina glanced at Kim, then nodded. "The last time I saw her, she was in the women's locker room."

"Thanks."

"Of course." The club mistress smiled. "Let me know if you need anything else. I'll be around." Katrina strolled off toward the bar, no doubt to continue making her rounds to ensure everything was ready for tonight.

Justin placed a hand on Kim's lower back and urged her toward the women's locker room.

"We're talking to Ali?" Kim asked.

"No. *You're* going to talk to Ali. I'm going to wait out here." He stopped in front of the entrance to the locker room.

Kim looked confused. He could see those wheels turning in her head again.

"I want you to talk to her about what happened earlier. I think you need to talk to another submissive, and since you're comfortable with Ali, she's the best choice."

He could see the urge to argue in her eyes, but she held her tongue. "Okay."

Justin closed the distance between them, tilted her chin up, and looked into her eyes. "Come find me when you're done." Then he placed a soft kiss on her lips and dropped his hand before turning on his heel and heading toward the bar.

He was hoping having Kim talk to another, more experienced, submissive would be good for her. Kim needed to get out of her own head if a D/s relationship was really what she wanted. Hopefully, Ali could help her with that.

Sliding onto one of the barstools, Justin waved to Brandon.

"You're here early."

"I wanted Kim to have a chance to talk to Ali before things got crazy."

Brandon nodded. "Beer?"

"I think I'll stick to water, for now."

The bartender fished out a bottle from under the bar and placed it in front of him. "Trouble with the new sub?"

Justin twisted the cap off the water bottle and took a long drink before answering. "She's having trouble getting into the right headspace. I'm hoping talking with Ali will help with that."

Brandon dumped a bucket of ice in the bin. "You know, I think a group of subs from the club meets once a week at Beth's café."

He recalled hearing about a new group that had formed in the past few months. Having more subs than only Ali to talk to could be good for Kim. That is, if she decided she wanted to continue this. "Thanks. I'll talk to her about it."

More people arrived. One couple went straight upstairs. He let his gaze linger on their ascent as he tried not to think about the conversation Kim and Ali were currently having.

⚜

"I screwed up, Ali." Kim plopped her butt down on the bench and immediately regretted it. Although her ass wasn't as sore as it had been earlier, it was still a little tender.

Ali stopped what she was doing and sat down next to her friend. "What happened?"

"Everything was great. We were kissing, then he told me to strip." Kim tried to pull her skirt down, to no avail. She still couldn't believe he hadn't allowed her to wear panties tonight. Okay, yes, she could. After what happened this afternoon, he probably wouldn't let her wear underwear again when they were together.

"Did you refuse?" Ali asked when her friend didn't continue.

"Not exactly." Kim met Ali's gaze. "I took my clothes off, but then he asked me to hand him my panties and instead of giving them to him, I asked him why."

"Oh."

"Yeah. He wasn't happy."

"I wouldn't think so." Ali grabbed Kim's hand. "What did he do?"

"He spanked me. And it wasn't like before." Last night when she'd told Ali about her one night with Justin, her friend had wanted details. Kim had shared with her how she'd liked it when he'd spanked her and how shocked she'd been at her body's reaction.

"It wasn't supposed to be. One was for pleasure. The other was for punishment."

"That's exactly what he said." Kim was pouting and she knew it.

Ali gave her a long, hard look. "Are you sure this is what you want?"

"What do you mean?"

Two women came into the locker room to change, so Ali stood and pulled Kim over to the far corner. It wasn't exactly private, but at least they wouldn't be in the way. "Submission is about giving up control and trusting your Dom."

"I trust Justin."

"Do you?"

"Yes," Kim said.

"Then why didn't you do what he asked you to do when he asked you to do it?"

That seemed to be the million-dollar question. "I just wanted to know why he wanted them. It seemed like an odd thing to want."

Ali shook her head. "The point is, it doesn't matter why he wanted them. You were playing. He's in charge. Your job is to trust him and to obey."

Kim opened her mouth to argue, but Ali cut her off.

"No buts. A good submissive obeys her Dom and trusts him to lead her. If you don't trust Justin as your Dom, then it isn't going to work."

She didn't respond right away. "What if I can't?"

Ali didn't sugarcoat it. "Then maybe this lifestyle isn't for you."

"But what about how my body reacted?"

"Maybe you just like a little kink in the bedroom." Ali stood again as more women came in. "That's not the same as a D/s relationship. You need to figure out what you want, and I would suggest you do it before you break Justin's heart."

What could she say to that? Deep down, she knew Ali was right. She'd been at the club for long enough to know how the dynamics between Dominants and submissives worked. The question was whether that was what she wanted in her own life.

"Think about it," Ali said. "Maybe try it out, see what giving up total control is like. You are at a BDSM club after all."

Kim laughed and pulled her friend in for a hug. "Thanks, Ali."

"Anytime."

She smoothed down her skirt and made sure nothing was showing that shouldn't be. "I should probably go find Justin."

"Good luck."

"Thanks."

Kim waved to a couple people as she left the locker room, but she didn't stop to talk. Justin had told her to talk to Ali and then come find him. She didn't want to disobey him again.

The club was filling up as she stepped out into the main room. Music was playing, and there was a couple already on the dance floor.

She scanned the room, looking for Justin. It took her a few moments to find him. He wasn't at the bar talking to Brandon like she thought he'd be. Instead, he was chatting with Lady Beth.

Kim debated whether to interrupt them, but Ali's words kept playing in her head. Deciding not to overthink it, she crossed the room and came to stand by Justin's side. He smiled, wrapped his arm around her waist, and pulled her against his side. She breathed a sigh of relief that she'd obviously chosen correctly this time.

"Beth was telling me about a group of subs from the club that meet at her café on Sunday afternoons."

"I'm sure they'd love to have you," Beth said. "Drew's there when he's not on shift at the firehouse. And Ali comes sometimes, too."

Ali had never mentioned going to a submissives group. Even after Kim had joined Serpent's Kiss. It made her wonder if Ali really didn't think Kim could be in a D/s relationship. "What time?"

She felt Justin's hand flex on her hip and wondered if she'd made another faux pas.

Beth smiled. "One o'clock. Since the café is closed on Sundays, there's complete privacy."

"I'll try to come. Thank you for inviting me."

"You're welcome. There are always some bumps in the road for a new submissive. Hopefully, having some other subs to talk to will help."

Kim wondered what Justin had told Lady Beth but decided to keep her thoughts to herself. "That would be good."

They spoke with Beth for a few more minutes before Justin's attention shifted and he asked Beth to excuse them.

It was on the tip of Kim's tongue to ask where they were going, but she forced herself to remain quiet. Ali told her to trust her Dom and she was going to try. What was the worst that could happen?

She found out the answer to that question a few minutes later as Justin led her upstairs to the second floor. This wasn't her first time upstairs, but it was her first time with a Dom. Her mind began swirling. Were they going to watch? Play? She could feel a mixture of panic and excitement settling in her stomach.

Justin headed for the end of the hall and opened the door on the right. It was a playroom like all the others she'd seen on this level. There were floggers, crops, whips, and several things she didn't have names for hanging up on the far wall. A spanking bench was tucked in the corner and Kim hoped that wasn't what he had in mind. She wanted to be able to sit down come Monday morning.

The sound of the door closing echoed in her ears. Was she in trouble again?

Kim watched as he moved around the room, coming to a stop in front of a long wooden table. He opened one of the drawers and removed what looked like a scarf of some kind. That didn't look too scary. Maybe he was going to tie her wrists like he'd done on that first night.

Her pulse kicked up a notch when he came behind her and brought the scarf over her head to cover her eyes. The urge to question him surged to her lips, but she managed to keep quiet. He secured a knot behind her head, and she was cast in total darkness.

"Tonight, we're going to work on trust."

She swallowed.

"Did you talk with Ali?" He was at her side now.

"Yes, Sir."

"Did you tell her about today?"

Kim closed her eyes out of habit, even though she already couldn't see anything. "I told her I screwed up."

His lips were at her ear. "And what did she say?"

Although it was a question, Kim was pretty sure he already knew what Ali had told her. It seemed to be the theme of the day. "She told me that if this was what I wanted, that I needed to trust you." That wasn't exactly what Ali had told her, but that was the gist of it.

"And is it what you want?" He'd stepped away again.

The not knowing where he was had her wanting to rip off the blindfold, but she resisted. "Yes. It's what I want. I'll try harder."

Then she felt something touch the back of her leg and she flinched.

"Tonight, we're going to work on trust. I want you to keep your hands at your side unless I say otherwise. Do you understand?"

"Yes, Sir." Kim blew out a breath and tried to prepare herself. She had to trust him.

He ran whatever it was up the back of her leg to the edge of her skirt, then moved to the other leg and did the same. It tickled a little when he reached the back of her knee, but she kept still. She could do this.

Once he'd reached her ankle, she felt him move around to her side, then a quick slap to the back of her thigh. It stung, but it didn't really hurt.

Then he came to stand in front of her and began sliding the object up the inside of her leg. Her skirt was higher in the front than in the back, and she was very aware of the fact that she wasn't wearing any underwear. She wanted to open her legs more but forced herself to remain still.

As he continued to touch her with the toy, she felt herself starting to relax. When he was finished with her legs, he moved to her arms. He brought the implement down to her hands, and she was tempted to use her fingers to explore and find out what it was he was using. But she was afraid if she did, he'd stop and she didn't want that.

Justin ran the object along her collarbone, then down her cleavage. She sucked in a breath as he skimmed over each of her nipples.

He hadn't said a word the entire time, and maybe that should have made her nervous, but it didn't. She could feel him there. Feel him watching her. Watching her reactions. It was turning her on in a way she hadn't imagined.

Kim knew the moment he stepped away and heard moving behind her. She waited to see what he would do next. The anticipation was building inside her and she wanted him to touch her.

When he returned to stand behind her, she could feel his heat radiating against her back. But instead of touching her, he ran something else along her leg. Whatever it was felt...fuller?

She wasn't sure if that was the right word, but it was all she could think of at the moment. Where the other toy had a single touching point, this seemed to have many. As she turned her mind off and allowed herself to feel, she was pretty sure it was a flogger. It felt completely different on her skin than the other toy—almost like a caress.

By the time he skimmed it along her stomach, Kim's entire body was tingling in anticipation. She didn't suspect what he would do next, but she wasn't sure she cared.

No sooner had that thought crossed her mind than she felt his finger trace a line down her chest and circle her right nipple. She hadn't been able to wear a bra with the shirt he'd chosen, so she knew he'd be able to see her body's reaction.

Still, he remained silent.

His fingers pinched and pulled her nipple through her shirt, making it hard. She bit the inside of her cheek to keep quiet. Heat rushed between her legs and she ached for more.

Then, before she'd realized what he was doing, the knot in the center of her top released, freeing her breasts. Cool air hit her warm skin, breaking some of the spell, and she gasped. Without thinking, her hands went to cover herself.

Chapter Sixteen

"Move your hands." The command was swift and direct. She'd been doing well, but her action didn't surprise Justin. The question was, would she choose to obey her Dom or would she dig in her heels and keep covering herself.

Her head turned toward the entrance to the room, even though she couldn't see anything with the blindfold on. She didn't move as she tried to decide what to do.

He waited. What she decided would give him a good indication as to whether a D/s relationship between them would work. As her Dom, there would be times when he'd ask her to do something she may be unsure about, especially at the club. She needed to trust that he could keep her safe and honor the limits she'd set for their play. If she couldn't do that, then this wouldn't work.

Several moments passed before she slowly lowered her arms, revealing her breasts to him once more. He saw her lip begin to tremble. He knew her well enough to know that she was on the verge of tears.

Justin cupped the side of her face, rubbing his thumb along her lower lip. "Tell me what's wrong."

"I just...people are watching me." Her voice was barely above a whisper.

"Why does that bother you?" he asked.

She leaned into his hand. "I'm not used to...being on display. It feels wrong somehow."

Her breathing was steadier now. She was calming down.

He brought his other hand up to palm one of her breasts. "You are beautiful. Every part of you."

Tilting her chin up, he brushed his mouth against hers, mimicking the motion of his thumb on her nipple. She let out a breathy moan.

The tension in her body eased, and he decided to continue with what he had planned. If there was another hiccup, they'd deal with it.

Lowering his head, he took her nipple into his mouth and sucked, worrying the tip between his teeth. The hard pebble on his tongue had him wondering how wet she was.

She arched her back, begging for more, seeming to have forgotten her worries of being watched. That was good considering his plans.

Not removing his mouth from her breast, he pushed her shirt from her shoulder and let it fall to the floor. Her reaction was minimal. He noticed her clench and release her hand before relaxing back into the feeling of his mouth on her flesh.

And it was glorious flesh. Kim had the most amazing tits. They weren't huge, but they were perfect for everything he wanted to do to them.

Once he was satisfied her breast was nice and tender, he moved on to the other one, giving it the same treatment. When he was happy with his progress, he captured her mouth with his again and reached for the zipper on her skirt.

The leather began separating as he slid the zipper lower. He felt her stiffen and waited to see what she would do.

"Please."

"Please, what?" he asked.

"I don't want everyone to see me naked."

"What did I tell you before?"

She pressed her lips together for a moment before she answered, "That every part of me is beautiful."

"That's right. Every part of you from your head to your toes." He paused. "Especially your beautiful pussy."

Justin saw her swallow and then nod. He finished unzipping her skirt and pushed it down her hips. The material pooled at her feet. Kneeling, he helped her step out of it and tossed it to the side.

The sight before him was stuff wet dreams were made of. Kim stood inches away from him, in nothing but a pair of black boots that ended an inch or so below her knees. She was the sexiest thing he'd ever seen.

Unable to resist, he spread her legs and took a long lick. "Hmm. Just as I thought. You're nice and wet for me."

Not wanting to push her too far tonight, but wanting to push the point home, Justin stood and lifted her into his arms.

She let out a little squeak and grabbed hold of his shoulders for a second before releasing him. "It's okay, baby. You can hold on to me."

Wrapping her arms around his neck, she held on tight as he brought her over to a low table set up near the spanking bench. It was lower than a standard table, making it the perfect height for sex or cunnilingus.

He set her down and reached into his pocket for a condom. "Unfasten my jeans."

While she may not have use of her sight, Kim didn't have issues finding the button on his jeans. With all her issues with being naked in front of an audience, she seemed not to have the same issue with him sans clothes.

As soon as his cock was free, he ripped the condom open and rolled it down his length. Holding the base, he lined himself up and pressed his hips forward.

Her muscles clenched around him and welcomed him into her warmth. He laid her back, pressing her into the table as he picked up the pace. This wasn't a slow seduction, nor was it meant to be. And for the first time since the scene began, he felt her attention was completely on him. She wasn't thinking about the potential people watching her or seeing her naked body. She was in the moment. With him.

Justin felt his body coil tight as his orgasm approached and snaked his hand between them. He circled her clit with his thumb, increasing the pressure until he felt her body tense. "Come for me."

He punctuated his words with several hard thrusts. Kim's head fell back against the table and her nails scraped his scalp as she found her release.

Dipping his head down, he captured one of her nipples in his mouth once more while he chased his own climax. A surge of energy raced up his balls moments before his orgasm hit him.

He rested his head against her chest as he caught his breath, then propped himself up on his elbows. She was breathing as hard as he was and she was still wearing the blindfold.

Grinning, Justin stepped back so he could slide out of her, took care of the condom in a nearby trashcan, and helped her from the table. Once she was on her feet again, he reached up and untied the blindfold, letting her see again.

Kim blinked several times as her eyes adjusted to the light. She looked at him, and then as if remembering where they were, her gaze shifted toward the door and the big picture window beside it. The window that he had darkened before he'd used the first toy on her to give them privacy.

She whipped her head back to look at him. "I thought..."

Justin tucked a lock of hair behind her ear. "Tonight wasn't about showing you off. It was about you learning to trust me as your Dom."

"I'm trying."

He pulled her into his arms and gave her a hard kiss. "Get dressed and we'll go downstairs and talk."

❧

After getting dressed, he'd taken hold of Kim's hand and escorted her to one of the many seating areas on the main floor of the club. He'd left her only long enough to retrieve two bottles of water from the bar before rejoining her on the couch. Kim took the bottle he handed to her and was about to unscrew the cap when he grasped her by the hips and lifted her onto his lap. The bottle slipped out of her hands, landing between two of the cushions.

Justin picked it up and handed it to her again. "Drink your water."

She was thirsty, so she downed almost half the bottle in one go. He brought his water to his lips and chugged the entire thing in one go. Her gaze drifted to the muscles in his neck and she had the urge to lick him. She would have thought her libido would have been satisfied, but apparently not.

"What are you thinking about?" he asked when he noticed her staring.

"I was thinking about what happened upstairs." That was true, but not exactly. Still, she really didn't want to talk about how she was becoming a sex maniac. "Am I in trouble again?"

"Do you think you should be?"

"I don't know. You did tell me to keep my arms down and I didn't."

He nodded. "This is true. Did you disobey me intentionally or was it an automatic reaction?"

She glanced down at the bottle she held in her hands. "I didn't intentionally disobey you."

Lifting her chin, he made her look at him. "I didn't think so. You covered yourself almost immediately once I opened your top."

"I wish I had known no one was watching." She wouldn't have freaked out if she'd known only he could see her.

Justin dropped his arm and sat back on the couch. He eased her weight back against him. "That would have defeated the purpose of the exercise."

He'd been testing her. She wasn't sure how she felt about that.

As if he could read her mind, or maybe it was the way her body tensed, he asked, "Does that upset you?"

"I'm not used to the guys I'm with being able to read me so well."

His chest vibrated beneath her. "A Dom needs to be able to read his sub. And it helps that we've known each other for a long time. I know your tells."

Kim took another sip of her water. She knew his tells as well. He had a muscle in his jaw that pulsated when he got angry. It didn't happen often.

He caressed the outside of her thigh as they sat there on the couch, her head resting against his shoulder. She continued to sip her water and listen to the music play in the background as people milled about around them.

Her eyes drooped, and then she noticed a woman looking at them from across the room. Kim had seen her around the club before, but she didn't know her. "Sir?"

"Yes?" He brushed some hair away from her face, sending tingles down her cheek.

"Who is that woman?"

He tilted his head to see who she was referring to. "Her name is Angela. She's a switch."

"What's a switch?" Kim had been around the club for three months and she'd never heard that term before.

"It's someone who switches from being a Dominant or a submissive depending on who they're playing with."

Kim thought about that for a few moments. She thought about Beth and Drew. "Are Lady Beth and Drew switches?"

Justin chuckled. "No. Beth is a Domme and Drew is her submissive. They don't ever switch. Not with each other and not with other people."

"But Angela does."

"Yes."

Kim pressed her lips together and debated whether to ask the question lingering in her mind. In the end, she decided she had to ask. "Has she ever played with you?"

His fingers drew circles on her bare thigh. "A couple of times."

She closed her eyes and tried not to let that bother her, but jealousy raced through her veins. Kim knew Justin had been with other women. He was thirty-four and a member of a kink club. But that didn't mean having one of the women right in front of her was an easy pill to swallow. She knew, however, that if they were to continue their relationship, she would have to get used to it.

To her surprise, he didn't try to placate her or explain away any interaction he'd had with Angela. "I'm one of three Doms she likes to play with when she's in a submissive frame of mind."

Three Doms.

Of course, Kim knew that Justin and Angela weren't in a relationship, but that didn't mean there wasn't anything there. On her side anyway.

When Kim opened her eyes again, the woman was still stealing glances in their direction, even though she was trying to be coy about it. "I think maybe it was more than just playing for her."

"It wasn't," he insisted.

Kim couldn't seem to let it go. "Then why does she keep looking over at us?"

Justin sat up, startling her. He waited until she'd gotten her bearings back and was looking at him. "I don't know why she's looking at us. Maybe she's curious about my new sub."

She opened her mouth to counter his assertion that Angela was only curious, but he cut her off.

"It doesn't matter. You are my submissive and while we're together, I won't be playing with anyone else and neither will you. Understood?"

"Yes, Sir."

"Good." Justin helped her onto her feet, then stood. "Ali's been gazing over here since we sat down. I'm sure she wants to talk to you and see how your first time upstairs went."

Kim glanced over to the far side of the room. Ali was looking at him, a mixture of curiosity and glee on her face.

They made their way over to where Ali was perched on the front of her seat, barely able to contain herself. Justin kept his fingers laced with hers as he addressed the group Ali was with. "Mind if we join you?"

"Of course not," Daniel said. He moved to another chair, freeing up the space next to Ali for them.

Justin sat down and motioned for Kim to take a seat next to him. She hadn't been sure if he'd want her to sit, but luckily, he hadn't made her guess. He leaned back, resting his arm on the back of the couch, and began playing with the hairs at the base of her neck. He'd made her put her hair up earlier, saying he wanted unfettered access to her neck. Considering she melted almost every time he touched or kissed her there, she'd have to find ways to wear her hair up when he was around more often.

"How's the shop?" Daniel asked.

"Good. We've been busy for the last few months. Our reputation seems to be growing."

The conversation turned to cars and Kim turned her attention to Ali. It wasn't that she disliked cars, but the talk of engines and fuel injectors was a foreign language to her.

As soon as she looked at her best friend, she knew the floodgates were about to open. "How did your brunch go? Did you spend all day together?"

"Okay, I guess. I mean, I've never done anything like that before with a guy. It was kind of strange talking about what you like and what you want to try." They were talking low, but she knew at least Justin could hear them if he was paying attention. He seemed too engaged in his conversation with Daniel and Jeff, though.

"It gets easier. The first time I went over my limit list with a Dom, I think I turned five shades of red," Ali confessed.

"Yeah. I don't know how many times I blushed."

"It's to be expected."

"I know. But it's still weird," Kim said.

Ali shifted a little closer. "So I know you said you got in trouble this afternoon, but you went upstairs. Did you just watch or did he take you into one of the playrooms?"

"One of the playrooms."

Her friend let out a little squeal. "How did it go?"

"I messed up again."

Ali frowned. "What happened?"

"It wasn't as bad as this afternoon, but he took my shirt off and I covered myself even though he'd told me to keep my hands down at my side." Kim sighed. "But as it turns out, no one could see me but him. He darkened the window to the room."

"You shouldn't be self-conscious. You have an amazing body. And if you haven't noticed, no one here is going to think you being naked as weird."

Kim followed Ali's gaze as she looked around the room at the other members of the club. Not five feet from them, a sub was sitting on her Dom's lap topless. From each nipple hung what looked like jewelry. "I know that. I'm just not used to being naked in front of people."

"You didn't seem to have issues being naked in front of Justin when you showed up at his house and offered yourself to him."

"That was different."

"How?" Ali asked. "You weren't in a relationship with him. You weren't even really friends. And yet, you didn't think twice about showing up on his doorstep in nothing but a trench coat and laying yourself bare for him like you were the main dish on a buffet."

Kim chuckled. "Nice visual."

Her friend shrugged. "Ultimately, it all comes back to the same thing. Trust. Did you put exhibitionism as a hard limit?"

"A soft limit."

She nodded. "Trust."

Kim knew her friend was right. Justin hadn't done anything to make her question her trust in him. Nothing he'd done had crossed any of her hard limits. Now all she had to do was get her brain to remember that every time they were playing together. Otherwise, her ass was going to be very sore.

Chapter Seventeen

Justin focused on talking to Daniel and Jeff, letting Kim and Ali have as much privacy as possible given where they were. Ali had been a member of the club before he joined, and he'd seen her play a few times. She knew how to submit to a Dom and what kind of mindset was required during a scene. Hopefully, she'd be able to help Kim.

"Sir?"

At the sound of Kim's question, he shifted in his seat, giving her his full attention.

She leaned in, lowering her voice. "I need to use the bathroom."

Pleased she'd asked before just walking off, he smiled and nodded his assent.

He watched as she and Ali strolled across the room to where the restrooms were located toward the back of the club. The skirt he'd chosen hugged her hips, framing her ass. Knowing she had nothing on under said skirt had him wanting to bend her over, lift the skirt, and take her from behind. It had been almost two hours since they'd come downstairs and his cock was itching to get inside her again.

"How are things going with the new sub?" Daniel asked. The older Dom had a lot more experience than Justin. He was in his fifties and had been in the lifestyle for over twenty years.

"As well as can be expected. She has a lot to learn, but she'll get there." Justin hoped, anyway.

"Ah, confidence. That's good, but don't get too cocky about it. She strikes me as being very stubborn."

Justin snorted. "She is."

Daniel nodded. "Ali will help her. She's a good submissive."

The pride in his voice piqued Justin's interest. "I've never seen you and Ali play together."

A solemn look took hold of the older Dom's features. "No, we've never played together."

Again, his tone had Justin wondering if maybe he was missing something, but he let it go. It wasn't any of his business in any case. "Have you ever trained a new sub? One who was new to the lifestyle, I mean?"

Daniel nodded. "I have. It can require a lot of patience."

"Can't disagree with you there," Justin said, remembering what happened earlier that afternoon.

Daniel grinned. "My best advice is to take it slow and don't try and throw a lot of new things at her all at once. When you do a scene, pick one thing to test the waters on and keep consistent. It all comes down to building that trust. Once she can let go, everything else will fall into place."

Very good advice and something he would have to keep in mind going forward. As much as he feared the reaction Mark, Davis, and Belinda would have to him and Kim being together, he wanted things between them to work. Which meant he had to take it slow. "Thanks. I'll keep that in mind."

"I'm here if you have any specific questions. And there are a few other Doms who have experience with new subs as well I can recommend if you'd like another perspective."

"I appreciate it."

Kim and Ali headed toward them, and Justin stood. He was ready to go home. That little taste of her he'd gotten earlier wasn't nearly enough.

He waited until Kim was within arm's reach. "Say goodbye to Ali."

She blinked up at him but turned and gave her friend a hug. "I'll call you tomorrow."

"You'd better." Ali gave him a knowing look as she embraced Kim, but he ignored it.

Justin took hold of Kim's hand, and they made their way to the foyer to get their coats. Given how little clothing she had on, he made sure she was buttoned up tight before they left the building. The temperature had taken a nosedive while they'd been inside the club. He felt her shiver as the wind zipped through the parking lot. He wrapped his arm around her, tucking her into his side as they rushed toward his car, trying to shield her from the wind as much as possible.

Once he'd helped her into the passenger seat, he reached into the back seat and grabbed the blanket he kept there for emergencies. It was as cold as everything else, but it would warm up quick enough. He unfolded it and draped it over her legs.

"Thanks." Kim shoved her hands underneath the blanket and pulled it higher to wrap around her middle.

Happy she was as warm as he could get her for now, he jogged around the car and slid behind the wheel. He put the key in the ignition and the engine roared to life. The sound never failed to bring a smile to his face.

"What are you smiling about?" Kim asked as she huddled deeper under the blanket.

"Thinking about all the work I did on this car."

"You're smiling about work?"

Justin chuckled. "Yep."

She was quiet for several minutes. "Was the car in really bad shape when you got it?"

He hadn't thought she'd be interested. She'd never shown interest in cars before. But he had to admit it pleased him that she'd asked. "Yes and no. The body was in great shape, but under the hood was a nightmare."

The temperature gauge was finally moving away from cold, so he turned the heater on full blast, hoping it would at least get the chill out of the car before they got back to his house. Warm air steamed out of the vents and Kim held her hands directly in front of one.

"Why was it a nightmare?"

He glanced over at her, and she genuinely looked interested. "The previous owner tried to soup up the engine."

"I'm guessing he didn't do it right?"

Justin snorted. To say he'd done a shitty job would be an understatement. "Not even close."

She turned in her seat so she could face him. The car was warming up and she wasn't shivering anymore. "He wanted you to fix it?"

"He did, but he underestimated what it would take. I think he almost had a heart attack when I gave him the price." Justin recalled how the man had gone pale, then beat red. He really had thought he was going to have to call an ambulance for the guy.

"So what happened? How did you end up with it?"

Justin pulled into his driveway and turned off the car. "He didn't like my price, but after taking it to ten other repair shops that refused to touch it, he didn't have many options."

"You offered to buy it from him."

His girl was smart.

Justin blew out a breath. She wasn't his girl. Not really. Not yet, anyway. They had to see if this could work first.

"Half the car would have to be taken apart, fixed, and then reassembled. It would take weeks, if not months to complete. The guy had already put a lot of money into the car and couldn't plow that much more into it, so I made him an offer." Justin ran a hand over the dashboard before reaching for the door handle. "One of the best business deals I've ever made."

Hopping out of the vehicle, he went to help Kim, then escorted her to the door. He'd left a light on for them, but it didn't do much considering how overcast it was. There was a storm moving in. They might even have snow on the ground come morning.

Letting them into the house, he removed his coat first before helping her. Kim rubbed her bare arms, trying to warm herself up. She was shivering again.

"Come here." He wrapped his arms around her, holding her tight against his chest.

She buried her face in the crook of his shoulder. Her nose was cold against his bare skin. "It wasn't this cold when we left."

"No, it wasn't. It has to have dropped at least twenty degrees."

Another ripple went through her body as she tried to suck up more of his heat.

Seeing how cold she was, his plans for her outfit were put on the back burner. "Let's get you into bed. Then I'll make sure you're warmed up."

She gazed up at him, a twinkle in her eyes. "Promise?"

Justin chuckled and pressed his lips to hers for a brief kiss. "Promise."

They were almost to his bedroom when his phone dinged, letting him know he had a new message. He ignored it and led her into his room. It was the first time she'd been there since the morning after their night together. Memories of her in his bed had lingered for weeks.

Pulling her into his arms once more, he covered her mouth with his in a lingering kiss. "Do what you need to do in the bathroom."

She nodded, then disappeared into the adjoining room.

Digging out his phone, he checked to see who'd messaged him.

Still on for tomorrow night? - Mark

All the conflicting feelings he had about what he was doing with Kim came to the surface again. How hard was it going to be to sit across from his best friend and not mention the fact that he was involved with his sister? Mark loved to talk about women, especially when he was drinking. Even though he didn't understand Justin's lifestyle, he was always asking about the women Justin dated. The problem was, Justin couldn't tell Mark anything this time.

For a moment, he thought about canceling, but then another wave of guilt hit. If this thing with Kim worked out, he couldn't hide from his best friend forever.

Yep. See you at 5. - Justin

He heard the shower turn on and thoughts of Kim naked and wet pushed all thoughts of Mark and the potential fallout from his mind. Leaving his phone on the dresser, he removed his clothes and headed into the bathroom.

Steam was already filling up the room when he let himself inside. Kim's head was tilted back as water streamed down her body. His cock stood at attention, aching to be inside her again.

Snatching a condom from the drawer next to the sink, he made his way to the shower and slid open the glass door.

⁂

Kim startled when she heard the shower door. She hadn't heard him come into the room.

He placed something on the ledge, then backed her against the wall. The cool tiles were a sharp contrast to the water that had been spraying on her a moment before. "Hi."

His body was flush against her and she could feel him hard against her stomach. "Feeling warmer now?"

Heat that had nothing to do with the shower took over. "Yes."

She'd barely gotten her answer out when his mouth descended, cutting off anything else she was going to say. He took control of the kiss, leaving her no doubt as to who was in charge.

Fingers slid into the wet heat between her legs. "Have you ever fucked in a shower before?"

His lips moved down to her neck, licking and sucking on her skin and sending her heart racing. She held tight to his shoulders. "No. I've never—"

Justin plunged two fingers into her pussy. He wasn't gentle about it, but for some reason that turned her on more. "Hmm. You like that, don't you?"

There was no reason to deny it. He could feel how wet she was. "Yes."

He added a third finger and positioned his thumb so it was bumping her clit with every upward thrust. She found herself pushing against his hand, trying to get more friction. Her orgasm was building, but it wasn't quite enough to push her over the edge. She needed more. "More. Please."

"Please what?" He didn't even sound winded.

How could he not know what she meant?

Then she realized her error. "Please, Sir, I need more. I want to come, but I need more."

Instead of giving her more, he pulled his fingers from her pussy. She didn't have time to protest, though, before he lifted her off her feet and placed her on the opposite side of the shower. Turning her around, facing away from him, he pressed on her back. "Bend over and put your hands on the seat."

There was a small bench built into the shower on the opposite side of the showerhead. Her hands were barely on the seat when she felt his hands on her hips. He lifted her up again and used his feet to spread her legs. She felt a little like a rag doll.

His hands left her body for several moments and she heard him moving around behind her. But before she could get too worried, he was back and this time it wasn't his fingers that were pressing against her sex.

Her eyes rolled back in her head as his length entered her, sending ripples of heat radiating through her body. He lined himself up and thrust into her with enough force that she almost lost her balance. She readjusted her stance and prepared to meet every one of his thrusts.

He wrapped one arm around her waist, using that as leverage to drive deeper, harder, into her. With his free hand, he reached down and pinched her nipple, sending sparks directly to her pussy. Her climax was building...fast. It wouldn't take much more to send her flying. Without thinking, she lifted one hand to rub her clit, needing release.

"Don't you dare touch your clit. Your orgasms belong to me. I decide when you come." He landed a firm smack on her ass.

Even though it hurt, it did nothing to calm her need to come. She was too far gone. If anything, his words had made it worse. Her entire body felt as if it were on fire.

Justin didn't relent. She had no clue how long he continued to pump in and out of her before he finally snaked a hand between her legs and gave her the release she was so desperate for. Her scream echoed inside the confined space, leaving her feeling spent.

He held on to her as she caught her breath. Her body felt as if it were vibrating and she wasn't sure she could walk or not.

"Sit down while I clean up." He helped her to turn around and made sure she wasn't going to dissolve into a puddle on the floor before stepping out of the shower to dispose of the condom.

Kim rested her head against the side of the shower. She could still feel him between her legs and yet felt the emptiness of him not being inside her anymore at the same time.

When he returned, he knelt in front of her and waited for her to meet his gaze. "How are you feeling?"

"Like someone just pounded my insides."

Justin released something between a laugh and a snort. He stood, lifting her up with him. She fell into him with an *omph*.

"Think you can walk, or do I need to carry you?" he asked.

That was a good question. She eased away from him, taking a tentative step to the side, and nearly fell on her face.

The next thing Kim knew, her feet were no longer on the ground. She clung to his neck as he carried her out of the shower and placed her on top of the vanity. He left her for no more than a second to grab a towel. She went to take it, but he ignored her and began drying her off himself.

"I can dry myself, you know?"

One side of his mouth lifted in a sexy smirk, but he didn't comment.

Once he'd wiped all the water from her body, he began working on her hair. He took his time, running his fingers through the strands and gathering any excess moisture into the towel. She let her eyes drift closed as he touched her. Never in all her fantasies over the years did she think she'd be sitting on Justin's bathroom counter while he took care of her like this.

With her body and mind slowly coming down from their high, she was getting sleepy. All she wanted to do was curl up in his very comfortable bed and fall asleep.

"Put your arms around my neck."

As soon as she wrapped her arms around him, he lifted her from the counter. Kim rested her head on his shoulder. A drop of water dripped from his hair onto his neck and she stuck out her tongue to lick it up.

Justin groaned. "Behave yourself."

"Can't help it." The words were mumbled, but it was the best she could manage.

He adjusted his hold on her, then she was being laid on the bed. When she didn't release her hold on him, he chuckled. "You can let go now."

"K." She let her arms fall to the bed, rolled over onto her side, and sighed as he pulled the covers over her.

Moments later, she felt the mattress dip as Justin climbed in beside her. He gathered her into his arms, tucking her into his side. She rested her head on his shoulder again, letting her nose graze his collarbone.

"Comfortable?" His chest vibrated under her cheek.

Kim felt his lips brush her forehead. "Hmm. Very." She was warm. She was comfortable. And most of all, she felt content.

Chapter Eighteen

Something warm against Justin's chest woke him the next morning. He'd been in such a deep sleep, he didn't register at first what it was, only that it felt good. But as the sleepy fog cleared, he realized someone was kissing their way down his chest, lower to his abdomen. Memories of the night before flooded his mind and his cock stood ready to continue where they'd left off.

She was heading south and he had no notion to stop her. Waking up to Kim in his bed was something he'd only dreamed about. The reality was proving better than any fantasy and he planned to take advantage of it. He laced his fingers through her hair, encouraging her to keep going to where he was aching for her.

Knowing he was awake, she scooted farther down the bed, her mouth hovering over his cock. She hesitated and glanced up to meet his gaze. "May I, Sir?"

He was pleased she'd asked permission. "Yes, you may. But don't make me come."

Her brow furrowed a little, then her eyes glazed over a bit, understanding that this was only the prelude. She was going to find out the benefits of not running from his bed first thing in the morning.

Kim's lips circled the head of his cock, licking the bead of pre-cum from the tip. He couldn't stop the groan that escaped at the feel of her tongue. If he'd thought he craved her before, it was nothing compared to now.

Justin closed his eyes as she sucked him in, using her mouth to pleasure him to the point where he wanted to explode. But coming down her throat wasn't what he had in mind. As great as her mouth felt, he wanted her hot little pussy wrapped around him, milking him dry.

Taking her by the shoulders, he hauled her up the length of his body and tossed her onto the bed beside him. She giggled as she landed on the mattress. "Did I do a good job sucking your cock, Sir?"

There was a twinkle in her eyes that he loved. And hearing her calling him Sir pulled at something deep within him. "You did a very good job sucking my cock, baby, and now I'm going to reward you by fucking you and making you come."

Her eyes darkened and a sound he could only describe as a purr emerged from her throat. "Yes, please."

Reaching over to the nightstand, he opened the drawer and grabbed a condom. She spread her legs wide, inviting him in as he rolled the protection down his length, and the sight of her sex open and wet beckoning him almost made him come all on its own.

He fell forward, bracing himself with one arm while he guided his erection to her entrance. "Wrap your legs around me."

She circled her legs around his waist and threaded her hands behind his head. He tilted his hips forward, sinking into her warmth. She was a little tight, probably because it was morning, but after a few shallow thrusts, she opened up to him and he sank into her balls deep.

Her breasts jiggled as he pumped his hips, pressing her into the bed. It was mesmerizing watching her hard nipples dance to the rhythm he set.

Unable to resist, he dipped his head down to capture one of the taut buds into his mouth. She released a contented sigh as he suckled her breast. Her head was thrown back and her eyes were closed. He could feel her nails as they dug into his scalp. The sensation sent shots of electricity to his cock and he knew he wasn't going to last much longer.

Taking hold of one of her hands, he brought it between them, guiding her to where they were joined. "Touch yourself."

She complied instantly, probably needing to come as badly as he did.

Justin sucked in a breath as her fingers brushed against his erection and he gave up on holding back. He rocked his hips faster...harder, picking up the pace.

Kim's eyes flew open and she began rubbing her clit in time with his thrusts. She lifted her hips, meeting his downward strokes with an upward one of her own. He knew she was close. So was he. The pressure building in his balls was about to explode.

"Come." He spoke the word a moment before he bit down on her nipple, sending a shot of pain through her already sensitive breasts.

It did exactly what he'd hoped. A spasm went through her body a moment before she let out a delicious scream. She rode out her orgasm as he drove into her until his own climax took hold.

He tumbled beside her on the bed, pulling her to onto her side. "You all right?"

Kim laughed. "I don't know."

"Broke you, did I?" He smiled. "How's your breast?"

Glancing down, she inspected her abused nipple. "Doesn't look like you broke the skin. I think I'll survive."

"A very good thing as I have plans for these beautiful tits of yours." He placed a gentle kiss on the red marks surrounding her nipple.

"Well, if they lead to more orgasms like that one, I won't object." She tucked her hands under her head. "I've never had so many powerful orgasms before."

"You like a little pain with your sex."

Kim frowned. "That sounds like it should be a bad thing."

Justin rested his hand on her hip, unable to keep from touching her. "Not at all. It's perfectly normal. Ask the submissives in your group today."

"That's different. They're into kinky stuff."

Justin's grin grew bigger. "Baby, I hate to break it to you, but so are you."

She was quiet for a few moments and he wondered what was going on in her mind. "I guess that's true, but I'm not sure I'm a very good submissive."

He'd been waiting for the right time to talk about last night. Ideally, they wouldn't be lying in bed naked, but he wasn't willing to let the moment pass. She wanted to talk, so they'd talk. "What makes you say that?"

"The submissives at the club seem so...submissive." He was about to point out the irony in that statement but remained quiet as she continued. "I mean, I know Ali isn't most of the time, but there she's different. And it isn't just her. All I have to do is watch someone for a few minutes and I can tell if they're a Dom or a sub in the way they interact with people." Kim sighed. "I'm just not sure I can do that."

"So you're not sure you can defer to your Dom?" He paused. "To me?" He tried not to let disappointment take over his thoughts. She was new to this and it would take time for her to figure it out. Heaven knew it had taken him a while to find his feet.

"I don't know." She met his gaze, sadness in her eyes. "I want to, but I'm afraid I'll disappoint you."

He ran a hand down the side of her face and tucked a lock of hair behind her ear. "Remember what I said last night about trust?"

She nodded.

"At the heart of it, that's what this lifestyle is. Trust. You don't have to trust every Dom you meet. You don't have to obey every Dom, either. But the connection you have with the one you choose to be your Dom should allow you to feel comfortable enough to give up control."

"What if I can't?" Her question was honest, and knowing her like he did, he could understand her concern.

"Let's just take one step at a time, okay?" She looked skeptical, but that was Kim. She liked to have a plan. "We agreed to give it a try for a month, right?"

She nodded. "I need to get out of my own head."

Justin placed a soft kiss on her lips. "Yes, you do. We're going to work on that."

A spark came into her eyes again, giving him hope. "I hope you know what you're in for."

He chuckled. "Oh, I think I have an idea." Palming her backside, he gave it a light slap. "I just hope your ass doesn't end up permanently red in the process."

She playfully pushed at his chest. "Sadist."

Justin laughed. He rolled away from her and tossed the covers off them both. "Come on, let's get some breakfast. I need to replenish my energy before I turn you over my knee again."

Kim picked up his pillow and threw it at him.

He caught it, threw it onto the floor, and reached for her. Her feet hit the floor for less than a second before he was slinging her over his shoulder, fireman style.

With her ass right in his face, he gave it another firm tap. "I thought I told you to behave."

Her response was to give his backside a slap right back.

He'd never had such a spunky submissive before, but he had to admit a part of him was looking forward to the challenge.

❧

AFTER PICKING HER UP, JUSTIN CARRIED HER INTO THE BATHROOM AND SET her on her feet. "Get dressed while I make us some food." He gave her a hard kiss, then turned on his heel and left her alone.

Kim blew out a loud breath and took a moment to center herself. So much had happened within the last twenty-four hours. She was in a D/s relationship with Justin. It may not last for more than a month, but their talk this morning had helped. Ali told her last night that Justin was really good with submissives, and that he'd help her get over her issues with giving up control.

Actually, what she said was that he'd help Kim get over her fear of giving up control.

At first, she'd balked at Ali's assertion. Kim wasn't afraid. She'd joined Serpent's Kiss, hadn't she?

But the more Kim thought about it, the more she knew Ali was right. Kim had learned early in her career to be assertive and to go after what she wanted. If she didn't, then someone else was going to get there first. She'd never be where she was at her job if she hadn't put her head down, worked her butt off, and made her intentions clear that she'd wanted the VP position.

That didn't mean she loved being in control of everything, though, did it? Especially when it came to sex, she liked when Justin took control. She liked that she didn't have to think of what would happen next. Or if she should move into a different position.

Kim did her business, washed her face, brushed her teeth, and dug out another one of Justin's shirts from the drawer. She debated throwing on a pair of his boxer briefs but decided against it. He seemed to like her without panties.

His back was to her when she strolled into the kitchen. The room smelled like bacon and her tummy rumbled in response. She'd worked up an appetite.

Walking up behind him, she circled her arms around his waist, resting her cheek on his back and taking in his scent. "Smells good."

Justin turned and circled his arms around her. "Stole another one of my shirts, I see." His hands went directly to her bottom and he groaned. "No underwear."

His response thrilled her. "I got the impression you liked it when I was missing that particular item of clothing."

"Hmm," he said, lowering his head to capture her mouth with his. "That I do."

The kiss was way too short, but she understood. He didn't want the food to burn. "Anything I can do to help?" she asked.

"You can set the table and get the milk and juice out of the fridge." He flipped the pancakes. "The food's almost done."

As she hurried to get the plates and silverware onto the table, Kim realized she was beginning to enjoy the feeling of not wearing any panties. At least, when she was in private with Justin nearby. She liked that at any time he could bend her over a chair and take her.

It was strange. She'd never had those kinds of thoughts before with a boyfriend. Of course, most of her boyfriends were rather docile compared to Justin, especially in the sexual aspect of their relationships. That is, if they got that far.

Yep, her sex life before Justin was rather boring.

"Watch yourself," Justin said as he brought the skillet of eggs over to the table and spooned a large portion onto each of their plates.

"Thanks."

He smiled, then made his way back to the stove to get the bacon and pancakes.

Everything tasted really good. She wasn't sure if that meant he was that good of a cook or if she was just that hungry. Either way, she was halfway through her plate of food before she came up for air. "Thanks for making breakfast."

His gaze raked over her from head to toe, lingering on her bare legs peeking out from the end of his long shirt. "I need to keep you fed, now, don't I?"

Heat rushed to her cheeks as a surge of feminine power flowed through her. No underwear was definitely the right decision.

They finished up their breakfast and loaded the dishwasher before heading back to his room to get dressed. In hindsight, that might not have been the best decision as they ended up back where they started...in his bed.

By the time they'd both showered and dressed, it was close to noon. "I should get back home and throw in a load of laundry before I have to pick up Ali."

"You're going to the submissive meeting today at Beth's Café?"

"Yeah." Kim grabbed her purse and placed it over her shoulder. "Ali thinks it would be good for me to talk to other submissives."

"It will be." Justin took hold of both her hands. "Remember, they've all been in your position at one time."

She blew out a breath and went to change the subject. "How is this thing with us going to work? I mean, I figure I'll see you on weekends at the club, but—"

"If you think I'm going to go a week without seeing you, you're crazy."

Warmth bloomed in her chest. She knew he'd agreed to give this thing between them a go for a month, but they hadn't really discussed what all that would entail outside of her being his submissive. "What did you have in mind?"

"Well," he said as he pulled her against his chest, "I thought maybe I could pick you up tomorrow night and we could go out to dinner."

"A date?"

"A date." He cupped her face and gave her a lingering kiss. "How does seven o'clock sound?"

Her happiness was dashed as soon as it came. "What if someone sees us?" The chances of them running into her brother while they were out to dinner were slim, but that didn't mean they wouldn't see someone they knew and it would get back to Mark.

"I told you before. I'm not going to hide you like a dirty secret, and I meant it."

She pressed her lips together and met his gaze. "I thought we were keeping things between us for a month."

He didn't answer right away, but he didn't let her go either. "I'm meeting your brother at O'Brien's tonight."

Kim took hold of his wrist and gave it a squeeze. She was asking him to keep a secret from his best friend. He'd agreed to it, but she also understood the dilemma he was facing. She'd gone through something similar when she hadn't shared with Ali that she'd slept with Justin. It had created some awkward moments and a lot of internal arguments with herself. Finally telling Ali had lifted a huge weight off her shoulders.

But things with Mark were different and both Justin and Kim knew it. The fact that Mark knew about Justin's preferences when it came to sex complicated things. How would her brother react to finding out Justin and Kim were an item?

She honestly didn't know.

"Your monthly hangout?" she asked.

"Yeah."

Kim waited for him to say something more, but he didn't. "You could cancel. Tell him something came up."

Justin shook his head. "Then I'd feel like even more of an asshole than I already do."

She furrowed her brow and scrunched up her nose. "Why do you feel like an asshole?"

"Because I'm fucking my best friend's sister."

Dropping her hands, she took a step back and he let his hands drop to his sides. "Have *you* changed your mind?"

The next thing she knew, she was pressed against a wall and being kissed to within an inch of her life. Kim clung to him, meeting the caress of his tongue with one of her own.

By the time they came up for air, her chest was heaving with each breath she took. She could feel him hard against her stomach, leaving her no doubt that he wanted her.

"Does that answer your question?" His voice was husky and deep. It sent delicious shivers down her spine.

She licked her lips and his gaze followed the movement.

"I'll pick you up tomorrow at seven. Dress in something comfortable."

"I have to work on Tuesday," she whispered against his lips.

"Mmm. So do I." His mouth descended again and she could already feel her body softening for him again. All thoughts of Mark pushed from her mind.

By the time he dropped her off at her house, her body was humming again. If not for the fact that she'd promised Ali she'd pick her up for the submissive meeting, Kim would have gladly spent the entire day in bed with Justin.

Chapter Nineteen

"Don't be nervous."

Kim glanced over at her best friend and frowned. "I'm not." When Ali gave her a skeptical look, she clarified. "Not much, anyway."

"There's nothing to be nervous about." Ali met her on the sidewalk and they began making their way toward Beth's Café.

"Can't be worse than my first night at the club, right?" Kim squared her shoulders as the café came into view. She'd never been to Beth's Café, but she'd heard about it from a few people at work. The muffins were supposed to be phenomenal. Too bad they were closed on Sundays. She'd have to come by during the week and try it out. Especially since she now knew the owner.

Ali scoffed and knocked on the door. "I would certainly hope not."

A few moments later, the door opened and Drew greeted them, dressed in kakis and a sweater. Kim didn't think she'd seen him in anything other than jeans and a T-shirt before. "Come on in, ladies."

"Thanks," Ali said as she stepped inside and stomped her feet on the welcome mat. It had snowed the night before, leaving almost an inch on the sidewalks. Luckily, nothing much had stuck to the roads.

Kim followed Ali inside and they both removed their coats.

"I'm glad you decided to come," Drew said to Kim. "Beth told me you might."

"Ali and Justin thought it would be good for me."

He nodded and gestured for them to follow him toward the back of the café where the rest of the group waited. "I'd been with Beth for a few months when she suggested it might be good for me to talk to other submissives away from the club and all the protocols there. I thought about trying to join another submissive group that meets locally, but after attending one meeting, I knew it wasn't a good fit for me. One of the perks of being a member of Serpent's Kiss is privacy. They were meeting in a popular restaurant at lunchtime."

"Not exactly private," Ali said.

"Not at all." Drew came to a stop in front of a table full of finger sandwiches and muffins. "Help yourselves. There are some benefits to meeting here. Namely, Beth's food."

Ali picked up a plate and began loading it up. "You're a lucky man."

Drew chuckled. "Yes, I am." He glanced over his shoulder. "I'm going to get things started. Once you have your food, come join us at the table and we'll make sure you know everyone."

Kim grinned and nodded, but the butterflies were back. She recognized everyone that was there from the club and she knew Drew and Jeff and Ali fairly well, but the others she'd only seen in passing. Kate, the submissive whose leash Justin had been holding on Kim's first night at the club, was there talking to Bridget. While Kim knew who Bridget was because she also watched the coat check like Ali did, she didn't know anything else about her.

"Relax," Ali leaned over and whispered in Kim's ear.

Taking a deep breath in and then slowly releasing it, Kim tried. The problem was that she didn't know what to expect. Neither Justin nor Beth had really explained what this meeting was exactly. And when she'd asked Ali on the way there, her friend hadn't provided a whole lot of information either. Kim didn't like to go into situations blind and that was kind of how she felt. When she had meetings for work, she'd sometimes prepare for weeks. Nothing was left to chance. If someone asked her a question, she'd be ready for it.

This lifestyle, however, seemed to be all about unpredictability. At least for the submissive end of the relationship. Out of everything, the not knowing what was going to happen next was probably the hardest part for her. She could take being tied up, spanked, and a host of other things...as long as she was prepared.

Their plates full of a variety of goodies, Kim and Ali made their way over to the group. Everyone else was already seated and nibbling on the food in front of them.

Drew cleared his throat. "We have someone new with us today. Kim joined

Serpent's Kiss a few months ago, so you all may have seen her around the club."

A few people around the table smiled. Others nodded. Everyone seemed friendly enough. Kim was glad the submissive she'd seen last night —the one who'd been staring her down as she sat on Justin's lap—wasn't present.

"Hi," Kim said, giving a half wave to everyone at the table.

"Why don't we all go around and say our names and how long we've been in the lifestyle," Drew said. "I'll go first. My name is Drew and I've been in the lifestyle for almost a year."

He turned to his right, prompting the next person to go. "I'm Bridget. I've been in the lifestyle for about six years."

Everyone went around introducing themselves. Jeff, Kate, Emma, Madison, Victoria, Haily, and Ali. Nine people in total. Kate had been in the lifestyle the longest...fifteen years. Kim was still trying to wrap her head around that, but given the little she'd seen of Kate's interaction with her husband at the club, she guessed that made sense.

Once the introductions were done, Drew asked if anyone had something they'd like to share. Jeff spoke up first. "Nicole has been researching the violet wand. I have to admit I'm a bit nervous about it. Have any of you had any experience with it?"

"I have," Kate said. "Master likes to play with it from time to time. It looks scarier than it is."

Jeff nodded. "Everything I've found said it feels getting shocked by touching a doorknob."

"Yes and no." Kate picked up a mini muffin from her plate. "Getting shocked by touching a doorknob is one sharp sensation. While the violet wand feels similar, it's not one big shock and it's gone." She paused. "It also depends on how high it's turned up as well."

He shuddered. "That doesn't sound all that pleasant."

Kate laughed. "Depends on your level of pain tolerance."

The conversation went on for a while and Kim wondered why someone would want to do something like that. She understood there were people who got off on pain. Hell, when she was teetering on the edge of orgasm this morning, all it had taken was a shot of pain from Justin biting her nipple and she'd gone flying. She understood that type of pain, but lying still while someone ran something along your skin, shocking you...she didn't see the appeal. And from the sound of it, neither did Jeff. But it appeared he was still going to do it.

Kim turned to Ali. "If he doesn't want to do it, then why not tell his partner that?"

Ali grinned, then turned to the group. "Kim has a question." Her friend looked at her and tilted her head toward the group, waiting.

Nothing like throwing Kim under the bus. "If you don't want to do something, then why not just say no?"

Kate was the one who answered. "Because what we get out of pleasing our Dom is greater than having to take a little pain."

She must have made a face because Drew jumped in to add his perspective. "Beth enjoys knife play. When she first told me, I wasn't all that thrilled about trying it, but I did because I trusted her and knew she was in control of the scene and would take care of everything."

Kim hadn't heard of knife play before outside of the checklist, and since both she and Justin had marked it as a hard limit, they had skipped over it. "So she likes to cut you?"

He smiled. "No. Although, some Dominants are into cutting. Beth is more into the mind play involved."

"I don't understand," Kim said. "Mind play?"

Bridget leaned forward, resting her forearms on the table. "She likes to mess with his head."

Kim was really confused now.

"I'm always blindfolded, so I can't see what she doing, and she makes sure before we start the scene that I've gotten a good look at what she's planning to use on me." Drew paused and one side of his mouth lifted, clearly remembering. "A lot of times she uses the knives to cut clothing from my body, or sometimes she'll even put a butter knife in some ice and use it to write on my skin. The cold makes it feel sharper than it is."

She knew she had to look like a deer caught in the headlines. "Why would she do that? Mess with your head, I mean?"

"Because it heightens your senses," Emma said, chiming in for the first time since the introductions.

Bridget nodded. "You'd be amazed how stuff like that can increase pleasure in other areas."

Kim was still reeling from the conversation when it shifted to anal play and butt plugs. She was only half listening, though. Her brain was still trying to process what Drew had shared.

He wasn't a small man. In fact, he was taller than his Domme by at least six inches. And he was fit. Even through the sweater he was wearing, she could see the outline of his muscles.

Yet, by his own admission, he allowed himself to be tied up and knives ran along his skin while he was blindfolded. Kim couldn't imagine the level of trust it would take to do that.

She remained quiet for the remainder of the meeting, thinking about all she'd learned and was still learning. Could she trust Justin like Drew trusted Beth or Kate trusted her husband?

Kim didn't know.

And then the question was…what if she couldn't? What happened then?

EVEN THOUGH JUSTIN HAD ENCOURAGED KIM TO GO TO THE SUBMISSIVE meeting, he spent the entire afternoon worrying. He was hoping talking to other submissives, not only Ali, would help her. She needed a support system. A place to ask questions and get opinions from others who'd been where she was.

That didn't make sitting on the sidelines any easier. He wanted their relationship to work. Waking up beside her that morning had been a dream come true and he wasn't even talking about the blow job she'd given him.

There was something about Kim that drew him in. They clicked in a way he hadn't experienced with any other woman. Having her in his arms felt right. Kissing her felt as if he were coming home and being lit on fire all at the same time. He'd suffer whatever consequences there were with Mark to have that with her for the rest of their lives. But they had to make it through their one-month trial first.

Justin spent the afternoon trying to keep himself busy. He drove to the shop to get some administrative stuff done. There was always paperwork to do for the business, especially with tax season right around the corner. But sorting through receipts and looking over payroll didn't keep his mind from wandering.

At four-thirty, he locked up the shop and headed toward O'Brien's, a sports bar downtown, a few blocks from Serpent's Kiss. He and Mark tried to meet there at least once a month for dinner and drinks. Their lives had taken very different directions. They didn't hang out with the same people anymore or go to the same functions. If they wanted to get together, they had to make an effort and so far, both of them felt it was worth it.

As Justin pulled into a parking spot and turned off the engine, he hoped his relationship with Kim didn't change things with his best friend. It would be his one regret, but he was hoping they could get Mark to understand and accept them being together. That is, if things between them went the way he wanted.

Climbing out of his car, he was reaching for the door handle when someone yelled his name. He turned to see Mark jogging toward him. "Perfect timing."

Mark smiled and ducked inside when Justin opened the door. "I wasn't sure how the roads were gonna be, so I left a little early."

It was almost completely dark, and the air temperature had plummeted. He wouldn't be surprised if tonight was even colder than last night had been. They were in a cold spell, and he was already over it. If he'd wanted cold weather, he would have moved to Minnesota.

A hostess greeted them and showed them to a table. She handed them menus and let them know their server would be by shortly.

Neither of them needed to look over the menu. They'd been there so many times, they knew exactly what they were going to order. "First time you've been out today?" Justin asked.

"Yeah. I had a shit ton of emails to go through for work."

"You do realize it's Sunday, right? Don't you get a day off?" Of course, he was one to talk. Justin had spent his Sunday afternoon working, too.

"I took yesterday off. Spent most of the day with a woman I've been seeing from the accounting department."

Their server stopped by to take their orders. Mark ordered a steak. Justin a burger. And they both ordered beers.

Once they were alone again, Justin picked up the conversation where they'd left off. "Dating someone from the office? Is that wise? You don't exactly have the best track record with women."

Mark waved away his concern. "She's an intern and only here for a few months."

That made sense. Mark wasn't exactly known for his long-term relationships. "How long have you been seeing her?"

The server returned with their beers, placing them on the table and then leaving them alone once more.

A sly grin appeared on Mark's face before he took a sip of his beer. "About a week."

More time than he'd officially been with Kim. "That new, huh?"

"Gotta keep things fresh. Getting tied down isn't my style. Too many fish in the sea and all that."

That was the difference between him and Mark. At least on the surface. Mark had no interest in a long-term relationship. Justin, on the other hand, wanted to settle down. He was all for marriage and kids. He just needed the right woman and for years the woman he wanted was off-limits.

"One of these days you're going to meet someone who'll change your mind about that," Justin said, lifting his beer bottle to his lips."

"You haven't found anyone yet, so there's little hope for me." Mark chuckled.

Justin let the comment go. He didn't want to talk about Kim. Not tonight.

To shift the subject away from women, Justin commented on the basketball game currently playing on one of the big screen televisions not far from their table. They spent the next hour commenting on the game, the players, and how St. Louis really needed to get a pro team again.

"Some guys from work are getting together next weekend to watch the game. You interested?" Mark asked as they put their coats on and got ready to leave.

"What time?"

Both Justin and Mark left a nice tip and the table, and they made their way toward the front. "Four o'clock next Sunday at my place."

The first thing that came to Justin's mind was Kim. He didn't know what her plans were, but he also didn't want to assume. They'd be together Friday and Saturday night at the club. After two days of playing, she'd probably need a break. "Sure. Want me to bring anything?"

"Bring that dip you make. It will go nicely with the wings I'm grilling."

They said goodbye at the door and Justin flipped up the collar of his coat as he walked to his vehicle. The wind had picked up again. He was already ready for spring, and it was only January.

When he arrived home, the first thing he did was check his messages to make sure he hadn't missed a call from Kim. Not that he was expecting her to call, but he'd kind of been hoping she would. His curiosity about her meeting earlier was eating at him.

Satisfied but a little disappointed that she hadn't called, he stripped out of his clothes and ambled into the bathroom to take a shower. His dinner with Mark had gone better than he'd expected. He hadn't spent the entire night dodging talk of who he was dating, but he knew that had a lot to do with the distraction the game had provided.

Mark loved sports, so if anything was going to get him off the topic of women, it was that. With playoffs right around the corner, his best friend had been invested in the outcome of the game.

If nothing else, it had given Justin some hope for the future. He and Mark could hang out without bringing Justin's relationship with Kim into it. All they had to do was get over a few rough hurdles first.

Chapter Twenty

The moment Kim walked through the door at work the next day, she was bombarded with issues. One of their clients decided they didn't like the marketing campaign they'd already signed off on and was supposed to begin running next week. She'd spent most of her morning on the phone trying to nail down what exactly the client didn't like and figuring out how to adjust it without having to scrap the whole thing.

By the time lunch rolled around, Kim needed a break. She grabbed her purse, let her assistant know she was going out, and rushed out of the building before someone could waylay her.

It was below freezing, but at least the sun had come out. All the snow from Saturday night had melted, so there weren't any issues walking to her favorite lunch spot in her heels.

Georgio's was a quaint Italian bistro three blocks from her office. She tried to make it there a couple of times a month if for no other reason than their fettuccine Alfredo. She'd once tried to make it herself at home, but it hadn't compared. Today, she was badly in need of comfort food.

The cozy atmosphere calmed her and the cappuccino she'd ordered warmed her from the inside. Kim pulled up a book she'd been reading on her phone and tried to spend her lunch break relaxing. She knew the moment she got back into the office it would be full steam ahead again. They still had a lot to do before the campaign could go live and less than a week to do it.

Her lunch was over too soon, and she trudged back to the office. At five o'clock, she sent her assistant home while she continued working with the account manager. There was so much to do and so little time. She thought briefly about texting Justin and canceling their dinner plans, but she didn't want to. After the day she'd had, she needed a break. So, at six, she and the account manager called it a night and headed home.

When she breezed through the door of her apartment, she began removing her clothes as she marched toward her bedroom. There was no time for a shower, but she needed to freshen up. Bracing her right leg on the edge of the bathtub, she turned on the water and lathered up her leg. She didn't want to have prickly hair on her legs for her date.

Kim was fastening her earring in her ear when the doorbell rang. Swiping her shoes from the closet, she hurried down the hall to answer the door.

Taking a quick peek first to make sure it really was Justin, she pulled the door open. He stood on her small porch looking as delicious as ever. His hair was still damp from his shower, and he looked downright edible. Did they really have to go out?

"We aren't going to get very far if you keep looking at me like that."

Kim took a step back, inviting him in. This was the first time he'd been in her apartment. When they'd stopped by on Saturday before going to the club, he'd stayed in the car while she ran inside to pack a bag.

It felt strange having him in her space. Her apartment wasn't huge, maybe half the size of his house, but it was perfect for her. Since she didn't have a roommate and she worked all the time, there wasn't a need for a second bedroom.

He took a look around, zeroing in on the pictures she had on the wall of her mom and dad. "I don't think I've seen this one before."

She came to stand beside him. "It's from when they were dating. Mom told me that Dad proposed a week later."

Justin turned to look at her but didn't say anything.

"What? Do I have dirt on my nose or something?" She went to rub her nose, but he captured her hand in midair. He pulled her to him and she fell against his chest with a little *omph*. As she gazed up at him, there was no mistaking the look in his eyes. Or what she was feeling behind his dark jeans.

Her body responded immediately. Blood pumped through her veins and she parted her lips, ready for the kiss she knew was coming.

But instead of kissing her, he put space between them. "Are you ready to go?"

Kim blinked, trying to shift her thinking and answer his question. "Um. Sure."

He moved toward the door, reaching for the knob. When he noticed she hadn't budged, he dropped his hand. "Something wrong?"

"No." Kim shook her head. "It's just...I thought." She blew out a breath. "I thought you were going to kiss me."

"I was."

"Oh." She was confused. "Then why—"

"We are way too close to a bed and if I kiss you right now, we aren't going anywhere but into it." The heat in his gaze told her he wasn't exaggerating.

"I wouldn't complain," she whispered.

He opened the door, letting the cold air into her apartment. "I know. But I promised you a date and I intend to keep that promise."

Sensing there was no use in arguing with him, Kim put on her coat. They exited the apartment and she locked the door behind them. Justin waited to the side, hands in his pockets. She turned toward the parking lot when he grabbed her arm, halting her progress. His lips were on hers before she knew what hit her.

The kiss was swift and hard...and over before she knew it. "I thought you decided not to kiss me."

One side of Justin's mouth pulled up and his eyes danced with amusement. He was enjoying throwing her off balance. "I changed my mind."

Placing a hand on the small of her back, he led her down the sidewalk to his car. He opened the door for her and held it open while she got situated in the passenger seat. She hadn't known where they'd be going tonight, but he'd said to dress in comfortable clothes, so she'd worn a pair of jeans and one of her favorite tops. Not exactly something she'd wear at the club, but the outfit accentuated her curves and made her feel sexy.

"How was your day?" he asked as he pulled out onto the highway.

"Crazy." She chuckled and leaned her head back on the headrest.

"Want to talk about it?"

She turned to look at him. "You don't want to hear about my day."

Justin frowned. "Why not?"

"Because." Kim noticed they were headed out of town. "It's not the type of thing you talk about on a date." When he didn't comment, she added, "You don't want to hear me complain about clients."

"Isn't that what boyfriends are for?"

Something fluttered in the pit of her stomach. "Is that what this is?"

Justin's fingers flexed on the steering wheel. "I thought I made it very clear this was a relationship. Last time I checked, that would put us into boyfriend/girlfriend territory."

Biting the side of her cheek, she watched the buildings go by as they drove. She didn't say anything for a long while and he let the silence in the car linger. "I went to the submissive meeting with Ali yesterday."

"I was gonna ask you about that." He glanced over at her. "How'd it go?"

Kim looked down at her hands. "I don't know if I can do this."

A different kind of quiet settled over the vehicle. "What makes you say that?"

"Just some of the stuff they said."

"Like?" He pulled into the parking lot of what looked to be a Mexican restaurant. Once he'd found a parking place, he removed his seat belt and shifted in his seat to face her.

She shook her head. "It wasn't anything specific. It was more...they act like it was perfectly natural to let their Dominants do whatever to them. Drew talked about Beth using knives on him and Nicole wants to use something called a violet wand on Jeff..."

Justin took hold of her hands and brought them to his lips. He placed a soft kiss on each of her palms, then made her look at him. "What is it about those things that scares you?"

The tone of his voice was soothing and helped to calm her a little. "I just don't know if I could ever trust someone that much and according to you and Ali, that's what I have to do."

"Trust isn't something that happens overnight. It's built over time." He cupped the side of her face and she leaned into his touch. "Step by step."

Moisture filled her eyes and she willed herself not to cry. "I want this to work so much."

"We have a month." His hand caressed the side of her face. "I know this is new to you. If it's what we both want, we'll figure it out. Let's not get ahead of ourselves, okay?"

She knew what he said made sense and, true to her character, she was trying to put the cart before the horse. They'd been together three days. They had a long way to go before they made any major decisions. "I'll try not to stress about it too much."

A slow smile spread across his lips before he leaned in to kiss her. "No more worrying for tonight."

Kim nodded and they made their way into the restaurant.

Justin spent the next hour trying to take Kim's mind off work and contemplating all the reasons she couldn't be a good sub. In the few times they'd been together, he knew by her body's responses that she was submissive. It was her head that was getting in the way.

Kim was the type of person who went after what she wanted. Case in point was the day she showed up on his doorstep, offering herself to him on a beautiful submissive platter. It was also what landed her the executive VP marketing position at one of St. Louis's most prestigious ad agencies. But she was going to have to let go and free herself of that need for control if she wanted to live this lifestyle with him.

Some Doms would tolerate their subs to top from the bottom. Justin did not.

In the past when a sub tried to top from the bottom, he'd put a swift and clear end to any notion they had that they were in control. With Kim, things were more complicated. She wasn't doing it to try and gain an advantage. He didn't even think she was doing it intentionally. It was a security thing for her. What he needed to do was to show her that keeping her safe was his responsibility.

"Can I get either of you some dessert? Fried ice cream, perhaps?" Their server had taken their dinner plates and was trying to tempt them with dessert.

Justin glanced at Kim to see if she wanted anything else. She held up her hand in a stop motion. "I'm good. I don't think I could eat any more if I tried."

Their server looked at Justin. "Just the check, please."

Placing the bill on the table, their server nodded. "I'll take it up when you're ready."

"I can't believe I ate all that food," Kim said, leaning back in the booth. "I'm going to have to put in some time at the gym this week."

"I don't think one meal is going to hurt." Just reached over and took her hands in his. "Besides, I happen to like all your curves."

"Is that so?"

Running a finger along the inside of her wrist, he met her gaze across the table. "Gotta have something to hold on to."

He saw color rise in her cheeks as his meaning registered. She glanced around the restaurant, confirming no one at the surrounding tables had heard him. It was going to be hard to leave her tonight.

After paying the bill, they donned their winter coats again and made their way back to his car. "Home?" she asked.

"Not quite yet." He put the key in the ignition and listened to the engine purr to life.

"Where else are we going?" she asked.

Justin grinned. She really did have a difficult time not being in control of things. "You'll see."

"Not even a hint?" She placed her hand on his thigh, a few inches below his crotch.

He removed her hand from his leg and placed it back in her lap. "Nope. You'll have to be patient and wait till we get there."

After his conversation with Daniel Saturday night at the club, he'd been thinking of different ways to build Kim's trust and get her to let go. Asking her on this date was a step in that direction. He didn't want a relationship with her that only revolved around sex, so being together and acting like a normal couple was important.

The second part of the evening, however, was about building that foundation of trust. The skating rink was five miles from the restaurant. Since it was a Monday night, it wasn't very busy. That was perfect for what he had in mind.

"We're going ice skating?" she asked as he helped her out of the car.

"Yep." He tucked her into his side as they headed inside. "Have you ever been ice skating before?"

"Not since I was six and I wasn't very good then."

Justin grinned and kissed the top of her head. He paid for their time on the ice and rented them both a pair of skates. His dad was a huge hockey fan, so Justin had spent a lot of time on the ice as a kid. He could skate almost as well as he could walk.

When they walked into the ice rink, there was only a handful of other people skating. There was a little girl and a woman he assumed was either her mother or her coach standing nearby, giving her instructions. The other three people were older and didn't look to be quite as steady on their feet.

He laced up his skates and waited for Kim to finish with hers. Then he reached for her hand and helped her up. Luckily, they only had a few feet to walk in order to reach the ice. Walking on ice skates wasn't his favorite thing in the world.

Bracing himself on the side edge of the rink, he removed the guard on his skates before stepping onto the ice. He held on to Kim's arm as she followed his lead.

As soon as she had both feet on the ice, she latched onto him, nearly landing them both on the ground. It was a good thing he was proficient on the ice. "Sorry."

He helped to steady her. "Better?"

"As long as I don't have to move."

Justin chuckled. "I think for it to be considered skating, you have to do more than stand in place."

"How about I stay right here by the wall, and you can skate to your heart's content?"

"Not a chance." He took a step back, putting a little distance between them, but not letting go of her arms.

"Don't let go!" Her voice was laced with panic. Her eyes pleaded with him, and her nails dug into his arm.

"I'm not going to let go. Relax." Before she could respond, he stalked backward, pulling her with him.

It was a small move, but like before, she overcompensated. "I'm going to fall."

"Look at me, not the ice." He waited for her to lift her gaze to meet his. "If you do what I tell you, you'll be fine."

She pressed her lips together but didn't comment.

Justin took her lack of response as agreement and continued with his lesson. "Tilt your hips forward a little." He watched as she complied. "Now slide your right foot forward."

Kim was holding on to him for dear life as he guided her step by step around the outside of the rink. She wasn't doing too bad. Every now and then, she'd wobble and grasp hold of him, but as they embarked on their second trip around the rink, she got steadier on her feet.

"Ready to move away from the edge?" Even though he asked the question, he changed their trajectory and moved them toward the interior of the ice.

She clung to him again, the fear he'd seen on her face earlier returning. "Maybe we should stick to the edge."

"Nope. You can handle this. I'm right here if you need me."

They spent another thirty minutes skating around before he led her over to the edge so they could remove their skates. Toward the end, she was skating with more confidence—he even noticed her smiling a little. She still wasn't steady enough to do it on her own, but she wasn't leaving claw marks in his arms either.

"You're really good," she said after handing in their skates. "I didn't know you could skate."

"My dad taught me. I think he was hoping I'd become a hockey player."

She slid into the passenger seat of his vehicle and waited until he was behind the wheel. "I think you're the only guy I know who's not really into sports."

He shrugged. "I like sports. I just don't eat and breathe them."

"I'm glad."

Justin glanced over at her before pulling out into traffic. "Why's that?"

"Because I'm not sure I could spend the next forty years listening to someone yell at the television every weekend."

Justin tried not to read too much into her statement. She wasn't saying she wanted to spend the rest of her life with him. But it was hard not to view it that way. "I'll keep that in mind."

Chapter Twenty-One

Kim didn't know where that came from, but she spent the remainder of the ride back to her apartment with her mouth firmly shut. They hadn't talked about more than one month, let alone forever. And she wasn't stupid enough to think they were anywhere near ready to have that type of a discussion either. There were too many obstacles they had to overcome first.

When they arrived at her apartment, Justin walked her to her door and waited as she took her key out and inserted it into the lock. "Did you want to come inside?"

He hesitated for a moment, then followed her in.

"I have some cake in the fridge and I can put some coffee on," she said, not sure what to do. Her day had ended much better than it had started, and she wasn't ready for it to be over yet, even though it was after ten.

"I'm good."

She stood on the threshold between her living room and kitchen, unsure what to do with herself. The urge to jump him was there, but she wasn't sure if that was appropriate in their agreement.

"Tell me," he said.

She lifted her gaze to meet his. "What?"

"You're thinking very hard about something. What is it?"

"Oh." She bit the inside of her cheek. "I was trying to decide whether jumping you was allowed."

He raised one eyebrow. "You think I'd be upset if you threw yourself at me?"

A smile spread across her face as the tension that had been building in her body eased. "Well, when you put it that way...no." She shook her head. "I feel constantly off balance and unsure of myself. Is that normal?"

"For someone who's used to being in control of things?" He left her hanging for a few moments before providing his answer. "Yes."

Her brow furrowed. "I'm not sure I like it."

Justin closed the distance between them, pulling her into his arms. The instant relief she felt from his touch was almost frightening. "I will never object to you trying to seduce me, baby."

"I'm allowed to initiate sex, even though I'm the submissive in the relationship?" Kim asked. She'd never seen that happen at the club, but she also knew things were different there.

"Of course." He ran his hands down her back to cup her ass and gave it a squeeze. "This lifestyle isn't meant to suppress your sexuality."

She was still confused about where the line was, but Ali had told her not to get too impatient. It was one of her faults, she knew. Kim wanted to know everything, and she wanted to know it now. Another reason why letting go was so difficult.

"You're thinking really hard again." He lifted her off her feet, startling her.

Kim grabbed hold of his shoulders as he carried her over to the couch. She'd been expecting him to sit down, but instead, he dumped her onto the couch and knelt in front of her. "Tonight, when you were gripping my arms to keep yourself steady, did you ever think I'd let you go and allow you to fall on your ass?"

"No." She'd never thought that. Not once. She knew he'd catch her if she started to fall.

"Why?" He settled between her legs, his hands resting on her thighs.

From the look on his face, she knew he was trying to make a point and it wasn't hard to figure out what it was. "I trusted you."

He nodded.

"But on the ice it's different," she insisted.

"No. It isn't." He sat back on his heels and looked her in the eyes. "You were completely focused on me. If I told you to move your right leg forward, you did. If I instructed you to bend your knees, you complied...because you trusted I would take care of you."

As much as she hated to admit it, she could see his point.

Justin stood and extended his hand, helping her up. "We both have to be up early tomorrow for work. Do you want me to leave?"

A zing that started somewhere in her chest went directly to her clit. It had only been two days since they'd had sex, but already she missed having him inside her. Plus, her bed had felt very empty the night before. She'd like to wake up beside him Sunday morning. Was it possible to get used to something after only experiencing it once?

Given their previous conversation, Kim decided not to hold back. "She wrapped her arms around his neck and brought her lips close to his. "I want you to stay."

He cupped the back of her head and kissed her hard. "You have five minutes to get yourself ready for bed and be waiting for me." Justin released her and headed toward the door.

"Where are you going?" she asked, still a little unsteady on her feet after the kiss.

"I need to grab my bag." He glanced at the clock on the wall. "And you're down to four minutes and twenty seconds."

Without another word, Justin disappeared out the door.

Kim glanced up at the clock. She figured she had four minutes left and she knew he wasn't kidding about the time limit. She turned off all the lights except for the one in the living room, checked the back door to make sure it was locked, then raced into her bathroom to take care of business and brush her teeth. She was glad she'd had the forethought earlier to shave because there was no way she could accomplish that in the short time she had left.

She had just finished kicking off her jeans when she heard him come back through the front door. As swiftly as she could, she finished removing her clothing and stood, naked, at the foot of her bed, waiting for him.

The house was quiet except for his footfalls, making them sound much louder than they actually were. Her heart pounded in anticipation. He hadn't said to get into bed or kneel or give her any instructions other than to be ready for him.

His frame filled the doorway to her bedroom, his shoulders nearly spanning the frame. He paused, taking in the view. His gaze started at her face and worked its way down, lingering on her breasts and hips.

He entered the room, but he walked over to the dresser instead of to her. Kim followed him with her gaze as he placed his bag on the chair and a mug of something on the dresser. Then he began unbuttoning his shirt.

It was a slow process. He took his time, not seeming to be in any rush to undress.

Kim wasn't sure what to do. She thought about helping him—see if she could speed things up—but decided against it. Even though her fingers were itching to touch him, she'd be patient. She could do that.

Justin peeled his shirt down his arms and tossed it onto the chair beside her dresser. His gaze met hers as he popped the button on his slack and lowered the zipper. His erection bulged from behind his underwear as he pushed the jeans down his legs and kicked them to the side.

Quirking a finger at her, he beckoned her to him. She couldn't get her feet to move fast enough. Memories of what he felt like...tasted like...had her wet and aching.

The urge to remove the last barrier of clothing separating them and giving in to her urges was tempting. She'd never denied herself with anyone but Justin. Then again, she'd never had more powerful orgasms than she'd had with Justin either. The irony wasn't lost on her.

As patiently as she could, she waited for him to tell her what he wanted.

Lifting a single finger to her breast, he traced around the outside, then around the nipple itself before taking the tiny bud between his thumb and forefinger. She closed her eyes as he rolled and pulled...pinched and twisted...her already sensitive nipple.

A low moan escaped her throat and the heat between her legs grew. She loved when he played with her breasts. Almost as much as when he played with her neck. For some reason, those two areas of her body seemed to have a direct line to her clit.

"Open your eyes." His voice was soft, yet firm. There was no doubt by his tone that it was a command, however.

Kim met his gaze and was struck by the depth of color in his green eyes. She loved it when he looked at her as if she were the only woman in the world he desired.

"Tonight, we're going to do a little breast play." He gave her nipple a hard pinch before releasing it and turning to reach into his bag. A second later, he held a pair of nipple clamps. He'd used them on her that first night and while they'd hurt, the pain had dissipated quickly. "Do you remember these?"

"Yes. Sir." She'd almost forgotten. Even though they weren't in the club or his playroom, they were still playing.

He grinned, letting her know she'd pleased him. For some reason, that made her happy. She wanted to please him.

Cupping her breast in one hand, he ran his thumbnail over the tip of her nipple, flicking it several times. It didn't hurt, but it wasn't a soft caress either.

She watched as her nipple darkened at the continual attention. It was becoming more sensitive.

Justin raised one of the clamps and positioned it over her nipple. After her first encounter with them, she'd done some research and learned they were called tweezer clamps. They were good for beginners because they allowed the user to adjust the level of pressure with a simple adjustment.

He watched her as he slid the metal bar higher to tighten the clamp. Kim sucked in a breath as pain shot through her nipple. She thought he'd stop, but he kept going a little further.

"That's it. Breathe through it. The pain will be worth it. I promise." He released the chain, letting it hang, and the weight sent more pain through her.

But her body seemed to be confused. Her sex pulsed, soft and ready for him, and her clit tingled in anticipation.

Moving to her other breast, he began playing with it the same as he had the other one. She felt...distracted. There was so much feeling going on that she didn't know how to process it all. When he clamped her left nipple, the pain almost startled her.

"How does that feel?" he asked, giving the chain connecting the clamps a little jerk.

"It hurts." She paused. "But I'm okay. Sir."

Justin pressed his lips to hers in a gentle kiss. "You're doing well. I'm proud of you."

A sense of pride filled her knowing she'd pleased him.

"I want you to put your arms behind your back."

She did as he asked and the new position thrust her chest forward, making her breasts more prominent.

He walked around behind her and adjusted the grip of her hands, so she was holding a little higher on her arms. It was a strange position, but it wasn't uncomfortable. His hands went to her hips. "Spread your legs a little. Not too much, though. I don't want you to lose your balance."

Once she was in the position he wanted, Justin moved around to stand in front of her again. "I told you we were going to do some breast play tonight. I'm going to have some fun with these tits of yours and you're going to stand there and not move. Do you understand?"

She couldn't anticipate what he was going to do. Fear and uncertainty raced through her. What if he did something she didn't like?

JUSTIN WAITED TO SEE WHAT SHE'D DO. HE COULD SEE HER THINKING. HER eyes had widened at his words, and he knew a hundred things were going through her head. As much as he wanted her to submit to him, he knew it had to be her choice. He couldn't...wouldn't force her. She had to trust him.

When she hadn't answered after several minutes, he lifted her chin and made her look at him. He didn't speak. Instead, he remained patient.

The muscles in her neck tensed and released as she swallowed. "Yes, Sir."

"You remember your safeword?" he asked. Not that he was expecting to push her to that point, but it was always good to check in.

"Yes, Sir." She sounded a little more confident this time.

"Very good. Let's get started, then."

Returning to his bag, Justin removed the first item he'd brought with him. The goal tonight was to build her trust in him while having some fun. He'd thought about bringing some rope but had decided against it. They'd get to rope play in due time.

Justin ran the black scarf through his fingers before holding it up so she could see it. When they'd played the first time, he'd blindfolded her, so this wasn't anything new. He moved behind her and secured the blindfold.

With a final check to make sure her eyes were covered, he went back to his bag. This time, he removed a single feather. He ran the feather along the outside of her breasts before grazing over one of her nipples. They looked perfect, all red as they were squeezed in the clamps. He was tempted to suck on them, but that would come later. First, he wanted to play.

Using only the very tip of the feather, Justin skimmed it ever so lightly over the sensitive flesh and she squirmed.

He removed the feather completely and admonished her, his tone expressing his displeasure. "Did I tell you that you could move?"

"It tickles."

Justin repeated himself. "Answer the question."

She was quiet for a long moment. "No, Sir."

"Do I need to restrain you on the bed, or can you control yourself?"

Again, it took longer than it should for her to answer. "You don't need to restrain me, Sir."

He had to give her credit. She was trying.

Removing the next item from his bag, he grazed the small flogger over the top of her breasts, letting the falls dip down over her nipples. He raised his hand and gave the flogger a gentle flick. The leather made contact an inch above the clamps.

Kim sucked in a breath but didn't move.

A smile spread across his face, and he repeated the action on the other breast.

This time, she was ready for it. Other than an intake of breath, there was no reaction.

He flipped the flogger over, using the handle to scrape against her left nipple. She tightened her hold on her arms, causing her breasts to thrust out more. "Do you like that?"

"I don't know what it is, Sir," she said in way of answering.

Justin chuckled. "You're not supposed to know. That's part of the fun." He moved to her right breast and did the same. "Answer the question. Do you like it?"

"Yes, Sir." She furrowed her brow. "It feels strange, but not in a bad way."

"These tits of yours look lovely in these clamps...so hard and red..." He leaned down and licked the nipple he'd been playing with.

"Yes." The word came out like a hiss.

He reached behind him and grabbed the little surprise he'd snatched from her freezer. After warming her nipple with his tongue, he pulled back enough to put the ice cube into his mouth. It was a decent size, so it should last for what he planned.

Returning to the same breast, he released the clamp and immediately sucked her nipple into his mouth. The pain from the clamp, combined with the hot of his mouth and the cold of the ice cube had her gasping and completely forgetting not to move.

Her fingers dug into his head. He wasn't sure whether she was trying to hold him to her or push him away. Either way, she was not obeying him and that needed to be rectified.

He stood, removed the ice cube from his mouth, and returned it to the mug. Kim dropped her arms. One clamp dangled from her left nipple.

She let out a little scream as he scooped her up without notice and laid her on the bed. "What did I tell you would happen if you did not remain still?"

This time, she answered him right away. "That you would restrain me." She pressed her lips together. "I'm sorry, Sir. It...what you did took me by surprise. I wasn't expecting—"

Justin had brought cuffs just in case. They were easier than rope and took up less space in his bag. He wrapped one wrist. "We need to work on your ability to follow instructions, but for now, these will keep you where I want you." Luckily for him, Kim's headboard had slats. It took a little maneuvering, but he was able to slip the chain around one before securing her other wrist.

Retrieving the mug and moving it to her bedside table, he removed his underwear before climbing onto the bed. He knelt between her legs, spreading them to accommodate him.

Before picking up where they left off, he gave her a thorough once-over. She was flushed and both her nipples were red and hard. Her pussy was also very wet. He could see it glistening and the musky scent had him wanting to bury his face in it.

"Are you ready to continue?"

"Yes, Sir." While she said the words, he sensed something was off.

"What's wrong?" He needed to know if there was an issue.

She shook her head. "Nothing."

Justin sighed and reached up to remove the blindfold. He needed her to look at him.

Kim blinked several times, her eyes adjusting to the light in the room. It was then he saw the moisture in her eyes. As much as he wanted to continue their sensory play, her mental well-being took priority.

"Take a deep breath in and hold it. I'm going to remove the other clamp."

"I'm okay. I—"

"I wasn't asking."

She closed her eyes but took in a breath and held it.

Bending, he held her breast with one hand, right above the nipple, and released the clamp. He soothed the pain with his tongue, sucking the abused flesh until he heard her breathing return to normal.

Next, he removed the cuffs. If she was a more experienced submissive, he might have had this conversation with her still restrained, but she wasn't.

He stood. "Get under the covers. I don't want you to get a chill. I'll be right back."

"Okay." Her voice was soft...almost childlike. He didn't like it.

As swiftly as he could, Justin went into the bathroom, dumped the ice, and refilled the mug with water. He was hard as a rock, but that couldn't be helped.

Running a hand through his hair, he headed back into the bedroom.

Chapter Twenty-Two

Kim pulled the covers up to her chin and waited for Justin to return. She'd screwed up again. How hard was it not to move? She knew she'd disappointed him, and she hated it, but she hadn't expected to react as she had. Tears had threatened to fall as he'd brought her over to the bed and bound her wrists.

It wasn't being cuffed that had caused the surge of emotion. He'd tied her up before. No, it was realizing she'd ruined their perfect night together.

After he'd taken her mind off her crappy day with dinner and ice skating, she'd wanted to give him her submission. She'd wanted it so badly, but in the end, she hadn't been able to do it. When she'd felt all the different sensations —pain from him removing the clamp—the heat of his mouth—and the cold from... Well, she didn't know what exactly.

Everything had hit her at once and she'd reacted before she was able to stop herself. She'd told him she could remain still on her own, but that hadn't been true.

As the seconds ticked by, her melancholy grew. She wasn't good at being submissive.

Justin strolled back into the room. She heard him approach the bed, but she was afraid to look at him. The mattress dipped with his weight as he sat down next to her. "I brought you some water."

"I'm okay," she whispered.

"Kim."

Reluctantly, she turned her head so she could see him. He was still naked.

Placing the mug on the nightstand next to her head, he took hold of her shoulders and lifted. She let out a little squeak as he moved her to a sitting position.

Kim gathered the blanket and once more attempted to cover herself. She wasn't sure why. It wasn't as if he hadn't seen every inch of her before.

She's barely gotten it over her breasts when he pulled it back down again. "No hiding."

"I'm not hiding."

"Really?" He tilted his head down and raised one of his eyebrows. "What are you doing, then?"

Not sure how to answer that, she deflected. "It's late and I'm tired."

"Is that your way of trying to kick me out?"

Was it? She wasn't sure. A part of her did want him to leave, but not because she didn't want him in her bed. She wanted him there. Always. But she also couldn't shake the feeling that she'd never be able to do the things he needed her to do. Hell, the things she wanted to do for him.

But she kept messing up. Her brain kept getting in the way. She'd watched enough submissives in the club to know how it worked.

When she didn't answer, he tilted her chin toward him and forced her to meet his gaze. "What happened tonight?"

"You know what happened."

He shook his head. "I'm not talking about you disobeying me." Justin rubbed his thumb along her cheek. "Why were you crying?"

"I wasn't crying." It was a weak denial and they both knew it. "I was just...upset."

"Why?"

"You know why."

Justin sighed. "This is going to be a very long conversation if you keep telling me I already know the answer to the question I asked. If I knew the answer, I wouldn't be asking." He paused. "Now, explain to me why you were upset."

"You told me not to move and I did. Twice. I thought I could do it. I thought I could remain still no matter what you did, but I couldn't."

Her response was met with silence. She didn't want to look at him and see the realization that she was a horrible submissive, but she couldn't help herself.

He was frowning. "Do you think the submissives at the club always obey their Doms' orders?"

Kim crossed her arms over her chest, but when his frown turned into a scowl, she dropped them again. She picked at the threads on her blanket to give her something to do besides look at him. "Yes."

Justin snorted, which caused her to glance up.

"What?" she asked.

"Even Kate, one of the best trained submissives I've ever met, disobeys her husband every now and then." He paused. "There are some harsh punishments involved for her not following his orders, but it does happen."

She didn't believe it. Granted, she didn't know Kate that well, but every time Kim had seen her at the club, she'd been a model submissive...something Kim doubted she'd ever be. "Like when?"

Justin chuckled. "Like when a repairman came by their house two days ahead of schedule and she answered the door."

"She isn't allowed to answer the door? Why?" Her voice had gone up an octave.

A knowing smile pulled at his lips. "Kate isn't allowed to wear clothes at home, so she had to put on a robe to answer the door."

"So, she has to ask permission to wear clothes inside the house?" For some reason, Kim felt angry on Kate's behalf.

He nodded.

That sounded...that was... "That's barbaric."

His eyebrows rose again. This time, in amusement. "Then I guess I shouldn't tell you what her punishment for disobeying was."

"He punished her?" Kim was sitting up. "For putting on a robe?" She wasn't sure what she was going to do, but she felt the urge to do something.

"Of course." He canted his head to the side. "Why are you angry? Kate knew what she was doing. She made a conscious choice to disobey her husband.

"But..."

The words died on her lips. But what? Justin was right. As much as she hated to admit it, he was right.

She met his gaze, pleading in her eyes. "I'll never be like that. I can't."

"Have I ever asked you to be like Kate?"

"No."

Justin took hold of her hand and brought it to rest against his thigh. He wasn't hard anymore, but that didn't mean she wasn't aware of him. How she could still be aroused after all this, she didn't know. "Kate and her husband negotiated their relationship the same way we did, but they have different kinks than we do. Kate gets off on her husband having total control over her in most aspects of their life."

That was hard to wrap her head around. She couldn't fathom someone wanting to give up that much control to their partner.

"That scares you, doesn't it?"

He was massaging the skin along her wrist, and it was distracting her. "Yes." She paused. "At the submissive group, Jeff mentioned Nicole wants to use a violet wand on him."

"I see." His tone was neutral, and Kim didn't like it. She couldn't get a read on him.

"He doesn't want to."

"You sure about that?" he asked.

Kim opened her mouth, but then closed it once more. Was she? He'd been unsure...nervous. But as she thought back to the conversation, she couldn't recall him ever saying he didn't want his Domme to use it on him.

Blowing out a tired breath, she admitted what he probably already knew. "No."

"There are safewords in this lifestyle for a reason." When she didn't say anything more, he turned the spotlight back on her. "Kim, I don't expect you to be perfect. You're new to this and you're going to mess up. Probably a lot." He shrugged. "We deal with it and move on."

"Deal with it?" She wasn't sure she liked that. Especially given their very recent conversation.

"If you break a rule, there are consequences. You know that." He paused. "And sometimes knowing you've disappointed your Dom is punishment enough."

She'd heard other submissives say that they'd disappointed their Doms at the club. Some of them had sounded as if the world were ending. Others seemed to brush it off as if it were no big thing.

Kim thought back to how she'd felt tonight after failing to hold still like Justin had asked her. Even though she hadn't been able to see his face, she'd known he was disappointed she didn't do what she'd assured him she could. The feeling of failure had overwhelmed her.

"I don't like disappointing you." The admission left her with mixed feelings.

He brought her hand to his lips and kissed her fingers. "I know."

Justin dropped her hand and stood. "Do you want me to stay tonight, or would you rather be alone?"

She pressed her lips together. He was letting her decide. Did she want him to stay or go?

Reaching over to the opposite side of the bed, she flipped the blanket down. "Stay."

He nodded, walked to the other side of the bed, and slid in next to her. She could feel his warmth and was drawn to it.

Justin reached for her, and she couldn't get into his arms fast enough. He tucked her head into his shoulder and kissed the top of her head. "Good night."

She nuzzled her nose against his collarbone. "Good night."

JUSTIN SPENT THE NEXT FEW DAYS THINKING ABOUT HOW HE COULD HELP Kim. He needed to build her confidence. While the advice he'd gotten from Daniel about introducing one thing at a time was sound, he was thinking he needed to break it down even further. Kim needed some wins, and it was his responsibility to help her achieve them.

He picked her up on Friday evening and headed to the club. The coat she wore covered whatever outfit she was wearing, which was both good and bad. It meant that whatever she was wearing was short and would give him easy access to her. But it also meant he couldn't see what was his.

"Hi," she said.

"Hello." His gaze raked over her from head to foot. "Unbutton your coat."

She opened her mouth to argue, then closed it again and began opening her coat.

Little by little, she revealed the red dress she was wearing. It looked to be soft...velvet maybe. The dress clung to her curves, then flared at the waist. He hadn't intended for them to start playing yet, but he couldn't resist. Besides, it was easy and would give him something to build on later. "Open your legs."

He heard her intake of breath a moment before she spread her legs.

They were still sitting in the parking lot in front of her apartment, so he needed to be discreet. As much as he'd love to finger fuck her right then, he didn't want to get caught by one of her neighbors. "Are you wearing panties?"

"No, Sir."

Pleased, he nodded. "Good girl." Then he removed the vibrator from his pocket and handed it to her. "Stick this in your pussy."

She took the vibrator from him. It was shaped like a small dildo with a flat end that had two wings. The wings were meant to go on either side of her clit.

Kim looked at him with wide eyes. "Here?"

He remained silent and waited to see what she'd do.

When she realized he was serious, she lifted her skirt, shifted in her seat, and placed the object where he'd instructed her to. When she removed her hand, he grabbed hold of it and inspected her fingers. He could smell her scent, which meant she was already wet.

Sucking two of her fingers into his mouth, he moaned at the small taste of her. It had been too long since he'd eaten her pussy. A problem he had every intention of rectifying tonight.

He released her fingers with a pop, not missing how her breathing had increased. "Put your seat belt on. We need to get going."

Once Kim was strapped in, he backed out of the parking lot and drove toward the club. They were a mile or so down the road before he slipped a hand into his pocket and turned on the device.

"Oh." Her shocked surprise brought a smile to his lips. He wanted her pussy dripping by the time they got to the club.

As they weaved their way through the city, he changed the vibrations. Every time she got too close to coming, he'd lower the setting.

By the time they reached the club, Kim was gripping the sides of her seat. Her chest was moving up and down with exaggerated breaths.

He switched off the toy and exited the vehicle. Kim didn't move when he opened the door for her. "Remove the vibrator and button your coat back up before you get out of the car."

Kim looked up at him as if only now realizing he was standing there. Her hand disappeared under her skirt as she removed the device. As she held it in her hand, he couldn't help but notice how wet it was as she tried to decide what to do with it.

"I'll take it," he said, holding out his hand.

She placed the vibrator in his palm and hurried to refasten her coat. Then, as if she was unsure her legs would hold her weight, she climbed out of the car.

A knowing grin bloomed on his face as he watched her find her feet. She narrowed her eyes at him. "This is your fault."

Justin laughed. "Come on. Let's get you inside. I have plans for you tonight."

"I'm not sure I can walk." She took a tentative step forward as he locked up the car.

"Here," he said, circling his arm around her waist. "I'll make sure you don't fall. Especially in those sexy heels you're wearing."

"I thought you might like them."

He hummed. "I'm going to enjoy fucking you in them later."

She stopped walking.

"Everything all right?" he asked.

"No."

He waited.

Blowing out a breath, she started moving again. "I'm so horny right now I feel like I'm going to explode and you talking like that isn't helping."

A deep belly laugh overtook him as they reached the club. He opened the door and ushered her inside. Swiping his membership card, he let them into the main foyer. "I'll keep that in mind for later." He winked at her before guiding her over to the coat check.

Ali was behind the desk tonight. "Hi, guys." She took their coats and hung them up in the large closet behind her.

"Are you working all night?" Justin asked.

"I'm supposed to. Did you need me for something?" Ali glanced at her friend, looking for anything amiss.

"No, but I wanted to know where you'd be if Kim needs you." He wasn't expecting Kim to need Ali tonight, but it was never a bad idea to have a backup plan.

Ali smiled. "Of course. And I'm sure Bridget will cover for me if I need her."

He tipped his head in Ali's direction, acknowledging her comment before turning his attention back to Kim. "Let's get inside."

Kim gave a little wave to Ali as Justin led her into the club. He guided her over to the bar. Chase, the other bartender, greeted them as they approached. "What can I get you tonight?"

His question was directed to Justin. Chase wasn't part of the lifestyle, but he'd been working at Serpent's Kiss long enough to know how it worked. "Two waters."

Chase grinned and ducked behind the bar to retrieve two bottles of water. He placed them on the shiny wood surface, and Justin handed over his membership card. After a quick swipe, Chase returned the card to its owner.

Justin adjusted both bottles in one hand, carrying them by their lids. Putting pressure on Kim's lower back, he turned them both toward the stairs.

"We're going upstairs?" she asked.

"Yes."

It was the only answer he gave her as they ascended the stairs to the second floor. As they neared the top, he could already hear the sounds of play. They were muted behind the doors of the playrooms, but it was hard to mask the sound of whips and floggers without soundproof rooms.

Several people were standing in front of various rooms, watching the play happening inside. Justin paused outside of the second room to his right when he noticed Daniel inside. He had Emma, an uncollared sub, secured to a St. Andrew's cross while he flogged her.

Since picking up on the interesting vibes between Daniel and Ali, he'd been paying more attention to the older Dom. As he watched the scene in front of him, he realized he'd never seen Daniel do anything with a submissive recently that involved more than tying them to a St. Andrew's cross and flogging them.

When Justin first joined the club, Daniel would play with subs often. He was very popular with the club's submissives for his expertise in flogging, even back then. But the scenes then would typically include more than flogging. Thinking back, he recalled a scene where Daniel had a sub laid out on a table, much like a gourmet meal, while he placed various food items on her body and licked them off. It had been extremely sensual to watch. But he hadn't seen Daniel do any scenes like that for at least the last year and he was now thinking that was because of Ali.

"Does that hurt?" Kim asked from beside him.

Justin looked over at her, then back at the scene. "Floggers tend to deliver more of a thud than a sting, but it depends on the type of flogger and the material it's made out of."

Not wanting to spend the entire night being a voyeur, he moved them away from the viewing window. They ended up in the same room they'd been in the week before. Justin had reserved the room because it was one of the few where the window could be blocked. Kim had marked exhibitionism as something she was unsure about. It wasn't something he wished to test this early on in their relationship.

This time, he allowed her to observe as he darkened the window, giving them privacy. Tonight was about building her confidence as a submissive, not only about building trust. He needed for her to see that she could be a good sub. It was just going to take time.

He selected a pillow from the corner and placed it in the middle of the room. "Remove your clothes and kneel. Leave the shoes on for now."

Kim pushed the narrow straps of her dress from her shoulders and shimmied it down her hips. He offered her a steadying hand as she stepped out of the dress. Kim handed the outfit to him and lowered herself to the floor onto the pillow. She bowed her head, spread her legs, and placed her hands in an upturned position on her thighs, awaiting his instructions.

Chapter Twenty-Three

Justin took in the sight before him...took in her positioning. He removed a hair tie from one of the drawers and moved to stand behind her. Gathering her hair, he secured it up and out of the way.

"Where did you learn to kneel like that?" He'd noticed her palms up the last time she'd knelt in front of him. At the time, however, he'd been too busy trying to convince himself not to take what she was obviously offering to comment on how she was presenting herself.

"Am I doing something wrong?" The sides of her mouth pulled down into a frown. "I did some research on the internet and it showed a woman kneeling like this."

"Kneeling with your palms up is a positioning common in a very specific practice of this lifestyle. I would prefer you to have your palms facing down, resting on your thighs."

Kim made the correction.

He smiled, even though she couldn't see him.

Taking his time, he walked around her, inspecting. While he didn't normally have subs spread their legs while kneeling, he had to admit he was enjoying the view. Still, if he told her to get into a kneeling position out on the main floor of the club, he didn't want there to be any confusion. "Bring your legs together. While I love the visual, holding that position for long periods of time may get uncomfortable for you."

She did as he asked.

Once he was satisfied she was kneeling the way he wanted her to, he stood in front of her and lifted her chin. "Whenever I tell you to kneel, this is how I want you."

"Yes, Sir."

He dropped his arm and moved to the far wall that contained a variety of implements. The scene tonight would need to be simple. He didn't want to overwhelm her.

Given her curiosity regarding the flogger, he selected one that most subs loved. It was heavy and the falls were soft. When welded correctly, it felt almost like a massage.

Justin pulled her head back using her ponytail. Her neck stretched as she met his gaze. "Since you were so fascinated by the flogger earlier, we're going to explore that tonight. You've never been flogged, correct?"

"No, Sir, I haven't."

He lifted the arm holding the flogger and glided it over the front of her, letting her feel the falls as they grazed her skin. Her eyelids fluttered a little as the toy rose over her chest and up her neck.

Taking his time, he ran the falls of the flogger over her arms, her legs, her back...everywhere he could reach while she was in her current position. He paid close attention to her breathing, noting it was slow and even. She was relaxed.

"Lean forward and place your hands on the floor. I want you on all fours."

Kim shifted her body weight and adjusted herself into the new position.

"Spread your legs a little more. I don't want you losing your balance."

As she opened her legs, his gaze was drawn to her sex. Her pink lips were wet and swollen...ready for him. His cock swelled even more in his pants, demanding attention. It would have to wait, however. He wanted to play first.

Again, he let the falls of the flogger skim over her back...her butt...her thighs. He wasn't in a hurry. They had plenty of time.

The first blow landed solid on the right side of her backside. Kim liked to be spanked, so he had no doubt she'd enjoy having her ass flogged.

She sucked in a breath, but other than that, she didn't react.

Justin repeated the motion on the other side. He gave her a moment to get used to the feel, then be began alternating his blows until her ass was a nice warm pink.

Kneeling, he inspected the abused flesh, now much more sensitive, and was pleased when Kim pushed back against his hand as he rubbed her cheeks. He reached between her legs, running his fingers through her wet heat. She rocked against his fingers as he circled her clit, trying to increase the pressure he was using. "Not yet, baby."

A soft whimper escaped her lips when he moved his hand away, not giving her the release she wanted.

He stood and landed a slightly softer blow to her upper back and shoulders. Once he'd warmed that part of her body, he moved back down, this time targeting her inner thighs. With each hit, the flogger would kiss her pussy lips.

As the session continued, he noticed sweat forming on her back and neck, and her breathing had picked up. She'd been in this position for more than twenty minutes and was often easing back, almost begging for more of the flogger. Kim was completely in the moment.

That was good, but his cock was in desperate need of attention. It was pressing painfully against his fly.

Laying the flogger down, he grabbed a chair and set it a foot or so from her face. Then he unfastened his pants, pushed them and his underwear down around his ankles, and sat. "Come here."

Her eyes were glazed over when she looked up at him. He held the base of his cock in one hand, and she crawled toward him.

Justin didn't need to tell her what he wanted. Kim's mouth engulfed his erection. She began bobbing her head with an enthusiasm he hadn't seen from her before.

Closing his eyes, he relished the feel of her lips and tongue as she sucked him. He liked blow jobs as much as the next guy, but it was close to an out-of-body experience every time she got her mouth on him. Justin knew it wasn't only her skill. It was because it was Kim.

He cupped the back of her head, guiding her movements. As his orgasm drew closer, he took hold of her ponytail and removed her lips from him. He needed to be inside her and he needed to be inside her now.

The chair fell as he stood, and he didn't care. He'd worry about that later.

Justin finished kicking off his jeans. Swiping a condom from the room's supply, he ripped it open and rolled it down his very hard length.

Kneeling behind Kim, he spread her legs even more, making room for himself. It was good Katrina had chosen a padded flooring for the playrooms. They came in handy when he didn't want to be bothered to move his submissive to a higher horizontal surface.

From his new position, he could smell her arousal. The desire to taste her was nearly overwhelming, but his need to feel her tight heat surrounding him took priority. There would be time for more later. It was still early and he planned to have her in his bed that night.

He coated his cock with her juices, teasing her clit before he lined himself up and thrust his hips forward. Her head dipped as he sank into her. She pushed back against him, urging him deeper. He relished the feeling of her muscles contracting around him, welcoming him inside.

Balls deep inside her pussy, he dug his fingers into her still rosy ass and began pumping his hips. He wasn't gentle about it, but he'd learned Kim liked it that way. She met him thrust for thrust and he was soon teetering on the edge again.

Snaking one hand around her middle, he found her clit. Wanting to draw it out, he was careful not to apply too much pressure. He wanted her to beg for it.

At first, she tried tilting her pelvis to increase the pressure. When that didn't work, she spread her legs more to get lower, closer to his hand. That didn't get the desired result, either.

She let out a high-pitched whimper. "Please."

He lifted the hand still on her ass and gave her skin a hard smack. "Please, what?"

"Please, let me come, Sir. I'm...I'm so close. I just need..."

"Tell me what you need, baby."

"More. Please rub my clit harder, Sir." Her voice was full of desperation.

Justin teased her a little more, then he gave her what she wanted.

It didn't take long. Within a matter of seconds, she was grinding on his hand and chanting *Please*. And it didn't take much longer until her interior muscles were clenching and milking his cock.

She came with a scream, one that in any other place would have had anyone who'd heard it coming to see if she needed help. Given their location, it was more likely to inspire envy from the other subs within earshot.

Feeling her pussy spasm around him was the final nail in the coffin for Justin's control. His climax hit him hard and seemed to go on forever. By the time it subsided, he felt spent. Completely content, but spent.

As soon as he was able, he pulled out, disposed of the condom, and moved to check on Kim. Her head was pressed against the floor, and she was still breathing hard.

"Are you okay?" he asked, brushing a loose strand of hair behind her ear.

"I don't know. I can't feel my legs again."

He lowered himself back to the floor and gathered her into his arms.

Kissing her temple, he cupped her face and met her gaze. "You did well, baby. I'm proud of you."

The smile that greeted him sent his heart racing in a completely different way. The fact that he was in love with Kim resonated in every bone in his body. He wasn't going to be able to give her up after their month was over. Seeing her look at him that way, knowing he'd put that smile on her face, did something to him. They had to figure it out. All of it. Including how they were going to tell Mark.

❦

KIM DIDN'T KNOW HOW LONG THEY SAT ON THE FLOOR OF THE PLAYROOM before they dressed and headed downstairs. She was feeling very clingy, which wasn't like her. Justin had gone to get them some more waters and she'd been left feeling somewhat lost.

He'd returned with two bottles of water and handed her one as he sat down beside her. "Drink. I don't want you getting dehydrated."

She was thirsty. He'd made her drink an entire bottle of water before they'd left the playroom, but her mouth still felt like it was full of cotton. "I don't understand why I'm so thirsty," she said.

Justin rested his arm along the couch behind her and she moved closer, wanting to be touching him. "I worked you hard. And you're not used to it."

Her gaze darted to the people around them, but no one seemed to be paying much attention to them. Granted, it was Beth, Drew, Nicole, Jeff, and Daniel, but that didn't make her any less embarrassed about it. Having sex in the club was strange enough. She wasn't ready to announce to the world what they'd done.

As she thought about it, she realized how it sounded. She'd joined a BDSM club where people had sex, often with other people watching, all the time. What they'd done upstairs was normal.

Actually, it wasn't normal. Their scene had been in private. No one had been watching them. Of course, her very loud scream as she came couldn't have gone completely unnoticed. Heat flooded her cheeks and she recalled how the sound had reverberated in the room.

Justin turned to whisper in her ear. "Remembering what we did upstairs?"

She tucked her head into his shoulder. "Yes. Please don't say anything."

He kissed the top of her head and combed his fingers through her hair. He'd removed the band that held it away from her face before they'd left the playroom, so her hair was flowing free once more. She closed her eyes, loving the feel of his hands threading through her locks. "You have nothing to be embarrassed about. No one here will judge you."

It was true. "I know." Kim took a deep breath. He smelled of sweat, and soap, and sex. It was a dangerous combination. At least it was for her. "I can't believe I did that."

His chest vibrated beneath her. "I will very happily give you orgasms like that every day."

"It's never been like that for me," she admitted. "Not like that."

He didn't seem shocked by her admission. "I doubt you've ever given up control like that before to your partner. You are submissive, baby. You just need to embrace it."

If a man had said that to her a year ago, it would have brought her hackles up. She was no one's doormat. But the more she learned about this lifestyle, the more she realized that wasn't what submission was at all.

She tilted her head to look at Drew where he sat on the floor at Beth's feet. More often than not, that was his position when they were sitting around talking with their friends at the club. He appeared to be completely relaxed as he chatted with Jeff, who was also kneeling on the floor beside his own mistress. It wasn't typical as far as the outside world was concerned, but here it fit.

And Drew wasn't a pushover. At their submissive meeting, he'd taken charge and led the conversation like a pro. She'd known he was a firefighter, but she'd learned from Ali he was a captain. He wouldn't have gotten in that position by letting people walk all over him.

Returning her attention to Justin, she brushed her lips against his neck, and he tightened his hold on her. "I'm trying."

They ended up staying for another hour before Justin decided he was ready to leave. While she wasn't feeling as needy anymore, that didn't mean she wanted the night to end.

Kim had expected him to head back to her place, but instead he drove in the opposite direction. She wasn't concerned as to where they were going, which said a lot. Her normal need for control would have had her asking questions.

Fifteen minutes later, they pulled into his driveway. "I should have had you pack a bag," he said before exiting the vehicle and coming to open her door.

"It's okay. With this coat, you can't tell what I'm wearing." She lowered her voice, knowing what it would do to him. "I won't have to worry about doing the walk of shame tomorrow."

Justin crushed her against him and gave her a lingering kiss. The air around them was cold, but her internal temperature was heating up as his lips moved against hers. "Let's get inside."

She laced her fingers with his and they made their way to the door. His thumb grazed across the skin of her wrist as he turned the key, letting them into his house. Given the incredible orgasm she'd had earlier, she couldn't believe how much she wanted him again.

He pushed the door open and led her inside before locking the door behind them. Tossing his keys down, his gaze met hers and her heartbeat kicked up another notch. He stalked toward her, pinning her against the wall. "You're wearing too many clothes again."

Kim met his gaze, loving the heat in his eyes. "Maybe you should do something about that."

His reaction had heat rushing to her core. He cupped her face with one hand as he captured her mouth with his. With his other hand, he began undressing her.

Her coat hit the floor first. Then her dress. His hands explored with every inch of skin he exposed. He was still fully dressed...coat and all...while she stood in his living room in nothing but her shoes. For some reason, that realization made her incredibly hot.

Justin's hand grazed over her abdomen as he slid lower until he cupped her sex. He hummed as he moved his fingers through her heat. "You're so wet, baby. I've been dying to taste you all night."

"Please."

He knelt on the floor in front of her and ran his nose along the neat patch of hair between her legs. "I love it when you beg me."

She threaded her fingers through his hair, closing her eyes and letting her head fall back against the wall with a thump.

Bang. Bang. Bang.

At first, the sound of someone banging on the door didn't register. She was too in the moment. It was only when Justin stood, leaving her, that she noticed.

Whoever it was, banged at the door again. It sounded as if they were trying to break through the door. After the third series of knocks, it was clear they weren't going away.

"Go to my bedroom. I'll get rid of whoever it is and we'll pick up where we left off."

Kim didn't bother to gather her clothes. She wouldn't need them until morning. Rushing down the hall, she ducked into his bedroom.

Mumbled conversation followed the sound of the door opening. She couldn't tell what they were saying, though. Not unless she opened the door. And given her current state of undress, she was afraid whoever it was would glance down the hall and see her.

Walking over to the bed, she sat down and waited, anxious for whoever it was to leave so she and Justin could pick up where they'd left off.

Chapter Twenty-Four

"Thank fuck you're here. Why aren't you answering your phone?"

Justin took a step back as Mark pushed his way into Justin's house. One look at his best friend told him something was wrong. "What's going on?"

Mark ran a frazzled hand through his hair. "Dad's been taken to the hospital, and I need to get there. I told mom I'd tell Kim, but she's not answering her phone. Ali isn't either, so they're probably together. I went by her house and her car's there, but she isn't, so I tried Ali's apartment. They aren't there either. I need to find her, but I don't know where else to look."

The euphoric high Justin had been on a few minutes before turned sour in his gut. "Back up. Davis is in the hospital? What happened?"

"He went out to the car to get something and slipped on some ice, Mom said. They think he may have broken his leg."

Okay, that wasn't as bad as he'd feared. Still, Kim would want to know and be there for her parents. Hell, he wanted to be there. But first, he needed to get Mark out of his house. His best friend finding Kim in Justin's house...especially in her current state...would only make things worse.

"I tell you what," Justin said. "You go to the hospital. Be with your mom. I'll find Kim and Ali. I know a few places they might have gone."

"Are you sure?" He could see Mark was torn.

"Of course." He moved toward the door.

It was then Mark noticed the discarded dress on the floor. "Oh, man. You're on a date. I'm sorry. I'll—"

"Stop. Davis and Belinda are more important than a date. She'll understand."

He looked skeptical but nodded and went to leave. It wasn't even a question that Justin would make sure Kim got to the hospital as soon as possible to be with her family. What was more of a concern to him was how she'd take the news.

"Thanks, man." Mark embraced Justin before walking out the door.

Justin waited until his friend had gotten into his car and driven off before gathering Kim's dress from the floor and padding down to the bedroom where Kim waited. She looked up when he walked through the door.

The look on his face must have been as telling as Mark's had been. "Who was it?"

"Your brother."

She paled. "What?"

"You need to get dressed. Your dad slipped and fell. They think he may have broken his leg, so they've taken him to the hospital."

Kim snatched the clothing from him. She had the dress on in a matter of seconds. "I need to go."

"Wait," he said, grabbing hold of her arm to stop her.

She looked up at him, her eyes wide.

"Unless you want your family to know we've been together tonight, you can't go racing off to the hospital minutes after your brother left my place."

It was as if the air had been let out of her sails. She pressed her lips together. Thinking.

"Your brother thinks you're with Ali." Her brow furrowed, so he supplied the additional information. "He tried to call you both, but you had your phones off." Before she could get too bogged down in the whys, he offered a solution. "I can call the club and let Ali know what's going on. We can swing by and pick her up, then head to the hospital. I told your brother I might know where you'd be, so it wouldn't be out of the question that I'd drive you."

Kim nodded and he dug his phone out of his pocket. He'd turned it off, the same as Kim, before they'd entered the club. While it was powering up, he helped her into her coat and escorted her to his vehicle. Before backing out of his driveway, he dialed the club's main number. The phone rang in both Katrina's office and the bar.

"Hello?" Chase answered the phone. Given the private nature of the club, they never answered with anything other than a plain greeting.

"Chase, it's Justin. I need to speak with Ali. It's an emergency."

"Sure. Just a minute."

Chase put him on hold as Justin drove toward the club. A few minutes later, Ali came on the line. "Justin?"

Justin filled Ali in on what was going on. She agreed to be waiting in the front foyer for them in ten minutes.

He pulled up to the curb in front of Serpent's Kiss and moments later, Ali emerged from the old building. She was still in her club clothes, but that was okay. He and Kim had talked on the way and decided it was best to be as honest as possible. She and Ali had been out clubbing. It would have been difficult to explain their attire with any other explanation.

It took another fifteen minutes to get to the hospital and another five to figure out where they needed to go. Kim's mom saw them first. She stood, drawing Mark's attention. His best friend stood, bracing his hands on his hips. "Where have you been?"

A flash of guilt swept across Kim's face. "Ali and I were at a club."

"And you couldn't answer your phone?" Mark asked.

"Stop it," Belinda said. "No one knew your father was going to get hurt. Kim's allowed to go out and have fun."

Mark didn't seem happy with the reprimand, but he let it go.

Belinda embraced her daughter. "I'm glad you're here."

"Thanks, Mom." Kim closed her eyes and held her mother close.

Justin decided to steer the conversation in a different direction. "How's Davis?"

"They took him to have his leg X-rayed about a half hour ago and they aren't back yet," Belinda said.

It took another forty minutes before someone came out to talk to them. Unfortunately, they'd only allow family members into the door, so Justin and Ali hung back.

"You doing okay?" Ali asked.

He glanced over at her. "I'm fine." His response was clipped, but it was the best he could do. All he'd wanted to do as they sat in the waiting room was to hold Kim's hand. Sadly, he'd been forced to sit there, hands folded in his own lap, while he'd watched Kim constantly fidget with anxiety. He hated being so close to her and yet so far away at the same time.

Ali flipped the page on the magazine she'd been perusing. "It's a good thing Mark's distracted tonight. You two aren't hiding it well."

"We haven't touched each other."

Grinning, Ali nodded. "True, but that doesn't mean you haven't been sending off signals."

"What are you talking about?"

She shrugged. "All the sly glances you've been shooting each other's way. And that longing look on your face when she left the room..."

Justin wanted to deny it, but he couldn't. He'd wanted to go with them and be the support Kim needed, but instead he was left sitting on his ass feeling useless.

Not able to stand sitting any longer, he stood. "Do you want anything from the vending machine?"

"No, I'm good," Ali said, going back to her magazine.

He strolled into the hall, heading for the elevators where the vending machines were located. He heard hushed, but agitated voices.

As he drew closer, he realized who it was. "Where were you tonight?" Mark demanded.

"I told you. I was at a club with Ali." He rounded the corner and nearly lost his shit. Mark was standing way too close to Kim. Her palms were pressed against the drywall, trying to put some space between them, but her chin lifted in defiance.

"What club? And how did Justin know where to find you?"

This wasn't good.

"Since when do I need to clear my whereabouts with you, big brother?"

"Since you show up to the hospital with your back covered in strange red marks."

Oh hell. He hadn't even thought about that. By morning, the evidence of the flogging he'd given her wouldn't be noticeable, but it had only been a couple of hours and that dress of hers left a good portion of her shoulders and upper back exposed. She'd had her coat on when they'd first arrived, but she'd obviously taken it off and it was impossible not to notice the marks. Justin could see them from here. He was going to have to intervene. "Everything all right? How's your dad?"

At the sound of his voice, the two siblings turned. Kim looked relieved. Mark looked annoyed.

It was Kim who answered him, though. "Dad's going to be okay, but he's going to have to have surgery. They have to put a pin in his leg."

"Could you give us a minute?" Mark asked, although, from his tone, he wasn't really asking.

"I'm not sure that's such a good idea."

His friend's eyes narrowed. "Why not?"

"Because you're acting like a jackass to your sister when she's already upset because of what's happening with your dad. You need to back off." Justin knew he was taking a chance coming between Mark and Kim, but he wouldn't let his friend berate his lover for something Justin did to her.

Mark took a step back and looked at his sister. Then to Justin. Blowing out a loud breath, he marched down the hall without another word.

"Thanks," Kim said, sagging against the wall.

"Come here." Justin opened his arms, inviting her into them.

She hesitated. "Someone might see."

"I don't care."

Kim collapsed into his arms.

He hugged her close. "Are you okay?"

"Yeah." Her answer was mumbled against his chest. "Everything was okay until I took my coat off. It was hot in the room, and I wasn't thinking."

Justin glanced down at the skin in question. The impact marks had faded a lot, but anyone who knew her would be able to spot the redness a mile away. Closer inspection would have made it clear it wasn't from her simply pressing against something.

He kissed the top of her head and tilted her head up. "Why don't you head back to the waiting room and keep Ali company for a while. I'll see if I can find Mark and"—Justin's gaze lingered on where his friend had disappeared down the hall—"see if I can smooth things over."

She nodded and stepped away from him.

Justin stayed put until she turned the corner, then he went to find Mark.

It was after one in the morning before they'd gotten her dad a room. Kim had wanted to wait until he was settled before leaving. Her mom hadn't wanted to leave, so the nurse had a cot brought in for her to sleep on.

"Are you sure you don't want me to stay, Mom?" Mark asked.

Belinda Langley shook her head. "There's nothing you all can do tonight. Go home and get some rest."

Kim embraced her mom. "I'll be back in the morning. Call me if you need anything."

"Thank you, honey." Her mom kissed her on the cheek before turning to hug Mark.

Justin and Ali hung back near the door. Once her dad had been assigned a room, they'd been able to see him. Not that he would likely remember them being there. He'd been given some strong pain relief and was currently snoring in his hospital bed.

After saying their goodbyes, the four of them made their way down the elevator to the parking lot. Mark had been acting strange around her ever since he'd returned to the waiting room with Justin. He hadn't mentioned her back again, but she'd made sure to retrieve her coat and keep it securely on her body.

Justin hovered close, but he hadn't spoken to her either since their embrace in the hall. She'd needed that hug. And while she wasn't remotely in the mood to pick up where they'd left off earlier that evening, she wanted the comfort of his arms around her. She wanted to fall asleep knowing he was right there, strong and sure.

The cold night air hit them in the face when they stepped outside. Mark turned to Justin. "Can you give Ali a ride home since her place is closer to yours?"

"Sure," Justin said. "I was planning to take both Ali and Kim home."

"I can take my sister."

"I don't think that's a good idea," Justin said.

Kim confirmed Justin's assessment. "Neither do I."

Her brother didn't seem happy his plans were being questioned. "Why not?"

"For what it's worth, I don't think it's a good idea, either." Everyone looked at Ali. She'd been quiet most of the evening, staying by Kim's side and supporting her. Holding Kim's hand when she needed it since Justin couldn't. "I don't know what's going on between the two of you and I don't care. It's been a long night and you both need rest. Whatever it is, you can figure it out tomorrow when everyone isn't so jumpy."

Kim silently mouthed *thank you* to her friend.

Mark rolled his shoulders. "Fine. We'll talk tomorrow." Then he turned on his heel and headed off toward where he'd parked his car.

"Okay then," Ali said.

Justin began walking again. "Let's get out of the cold."

They piled into Justin's car and made their way toward Ali's apartment. Ali made herself comfortable in the back seat. "You two are going to need to come clean soon. Mark's going to figure it out before too long."

Justin flexed his fingers on the steering wheel but didn't comment. Neither did Kim.

Everyone was quiet for the rest of the drive. They parked in front of Ali's apartment, and she flipped the hood up on her coat. "Call me tomorrow morning and I'll go to the hospital with you."

"Thanks, Ali."

Her best friend placed a comforting hand on Kim's shoulder, then exited the vehicle.

They waited for her friend to go inside and turn on the lights before leaving. Ali's mom was still there and driving Ali crazy, but she wouldn't say anything about Ali getting in late. She may not even be in yet herself. Zelda had moved into her find another man stage.

Justin maneuvered out of the small parking lot and headed back to her apartment. He pulled into the parking spot nearest to her door and turned off the engine.

No words were said as they got out of the vehicle and made their way up the sidewalk. Justin waited behind her as she put the key in the lock and turned. He helped her with her coat before removing his own, then hanging them both in the closet. She'd wondered if she would need to ask him to stay, but he showed no signs of going. She fell into his arms, burying her face in his chest as she'd wanted to do for the last few hours.

The feel of his hands running along her back made her feel safe. She knew her dad would be okay, but seeing him lying in that hospital bed looking pale and not his usual energetic self had been a wake-up call. He wasn't going to be around forever. None of them were and they all had to make the most out of the time they had.

Leaning back, he cupped her face in both his hands and kissed her lips with the softest pressure. "Go get ready for bed. I'll lock up."

Kim didn't argue. She stopped in her small bathroom to take care of business and brush her teeth before heading into the bedroom.

Everything was how she left it. She'd had trouble deciding what to wear to the club. There were several outfits draped over the end of her bed. She picked them up and threw them into the corner. It was too late and she was too tired to worry about them tonight.

Water turned on in the bathroom as she removed her dress and threw it into the dirty clothes hamper before kicking off her heels. Her feet were killing her. At the club, she'd known she'd be sitting or kneeling most of the time, so wearing the heels hadn't been a big deal. The hospital floors, however, had not been kind to her feet. She'd spent way too much time walking and standing on the hard floors.

She was sitting on the edge of the bed, rubbing her poor feet, when Justin strolled into the room. He crossed the room and sat down at the end of the bed, more than a foot away from her. "Get into the bed and I'll rub your feet for you."

Kim didn't have the energy to argue. She pushed herself higher on the bed and he placed her feet in his lap.

The first few touches were almost painful as he worked the knots out of her feet. But slowly the pain began to ease and what he was doing felt so good. She rested her head on her pillow and closed her eyes, letting the feel of his fingers caressing her lift the tension in not only her feet but her entire body.

Chapter Twenty-Five

Kim's eyes fluttered open. Light was streaming through the curtains. She stretched, then sat up, looking around her room. The other side of the bed was empty, but the crinkled sheets confirmed he'd stayed. She paused to listen and heard the faint sounds of movement in her kitchen.

Swinging her legs around, she lowered her feet to the floor and stood. Her brain felt full of fog. She glanced at the clock to see how late it was and was shocked to see it was after eleven. She'd slept for nine hours. That wasn't like her. A solid seven and she was good to go.

After another good stretch, she threw on a robe and crossed the hall to the bathroom. She splashed some water on her face, brushed her teeth, and took care of business before going in search of Justin.

The smell of coffee hit her and her stomach growled. She hadn't eaten anything since before they'd gone to Serpent's Kiss.

He heard her and glanced up from where he sat at her kitchen table. He was dressed in different clothes than he'd worn the night before. She frowned. Had he gone home last night? "You changed?"

Justin looked down at his clothes, then back at her. "I keep a change of clothes in my trunk in case I get grease on them. I never know when I need to be presentable in front of a client."

"Oh. Okay." She padded to the counter to pour herself a cup of coffee.

The sound of a chair scraping across the floor was followed by the feel of him behind her. His breath tickled her ear. "You thought I left?"

She shook her head. "I didn't think so, but then I saw your clothes."

He turned her around to face him. "I wasn't going to leave you alone last night."

Suddenly, coffee wasn't as important as feeling his arms around her. She collapsed into him, circling her arms around his waist. "Thank you. I'm so glad you were there with me last night, even though we had to keep our distance."

He rested his cheek on her head and held her close. "Ali's right. We aren't going to be able to hide our relationship for much longer."

"We said we'd give it a month." She met his gaze. "It's only three more weeks."

She saw something flash across his face, but it was gone too fast for her to get a read on what he was thinking. He kissed the tip of her nose and took a step back. "I made breakfast."

It was then she noticed the eggs and sausage on the stove. "It smells good."

Kim twisted to get a mug from the cabinet and resumed getting her coffee. The caffeine hit her tongue and she sighed. After a few sips, the fog dissipated and she could think clearly again.

As she sat down with her eggs and sausage, she couldn't shake the feeling that she'd upset Justin with her response. Was he ready to announce to her family that they were together? Did he no longer care about Mark and her parents finding out? Was she?

After her brother's reaction last night, Kim was afraid of how he was going to take the news. She was hoping since he knew Justin, trusted him, that it wouldn't be bad, but she wasn't holding her breath.

She took a few bites of her food, making her stomach happy. "Does Mark know about you being a Dom?"

Justin set down his coffee. "Yes."

Pressing her lips together, she met his gaze. The food she'd already eaten began to churn in her stomach. "How much does he know?"

"Enough to want to kick my ass when he finds out you're my submissive."

She wanted to disagree about Mark's likely reaction, but she knew Justin was right. It wouldn't be the first time her brother had laid someone out on her behalf. He'd done it once before when they were in high school. She'd been a freshman and one of the senior football players had cornered her in the hall outside the boys' locker room. She'd been there waiting on Mark to drive her home. Her brother had come out to find Toby Green snaking his slimy hand up her shirt right there in the hallway. Mark had broken Toby's nose and gotten suspended for a week. He'd viewed it as a win, though, because Toby hadn't bothered her again after that.

Kim finished the rest of her breakfast and her coffee. "I'm gonna call Mom and check in."

"I'll clean up." He stood and went to the sink and began rinsing the dishes.

Making her way out of the kitchen, she realized her phone was still in her coat. Rushing over to the closet, she fished her phone out of her coat pocket and saw she had three missed calls. One was from her mom, one from Ali, and one from her brother.

Crap.

Taking her phone into her bedroom, she dialed her mom first.

"Good morning, honey." Her mom sounded tired.

"Is Dad okay?" Kim asked, concerned something may have happened overnight.

She could hear movement through the phone before her mom answered. "Nothing much has changed since you and your brother left last night. The surgeon came in to see him early this morning. They've scheduled the surgery for this afternoon at three o'clock."

Kim glanced at the clock again. It was noon already. "I'll be there soon. Did you want me to pick up anything on the way?"

"Would you mind swinging by the house and bringing me a change of clothes?"

"Sure." Kim glanced at herself in the mirror and ran a hand through her hair. She should have taken a brush to it earlier. "Did you want me to grab anything specific?"

"Just a pair of jeans, a long-sleeved shirt, and a sweater. It's been a little chilly in at times."

"No problem." Kim picked up her brush and began dragging it through her hair. "What about food? Have you eaten anything?"

"I had a muffin and some fruit this morning from the cafeteria."

"That had to be hours ago, Mom. I'll pick you up a sandwich on my way." She reached for a tie to pull her hair back. "I should be there before one."

"Don't rush. Your dad and I are just watching some television while we wait."

After saying goodbye to her mom, Kim removed a pair of jeans and a sweater from her closet and grabbed a bra and underwear from the dresser. She put her phone on speaker after dialing Ali's number and began getting dressed.

Her friend answered on the second ring. "Hey."

"Hey, yourself." Kim stepped into her jeans and pulled them up her legs and over her hips. She told Ali about her dad's surgery and that she would be heading to the hospital soon.

"Do you want me to go with you?" Ali asked.

Kim retrieved her most comfortable shoes and sat on the edge of her bed to put them on. "I don't know how long the surgery is going to last. Don't you have to work tonight?"

"I called Katrina this morning and let her know what was going on. She knows I might not be there."

Justin appeared in the doorway as Kim finished tying her shoes. "Was she upset?"

Her friend snorted. "No. Of course not. Why would she be upset?"

"I don't know." Kim didn't really know Mistress Katrina that well, but the woman intimidated the hell out of her.

"What time are you heading to the hospital?" Ali asked.

"Soon. I have to stop at Mom and Dad's first and get Mom a change of clothes. Then I told her I'd stop and get her a sandwich."

"I'll stop and get some lunch for all of us. You just worry about the clothes," Ali said.

Kim's gaze met Justin's. He was leaning casually against the frame of her door. "Thanks."

Disconnecting the call, she lowered the phone into her lap. He strolled into the room and sat down on the bed beside her. "How's your dad?"

"His surgery is at three. I need to pick Mom up a change of clothes, and then I'm going to head to the hospital."

He nodded. "Your brother just called me. Asked if I knew where you were because you weren't answering your phone."

"What did you say?"

"I told him you were probably either sleeping or on your way to the hospital." Justin sighed. "I don't like lying to him." He paused. "To any of them."

"It's only a little longer. We still don't know if it's gonna work between us." As soon as she said it, she regretted the words, but it was too late. They were out there, and she couldn't take them back.

His gaze lingered on her face before he averted his eyes and stood.

Kim knew she'd hurt him, and it tore her up inside. She felt as if she'd been punched in the gut. "I didn't mean—"

Justin held up his hand. "I know."

Not willing to let it go, she went to him. "No, you don't."

He looked at her and she could see that same look in his eyes again. It was a mix of sadness and hurt. She knew she had to fix it. It wasn't as if she didn't want to be with him.

Circling her arms around his neck, she pulled herself up on her tiptoes and brushed her lips against his. He placed his hands on her waist, holding her to him. "I want us to be together. For so long I've dreamed about being yours and the reality is so much better than any of my fantasies." She licked his bottom lip with the tip of her tongue. "But this thing between us isn't that simple."

She felt his cock growing against her belly and her body was warming, preparing for him. But they didn't have time for that. Not now. Still, she wasn't willing to let him think she wasn't sure about them.

"You deserve someone who can be everything you need and I'm still not sure I can."

He frowned and she knew what was coming. "You're submissive. You just need time and training."

"Maybe."

"No maybe." He crushed her against his body and kissed her hard, holding the back of her head. "If we didn't need to get to the hospital, I'd show you exactly what I mean, but that would take more time than we have. Plus, I don't want your brother getting any ideas and showing up on your doorstep." He kissed her again. This time, she could feel it all the way down to her toes. "Go to the hospital. Be there for your family."

"You're not coming?" she said when he stepped back, putting distance between them.

"I told your brother I'd be there around two."

Kim nodded. They needed to talk more, but he was right. This wasn't the time.

JUSTIN HATED TO LEAVE HER, BUT IT COULDN'T BE HELPED. UNLESS THEY were going to make their relationship public, they had to arrive separately and act as if they weren't more than longtime acquaintances. It fucking sucked.

Mark wasn't exactly in the best mood when he'd called Justin that morning. A night of sleep hadn't helped to calm his friend down. When he'd caught up to him at the hospital, Mark told him about the marks on Kim's back. He was convinced they weren't from her leaning up against something as she'd told him...that instead, someone had done something to her. It was an awkward conversation where Justin felt like he was dodging arrows aimed directly at him.

After kissing Kim goodbye and promising to see her at the hospital, he drove back to his house, showered, and changed again. He didn't really need to take a shower, but it was something to pass the time and it kept him from dashing off to the hospital.

Kim wanted to stick to their original agreement and even if it killed him, he'd respect her wishes. She said it was her uncertainty about being a good submissive for him, and even though he believed her, it still hurt. He was tired of hiding. He'd been burying his feelings for her for too long already. They could never get that time back.

At one-forty-five, Justin arrived at the hospital and sent a text to Mark. **Hey, man. I'm here.**

In Dad's room. -Mark

Justin pocketed his cell phone and made his way to the elevator. The ride up to the sixth floor was slow. He stood toward the back of the elevator as people entered and exited on their way to see patients. By the time he reached Davis's room, Mark, Kim, and Belinda were all standing out in the hall.

Concern that something may have happened caused his chest to clench. "Hey."

Kim's gaze met his and Justin ached to hold her. It had been less than two hours, but the worry was etched on her face. He almost said screw it, but he held back because he knew that was what she wanted.

Belinda embraced him, and he held tight to the woman who had been a second mother to him. "Thank you for coming."

"I wouldn't be anywhere else." He released her and met Mark's gaze. "How is he?"

"They're prepping him for surgery. We're going to follow him down to pre-op, and then it's a waiting game." Mark looked calm on the surface, but he knew his friend better than most. He was worried.

Any additional conversation was cut short when the orderly rolled Davis into the hall. Justin hung back, letting Belinda, Mark, and Kim go first. They all made their way down to the second floor, where they were forced to say goodbye to Davis and were directed to a nearby waiting room.

The surgery would take one to two hours, so they had time to kill. Ali texted Kim not long after they got to the waiting room and Kim went to meet her friend and bring her to join the rest of the group.

It was a long two hours. Ali stayed by Kim's side and Justin kept an eye on Mark as he hovered over his mom.

"Mom."

Belinda looked over at her daughter, then followed Kim's gaze across the room. Davis's doctor ambled toward them, looking relaxed. Mark must have noticed it too because he felt some of the tension ease from his best friend.

The doctor approached all of them and they stood. "Everything went well. He's being moved to recovery, and once he's awake, they'll take him back to his room."

"When can he come home?" Belinda asked.

"If all goes well tonight, he should be able to go home tomorrow. He'll have to take it easy for a few weeks, but everything should heal just fine."

"Thank you, Doctor." Mark extended his hand to the surgeon.

The doctor shook Mark's hand and nodded. "You might want to take this time to get some dinner. He'll be in recovery for at least an hour." He looked directly at Belinda. "We have your number if we need to get ahold of you."

"I think that's a great idea," Mark said. The doctor walked away, and he turned his attention to his mother. "Come on, Mom. Let's get you something to eat."

Justin thought she was going to argue—it hadn't been that long since they'd eaten the sandwiches Ali had brought—but she nodded and gathered her things to leave. They didn't end up going far. One of the nurses had recommended a restaurant within walking distance from the hospital.

They were seated at a round table, so Justin made sure to take a seat next to Kim. Ali sat on her other side, next to Belinda. It wasn't as if they were close, but he felt better knowing Kim was at least within reach.

Mark sat on his other side, keeping a very close eye on his sister. Now that they knew his father was going to be okay, Mark's attention returned to Kim. Instead of addressing her, though, his gaze fell on Ali. "We haven't seen you that much lately."

"Life has been a little crazy. Work is keeping me busy. And, of course, my mom was in town for a while."

Belinda took a drink of her water. "Has she moved out already?"

Ali shook her head. "Not yet. She met the love of her life." She made quote marks with her fingers. "At a bar on Wednesday night and he's going to take her on a road trip to see The Grand Canyon. She wants to make love under the stars. They're leaving tomorrow."

"Davis and I went there before you kids were born." The look on Belinda's face said more than her words.

"Mom!"

"Way to go," Ali said with a grin.

Mark scrunched up his nose. "Ew, Mom."

Justin chuckled. "I think it's great."

"Yes, well…"

Luckily, the server arrived with their meals and everyone focused on their food. When the conversation picked up again, it changed to Davis's recovery. He was going to need help getting around for a while. A plan was made to cover showers, dressing, and keeping up with things around the house. Even though Justin and Ali weren't technically members of the Langley family, they'd both eagerly jumped in to offer to do their part.

Kim laid her fork down on her plate and pushed away from the table. "I'm gonna hit the bathroom before we head back."

"That sounds like a good idea." Justin stood and followed her to the front of the restaurant. As soon as they disappeared around the corner, he reached for her hand and squeezed. She leaned into him and rested her head on his shoulder for a few seconds.

They walked the rest of the way to the restrooms holding hands, separating at the last minute. He waited until she went into the ladies' room before ducking into the men's.

He was washing his hands when Mark strolled into the bathroom. "Something's going on with Kim and I think you know what it is."

Chapter Twenty-Six

Justin froze for a long moment before turning off the water and turning away from his friend to dry his hands. "Why would I know what's going on with her?"

"You knew where to find her last night."

After drying his hands, Justin moved to exit the bathroom. "That's a big leap to me knowing what's going on with her."

Mark followed him out. "I think she's seeing someone."

Keeping his gaze straight ahead, he continued to make his way back toward their table. "You do realize your sister's an adult, right? As much as you don't like to think about it, she does date. I'm sure she has sex, too."

His friend didn't respond right away, so Justin was thinking he was going to let it go. Instead, Justin felt Mark's hand wrap around his arm, his fingers digging into Justin's flesh. It wasn't painful, but it was meant to get his attention.

He turned and looked at his friend. Mark's breathing was more labored than it should have been for the pace they were walking. "Someone hit her last night."

Justin's eyes widened. "What do you mean someone hit her? She looked fine to me."

"I told you about the marks on her back. Someone did that to her." Mark took a step closer and lowered his voice. "I think they were from a rope or...what do you call it...a crop or something. I should have had you look at them."

Swallowing, Justin tried not to react to the disdain in his friend's voice. He knew Mark didn't understand his lifestyle, but he'd never heard him react this way. Then again, they'd never been talking about his sister before. "Maybe she likes that sort of thing."

Mark's brow furrowed, and he released his hold on Justin's arm. "She can't like that stuff, man. Kim's too..."

"Too what?"

His friend shook his head. "I just don't want to think about her into that kind of stuff."

He was getting irritated with Mark. Even if he didn't realize it, what he was saying was kind of insulting. "Kinky stuff, you mean."

"Yeah." Then he must have realized how what he was saying sounded. "I know that's your thing, man, and that's cool. But Kim..."

"Is a grown woman and able to make her own decisions."

Mark blew out a breath. "She's my little sister."

Justin just looked at him, not trusting himself to speak.

Running a hand through his hair, Mark averted his gaze. "What if she gets hurt?"

He wanted to say something along the lines of *I'd never hurt her*, but of course he couldn't say that. "I hate to break it to you, but you can't always protect her."

"I can break the bastard's nose."

Justin tried not to react. Luckily, Mark wasn't paying attention to him. His gaze had drifted to Belinda, Kim, and Ali as they made their way toward them. Apparently, they'd gotten tired of waiting for them to return.

"We were wondering if you two got lost," Kim said, eyeing both of them.

"Nope," Justin said. "You ready to go?"

Belinda finished doing up the buttons on her coat. "Hopefully, they have Davis back in his room. I'll feel better once I see him."

Once again, he took up the rear as they walked the short distance back to the hospital. Davis was propped up in his bed. He was a bit groggy but otherwise seemed okay. The nurse advised us not to stay long so he could get some rest.

Ali and I stood by the door and let Belinda, Mark, and Kim have a moment with the family patriarch.

"Did Mark grill you?" Ali asked, in not much more than a whisper.

Justin shrugged. He wasn't sure what he'd call his conversation with Mark.

His friend was worried about his sister. He understood that. But Mark took his protective streak too far sometimes. Kim wasn't a little girl anymore and Mark needed to come to terms with that.

"Go home and get some rest, sweetheart. I'll be fine. The nurses will take care of me."

Belinda didn't want to leave his side. "I can sleep on the cot like I did last night."

"You couldn't have gotten a lot of rest on that thing, Mom," Kim said. "Go home. Get some sleep. Dad will be fine for one night and he'll get to go home tomorrow."

Mark placed a hand on his mom's shoulder. "Kim's right. You need to take care of yourself."

Realizing she was outnumbered, Belinda nodded. "Okay. But we're making sure the nurse has my number."

"Of course, Mom." Mark stood next to his mom as she kissed her husband goodbye, then walked with her to the nurse's station to make sure they had all her contact information.

Kim leaned over and kissed her dad on the cheek. "I'll see you tomorrow, Dad."

He gave her arm a squeeze and smiled up at her.

Justin and Ali both said their goodbyes to Davis, then left him to get some rest.

It was after eight o'clock by the time Justin pulled into his driveway. Kim was taking her mom home, and he was hoping after that she'd be coming to his place. These long days of having her so close but not being able to touch her were wearing on him.

His conversation with Mark was also weighing on his mind. They weren't going to make it the three weeks. He knew it in his gut. But Kim was still reluctant to take that final step. He knew she could be a good submissive for him, but he had to get her to see it as well.

He was putting a load of laundry in the wash when he heard a car door slam shut. His heart rate kicked up a notch at the thought of seeing her. It had always been that way to a certain extent, but it was different now. Before, it had been mixed with dread because he couldn't do anything about his feelings. That wasn't the case anymore.

She didn't get a chance to knock before he opened the door and gathered her into his arms. He buried his face in her hair, absorbing her warmth...her scent.

Her lips grazed his neck, and he felt a shiver travel down his spine. His love for this woman filled his chest and he wanted so badly to be able to tell her.

Taking her face in his hands, he lowered his mouth to hers. The kiss wasn't rushed. It was soft, yet firm. Loving, yet possessive. Her lips glided against his.

Justin ran his tongue along the seam of her lips, and she opened her mouth, allowing him inside. His tongue caressed hers, dancing, playing. He loved kissing her.

Kim snaked her hand between them and began unzipping her coat. Once the zipper was free, he helped her push it off her shoulders and onto the floor. "That's better," she mumbled against his lips.

He hummed and kissed his way down her jaw to her neck. "Much."

She canted her head to the side, giving him better access as she threaded her fingers through his hair. "Make love to me."

He hadn't planned on having sex tonight. Yes, he wanted to, but he always wanted to have sex with Kim. "You're sure, baby?"

"Yes." She gazed up at him. "I need to feel you inside me. I want to forget about everything but you."

Placing another kiss on her lips, he released her. "Get yourself ready for bed. I'll be there in a minute."

Kim nodded and made her way down the hall to his bedroom.

He took his time checking the doors and turning off all the lights, needing to calm down a little. The last thing she needed tonight was for him to jump her. She'd asked him to make love to her, not fuck her senseless.

The sight of her lying naked on his bed was something he wasn't likely to forget anytime soon. He'd expected to find her in his bed, under the covers, preferably naked. But she wasn't in his bed. She was on his bed. Laid out like a dish waiting to be devoured.

Kicking his shoes into the corner, he crossed his arms at the waist and lifted his shirt up his torso and over his head. He threw it onto the floor and crossed to the bed. The mattress dipped under his weight as he crawled on top of her, bracing his weight with his arms. "I thought you'd be in bed."

She gazed up at him without an ounce of shyness. "I was waiting for you. I was afraid if I got under the covers, I'd fall asleep."

Her hands grazed his chest, gliding over his nipples before she circled her arms around his neck. He gazed down at her, his erection pressing painfully against his jeans. "And you don't want to sleep."

Kim shook her head, the motion causing strands of her hair to tickle his forearms. "No. I don't want to sleep. Not yet."

His cock pulsed at her words. He eased himself on top of her and captured her mouth with his.

THERE WERE SO MANY TIMES TODAY WHEN KIM HAD WANTED TO TOUCH Justin. Her dad rarely got sick, and seeing him in a hospital bed, hooked up to monitors, was difficult to process. It was as if all at once she was hit with the fact that he wouldn't always be there.

Sadness had gripped her and all she wanted was to fall into Justin's arms and have him tell her everything would be okay. Given how independent she usually was, it felt wrong to need someone like she felt she needed him.

But as he pressed her body into the mattress, the comfort she'd been seeking warmed her body in ways she never thought possible. She'd had boyfriends before, but never once had she felt connected to them the way she did Justin. Wanting to see him...talk to him...feel him...was a new experience for her when it came to men.

She turned her head to give him access to her neck as he licked his way down the column of her neck, and then back up to take her earlobe into his mouth. He suckled it and worried it between his teeth, sending little tingles shooting down her body. She'd never had someone play with her earlobes before and she found she liked it. At least from him.

Her hips lifted off the bed of their own accord, seeking the friction she so badly desired. She could feel his length, hard and firm against her thigh.

"Patience, baby."

"I want you. I want to feel you inside me." She paused as an overwhelming rush of emotion came over her. "I need you."

He skimmed his hand down the length of her body, resting it on her hip, and lifted his head to meet her gaze. She had no idea what he saw, but he placed a firm kiss on her lips and scurried off the bed.

She watched as he removed his jeans and socks, kicking them to the side. Then he opened the drawer in his nightstand and fished out a condom. It only took a few seconds for him to tear the package open and roll the protection down his length.

Justin stood beside the bed, looking down at her. He brushed the hair away from her face and trailed the back of his hand along her cheek. "Push yourself up onto the pillows."

Doing as he asked, she lowered her head onto the soft pillow and sighed in contentment as he positioned himself between her legs. He placed two fingers at her entrance, circling before pressing them inside.

Kim closed her eyes and arched her back as he massaged her inner walls. She was wet and ready for him.

The mattress moved under his weight, but it wasn't his cock she felt next. It was his mouth. He slid his fingers in and out of her as he licked her swollen flesh. She wanted his cock inside her, but this felt so good, too.

His tongue began to circle her clit and she felt her orgasm building. She reached down, fisting his hair, not sure if she wanted him to stop or keep going.

With his free hand, he removed her hand and placed it on the bed. "Keep your hand on the bed. I'm not stopping until you come all over my face."

Heat zinged through her and zeroed in on her clit. She arched her back, silently begging for more.

He traced her lips with the tip of his tongue before returning to her clit. It seemed to go on and on and her chest was heaving with her exaggerated breaths. She was so close, but she needed a little more. Just a little more pressure to her clit and she'd be flying.

Sweat beaded on her body and she gripped the sheets with white knuckles. Her entire body was vibrating.

Then he took her clit into his mouth and sucked as if his life depended on it.

Her body collapsed in on itself. Something between a cry and a scream left her lips as she rode out her climax. Wave after wave hit her, prolonging her release.

Then she felt him. Not his fingers. Not his mouth. He thrust his cock into her in one fluid motion, sending another shock wave through her system.

"Breathe, baby." His lips hovered over hers and she could smell herself. Her scent wafted off him, marking him as hers, and a sense of possession gripped her. He was hers.

She needed to touch him. To show him how she felt because she wasn't sure she could put it into words. No man had ever made her feel the things he did. "I want. To touch. You."

Her words were broken up between her ragged breaths, but it didn't matter. He licked across her bottom lip and whispered, "Touch me."

Kim wrapped her legs around his waist and ran her hands up his muscular back. He kissed her, plunging his tongue deep into her mouth as he pumped his hips, driving his cock into her sex. They couldn't get any closer, and yet she couldn't seem to get close enough. She wanted more. Always more of him.

His lips never left hers as his hand moved lower, bracketing her hip, holding her exactly where he wanted her. He ground his pelvis against her clit, and she felt another orgasm building.

This one didn't hit her with as much force as the first, but that didn't lessen its impact. He swallowed her screams as she rode out her climax before grunting his own release.

Justin rolled over and pulled her onto his chest. He was breathing as hard as she was and she closed her eyes, not wanting to let go of the moment.

They lay there as their breathing returned to normal. His fingers brushed through her hair, relaxing her even more. "I need to go clean up."

"Okay." She didn't move.

He chuckled. "That means I need to get up."

Reluctantly, she let him go.

Kim rolled over and watched him stroll into the bathroom. Once he was out of sight, she flopped onto her back and sighed. The man made her feel as if she had no bones left in her body every time they were together. It didn't matter if the sex was hard and fast or if it was slow and gentle. Her body would take him any way it could get him.

As that thought resonated through her post-orgasmic brain, her worries surfaced again. She wanted a future with him. Wanted it more than anything she'd ever wanted in her life. But the fear that she couldn't be everything he needed still plagued her. He deserved a submissive who could serve him without overthinking everything.

Was she able to do that?

Justin emerged from the bathroom in all his naked glory. He sat down on the edge of the bed next to her and reached for her hand. "How are you feeling?"

That was a good question. But he wasn't asking her about her mental state. Or at least not in regards to the thoughts currently swirling around in her head. "Tired."

"Your dad's going to be all right. He's strong." That grin that did things to her insides pulled at his lips. "And stubborn."

She squeezed his hand. "I know. I'm glad it wasn't worse. Sometimes he doesn't realize he's not as young as he used to be."

He smiled and brought her hand to rest on his thigh. "I know the timing might not be perfect, but I'd like to take you away for a couple of days. Just the two of us."

So many emotions hit Kim at once. Her first thought was *yes, please*. But it was quickly followed by worry about leaving her dad.

Before she could come up with a coherent response, he continued. "I don't think Mark is going to let this go. You know how he is. He's not likely to let this mystery go unsolved." Justin met her gaze. "It will be so much worse if he finds out on his own. I don't want to wait for that to happen."

"And you think the two of us disappearing for a few days is going to fix that?" She was trying to follow his train of thought, but his logic wasn't making sense.

"I don't think it's going to take him three weeks to figure out that you and I are seeing each other. He's already come close to catching us once."

She hadn't known at the time it was Mark, but the thought of her brother walking in on her, naked, in Justin's bedroom had her pulse kicking up a notch and not in a good way. "You don't want to wait the three weeks." It wasn't really a question. He'd hinted at it before.

"I don't." He lifted her hand to his lips and kissed the tips of her fingers. "The month was to figure out if you can be a good submissive for me."

He held her gaze, waiting for her to nod her agreement.

"I want to prove to you that you can."

Kim sat up, feeling strangely at a disadvantage lying down. "How?"

"We go away for the weekend. I'll pick you up from work Friday night and we can spend two days alone, just us."

"And we'd be playing the whole weekend?" she asked.

"Yes."

Kim wasn't sure what to say, so she took a moment to process what he was saying. She couldn't argue with his logic, but could she submit to him for two days straight? The whole problem was that, according to Ali, she couldn't get out of her own head. How were two days away going to change that?

On the other hand, maybe it would answer the question that was looming over their relationship. Could she be a good submissive for him?

It was the one thing holding their relationship back. He was right about that. The sex was amazing. And they had no issues out of bed either. The only sticking point—the only thing standing between them and a future together—was whether she could live a D/s lifestyle with him.

Justin stood. "Think about it and let me know by Wednesday so I can make the arrangements."

"Where would we go?"

He didn't seem bothered by her question...or surprised. "A friend of Katrina's owns a cabin about an hour from here. It will give us privacy and your brother doesn't know about it."

Two days in a cabin alone with Justin. Her sex pulsed at the thought.

Releasing her hand, he stood and walked around to the other side of the bed. He slid in beside her and gathered her into his arms as if their conversation hadn't happened.

Kim snuggled against his chest, letting what he'd said permeate her brain. The chances of keeping their relationship a secret from her brother for the next three weeks were slim. Justin was right about that. And it was only her concern about submitting to him that was holding her back. Every cell in her body wanted to be with him. It was only the fallout if things didn't work out that she feared. She knew that if push came to shove, her brother would choose her, and she didn't want him to lose his best friend.

She propped herself up on her elbow so she could look at him. "Two days?"

"Yes." He grazed his knuckles over her cheek and waited.

As much as the thought of giving over control to him for two whole days terrified her, she knew she needed to try. Their future depended on it. "Okay. I'll go away with you this weekend."

"And be my submissive?"

She swallowed. "And be your submissive. You'll be in control."

A wicked smile bloomed on his face and he brought her lips to his. "We are going to have so much fun, baby."

Chapter Twenty-Seven

Kim said goodbye to her assistant Friday afternoon and made her way to the elevator that would lead her to the parking garage. Originally, Justin was going to pick her up from work, but she didn't want to leave her car in the parking garage the entire weekend.

Over the course of the week, she'd talked to Ali more times than she could count. To say Kim was nervous about this weekend was putting it mildly. She was going to be giving up control of everything to Justin for two whole days. While that might not seem like a big deal to some people, for her it was huge.

As if reading her mind, Ali's ringtone filled her vehicle as she pulled out of the parking garage. "How you holding up?"

The hint of amusement in her best friend's voice had her rolling her eyes. "I'm not going to chicken out, if that's what you're asking."

"Didn't think you would."

A horn honked somewhere behind her. It was a quarter after five on a Friday afternoon in downtown St. Louis. Traffic was horrible. Normally, Kim didn't make it out of the office until after six, which meant she missed the worse of the traffic. Maybe she should have told Justin to pick her up later. "I want this to work, Ali.

"It will. Just try not to overthink it. Trust him to take care of you and let everything else go. You might surprise yourself. I mean, look at Drew. He's in charge at his job, but he submits to Beth. You've seen them together." Another horn sounded, but this time it was through the phone. "Learn to use a turn signal."

Kim chuckled.

"I hate Friday traffic," Ali mumbled.

The exit Kim was looking for finally appeared and she eased her vehicle into the lane she needed. "I'm not used to it anymore. I'm usually still at the office."

"You work too much."

"I have to or someone else will end up in my job." It was a sad reality that to be at the top of her profession, she had to put in a lot of hours. Most days, she arrived before seven and left after six. She did try to take weekends off, but sometimes she didn't even get that.

"Well, try not to worry about work while you're with Justin."

Kim breathed a sigh of relief when she turned onto her street. One of the advantages of living in the city was that she didn't have a long commute. "Something tells me I won't have a choice."

Ali giggled. "True."

When Kim pulled into her parking spot outside of her apartment, she spotted Justin already there waiting. "He's here."

"Hey." Kim looked away and turned off her engine. "Stop stressing and have fun."

Taking a deep breath in, she released it. "I'll do my best."

"Love you."

"I love you, too," Kim said. "I'll call you when I get back."

"You'd better. I want all the details. Not like I'm seeing any action lately." Before Kim could comment on that, Ali added, "Later," and ended the call.

Kim snatched her purse from the passenger seat and stepped out of the car. Justin exited his vehicle and followed her up the walkway. As she put her keys in the lock, she felt his body press against her back. She closed her eyes and turned the key, wanting to get inside so she could get her hands on him. It had been three days since they'd seen each other. Sure, they'd talked and texted since then, but it wasn't the same.

She pushed the door open and hurried inside. Within seconds, he was on her. Justin backed her against the wall and kissed her hard. By the time he came up for air, she was ready to cancel their plans and spend the entire weekend there in bed with him.

"Are you ready to go?"

It took a moment for her to register what he'd said. "Yeah. My bags are in my room."

He gave her another quick kiss, then headed toward her bedroom, leaving her leaning against the wall, still trying to catch her breath.

It felt like only seconds had gone by when he returned carrying the two suitcases she'd packed. "You do realize we're only going to be gone for two days, right?"

"I wasn't sure what to bring. You didn't tell me anything besides we're going to be staying in a cabin."

Justin grinned and opened the door once more. He gestured for her to go first, so she pushed off the wall and walked back outside.

After locking up and loading her bags into his car, he drove east toward Illinois. She sat back and tried to relax as the city gave way to open fields.

With the city lights behind them, she needed to fill the silence with something. The silence was killing her. "Have you ever seen Ali play with a Dom at the club?" Kim had been a member for almost four months now and she'd never seen her friend do anything but hang out and work.

"I have."

When he didn't elaborate, she pressed him for more information. "Who?"

Justin glanced over at her, then back at the road. "She's played with a handful of Doms. No one recently, though."

"Why?" She was pretty sure she knew why, but she wanted to get his opinion.

He shrugged.

"Come on. You've been there longer than I have. Isn't it odd that she's a member of the club and hasn't played with anyone in months?"

Again, he glanced over at her. "Have you asked Ali?"

She hadn't. Ever since Kim had joined the club, the focus had been on her. And then on her and Justin. She hadn't thought to ask her friend why she didn't play with anyone. "It hasn't come up."

They lapsed back into silence again as they continued to drive. Justin turned off the highway and they drove another twenty minutes before he turned down a two-lane road with no lines. "Are we almost there?"

He grinned. "Almost."

Five minutes later, they turned down a gravel road. There were no lights anywhere to be seen, which was something she wasn't used to. Even at her parents' house in the suburbs, there were streetlights, lights on houses, and from cars going past. Here there was nothing but trees and it was so dark she couldn't see the ones illuminated by the headlights.

The road curved, and then, as if by magic, a cabin appeared. It was surrounded by trees and about a fourth the size of her parents' house from what she could see in the dark. He stopped a few feet from a set of steps that led up to a small porch and turned off the car.

Justin opened his door, then went to the back to get their luggage. She followed his lead and exited the vehicle. It was so dark. Since he'd turned off the car, the only light that shone was from the moon overhead and the few stars that were visible in the sky.

He came up beside her and she jumped.

"Sorry." He didn't sound all that sorry.

"Don't sneak up on me like that."

Chuckling, he motioned toward the door. "Let's get inside before some creature decides to come out of the woods and eat us."

"Not funny," she said.

Kim took a tentative step on the first step, making sure it was solid before ascending the rest of the way to the small deck. She stood to the side as Justin set the bags down at his feet, then removed a key from his pocket.

She scanned the forest as he unlocked the door and hurried inside the moment it was open. His soft chuckle told her what he thought of her fears. "It's not funny. I'm a city girl. I'm not used to being out in the woods like this."

He brought the bags inside and carried them over to what she assumed was the bedroom...if you could call it that. The cabin was one big room with a small kitchen area on one end and a large bed on the other. It had a small table with four chairs and a couch directly opposite a fireplace.

It was then she noticed the door next to the kitchen. A bathroom, maybe? She could only hope. Kim wasn't sure how she'd fare if she had to go outside to use an outhouse in the middle of the night.

❦

JUSTIN WAS TRYING NOT TO LAUGH AT THE LOOK ON KIM'S FACE. HIS reasons for picking this location were because it was close and there was plenty of privacy. The nearest neighbor was over a mile away and the only person who knew where they were was Katrina, who had generously given him Garrett's phone number so he could make the arrangements. It hadn't crossed his mind that Kim would be terrified of the animals that might be hiding in the woods.

Garrett used the cabin for fishing trips during the summer, so he'd been more than happy to lend it to Justin. Especially after he'd explained to the other Dom the situation.

Putting some wood in the fireplace, Justin busied himself with getting a fire started. While it wasn't freezing in the cabin, it wasn't exactly toasty warm either and he had plans for Kim. Naked plans. And he didn't want her focused on how cold she was. He wanted her focused on him.

This weekend, they were going to start at the beginning and work their way up from there. He'd spent the week reviewing her limits list again and producing a loose plan on what he wanted to accomplish. Depending on her responses, it would have to be adjusted, but he was okay with that. Kim might not be sure she was a submissive, but he was. He'd seen the way she reacted to being dominated. He'd noticed the way her eyes dilated when she'd watched interactions between Doms and subs at the club. Now, he had to get her to see it and embrace that part of herself.

Once the fire was going, he stood and surveyed the room. He'd never been here before, but Garrett had given him a good description. The other Dom had also arranged to have groceries delivered earlier that day. They were stocked and ready to go for the weekend.

Justin walked over to Kim and ran his hands up and down her arms. "Warming up?"

She nodded. "I don't think I'm ready to take my coat off yet, though."

He grinned. "How about some dinner? Hopefully, by the time we're finished eating, the fire will have the room warmed up."

They moved into the kitchen, and he instructed her to sit before he began opening doors and finding what he needed. "I can help."

"That's all right. I want you to conserve your strength." He winked at her, and she blushed. He loved to make her blush. In some ways, Kim was very innocent. In others, she was a vixen. Kim was both comfortable in her body and shy at the same time. It was something he was excited to explore.

That thought brought a smile to his face. He had a million things he wanted to explore with her. Showing her off was only one of them.

"How was your day?" he asked as he moved about the kitchen. The list of grocery items he sent Garrett's property manager was simple. He didn't want to spend all weekend in the kitchen, so he'd opted for three meals they could eat throughout their two days at the cabin.

By the time he finished the pasta and salad, Kim had removed her coat. He dished out their plates of food and carried them over to the table.

"Thanks," Kim said, picking up her fork.

Justin took a bite. It wasn't anything fancy, just pasta and sauce, but it hit the spot on the cold evening. "How was your day?"

"Busy. I felt a little guilty leaving early when we have a campaign launching on Monday." She glanced up at him. "But I have confidence the account manager can finish it up and have it ready to go on time."

"I'm sure they can. You wouldn't put someone in charge of an account who couldn't handle it."

She smiled. "What about you?"

He shrugged. "I tore out an engine. Spent six hours getting the thing out, then found out we won't get the part we need for two weeks." He paused as he took another bite. "Luckily, this isn't the customer's primary vehicle, so they're in no rush for it."

"That's good."

They chatted a little more about work while they finished their dinner. He'd phoned Daniel last night and picked his brain about a few things and the other Dom stressed again to keep it simple. No hanging her from the rafters or anything.

Justin could feel her tension returning once she finished eating. "Did you want me to clean up?"

"No." He'd planned to have her too exhausted to worry about dishes this weekend.

Kim placed her hands in her lap and waited, at least sensing, if not knowing what was coming next.

Pushing his plate aside, he leaned back in his chair. "From now until we leave this cabin, you are to obey me. No talking back, or second-guessing my commands. Do you understand?"

He saw the muscles in her neck constrict and release as she swallowed. "Yes, Sir. I understand."

"Good." He pushed away from the table and stood. "While I clean up, I want you to remove all your clothes and lie on the bed. You're going to give me a show while I work."

She was halfway out of her chair when she paused and stared at him. "A show?"

Justin couldn't help but grin at the look on her face and the reaction he knew he'd get at his next words. "Yes. You're going to masturbate for me."

Her eyes went wide and her breathing picked up. He wasn't sure if that was due to excitement or nerves. He'd always been the one to get her off when they'd been together, but he had no doubt she had plenty of experience touching herself. For years, he'd jacked off to the vision of her bringing herself to release. Tonight, he was going to see it first-hand.

When she didn't immediately comply, he raised an eyebrow, letting her know he was waiting. Justin wondered if she would protest, but after a few moments, she crossed the room to the bed and began stripping. It took effort for him to pull his gaze away so he could begin cleaning up.

He gathered all the dishes and turned on the water. Getting the dishes rinsed and loaded into the dishwasher couldn't happen fast enough, but he also didn't want to rush it.

Kim climbed onto the bed and lay with her head on one of the pillows. She spread her legs wide, putting her pussy on display for him. His cock strained in his jeans at the sight. Her pretty pink lips called to him, begging to be tasted, but he resisted. The end result would be worth it.

She started off slowly, rubbing up and down her sex, gathering her moisture. He watched as she swirled her index finger around her clit, letting out the sweetest sigh as she began rubbing the sensitive flesh.

Justin forced himself to look away long enough to finish what he was doing. He'd never loaded a dishwasher so fast in his life.

After placing all the dishes inside, drying his hands, and turning it on, he made his way over to the bed. She looked up at him, her eyes telling him all he needed to know.

He glanced down at her hands between her legs, watching as her fingers moved. Her nipples were hard, sticking up like beacons begging for his attention. She was beautiful. And she was his.

Moving down the bed, he positioned himself so he could have an unobstructed view of her pussy. Her opening was calling to him, glistening with her arousal. He leaned in to get a whiff, then dipped his finger inside.

When he removed it a moment later, it was covered in her juices. He brought it to his mouth and sucked, savoring her flavor. It wasn't as good as getting it directly from the source, but it was damn good. And by her reaction, she liked watching him tasting her as well.

"Someone's being a very naughty girl, making herself all wet." He was curious as to how she would react. They hadn't gone down this road before.

But she responded how he'd hoped. "Yes, Sir. I'm a very naughty girl."

Justin couldn't hide his smile. "Well, I guess we should take advantage of that, shouldn't we? Don't stop touching yourself."

If anything, she picked up the pace as she rubbed her clit while he removed his clothes. Instead of seating himself between her legs, he cupped the back of her head with one hand and held his erection in the other. He placed his cock between her lips, and she opened for him, sucking him into the warmth of her mouth.

He began to thrust his hips, keeping pressure on the back of her head, moving it the way he desired. Each time her tongue rubbed the underside of his head, he felt his balls tighten. He alternated between watching his cock slide in and out of her mouth and her hand where it continued to pluck her clit in time with each of his thrusts.

"Does my naughty girl want to come?" he asked, feeling his own orgasm building.

She hummed against his cock, and he nearly lost it.

"Let me see you come."

In less than a minute, she was moaning and arching her back. He pumped into her mouth faster, her gag reflex kicking in, but it didn't seem to take away the moment. If anything, it seemed to trigger her climax. She came, sucking on his cock with a renewed vigor, and he couldn't hold back any longer.

Chapter Twenty-Eight

The first thing that registered in Kim's brain as she awoke the next morning was the smell of food. She ran her hand over the space beside her, recalling what had transpired last night...and this morning. Well, she thought it was morning anyway. So far, she hadn't seen any clocks in the cabin.

A smile pulled at her lips as she remembered him waking her up. He'd already been posed between her legs, his cock pressing against her opening, when her eyes fluttered open. Justin had waited for her gaze to meet his before he pushed his hips forward and entered her.

When she'd reached for him, he'd held her arms above her head and continued to move in and out of her pussy. He didn't take his eyes off her, but there was also a sense that she was being used for his pleasure. For some reason, that thought appealed to her. She knew it shouldn't, but it did. She wanted to be the one who brought him pleasure. And knowing he woke up in the middle of the night, wanting her, and then taking what he wanted, was a huge turn-on.

"You're awake." Sometime during her mental drift, Justin had walked over to her. "I was beginning to think I'd have to wake you up again."

The wicked grin on his face had her internal muscles tightening and heat rushing to her sex. She sat up, clutching the sheet to her chest.

Justin wasn't having it. He yanked the sheet down, exposing her. "There will be none of that this weekend. Ever, if I have anything to say about it." His gaze lingered on her breasts before returning to her face. Then he extended his hand, offering to help her up.

She placed her hand in his and twisted to place her feet on the ground. The floor was cold and she pulled her feet up to hover an inch from the ground.

"Did you bring some slippers or socks with you?"

"They're in my bag." Which was by the door.

He released his hold on her and went to get her bag. Justin was barefoot and didn't seem bothered by the cool floor. Then again, she rarely ran around without something on her feet.

Returning with her bag, he placed it on the bed beside her. "Put something on your feet, use the bathroom if you need to, and join me in the kitchen."

She nodded and waited until he'd gone back into the kitchen before digging through her bag to find her fuzzy, lounge around for the day, socks.

After slipping them on, she lowered her feet to the floor once more and stood. The urge to grab the quilt off the bed and wrap it around herself was hard to resist. She wasn't used to running around naked, but something told her that if she and Justin stayed together, it was going to become a regular occurrence.

She made a detour in the small bathroom before joining him. A huge stack of pancakes, a plate of sausage, and a bowl of scrambled eggs greeted her when she approached the table. "What would you like to drink?" he asked. "We've got milk, orange juice, coffee, or water?"

"Coffee, please." She needed her coffee first thing in the morning. Especially since she didn't know what the day would hold.

Justin poured two cups of coffee and in one he added milk and sugar. He carried them over to the table, placing them both side by side, and sat down. It was only then that she realized there was only one place setting, and all the food was on his side of the table.

He turned toward her, his legs spread wide. "Come eat before it gets cold."

Surely, she had to be missing his meaning. Did he really want her to sit on his lap while they ate breakfast?

But it quickly became obvious that it was exactly what he wanted. He sat there, waiting.

Still, she needed to be positive. "You want me to sit on your lap?"

"Yes." When she didn't move, he quirked an eyebrow at her in that way to let her know he expected her to act or respond.

She walked over to him and sat down on his leg, her pussy rubbing against the coarse material of the jeans he wore.

Justin lifted her, brought both his legs together, and sat her back down on his lap. Her feet dangled on the other side of the chair.

"I thought you'd be hungry," he said when she didn't move. "I know I'm starving."

It still felt odd to be sitting on his lap like this, but she began loading food on the plate.

"More."

She glanced at him, not understanding.

"That's not enough for both of us."

One plate. They were going to be sharing.

Kim placed four more pancakes onto the plate before loading it up with sausage and eggs. There was almost nothing left in the serving trays once she was done. If he knew they were going to be sharing, why didn't he just use the one plate instead of dirtying more dishes?

Kim thought she got her answer a moment later. "You will feed me a bite, then feed yourself."

"I'm feeding you?" she asked.

He ran a hand down her thigh, and it sent a warm rush of moisture to her center. She'd never fed a guy before, but if that was what he wanted from her, she could do it.

She plunged her fork into the eggs, making sure they were secure enough they wouldn't fall off, and lifted them to his mouth. His lips closed over the fork and she pulled the fork away. Then she gathered some eggs for herself and took a bite. They were fluffy and perfect.

Everything was going well until she dropped some syrup onto his chest. He glanced down at it, then at her. "You made a mess. I think you should clean it up."

Kim twisted to get up, but he held her firmly. She looked at him, unsure at first what he wanted.

Then she caught the look in his eyes. Given how their weekend had gone so far, sexy and sensual seemed to be on the top of the menu. Lowering her head, she used her tongue to lick the rogue syrup from his chest.

His response sent a thrill through her. A deep rumble sounded from his throat and his fingers dug into her hip. She was kind of liking this level of power she had over him.

Justin's hand came up to grab the back of her head and brought her lips to his. He captured her mouth and thrust his tongue inside. The taste of pancakes and syrup filled her senses as he sucked on her tongue.

All too soon, he ended the kiss and she released a quiet whine in protest. Justin chuckled. "Patience, baby. Let's get through breakfast and we can play."

"What if I want to play now?" she asked, dipping her head a little and giving him her most seductive look.

He gave her nipple a hard pinch. "Behave."

She gave a yelp. "Not fair. You can't kiss me like that, then leave me hanging."

"Yes, I can. I'm your Dom, remember?"

Kim blew out a breath and willed her body to calm down. It wasn't easy to do either with her being naked on his lap and his erection pressing into her leg. He was as worked up as she was, but she did as he wanted and turned her attention back to the food.

Everything was going okay until she placed the last bite of food into his mouth. She'd stopped eating a few minutes before, already having eaten more than she normally would. He was still hungry, of course, and ended up polishing off the rest of the pancakes, eggs, and most of the sausage.

Before he'd finished chewing, he repositioned her like she weighed nothing, placing her legs on the outside of his and her back to his chest. She was about to ask him what he was doing when she got her answer. His mouth went to her neck and his hands cupped her breasts. His teeth nibbled at the sensitive flesh between her ear and shoulder while his hands massaged her chest. She'd never thought of her nipples being overly sensitive until the first time they'd slept together. Now she knew it was because the guys she'd been with before had been too gentle...too careful. Afraid of hurting her.

Justin didn't shy away from inflicting a little pain. But she found she liked it. At least, her body did. A shot of electricity went straight to her clit every time he tortured her nipples.

"Are you wet for me yet?"

His whispered words did nothing to cool her down. She wanted to touch him, but in her current position, her access to him was limited. "Yes."

He smacked her breasts. "That's not how you address me when we're playing."

"Yes, I'm wet for you, Sir." Why did him reminding her they were playing make her even hotter?

Justin hummed against her skin, and she felt it all the way down to her toes. "I do love it when you call me Sir."

One of his hands left her breast and trailed down her stomach to her legs. She leaned back into him as his fingers skimmed over her lips and dipped into her sex.

"Such a good girl. You are getting all wet and ready for your Dom."

"Yes, Sir. I'm ready for you." She was always ready for him."

His lips brushed over her ear. "That's good, because you're going to come all over my fingers, and then you're going to ride my cock like the naughty girl you are."

⁂

KIM SUCKED IN A BREATH AT HIS WORDS, AND HE FELT HER INNER MUSCLES react to his words, which stifled his own groan. His cock was painfully hard, confined in his jeans, but he knew if he hadn't been dressed, he'd already be buried deep inside her. As wonderful as that sounded, it wasn't what he wanted.

Bringing his other hand down between her legs, he began playing. He wanted to have a little fun, so he set out to tease her but not give her enough to find release. The benefit was seeing her reaction. Justin learned what she liked and what she loved. Like the fact that her muscles tightened and her breathing sped up when he'd played with the skin between her pussy opening and her asshole. Most guys enjoyed being stimulated there, but it wasn't an area that got a lot of attention on women.

He continued to test it and after a while, he wondered if it was the area itself or what it hinted at that contributed to her reaction. Was it the fact that she didn't know if he was going to go lower? She'd marked anal sex as a soft limit and that she'd never tried it on her list. Given her reaction, he was going to have to add that to the things for them to try and soon. The thought of plunging his cock into her ass had him nearly coming on the spot.

It meant it was a good time to end this game and bring them both some relief. "Are you ready to come, baby?"

"Yes, Sir."

She'd barely gotten the words out before he moved his fingers where he wanted them. One was poised directly on her clit, while the other thrust in and out of her hot sex. He had her so lubed up and ready for him, he couldn't wait to drive his cock into her.

Kim's orgasm built fast. She clutched at the chair, her legs, anything she could reach. "Put your arms around my neck."

Her immediate compliance meant she was rewarded as he sucked the skin of her neck into his mouth. She arched her back, thrusting her tits up and giving him a perfect view of her hard nipples. He wanted them in his mouth, but that would have to wait until later.

Her climax came the moment he bit down on her neck hard enough to leave a mark. Her arms pressed against the back of his head as a high-pitched squeal surged from her lips. She rode his fingers until the shock waves subsided, then collapsed against him.

Justin gave her a few moments to catch her breath, then he picked her up by the waist and turned her so she was straddling his lap. He took possession of her mouth and was pleased when she met him with equal enthusiasm. "Unfasten my jeans, baby. I want to fuck you."

Kim's fingers tickled the skin along his waist as she worked the button free. Once she'd pulled the zipper down, he lifted his hips enough to push the fabric out of the way. He hadn't bothered with underwear this morning, which turned out to be a great idea.

Grabbing the condom he'd left on the table within reach, he handed it to her. While he was used to using protection with his partners, he hated it with her. It was an inconvenience he didn't want. She was on birth control, so he could forgo it, but it was an extra layer of protection he'd always employed when it came to sex. And as much as he wanted to say fuck it, he would suck it up until she made her decision. Once she was really and truly his for the long term, there would be nothing between them.

With the protection in place, he lifted her and brought her entrance in line with his cock. He lowered her down in one fluid motion, not stopping until every inch of his cock was buried inside.

They both groaned as her pussy hugged his length. He gave her another hard kiss. "Put your hands on my shoulders and ride me, baby. I want to see your tits bounce as you fuck my cock."

Kim braced herself, then began to move. He held on to her hips, helping to guide her movement as she slid up and down his length. The urge to take over was strong, but he let her control the movements. Plus, it gave him the opportunity to take in the view.

He'd never seen a more beautiful sight. Kim's head was back, her eyes closed as she concentrated on what she was doing and feeling. Her breasts were calling to him as they jiggled each time she lifted and lowered onto his cock. Justin could already feel the energy growing in his balls and knew it wouldn't take much longer before he exploded. But he needed to get her there first.

Dipping his head, he captured one of her nipples into his mouth. She gasped and her nails dug into his shoulders. He felt his orgasm building and knew he wouldn't be able to hold it at bay for much longer.

Justin increased the suction on her nipple, giving it a few playful nips as he positioned his other hand around her waist. Turning his hand, he placed his thumb directly over her clit.

She reacted exactly the way he'd wanted her to. Kim tried to pick up her pace, but her movements were erratic as she climbed higher toward her climax.

He used his other hand to guide their movements, helping her with the pace. Lifting his hips, he drove deeper, harder, aiding in the goal. Needing that release as much as she did. "Let go, baby. Let me feel you come on my cock."

"Justin." The sound of his name in that begging tone had him driving into her harder. He'd made plenty of women beg over the years, but none of them had affected him the way she did.

Then he felt it. Her interior muscles clamped down on him, released, and then clamped down again in rapid succession. He bit down on her nipple, knowing it would increase her pleasure, and was rewarded with the scream he'd been waiting for. It was his signal that he could let go.

His own orgasm hit him hard and felt as if he was giving her part of himself. If he hadn't known before that he was in love with Kim, he would be a fool to deny it now. He might be her Dom, but she owned him, and it would kill him if she chose to walk away.

"You okay?" He kissed the side of her head. After she'd come, Kim had leaned forward to rest her head on his shoulder.

"I think so. Just don't ask me to move anytime soon. I don't think I can stand anymore."

He chuckled and stood, palming her ass to hold her up.

Kim wrapped her arms around his neck. "What are you doing?"

It wasn't the easiest to walk with his jeans around his ankles, but he could manage. Besides, he wasn't going far.

The couch was only about ten steps away, but it took him twice that since he couldn't do more than shuffle given his current clothing situation. As they'd made their way to the seating area, his cock slipped out of her, driving home the fact that he needed to go clean up.

Justin placed her on the couch and draped a blanket over her. "I'll be right back."

She huddled under the cover, a look of tranquility on her face.

He bent over to pull his jeans up far enough that he could walk, then headed for the bathroom.

After disposing of the condom, going to the bathroom, and washing his hands, he went to join her. They had nothing to do today except hang out and have as much sex as they both could handle. He didn't want to overwhelm her, but he was going to push her limits a little. At some point, he wanted to play with a few of the toys he'd brought with him. But for now, he was content to sit with her, talk, and watch the fire. Besides, he needed a little recovery time of his own.

Chapter Twenty-Nine

Kim wasn't sure she'd ever been more relaxed. And she couldn't remember the last time she was this happy.

They hadn't bothered to get dressed. When Justin had come out of the bathroom, he'd quickly cleaned up from their breakfast, then joined her on the couch. He'd gathered her in his arms, holding her as if she were the most precious thing in the world to him.

She circled her index finger around his nipple as she rested her head on his chest. His heartbeat was steady under her ear and the fireplace kept them warm.

"And what are you grinning about?" he asked. They'd been talking on and off, but it had been nice to lie there together in front of the fire, watching the flames dance around.

"I was thinking how much I like this. Being here with you."

He pressed his lips to the top of her head. "I love being here with you."

She didn't miss that he'd used the word love instead of like. Kim knew he cared about her. Hell, they never would have embarked on this experiment if there was nothing there. Physical attraction alone wasn't worth the potential fallout.

Lifting her head, she met his gaze, searching to see if she was reading too much into his words.

What she saw had her breath catching in her throat. Every logical part of her brain argued with her that it was too soon, or that it was the sex. But

Justin was as naked as she was, which meant she could feel every inch of him. He wasn't aroused at the moment. What she saw in his eyes had nothing to do with sex.

And it wasn't as if they were strangers. They'd also known each other for half their lives. The only people who knew her better were her family and Ali.

She lowered her mouth to his, then hesitated, remembering where they were and why. "May I kiss you, Sir?"

He smiled and threaded his fingers in her hair. "You may."

With permission granted, Kim covered his lips with hers. She kept the kiss light, keeping her mouth closed.

His hand tightened in her hair, but he didn't deepen the kiss.

She looked up to meet his gaze. "I love being with you, too."

Justin shifted beneath her. He brought his other hand up to caress her cheek. It was his turn to search her eyes. "Are you ready to be mine? No more doubts? No more waiting?"

Kim lowered her gaze. Her fears were still there. Not about her family. She could deal with her brother, and she had a feeling her parents would be thrilled. Her mom had been wanting her to find a good man to settle down with. Justin was a good man.

No, her concerns rested on whether she could be his submissive.

So instead of answering his question, she asked one of her own. "I don't know if I can be the perfect submissive."

"Baby, there's no such thing."

She bit the inside of her cheek. "I don't want to disappoint you."

His fingers massaged the back of her head, sending delicious tingles down her neck. She felt like purring. "I think you're a better submissive than you think."

Kim met his gaze again. "What do you mean?"

"You want to please your Dom."

It was true. But was that enough? "What if I screw up?"

His other hand joined the first, and she had to struggle to keep her eyes open. "I'm sure you will."

"But—"

"So will I."

She leaned into his hands. "You've been doing this for years. Why would you mess up?"

"Because I'm not perfect either." One of his hands left her hair and trailed down her neck. Her body was beginning to soften again...prepare itself for him. "But when either of us makes a mistake, we deal with it. That's how a relationship works. Even the D/s ones."

It was hard to argue with his logic. "It's hard to concentrate with you doing that."

"Doing what?" he asked with way too much innocence. She could feel his cock growing hard once more. He wasn't unaffected by what he was doing to her.

She tilted her head back, exposing more of her neck.

Justin took advantage. He guided her flesh to his lips and drew the skin into his mouth. Heat rushed to her sex, and she squirmed against him.

He nibbled his way down to her collarbone, then back up to her ear. "Are you mine?"

Even with her body warming and her need for him to be inside her again increasing with each passing second, she knew what he was asking. "I'm yours."

His hand tightened on her hair. "Again."

"I'm yours, Sir. Only yours."

He dragged her mouth to his and kissed her hard. She gasped, and he took advantage, thrusting his tongue inside. The kiss wasn't gentle, but it wasn't meant to be. This was about possession. She belonged to him. She'd always belonged to him.

Justin spread her legs and positioned himself at her entrance. Kim felt the tip of his cock rubbing against her sensitive flesh and moaned. She needed him inside her.

As if he knew what she'd been thinking, he ripped her mouth away from his and made her look at him. "No more stalling. No more uncertainty."

She nodded.

His green eyes darkened as his pupils dilated. "Mine." He pushed her down onto his erection, not stopping until she took all of him.

One of his hands dug into her hip, helping to guide the movement. He lifted his hips up while driving her down. She moved with him, needed to feel every inch of him claim her as his.

And that was what this was. There was no mistaking that. She was his and he was making sure there was no doubt in either of their minds.

Their mouths came together again as he continued to take her. Her nipples brushed against his chest with the movement, sending sparks through her breasts directly to her clit. Before him, she'd never given much time or thought to her nipples, but now they craved to be touched...played with.

He moved his mouth to her neck once more and she arched her back, silently begging him to go lower...to suck on her breasts.

Justin nipped at her collarbone. "What do you want, baby? Tell me."

"Please suck on my nipples, Sir."

"That's my good girl." A moment later, his lips clamped around her right nipple.

"Yes!" She held his head to her breasts, not wanting him to stop.

With both his hands on her hips, he drove her down onto his cock with almost painful force. He'd bent his legs to provide more leverage and while it felt great, she needed more.

Kim wanted to touch herself, but she knew she couldn't. Not unless he told her she could. And for some reason, that sent a thrill through her. Maybe he was right. Maybe she was more submissive than she'd thought. "May I touch myself, Sir?"

He released the nipple he'd been torturing and turned his attention to the other side. He gave the nipple a bite hard enough to make her yelp. "Yes. Make yourself come, and then I'm going to come inside my pussy."

Her breath caught in her throat again, but this time for an entirely different reason. He wasn't wearing a condom. And while she was on birth control, she knew the significance. She was his.

Snaking her hand between them, she slid her fingers through her wetness to find her clit. She brushed against him as he moved in and out of her and he groaned. "Get to playing with your clit, you naughty girl, or I'll have to turn you over my knee again."

Heat rushed to her center, and she began rubbing her clit. It was swollen and sensitive. She dug her nails into his shoulder, trying to anchor herself. Between Justin fucking her, sucking on her breast as if his life depended on it, and her rolling and plucking her clit, she was ready to fly.

Her orgasm hit her, and she screamed. Ripple after ripple of pleasure coursed through her body.

"Fuck!"

A moment after the word tore from Justin's throat, she felt his cock pulse within her, shooting his cum inside her. He held her hips down against his pelvis, securing her to him until he'd emptied every last drop.

Justin licked his way up her chest to her throat before capturing her lips again. He made no move to separate them and to be honest, she wasn't in any hurry either.

He caressed the side of her face with the back of his hand. "How about a shower?"

"I thought you were in charge."

She felt a sharp pinch to her ass. "I was trying to be nice, but if you insist..."

The next thing Kim knew, he was on his feet, striding toward the bathroom.

⊷❧⊶

They spent the rest of the weekend in various stages of undress. Well, he did. She wasn't allowed more than socks and the occasional blanket to cover up with when she was cold. Kim had never spent so much time naked before. But considering how often they were having sex, or he was playing with her in some way, clothes would have just gotten in the way.

Sunday afternoon came way too soon. Kim wasn't ready to go back. She wanted to stay in their cocoon for a while longer.

"Got everything?" He came up behind her and placed a kiss on her neck. She was going to need to dig into her makeup drawer to find some concealer. Her neck was not only red, but there were a few hickeys as well. She loved it when he sucked on her neck, though.

"Yeah. I think I've got everything."

He picked up their bags, and she took one last look around. It had been less than two days, but so much had happened. She didn't want to leave.

"Kim?"

She shook herself out of it and joined him at the door. "Sorry. I just..."

"We can always come back. Maybe for a long weekend next time. I'm sure Garrett wouldn't mind." He opened the door, letting the cool air in. Justin had doused the fire an hour ago, wanting to make sure it was out before they left, so there wasn't anything to ward off the cold outside air.

Justin had told her more about the cabin's owner. He was from Chicago but came down to the cabin to get away from the city. "I'd like that."

After loading the bags into the trunk of his car, Justin slid behind the wheel. The car was nice and warm already, which she was grateful for. Since they were in the middle of nowhere, he'd started the car and let it warm up before they'd left—something he wouldn't be able to do in St. Louis.

They hadn't been outside the cabin since they arrived, so this was the first time she was getting to see their surroundings in the daylight. While the trees had looked ominous in the dark, they were tall and majestic with the sun shining down on them. As they drove down the drive to the main road, she almost felt sheltered by them. Safe. Of course, that might have something to do with the person sitting beside her as well.

Kim rested her head on the headrest and smiled. She'd been so worried about their weekend, but it had turned out better than she'd hoped. Not only was she feeling better about her submissive role, she was beginning to embrace it. She loved seeing his reaction when she called him Sir. Or the way his breath hitched when she ran her tongue along the underside of his erection.

She was so lost in her sexy memories that she almost missed the fact that he'd said something. "I'm sorry, what did you say?"

He chuckled. "I won't ask what you were thinking about over there, you naughty girl, but I asked when you wanted to tell your family. Did you want to see if we can get together for dinner sometime this week?"

The thought of telling her family was a sure way to throw a cold bucket of water on her libido. "I'll call my mom when we get home and see what her schedule is."

"Let me know and I'll be there." He paused. "I want to get this over with."

It should be funny, but it wasn't. Them announcing they were a couple was a big deal and one that would change a lot of things. Justin had been part of their family for almost two decades as her brother's best friend. She was hoping he'd still be that but going forward he would also be hers.

"I think Mom will be pleased. She likes you."

He glanced over at her, then back at the road. They were on the highway now and already halfway home. "It's not your mom I'm worried about." Then he corrected himself. "I am, but your dad and brother are the wild cards here. I think we can win your dad over, but I don't know how bad your brother is going to react. He's going to feel betrayed, and I can't do anything to fix that." Justin reached for her hand and laced their fingers together. "I'm not letting you go."

That warm feeling bloomed in her chest. "I'm not letting you go, either."

Justin brought their fingers to his lips and gave the back of her hand a kiss before lowering them to rest on his thigh. They drove the rest of the way in silence as they made their way back into the city.

JUSTIN PARKED IN FRONT OF HER APARTMENT AND TURNED OFF HIS CAR. HE wanted to go inside with her. Hell, he never wanted to spend a night without her again. That right there told him how head over heels he was for her.

"Move in with me." The words were out before he could stop them.

"What?"

He turned to face her, taking both her hands in his. "I want you in my bed. Always."

The muscles in her neck contracted as she swallowed, and she pressed her lips together. "Don't you think it's too soon?"

"No. We've waited seventeen years. I'd say it can't happen soon enough. Besides, if you're in my bed, I can have my wicked way with you any time I want."

He was hoping to make her laugh, and it worked. Sort of. She let out the cutest little snort. "My lease isn't up for another two months."

"That's too long."

Kim held his gaze for a long moment. "You're serious."

"I am." He squeezed her hands. "I'm done waiting. I want a life with you, and I want it now. Not in two months. Not in two weeks."

She released a loud breath. "That's a big step."

"Not as big as me asking you to marry me."

Her eyes went wide.

"I'm not asking. Yet." He ran his thumb along the inside of her wrist. "Move in with me. Share my bed. My home."

He wasn't sure what she was going to say. Kim didn't make rash decisions. She was a planner. He knew he'd thrown her a curveball, but he was hoping she'd take the chance.

Kim looked toward her apartment, and he felt his hopes sink. She wasn't ready.

"I'll need boxes."

It took him a moment to register what she'd said. When he did, he could barely contain his joy. "Is that a yes?"

She bit her lower lip and nodded.

Justin nearly leaped into her lap and kissed her. "I love you."

When she froze, he pulled back, concerned something was wrong.

He searched her face. "What is it?"

"That's the first time you've told me you love me."

He hadn't thought about it, but it was true. Holding her face between his hands, he brushed his lips against hers. "I love you."

Kim looked as if she were blinking back tears. She rested her forehead against his and held his gaze. "I love you, too. I have for a long time."

"I know," he said, tucking a lock of hair behind her ear. "We've wasted so much time. No more waiting."

She smiled. "No more waiting."

Chapter Thirty

Justin ended up spending the night at Kim's apartment and she had to admit she could get used to sharing a bed with him. She liked waking up beside him. Of course, that also meant morning sex, which she wasn't complaining about.

"I'll meet you here at seven and we'll start packing." He crushed her against his body, his hands going directly to her ass. "I'll bring pizza."

Kim couldn't believe they were really doing this. She'd lived by herself since graduating from college. It would be a huge change to share her space with someone else again. She was equal parts excited and nervous. He was right, though. They'd waited long enough. "I'll throw together a salad."

He scrunched up his nose. "If you must."

She laughed. "Vegetables won't kill you."

"Guess I'll have to get used to eating more of those, huh?" He gave her butt a squeeze as he lowered his mouth to hers.

"Definitely."

She circled her arms around his neck as their tongues tangled together. He tasted like coffee mixed with her mint toothpaste.

He released her and sighed. "I need to get going. I'll see you tonight."

Kim nodded.

After one more quick kiss goodbye, he jogged out to his car and drove away.

Heading back to her bedroom, Kim laid her clothes out on the bed and crossed the hall into her small bathroom. It was hard to believe she was leaving this place.

She turned on the water and began going through her morning routine. They'd gotten up a half hour early so he could run home before he went to the shop. As it turned out, he was barely going to make it to work before they opened because he'd convinced her they should shower together.

A huge smile grew on her face as she remembered the details of that shower. He'd made her come twice, and that was on top of the orgasm she'd had before they'd made it out of bed. She'd never come so much in her life. Before him, she'd thought multiple orgasms with a guy were a myth.

Reaching for her makeup bag, she began applying concealer to her neck. He really did love to mark her. She'd even noticed a couple of spots on her breast.

By the time she finished applying her makeup, did her hair, and dressed, it was almost seven-thirty. It was a good thing she only lived fifteen minutes from the office. Otherwise, she'd be late. And she hated to be late.

Kim strolled into the office with five minutes to spare. Her assistant was already at her desk. "Good morning, Brenda. How was your weekend?"

"Good." Her assistant tilted her head, looking at her.

"Everything all right?" Kim asked. She was tempted to touch her neck, fearing she'd missed a spot, but willed her hands to remain at her sides. It wasn't as if she could feel a hickey.

"Yeah. Fine." Brenda averted her gaze. "Um, you just missed a call from your brother. He wants you to call him."

The last time Mark had called her at work was when he'd gotten a promotion. Given it was only eight on a Monday morning, she highly doubted that was the case this time. "Thanks."

Kim flipped the light on in her office and took a seat at her desk. After placing her purse in the bottom drawer of her desk, she picked up her phone and dialed.

Her mom answered on the second ring. "Hi, honey. How was your trip?"

She'd told her mom she was going out of town, but given her job, it wasn't uncommon for her to have to travel to New York or Chicago, her mom hadn't asked for details. "It was good. How's Dad doing?"

"Going stir-crazy." Her mom chuckled. "He wants to get up and do things. The doctor told him not to overdo it, but you know your dad. He's not used to sitting around the house doing nothing. It's driving him crazy."

Her dad wasn't a big television or movie watcher. He preferred to be doing things. He liked to garden and tinker in his garage. "Maybe he can find something to do in the garage that doesn't take a lot of movement."

"We are talking about the same man, right?"

Kim laughed. Her mom was right. Her dad would never sit still. He'd find something he had to get or do that would require him to defy the doctor's orders. "Sorry, Mom. When does he go back to the doctor?"

"Tomorrow." Her mom blew out a breath.

"Sorry, Mom." Kim bit the inside of her cheek. Maybe dinner with her family this week wasn't such a good idea. "Is there anything I can do?"

"No, honey. It is what it is. We're okay." Her mom paused. "I'm sure your dad would love to see you if you have time this week."

Well, that was an opening if she ever saw it. "Why don't we all get together on Wednesday? Justin can join us. I have some news I want to share with everyone."

Her mom didn't answer right away, and Kim was wondering if her mom radar was going off. Should she not have mentioned Justin? But then it would have seemed odd if he'd shown up.

"That sounds like a great idea," Belinda said. "I'll throw together a roast. Justin has always loved my roast."

It was true. Justin always raved about her mom's cooking. Then again, his mom didn't cook all that much. A home-cooked meal to her was usually a frozen dinner she threw in the oven. "Do you want me to bring anything? Dessert?"

"No worries. I'll make some cupcakes or something. It will keep me busy."

"Okay. Well, call me if you need anything."

She hung up with her mom and debated whether to call her brother right away. Mark was not on her list of favorite people right now. He'd been a jackass at the hospital and he'd yet to apologize for it. She got why he was so protective, but his response was over-the-top. He needed to realize she wasn't a little girl anymore and she could take care of herself.

Deciding not to put it off, she dialed her brother's office. "Mr. Langley's office."

"Hi, Meg. It's Kim. Is my brother in?"

"Hi, Kim. Yep, your brother's in. Let me make sure he's not on the phone." There was a long pause. "Nope. Okay, hold on and I'll put you through."

It took almost a minute for her brother to pick up the line. "I wasn't sure if you were going to call me back or not."

Kim leaned back in her chair. "Does that mean you're calling to apologize?"

She heard a chair squeaking in the background, and then her brother sighed. "I'm sorry if I overreacted. I just...I worry about you. And when I saw those marks, I freaked. I don't like the idea of someone hurting you."

"No one hurt me." She needed him to know that. And he was going to have to get used to seeing marks like that on her from time to time. She'd really liked it when Justin had flogged her.

"Are you..."

When he didn't finish his sentence, she wondered what was going through that head of his. Probably the worst-case scenario. She only hoped his worst-case scenario wasn't her dating Justin. That might make Wednesday's dinner more eventful than she wanted it to be.

She decided to change the subject. "Can you come to dinner at Mom and Dad's on Wednesday night? Justin's invited, too." Again, she decided to add that, so it wouldn't be weird right off the bat for him to be there. She wanted to tell her family when everyone was calm and happy.

The other end of the line was quiet, and she wondered what he was thinking. "Are we going to find out about this new guy?" Mark asked.

"How do you know if there's a new guy?"

He snorted. "Please. You haven't been at your apartment the last two times I've stopped by, you had red marks all over your back at the hospital after you said you were out clubbing with Ali, and you disappeared this weekend."

She rolled her eyes. "Guess you're just going to have to come to dinner on Wednesday and find out what my news is."

"So, there is news."

"There is. And if you want to know what it is, then you'll be there."

"I'll be there."

Kim reached for the stack of papers in her inbox that needed her attention. "Good. Now, be a good brother and apologize for being a big jerk."

"I'm not a jerk." When she didn't respond in any way, he chuckled. "Fine. I'm sorry for being a jerk. Are you happy now?"

"Yes. Very." She scanned over the page in front of her. "Now, I have work to do. I'll see you Wednesday night."

"Later, Sis."

Kim rolled her eyes again. "Later."

JUSTIN WAS HAVING THE DAY FROM HELL. THE MOMENT HE WALKED IN THE door, Sandi had pounced. A customer had come in on Saturday for an oil change and tire rotation, but when he was told he also needed some major front-end work, he'd gone off on the tech. And Sandi. The customer had only left when she had threatened to call the police.

If that wasn't bad enough, he found out the parts he'd been waiting on for two months weren't coming. His supplier couldn't source them, and so he'd had to spend three hours on the phone looking for new parts.

By the time he arranged for the parts with a new vendor and called to update the client, he knew it was going to be a late night. There was no way he was going to make it to Kim's apartment to help her pack. That only soured his mood more.

Then there was the text he'd gotten from Mark inviting him to dinner with the family on Wednesday night.

Family dinner Wednesday night. Can you come? - Mark

Justin kept his response short, not wanting to give his friend anything to read into.

Sure. What time? - Justin

The answer came back right away.

6 - Mark

Justin was relieved they weren't drawing this out, but that didn't mean he wasn't nervous about it. Kim didn't think her parents would have an issue with them being together and maybe she was right. Davis and Belinda liked him. But he still didn't want them to feel as if he were betraying their trust by defiling their daughter. He could only hope they'd realize how he felt about Kim and at least be okay with it. Especially once they found out Kim was moving in with him.

No, it wasn't Davis and Belinda that most worried him. It was Mark and there was no amount of stressing or planning or prepping that was going to alter his best friend's reaction. He was only hoping they could work through it and remain friends.

Wiping the grease off his hands, Justin noticed the time. It was almost five and not only was he not even close to being finished for the day, but he hadn't eaten anything outside of the candy bar he'd gotten from the vending machine in the lobby two hours ago.

He dug his phone out of his pocket and dialed Kim. She answered on the first ring. "Hi, sexy."

Justin laughed and it felt good. "Shouldn't that be my line?"

A door closed in the background, and he wondered if it was a car door or if she was still in her office. "I think it fits you more than me."

He leaned back on the toolbox behind him and took what felt like his first full breath since he'd arrived that morning. "I beg to differ."

She giggled.

The sound sent all kinds of warm tingles through his body. He opened his mouth to say something dirty but caught sight of one of his techs striding toward him. His heart sank and he held up a finger, letting the tech know to give him a minute.

"Hey, baby, I'm not going to make it over tonight. Today's been a nightmare and I have no idea when I'm gonna get out of here."

"That's okay. I can pack some things up on my own."

"I'm sorry." He was the one who'd suggested they move in together and he should be there to help her pack up her things. Plus, he was supposed to be bringing the boxes. "I'll do my best to get out of here early tomorrow."

"It's okay. Really. I'll be fine. I should probably sort through my closet first anyway. No need to move stuff I never use."

He could see his tech shifting on the balls of his feet twenty feet away and sighed. "I need to go. I'll call you later tonight." He paused. "I love you."

"I love you, too."

Justin hadn't wanted to hang up. Talking to her was the bright spot in his shitty day and from the look on his tech's face, there was another issue that needed his attention.

The last customer left at six and his techs not long after that. It had been a bad day all around and he couldn't blame his guys for wanting to hightail it out of there as fast as they could.

"Did you need anything before I go?" Sandi asked, peeking her head into the shop.

"No, I'm good. Just glad for the quiet. Hopefully, I can get this engine finished up."

Sandi nodded. "Don't stay too late. You need your rest, too."

He smiled. "I won't. Have a good night."

She waved and closed the shop door behind her. He listened as she walked out the front door and locked it behind her. Then there was nothing. Utter silence. It was bliss.

Justin turned back to the engine he'd been working on for what felt like forever and got to work. It was only at night when he was able to really settle into what he was doing. He loved working on cars. That was why he'd become a mechanic. But it was only at night when he was there by himself that he could let go and enjoy the process. During the day there were too many people needing his opinion, or customers to deal with.

Time fell away and he got lost in the work, which was why it took him a while to hear the tapping sound coming from outside.

He grabbed a clean towel, wiped his hands, and walked around the car to the bay door. There on the other side was Kim...holding a pizza box.

Justin hit the button to raise the door and as soon as it was waist high, Kim ducked underneath. He quickly hit the reverse button. It wasn't as cold as it had been outside, but it was still January in St. Louis.

"What are you doing here? I thought you were home packing?"

"I thought you might be hungry," she said, holding up the pizza.

He was starving, but now that she was inside in the light, he got a good look at what she was wearing. "That's not what you were wearing this morning."

She grinned and he saw mischief in her eyes. His groin tightened. "I stopped home and changed into something more comfortable."

More comfortable. Not exactly the words he'd choose to describe the skirt and sweater she was wearing. The skirt ended four inches above her knees. It wasn't tight-fitting, but that meant it wouldn't take much to flip it up and out of the way. The sweater, in comparison, clung to her chest, hugging her tits. His mouth was watering, and he wasn't sure which was causing more of the moisture: the pizza or her outfit.

He took the pizza from her and carried it to the bench he used. Clearing off a space, he set it down, then went to wash his hands in the sink.

Kim pulled up a stool and sat down. His gaze drifted to her legs, and he had to will his libido to calm down. As much as he wanted her, he also needed food. He didn't want to get lightheaded or faint while he was taking her.

And take her he would. One of his long-time fantasies had involved her on the hood of a car. She was here. They were alone. And he was going to make that fantasy come to life tonight.

Chapter Thirty-One

"You look tired," Kim said as they dug into the pizza.

"Long day." He took a bite of pizza and met her gaze. "It's much better now."

"Because of me or the pizza?" She was teasing him, and it felt great.

"Both." His gaze trailed over her body before returning to her face. "Definitely both."

He scarfed down the first slice of pizza and took another, biting into it as if he hadn't eaten in days. "Did you eat lunch today?" she asked.

"I had a candy bar around one."

She frowned. "That's not lunch."

Justin shrugged. "It was all I had time for, and I barely got that down before I had to put out the next fire."

"I'm sorry you had a bad day." It was a complete contrast to hers. After her phone call with Mark, she'd had two client meetings and an executive lunch. The rest of her day had been spent catching up on emails and returning calls.

"It happens." He polished off his second slice of pizza, then smiled at her. "Part of owning my own business. Besides, if I remember correctly, you had a not so stellar day last week that I helped you forget." His wicked grin returned, and he was no longer paying attention to the pizza.

Kim slid off the stool and onto the floor. Luckily, there was a mat where they were sitting, and she didn't have to be on the concrete floor. She knelt in front of him and ran her hands along the legs of his jeans. "Would you like me to help you forget, Sir?"

He nodded and her hand went to the button on his jeans. She released it, then lowered the zipper. He was wearing underwear today, but she could work with it.

Lifting his hips, he helped her move his jeans out of the way. Without the constricting fabric of his pants, his erection stretched the fabric of his underwear. She pressed her lips against the bulge, and he groaned. "You're gonna pay for teasing me, baby."

"You don't like it when I tease you, Sir?"

Justin chuckled. "I didn't say that."

Deciding to push her luck, Kim skimmed her nose along his length before pulling the fabric out of the way. His erection sprang free, standing proud and begging for her attention. She met his gaze as she closed her mouth on the head of his cock.

The rumble that sounded deep in his chest went straight to her clit.

For some reason, she wanted to tease him. She wanted to drive him crazy. So instead of taking more of him in her mouth, she concentrated on the tip. She ran her tongue around the ridge and massaged his hole, all the time providing gentle suction with her mouth.

His hands went to her head. He fisted her hair, sending a shot of pain through her skull. She noticed he didn't tell her to stop, though.

Taking a little more of him into her mouth, she flattened her tongue along the underside of his shaft, dragging it up, and then returning her attention to his head. She did this over and over and his hold on her hair tightened. Giving a blow job had never been so much fun. Or had made her this hot.

She'd been about to take him to the back of her throat when he ripped her mouth away. His cock was glistening from her mouth, but she didn't get to look at it for long. Justin lifted her by the arms and set her on her feet. Then he flipped her around and bent her over his lap.

Kim knew what was coming before his hand connected with her ass. The sting was an electric shot to her system that sent liquid heat to her sex.

He massaged her butt before he spanked her again. "No panties?" Smack. "You deserve this spanking even more than I thought." He landed three more blows in quick succession. "You like teasing your Dom, don't you?"

"Yes, Sir."

More smacks and Kim began squirming against him, needing friction. She wanted him to touch her clit. She wanted him inside her. She wanted...more.

"My needy girl wants to come, does she?"

"Please, Sir."

But he didn't let her come. Instead, he continued to smack her ass until it was burning. Then he put her back on her feet and dragged her across the room to stand in front of a car that looked older than she was.

He left her long enough to flip the light switch on the wall behind them, cloaking them in darkness. The only light came from over his work bench twenty feet away. She could still see him, but anyone who happened to be outside wouldn't be able to see more than shadows.

Justin returned to stand in front of her. He slipped his hands under her skirt and cupped her bare cheeks. The next thing she knew, her feet were off the ground again.

Kim grabbed his shoulders as she was lifted. But before she could wrap her legs around his waist, he deposited her onto the hood of the car—the cool metal soothing the abused skin of her ass.

She didn't have a lot of time to think about that, however, before he lowered himself on top of her and captured her mouth with his. He hitched her leg up until it was braced on his shoulder. She was open and exposed and completely and totally ready for him. Her sex pulsed in anticipation of him filling her.

He probed her opening before pushing two fingers inside. His tongue mimicked the movement of his fingers, plunging in and out, twisting and massaging. She was so close to coming. All she needed was a little pressure to her clit and she'd be flying.

But he didn't give her what she wanted. Instead, he moved lower, rimming her asshole with his finger. "Once you're in my bed permanently, I'm going to start plugging your ass. I want you nice and ready for me when I take you here."

She sucked in a breath. They'd talked a little about anal sex when they'd gone over their lists, but she hadn't thought too much about it. Anal sex was one of many things she'd never tried, but she'd seen it at the club. It was something that both intrigued her and made her nervous to try. "Will I like it, Sir?"

"Based on your reaction to me just doing this..." He ran his finger once more around the outside of her hole, then pushed the tip inside.

She sucked in a breath. It wasn't painful, but it felt weird and so...forbidden.

"But not tonight." His hand moved to her hip. He reached between them, and then she felt the tip of his cock.

When he didn't move, she arched her back, trying to encourage him.

He slapped her hip in response. The sting heated her skin even more. "Stop being so impatient. You'll get my cock when I say and not a moment before, understand?"

"I'm sorry, Sir. It's just that I've been dreaming about this all day, and I want to feel you inside me."

Justin groaned and he shifted. He pushed them higher onto the car until they were both on top of the hood.

The movement had pushed her clothing up even more. Her sweater was bunched up around her armpits. She debated whether to wear a bra or not when visiting him. Going without panties was one thing, but no bra was another thing entirely. She wasn't a big girl in that respect, but she wasn't tiny either.

In the end, she'd left her bra at home. A decision she was now very happy about. Justin's gaze lowered to her breasts and without a word, he sucked her nipple into his mouth.

Kim moaned and threaded her fingers into his hair. She'd never been a big fan of men playing with her nipples before, but now she was realizing that was because they were too gentle. There was no light suction or licking. Justin went all in when it came to sex and that included playing with her breasts.

He grabbed her wrists and brought them above her head—pinning her hands against the windshield. Heat rushed to her pussy. She loved it when he held her down like this. There was something about it that sent her pulse racing in the best possible way.

Then he flexed his hips and thrust into her. His cock filled her, pushing inside until he couldn't get any farther. She felt full and hot and needy. "Please, fuck me, Sir. I need your cock."

Justin groaned, pulled out, and plunged deep into her. He released her nipple and devoured her mouth instead. The hard surface of the car was a sharp contrast to his body as he took her. Her ass was still burning, but it was all sensation and she welcomed it.

He began rolling his hips each time he thrust, giving her clit the friction it so desperately needed. She was so close. All she needed was a little...

Her orgasm hit her, and she couldn't stop the scream that tore through her. He attempted to swallow her cries, but they echoed in the spacious room.

As she was coming down from her high, she felt him shudder as he found his own release. His groan sent another shock wave of pleasure through her system, and she treasured it. He was hers.

"What the fuck?"

IT TOOK JUSTIN A MOMENT TO REGISTER THE WORDS. HE'D BEEN SO CAUGHT up in Kim that nothing else had mattered. When he turned his head, though, all the pleasure he'd felt was replaced with dread. There, standing on the other side of the bay, was Mark.

Justin released Kim's wrists, but that was about as far as he got before Mark was on him. His best friend grabbed him by the back of the neck and pulled him off Kim. He stumbled, the jeans constricting his ability to find his balance, and he hit the floor with a solid thud.

Scrambling to his feet, his gaze went to Kim. She was staring wide-eyed at her brother, who was advancing on Justin. Her clothes were still in disarray, and she seemed more concerned with the situation than with her current state of undress.

It was because he was focused on Kim that he hadn't seen Mark's fist coming. A jolt of pain surged through his jaw.

He shuffled back a few steps, then stood to his full height, rubbing his jaw. Nothing felt broken, but it was going to leave a bruise.

Mark took a step forward, but Justin was ready for him this time. "You caught me off guard before. Try it again and I'll put your ass on the ground."

It wasn't an idle threat. Justin had at least forty pounds on Mark and was in better shape. In a real fight, there was no doubt which one of them would win. Justin didn't want to fight his best friend, but he wasn't going to be his punching bag either.

Conflict in his eyes, Mark seemed to be considering his options. "What the hell are you doing to my sister?"

"Mark—"

Mark whirled around, facing Kim for the first time. "Fuck! Kim, are you all right? He didn't hurt you, did he?"

She adjusted her clothes, covering herself. "I'm fine." She slid off the hood of the car. "At least I was before you showed up and decked my boyfriend." Her hands went to her hips, and she stared her brother down.

Pride filled him. His woman was a spitfire. It only made her willing submission to him more meaningful.

Justin took the opportunity to put his jeans back in place while Mark's attention wasn't on him. He wasn't worried about Mark hurting Kim. Yell at her? Get in her face? Yeah, maybe. But Mark was usually more bluster than action. He had to be really worked up for it to come to blows and he would never hit a woman.

"Your boyfriend?" Mark's voice went up an octave.

Kim stood up straight and met her brother's gaze. "Yes. My boyfriend."

When Mark turned back to Justin, he didn't look anywhere close to pacified. "What are you doing with my sister?"

"Mark—"

"I'm asking him, Kim." Mark narrowed his eyes at Justin. "You have no idea the twisted games he likes to play with women. What he likes to do to them. What he gets off on. You probably don't know that he's—"

This time, she cut him off. "He's a Dominant."

Mark's head whipped back around, and his eyes widened. Justin could see the wheels turning in his friend's head as he put the scene he'd walked in on into perspective. "You can't…"

Kim stalked toward her brother and pointed a finger at his chest. "You don't get to tell me what I can and can't do, big brother. I'm thirty-two years old. I can have sex with whoever I want, any way I want. Got it?"

Silence hung in the air for what felt like forever. Justin wanted to go to Kim, pull her into his arms, and make the last few minutes go away. Her showing up at the shop had been a bright light to the otherwise miserable day. And loving her was the icing on the cake. It made everything that had gone wrong seem unimportant. When she was with him, the rest of the world didn't matter.

But had he known the evening would end like this, he would have left his work and followed her home. They could have warmed up the pizza, and she wouldn't be standing in the middle of his shop having a stare down with her brother.

Mark finally got his voice back. "You're not submissive."

"How would you know what I like in the bedroom?" She wasn't backing down and Justin felt a smile tug at his lips.

Again, his friend was tongue-tied.

Justin wanted to go to Kim, but that would mean he'd have to get within arm's reach of Mark, and he was trying to prevent a fight. Kim didn't need to see that.

Then Mark walked over to the wall and leaned against it. Justin wasted no time going to Kim's side. He wanted to hold her, but he kept his hands to himself for now.

Mark ran a hand over the top of his head. "How long?" He swallowed. "How long have you been fucking my sister?"

Justin blew out a breath. Before he answered, he circled his arm around Kim's waist, staking his claim. "Officially, a little over two weeks ago."

His friend snorted. "What about unofficially?"

Kim answered this time. "About four months."

Mark's eyes narrowed and he stared at Justin. Then his gaze moved to Kim. They weren't as hostile, but they weren't overly friendly either. "This is what you wanted to tell the family Wednesday."

It wasn't a question, but Kim answered anyway. "Yes." She looked up at Justin, her eyes softening. "We want to be together, and we're tired of hiding."

"You shouldn't have hidden it in the first place," her brother snapped.

Justin pulled his gaze away from Kim's and looked at Mark. "You would have been okay with it if we'd announced our intentions first?"

"Hell no!" Mark pushed himself away from the wall. "I can't believe you would betray me...our friendship like this."

"My relationship with Justin has nothing to do with your friendship," Kim said.

"Of course it does." Mark shook his head as if trying to clear it. "He's told me about some of the things he's done to the women he's been with. I can't...I can't think about him doing that kind of stuff to you."

Kim started to respond, but Mark held up his hand to stop her. "I can't do this right now. I need to think."

Mark started to the door and Kim made to go after him.

Justin held her back. "Let him go."

"But—"

"He's right. He needs time to process everything. Let's give him that."

Justin thought she might argue, but she nodded and turned to rest her head on his chest. After a moment, she lifted her hands to his face. "How's your jaw?"

"Sore. It'll be bruised by morning."

She rose on her tiptoes and placed a soft kiss on his skin. "He shouldn't have hit you."

Justin shrugged. "I'm sleeping with his sister. It could have been worse."

Kim didn't look any happier. "We should put some ice on it."

"I've got some at home." He cupped her face and rubbed his thumb over her bottom lip. It was still swollen from his kisses.

She leaned into his touch. "I didn't want Mark to find out this way."

"Neither did I, but what's done is done. We can't change it." He let his arm fall to his side. "Give me a minute to lock things up, and then we'll get out of here."

It took a little longer than that to make sure everything was secure and make their way out to their vehicles. He gave her a soft kiss before she climbed behind the wheel of her car. "I'll see you at home," she said before closing the door.

Home. Their home. He really liked the sound of that.

Chapter Thirty-Two

It had been two days since Mark had walked in on them at Justin's shop. Kim had thought that maybe he'd call or text her, but there'd been nothing. She wasn't sure if that was good or bad.

Justin hadn't heard from Mark either. He'd sent him a text Tuesday morning saying they needed to talk, but Mark hadn't replied.

There'd also been no spontaneous calls from either of her parents, so she was assuming Mark hadn't gone to them and spilled the beans. Her mom had texted her and Justin individually to confirm they were both coming to dinner, but there was no indication that she knew what was going on. Kim only hoped her parents took the news of her relationship with Justin better than her brother had.

The door opened and Justin rushed inside. "Hi, honey, I'm home."

Kim laughed. "You're late."

"One of my guys wanted to adjust his schedule for next week. Took way longer than I expected." He picked her up, gave her a kiss that was full of promise, and set her feet back on the ground. "Give me five minutes to clean up, and I'll be ready to go."

She nodded and watched as he raced down the hall to his bedroom.

Kim grabbed her coat and purse from his closet and sat down on the couch to wait. For all intents and purposes, she'd already moved in. He'd cleared out space in his closet and two drawers for her and she was slowly moving her things out of her apartment. Barring any unforeseen obstacles, she was hoping to have everything done by the end of the month.

As promised, Justin reappeared five minutes later, hair damp from his shower and wearing a green button-down shirt and a pair of black jeans. He looked good enough to eat, and she had to remind herself of where they were going tonight. No matter how delectable he looked, she needed to keep her hands to herself.

She stood, slipped her coat on, and headed for the door. Justin stopped her and pulled her against him. "No matter what happens tonight, remember I love you."

"I know." Kim brushed her fingers over his bruised jaw. He looked as if he'd been in a barroom brawl. They'd put ice on it as soon as they got back to his house, but it had still turned black and blue. Her brother hadn't been playing when he'd landed that punch.

He took her hand in his and kissed the inside of her palm. "We need to go."

Kim nodded and let him lead her out to the car. They'd decided to ride together. In less than an hour, her entire family would know about their relationship.

Justin held her hand on the drive to her parents. He was quiet and she let the silence fill the small space. They were both worried. Not only about her parents' reactions to their news, but neither of them had any idea if Mark would be there. And if he was, what he would say or do.

They got part of their answer when they pulled up in front of Kim's parents' house. Mark's car was parked in the driveway.

Looking over at her, Justin squeezed her hand. "Ready?"

She wasn't, but there was no point in delaying it. "Yeah."

He got out of the vehicle and came around to open her door. She let him help her out and leaned into him when he reached for her hand again as they walked to the front door. They separated before Kim opened the door and let them inside.

The house smelled of food. They weren't greeted by screaming or fists flying, so she counted that as a good sign.

Then they rounded the corner. Mark was sitting in her dad's recliner with a beer in his hand. He stared at them for several long moments before getting to his feet.

Justin moved her behind him, bracing himself for whatever it was Mark was going to dish out. The tension in the room was thick. "I think we need to talk," Justin said.

Her brother downed the rest of his beer, then set it down on the coffee table with a little more force than necessary. "Yes, let's talk." But instead of talking to Justin, he turned his attention to Kim. "He's the one who put those marks on your back, isn't he?"

She wasn't going to lie and maybe this was a good thing. They needed to clear the air. Although, she would rather not be doing it in her parents' living room. "Yes."

"How could you let him hurt you?" His voice was a mixture of disbelief and hurt.

She moved toward her brother. Justin didn't stop her, but she felt his gaze on her. "He didn't hurt me."

"I saw the marks. He hurt you."

Kim shook her head. "That's not the way it is. You must know that. You know Justin. He wouldn't hurt me."

Mark shook his head, but the conversation was cut short when her dad hobbled into the room on a pair of crutches. "I thought I heard voices in here. You two must have snuck in."

"I need another beer," Mark mumbled before fleeing the room.

Her dad raised an eyebrow, but she ignored it.

"Hi, Dad." Kim gave her dad a hug. "How are you doing?"

He returned the embrace as best as he could. "Hi, honey." Davis Langley looked over Kim's head and nodded his greeting to Justin. "Doctor says the leg's healing up fine. Another two or three weeks and I should be able to lose the crutches."

"That's great news, Dad."

They made their way into the kitchen to find her mom. Belinda was setting the food on the table. "Oh good. I thought I heard voices." She looked at her husband. "I told you I wasn't hearing things."

Kim placed a kiss on her mom's cheek. "Need help with anything?"

"Nope. Everything's pretty much done. All we're waiting on is for the rolls to come out of the oven."

They all took a seat. It was then her mom noticed her brother was missing. "Where's Mark?"

"He said he was going to get another beer," Davis said. "Maybe he went down to the basement."

Justin stood. "I'll go find him."

His gaze met Kim's and held for a long moment before he headed down the stairs to the basement to find Mark.

When Kim turned her attention back to her parents, her mom tilted her head to one side and gave her a little smirk. "Something you want to tell us?"

Kim swallowed. This wasn't exactly how she'd envisioned telling them, but she supposed now was as good a time as any. And besides, maybe it was better if it was only her and her parents. Especially with the way Mark was acting. "Justin and I are...dating."

Her dad had been about to take a drink of his water but stopped mid sip. He didn't say anything right away, though. His gaze went to the stairs Justin had disappeared down, then back to her. "How long has this been going on?"

His voice was even and monotone. That wasn't always a good sign. "It started about four months ago." No need to go into detail that it all started with what was supposed to be a one-night stand.

Her mom's eyebrows rose almost to her hairline. "Four months?"

Kim nodded. "We wanted to make sure before we told anyone." She paused. "Especially Mark."

Belinda Langley frowned. "I guess that explains your brother's sour mood."

"He sort of...walked in on us together." She chanced a glance at her dad. His face was unreadable, and it was making her nervous. "He punched Justin."

Her mom's eyes held a mixture of shock and concern. She seemed to be taking it all in.

"You were together at New Year's?" her dad asked.

This was where it got complicated. "Not exactly. We were trying to figure things out. But a few weeks ago we decided to really give a relationship a try."

"A few weeks? I thought you said you've been together for four months?" Her dad's tone had darkened.

She needed to turn the conversation around before both males in her family lost their heads over her relationship. "Things between us first started four months ago, but we both struggled with whether to get serious."

"And now it's serious?" her father asked.

"Yes." Kim met her dad's gaze. "We're moving in together."

Her dad began to stand, then faltered.

Both women shot out of their chairs and reached out to prevent him from falling. He pushed them away. "I'm fine."

Then their attention was pulled away by the sound of a crash coming from the basement.

JUSTIN WASN'T SURE WHAT HE'D FIND WHEN HE WENT DOWNSTAIRS. HE AND Mark had been friends for a long time, so it wasn't the first fight they'd had. But this was different.

It was dark when he got to the bottom of the stairs. Mark hadn't bothered to turn on the lights. Justin flipped the switch on the wall and scanned the room, looking for his friend.

It took him a few seconds, but he spotted him sitting on the couch along the far wall. His hands rested on his knees and his head was leaning back.

"Hey," Justin said from the bottom of the stairs.

Mark opened his eyes and sent a death stare in Justin's direction. Not exactly encouraging.

Justin took a couple of steps into the room. "Can we talk?"

"Nothing to talk about."

"Of course there is."

His friend stood and walked over to the bookcase to his right. It was full of family photos. "I shouldn't have stopped with one punch. You deserved much more for hurting Kim."

"I didn't hurt her. I love her."

"Bullshit!" Mark whirled to face him. "I saw the marks."

Justin blew out a breath. "They were from a flogger."

Mark nodded. "You hit her. I knew it wasn't from her pressing against something. You fuckin' hit her." His voice rose in volume and Justin hoped it didn't carry up the stairs.

"It's not like that and you know it."

"Isn't it?" Mark narrowed his eyes once more and took an aggressive step forward. "Isn't that what you do as a Dominant? Cause your submissives pain?" He let out something close to a growl. "You hurt Kim and then got off on it."

If this wasn't Mark and they weren't talking about Kim, Justin would have decked his friend. "I don't do anything to the women I play with that they don't want me to do."

"So you're saying Kim was asking for it?"

This was so not going the way he'd hoped. "Stop making it sound like I'm abusing her. I'm not knocking her around."

"You're just using toys"—he put the word toys in air quotes—"to get your rocks off."

"You are such an ass sometimes, Mark, do you know that?" Justin blew out a breath. "Kim has found she likes certain things when it comes to sex. Things I enjoy as well. She has her safewords if she ever needs or wants me to stop our play."

If looks could kill, Justin would be a dead man. Then, without any warning, Mark lunged.

Justin fell backward, right into the large square coffee table in the center of the room. The corner jammed into his back, sending a jolt of pain down his side. He couldn't focus on it for long because Mark was on top of him. The next thing he knew, Mark's fist was on a collision course with his face. He managed to block it, but not well enough. Mark's elbow hit Justin's lip and an instant later, he felt the coppery taste of blood.

Using his body weight, Justin flipped them over and pinned Mark beneath him. His friend struggled and it took all Justin's strength to keep him down.

"What's going on down here?" Belinda's voice came from the stairs.

He glanced up to see Kim, followed closely by her mom, descending the stairs. Both women looked frantic, no doubt coming to investigate the noise.

"Mark Jacob, what are you doing?" It was his mother's voice that finally got Mark's attention.

Fairly confident fists weren't going to start flying again, at least not with Belinda and Kim standing there, Justin released Mark's wrists and rolled off him. He got to his feet, not wanting to be caught in a vulnerable position should Mark decide to resume.

"I'm waiting on answers." Belinda was looking at both Justin and Mark.

Mark blew out a breath. "We're just having a...disagreement."

"Does this have something to do with your sister and Justin dating?"

His friend snorted. "Yeah. It has to do with them *dating*." He put extra emphasis on the word dating.

Belinda didn't respond right away. She seemed to be considering her answer. "I have to say that I'm a bit shocked with the news, but I don't think that justifies you two breaking my furniture. You will clean this up." She looked at Justin as well. "Both of you. And then you will come upstairs and have dinner with the family like civilized adults. Do you understand?"

"Yes, ma'am," Justin said, tentatively touching his now bloody lip. He was going to need more ice.

Mark sent Justin another scathing look. "Yes, ma'am."

Belinda straightened her shoulders, took hold of Kim's hand, and turned toward the stairs. "Come on. Let's leave these two *men* to clean up."

Kim sent a concerned glance Justin's way. He nodded, and she disappeared up the steps with her mom, leaving Mark and Justin alone again.

Justin shoved his hands into his pockets and faced Mark. "Look, I know you don't like the idea of me dating your sister."

He snorted.

"Okay, you don't like the idea of me having sex with your sister, especially in the way I like to have sex." Justin paused. "But like it or not, she's an adult, and she can have sex with whoever she wants however she wants. You don't have to like it."

"You're supposed to be my friend."

"I am your friend. That doesn't have to change." Justin waited.

"I don't know if I can stand the idea of you doing that kind of stuff with her. It was one thing when you were telling me about it when it was women I didn't know, but Kim..."

Justin thought about how to approach this. It really wasn't any of Mark's business, but he also felt compelled to plead his case. "Kim came to me."

Mark's head snapped up and Justin knew he had his full attention.

"I'm not going to go into details, but she came to me and asked if I'd introduce her to the lifestyle." He paused. "I won't hurt her, man. I love her, and...we're moving in together."

His friend took a step forward, then stopped himself. "You're serious."

"I'm serious." Justin removed his hands from his pockets and moved closer. "We've had feelings for each other for a while, but both of us were holding back. We didn't want to upset things. You or Belinda or Davis. I get that it's sudden for you, but it's not for us. This has been a long time coming."

Mark's shoulders relaxed, and Justin figured the storm was over. At least for now. "I'm just not sure. It feels wrong."

"Maybe you should talk to your sister." Justin paused. "And by talk I mean listen to what she has to say. She wants this as much as I do. Also, do you really think your sister would let me do something to her she didn't want me to? She's not exactly the passive type. She knows what she wants and she goes after it."

After a long moment, Mark nodded, then looked at the mess on the floor. The coffee table was on its side and everything that had been on it was now scattered across the floor. "We should probably clean things up before Mom comes back down."

Justin grabbed one end of the table, while Mark gripped the other. They picked it up and set it back in its place. Luckily, nothing appeared to be broken.

Once everything was where it was supposed to be, they made their way upstairs. But they weren't greeted by the serene family scene they'd expected. Davis was balancing on his crutches and Belinda and Kim were standing on the other side of the table. From the looks of it, there was another storm brewing, and they hadn't even had dinner yet.

Chapter Thirty-Three

Kim had about had it with all the testosterone. It was bad enough her brother was acting like an idiot. Now her dad was grilling her as well. He'd paused long enough to confirm no one downstairs was missing any limbs, then started in. "Now, finish explaining to me how you and Justin are moving in together."

"It does seem rather fast, honey." Her mom didn't look upset, just concerned.

She understood that to them it might seem that way. "It's been seventeen years."

"You haven't been dating for seventeen years," her father said.

"No, Dad. But we've known each other. It's not like he's a stranger."

Her father stared at her for a long moment. "I still think you should wait."

She opened her mouth to respond, but her attention was drawn to Justin and Mark coming into the room. Justin's lip was busted, the area around it already swelling.

Kim narrowed her eyes at her brother and crossed the room to Justin. She skimmed her fingers over his face before turning toward her brother. "Can't you manage to talk without using your fists?"

Mark didn't seem overly concerned with her chastisement. "He's lucky I didn't do more than that."

She blew out a frustrated breath. "Unbelievable."

Justin cupped the side of her face, then rested his hand on her shoulder before addressing her parents. "I know our news caught you all off guard, but it's not going to change how we feel."

Her mom walked over to place a hand on Justin's arm. "It's not the fact that you're dating." Her mom paused. "I mean, we're a little surprised, but it's the moving in together. That's a big step."

"Yes, it is."

No one said anything as that hung in the air for several long moments. It was her dad who broke the silence. He looked Kim in the eyes. "I don't like it. I wish you'd wait. For another year at least. But you're an adult, and I can't stop you."

"Dad, we've waited too long already," Kim said.

Justin gave her shoulders a squeeze, then looked at Davis. "I'll take care of her. I promise you."

Her dad lowered himself into his chair, propping his crutches against the wall behind him. "You'd better. I won't be using these damn things forever."

"Understood, sir."

Davis Langley nodded once, then turned to his wife. "Do you have an ice pack or something for Justin's lip? Looks like a nasty cut he's got there." Then he scooped up a heaping spoonful of mashed potatoes and deposited them onto his plate as if they'd been discussing the weather.

Her mom retrieved an ice pack from the freezer and wrapped it in a towel before handing it to Justin. He winced as he pressed it against his face. Kim didn't miss her brother's smirk.

Everyone took a seat around the table and for a while, the only sound was the scraping of dishes as food was piled on plates. Justin sat between her and her mom, which was the safest place at the table for him. Kim still didn't trust the men in her family to behave themselves.

Eventually, her mom approached the elephant in the room again. "I don't want any more fighting." She glared at her son and husband. "But when are you two planning to move in together?"

Kim met Justin's gaze before answering her mother's question. "I've already begun moving some of my things, but there's not a huge rush. I have the apartment until the end of next month."

"That's where you were the night of Dad's accident," Mark said. "You two were together." He paused, seeming to process the information he now knew, then narrowed his eyes at Justin. "She was the woman."

She knew exactly what was going through her brother's mind. The discarded dress she'd left on Justin's living room floor painted a pretty good picture of the situation. Justin answered her brother, but not in the way she'd thought. "Of course she was. I don't cheat. Kim's the only woman I've dated since we started seeing each other four months ago."

Kim looked over at him and hoped she didn't look as surprised as she felt at the news. She hadn't been with anyone since that first night, but she hadn't known if he had. Their first night had been a no strings type deal. They'd made no commitments. No promises. But she couldn't deny she liked this new information.

Mark stabbed a piece of meat on his plate and shoved it into his mouth. She guessed that was better than him leaping over the table to take yet another shot at Justin.

"I'm not going to lie," her father said. "This is going to take some getting used to." He looked at Justin. "It's not that I don't like you. Hell, you've been like a second son to us, but I've never gotten a hint from either of you before tonight that you saw each other this way."

Justin placed a hand on her knee under the table. "We were really good at hiding it."

Her mom speared a carrot. "What I don't understand is why." She waved her fork in the air. "I mean, obviously these two aren't thrilled about it, but if you both felt this way for so long..."

She let that trail off, obviously expecting an answer. Kim met her mother's gaze. "I didn't know he saw me as anything more than Mark's sister. I thought my feelings were one-sided." Kim glanced over at Justin. "We both did."

Belinda shook her head. "You're not exactly like any of Kim's previous boyfriends."

Justin snorted, then winced. He was trying to eat, but she could tell it hurt to chew. He was eating more of the mashed potatoes than anything else.

"No, he's not, but that's a good thing. There's a reason why my other relationships didn't work out." She wasn't going to mention that the main reason they didn't work out was because she'd realized she was a submissive and she needed a man who could take control in the bedroom. That was the type of information her mother didn't need.

Conversation was stark for the rest of the meal. Her brother kept sending glares across the table at Justin, while her dad appeared extremely interested in the food on his plate. It was one of the strangest family dinners they'd ever had.

Kim breathed a sigh of relief when her dad asked Mark to help him with something in the garage. Normally, Justin would have gone with them, but he stayed back. She couldn't blame him. He'd had a rough few days with the men of her family.

"Do you need some help cleaning up?" Justin asked her mother.

"No, but thank you for asking. I've got it. There isn't much to clean up in any case." She inspected his face. "You should keep putting ice on that throughout the night to keep the swelling down." She smiled. "Maybe Kim can help you with that."

"You're okay with this? Us being together?" Justin asked.

"As long as you make my girl happy, I'm happy." Belinda took hold of his free hand. "Be good to her."

"Yes, ma'am." He tried to smile and winced again.

Kim gave her mom a hug. "Thanks, Mom. For everything."

"You're very welcome, honey." Belinda released her daughter and took a step back. "Now go home and take care of your man. He needs your attention more than I do tonight."

"Do you think it's safe to say goodbye to Dad?" Kim asked, eyeing the door that led to the garage.

"I think maybe you should give your dad a day or two to adjust."

After giving her mom another hug, Kim and Justin retrieved their coats and made their way to the car. "Do you want me to drive?" Kim asked.

He opened the passenger door and motioned for her to get inside. "I'm not hurt that bad."

Kim shook her head and waited until he got behind the wheel. "You don't have to be all macho with me. I know it hurts. I saw you wincing at dinner."

The engine purred to life, and he pulled away from the curb. "I've had worse."

"Still. He shouldn't have hit you." She paused. "Again."

"He's your brother." Justin shrugged. "It could have been worse."

"You keep saying that."

He glanced over at her, then pulled away from the curb. "Because it's true."

She thought about that for a moment. While she hated to admit it, Justin was probably right. "He needs to get over it."

Justin reached for her hand and tucked it against his thigh. "It doesn't matter."

Kim wasn't sure she agreed with him. If her brother tried to deck Justin every time they saw each other, it would make family gatherings impossible. She didn't want that. She wanted her family—all her family—to accept her decision. Was that so much to ask?

At least her mom seemed to be in their corner.

The next couple days passed with no word from Mark or Davis. Kim had spoken to her mom, but the two Langley men were staying silent. Justin supposed that was better than the alternative.

The bruising on his face was going down. He still had a busted lip, which meant he'd been unable to really kiss Kim...or suck on her nipples the way he wanted. It was making him cranky.

It was Friday evening, and he was more than ready to head to the club. He needed to put everything else out of his head for a while and be Kim's Dom.

They were halfway to the vehicle when they noticed Mark's car parked behind them. Justin blew out a loud breath. "We don't need this tonight."

Kim placed her hand on his chest. "Maybe it's a good thing."

Mark got out of the car and strode toward them. Justin wrapped his arm around Kim's waist. Luckily, it wasn't too cold out. He hadn't planned for them to be outside for long and the outfit he'd chosen for Kim to wear wasn't exactly made for warmth.

Stopping a few feet from them, Mark shoved his hands in his pockets. "You're heading out."

It wasn't said as a question, but Justin answered anyway. "We are."

Mark nodded.

When he didn't say anything more, Justin grew impatient. "Was there a reason you stopped by?"

"Mom says I need to apologize." Mark ran a hand over the top of his head, then looked at Kim. "She thinks I was out of line thinking I have a say in who you can date. But she doesn't understand everything and it's not the kind of thing I want her to know."

Justin felt Kim stiffen in his arms. "My relationships are none of your business."

"You're not submissive, Kim." His voice was pleading. "You don't know some of the things he'd done to women he's..." Mark paused. "Played with."

"I don't need to know what he's done with other women. All I care about is what's happening now and what we do together."

Mark shook his head. "That's not how it works."

"What do you mean that's not how it works?" she asked.

Her brother pulled at his hair, something he only did when he was really frustrated. "He's the one in control. He gets to decide."

Justin wanted to step in, but he knew this had to come from Kim. He could talk until he was blue in the face—tell Mark that all play was negotiated ahead of time—but he doubted his friend would believe him.

"No," she said. "I get to decide."

Mark shook his head and opened his mouth to argue, but Kim didn't let him get a word in.

"Justin gets to decide *when* we do things, but he doesn't do anything I haven't said is okay. I've talked more about sex with Justin than I have with any other man I've dated. He knows what I like, what I don't like, and what I'd like to try."

Her brother scrunched up his nose when she mentioned sex, but that was his only reaction to what she'd said.

Kim lowered her voice and looked her brother in the eye. "Justin's who I want to be with, and you need to respect my decision."

"And if I can't?" Mark asked.

"Then you need to at least keep your opinions to yourself." Kim glanced up at Justin, then back at her brother. "And stop hitting people."

Mark sighed. "As much as I hate to admit it, you're right. It's not my decision. But that doesn't mean I don't worry about you. You're my little sister."

Kim walked over to her brother, and Justin flexed his fist before dropping it to his side. "While I appreciate that you want to protect me, you don't have to protect me from Justin."

He glanced between them. "I'll try to"—he paused—"keep that in mind."

Going up on her tiptoes, she circled her arms around her brother's neck and kissed his cheek. "Thank you."

He returned the embrace. "I still don't like it, though."

Kim chuckled. "You don't have to like it. Just keep your mouth shut about it."

Mark snorted, then he ran his hands along her back. "Are you wearing anything under that coat?"

She took a step back and raised a sassy eyebrow at him. "You sure you want to know the answer to that question?"

Her brother paled and Justin couldn't help but grin when Mark threw his hands up in surrender. "No. Definitely not."

"Good answer," she said.

Mark looked up at Justin. Their gazes held for a long moment, then Mark nodded. "I'm gonna head out."

"Good night." Kim smiled and waved.

Walking up behind her, Justin placed a hand on her hip. "Come on. Let's get you in the car. I think we've tortured your brother enough for one night."

She giggled but let him lead her to the car. "I couldn't help it. His holier than thou attitude is getting old."

"I can't disagree, but taunting him probably isn't going to give us the end result we want."

"True."

They arrived at the club twenty minutes later, having been waylaid in some lingering downtown traffic. It was a nice night for January, and people were taking advantage. That also meant the club was likely to be busy.

Justin parked the car in the small parking lot next to the club and walked around to the passenger side to help Kim. When she placed her boots on the ground and stood, it was like a wet dream come to life. The black boots came up over her knee, and all he could think about when he saw those four-inch heels were how they tilted her ass into the perfect position for him to pound into her.

Kim took his hand, allowing him to help her to her feet, giving him a knowing smile. She knew exactly what he was thinking. That probably had something to do with the fact that he'd pulled her against his crotch before they left and mentioned how much he liked her new boots.

As he removed his keycard from his pocket, his fingers brushed against the other item he had tucked inside. Kim's collar. He'd thought about presenting it to her at home, but the club had been where everything started for them. It was where she'd first seen him as a Dom and decided to approach him. And it was where they'd both decided to give a relationship between them a go. It seemed fitting to being the next stage of their D/s relationship there as well.

After leaving their coats with Bridget, they headed into the club. Justin took a quick look around and found Ali exactly where he expected her to be.

He placed his hand on Kim's lower back and steered her in Ali's direction. Her friend saw her and smiled. "I wasn't sure if you two would be here tonight with the moving and all."

Justin motioned for Kim to take a seat next to her friend. "I'll leave Kim to fill you in. I'm going to get us some drinks."

"So?" Ali asked as he turned away and weaved his way to the bar. He figured he'd give them a few minutes alone. Since he and Kim had gotten together, she and Ali hadn't had much girl time. He was going to have to rectify that.

Brandon greeted him with a smile. "I heard you checked out Garrett's cabin last weekend."

"Word travels fast." Justin chuckled.

"I may have been around when you called Katrina for Garrett's number."

Justin raised an eyebrow.

Brandon waved a dismissive hand. "Nothing like that. We were going over ordering. As great as Katrina is, she's not my type."

The bartender was a Dominant. Justin had never seen him bottom for anyone. And in the two years he'd been coming to the club, he'd never known Mistress Katrina to bottom for anyone either. The image of the two of them trying to play together was almost comical. All he could picture was each of them trying to top the other.

Justin shook his head and chuckled. "No, she isn't."

Brandon grinned. "So what can I get you"—he glanced behind Justin toward the couch where Kim and Ali had their heads together—"and your lady this evening?"

"Two waters for now."

Within seconds, Brandon placed two bottles of water onto the polished wood.

Justin handed over his membership card, and after a quick swipe, he thanked Brandon and made his way back to Kim. He placed the waters on the table beside the couch, sat down next to Kim, promptly picked her up, and settled her on his lap. "How are you doing tonight, Ali?"

She smiled. "Not as good as you two."

Reaching for their waters, he handed one to Kim. "No argument there."

He made himself comfortable and listened while Kim and Ali continued to talk, content to hold her for a while. As the night wore on, however, he couldn't keep himself from touching her. He ran his hand up her thigh and under the hem of her skirt. It was blue tonight. Midnight blue to match the corset he'd picked out. He wanted to finger her, but he knew she wasn't ready for that.

Leaning in, he brought his lips to her ear. At the same time, he skimmed his fingers along the inside of her thigh. "Tell Ali you'll talk to her later."

Kim's breath hitched, and then she licked her lips. "I'll talk to you later, Ali."

Not waiting, Justin stood, bringing Kim with him. He steadied her on her feet, making sure she was stable, then took hold of her hand as he led her up the stairs to the second floor.

Chapter Thirty-Four

Kim had told Ali what had happened with her dad and brother. Her best friend had been sympathetic. "They'll come around. It's just going to take some time."

She really hoped that was true.

Thoughts of Ali and her family were pushed to the back of her brain as she and Justin reached the second floor of the club. It was almost nine and the club was in full swing. That meant the second floor was busy. Individuals and couples lingered in the wide hallway, peering into the rooms, watching the play taking place inside.

The sound of a paddle smacking against skin drew her attention to a room on the left as they passed by. Justin hadn't used anything but his hand on her, but she figured he would eventually. And the woman on the other side of the glass didn't seem to be complaining. In fact, Kim thought she heard the woman moan.

One of the first things Kim had learned when she joined the club and ventured up to the second floor was that the walls were thin. Or at least there'd been no effort to deaden the sound. While those in the hall typically couldn't hear the words that were being spoken between the people playing, the sound of paddles, whips, and floggers carried.

Justin paused and pulled her over to the window. She gazed inside and sure enough, a woman was tied to a spanking bench with her bare ass showing for all the world to see. Her Dom stood with a long wooden paddle in his right hand, getting ready to land another blow to the submissive's already rosy backside.

When the Dom's arm came down and the paddle landed solid on the submissive's flesh, Kim felt Justin move to stand behind her. His lips pressed against her ear. "She seems to be enjoying her Dom's paddle."

A second later, the Dom reached between the submissive's legs, moving his fingers through her folds several times. Then he brought his fingers to his mouth and sucked.

Kim's interior muscles clenched. Justin had done that, dipping his fingers into her center and tasting her after he's spanked her. She didn't understand why being turned over his knee and disciplined like a child turned her on so much, but it did. And she was learning that her reactions weren't so strange, after all. Other women liked to be spanked, too. "Yes, Sir."

Justin's hand grazed the outside of her hip and moved lower until he reached the hem of her skirt. Her breath caught again when he began moving his hand upward. This time, there was no clothing between her and his fingers.

She glanced around, nervous about someone seeing, but no one was paying attention to them. The hallway was dim, and people were either watching what was going on inside the rooms or they were on their way to a room themselves.

Then his fingers brushed over her lips. Heat and moisture rushed to her sex.

"Relax and watch the naughty girl get spanked." His whispered words were punctuated by a gentle tug of her clit.

Kim couldn't stop the soft moan that escaped. His fingers felt so good and she found she was less worried about who might see them than the need for him to keep touching her. As the Dom behind the glass turned the submissive's ass a nice shade of red, Justin continued to play. His fingers massaged and tugged at her skin and she could already feel the wetness dripping down the inside of her thighs.

When the Dom finally laid the paddle down, he swiped a condom from a large bowl next to the door. He dropped his pants around his ankles, rolled the protection on, then spread the submissive's cheeks. But instead of driving into her pussy, he reached for a bottle on a nearby table. He squeezed and drizzled what she realized had to be lube down her crack.

It was then Kim realized what he was going to do. She watched in fascination and a little trepidation as he swirled the lube around her hole, then pushed his fingers inside. He pumped them several times before lining up his cock and thrusting his hips forward.

His hips slapped against her red ass and Kim heard her moan. Her body clenched as heat coiled in her belly watching the scene. Had Justin planned this? They'd been talking about anal since they came back from their weekend away. She was nervous about it but seeing this was changing her mind. The submissive didn't seem to be in pain. If anything, she looked as if she were about to burst with pleasure.

Then the Dom reached for a small vibrator that looked no bigger than a finger. He turned it on and held it between the sub's legs, directly on her clit. The sub cried out and Kim's sex pulsed in response.

Justin moved his fingers onto her clit and began circling. "Alexander and Grace love anal sex. It's one of her favorite things and he gives it to her often."

Kim blinked and focused on the couple before her. She knew who Alexander and Grace were. They'd given an anal sex demonstration before the entire club on her first night as a member. She hated to admit it, but she hadn't watched much of it, afraid of what she might see. But this was...hot. Sexy. And with Justin playing with her clit, she was close to coming.

"She's going to come," Justin whispered in her ear.

Grace's entire body was flushed all the way down to her toes. She was moaning and her fingers gripped the soft pads of the bench. Then, less than thirty seconds later, she screamed out her release.

Justin dropped his fingers, leaving Kim aching. He turned her around to face him, cupped the side of her face, and kissed her hard.

Her head was spinning when he released her and she almost tripped over her own feet when they started walking again. He kept his arm around her waist, though, apparently aware of her precarious balance situation.

They entered the room they'd played in twice before and she looked around. There was already a pillow on the floor in the center of the room. He shut the door behind them and lowered the blinds on the window.

She stood, waiting. They'd never played with clothes on before, but he hadn't instructed her to remove them. While she might not be the best submissive yet, she knew it was best not to do anything until he told her what he wanted her to do.

Justin turned and smiled. He extended his hand, and she took it.

They walked to the middle of the room, the pillow next to her feet, but he didn't tell her to kneel. Instead, he dropped her hand and stood in front of her. He looked serious and she wondered if she'd done something wrong again.

"I wanted to do this at the club because this is where everything began. It's where you first saw me and decided you wanted me to be the one to show you what it was like to submit. It's also where we decided to give a relationship between us a go."

Warmth grew in Kim's chest as she listened to his words. Justin could talk dirty to her and send her body flying, but there was something about hearing him talk about how their relationship started that pulled at her heart.

He removed something from his pocket and held it out so she could see it. In his palm lay a silver chain. It was simple and plain. "I wanted something you could wear, even at work." His gaze held hers. "Once I put this on you, I never want you to take it off."

Kim swallowed. Even though he hadn't said it, she knew exactly what it was. He wanted to collar her. To make her his.

The thing was, she was already his. She always had been. Even before their one night together. It was why no other man had measured up. She'd always been Justin's.

He held it up in front of her. "Will you wear my collar, Kim?"

She couldn't stop herself from smiling. "Yes, Sir."

Justin grinned back at her and came around behind her. "Lift your hair."

Kim gathered her hair and held it off her neck.

His fingers skimmed her neck and collarbone as he placed the collar around her neck and secured it. He placed a kiss on her shoulder, his lips lingering on her skin. "You look beautiful wearing my collar."

She released her hair and brought her hand up to touch it as it lay flat at the base of her neck. "Thank you, Sir."

"Thank you, baby." He brushed her hair aside and continued to place kisses along the back of her neck, following the line of her new collar. "I plan on making you a very, very naughty girl. Are you ready for that?"

The seriousness of the moment turned in an instant to anticipation. "Yes, Sir. I'm ready."

And she was. Very ready. Whatever they had to face, it would be okay if they did it together. Everything felt right when she was with Justin.

He turned her in his arms and crashed his lips over hers. "I love you, Kim. I always have and I always will."

Kim gazed up at him, seeing the love in his eyes. "I love you, too, Sir. I wish we hadn't waited so long."

Tucking her hair behind her ears, he kissed the tip of her nose. "It doesn't matter. We're together now and I plan on keeping you."

"What if I want to keep you?" She knew she was playing with fire, but she didn't care.

A wicked look came into Justin's eyes and before she knew it, she was being hoisted over his shoulder and carried over to the spanking bench. She guessed it was time for him to discipline his naughty girl.

Epilogue

Mark strolled into the kitchen carrying two more boxes. He placed them on the table and turned to his sister. "I think this is all of it."

"Did you get the boxes that were in the front seat?" Kim asked.

"Yep. Dad and I put them in the living room. Did you want me to bring them in here?"

Kim shook her head. "I'll go through them later. They're mainly knickknacks."

Mark glanced around the room, then behind him. Ali frowned. She knew what he was doing—looking for Justin. As far as she knew, the two hadn't spoken since the family dinner. They also hadn't fought either, so there was that. And Mark and Kim's dad had shown up to help today, bearing cookies from Belinda. Ali had needed the sugar. She hadn't been sleeping well for the last week.

"Justin's in the back bedroom with Drew and Daniel setting up my old bed if you guys want to help," Kim said to her brother as her dad came into the room. It had been about six weeks since Davis's fall and he was getting around a lot better. He'd ditched the crutches for a cane as soon as his doctor had given him the okay, but still seemed irritated at his limited mobility. She couldn't exactly blame him.

Shoving his hands in his pockets, Mark rocked back on his heels. "Did you need help with anything else, Sis?"

It was Kim's turn to frown, disappointment clear on her face. Her friend had hoped her family would have come around by now. At least they'd shown up to help today. Ali hadn't been sure about that. Neither had Kim. "No. We're about finished in here and all the furniture's either here or in storage."

Mark nodded and glanced over at Davis. "I think Dad and I are going to take off then, if you don't need us anymore."

Kim sighed. "Okay."

Davis limped over to give his daughter a hug and kiss her cheek.

"Thanks for coming, Dad," Kim said.

"Of course."

The two men exited the room and Kim's shoulders slumped at the sound of the door closing behind them. Ali's heart went out to her. Kim was close with her family and to have them react like this to such a major decision in her life was hard. Davis seemed to be slowly coming around. He'd even said hi to Justin when they'd all met at Kim's apartment that morning.

It took them another half hour to empty the new boxes Mark had brought. Ali removed the last mug from the box and placed it in the cabinet to the right of the refrigerator. "Is that everything?"

Kim glanced around the kitchen. "Yeah, I think so. In here at least." She gathered the empty boxes from the table. "We should probably go see if the guys need any help."

Justin, Drew, and Daniel were tackling the bigger stuff while Davis and Mark had carried in the smaller boxes. Kim and Ali had worked to put things away. It was the best division of labor considering the tension and Davis's injury.

Ali and Kim made their way down the hallway to the spare bedroom. "Not sure we're going to be much help carrying furniture." Ali yawned.

"That's the third time you've yawned in the last hour. What's up with you?" Kim bumped Ali's shoulder.

"Nothing. I just haven't been getting a lot of sleep lately."

"Oh?" Kim asked. "Someone been keeping you up at night?"

Ali snorted. "I wish."

They made their way to the spare bedroom. "What then?"

As they walked into the room at the far end of the hall, the sight of Drew's backside as he bent over to connect the footboard to the rest of the frame greeted them. Daniel was facing him, holding the metal part, and Justin was on the other side of the bed, trying not to laugh.

"Need some help?" Kim asked.

Justin looked up and smiled when he saw her. "I think we've almost got it."

Drew grunted as the frame finally slipped into the slot and stood. "That was more challenging than I thought it would be."

"It was sticking when we took it apart the other day," Justin said.

Daniel shook his head. "Hopefully, you won't be needing to take it apart again for a very long time."

Kim ran her hand over the dark wood. "I don't plan on going anywhere anytime soon."

"Damn straight." Justin grabbed her hips and pulled her back against him.

She chuckled and wiggled her ass into him.

Ali grinned. It was nice seeing Kim and Justin happy together. "Is there anything else that needs brought in or put away?"

"Are you ladies finished in the kitchen?" Justin asked.

Kim tilted her head to the side so she could look up at him. "Yep. All done."

"Then I think that's everything." Justin kissed the tip of her nose. "You're officially all moved in."

Daniel cleared his throat. "And with that, I think it's time we said goodbye."

"You don't have to run off."

Justin cut Kim off. "Yes, they do."

Drew and Daniel both chuckled and Ali shook her head.

They all made their way to the living room. Daniel helped Ali with her coat, and she had to suppress her reaction to his fingers as they brushed the back of her neck. He didn't feel that way about her. They were friends.

Her body, however, had trouble remembering that. Every time he touched her, it sent tingles down her arm or her leg or wherever they connected. She'd been attracted to him from the start. Everything about him turned her on, from his lips to his hands to the way he took care of her. She wanted to be his.

But that wasn't going to happen. He wouldn't even play with her at the club. The few times she'd mentioned wanting to play, he'd found another Dom for her to play with.

"Everything all right?" Daniel asked as they headed to their vehicles.

"I'm fine. Just a little tired."

He stopped them both and frowned. "Why?"

This was what was so frustrating. Sometimes he acted as if he were her Dom, but then it never went anywhere.

Daniel waited for an answer.

"I've got new neighbors."

He furrowed his brow in concentration. "They're keeping you up?"

She nodded as she stifled yet another yawn.

"Did you report them to your complex management?" he asked.

"I can't."

Daniel crossed his arms. "If they're making noise at all hours of the night, you should report them."

"It's not..."

"What?"

Ali glanced around, but they were alone. Justin and Kim had stayed in the house and Drew had already left. She sighed. "They have very loud sex."

He raised an eyebrow.

"She's very vocal and he's...well, he's not quiet either." She felt her face flush. "I can't exactly call management and report my neighbors for having sex."

Daniel thought about it for a long moment. "When's your lease up?"

"Not for another six months." Ali rubbed her hand on her forehead. "It'll get better." She hoped.

It took him a while to respond. When he did, it wasn't how she'd expected.

He took hold of her elbow and walked her to her car. "I'll follow you home."

"Why?" Was he going to talk to her neighbors? She wasn't sure how she'd feel about that.

"Because you're going to pack a bag and come home with me."

Her eyes went wide and she opened her mouth to argue.

He cut her off. "Just for a night. I'm sure I can find you something tomorrow."

"But what about my lease? I can't afford to pay rent on two places."

"Don't worry about it." He opened her car door and gestured for her to get in. "I'll figure something out."

"Daniel, you don't need to. I'll be fine."

He braced himself on the car and leaned in. Her gaze was drawn to the silver at his temples. It made him look distinguished. "You are not fine. Your eyes are bloodshot and you're slouching. You never slouch."

Out of habit, Ali straightened. He was right. She'd been slouching.

"That's not to even mention how many times you've yawned since we've been here."

Had she really yawned that much? She didn't think so. At least not when he'd been around.

When she didn't answer, he stood and met her gaze once more. "Do you feel awake enough to drive?"

She nodded. "Yes."

He gave a curt nod. "If that changes, pull over. Understand?"

Again, he was acting like he was her Dom. It was all so confusing, but she was too tired to argue. "Yes."

True to his word, Daniel stayed behind her while she drove to her apartment. She got out of her vehicle and within seconds, he was beside her. "Do you want some help?"

Ali shook her head. "No. I'll only be a few minutes." She wasn't sure she could handle him being in her space. Eventually, she'd have to come back here. She didn't need images of him leaning against her bedroom door filling her head.

In less than ten minutes, she had a suitcase packed with all her essentials and enough clothes for a week. Maybe after she got some rest, she'd be able to think clearer about her situation.

With her bag in hand, she stepped outside and turned to lock her door. Ali felt Daniel come behind her, and she bit her lip when she heard his voice so close. "I'll take your bag for you."

She handed him her bag without protest. But instead of going to her car, he continued walking to his. "Um?"

Daniel turned. "I'll bring you back to your car later. Right now, you're not alert enough to be driving."

"I made it home, didn't I?" Even that sounded lame to her own ears.

"Do you really want to stand here and argue about your driving?"

No, she didn't.

Resigned, she made her way to his car. He opened the door for her and she got in. The plush leather seats were soft against her skin, cradling her. They were warm, as if someone else had been sitting there.

She sighed and closed her eyes. Seat warmers were a wonderful thing. He must have had it on during the drive to her apartment, so it would be warm for her.

The driver's side door opened, then closed. A faint hint of his cologne or soap tickled her nose. It had her entire body relaxing.

"Are you comfortable?" he asked as he started the car.

"Hmm."

He turned on some soft instrumental music. The melody soothed her, making her entire body feel heavy.

She was in Daniel's car. She was going home with him.

Snuggling down in the seat, she let herself enjoy the moment. Even though she may never have him as her Dom, he was her friend, and she knew he'd take care of her.

A soft smile tugged at her lips as she drifted off to sleep.

***

Read Daniel and Ali's story in **CLAIMING HIS KISS**. Available Now!

CAN'T WAIT FOR SHERRI HAYES' NEXT BOOK?

Let her know by leaving a review and telling her what you liked about
BOUND BY DESIRE (SERPENT'S KISS, VOL. 1)

Also by Sherri Hayes

Finding Anna

Slave (Finding Anna, Book 1)

Need (Finding Anna, Book 2)

Truth (Finding Anna, Book 3)

Trust (Finding Anna, Book 4)

Change (Finding Anna, Book 5)

Indulge: A Finding Anna Novelette

The Daniels Brothers

Behind Closed Doors

Red Zone

Crossing the Line

What Might Have Been

Daniels Brothers Box Set (Books 1-4)

Serpent's Kiss

Welcome to Serpent's Kiss

Burning for Her Kiss

Longing for His Kiss

His Forbidden Kiss

Claiming His Kiss

Tangled In His Embrace

Liberty Crossroads

Seducing Janey

Strictly Professional

Strictly Professional

A Christmas Proposal

<u>**Box Sets**</u>

Daniels Brothers Box Set (Books 1-4)

Bound by Desire (Serpent's Kiss Vol. 1)

Boys In Blue: Everyday Heroes

Acknowledgments

Writing a book is always a journey and I'm lucky to have had some wonderful people along for the ride on this one.

Thank you to my beta reader, Riane Holt. I'm not sure how she does it, but somehow she's able to find the littlest inconsistency within a story. Her eagle eyes never cease to amaze me.

Editors and proofreaders are the unsung heroes of the book world. Without them, our books wouldn't be nearly as good. They painstakingly go through each and every word to help us clean up and polish our work. Thank you to my editors, Wyndy, Andrea, and Emily Lawrence, and to my proofreaders Angela and DeAnne Taylor for helping make my book the best it could be.

Thank you to Sara Eirew, the photographer and cover designer for the first two books in the series. Her beautiful pictures help to bring the characters to life. And to Amy with Qdesigns for her beautiful cover for His Forbidden Kiss.

Covers are often the first thing a reader notices about a book, so a great cover design is important. A huge thank you Miblart for tackling the design of Bound by Desire. I wanted something that captured all three books, but also fit with the vibe of the series. They nailed it!

About the Author

Sherri picked up her first romance novel when she was twelve and immediately she was hooked. She would stay up reading long after everyone else in her house had gone to bed, needing to see the hero and heroine get their happily ever after. But Sherri never imagined becoming an author.

At the age of thirty, all that changed. After getting frustrated with the direction a television show was taking two of its characters, Sherri decided to try her hand at writing an alternative ending to give the characters the happy ending they deserved.

Since then, writing has become a creative outlet that allows her to explore a wide range of emotions, while having fun taking her characters through all the twists and turns she can create.

www.ingramcontent.com/pod-product-compliance
Lightning Source LLC
Chambersburg PA
CBHW071954190726
48293CB00001B/12